THE
CLASS

BOOKS BY ERICH SEGAL

NOVELS

Love Story
Oliver's Story
Man, Woman and Child
The Class

FOR CHILDREN

Fairy Tale

ACADEMIC BOOKS

Roman Laughter: The Comedy of Plautus
Euripides: A Collection of Critical Essays (Ed.)
Plautus: Three Comedies (Ed. and Trans.)
The Oxford Readings in Greek Tragedy (Ed.)
Caesar Augustus: Seven Aspects (Co-ed.)
Plato's Dialogues (Ed.)

THE CLASS

ERICH SEGAL

BANTAM BOOKS
TORONTO · NEW YORK · LONDON · SYDNEY · AUCKLAND

PUBLISHER'S NOTE

This is a novel about fictional members of The Harvard Class of 1958. The author has included the Eliot family in the background for his story because that distinguished family has a long and proud relationship with Harvard University. But the fictional character of Andrew Eliot is not intended to portray or refer to any actual member of the Eliot family, whether living or dead. All of the main characters in this novel are creations of the author's imagination. These characters illustrate some of the divergent directions taken by young men of this generation into the fields of politics, the arts, intellectual life, or in voyages of self-discovery. In tracing their years at Harvard, and thereafter until their 25th Reunion, the author portrays a number of events in which public figures from American political and artistic life appear. He has included portrayals of these public personalities as symbols of certain influences of the past twenty-five years. The reader should understand that the specific conversations and incidents involving these personalities are the author's own creations.

THE CLASS

A Bantam Book / May 1985

ALL RIGHTS RESERVED

Library of Congress Cataloging in Publication Data

Segal, Erich, 1937–
The class.

I. Title.
PS3569.E4C4 1985   813'.54   84-91725
ISBN 0-553-05084-2

Published simultaneously in the United States and Canada

PRINTED IN THE UNITED STATES OF AMERICA

FG   0 9 8 7 6 5 4 3 2 1

For Karen and Francesca
The class in my life

There must be . . . some possible ground in
reason for one's boiling over with joy that
one is a son of Harvard, and was not, by some
unspeakably horrible accident of birth,
predestined to graduate at Yale or at Cornell.

WILLIAM JAMES,
M.D., 1869

THE
CLASS

ANDREW ELIOT'S DIARY

May 12, 1983

My Harvard Twenty-fifth Reunion is next month and I am scared to death.

Scared to face all my successful classmates, walking back on paths of glory, while I have nothing to show for my life except a few gray hairs.

Today a heavy, red-bound book arrived that chronicles all the achievements of The Class of '58. It really brought home my own sense of failure.

I stayed up half the night just staring at the faces of the guys who once were undergraduates with me, and now are senators and governors, world-famous scientists and pioneering doctors. Who knows which of them will end up on a podium in Stockholm? Or the White House lawn?

And what's amazing is that some are still married to their first wives.

A few of the most glittering successes were close friends of mine. The roommate I once thought of as a fruitcake is the candidate likeliest to be our next Secretary of State. The future President of Harvard is a guy I used to lend my clothes to. Another, whom we barely noticed, has become the musical sensation of our age.

The bravest of them all laid down his life for something he believed in. His heroism humbles me.

And I return, resplendent in my disappointment.

I am the last Eliot of a great line to enter Harvard. My ancestors were all distinguished men. In war, in peace, in church, in science, and in education. As recently as 1948, my cousin Tom received the Nobel Prize for Literature.

But the brilliance of the family tradition has grown dim with me. I don't even hold a candle to Jared Eliot (Class of 1703), the man who introduced rhubarb to America.

1

Yet I do have one tenuous connection with my noble forebears. They were diarists. My namesake, Reverend Andrew Eliot, '37, while bravely tending his parishioners, kept a daily record—still extant—describing what the Revolutionary War was like during the siege of Boston in 1776.

The moment the city was liberated, he hurried to a meeting of the Harvard Board of Overseers to move that General George Washington be given an honorary doctorate.

His son inherited his pulpit and his pen, leaving a vivid account of America's first days as a republic.

Naturally, there's no comparison, but I've been keeping note-books all my life as well. Maybe that's the single remnant of my heritage. I've observed history around me, even if I didn't make any of it.

Meanwhile, I'm still scared as hell.

COLLEGE

YEARS

We took the world as given. Cigarettes
Were twenty-several cents a pack, and gas
As much per gallon. Sex came wrapped in rubber
And veiled in supernatural scruples—call
Them chivalry. . . .

Psychology was in the mind; abstract
Things grabbed us where we lived; the only life
Worth living was the private life, and—last,
Worst scandal in this characterization—
We did not know we were a generation.

JOHN UPDIKE
CLASS OF 1954

They glanced at one another like tigers taking measure of a menacing new rival. But in this kind of jungle you could never be sure where the real danger lurked.

It was Monday, September 20, 1954. Eleven hundred sixty-two of the best and brightest young men in the world were lined up outside that monstrous Victorian Gothic structure known as Memorial Hall. To register as members of the future Harvard Class of '58.

Running the sartorial spectrum from Brooks Brothers to hand-me-downs, they were variously impatient, terrified, blasé, and numb. Some had traveled thousands of miles, others a few blocks. Yet all knew that they were now merely at the beginning of the greatest journey of their lives.

Shadrach Tubman, son of the president of Liberia, flew from Monrovia via Paris to New York's Idlewild Airport, whence he was driven to Boston in his Embassy's limousine.

John D. Rockefeller, IV, unpretentiously took the train up from Manhattan and splurged on a taxi from South Station to the Yard.

Apparently the Aga Khan simply epiphanized. (Other rumors had it that he'd flown there on a magic carpet—or a private jet.) In any case, he stood in line waiting to register just like any mortal.

These freshmen had arrived already luminaries. They had been born directly into the limelight.

But on this last day of summer 1954, more than a thousand other potential comets were waiting to burst from dark anonymity to light up the sky.

Among them were Daniel Rossi, Jason Gilbert, Theodore Lambros, and Andrew Eliot. They—and a fifth, still half a world away—are the heroes of this story.

DANIEL ROSSI

I thought the sparrow's note from heaven,
Singing at dawn on the alder bough;
I brought him home, in his nest, at even;
He sings the song, but it cheers not now,
For I did not bring home the river and the sky.

RALPH WALDO EMERSON
CLASS OF 1821

From earliest childhood Danny Rossi had a single, desperate ambition—to please his father. And one single haunting nightmare—that he never could.

At first he believed there was a legitimate reason for Dr. Rossi's indifference. After all, Danny was the slender, unathletic brother of the toughest fullback in the history of Orange County, California. And all the time that Frank Rossi was scoring touchdowns and attracting college scouts, Dad was too involved with him to pay attention to his younger son.

The fact that Danny got good grades—which Frank never did—made no impression whatsoever. After all, his brother stood a mighty six feet two (a head taller than Danny), and his mere entrance on the field could bring a stadium of cheering people to their feet.

What could little bespectacled red-haired Danny do that earned applause? He was, or so his mother constantly reported, a gifted pianist. Almost a prodigy. This would have made most parents proud. And yet Dr. Rossi never once had come to hear him play in public.

Understandably, Danny felt enormous pangs of envy. And a resentment growing slowly into hatred. Frank is not a god, Dad. I'm a person, too. Sooner or later you're going to notice me.

But then in 1950, Frank, a fighter pilot, was shot down in Korea. Now Danny's pent-up jealousy transformed, in painful

6

stages, first to grief and then to guilt. He somehow felt responsible. As if he'd wished his brother's death.

At the ceremony in which they named the school athletic field for Frank, his father wept uncontrollably. Danny looked with anguish at the man he so admired. And he vowed to bring him consolation. Yet, how could he give his father joy?

Even hearing Danny practice annoyed Arthur Rossi. After all, a dentist's busy day was orchestrated to the grating noise of drills. And so he had a cork-lined studio built in the cellar for his sole surviving son.

Danny understood this was no act of generosity, that his father wished to be freed from the sight as well as the sound of him.

Yet, Danny was determined to keep fighting for his father's love. And he sensed sport was the only way for him to rise from the cellar of paternal disapproval.

There was just one possibility for a boy of his size—running. He went to see the track coach and asked shyly for advice.

He now got up at six each morning, slipped on sneakers, and left the house to train. His excessive zeal during those early weeks made his legs sore and heavy. But he persevered. And kept it all a secret. Till he had something worth telling Dad.

On the first day of spring, the coach made the entire squad run a mile to gauge their fitness. Danny was surprised that he could actually stay near the real runners for the first three quarters.

But suddenly his mouth was parched, his chest aflame. He started to slow down. From the center of the field he heard the coach call out, "Hang in there, Rossi. Don't give up."

Fearing the displeasure of this surrogate father, Danny drove his weary body through the final lap. And threw himself, exhausted, onto the grass. Before he could catch his breath, the coach was standing above him with a stopwatch.

"Not bad, Danny. You sure surprised me—five minutes forty-eight seconds. If you stick with it, you can go a heck of a lot faster. In fact, five minutes can sometimes cop third place in our dual meets. Go to the supply desk and get a uniform and spikes."

Sensing the proximity of his goal, Danny temporarily abandoned afternoon piano practice to work out with the team. And that usually meant ten or twelve grueling quarter-miles. He threw up after nearly every session.

*　　*　　*

Several weeks later, the coach announced that, as a reward for his tenacity, Danny would be their third-miler against Valley High.

That night he told his father. Despite his son's warning that he'd probably get badly beaten, Dr. Rossi insisted on attending.

That Saturday afternoon, Danny savored the three happiest minutes of his childhood.

As the fidgety runners lined up at the middle of the cinder track, Danny saw his parents sitting in the first row.

"Let's go, son," his father said warmly. "Show 'em the good old Rossi stuff."

These words so ignited Danny that he forgot the coach's instructions to take it easy and pace himself. Instead, as the gun went off, he bolted to the front and led the pack around the first turn.

Christ, thought Dr. Rossi, the kid's a champion.

Shit, thought the coach, the kid's crazy. He'll burn himself out.

As they completed the first lap, Danny glanced up at his father and saw what he had always thought impossible—a smile of pride for him.

"Seventy-one seconds," called the coach. "Too fast, Rossi. Much too fast."

"Looking good, son!" called Dr. Rossi.

Danny soared through the next four hundred yards on wings of paternal approval.

He passed the halfway mark still in the lead. But now his lungs were starting to burn. By the next curve, he had gone into oxygen debt. And was experiencing what runners not inaccurately call rigor mortis. He was dying.

The opposition sped past him and opened a long lead. From across the field he heard his father shout, "Come on, Danny, show some *guts*!"

They clapped when he finally finished. The sympathetic applause that greets the hopelessly outclassed competitor.

Dizzy with fatigue, he looked toward the stands. His mother was smiling reassuringly. His father was gone. It was like a bad dream.

Inexplicably, the coach was pleased. "Rossi, I've never seen a guy with more guts. I caught you in five minutes fifteen seconds. You've got real potential."

"Not on the track," Danny replied, limping away. "I quit."

He knew, to his chagrin, that all his efforts had only made matters worse. For his embarrassing performance had been on the track of Frank Rossi Field.

Humiliated, Danny returned to his previous life. The keyboard became an outlet for all his frustrations. He practiced day and night, to the exclusion of everything else.

He had been studying since he was six with a local teacher. But now this honorable gray-haired matron told his mother candidly that she had nothing more to give the boy. And suggested to Gisela Rossi that her son audition for Gustave Landau—a former soloist in Vienna, now spending his autumnal years as music director of nearby San Angelo Junior College.

The old man was impressed by what he heard and accepted Danny as a pupil.

"Dr. Landau says he's very good for his age," Gisela reported to her husband at dinner. "He thinks that he could even play professionally."

To which Dr. Rossi responded with a monosyllabic, "Oh." Which meant that he'd reserve all judgment.

Dr. Landau was a gentle if demanding mentor. And Danny was the ideal pupil. He was not only talented but actually eager to be driven. If Landau said go through an hour of Czerny's keyboard exercises every day, Danny would do three or four.

"Am I improving fast enough?" he'd ask anxiously.

"*Ach,* Daniel, you could even work yourself a little less. You're young. You should go out some evenings and have fun."

But Danny had no time—and knew nothing that would bring him "fun." He was in a hurry to grow up. And every waking moment when he was not in school, he spent at the piano.

Dr. Rossi was not unaware of his son's antisocial tendencies. And it upset him.

"I'm telling you, Gisela, it's unhealthy. He's too obsessive. Maybe he's trying to compensate for his shortness or something. A kid his age should be going out with girls. God knows Frank was a real Casanova by this time."

Art Rossi was distressed to think that a son of his could have turned out to be so . . . unmanly.

Mrs. Rossi, on the other hand, believed that if the two men were a little closer, her husband's qualms might disappear.

And so at the end of dinner the next evening, she left them on their own. So they could chat.

Her husband was perceptibly annoyed, since he always found talking to Danny a disquieting experience.

"Everything okay at school?" he inquired.

"Well, yes and no," Danny replied—just as uneasy as his father.

Like a nervous infantryman, Dr. Rossi feared he might be crossing into a minefield.

"What seems to be the matter?"

"Dad, everybody at school sort of thinks I'm weird. But a lot of musicians are like me."

Dr. Rossi began to sweat. "How is that, son?"

"Well, they're really passionate about it. I'm that way, too. I want to make music my life."

There was a brief pause as Dr. Rossi searched for an appropriate response.

"You're my boy," he said at last, as an evasive alternative to an expression of sincere affection.

"Thanks, Dad. I think I'll go down and practice now."

After Danny left, Art Rossi poured himself a drink and thought, I guess I should be grateful. A passion for music was better than several others he could have imagined.

Just after his sixteenth birthday, Danny made his debut as a soloist with the Junior College Symphony. Under the baton of his mentor, he played Brahms's arduous Second Piano Concerto before a packed auditorium that included his parents.

As Danny stepped on stage, pale with fright, his glasses caught the glare of the primitive spotlight, nearly blinding him. When at last he reached the piano, he felt paralyzed.

Dr. Landau walked over and whispered, "Don't worry, Daniel, you are ready."

Danny's terror magically dissipated.

The applause seemed to go on forever.

As he bowed and turned to shake his teacher's hand, Danny was startled to see tears in the old man's eyes.

Landau embraced his protégé.

*   *   *

"You know, Dan, you made me real proud tonight."

Ordinarily, a son so long starved for paternal affection would have been ecstatic to get such a compliment. But that evening Daniel Rossi had been intoxicated by a new emotion: the adoration of a crowd.

From the time he entered high school, Danny had his heart set on going to Harvard, where he could study composition with Randall Thompson, choral master, and Walter Piston, virtuoso symphonist. This alone gave him the inspiration to slog through science, math, and civics.

For sentimental reasons, Dr. Rossi would have liked to see his son at Princeton, the university celebrated by F. Scott Fitzgerald. And which would have been Frank's alma mater.

But Danny was impervious to all persuasion. And finally Art Rossi stopped his campaign.

"I can't get anywhere with him. Let the kid go where he wants."

But something occurred to shake the dentist's laissez-faire attitude. In 1954, the zealous Senator McCarthy was focusing his scrutiny upon "that Commie sanctuary Harvard." Some of its professors would not cooperate with his committee and discuss their colleagues' politics.

Worse, the President of Harvard, the stubborn Dr. Pusey, then refused to fire them as Joe McCarthy had demanded.

"Son," Dr. Rossi asked with growing frequency, "how can anyone whose brother died protecting us from communism even dream of going to that kind of school?"

Danny remained taciturn. What was the point of answering that music isn't political?

As Dr. Rossi persevered with his objections, Danny's mother tried desperately not to take sides. And so Dr. Landau was the only person with whom Danny could discuss his great dilemma.

The old man was as circumspect as possible. And yet he confessed to Danny, "This McCarthy frightens me. You know, they started out in Germany like this."

He paused uneasily, now pained by unhealed memories.

Then he continued softly, "Daniel, there is fear throughout the country. Senator McCarthy thinks he can dictate to Harvard, tell them whom to fire and so forth. I think their president has shown enormous bravery. In fact, I wish I could express to him my admiration."

"How could you do that, Dr. Landau?"

The old man leaned slightly toward his brilliant pupil and said, "I would send them you."

The Ides of May arrived and with them letters of acceptance. Princeton, Harvard, Yale, and Stanford all wanted Danny. Even Dr. Rossi was impressed—although he feared his son might make a fatal choice.

Armageddon came that weekend when he summoned Danny to his cordovan-upholstered study. And asked the crucial question.

"Yes, Dad," he answered diffidently, "I'm going to Harvard."

There was a deathly silence.

Up till now, Danny had cherished the unconscious hope that when his father saw the strength of his conviction, he would finally relent.

But Arthur Rossi was as adamant as stone.

"Dan, this is a free country. And you're entitled to go to whatever college you desire. But I'm also free to express my own dissent. And so I choose not to pay a penny of your bills. Congratulations, son, you're on your own. You've just declared your independence."

For an instant Danny felt confused and lost. Then, as he studied his father's face, he began to comprehend that this McCarthy business was just a pretext. Art Rossi simply didn't give a damn for him at all.

And he realized that he had to rise above his childish need for this man's approbation.

For now he knew he'd never get it. Never.

"Okay, Dad," he whispered hoarsely, "if that's the way you want it. . . ."

He turned and left the room without another word. Through the heavy door, he heard a timpani of punches pounding savagely on his father's desk.

Yet strangely he felt free.

JASON GILBERT, JR.

joy was his song and joy so pure
a heart of star by him could steer
and pure so now and now so yes
the wrists of twilight would rejoice.
. . . .
his flesh was flesh his blood was blood:
no hungry man but wished him food;
no cripple wouldn't creep one mile
uphill to only see him smile.

e.e. cummings
CLASS OF 1915

He was the Golden Boy. A tall and blond Apollo with the kind of magnetism women loved and men admired. He excelled at every sport he played. His teachers adored him, for despite his universal popularity, he was soft-spoken and respectful.

In short, he was that rare young man whom every parent dreams of as a son. And every woman dreams of as a lover.

It would be tempting to say that Jason Gilbert, Jr., was the American Dream. Certainly a lot of people thought so. But beneath his dazzling exterior there was a single inner blemish. A tragic flaw he had inherited from generations of his ancestors.

Jason Gilbert had been born Jewish.

His father had worked hard to camouflage the fact. For Jason Gilbert, Sr., knew from the bruises of his Brooklyn childhood that being Jewish was a handicap, an albatross around the soul. Life would be far better if everyone could simply be *American*.

He had long considered disposing of the liability of his last name. And finally, one autumn afternoon in 1933, a circuit court judge gave Jacob Gruenwald a new life as Jason Gilbert.

Two years later, at his country club's spring ball, he met

13

Betsy Newman, blond, petite, and freckle-faced. They had a great deal in common. Love of theater, dancing, outdoor sports. Not least of all, they shared a passionate indifference to the practices of their ancestral faith.

To avoid the pressures from their more religious relatives to have a "proper" ceremony, they decided to elope.

Their marriage was a happy one whose joy was magnified in 1937 when Betsy gave birth to a boy, whom they named Jason, Jr.

The very moment that he heard the splendid news, in the smoke-filled waiting room, the elder Gilbert made a silent vow. He would protect his newborn son from suffering the slightest hardship because he was of nominally Jewish parents. No, this boy would grow up and be a first-class member of American society.

By this point Gilbert, Sr., was executive vice-president of the rapidly expanding National Communications Corporation. He and Betsy were living on a lush three-acre homestead in growing—and unghettoed—Syosset, Long Island.

Three years later, baby sister Julie came along. Like her brother, she inherited her mother's blue eyes and blond hair—though only Julie got the freckles.

Their childhood was idyllic. Both seemed to thrive on the regimen of self-improvement that their father had devised for them. It began with swimming and continued with riding and tennis instruction. And, of course, skiing on their winter holidays.

Young Jason was prepared with loving rigor to become a demon of the tennis courts.

First he was tutored at a nearby club. But when he showed the promise that his father had fully expected, each Saturday the elder Gilbert personally drove his budding champion to Forest Hills for coaching by Ricardo Lopez, former Wimbledon and U.S. champion. Dad watched every minute of the sessions, shouting encouragement and reveling in Jason's progress.

The Gilberts had intended to bring up their children with no religion at all. But they soon discovered that, even in a place as easygoing as Syosset, no one could exist in unaffiliated limbo. It was worse than being . . . something second rate.

Fortune dealt them yet another ace when a new Unitarian church was built nearby. They were accepted cordially, though their participation was sporadic, to say the least. They hardly ever went on Sundays. At Christmas they were on the slopes and Easter on the beach. But at least they belonged.

Both parents were intelligent enough to know that trying to raise their children as Mayflower WASPs would ultimately cause them psychological perplexities. And so they taught their son and daughter that their Jewish background was like a little rivulet that poured from the Old Country to join with the mighty mainstream of American society.

Julie went away to boarding school, but Jason opted to remain at home and attend Hawkins-Atwell Academy. He loved Syosset, and was especially reluctant to give up the chance of dating girls. Which, next to tennis, was his favorite sport. And in which he was equally successful.

Admittedly, he was no whirlwind in the classroom. Still, his grades were good enough to all but guarantee admission to the university he and his father dreamed of—Yale.

The reasons were both intellectual and emotional. The Yale man seemed a tripartite aristocrat—gentleman, scholar, and athlete. And Jason simply *looked* like he was born to go there.

And yet the envelope that arrived on the morning of May 12 was suspiciously underweight, suggesting that its message was short. It was also painful.

Yale had rejected him.

The Gilberts' consternation turned to rage when they learned that Tony Rawson, whose grades were certainly no better than Jason's, and whose backhand most assuredly was worse, had been accepted at New Haven.

Jason's father insisted on an immediate audience with the school headmaster, himself an old Yalie.

"Mr. Trumbull," he demanded, "can you possibly explain how they could reject my son and take young Rawson?"

The gray-templed educator puffed at his pipe and replied, "You must understand, Mr. Gilbert, Rawson is a Yale 'legacy.' His father and grandfather were both Old Blues. That counts for a lot up there. The feeling for tradition runs extremely deep."

"All right, all right," the elder Gilbert responded, "but could you give me a plausible explanation of why a boy like Jason, a real gentleman, a great athlete—"

"Please, Dad," Jason interrupted, increasingly embarrassed.

But his father persisted. "Could you tell me why your alma mater wouldn't want a man like him?"

Trumbull leaned back on his chair and replied, "Well, Mr. Gilbert, I'm not privy to the actual deliberations of the Yale committee. But I do know that the boys in New Haven like to have a 'balanced mix' in every class."

"Mix?"

"Yes, you know," the headmaster explained matter-of-factly, "there's the question of geographical distribution, of alumni sons—as in Tony's case. Then there's the proportion of high school and prep school students, musicians, athletes. . . ."

By now Jason's father knew what Trumbull was implying. "Mr. Trumbull," he inquired with all the restraint he could still muster, "this 'mix' you refer to, does it also include—religious background?"

"In fact, yes," the headmaster answered affably. "Yale doesn't have what you would call a quota. But it does, to some extent, limit the number of Jewish students it accepts."

"That's against the law!"

"I should hardly think so," Trumbull replied. "Jews are—what?—two and a half percent of the national population? I'd wager Yale accepts at least four times that number."

Gilbert, Sr., was not about to wager. For he sensed that the older man knew the exact percentage of Jews accepted annually by his alma mater.

Jason feared an angry storm was brewing and longed at all cost to avert it.

"Look, Dad, I don't want to go to a school that doesn't want me. As far as I'm concerned, Yale can go to hell."

He then turned to the headmaster and said apologetically, "Excuse me, sir."

"Not at all," Trumbull responded. "A perfectly understandable reaction. Now let's think positively. After all, your second choice is a very good school. Some people even think Harvard is the best college in the country."

TED LAMBROS

Great God, I ask thee for no meaner pelf
Than that I may not disappoint myself,
That in my action I may soar as high,
As I can now discern with this clear eye.

HENRY DAVID THOREAU
CLASS OF 1837

♦

All sensible people are selfish.

RALPH WALDO EMERSON
CLASS OF 1821

He was a commuter. A member of that small and near-invisible minority whose finances were not sufficient to allow them the luxury of living with their classmates on campus. Thus, they were Harvard men only by day—a part and yet apart—forced to return at night by bus or subway to the real world.

Ironically, Ted Lambros had been born almost in the shadow of the Yard. His father, Socrates, who had come to America from Greece in the early thirties, was the popular proprietor of The Marathon restaurant on Massachusetts Avenue, a brisk walk north from Widener Library.

In his establishment, as he would frequently boast to members of his staff (in other words, his family), more great minds would nightly gather than ever had "symposiazed" at the Academy of Plato. Not just philosophers, but Nobel Prize winners in

17

physics, chemistry, medicine, and economics. And even Mrs. Julia Child, who had pronounced his wife's lamb in lemons "most amusing."

Moreover, his son Theodore attended Cambridge High and Latin School, so very near the sacred precinct that it was almost part of the college itself.

Since the elder Lambros held the members of the faculty in a reverence bordering on idolatry, it was natural that his son grew up with a passionate desire to go to Harvard.

At sixteen, the tall and darkly handsome Theodore was promoted to full waiterhood, thus bringing him in closer contact with these academic luminaries. Ted felt a thrill when they merely said good evening to him.

He wondered why. Just what was this Harvardian charisma he could sense even in the briefest motion of depositing a plate of Kleftiko?

One apocalyptic evening, it at last became clear. They had such uncanny confidence. Self-assurance emanated from these dignitaries like a halo—whether they were discussing metaphysics or the merits of a new instructor's wife.

Being the son of an insecure immigrant, Ted especially admired their ability to love themselves and treasure their own intellects.

And it gave him a goal in life. He wanted to become one of them. Not just an undergraduate but an actual professor. And his father shared the dream.

Much to the discomfort of the other Lambros children, Daphne and Alexander, Papa would often rhapsodize at dinner about Ted's glorious future.

"I don't know why everybody thinks he's so great," young Alex would grudgingly retort.

"Because he is," said Socrates with mantic fervor. "Theo is this family's true *lambros*." He smiled at his pun on their last name, which in Greek meant "gleam" or "brilliance."

From Ted's small room on Prescott Street, where he grinded well into the night, he could see the lights of Harvard Yard barely two hundred yards away. So close, so very close. And if his concentration ever flagged, he would rouse himself by thinking, "Hang in, Lambros, you're almost there." For, like Odysseus in the swirling sea around Phaeacia, he could actually perceive the goal of all his long and mighty struggles.

Consistent with these epic fantasies, he dreamed about the maiden who'd be waiting for him on this magic isle. A golden-haired young princess like Nausicaa. Ted's Harvard dreams embraced the Radcliffe girls as well.

Thus, when he read the *Odyssey* for senior English honors class and reached book 6—Nausicaa's great infatuation with the handsome Greek washed up on her shore—he saw it as an augury of the delirious reception he would get when at last he arrived.

But Ted's straight A in that English course was one of the very few he received all year. In fact, most of the time he earned solid if not brilliant B-pluses. He was more plugger than slugger. So could he dare hope to be admitted to Fair Harvard?

He stood merely seventh in his class, with College-Board scores only slightly higher than average. True, Harvard usually sought out well-rounded individuals. But Ted adjudged himself to be a square. For after studying and waitering, where was the time to learn the harp or go out for a team? He was somberly objective and kept trying to persuade his father not to expect the impossible.

But Papa Lambros was unswervingly optimistic. He was confident that Ted's letters of recommendation from the "gigantic personalities" who dined at The Marathon would have a magical effect.

And in a way, they did. Ted Lambros was accepted—albeit without financial aid. This meant he was condemned to remain in his cell on Prescott Street, unable to taste the joys of Harvard life beyond the classroom. For he would have to spend his evenings slaving at The Marathon to earn the six-hundred-dollar tuition.

Still Ted was undaunted. Though he was only at the foothills of Olympus, at least he was there, ready to climb.

For Ted believed in the American dream. That if you wanted something badly enough and devoted your heart and soul to it, you would ultimately succeed.

And he wanted Harvard with the same "unperishable fire" that drove Achilles till he conquered Troy.

But then Achilles didn't have to wait on tables every night.

ANDREW ELIOT

No! I am not Prince Hamlet, nor was meant to be;
Am an attendant lord, one that will do
To swell a progress, start a scene or two,
Advise the prince; no doubt, an easy tool,
Deferential, glad to be of use,
Politic, cautious, and meticulous;
Full of high sentence, but a bit obtuse. . . .

T.S. ELIOT
CLASS OF 1910

The newest Eliot to enter Harvard continued a tradition that began in 1649.

Andrew had a privileged childhood.

Even after they had gracefully divorced, his parents lavished on him all a growing boy could wish for. He had an English nanny and a horde of teddy bears. And from as early as he could recall, they sent him to the most expensive boarding schools and summer camps. They established a trust fund, making his future secure.

In short, they gave him everything except their interest and attention.

Of course they loved him. That went without saying. Perhaps that is why they never actually said it. They simply assumed he would know that they appreciated what a fine and independent son he was.

Yet, Andrew was the first of his entire family to feel himself unworthy of admission to Harvard. As he often joked self-deprecatingly, "They let me in because my name was Eliot and I could spell it."

Clearly, his ancestry cast giant shadows on his confidence. And, quite understandably, what he regarded as a lack of creativity only magnified his innate inferiority complex.

Actually, he was a rather bright young man. He had a modest way with words—as witnessed by the diary he kept from prep school onward. He played soccer well. He was a wing whose corner kicks helped many a center-forward score.

That was an index of his personality—he was always happy when he could assist a friend.

And off the field he was kind, thoughtful, and considerate.

Most of all, though he would not have arrogated such a distinction for himself, he was considered by his many friends a *darn nice guy.*

The university was proud to have him. But, Andrew Eliot '58 had a quality that set him apart from every other member of his Harvard class.

He was not ambitious.

Just after 5:00 A.M. on September 20, a Greyhound bus reached the dingy terminal in downtown Boston and disgorged, among its passengers, a tired and sweaty Daniel Rossi. His clothing was a mass of wrinkles and his reddish hair unkempt. Even his glasses were fogged with transcontinental grime.

He had left the West Coast three days earlier with sixty dollars in his pocket, of which he still had fifty-two. For he had all but starved his way across America.

Totally exhausted, he was barely able to drag his single suitcase (full of music scores he'd studied on the journey, and a shirt or two) down to the subway for Harvard Square. First he trudged to Holworthy 6, his freshman lodgings in the Yard, then registered as quickly as possible so that he could return to Boston and transfer from his California branch to Local No. 9 of the Musicians Union.

"Don't get your hopes up, kid," cautioned the secretary. "We got a million piano players out of work. Actually, the only keyboard jobs available are holy ones. You see, the Lord just pays the union minimum." Pointing her long, vermilion-painted fingernail toward the small white notices pinned on a bulletin board, she added wryly, "Choose your religion, kid."

After a careful study of the possibilities, Danny returned with two scraps of paper.

"These would be great for me," he said. "Organist on Friday night and Saturday morning at the temple in Malden, and Sunday morning at this church in Quincy. Are they still available?"

"That's why they're hangin' there, kid. But, as you can see, the bread they're offering's more like Ritz crackers."

"Yeah," Danny replied, "but I can really use whatever money

I can get my hands on. Do you get many Saturday-night dance gigs?"

"Gee, you sure seem hungry. Got a big family to support or somethin'?"

"No. I'm a freshman at Harvard and need the dough for tuition."

"How come those rich guys in Cambridge didn't give you a scholarship?"

"It's a long story," Danny said uneasily. "But I'd be grateful if you'd keep me in mind. In any case, I'll stay in touch."

"I'm sure you will, kid."

Just before eight the preceding day, Jason Gilbert, Jr., had awakened in Syosset, Long Island.

The sun always seemed to shine more brightly in his bedroom. Perhaps it was reflected from his many glittering trophies.

He shaved, put on a new Chemise Lacoste, then hauled his luggage, as well as assorted tennis and squash rackets, down to his 1950 Mercury coupé convertible. He was looking forward to roaring up the Post Road in the buggy he had lovingly rebuilt with his own hands, souping it up and even adding a dual fiberglass exhaust.

The entire Gilbert household—Mom, Dad, Julie, Jenny the housekeeper and her husband Maxwell the gardener—were waiting to see him off.

There was much kissing and embracing. And a short valedictory from his father.

"Son, I won't wish you luck because you don't need it. You were born to be number one—and not just on the tennis court."

Though Jason did not show it, these parting words had the opposite of their intended effect. For he was already uneasy at the prospect of leaving home and testing his mettle against the real big leaguers of his generation. That last-minute reminder of Dad's high expectations made him even more nervous.

Still, he might have taken comfort had he known that his adoring father's speech had been echoed several hundred times that day by several hundred other parents who were also sending their uniquely gifted progeny off to Cambridge, Massachusetts.

Five hours later, Jason stood outside his assigned freshman dormitory, Straus A-32, on which a scrap of torn yellow paper was taped.

To my roommate: I always nap in the afternoon,
so please be quiet.
                    Thank you.

It was signed simply "D.D."

Jason quietly unlocked the door and carried his baggage practically on tiptoe into the one free bedroom. After placing his suitcases on the metal bed (it creaked slightly), he glanced out the window.

He had a view—and all the noise—of hectic Harvard Square. But Jason didn't mind. He was actually in a buoyant mood, since there was still enough time left to stroll to Soldier's Field and find a pickup game of tennis. Already dressed in white, he merely grabbed his Wilson and a can of Spauldings.

Luckily, he recognized a varsity player who had defeated him in a summer tournament two years earlier. The guy was happy to see Jason again, agreed to hit a few, and then quickly learned how much the new arrival had improved.

When he got back to Straus Hall, there was another yellow note on the door, announcing that D.D. had gone to dinner and would then proceed to the library (the *library*—they hadn't even registered!) to study, and would be back just before 10:00 P.M. If his roommate planned on coming in after that, would he be kind enough to be as quiet as possible.

Jason showered, put on a fresh Haspel cord jacket, grabbed a quick bite at a cafeteria in the Square, then tooled up to Radcliffe to scout the freshman girls. He returned about ten-thirty and was duly respectful of his unseen roommate's need for rest.

The next morning he woke to find yet another note.

I have gone to register.
If my mother calls, tell her I had a good
dinner last night.
                    Thanks.

Jason crumpled up this latest communiqué and marched off to join the line that now stretched well around the block outside Memorial Hall.

The high intentions of his message notwithstanding, the elusive D.D. was not by any means the first member of The Class to register. For at the very stroke of nine, the large portals of Memorial Hall had opened to admit Theodore Lambros.

Three minutes earlier, Ted had left his home on Prescott Street to stride over and claim a tiny but indelible place in the history of the oldest college in America.

To his mind, he had entered Paradise.

A ndrew Eliot's father drove him down from Maine in the family's vintage station wagon, laden with carefully packed trunks containing tweed and shetland jackets, white buck shoes, assorted moccasins, rep ties, and a term's supply of button-down and tab-collar shirts. In short, his school uniforms.

As usual, father and son did not speak much to each other. Too many centuries of Eliots had gone through this same rite of passage to make conversation necessary.

They parked by the gate closest to Massachusetts Hall (some of whose earlier occupants had been George Washington's soldiers). Andrew ran into the Yard and rushed up to Wig G-21 to enlist the aid of his former prep school buddies in hauling his gear. Then, as they were toting barge and lifting bale, he found himself momentarily standing alone with his father. Mr. Eliot took the occasion to impart a bit of worldly advice.

"Son," he began, "I would be very grateful if you did your best not to flunk out of here. For though there are innumerable secondary schools in this great land of ours, there is only one Harvard."

Andrew gratefully acknowledged this astute paternal counsel, shook his father's hand, and raced off to the dorm. His two roommates had already begun to help him unpack. Unpack his liquor, that is. They were toasting their reunion after a summer of self-styled debauchery in Europe.

"Hey, you guys," he protested, "you could at least have asked me. Besides, we've got to go register."

"Come off it, Eliot," said Dickie Newall as he took another swig. "We walked past there just a while ago and there's a line around the goddamn block."

"Yeah," Michael Wigglesworth affirmed, "all the weenies want to get there first. The race, as we well know, is not always to the swift."

"I think it is at Harvard," Andrew politely suggested. "But in any case, it isn't to the smashed. I'm going over."

"I knew it." Newall sniggered. "Old Eliot, my man, you've got the makings of a first-class wonk."

Andrew persisted, undaunted by this preppie persiflage. "I'm going, guys."

"Go on," Newall said, dismissing him with a haughty wave. "If you hurry back we'll save you some of your Haig & Haig. By the way, where's the rest of it?"

And so Andrew Eliot marched through Harvard Yard to join the long, winding thread of humanity—and ultimately to be woven into the multicolored fabric called The Class of '58.

B y now The Class was all in Cambridge, though it would take several hours more for the last of them to be officially enrolled.

Inside the cavernous hall, beneath a giant stained-glass window, stood the future leaders of the world. Nobel Prize winners, tycoons of industry, brain surgeons, and a few dozen insurance salesmen.

First they were handed large manila envelopes with all the forms to be signed (in quadruplicate for the Financial Office, quintuplicate for the Registrar, and, inexplicably, sextuplicate for the Health Department). For all this paperwork they sat side by side at narrow tables that stretched forever and seemed to meet only in infinity.

Among the questionnaires to be completed was one for Phillips Brooks House, part of which asked for religious affiliation (response was optional).

Though none of them was particularly pious, Andrew Eliot, Danny Rossi, and Ted Lambros marked the boxes next to Episcopal, Catholic, and Greek Orthodox, respectively. Jason Gilbert, on the other hand, indicated that he had no religious affiliation whatsoever.

After the official registration, they had to run an endless gauntlet of wild, paper-waving proselytizers, all vociferously urging Harvard's now-official freshmen to join the Young Democrats, Republicans, Liberals, Conservatives, mountain climbers, scuba divers, and so on.

Countless irrepressible student hucksters noisily cajoled them to subscribe to the *Crimson* ("Cambridge's only breakfast-table daily"), the *Advocate* ("so you can say you read these guys before they got their Pulitzers"), and the *Lampoon* ("if you work it out, it comes to about a penny a laugh"). In short, none but the most determined misers or abject paupers emerged with wallets unscathed.

Ted Lambros could sign up for nothing as his schedule was already fully committed to courses academic by day and culinary by night.

Danny Rossi put his name down for the Catholic Club, assuming that religious girls would be a little shier and therefore easier to meet. Maybe they would even be as inexperienced as he.

Andrew Eliot made his way through all this welter like a seasoned explorer routinely hacking through dense foliage. The kind of social clubs that he'd be joining did their recruitment in a more sedate and far less public fashion.

And Jason Gilbert, except for buying a quick subscription to the *Crimson* (so he could send the chronicles of his achievements home to Dad and Mom), strode calmly through the phalanx of barkers, much like his ancestors had traversed the Red Sea, and returned to Straus.

Miracle of miracles, the mysterious D.D. was actually awake. Or at least his bedroom door was open and someone was lying on the bed, face enveloped by a physics text.

Jason hazarded direct discourse. "Hi there, are you D.D?"

A pair of thick, horn-rimmed spectacles cautiously peeked above the book.

"Are you my roommate?" a nervous voice responded.

"Well, I've been assigned to Straus A thirty-two," Jason answered.

"Then you're my roommate," the young man logically concluded. And after carefully marking with a paper clip the line where he had left off reading, he put down his book, rose and offered a somewhat cold and clammy hand.

"I'm David Davidson," he said.

"Jason Gilbert."

D.D. then eyed his roommate suspiciously and asked, "You don't smoke, do you?"

"No, it's bad for the wind. Why do you ask, Dave?"

"Please, I prefer to be called David," he replied. "I ask because I specifically requested a nonsmoking roommate. Actually I wanted a single, but they don't allow freshmen to live alone."

"Where are you from?" Jason inquired.

"New York. Bronx High School of Science. I was a finalist in the Westinghouse Competition. And you?"

"Long Island. Syosset. All I've been is finalist in a couple of tennis tournaments. Do you play any sport, David?"

"No," the young scholar replied. "They're all a waste of time. Besides, I'm pre-med. I have to take things like Chem Twenty. What's your chosen career, Jason?"

God, thought Jason, do I have to be interviewed just to be this wonk's cellmate?

"To tell the truth, I haven't decided yet. But while I'm thinking about it, shouldn't we go out and buy some basic furniture for the living room?"

"What for?" D.D. asked warily. "We each have a bed, a desk, and a chair. What else do we need?"

"Well," said Jason, "a couch might be nice. You know, to relax and study in during the week. We could also use an icebox. So we'd have something cold to serve people on the weekends."

"People?" D.D. inquired, somewhat agitated. "Do you intend to have parties here?"

Jason was running out of patience.

"Tell me, David, did you specifically request an introverted monk as your roommate?"

"No."

"Well, you didn't get one. Now, are you going to chip in for a second-hand couch or not?"

"*I* don't need a couch," he replied sanctimoniously.

"Okay," said Jason, "then I'll pay for it myself. But if I ever see you sitting on it, I'll charge you rent."

◆

Andrew Eliot, Mike Wigglesworth, and Dickie Newall spent all that afternoon scouring the furniture emporia in and around the Square and procured the finest leatherette pieces available. After expending three hours and $195, they stood at the ground floor of G-entry with all their treasures.

"God," Newall exclaimed, "I shudder to think how many lovelies will succumb on this incredible chaise longue. I mean they'll just take one look at it, disrobe, and hop right on."

"In that case, Dickie," Andrew interrupted his old buddy's reverie, "we'd better lug it up the stairs. If a Cliffie passes while we're standing here you might just have to perform in public."

"Don't think I couldn't," Newall answered with bravado, quickly adding, "come on let's get this paraphernalia up the stairs. Andy and I'll take the couch." And then, turning to the largest member of their trio, he called out, "Can you manage that chair by yourself, Wigglesworth?"

"No sweat," the tall athlete replied laconically. And with that he lifted the huge armchair, placed it on his head as if it were a large padded football helmet, and started up the stairwell.

"That's our mighty Mike," Newall quipped. "Fair Harvard's future crew immortal and the first man from this college who'll play Tarzan in the movies."

◆

"Just three more steps. Please, you guys," Danny Rossi implored.

"Hey, listen, kid, the deal was we'd *deliver* it. You didn't say there would be stairs. We always take pianos in an elevator."

"Come on," Danny protested, "you guys knew that they don't have any in Harvard dorms. What's it going to take for you to deliver this up just three more steps into my room?"

"Another twenty bucks," replied one of the burly delivery men.

"Hey, look, the damn piano only cost me thirty-five."

"Take it or leave it, kid. Or you'll be singin' in the rain."

"I can't afford twenty bucks," Danny moaned.

"Tough titty, Harvard boy," growled the more talkative of the two movers. And they ambled off.

Danny sat there on the steps of Holworthy for several minutes pondering his great dilemma. And then the notion came to him.

He placed the rickety stool in position, lifted the lid of the ancient upright, and began, first tentatively and then with increasing assurance, to animate the fading ivories with "The Varsity Drag."

Since most of the windows in the Yard were open because of the Indian Summer weather, it was not long before a crowd surrounded him. Some spirited freshmen even began to dance. To get in shape for conquests up at Radcliffe and on other social battlefields.

He was terrific. And his classmates were genuinely thrilled to discover what a talent they had in their midst. ("The guy's another Peter Nero," someone remarked.) At last Danny finished—or thought he had. But everybody clapped and shouted for more. So he started taking requests for pieces as varied as "The Saber Dance" and "Three Coins in the Fountain."

At last, a university policeman happened on the scene. It was just what Danny had been hoping for.

"Listen," the officer growled, "you can't play a pianer outside in the Yard. You gotta move this here instrument into a dorm."

The freshmen booed.

"Hey, listen," Danny Rossi said to his enthusiastic audience. "Why don't we all bring this piano up the stairs to my room and then I'll play all night."

There were cheers of assent as half a dozen of the strongest present started carrying Danny's upright with festive alacrity.

"Wait a minute," the cop warned, "remember, no playing after ten P.M. Them are the rules."

More hisses, boos, and grunts as Danny Rossi politely answered, "Yes, sir, Officer. I promise I'll only play till dinnertime."

◆

Though he, of course, was not privileged to be moving from the cubicle he'd occupied throughout his high school days, Ted Lambros nonetheless spent much of that afternoon purchasing essential items in The Coop.

First and foremost, a green bookbag, a must for every serious Harvard man—a utilitarian talisman that carried the tools of your trade and identified you as a bona fide scholar. He also bought a large, rectangular crimson banner whose white felt letters proudly boasted "Harvard—Class of 1958." And, while other freshmen were hanging identical chauvinistic fabrics on the walls of their dormitories in the Yard, Ted hung his over the desk in his tiny bedroom.

For good measure, he acquired an impressive-looking pipe from Leavitt & Pierce, which he would someday learn to smoke.

As the afternoon waned, he checked and rechecked his carefully purchased secondhand wardrobe and inwardly pronounced himself ready to meet tomorrow's Harvard challenge.

And then, the magic aura broken, he headed up Massachusetts Avenue to The Marathon, where he would have to don the same old hokey costume in order to serve lamb to the lions of Cambridge.

♦

It was a day of standing on lines. First in the morning at Memorial Hall, and then just after 6:00 P.M., when the dinner column began to form at the Freshman Union, winding outside, down its granite steps, and almost into Quincy Street. Naturally, each freshman wore a tie and jacket—although the garments varied in color and quality, depending on the means and background of the wearer. The rules explicitly proclaimed that the only civilized attire in which a Harvard man could take a meal.

But these formally accoutred gentlemen were in for a rude surprise. There were no dishes.

Instead, their food was scooped out into a tan plastic doggy bowl divided into unequal sections of undetermined purpose. The only rational compartment was the cavity within the hub of this contraption, which could hold a glass of milk.

Ingenious as it was, it could not hide the fact that freshman food was absolutely wretched.

What was that gray sliced stuff slapped at them at the first station? The serving biddies claimed it was meat. It looked like innersoles to most and tasted much that way to all. It was no consolation that they could eat all they wanted. For who would ever want more of this unchewable enigma?

The only real salvation was the ice cream. It was plentiful and filling. And to an eighteen-year-old this can compensate for almost any culinary lapse. And did so in prodigious quantities.

No one really bitched in earnest. For, although not all of them admitted it, they were excited just to *be* there. The tasteless food gave every person in The Class an opportunity to be superior to *something*. Nearly all of them were used to being number one in some domain. The Class contained no fewer than 287 high school valedictorians, each painfully aware that only one of them was good enough to match that achievement at Harvard.

By some uncanny instinct, the jocks had already started to discover one another. At one round table in the outer circle, Clancy Roberts was subtly campaigning for the freshman hockey captaincy. At yet another, football linemen, who had met an hour earlier at Dillon Field House, savored what would be among the last meals they would be obliged to take with the plebs. For, once the pads were on, they'd be dining at the training table in the V-Club, where the meat, though no less gray, would be served twice as thick.

The huge, wood-paneled hall reverberated with the loud chatter of nervous freshmen. You could tell who had gone to high schools and who to prep schools. For the latter dressed in matching plumage—shetland jackets and rep ties—and ate in larger groups, whose conversation and laughter were homogenized. The would-be physicist from Omaha, the poet from Missouri, and the future lawyer-politician from Atlanta ate alone. Or, if after twenty-four hours they could still stand them, with their roommates.

Harvard did not choose your living companions without much deliberation and analysis. Indeed, some keen sadistic genius must have spent innumerable hours on this strange apportionment. And what a task it was—a smorgasbord containing eleven hundred wholly different dishes. What would you serve with what? What would go well and what give interpersonal dyspepsia? Someone in the administration knew. Or at least thought he did.

Of course, they asked you for your preferences. Nonsmoker, athlete, interested in art, et cetera. Preppies naturally requested and received accommodations with their buddies. But then, they were the few conformists in this monstrous colony of oddballs, where exceptions were the norm.

What, for example, could they do with Danny Rossi, whose singular request had been a dormitory as near as possible to Paine Hall, the music building? Put him with another music type? No, that might risk a clash of egos. And what Harvard wanted was harmonious tranquility among its freshmen, who that week were in the process of receiving the most agonizing lesson of their lives. They were about to learn that the world did not spin uniquely around them.

For reasons inexplicable to everyone except the college powers, Danny Rossi was assigned to share his rooms in Holworthy with Kingman Wu, a Chinese future architect from San Diego (perhaps the link was California), and Bernie Ackerman, a mathematics whiz and champion fencer from New Trier High School in a suburb of Chicago.

As they all ate dinner at the Union that evening, it was Bernie who tried to puzzle out why they three had been thrown together by the mandarins of Harvard roommate-ism.

"It's the stick," he offered as a solution. "That's the only symbol that connects us three."

"Is that supposed to be profound or just obscene?" asked Kingman Wu.

"Hell, don't you see it?" Ackerman persisted. "Danny's going to be a great conductor. What do those guys wave at an orchestra? Batons. Me, I've got the biggest stick, 'cause I'm a fencer. Get it now?"

"And me?" asked Wu.

"What do architects most often draw with? Pencils, pens. There's the three sticks and the solution to the mystery of our being put together."

The Chinaman was not impressed. "You've just awarded me the smallest one." He frowned.

"Well, you know where to stick it, then," Ackerman suggested with a self-congratulatory chuckle.

And thus the first eternal enmity among The Class of '58 was born.

◆

In spite of his outward self-assurance, Jason Gilbert was nervous about going to the Union on his own for that inaugural repast. So desperate was he that he actually sought out D.D. in order to propose they go together. Alas, his roommate was already back before Jason had even dressed.

"I was the third on line," he boasted. "I had eleven ice creams. That'll really please my mom."

So Jason ventured out alone. As luck would have it, near the steps of Widener Library he ran into a guy he'd played (and beaten) in the quarter finals of the Greater Metropolitan Private Schools Tourney. The fellow proudly introduced his quondam rival to his current roommates as "the S.O.B. who's going to knock me off for number one. Unless that guy from California beats us both."

Jason was happy to join them, and the talk was mostly of the tennis court. And the wretched food. And doggy bowls, of course.

September 21, 1954

My roommates and I celebrated our first night at Harvard by not eating there. We elected instead to go into Boston, have a quick meal at the Union Oyster House, and then move on to Scollay Square, the sole oasis of sleaze in the city's desert of puritanical decency.

Here we attended the edifying spectacle at the Old Howard. This venerable burlesque theater has housed the legendary strippers of the age, not least of whom was tonight's attraction, Irma the Body.

After the performance (if that's the word for it), we all dared one another to go backstage and invite the leading lady to join us sophisticates for a drop of champagne. First we thought of composing an elegant epistle ("Dear Miss Body . . ."), but then decided a live emissary would be more effective.

At this point there were huge piles of braggadocio being hurled back and forth. Each of us showed our tremendous latent courage by pretending to be on our way in. Yet no one took more than two steps toward that stage door.

I then came up with a brilliant solution: "Hey, why don't we *all* go?"

We all eyed one another to see who'd be first to respond. But no one did.

Then, in a sudden, inexplicable fit of conscientiousness, we unanimously decided that discretion bade us get some sleep to prepare us for the rigors of a Harvard education. The spirit, we reasoned, must take precedence over the flesh.

Alas, poor Irma, you don't know what you missed.

Twelve freshmen stood in a straight line, stark naked. They were of varying somatotypes, ranging from corpulent to frail (Danny Rossi was among them). Their physiques were as disparate as Mickey Mouse and Adonis (Jason Gilbert was also among the dozen). Before them stretched a wooden bench some three feet off the ground, and behind it an imperious gymnasium official who had menacingly introduced himself as "Colonel" Jackson.

"Awright," he barked. "You freshmen are about to take the famous Harvard Step Test. Which, as you don't have to be a Harvard man to figger out, involves the stepping up and stepping down on this here step. Clear so far? Now, this here test was devised during the war so's we could check our G.I.s' fitness. And it must have worked, 'cause we beat Hitler, didn't we?"

He paused to await some expression of patriotic enthusiasm on the part of his charges. But, losing patience, he continued laying down the rules.

"Okay, when I blow my whistle, you start climbing on and off the bench. We'll be playing an LP and also I'll be beating time with this here stick. Now this procedure will continue for five entire minutes. And I'm watching all of you, so don't goof off or miss a step or you'll be majoring in P.T. exercises the whole darn year."

Danny trembled inwardly as this officious ogre rambled on. Shit, he told himself, these other guys are so much taller than I. For them it's just like stepping on a curb. For me this lousy bench is like Mount Everest. It isn't fair.

"Awright," Colonel Jackson snapped. "When I say go, you start stepping. And keep in time!"

Go!

And they were off.

As an LP blared stridently, the monster pounded his stick with relentless, debilitating regularity. *Up*-two-three-four, *up*-two-three-four, *up*-two-three-four.

After a few dozen steps, Danny was beginning to tire. He wished the colonel's beat would slacken even slightly, but the man was an infernal metronome. Still, at least it would soon be over—he prayed.

"Half a minute!" Jackson called out.

Thank God, thought Danny, just a little more and I'll be able to stop.

But an agonizing thirty seconds thereafter, the official bellowed, "One minute down, just four to go!"

No, thought Danny, not *another* four minutes. I can barely breathe. Then he reminded himself that if he quit, he'd have to take a gym class with this sadist in addition to his other courses! And so he mustered all his inner fortitude, the courage that had once fueled him on the running track, and fought beyond the limits of his pain.

"Come on, you puny carrot top," the torture master bellowed. "I can see you're skipping steps. Keep going, or I'll make you do an extra minute."

Sweat was pouring down all of the dozen freshmen's limbs. And even splashing onto their neighbors.

"Two minutes. Just three more to go."

Now Danny sensed in desperation that he'd never make it. He could barely lift his legs. He was sure he'd fall and break an arm. Farewell to concertizing. All because of this ridiculously useless exercise in animality.

Just then a quiet voice next to him said, "Take it easy, kid. Try to breathe normally. If you miss a step, I'll do my best to block you."

Danny wearily looked up. It was a blond and muscular classmate who had uttered this encouragement. An athlete in such splendid shape that he had breath enough to give advice while he was stepping regularly up and down. All Dan could do was nod in gratitude. He steeled himself and persevered.

"Four minutes," cried the Torquemada in a sweatshirt. "Only one to go. You guys are doing pretty good—for Harvard men."

Danny Rossi's legs were suddenly rigid. He couldn't take another step.

"Don't quit now," his neighbor whispered. "Come on, babe, just another lousy sixty seconds."

Then Danny felt a hand reach underneath his elbow and pull him up. His limbs unlocked, and stiffly he resumed the grueling climb to nowhere.

And then at last, deliverance. The whole nightmare was over.

"Awright. Everybody sit down on the bench and put your hand on the neck of the guy on your right. We're going to take pulses."

The freshmen, now initiated in this sweaty rite of passage, gladly collapsed and struggled to regain their breath.

When Colonel Jackson had recorded all pertinent fitness information, the twelve exhausted freshmen were instructed to take showers and proceed, still in their birthday suits, down two flights of stairs to the pool. Because, as the overbearing instructor so aptly expressed it, "Whoever cannot swim fifty yards cannot graduate this university."

As they stood side by side under the showers washing off the sweat of persecution, Danny said to the classmate whose magnanimous assistance would allow him countless extra hours at the keyboard, "Hey, I can never thank you enough for saving me out there."

"That's okay. It's a stupid test to start with. And I pity anyone who'd have to listen to that ape give orders for a whole semester. What's your name, by the way?"

"Danny Rossi," said the smaller man, offering a soapy hand.

"Jason Gilbert," the athletic type replied, and added with a grin, "can you swim okay, Dan?"

"Yes, thanks." Danny smiled. "I'm from California."

"California, and you're not a jock?"

"My sport is the piano. Do you like the classics?"

"Nothing heavier than Johnny Mathis. But still, I'd like to hear you play. Maybe after dinner sometime in the Union, huh?"

"Sure," Danny said, "but if not, I promise you a pair of tickets for my first public performance."

"Gee, are you that good?"

"Yes," said Danny Rossi quietly, without embarrassment.

Then they both descended to the pool and, in adjoining lanes, Jason with flamboyant speed, Danny with deliberate caution, swam the obligatory fifty yards that marked their final physical requirement for a degree at Harvard.

ANDREW ELIOT'S DIARY

September 22, 1954

Yesterday we had the stupid Harvard Step Test. Being in reasonable shape for soccer, I passed it with no sweat. (Or to be more accurate, a lot of sweat, but very little effort.) The only trouble came when "Colonel" Jackson made us reach over to feel the neck artery of the guy next to you, my neighbor was so slippery with perspiration that I couldn't find his pulse. So when that Fascist character came by to write it down, I just made up a number that popped into my head.

When we got back to the dorm, the three of us reviewed this fairly degrading experience. We all agreed that the most undignified and unnecessary aspect was the damn posture picture just before the Step Test. Imagine, now Harvard has a personal file of everyone—or perhaps more accurately, every member of The Class—standing naked in front of the camera, ostensibly to test our posture. But probably so that when one of us becomes President of the United States, the phys. ed. department can pull out his picture and see what the leader of the greatest nation in the world looks like in the raw.

What really bugged Wigglesworth was that some thief could break into the IAB, filch our photographs, and sell them for a fortune.

"To whom?" I asked. "Who'd pay to see the pictures of a thousand naked Harvard freshmen?"

This gave him pause for thought. Who indeed would treasure such a portrait gallery? Some horny Wellesley girls, perhaps. Then something else occurred to me: do Cliffies have to take these pictures too?

Newall thought they did. And I conceived this great idea of sneaking into the Radcliffe gym to steal *their* pictures. What a show! Then we'd know what girls to concentrate our efforts on.

At first they really liked my plan. But then their courage sort of evanesced. And Newall argued that a "real man" should be able to find out empirically.

So much for bravery. I would have liked that midnight raid. I think.

S tudy cards were due in at 5:00 P.M. on Thursday. This gave The Class of '58 a little time to shop around and choose a balanced program. They'd need courses for their majors, some for distribution, and some perhaps for cultural enrichment. And, most important, a gut. At least one really easy course was absolutely necessary for those who were either preppies or pre-med.

For Ted Lambros, who was certain he'd be majoring in classics, the selection was fairly straightforward: Latin 2A, Horace and Catullus, and Nat. Sci. 4 with the pyrotechnic L. K. Nash, who regularly blew himself up several times a year.

Both as a gut and a requirement, he took Greek A, an introduction to the classical version of the language he had used since birth. After two semesters he would be able to read Homer in the original. And in the meantime, as a fourth course, he would read the famous epics in translation with John Finley, the legendary Eliot Professor of Greek Literature. "Hum 2," as it was affectionately known, would provide stimulation, information, and, as everyone at Harvard knew, an easy grade.

Danny Rossi had already planned his schedule during his cross-country trek. Music 51, Analysis of Form, an unavoidable requirement for every major. But the rest would be pure joy. A survey of orchestral music from Haydn to Hindemith. Then, beginning German, to prepare him to conduct the Wagner operas. (He'd start Italian and French later.) And, of course, the college's most popular and inspirational free ride—Hum 2.

He had wanted to take Walter Piston's Composition Seminar, and had assumed that the great man would admit him even though Danny was a freshman and the class had mostly graduates. But Piston turned him down "for his own good."

"Look," the composer had explained, "the piece you handed in was charming. And I really didn't have to see it. Gustave Landau's letter was enough for me. But if I take you now, you might be in the paradoxical position of—how can I put it?—being able to sprint and not to walk. If it's any consolation, when Leonard Bernstein was here we forced him to do his basic music 'calisthenics' just like you."

"Okay," Danny said with polite resignation. And as he left thought, I guess that was his way of saying my piece is pretty juvenile.

◆

Freshmen who are preppies have a great advantage. Through their network of old graduates familiar with the Cambridge scene, they learn precisely what the courses are to take and which ones to avoid.

The Harris Tweed underground imparts to them the secret word that is the key to making good at Harvard: *bullshit*. The greater the opportunity for tossing the verbiage like so much salad (unimpeded by the need for such trivia as facts), the more likely the course would be a snap.

They also arrived at college well versed in the techniques of the essay question, and could pad their paragraphs with such useful phrases as "from a theoretical point of view," or "upon first inspection we may seem to discern a certain attitude which may well survive even closer scrutiny," and so forth. This sort of wind can sail you halfway through an hour test before you have to lay a single fact on paper.

But you can't do that in math. So for God's sake, man, stay away from science. Even though there's a Nat. Sci. requirement for course distribution, take it in your sophomore year. By then you'll have perfected your prose style so that you might even be able to argue that, from a certain point of view, two and two might just possibly equal five.

The program Andrew Eliot selected was a preppie's dream. First, Soc. Rel. 1, because the name—Social Relations—was itself an invitation to throw bull. Then English 10, a survey from Chaucer to his cousin Tom. It was fairly rigorous but he'd read most of the stuff (at least in Hymarx outlines) in senior year at prep school.

His choice of Fine Arts 13 also showed astuteness. Not much reading, little taking down of notes. For it meant mostly watching

slides. Moreover, the noon hour of its meeting and the semidark-
ness of its atmosphere were most conducive if one needed a short
nap before lunch. Also, Newall pointed out, "As soon as we find
girlfriends at the Cliffe, that auditorium will be the perfect spot
for making out."

There was no problem about his final course. It had to be
Hum 2. In addition to its many other attractions, since the instructor held the chair endowed by Andrew's ancestors, he looked
upon Professor Finley as a sort of family retainer.

The night they handed in their study cards, Andrew, Wig,
and Newall had a gin-and-tonic party to honor their official
course commitment to self-betterment.

"So, Andy," Dickie asked after his fourth, "what do you
want to be when you grow up?"

And Andrew answered, only half in jest, "Frankly, I don't
think I really want to grow up."

ANDREW ELIOT'S DIARY

October 5, 1954

The occasions that we thousand-odd will meet together as a class in our entire lifetime are extremely rare.

We gather three times while we are in college. First at the Freshman Convocation—sober, serious, and boring. Then at the notoriously gross Freshman Smoker—just the opposite. And, finally, after jumping all the necessary hurdles, one June morning four years hence when we'll receive diplomas.

Otherwise, we go through Harvard on our own. They say our most important meeting is a quarter-century after we all graduate. That would be 1983—impossible to think that far away.

They also say that when we come back for our Twenty-fifth Reunion we'll be feeling something vaguely like fraternity and solidarity. But for now, we're much more like the animals on Noah's Ark. I mean, I don't think the lions had too much to chat about with the lambs. Or with the mice. That's just about the way me and my roommates feel about some of the creatures that are on board with us for this four-year voyage. We live in different cabins and sit on different decks.

Anyway, we gathered all together as The Class of '58 tonight in Sanders Theater. And it was pretty solemn.

I know Dr. Pusey isn't everybody's hero nowadays, but when he talked tonight about the university's tradition of defending academic freedom, it was kind of moving.

He chose as an example A. Lawrence Lowell, who at the beginning of this century succeeded my great-granddad as President of Harvard. Apparently, right after World War I, a lot of guys in Cambridge had flirtations with the Socialists and Communists—then preaching hot, new stuff. Lowell was under tremendous pressure to dismiss the lefties from the faculty.

Now, even guys as dim as I caught Pusey's tacit parallel with Senator McCarthy's unrelenting war on him when he quoted

Lowell's great defense of professors in the classroom being absolutely free to teach "the truth as they see it."

You have to hand it to him. He's demonstrated courage as Hemingway defined it, "grace under pressure." And yet The Class of '58 did not give him a standing ovation.

But something tells me that when we're older and have seen more of the world, we'll feel ashamed that we didn't acknowledge Pusey's bravery tonight.

"Where you going, Gilbert?"

"Where does it look like, D.D.? To breakfast, obviously."

"Today?"

"Sure, why not?"

"Come on, Gilbert, you should know better. Don't you realize it's Yom Kippur?"

"So?"

"Well, don't you know what it is?"

"Of course, the Day of Atonement for Jews."

"Gilbert, you should be fasting today," his roommate admonished. "You talk as if you're not Jewish."

"Well, D.D., as a matter of fact, I'm not."

"Don't give me that. You're as Jewish as I am."

"On what evidence do you base that categorical statement?" Jason said good-humoredly.

"Well, to begin with, haven't you noticed that Harvard always assigns Jews to the same rooms? Why else do you think they put you with me?"

"I wish I knew," Jason said jocularly.

"Gilbert," D.D persisted, "do you actually stand there and deny that you are of the Jewish faith?"

"Look, I know my grandfather was a Jew. But as far as faith is concerned, we belong to the local Unitarian church."

"That doesn't mean a thing," D.D. retorted. "If Hitler were alive he'd still consider you a Jew."

"Listen, David," Jason answered, unperturbed, "in case you haven't heard, that bastard's been dead for several years now. Besides, this is America. You do recall that bit in the Bill of Rights about freedom of worship. In fact, the grandchild of a Jewish man can even have breakfast on Yom Kippur."

But D.D. was far from conceding defeat.

"Gilbert, you should read Jean-Paul Sartre's essay on Jewish identity. It would wake you up to your dilemma."

"I didn't realize that I had one, frankly."

"Sartre says that someone's Jewish if the world *regards* him a Jew. And that means, Jason, you can be a blond, eat bacon on Yom Kippur, wear your preppie clothes, play squash—it doesn't change a thing. The world will still consider you a Jew."

"Hey, look, so far, the only guy that's ever given me grief on this whole business has been you, my friend."

And yet Jason realized inwardly that what he'd just stated was not quite the truth. For had he not experienced a little "problem" vis-à-vis the Yale Admissions Office?

"Okay," D.D. concluded as he buttoned up his coat, "if you want to go on living like an ostrich, it's your privilege. But sooner or later you'll learn." And in parting, he added sarcastically, "Have a good breakfast."

"Thanks," Jason called cheerily, "and don't forget to pray for me."

The old man gazed at the wine-dark sea of students reverently awaiting his comments on Odysseus' decision to sail homeward after ten years of breathless encounters with women, monsters, and monstrous women.

He was standing on the stage of Sanders Theater, the only Harvard building large enough—or indeed appropriate—to house the lectures of Professor John H. Finley, Jr., chosen by Olympus to convey the glory that was Greece to the hoi polloi of Cambridge. Indeed, such was his charismatic eloquence that many of the hundreds who entered Humanities 2 in September as philistines emerged by Christmas as passionate philhellenes.

Thus it was that on Tuesdays and Thursdays at 10:00 A.M., fully one-quarter of the entire population of Harvard College gathered to hear the great man's lectures on the Epic from Homer to Milton. Everyone seemed to have a favorite vantage point for viewing Finley. Andrew Eliot and Jason Gilbert preferred the balcony. Danny Rossi, killing two birds with one stone, would alter his position frequently since he wanted to master the acoustics of the hall, venue for Harvard's major concerts and even the occasional visit by the Boston Symphony.

Ted Lambros always sat in the first row, lest he miss a single winged word. He had come to Harvard already wanting to major in Latin and Greek, but Finley's survey endowed the prospect with mystical grandeur that filled him with euphoria as well as ethnic pride.

Today Finley was discussing Odysseus' departure from the enchanted isle of the nymph Calypso, despite her passionate pleas and promises to grant him eternal life. "Imagine—" Finley breathed to his rapt auditors. He then paused while all wondered what he would ask them to conjure.

"Imagine our hero is offered an unending idyll with a nymph who will remain forever young. Yet, he forsakes it all to return to a poor island and a woman who, Calypso explicitly reminds him, is fast approaching middle age, which no cosmetic can embellish. A rare, tempting proposition, one cannot deny. But what is Odysseus' reaction?"

He then paced back and forth, and recited without book, clearly translating from the Greek as he went along:

"Goddess, I know that everything you say is true and that clever Penelope is no match for your face and figure. But she is after all a mortal and you divine and ageless. Yet *despite all this* I yearn for home and for the day of my returning."

He stopped pacing and walked slowly and deliberately to the edge of the stage.

"Here," he said, at a whisper that was nonetheless audible in the farthest corner, "is the quintessential message of the *Odyssey*. . . ."

A thousand pencils poised in readiness to transcribe the crucial words to come.

"In, as it were, leaving an enchanted—and one must presume pleasantly tropical—isle to return to the cold winter winds of, shall we say, Brookline, Massachusetts, Odysseus forsakes immortality for—identity. In other words, the imperfections of the human state are outweighed by the glory of human love."

There was a brief pause while the audience waited for Finley to draw breath before daring to do so themselves.

And then applause. Slowly the spell was broken as students marched out the various Sanders Theater exits. Ted Lambros was close to tears and felt he had to say something to the master. But it took him a few seconds to gather his courage. By this time, the nimble academic had donned his tan raincoat and fedora and had reached the tall arched gateway.

Ted approached him diffidently. As he did he was amazed that, on terra firma, this man of such great stature was actually of normal height.

"Sir, if you'll permit me," he began, "that was the most inspiring lecture I've ever heard. I mean, I'm just a freshman, but I'm going to major in classics, and I'll bet you've made a thousand converts in there . . . uh, sir."

He knew he was rambling gauchely, but Finley was accustomed to such reverential clumsiness. And in any case he was pleased.

"A freshman and already decided on the classics?" he inquired.

"Yes, sir."

"What is your name?"

"Lambros, sir. Theodore Lambros, '58."

"Ah," said Finley, " 'Theo-doros,' gift of God, and 'lampros'—a truly Pindaric name. One thinks of the famous verses in *Phythian* 8—*Lampron phengos epestin andron,* 'radiant light that shines on men.' Do come and see us for Wednesday tea at Eliot House, Mr. Lambros."

Before Ted could even thank him, Finley turned on his heels and marched off into the October wind, reciting Pindar all the way.

J ason awoke at the sound of someone in great distress.

He glanced quickly at his night table. It was just after 2:00 A.M. From across the suite, he heard muffled sobbing and frightened cries of, "No, no!"

He leapt out of bed and rushed across to D.D.'s door, the source of all those tormented noises.

Knocking softly, Jason asked, "David, are you okay?"

The sobbing stopped abruptly and there was only silence. Jason knocked again and rephrased his question.

"Are you all right in there?"

Through the closed door came the curt response, "Go away, Gilbert. Leave me alone." But it was in a strangely anguished tone of voice.

"Listen, D.D., if you don't open up I'm going to break in."

After a second he heard the scraping of a chair. A moment later the door opened a crack. And his roommate peeked out nervously. Jason could perceive that he had been at his desk studying.

"What do you want?" snapped D.D.

"I heard noises," Jason replied. "I thought you were in some kind of pain."

"I just fell asleep for a minute and had a sort of nightmare. It's nothing. And I'd be grateful if you'd let me study." He closed the door again.

Jason still would not retreat.

"Hey, listen, D.D., you don't have to be pre-med to know that people can go nuts from not sleeping. Haven't you studied enough for one night?"

The door opened again.

"Gilbert, I couldn't possibly go to bed if I thought any of my competition were still awake studying. Chem. Twenty is the survival of the fittest."

"I still think a little rest would make you fitter, David," Jason said softly. "What was your nightmare, by the way?"

"You wouldn't believe me even if I told you."

"Try me."

"It's silly," D.D. laughed nervously, "but I dreamed that they handed out the bluebooks—and I didn't understand the questions. Stupid, ha? Anyway, you can go to bed now, Jason. I'm perfectly okay."

The next morning, D.D. made no mention whatsoever of the trauma of the night before. In fact, he was exceptionally obnoxious, as if unconsciously informing Jason that what he had seen a few hours earlier was just a one-time aberration.

Still Jason felt duty-bound to say something to the dorm proctor, who was nominally supposed to be responsible for their welfare. Besides, Dennis Linden was a medical student and might understand the whole phenomenon that Jason had witnessed.

"Dennis," cautioned Jason, "you've got to give me your word that this is strictly confidential."

"Absolutely," the soon-to-be-M.D. replied. "I'm glad you called this thing to my attention."

"Seriously, I think D.D. will go bonkers if he doesn't get all A's. He's got this wild obsession that he has to be first in The Class."

Linden puffed his Chesterfield, blew rings into the air, and answered casually, "But, Gilbert, we both know that's an impossibility."

"What makes you so sure?" Jason inquired, puzzled.

"Listen, let me tell you something in confidence. Your roommate wasn't even number one in his own high school, which sent half-a-dozen guys here with much higher averages and board scores. In fact, the Admissions Office only rated him a little over 10.5."

"What?" Jason asked.

"Look, as I said, this stuff is really classified. But Harvard calculates the future standing of each student they accept—."

"In advance?" Jason interrupted.

The proctor nodded and continued. "And what's more, they're almost never wrong."

"You mean to tell me that you know what grades I'm going to get this January?" Jason asked with stupefaction.

"Not only that," the future doctor answered, "we know pretty much just where you'll graduate."

"Why not tell me now, so I won't bother studying too hard," Jason said, only barely joking.

"Now come on, Gilbert, what I said is absolutely off the record. And I only told you so you could be ready to support your roommate when he wakes up to discover that he isn't Einstein."

Jason suddenly erupted with angry resentment.

"Hey, listen, Dennis, I'm not fit to act as a psychiatrist. Can't we do something to help this guy now?"

The proctor took another puff and answered, "Jason, young Davidson—who, between the two of us, I find a little twerp—is here at Harvard precisely to learn his limitations. That is, if I may say so, one of the things that we do best. Let this ride till midterm. If the guy's unable to deal with the fact that he's not on top of the mountain, then maybe we'll arrange for him to talk to someone in the Health Department. Anyway, I'm glad that you called this to my attention. Don't hesitate to come again if he starts acting weird."

"He's always acted weird," Jason responded with a half-smile.

"Gilbert," said the proctor, "you've got no idea what whackos they accept at Harvard. D.D. is a damn Gibraltar compared to some of the nutcases I've seen."

ANDREW ELIOT'S DIARY

October 17, 1954

I never thought I was a good student and I didn't mind getting C's for all my hour exams. But I did think of myself as a pretty good soccer player. And that illusion's just been dispelled.

The damn freshman team is so packed with all kinds of international big gunners that I could barely get a chance to put my toe in.

Still, there is a little solace in this truly Harvard lesson in humility. As I sit there on the bench awaiting my dispensation of three or four minutes' play during the final moments (if we're leading by enough), I can console myself with the reminder that the guy who plays ahead of me is no ordinary jock.

Maybe his corner kicks are so lofty because he is descended from the Almighty.

Still, if I have to be a second stringer it might as well be to the likes of Karim Aga Khan, who is, as Professor Finley put it, "the great, great, great, great, and ad infinitum grandson of God."

And he's not the only dignitary who has relegated me to being practically a spectator. Our center forward is another divinity—a genuine Persian prince. And we've got ringers from places as exotic as South America, the Philippines—and even public high schools. All of whom have contributed to my sedentary status.

But at least we're undefeated. There's some comfort to be found in that. And if I get to play another seven minutes, I'll have earned my freshman numerals.

As if the flower of my confidence has not been sufficiently wilted by the heat of these guys' talent on the field, I grit my teeth as I report that Bruce Macdonald, the best player of them all, is perhaps the greatest genius in the whole damn Class.

He graduated number one at Exeter, was captain and high

scorer of their soccer team, ditto for lacrosse in springtime. And just to keep him busy in the evenings, he's so terrific with a violin that, as a freshman, he's been chosen concertmaster of the Harvard-Radcliffe Orchestra!

Thank God I arrived here with a well-developed feeling of inferiority. Because if I had come as cocky as most guys were on the first day we were kicking soccer balls, I would have thrown myself into the Charles.

The rabbi stood at the podium and announced:

"After the concluding hymn, the congregation is cordially invited to the Vestry Room for wine, fruit, and honeycake. Now let us turn to page one hundred two and join in the singing of 'Adon Olam, Lord of the Universe.'"

In the organ loft above, Danny Rossi picked up his cue and struck the opening chords with a gusto that delighted the worshippers.

> Lord of the Universe, who reigned
> Ere earth and heaven's fashioning,
> When to create a world he deigned
> Then was his name proclaimed King.

After the rabbi's benediction, they filed out as Danny played the recessional. The moment he finished, he grabbed his jacket and hurried downstairs.

He entered the Vestry Room unobtrusively and headed for the abundantly laden tables. As he was filling a paper plate with slices of cake, he heard the rabbi's voice.

"How good of you to stay on, Danny. It's certainly beyond the call of duty. I know how terribly busy you are."

"Oh, I enjoy being involved in everything, Rabbi," he replied. "I mean, it's all very interesting for me."

Danny was being quite sincere. Although he did not mention that what he most appreciated about the Jewish festivals was the plentiful food, which usually enabled him to skip lunch.

This particular Saturday would be especially hectic for him, since the youth group of the Congregational church in Quincy, which he also served, was holding its Fall Hop. And he had persuaded the minister to hire "his" trio (quickly calling the Union for a young drummer and bassist). It would be tiring, but that fifty-buck fee would be a great consolation.

It seemed pointless to go all the way back to Cambridge to pass the time between sacred and secular gigs, especially since Harvard would be caught up in Saturday football mania and it would be too noisy to work anyway. So Danny took the MTA to Copley Square and spent the afternoon studying in the Boston Public Library.

There was a plumpish brunette sitting at the end of his table, with several notebooks emblazoned BOSTON UNIVERSITY. This gave the timid Casanova a clue of how to engage her in conversation.

"Do you go to B.U.?"

"Yeah."

"I go to Harvard myself."

"That figures," she said dismissively.

With a sigh of anticipated defeat, Danny returned to Hindemith's *Craft of Musical Composition*.

When he emerged, a chilly darkness had descended upon the city. As he strolled through Boston's version of Venice's Piazza San Marco, he pondered a vital theological dilemma.

Would the Congregationalists serve food?

Better not take too big a leap of faith, he told himself. Hedge your bets. So he grabbed a quick tuna on rye before beginning the journey south to Quincy.

The best part of the dance was that the drummer and the bass player turned out to be young college students like himself. The worst part was that he had to spend the entire evening at the piano, trying not to ogle the well-developed high school girls in their tight sweaters gyrating to the beat his hungry fingers produced on the keyboard.

When the last couples finally straggled off the floor, an exhausted Danny looked at his watch. God, he thought, eleven-thirty and it'll take me at least an hour to get back to Harvard. And I've got to be back here before nine.

For an instant he was tempted to sleep upstairs on an isolated pew. No, don't risk your job. Better haul yourself back home.

*   *   *

When he finally entered Harvard Yard, nearly every window was dark. Yet, as he approached Holworthy, he was stunned to find his roommate, Kingman Wu, perched on the stone steps.

"Hi, Danny."

"King, what the hell are you doing out here? It's freezing."

"Bernie bounced me," his friend replied forlornly. "He's practicing his fencing and claims he's got to be alone to concentrate."

"At this hour? The guy's a maniac."

"I know," said Kingman miserably. "But he's got a sword, so what the heck could I do?"

Perhaps the state beyond exhaustion dissipates all fear, for Danny felt strangely brave enough to deal with this emergency.

"Come on, King, maybe the two of us can bring him to his senses."

As they headed in, Wu muttered, "You're a real pal, Danny. I only wish you were six feet tall."

"So do I," Danny said wistfully.

Fortunately, the mad musketeer had gone to sleep. And a weary Danny Rossi followed almost instantly thereafter.

"Od, there's this Jewboy going out for squash who's
unbelievable."

Dickie Newall was giving his roommates a detailed account
of tryouts for the sport at which he'd excelled from the moment
he was old enough to hold a racket.

"Is he going to beat you out for number one?" asked Wig.

"Are you kidding?" Newall groaned. "He could cream half
the varsity. His drop shots are absolutely uncanny. And what
really gets my goat is that the guy's real neat. I mean, not just for
a Jew—for a person."

At which point Andrew inquired, "What makes you think
Jews aren't people?"

"Aw, come on, Eliot, you know what I mean. They're usually
these dark, brainy, aggressive guys. But this one doesn't even
wear glasses."

"You know," Andrew commented, "my father always had a
special admiration for the Jews. In fact, they're the only doctors
he'll see for anything."

"But how many of them does he see *socially*?" Newall volleyed back.

"That's different. But I don't think he avoids them as a
policy. It's just the circles that we move in."

"You mean it's mere coincidence that none of these great
physicians get put up for any of his clubs?"

"All right," Andrew conceded. "But I've never heard him
make a racial slur of any sort. Even about Catholics."

"But he doesn't mix with those guys either, does he? Not
even our new mackerel-snapping senator from Massachusetts."

"Well, he has done some business deals with Old Joe
Kennedy."

60

"Not over dinner at the Founders' Club, I'll bet," Wig interposed.

"Hey, look," Andrew replied, "I didn't say my dad's a saint. But at least he taught me not to use the kind of language Newall enjoys so much."

"But, Andy, you put up with my colorful epithets for years."

"Yeah," Wig agreed. "What's suddenly made you such a Goody Two-Shoes?"

"Listen, guys," Andrew responded. "In prep school we had no Jews or Negroes at all. So who cared if you went on about the 'lower orders.' But Harvard's full of all types, so I think we should learn to live with them."

His roommates glanced at one another quizzically.

And then Newall complained, "Knock off this preaching, huh? I mean, if I'd said this guy was short or fat, you wouldn't have given me any heat. When I refer to someone as a Hebie or a coon, it's just a friendly way of typing him, a sort of shorthand adjective. I mean, for your information, I've invited this guy Jason Gilbert to our blast after the football game on Saturday."

Then he looked at Andrew with mischief in his eyes and added, "That's if you don't mind actually mixing with a Jewboy."

Although it was only the first week of November, the air at six o'clock was glacial and as dark as any winter evening. As Jason was dressing after squash practice, he discovered, to his annoyance, that he'd forgotten to bring a tie. He'd now have to return to Straus to get one. Otherwise, that Irish Cerberus who stood checking necks at the Union doorway would gleefully bounce him. Damn. Damn.

He trudged back across the chilly, leafless Yard, climbed the stairs to A-32, and fumbled for his key.

The moment that he pushed the door ajar, Jason noticed something odd. The place was dark. He glanced at D.D.'s room. No light from there either. Maybe he was sick. Jason rapped softly and inquired, "Davidson, are you okay?"

There was no reply.

Then, breaking the ironclad house rules, Jason opened the door. First he noticed the ceiling, where the electric wires had been torn out. Then he glanced quickly at the floor. Where he saw his roommate in a heap, motionless—a belt around his neck.

Jason was vertiginous with fear.

Oh God, he thought, the bastard's killed himself. He knelt and turned D.D. over. This gesture elicited the faintest semblance of a groan. Quick, Jason, he urged himself, fighting to keep his wits, call the cops. No. They might not come in time.

He swiftly removed the leather belt from his roommate's lacerated throat. He then heaved him up onto his shoulders like a fireman, and rushed as quickly as he could to Harvard Square, where he commandeered a taxi, ordering the driver to tear-ass to the infirmary.

*   *   *

"He'll be all right," the on-duty physician assured Jason. "I don't think Harvard sockets are wired well enough for suicide. Although, God knows, there are some kids who actually succeed in their ingenious ways. Why do you think he did it?"

"I don't know," said Jason, still somewhat deadened from the shock.

"The young man had a bit too much invested in his grades," Dennis Linden pronounced. He had arrived on the scene in time to offer a professional analysis of the young freshman's desperate action.

"Did his behavior give you any hints that this was coming?" asked the Health Service doctor.

Jason shot a glance at Linden, who continued to pontificate, "Not really. You can never figure out which egg is going to crack. I mean, the freshman year's so fraught with pressure."

As the two doctors continued chatting, Jason fixed his gaze on his shoes.

Ten minutes later, Jason and the proctor walked together out of the infirmary. It was only then that he realized that he had no coat. Or gloves. Or anything. Panic had inured him to the cold. Now he was shivering.

"You need a lift, Jason?" Linden asked.

"No, thanks," he answered sullenly.

"Come on, Gilbert, you'll freeze to death walking back like that."

"Okay," he relented.

During the short ride up Mount Auburn Street, the proctor tried to justify himself.

"Look," he rationalized, "this is what Harvard's all about—it's sink or swim."

"Yeah," Jason mumbled half-aloud, "but you're supposed to be the lifeguard."

At the next red light he climbed out of Linden's car and slammed the door.

His anger again made him oblivious to the bitter cold.

He walked on toward the Square. At Elsie's he consumed two Roast-Beef Specials to replace the dinner he had missed, then went over to Cronin's, cruising by the wooden booths to find a friendly face so he could sit down and get drunk.

*   *   *

Jason was awakened rudely the next morning by a rapping on the door that made his headache even worse. It was only when he started groggily toward it that he noticed he was still in last night's clothing. Anyway, his soul felt wrinkled. So they matched.

He opened the door.

A stocky, middle-aged woman, wearing a green floppy hat, was planted solidly outside.

"What did you do to him?" she demanded.

"Oh," Jason said quietly, "you must be David's mother."

"A real genius you are," she muttered. "I'm here to get his clothes."

"Please," Jason said, immediately ushering her in.

"It's freezing on that landing, if you didn't notice," she remarked while entering the suite and glancing hawk-eyed into every corner.

"Foo, it's a real pigsty. Who cleans up this place?"

"A student porter vacuums once a week and swabs the john," said Jason.

"Well, no wonder my poor boy's ill. Whose filthy clothes are these all over everywhere? They carry germs, you know."

"They're David's," Jason answered softly.

"So how come you threw my David's clothes all over everywhere? Is that your rich boy's idea of a little fun?"

"Mrs. Davidson," Jason said patiently, "he dropped them there himself." After which he quickly added, "Would you like to sit down? You must be very tired."

"Tired? I'm exhausted. Do you know what that night train is like—especially for a woman my age? Anyway, I'll stand while you explain why it's not your fault."

Jason sighed. "Look, Mrs. Davidson, I don't know what they've told you down at the infirmary."

"They said that he was very sick and has to be transferred to some god-awful . . . hospital," she paused, and then she gasped, "a mental hospital."

"I'm really sorry," Jason answered gently, "but the pressure here can be ferocious. To get grades, I mean."

"My David always got good grades. He studied day and night. Now suddenly he leaves my house and comes to live with you and he collapses like he had no yeast. Why did you disturb him?"

"Believe me, Mrs. Davidson," Jason insisted, "I never bothered him. He—" Jason worked up the courage to complete his sentence "—sort of brought it on himself."

Mrs. Davidson slowly absorbed this allegation.

"How?" she asked.

"For reasons that I simply cannot fathom, he just felt he had to be the best. I mean, the very best."

"What's wrong with that? I brought him up that way."

Jason felt a surge of retrospective pity for his erstwhile roommate. Obviously his mother rode him like a racehorse in a never-ending homestretch. He wouldn't have to be Humpty Dumpty to crack under that kind of strain.

Then suddenly, without warning, she flopped onto their couch and began to sob.

"What did I do? Didn't I sacrifice my life for him? This isn't fair."

Jason touched her tentatively on the shoulder. "Look, Mrs. Davidson, if David's going to a hospital he'll need his clothes. Why don't I help you pack?"

She gazed up at him with a look of helplessness. "Thank you, young man. I'm sorry that I yelled, but I'm a bit upset, and I've been on the train all night."

She opened her purse, took out a handkerchief already moist, and dabbed her eyes.

"Hey, look," Jason said softly. "Why don't you rest here. I can boil some coffee. Meanwhile, I'll pack his stuff, go get my car, and drive you to . . . wherever David is."

"A place called Massachusetts Mental Health, in Waltham," she replied, choking on nearly every syllable.

In the bedroom, Jason grabbed a suitcase and tossed in garments he thought would be appropriate. Instinct told him that the hospital would not require ties and jackets.

"What about his books?" his mother called out.

"I don't think he'll need his school stuff right away, but I'll hold on to it and bring him what he wants."

"You're very kind," she said again. And blew her nose.

One suitcase packed, Jason cast a quick eye around the room to see if he'd missed anything essential. At that moment he caught sight of something lying on top of the desk. Even as he reached out, he had ominous forebodings of what it would be.

Yes, he was right. It was the bluebook from D.D.'s Chem. 20 midterm. And his roommate's nightmare had turned out to be prophecy. He had received a mere B-minus. As casually as possible, he folded the exam and stuffed it in his back pocket.

"Wait here, Mrs. Davidson. My car's a few blocks away. I'll run and get it."

"I must be keeping you from your classes," she said meekly.

"That's okay," he answered. "I'm just happy I can do something for David. I mean—he's a real nice guy."

Mrs. Davidson looked into Jason Gilbert's eyes and murmured, "You know, your parents should be extremely proud."

"Thank you," Jason Gilbert whispered. And ran off, a dull ache in his heart.

November 3, 1954

One of the great joys of living away from home and not at prep school is being able to stay up all night. Now and then it's actually for something serious like finishing a paper that's due the next day.

Mike Wigglesworth is an expert at this technique. He sits down at his typewriter at around seven in the evening with a few notes and a half-dozen Budweisers. He pecks out a first draft before midnight and then spends the wee small hours mixing in an appropriate quantity of bullshit. For the latter process he stokes up with coffee. Then he goes to breakfast, eats a dozen eggs and bacon (he's a crew star, after all), and drops off his paper. Then he goes to sleep until the afternoon, when he gets up to go down to the Boathouse.

But last night all three of us had a respectable reason for staying up. To hear the outcome of the national elections. Not that any of us really gives a damn for politics. It's just a nice excuse for getting gently plowed.

Typical of that provincial rag, this morning's *Crimson* focused on the quantity of Harvard men who'd been elected. No fewer than thirty-five of the new congressmen went to our humble college, not to mention four of the new senators. Now, when the nation's problems get too heavy for them, they can join Jack Kennedy in the Senate men's room and all sing Harvard football songs.

As I sat at breakfast reading through the *Crime,* a sudden notion struck me. Maybe that unprepossessing guy at the next table eating Wheaties will someday be a senator. Or even President. The thing is that you never know who's going to make it. Dad once told me that FDR was pretty kooky as an undergraduate. So much so, he was blackballed by the Final Club that took his cousin Teddy.

The Harvard freshmen are still sort of formless caterpillars. It really takes some time to find out who'll become the rarest butterfly of all.

The only thing I'm certain of is that I'll remain a caterpillar all my life.

From the *Harvard Crimson* of January 12, 1955:

GILBERT TO LEAD YARDLING SQUASH TEAM

Jason Gilbert '58 of Straus Hall and Syosset, Long Island, has been elected Captain of the Freshman Squash Team. Gilbert, who attended Hawkins-Atwell, where he captained both the squash and tennis teams, is undefeated at the number-one slot thus far this season. He is also seeded seventh in the Eastern States Junior Tennis rankings.

"Gilbert, you deserve a medal," Dennis Linden remarked. "If you hadn't thought so quickly, that little nerd D.D. might actually have killed himself."

The proctor had called him in not merely to commend Jason for his paramedical heroics, but to share with him a fresh dilemma. In other words, to impart some dubiously good news.

"We've got another roommate for you," Dennis announced. "I personally chose him at a meeting of the proctors—because I really feel you could be a stabilizing influence on him."

"Hey, this isn't fair," Jason protested. "Do I have to be a nursemaid again? Can't I just have someone normal?"

"Nobody at Harvard is normal," Linden philosophically replied.

"All right, Dennis," Jason answered, with a sigh of resignation. "What's *this* guy's problem?"

"Well," the proctor started nonchalantly, "he's a teeny bit . . . aggressive."

"Well, that's okay. I've taken boxing lessons."

Linden coughed. "The problem is—he fights with swords."

"What is he, some foreign student from the Middle Ages?"

"Very witty." Linden smiled. "No, actually he's a hotshot on the fencing team. His name's been in the *Crimson* now and then—Bernie Ackerman. He's terrific with a saber."

"Oh great. Who's he tried to kill so far?"

"Well, not exactly kill. He's living in Holworthy with a very sensitive Chinese fellow. And every time they have the slightest argument, this Ackerman gets out his sword and waves it at the little guy. The kid is now so petrified, the Health Department had to give him pills to sleep. So, clearly, we've just got to separate them."

"Why the hell can't you give me the Chinaman?" Jason complained. "He sounds like a sweet guy."

"No. He gets along okay with roommate number three—a music type. So the proctors figured we'd let well enough alone. Besides, I had the notion that a guy like you could teach that character a lesson."

"Dennis, I'm here to take courses, not teach manners to Ivy League hoodlums."

"Come on, Jason," the proctor cajoled, "you'll turn this guy into a pussycat. And you can count on getting something positive put on your record."

"Dennis," Jason said in valediction, "you're all heart."

January 16, 1955

Jason Gilbert had us all in stitches yesterday at our pre-midyear blast. We recruited some carefully selected lovelies from the local junior colleges with the best reputation for their students' promiscuity. (Newall claims he scored as he drove one of them back to Pine Manor, but we only have his word for it. Really clever guys can bring back evidence.)

Old Gilbert has a way of taking charge of every party. First of all, he's so damn handsome we have trouble keeping our own dates' attention. And then when he starts telling stories, we're all rolling on the floor. Apparently, he's just gotten a new roommate (he won't say what happened to the other one), and the guy's a sort of maniac.

As soon as Jason tries to go to sleep, this nut pulls out a sword and jumps around the living room like Errol Flynn.

Anyway, by the first week the guy'd already slashed their sofa practically to shreds. What was even worse was the noise. It seems every time he scored, which was no problem since the couch could not fight back, he'd yell out, "Kill!" Which was driving Jason absolutely up the wall.

And so last night they had a showdown. Gilbert faced this character with just a tennis racket, and as quietly as possible asked what the hell he thought he was doing. The guy responded that he needed extra practice for the Yale meet.

Jason then said if he really needed practice, he'd be happy to provide it. Only they would have to fight until one of them was dead. Understandably, at first the guy thought Gilbert was just bluffing. But to lend his challenge credibility, Jason smashed what was left of the couch into splinters with his tennis racket. After which he turned to his opponent and explained that that was what he'd make of *him* if he should lose the match.

Unbelievably, the swordsman dropped his blade and made a fast retreat into the bedroom.

Not only did that put an end to all the mayhem, but the swashbuckler went out the next day and bought them a new couch.

Life in Gilbert's suite was pretty quiet after that. In fact, completely quiet. Apparently the guy's too scared even to talk to Jason now.

Like his famous forebear in antiquity, Socrates Lambros was uncompromising in his way of life. This meant that no excuse could absolve his son Ted from evening duties at The Marathon. Hence, Ted had not been permitted to join The Class on the September evening when President Pusey had preached so eloquently in defense of academic freedom.

And since he remained imprisoned from the moment he left classes, Ted never got to see a football game and sit in Soldier's Field amid his fellow freshmen simultaneously yelling themselves hoarse and drinking themselves sick.

This was among the myriad reasons why he did not feel emotionally a full-fledged member of The Class of '58. He longed to be assimilated with his brethren.

Hence, when the Freshman Smoker was announced, he begged his father for a dispensation to attend this one occasion in a Harvard man's career that is avowedly devoted to frivolity.

Socrates was adamant, but Thalassa took her son's side.

"The boy, he works all the time so hard. Let him have one free evening. *Parakalo,* Socrates."

"Okay," the patriarch at last relented.

And Demosthenes could not have eulogized a leader with more grateful eloquence than young Ted Lambros lavished on his father.

Thus, on the eve of February 17, Ted Lambros shaved, put on a new J. August shirt and his very best tweed jacket (secondhand, but almost new), and strode to Sanders Theater. He paid his dollar, which gave him not only entry to the show and all the beer he could consume thereafter, but also door prizes, which ranged from corncob pipes to sample packs of Pall Mall cigarettes.

Deo Gratias, he was really one of them at last.

At half past eight, an overly made-up master of ceremonies walked nervously on stage to start the evening's entertainment. He was welcomed by a tidal wave of grunts and groans and unimaginable obscenities from the sophisticated Harvard men.

The first attraction was the Wellesley Widows, a dozen prim young singers from the nearby ladies' college.

They had scarcely sung a note when from all corners of the theater came a hail of pennies and shouts of, "Get naked!"

The announcer counseled the women to make a hasty retreat. Subsequent performers met similar fates.

The stage show, such as it was, was merely grace before dinner. The real part of the Smoker was waiting, across the corridor in Memorial Hall, where three hundred kegs of beer had been trucked in to quench the freshmen's thirst.

The men were chaperoned, of course. Four deans were present, as were all the proctors and ten members of the university police. The cops had been astute enough to wear their raincoats. And they really needed them.

In no time Mem Hall—scene of so many solemn university events—was ankle deep in beer. Fights broke out. The proctors who attempted to make peace were rudely punched and shoved onto the liquid floor.

Ted Lambros stood watching this melee in total disbelief. Was this really a gathering of the future leaders of the world?

Just then he was accosted.

"Hey, Lambros," someone shouted, "you're not even drunk."

It was Ken O'Brien, who had gone to Cambridge Latin with him, and who was both soaked and sloshed.

Before Ted could respond, he felt a gush of wetness on his head. A baptism of beer. As the liquid oozed slowly down onto his best tweed jacket, Ted angrily lashed out at Ken, catching him squarely on the chin. But in doing so he lost his balance and fell to the ground. Or, as it had become, a lake of beer.

He couldn't stand it any longer. Although O'Brien, whom he'd knocked onto his knees, kept calling almost amicably to please continue fighting, Ted splashed, sick at heart, out of Mem Hall. Never looking back.

The Harvard-Radcliffe Orchestra holds an annual concerto contest to determine the most talented soloist in the community. The competition is held in the winter so that the victor, usually a senior or grad student, can highlight the orchestra's spring concert.

But there are always eager beavers who try to get their names down early. And Don Lowenstein, the president, has to employ tactful diplomacy to discourage them from screwing up in public.

But his freshman visitor this afternoon, slight, bespectacled, and red-haired, would not be dissuaded.

"Look," Lowenstein somewhat condescendingly explained, "our soloists mainly go on to be professionals. I'm sure you were a whiz in high school, but—"

"I'm a professional," interrupted Danny Rossi '58.

"Okay, okay, don't get excited. It's just this competition's unbelievably intense."

"I know," Danny answered. "If I don't measure up, that'll be my problem."

"Let's settle this right now. Come downstairs and let me listen to you."

When he returned nearly an hour later, Donald Lowenstein was in a mild state of shock. Sukie Wadsworth, the vice-president, was now in the office and looked up as he walked in and flopped behind his desk. "Sukie, I've just heard this year's concerto winner. And let me tell you, this freshman Rossi is a genius."

Just then the subject of his praise walked in.

"Thanks for your time," Danny said. "I hope you think I'm good enough to join the competition."

"Hello," said the Radcliffe girl, taking the initiative. "I'm Sukie Wadsworth, the orchestra V.P."

"Uh—nice to meet you." He hoped she didn't notice how he was staring at her from behind his lenses.

"I think it's very exciting that we'll have a freshman in the contest this year," she added brightly.

"Well," Danny said shyly, "I may just end up embarrassing myself."

"I doubt it." Sukie smiled, dazzling him further. "Don tells me that you're very good."

"Oh. Well—uh—I hope he's not just being polite."

There was a sudden awkward pause. And in that briefest of intervals, Danny resolved to make a heroic attempt at impressing this lovely creature.

Of course he'd fail, as usual. But then he tried to tell himself that the law of averages might be on his side.

"Uh, Sukie, would you like to hear me play?"

"I'd love to," she replied enthusiastically, and took Danny by the hand as they went out to find a practice room.

He played a Bach partita and a lightning-fast Rachmaninoff. Inspired by the feminine proximity, his technique was even more impressive than before, but he didn't glance at her for fear of losing concentration.

And yet he sensed her presence. Oh, how he sensed her presence.

At last he looked up. She was leaning over the piano, her low-necked blouse offering a view of great aesthetic interest.

"Was I any good?" he asked, slightly breathless.

A broad smile crossed her face.

"Let me tell you something, Rossi," she began, moving close enough to place her hands on his shoulders. "You are without doubt the most fantastic guy I've ever had the pleasure of being in a room with."

"Oh," said Danny Rossi, looking up at her, nervous raindrops forming on his brow. "Say—uh—would you like to have a cup of coffee sometime?"

She laughed.

"Danny, would you like to make love right now?"

"Right here?"

She began to unbutton his shirt.

*   *   *

Danny had always hoped that women ultimately would discover that his brilliant execution of a keyboard passage could be just as stimulating as the execution of a gridiron pass. At last it had happened.

And football players never get to play encores.

March 6, 1955

What makes Harvard—and, I have to admit, Yale—different from every other university in America is its so-called college system.

Around 1909, Cambridge was turning from a village into a real city, and though some students lived in dorms, Harvard men were scattered everywhere across town. The poorer guys rented cheap hovels along Mass. Avenue, while the overprivileged ones (like my father) lived in really posh apartments in the area then called the Gold Coast (near Mt. Auburn Street). This dispersion was symptomatic of a rigid social separation that perpetuated lots of prejudice.

President Lowell thought that it was wrong for undergraduates to live in these hermetic cliques. So he championed the idea of copying Oxford and dividing the university into smaller colleges that would be a mixture of all types.

The process works like this. First they admit all of us freshmen into dormitories in the Yard so that—in principle—we get to meet the different kinds of guys that make up one whole class. After a year of this enlightening experience we're supposed to have found our new diverse and fascinating friends. At which point we'll be ready to spend our next three years down by the river in those exciting little colleges that Harvard snobbishly calls simply "houses."

Actually, for some guys this arrangement has some educational value. Jocks from Alabama find themselves applying to a house along with pre-med types, philosophers, and would-be novelists. And when it does work, this setup really can enrich a person's life as much as any academic course.

But this is far less true where preppies are concerned. Variety is not the spice of our lives. We're like bacteria (though slightly brighter). We flourish in our own special environment. So I'm sure the university was not surprised when Newall, Wigglesworth, and I decided to perpetuate our roommatehood for three more years.

Originally, we had wanted to have Jason Gilbert join with us as a foursome. He's a really good guy and would help to keep things lively. Also, Newall figured we might profit from the surplus of his feminine admirers. But that was secondary.

Dick asked him on the bus back from the squash match against Yale (which we won). But Jason was reluctant. He had had such unbelievable bad luck with roommates that he'd made up his mind to apply to live alone next year. Though sophomores rarely get this privilege, Gilbert's proctor promised to write a letter of support for him. And Jason suggested that we all select the same house as our first choice so that we could have our meals together and he'd be nearby for our multitudinous impromptu parties.

Now our only problem was where to apply.

Though there are seven houses, only three of them are really socially acceptable. For despite this bull about democracy, most of the masters want to give their house a distinctive tone, and thus try to select a preponderance of certain types, who reciprocally gravitate toward them.

A lot of guys choose Adams House (named after good old Johnny, Class of 1755, the second U.S. President), perhaps because it had once been Gold Coast apartments. Also, not inconsequentially, it has a chef who once worked in a fancy New York restaurant (a factor not to be ignored when you consider three full years of breakfast, lunch, and dinner).

Then there's Lowell House, a Georgian masterpiece, convenient to the Final Clubs, whose master is more English than the queen. Withal, a very tweedy place.

But Harvard's undisputed preppie paradise is . . . Eliot House. Needless to say, both Wig and Newall want to make it their first choice. But I'm a bit uneasy at the prospect of inhabiting this rather awesome red-brick monument to my great-grandfather (his statue's even in the courtyard).

Still, Wig and Newall were really hot to go where most of our friends already are ensconced. We had the makings of a real dilemma, till an unexpected visitor surprised us fairly late one evening.

Fortunately, no one was too drunk to hear the knocking at the door.

Newall stood up unsteadily to greet our nocturnal guest. I suddenly heard him cry out, "Jesus Christ!" and hurried to the door to hear our visitor reply, "Not quite, young man, I'm just His humble servant."

It was none other than Professor Finley. I mean the man himself—in our own dorm!

He happened to be passing by on his late evening promenade, and thought he'd take the liberty of popping in to ask where we'd be applying for next year. And especially if Eliot was "privileged" to be among our choices.

We quickly assured him that it was, although he sensed that I myself had qualms about being Andrew Eliot in Eliot House, whose master was the Eliot Professor of Greek.

In fact, he'd come to reassure me.

He did not expect me to translate the Bible for the Indians, or become the President of Harvard. And yet he was certain that in my own way I'd make my mark somehow.

I don't know if I was more stunned or just moved. I mean, this great professor thought that I might actually develop into—I don't know—something.

The next morning I was still not really sure that John H. Finley actually had come in person to our room.

But, even if it was a dream, the three of us are going to go to Eliot. Because even the ghost of Finley—if it was only that—is good enough to spellbind anyone.

When Jason Gilbert picked up the *Crimson* outside his door each morning, he turned his immediate attention to the sports page to see if any of his exploits had been mentioned. After that, he read the front page to learn what was happening around the college. Finally, if he had time, he checked the world news, which was always briefly outlined in a corner.

For this reason he failed to notice a brief item reporting that, for the first time in memory, a freshman had won the annual concerto contest of the Harvard-Radcliffe Orchestra.

On the evening of April 12, 1955, Daniel Rossi '58 would be playing Liszt's E-Flat Concerto.

Jason learned of this only three days later, when an envelope was slipped under his door.

> Dear Gilbert,
>
>   If you hadn't helped me with the Step Test, I probably would never have been able to practice enough to win.
>
>   Here, as promised, are two tickets. Bring a friend.
>
>   Regards,
>   Danny

Jason smiled. That freshman-week experience was such a distant memory, he'd never given Danny's words a second thought. But now he could invite Annie Russell, the most sought-after girl at Radcliffe. Jason had long been looking for a suitable occasion. And this was a great one.

*   *   *

On the night of April 12, all of Harvard's talent watchers crowded into Sanders Theater to examine what had been predicted as a new comet entering their galaxy.

No one was more aware of the impending scrutiny than the soloist himself. Danny stood in the wings, watching with mounting anxiety as the hall continued to fill with intimidating personalities. Not only were his Harvard professors present, but he recognized important figures from the city's famous conservatories. My God, even John Finley was there.

During the exhilarating weeks of rehearsal he had looked forward with a kind of manic joy to this grand occasion—the moment to parade his pianistic talents before a thousand bigwigs. He had suddenly felt like a giant.

That is, until last night. For on the eve of what he had been sure would be his Harvard coronation, he could not get to sleep. He tossed. He turned. He fantasized catastrophe. And moaned as if it were inevitable.

I'll be a laughingstock, he thought. I'll faint when I walk out on stage. Or else I'll trip. Or maybe play my entrance much too soon. Or too late. Or completely forget the music.

They'll be rolling in the aisles. And not just Orange County ladies, but a thousand of the world's most knowledgeable people. What a disaster. Why did I ever go out for this goddamn contest anyway?

He felt his forehead. It was hot and moist. Maybe I'm sick, he thought. He hoped. Maybe they'll have to cancel my appearance. Oh please, God, make me have the flu. Or even something fairly serious.

To his increased distress, the next morning he felt reasonably healthy. And thus resigned himself to face the evening guillotine in Sanders Theater.

He stood backstage all alone, wishing he were somewhere else.

Don Lowenstein, who was conducting, came back to ask him if he was ready. Danny wanted to say no. But something autonomic made him nod.

He took a breath, said inwardly, "Oh shit," and walked on stage, his eyes fixed on the floor. Just before sitting at the piano, he bowed slightly to the audience, acknowledging their polite applause. Mercifully, the spotlights blinded him and he could see no faces.

Then an uncanny thing occurred.

No sooner was he at the keyboard than his fear transformed into a new sensation. Excitement. He was burning to make music.

He signaled readiness to Don.

The motion of the opening baton put Danny in a strange, hypnotic trance. He dreamed that he was playing flawlessly. Far better than at any prior moment in his life.

The sounds of "Bravo!" flew at him from every corner of the hall. And applause that seemed without diminuendo.

The atmosphere surrounding Danny afterward reminded Jason of the finals of a tennis championship. They did everything but pick him up and carry him around the theater on their shoulders. Gray eminences of the music community were lined up like fans to shake his hand.

Yet, the moment Danny noticed Jason, he broke free and hurried to the edge of the stage to greet him.

"You were fantastic," Jason warmly hailed him. "We were really glad to get the tickets. Oh, I'd like to introduce my date, Miss Annie Russell, '57."

"Hi." Danny smiled. "Are you at The Cliffe?"

"Yes," she answered, beaming. "And can I be the millionth person to say you were absolutely fabulous tonight."

"Thanks," said Danny. And then quickly added in apologetic tones, "Hey look, I'm really sorry, but I've gotta go shake more professors' hands. Let's get together for a meal sometime, huh, Jason? It was nice to meet you, Annie."

He waved goodbye and sprinted off.

The next afternoon, buoyed by her vivacious attitude all evening, Jason telephoned Annie to invite her to the football game next Saturday.

"I'm really sorry," she replied, "I'm going down to Connecticut."

"Oh, a date at Yale?"

"No. Danny's playing with the Hartford Symphony."

Shit, thought Jason as he hung up, bursting with frustration. That's a lesson for you.

Never help a Harvard classmate—even up a step.

On Tuesday, April 24, 1955, winter was still very much in the Cambridge air. Yet, official administrative statistics suggest that a metaphorical ray of sunlight shone into the lives of 71.6 percent of Harvard's 322d freshman class. For this elated majority had been accepted by the house of their first choice.

To the trio in Wig G-21 it came as no surprise, since their admission had been heralded a month earlier by the visitation of a distinguished archangel. But they were delighted to learn that they had been assigned a suite that enjoyed a river view. Not many sophomores got such choice accommodations.

Nor did many sophomores get the privilege of living in a single room. But Jason Gilbert, Jr., was so honored (for services rendered). His private lodgings were situated across the Eliot courtyard from his three aristocratic friends.

He conveyed the good news to his father in their weekly phone conversation.

"That's terrific, son. Why, even people who've only barely heard of Harvard know that Eliot House has the cream of under-graduate society."

"But everybody here is supposed to be cream, Dad," Jason answered good-humoredly.

"Yes, of course. But Eliot's the crème de la crème, Jason. Your mother and I are really proud of you. I mean, we always are. By the way, have you been doing those new exercises for your backhand?"

"Yes, Dad. Absolutely."

"Say, I read in *Tennis World* that all the big guns are going heavier on the road work—just like boxers in the morning."

"Yeah," said Jason, "but I really haven't got time. My course work is incredible."

"Of course, son. Don't do anything to compromise your education. Speak to you next week."

"So long, Dad. Love to Mom."

◆

Danny Rossi, on the other hand, was outraged. His first choice had been Adams House, because so many musical and literary types lived there. You could practically knock on your left and right and have enough participants for chamber music.

So certain had he been of acceptance into Adams that his alternate second and third selections were scribbled down without the slightest forethought. He had merely listed two other houses as they appeared in alphabetical order on the application, namely Dunster and Eliot.

And it was his *third* choice, Eliot, to which he was assigned.

How could they do this to him—someone who had already distinguished himself in the college community? Wouldn't Adams House someday be proud to boast that Danny Rossi had once lived there?

Moreover, he didn't relish the prospect of being stuck for three years in Eliot with a bunch of smug preppies.

The man to whom he chose to voice his complaint was Master Finley. Such was his respect for the great man after Hum 2 that he felt he could honestly convey his disappointment to the master of the house he didn't want to be in.

But even more astonishing was his reaction when Finley candidly confessed. "I wanted you very badly, Daniel. I had to trade the master of Adams two football stalwarts and a published poet just to get him to relinquish you."

"I guess I should be flattered, sir," said Danny, quite off balance at the news. "It's just that—"

"I know," the master said, anticipating Danny's misgivings, "but despite our reputation, I want Eliot to be outstanding in all the disciplines. Have you visited the house before?"

"No, sir," Danny admitted.

A moment later Finley was conducting Danny up a winding staircase in the courtyard tower. The young man was out of breath, but the dynamic Finley had sprinted up the steps. And now opened a door.

The first thing Danny saw was an astonishingly beautiful view of the Charles River through a large circular window. Only seconds later did he realize that there was a grand piano placed before it.

"What do you think?" asked Finley. "All the great minds of the past found inspiration in elevated places. Think of your own Italian genius Petrarch ascending Mont Ventoux. A most platonic gesture."

"This is unbelievable," said Danny.

"A man could write a symphony up here, could he not, Daniel?"

"I'll bet."

"Which is why we wanted you at Eliot House. Remember, all of Harvard welcomes genius, but here we cultivate it."

The living legend held his hand out toward the young musician and remarked, "I look forward to your coming here next fall."

"Thank you," said Danny, quite overwhelmed. "Thank you for bringing me to Eliot."

◆

Yet, for certain members of The Class of '58, April 24 was just like any other day.

Ted Lambros was one of those unhappy few. For, being a commuter, he had not applied to any house and hence was completely unaffected by the news conveyed to all those living in the Yard.

He went to class as usual, spent the whole afternoon grinding in Lamont Library, and at five headed for The Marathon.

Still, he could not help being aware that the more privileged of his classmates were rejoicing at the prospect of spending the next three years along the river as members of a unique housing arrangement.

Having garnered an A-minus and three B's at midterms, he had been reasonably confident of obtaining a scholarship—large enough, in fact, to permit him to live at the college.

But to his chagrin, he had received a letter from the Financial Aid Office, which took great pleasure in informing him that he had been granted a stipend of eight hundred dollars for next year.

This would normally seem like cause for at least some modest rejoicing. But Harvard had just recently announced a rise in its basic tuition to precisely that amount.

Ted felt frustrated as hell. Like a runner sprinting madly on a treadmill.

He still did not really belong. Yet.

There had not merely been members of the academic community at Danny Rossi's Sanders Theater concert. Unknown to the soloist, Professor Piston had invited Charles Munch, the distinguished conductor of the Boston Symphony. The maestro wrote Danny an encomiastic letter, in his own hand, commending his performance and inviting him to spend the summer working for the famous Tanglewood Music Festival.

> The tasks are not exalted, but I feel that you would benefit from the proximity to all the great artists who come visit us. And I would personally welcome you to sit in on our orchestra rehearsals, since I know you aspire to a professional career.

> Yours sincerely,
> Charles Munch

This invitation also solved a touchy family dilemma. For, in her weekly letters, Gisela earnestly assured her son that if he came back home that summer she was certain that his father would destigmatize him. And they could build a new relationship.

And yet, although he longed to see his mother—and to share his great success with Dr. Landau—Danny simply could not risk another confrontation with Arthur Rossi, D.D.S.

♦

Then suddenly, almost abruptly, freshman year was at an end.

The month of May began with Reading Period for exams.

These special days were theoretically for extra, independent study. But for a lot of Harvard men (like Andrew Eliot and company), it meant sitting down to do a whole semester's work, beginning with the very first assignments in their courses.

The athletic season culminated with the many confrontations against Yale. Not all the clashes went in Harvard's favor. But Jason Gilbert led the tennis team to victory. And took particular delight in watching the Yale coach's face as he unmercifully destroyed their number-one man, and returned with Dickie Newall in the doubles for another round of sweet revenge.

Now even Jason had to settle down and do some heavy studying. He drastically reduced his social life, restricting it to weekends only.

Meanwhile, in Harvard Square the sales of cigarettes and NōDōz pep pills rose dramatically. Lamont was packed around the clock. Its modern ventilation system spewed back all the scents of unchanged shirts, cold sweat, and naked fear. Yet no one noticed.

Examinations actually were a relief. For The Class of '58 learned to its great delight that the old proverb about Harvard was quite true: The hardest part was getting in. You had to be a genius *not* to graduate.

And yet, as freshman dorms were emptied—to make room for the ancient graduates of twenty-five years previous who would be living in them once again during Commencement Week—some members of The Class were leaving, never to return.

A tiny number had actually accomplished the impossible and flunked out. Some honestly conceded that they could not bear the prospect of more pressure from such unbelievably ambitious peers. And thus, capitulating to preserve their sanity, elected to transfer to universities near home.

Some went down fighting. And lost their minds in doing so. David Davidson (still in the hospital) was not the last. In fact, at Easter there had been a suicide compassionately misrepresented by the *Crimson* as an auto accident (although Bob Rutherford of San Antonio had actually been parked in his garage when death occurred).

And yet, as certain rugged members of The Class would argue, was this not something of a lesson to both the victims and the survivors? Would life at the very top be any easier than the self-inflicted torture chamber that was Harvard?

But the more sensitive of them recognized that they still had another three years to survive.

October 1, 1955

Last August when we were all up at the family house in Maine—
where I spent most of the time getting to know my new step-
mother and her kids—Father and I had our annual lakeside chat.
First he congratulated me for squeaking by in all my courses.
Indeed, the prospect of my actually staying in one school for four
entire years now seemed to him a pleasant possibility.

Further in an educational vein, he expressed his determination that I should not suffer from the handicap of having been
born rich. His message was that although he would gladly pay my
tuition fees and board, he was stopping my pocket money for my
own good.

Therefore, if I wished—as he hoped I did—to join a Final
Club, to go cheer Harvard at football games, to take young
eligible ladies to Locke-Ober's, etc., I would have to seek gainful
employment. All of this was, of course, to teach me Emersonian
self-reliance. For which I thanked him politely.

Upon my return to Cambridge for sophomore year, I went
straight to the Student Employment Center and found that the
really lucrative jobs had already gone to scholarship students who
needed the dough more than I. Thus, I could not have the enlightening experience of washing plates or dishing out mashed potatoes.

Just when things looked bleakest, however, I ran into Master
Finley in the courtyard. When I told him why I was back so early,
he commended my father's desire to inculcate good Yankee values.
Surprisingly, as if he had nothing better to do, he marched me
straight to the Eliot House library, where he persuaded Ned
Devlin, the head librarian, to sign me on as one of his assistants.

Anyway, I've got this really good deal. Three nights a week I
get seventy-five cents an hour for just sitting at a desk from seven
till midnight watching guys read books.

Actually, Master Finley must have known what he was doing,

because the job is so undemanding that, for lack of something better to do, I study.

Once in a great while, a guy interrupts me to take out a book—so I rarely have to look up from the page—except if somebody's talking too loud and I have to shut him up.

But last night was different. Something actually *happened* in the Eliot House library.

At about nine o'clock I lifted my eyes just to survey the scene. The place was dotted with studying preppies in their usual uniform, button-down shirts and chinos.

But at a table in the far corner I noticed something strange on the back of a well-built guy. It was, I thought, my own jacket. Or, more accurately, my own former jacket. Normally I wouldn't know the difference, but this was a tweed job with leather buttons that my folks had brought me from Harrods in London. There weren't many of those around.

Not that this in itself should be surprising. After all, I had sold it last spring to that famous used-clothes merchant, Joe Keezer. He's a Harvard institution, and most of my friends, when in need of extra cash for such necessities as cars, liquor, and club dues, have flogged their fashionable rags to old Joe.

But I don't know a single guy who ever *bought* from him. I mean, it doesn't work that way. So, strictly in my professional capacity as librarian, I was confronted with a problem. For possibly, indeed quite probably, there was an infiltrator in the library disguised as a preppie.

The guy was good-looking—dark and handsome. But he was a little *too* kempt. I mean, although the room was kind of stuffy, not only did he keep the jacket on, but I could see he didn't even open up his collar. Also, he seemed to be cramming like a demon. He was buried in his book, moving only now and then to check a dictionary.

Now, all of this is not against the law. And yet it's not the *norm* for anyone I knew in Eliot House. And so I figured I had better keep my eyes on this possible interloper.

At eleven-forty-five, I usually start extinguishing lights to give the guys a hint that I am closing shop. By chance last night the library was already empty—except for this stranger in my former jacket. This gave me a chance to solve the mystery.

I casually approached his table, pointed toward the large lamp in the middle, and asked if he minded if I shut it off. He looked up, startled, and said, kind of apologetically, that he hadn't realized it was closing time.

When I answered that by house rules he officially had fourteen minutes more, he got the message. He stood up and asked me how I'd guessed he wasn't from Eliot. Was it something in his face?

I answered candidly that it was only something in his jacket.

This embarrassed him. As he started to examine it, I explained that it was a former possession of mine. Now I felt shitty for mentioning it, and quickly assured the guy that he could use the library anytime I was there.

I mean, he was at Harvard, wasn't he?

Yeah. It turns out he's a sophomore commuter. Named Ted Lambros.

On October 17, there was a small riot in Eliot House. More specifically, a demonstration against classical music. Still more specifically, a demonstration against Danny Rossi. To be extremely precise, the actual aggression was not against the man but his piano.

It all started when a couple of clubbies began an early cocktail party. Danny usually practiced at Paine Hall, except when he had exams or a paper due. Then he used the secondhand upright in his room.

He was at it hot and heavy that afternoon when some of the jolly tipplers decided that Chopin was not suitable background music for getting smashed. It was simply a matter of taste. And, of course, in Eliot House, taste was the supreme law. It was therefore decided that Rossi had to be silenced.

At first they tried diplomacy. Dickie Newall was dispatched to tap politely on Rossi's portal and respectfully request that Danny "quit playing that shit."

The pianist replied that house rules allowed him to practice a musical instrument in the afternoon. And he would stick to his rights. To which Newall responded that *he* didn't give a flying fig for rules, and that Rossi was disturbing a serious symposium. Danny then asked him to go away. Which he did.

When Newall returned to report the failure of his mission, his co-imbibers decided that physical action was necessary.

Four of Eliot's staunchest and drunkest legionnaires marched resolutely across the courtyard and up to Rossi's room. They knocked politely on the door. He opened it slightly. Without another word, the commandos entered, surrounded the offending instrument, lugged it to the open window, and—hurled it out.

Danny's piano fell three floors to the courtyard, smashing

and disintegrating on the pavement below. Fortunately, no one was passing by at the time.

Rossi feared he'd be the next to be defenestrated. But Dickie Newall simply remarked, "Thanks for your cooperation, Dan." And the band of merry men departed.

In a matter of seconds there was a crowd around the dismembered instrument. Danny was the first to arrive and reacted as though someone in his family had been murdered.

("Christ," Newall reported, "I've never seen a guy get so upset about a piece of wood.")

The perpetrators of the assault were immediately convoked in the senior tutor's office, where Dr. Porter threatened them with expulsion and ordered them to pay for a new piano as well as for the broken window. Moreover, they were commanded to march over and apologize.

But Rossi was still in a fury. He told them they were a bunch of uncivilized animals who didn't deserve to be at Harvard. Since Dr. Porter was right there, they grudgingly agreed with him. As they departed, the clubbies vowed revenge on the "little Italian wimp" who had caused them so much embarrassment.

That night at dinner, Andrew Eliot (who had been warming the varsity soccer bench during that afternoon's debacle) saw Danny sitting all by himself at a corner table, picking at his food and looking really miserable. He walked over and sat down across the table.

"Hey, Rossi, I'm sorry to hear about your piano."

Danny lifted his head. "Who the hell do they think they are?" he suddenly exploded.

"You want the truth?" Andrew asked. "They think they're God's gift to sophistication. But actually they're just a bunch of empty-headed preppies who wouldn't even be here if their parents hadn't sent them to expensive schools. A guy like you makes them feel insecure."

"Me?"

"Yeah, Rossi. *You're* what this place is all about. You've got one thing they can't buy, and it galls the hell out of them. They're jealous because you've got real talent."

Danny was quiet for a moment. Then looked at Andrew and said softly, "You know, Eliot, you're a really good guy."

Ted could not concentrate on Helen of Troy. Not that Professor Whitman's remarks about her appearance in Book Three of the *Iliad* were not fascinating. But Ted was distracted by something even more divine than the face that launched a thousand ships.

For more than a year now he had been staring at this girl. They had both started Ancient Greek together the previous fall, and Ted could still remember his first sight of her, as the soft morning sun shone through the windows of Sever Hall irradiating her amber hair and delicate features. She seemed like an image carved on an ivory brooch. The tasteful, unostentatious manner of her dress made him think of the nymph in Horace's ode— *simplex munditiis*—embellished in simplicity.

He could recall the day—now thirteen months ago—when he had first noticed Sara Harrison. Professor Stewart had asked for someone to conjugate *paideuo* in the imperfect and first aorist, and she had volunteered. She had been sitting timidly by the window in the very last row—quite the opposite of Ted, who always sat front and center. Though she had been reciting correctly, her voice was so soft that Stewart had to ask her politely to speak louder. It was at this precise moment that Ted Lambros had turned his head and seen the girl.

From then on, he altered his seating position to the far right of the first row so that he could both gaze at Sara and still be conspicuously placed to gain academic points. He had a copy of the *Radcliffe Register* in his desk at home, and like a secret drunk he periodically indulged himself by taking it out and gazing at her picture. He also studied the meager information printed with it. She was from Greenwich, Connecticut, and had attended Miss

Porter's. She lived in Cabot Hall—in the unlikely event that he should ever get the courage to call her.

In fact, he wasn't brave enough even to attempt small talk with her after class. He had gone through two terms like this, concentrating equally on the intricacies of the Greek verb and the delicacies of Sara's face. But whereas he was aggressively bold when it came to answering grammatical questions, he was pathologically shy about saying *anything* to the angelic Sara Harrison.

But then, something unprecedented occurred. Sara was unable to answer a question.

"I'm sorry, Mr. Whitman, I just can't get the hang of Homer's hexameter."

"You'll catch on with a little practice," the professor replied kindly. "Mr. Lambros, would you scan the line please."

That is how it all began. For after class, Sara came up to Ted.

"Gosh, you scan so easily. Is there some secret to it?"

He barely had the courage to reply.

"I'd be glad to help you if you'd like."

"Oh, thank you. I'd really appreciate that."

"How about a cup of coffee at The Bick?"

"Great," said Sara.

And they walked out of Sever Hall side by side.

Ted found her problem at once. She had neglected to take account of the digamma, a Greek letter that existed in Homer's alphabet but which had since been dropped and was not printed in the text.

"You just have to imagine where a word might have an invisible *w* in front of it. Like *oinos,* which would become *woinos,* and would remind you more of 'wine,' which is what it actually means."

"You know, Ted, you're a terrific teacher."

"It helps to be Greek," he said with uncharacteristic shyness.

Two days later, Professor Whitman again called on Sara Harrison to scan a Homeric hexameter. She did it perfectly, and after doing so smiled gratefully across the room at her proud tutor.

"Thanks a million, Ted," she whispered as they walked from class. "How can I repay you?"

"Well, you could join me for another cup of coffee."

"With pleasure," she replied. And her smile made him slightly weak at the knees.

From then on, their meetings after class became a ritual to which Ted looked forward like a pious monk anticipating matins. Of course the talk was general—mostly about their classes and especially Greek. Ted was too shy to make the slightest move that might change their relationship and lose this platonic ecstasy.

Still, they were helping each other with Whitman's course. Ted was understandably stronger on the linguistic side, but Sara knew the secondary literature. She had read Milman Parry's *"L'epithète traditionnelle dans Homère"* (which did not exist in English), and could give Ted a fuller comprehension of Homer's formulaic style.

They both got A's and moved triumphantly to Greek Lyric Poetry with Professor Havelock. But the subject matter only intensified Ted's emotional state.

It began with the passionate verses of Sappho, which they took turns reading and translating as they sat across the scratched laminated table.

" 'There are those that say that the most beautiful thing on the dark earth is a multitude of horsemen' "

" 'Others say it is an armada of ships.' "

" 'But I say it is the one you love.' "

And so on all the way through Sappho Fragment 16.

"That's fantastic, isn't it, Ted?" exclaimed Sara. "I mean, the way a woman expresses her emotion by saying that it surpasses all things that are important in the world of men. It must have been pretty revolutionary stuff in those days."

"What amazes me is how she can display her feelings without any embarrassment. That's tough for anybody—man or woman." He wondered if she sensed that he was also speaking of himself.

"More coffee?" he asked.

She nodded and rose. "It's my round."

As she started toward the counter, Ted thought fleetingly of asking her to have dinner some night. And then immediately lost heart. Besides, he was indentured to The Marathon from five till ten-thirty every day of the week. And he was certain she had a boyfriend. A girl like that could have her pick of anyone.

*   *   *

To welcome the arrival of spring, Professor Levine gave Ted's Latin class an unscheduled reading of the glorious hymn *Pervigilium Veneris*. Though celebrating a new springtime for all lovers, it ends on a touching elegiac note. The poet laments:

Illa cantat, nos tacemus: quando ver venit meum?
Quando fiam uti chelidon ut tacere desinam?

Songbirds sing, must I be silent? When I pray will my
    spring come?
When will I be like the swallow, singing forth no longer
    dumb?

November 4, 1955

Long before I came to Harvard I dreamed of being a chorus girl.

Not only is it a lot of laughs, but it's also a great way to meet women.

For over a century now the Hasty Pudding Club has been producing an annual all-male musical comedy. The authors are usually the best wits in the college (that's how Alan J. Lerner '40 trained to write *My Fair Lady*).

But the show's legendary status is not due to the quality of the script, but rather the quantity of the chorus line. For this unique corps de ballet is peopled by brawny preppie jocks in drag, kicking up their hairy muscular legs.

After its Cambridge run, this mindless and fairly gross extravaganza makes a brief tour of cities selected for the hospitality of their alumni and, most important, the nubility of their daughters.

I remember years ago, when my dad first took me to one of these productions, thinking the thundering hoof beats of the can can guys would quite literally bring down the house. They made that whole wooden building on Holyoke Street tremble.

This year's production (the 108th) is called *A Ball for Lady Godiva*—which should give you some idea of the refined level of its humor.

Anyway, the first afternoon of tryouts looked like an elephants' convention. I mean, some of the football players made a crewman like Wigglesworth seem sylphlike by comparison. There was no question that all these mastodons were dying to be one of Lady Godiva's chambermaids—which is how they were going to dress this year's Rockettes.

I knew the competition would be rough, so I worked out with weights (toe raises and squats) to beef up my leg muscles in hopes of getting them to look incongruous enough to make the grade.

We each got about a minute to sing something, but I think the whole issue was decided in the split second when we were asked to roll up our trousers.

They called us alphabetically, and, with knees knocking, I walked up on stage to sing a snatch of "Alexander's Ragtime Band" in my very lowest baritone.

I sweated for two days waiting for them to post the cast list this afternoon.

It contained two surprises.

Neither Wig nor I got to be chambermaids. Mike—to his eternal glory—captured the coveted role of Fifi, Lady Godiva's debutante daughter.

And I—O shame!—was cast as *Prince* Macaroni, one of the suitors for his hand.

"Great," Mike enthused, "I'm actually rooming with one of my costars."

I was not amused. I was thinking that I'd failed again.

I wasn't even man enough to be a girl.

It was the usual Friday night at The Marathon. Every table was packed with chattering Harvard men and their dates. Socrates urged his staff to hurry along since there was a vast crowd of people standing outside waiting their turn. Up front near the cashier's desk there seemed to be some argument going on. Socrates called across to his elder son in Greek, "Theo, go and help your sister."

Ted hastened to the rescue. As he approached, he could hear Daphne protesting, "Look, I am terribly sorry but *you* must have misunderstood. We never take reservations on the weekends."

But the tall, supercilious preppie in the Chesterfield coat seemed quite adamant that he had booked a table for 8:00 P.M. and was not about to stand outside on Mass. Avenue with (in so many words) the hoi polloi. Daphne was relieved to see her brother arrive.

"What's going on, sis?" Ted asked.

"This gentleman insists he had a reservation, Teddy. And you know our policy about weekends."

"Yes," Ted responded, and turned immediately to the protesting client to explain, "we would never—"

He stopped in mid-sentence when he noticed who was standing next to the irate, distinguished-looking man.

"Hi, Ted," said Sara Harrison, who was manifestly embarrassed at her escort's rudeness. "I think Alan's made a mistake. I'm terribly sorry."

Her date glared at her.

"I don't make such errors," he stated emphatically, and immediately turned back to Ted. "I called yesterday evening and spoke to some woman. Her English wasn't very good so I was quite explicit."

"That must have been Mama," Daphne offered.

"Well, 'Mama' should have written it down," insisted the punctilious Alan.

"She did," said Ted, who now had a large reservations book in his hand. "Are you Mr. Davenport?"

"I am," said Alan. "Do you see my reservation for eight o'clock?"

"Yes. It's listed for last night, Thursday—when we *do* accept reservations. Look." He offered the document.

"How can I read that, man? It's in Greek," he protested.

"Then ask Miss Harrison to read it to you."

"Don't involve my date in your mess-up, waiter."

"Please, Alan, he's a friend of mine. We're both in classics. And he's right." Sara pointed to the approximation of "Davenport" scribbled by Mrs. Lambros for eight o'clock the previous night. "You must have forgotten to tell her it was for the next day."

"Sara, what on earth is the matter with you?" Alan snapped. "Are you taking some illiterate woman's word against mine?"

"Excuse me, sir," said Ted, reining in his temper as best he could. "I'm sure my mother is no less literate than yours. She just happens to prefer writing in her native tongue."

Sara tried to end the increasingly bitter dispute.

"Come on, Alan," she said softly, "let's go for a pizza. That's all I wanted in the first place."

"No, Sara, there's a matter of principle involved here."

"Mr. Davenport," Ted said quietly, "if you'll stop blustering I'll give you the next available table. But if you persist in this obnoxious behavior, I'll throw you the hell out."

"I beg your pardon, *garçon*," Alan responded. "I happen to be a third-year law student, and since I am in no way inebriated, you have no right to eject me. If you try, I'll sue the pants off you."

"Excuse *me*," Ted replied. "You may have learned a lot of fancy concepts at Harvard Law, but I doubt if you studied the Cambridge city ordinances that allow a proprietor to kick out somebody—inebriated or not—if he's making a disturbance."

By now Alan had sensed that this was turning into a jungle duel, with Sara as the prize.

"I dare you to throw me out," he snapped.

For a second nobody moved. Clearly, the two antagonists were squaring off for a battle.

Daphne sensed that her brother was about to imperil their whole livelihood and whispered, "Please, Teddie, don't."

"Would you care to step outside, Alan?" said a voice.

Alan was startled. For it was Sara who had spoken these words. He glared down at her.

"No," he retorted angrily. "I'm going to stay here and have dinner."

"Then you'll eat it alone," she replied, and marched out.

As Daphne Lambros thanked God many times under her breath, Ted stormed into the kitchen, where he began to pound his fists against the wall.

In an instant his father arrived. *"Ti diabolo echeis,* Theo? What's this ridiculous behavior? The house is full, the customers are complaining. Do you want to ruin me?"

"I want to die," Ted shouted, continuing to attack the wall.

"Theo, my son, my eldest, we have a living to earn. I beg you to go back and take care of tables twelve through twenty."

Just then Daphne stuck her head through the kitchen door.

"The natives are getting restless," she said. "What's the matter with Teddie?"

"Nothing!" Socrates growled. "Get back to the cash register, Daphne!"

"But, Papa," she replied timorously, "there's a girl who wants to speak to Theo—the one who sort of refereed the fight."

"Omigod!" Ted gasped and took one step toward the men's room.

"Where the hell are you going now?" Socrates barked.

"To comb my hair," said Ted as he disappeared.

Sara Harrison was standing shyly in a corner, shivering slightly in her coat, even though the place was overheated.

Ted walked up to her. "Hi," he said with the casual expression he had frantically rehearsed in front of the mirror.

"I can't tell you how sorry I am," she began.

"That's okay."

"No, let me explain," she insisted. "He was an insufferable bore. He was like that from the minute he picked me up."

"Then why do you date a guy like that?"

"Date? That creature was a fix-up. His-mother-knows-my-mother sort of thing."

"Oh," said Ted.

"I mean filial duty has its limits. If my mother ever tries that again, I'll say I'm taking holy vows. He was the pits, wasn't he?"

"Yes." Ted Lambros smiled.

Then there was an awkward pause.

"Uh—I'm sorry," Sara repeated, "I guess I'm keeping you from your work."

"They can all starve, for all I care. I'd rather talk to you."

Omigod, he thought to himself. *How did* that *slip out?*

"Me too," she said shyly.

From the vortex of the busy restaurant his father called out in Greek, "Theo, get back to work or I'll put my curse on you!"

"I think you'd better go, Ted," Sara murmured.

"Can I ask just one question first?"

"Sure."

"Where's Alan now?"

"In hell, I suppose," Sara replied. "At least that's where I told him to go."

"That means you haven't got a date tonight," Ted grinned.

"Theo!" his father bellowed. "I will curse you and your children's children."

Ignoring the increased paternal threat, Ted continued, "Sara, if you can wait another hour, I'd like to take you to dinner."

Her reply was a single syllable: "Fine."

The cognoscenti knew that the Newtowne Grill, beyond Porter Square, served the best pizza in Cambridge. This is where, at eleven o'clock, Ted brought Sara (in the family's beat-up Chevy Biscayne) for their first dinner date. He had finished his chores at The Marathon with extraordinary speed, for there were wings on his heart.

They sat at a table by the window, where a red neon sign flashed periodically on their faces, giving the whole atmosphere the feeling of a dream—which Ted still half-believed it was. While waiting for their pizza they each sipped a beer.

"I can't understand why a girl like you would even dream of accepting a blind date," said Ted.

"Well, it's better than sitting home studying on a Saturday night, isn't it?"

"But you must be besieged with offers. I mean, I always imagined you were booked up through 1958."

"That's one of the great Harvard myths, Ted. Half of Radcliffe sits around feeling miserable on Saturday night because everybody at Harvard just *assumes* somebody else has asked them out. Meanwhile, all the girls at Wellesley have roaring social lives."

Ted was amazed. "I wish to hell I had known. I mean, you never mentioned. . . ."

"Well, it's not the sort of thing you bring up over Greek verbs and English muffins," she replied, "although I sometimes wished I had."

Ted was nearly bowled over.

"Do you know, Sara," he confessed, "I've been dying to ask you out since the very first minute I saw you."

She looked at him with sudden brightness in her eyes.

"Well, what the hell took you so long—am I that intimidating?" she asked.

"Not anymore."

He parked the Chevy in front of Cabot Hall and walked her to the door. Then he put his hands on her shoulders and looked her straight in the eyes.

"Sara," he said firmly, "I've waded through a year of English muffins for this."

And he kissed her with the passion that he'd stored up in a million fantasies.

She responded with an equal fervor.

When at last he started home, he was so intoxicated that he barely felt his feet make contact with the ground. Then suddenly he stopped. Oh shit, he thought, I left the car in front of Cabot Hall! He dashed back to retrieve it, hoping Sara would not notice his idiotic error from her window.

But at that moment, Sara Harrison's eyes were not focused on anything. She was simply sitting motionless on her bed, staring into space.

The final lyrics of Greek 2B were by an author not generally known for amorous verse—Plato.

"It's ironic," Professor Havelock remarked, "but the philosopher who banished poetry from his Ideal Republic was himself the author of perhaps the most perfect lyric ever written." And he then read out in Greek one of the famous *Aster* epigrams.

> Star of my life, to the stars your face is turned;
> Would I were the heavens, looking back at you with
> ten thousand eyes.

Appropriately enough, the bells of Memorial Hall tolled the end of the class. As they walked out the door together, Ted whispered to Sara, *"I* wish I were the heavens."

"Nothing doing," she replied. "I want you right nearby."

And they walked toward The Bick hand in hand.

November is the cruelest month —at least for ten percent of the sophomore class. For it is then that the Final Clubs (so called because you can belong to only one) make their definitive selections. These eleven societies exist merely on the edge of Harvard life. But it is, one may say, the gilt edge.

A Final Club is an elite, if homogeneous, institution where rich preppies can go and have drinks with other rich preppies. These gentlemanly sodalities do not intrude on college life. Indeed, the majority of Harvard men barely know they exist.

But, needless to say, November was a busy month for Messrs. Eliot, Newall, and Wigglesworth. Their suite was a veritable mecca for tweedy pilgrims, flocking to implore them to join *their* order.

Like modern musketeers, the three decided they'd stick together. Though they got invited to punches for most of the clubs, it was pretty clear that they'd go to either the Porcellian, the AD, or the Fly.

In fact, if all got asked, they knew they'd join the Porc. If you're going to bother with these things, it might as well be the undisputed number one, "the oldest men's club in America."

Having been included in the P.C.'s last-cut dinner, they assumed they were in.

Back at Eliot, they were still in their penguin suits, nursing a final *digestif,* when there was a sudden knock at the door.

Newall quipped that it might be some desperate emissary from another club—perhaps the AD, which took Franklin D. Roosevelt when the Porcellian blackballed him.

It turned out to be Jason Gilbert.

"Am I disturbing you guys?" he asked somberly.

"No, not at all," Andrew responded. "Come in and join us for a brandy."

"Thanks, but I never touch the stuff," he replied.

His glance made them curiously self-conscious about their attire.

"The final dinner, huh?" he inquired.

"Yeah," Wig replied casually.

"The Porc?" he asked.

"Right the first time," Newall sang out.

But neither Mike nor Dick sensed the tinge of bitterness in Jason's voice.

"Was it a tough decision, guys?" he asked.

"Not really," said Wig. "We had a couple of other options, but the P.C. seemed the most attractive."

"Oh," said Jason. "It must feel great to be wanted."

"You ought to know," Newall quipped. "Every lovely at The Cliffe burns incense to your picture."

Jason didn't smile. "That's probably because they don't realize I'm a leper."

"What the hell are you talking about, Gilbert?" Andrew asked.

"I'm talking about the fact that while almost every guy I know got at least one invitation to the first punch of a club, I wasn't even asked by the lowly BAT. I never realized I was such an asshole."

"Come on, Jason," Newall said reassuringly. "Final Clubs are a bunch of crap."

"I'm sure they are," he replied. "Which is why you guys are all thrilled to be joining one. I just thought that being tuned to the club mentality, you might have some notion as to what precisely they found so obnoxious about me."

Newall, Wig, and Andrew looked uncomfortably at one another, wondering who would have to explain to Jason what they had assumed was obvious. Andrew could see that his roommates weren't up to it. So he made a stab at the not-so-commendable facts of Harvard life.

"Hey, Jason," he began. "Who are the guys that mostly get asked to the clubs? Preppies from St. Paul's, Mark's, Groton. It's kind of a common bond. You know, birds of a feather flocking together and so forth. You can see what I mean?"

"Sure," Gilbert retorted ironically. "I just didn't go to the right prep school, huh?"

"Yeah," Wig quickly agreed. "Right on target."

To which Jason replied, "Horseshit."

There was a deathly silence in the room. Finally Newall grew annoyed that Jason had broken their mellow mood.

"For Christ's sake, Gilbert, why the hell should a Final Club have to take Jews? I mean, would the Hillel Society want *me?*"

"That's a religious organization, dammit! And they wouldn't want me. I mean, I'm not even—"

He stopped, his sentence half-completed. For a moment, Andrew thought that Jason had been about to say he wasn't Jewish. But that would be absurd. Could a Negro stand there and suggest he wasn't black?

"Hey, listen, Newall," Wigglesworth piped up, "the guy's our friend. Don't piss him off more than he is."

"I'm not pissed off," Jason said in a quiet fury. "Let's just say I'm uncomfortably enlightened. Good night, birds, sorry to have interrupted your flocking together."

He turned and left the room.

That called for another round of brandy and a philosophical observation from Michael Wigglesworth. "Why's a neat guy like Jason that defensive about his background? I mean, there's nothing so bad about being Jewish. Unless you really care about stupid things like Final Clubs."

"Or being President of the United States," added Andrew Eliot.

◆

November 16, 1955

Dear Dad,

I didn't get into a Final Club. I know in the scheme of things it's not that important, and I really don't care that much about having another place to go and drink.

Still, what really bothers me is that I wasn't even considered. And most of all the reason why.

When I finally worked up the guts to ask some of my friends (at least I always *thought* they were my friends) for an explanation, they didn't pussyfoot around. They just came straight out and told me that the Final Clubs never take Jews. Actually, they put it in such a genteel way that it hardly sounded like prejudice.

Dad, this is the second time I've been rejected for something simply because people regard me as Jewish.

How do you reconcile this with the fact that you've always told me we were Americans "just like everybody else"? I believed you—and I still want to. But somehow the world doesn't seem to share your opinion.

Perhaps being Jewish is not something you can remove like a change of clothing.

Maybe that's why we're getting all of the prejudice and none of the pride.

There are lots of really gifted people here at Harvard who think being Jewish is some kind of special honor. That confuses me as well. Because now more than ever I'm not sure exactly what a Jew *is*. I just know lots of people think I'm one.

Dad, I'm terribly confused and so I'm turning for help to the person I respect most in the world. It's important that I solve this mystery.

Because until I find out what I am, I'll never find out *who* I am.

Your loving son,
Jason

His father did not answer this disturbing letter. Instead, he canceled a full day of business meetings and took the train straight up to Boston.

When Jason walked out of squash practice he could hardly believe his eyes.

"Dad, what are you doing here?"

"Come on, son, let's go to Durgin Park and have one of their super steaks."

In a sense, the choice of restaurant said everything. For the world-famous chophouse near the abattoirs of Boston had no booths or private corners. With its inverted snobbery, it placed bankers and busmen at the same long tables with red checkered cloths. A kind of forced democracy of the carnivorous.

Perhaps the elder Gilbert was sincerely unaware that intimate communication was impossible in such a setting. Perhaps he chose it merely out of an atavistic feeling of protectiveness. He'd feed his boy to somehow compensate for all the hurt he felt.

In any case, amid the clatter of heavy china plates and shouting from the open kitchen, all that Jason came away with was the fact that Dad was there to back him up. And he'd always be. Life was full of disappointments. The only way to deal with minor setbacks was to fight back harder still.

"Someday, Jason," he had said, "when you're a senator, the boys who turned you down now will be mighty sorry. And believe me, son, this painful incident—and hey, I really hurt with you—won't mean a thing."

Jason accompanied his father to South Station for the midnight train. Before he climbed aboard, the elder Gilbert patted Jason on the shoulder and remarked, "Son, there's no one in the world I love more than you. Always remember that."

Jason walked back toward the subway feeling strangely empty.

"**N**o."
"Yes."
"No!"

Sara Harrison sat bolt upright, her face flushed.

"Come on, Ted. How many times in your life have you refused to make love to a girl?"

"I take the Fifth Amendment," he protested.

"Ted, it's dark here and you still look embarrassed as hell. I don't care how many girls you've slept with before me. I just wish you'd let me join the club."

"No, Sara. It just doesn't seem right in the back of a Chevrolet."

"I don't mind."

"Well, I do, dammit. I mean, I want our first time to be somewhere a little more romantic. You know, like the banks of the Charles."

"Are you crazy, Ted? It's freezing! What about the Kirkland Motel? I've heard their policy is pretty lax."

Ted sat up and shook his head. "No go," he sighed despondently. "The guy that owns it is a family friend."

"Which brings us back to this lovely Chevrolet."

"Please, Sara, I want this to be different. Look—next Saturday we can drive to New Hampshire."

"New Hampshire? Have you lost your mind? You mean from now on we'll have to drive a hundred miles every time we want to make love?"

"No no no," he protested. "Just till I can find a decent place. God, if ever I wished I lived in a House, it's now. At least those guys can have women in their rooms in the afternoons."

"Well, you don't, and I'm stuck in a Radcliffe dorm that only lets men visit once in a blue moon. . . ."

"Well, when's the next blue moon?"

"Not till the last Sunday of next month."

"Okay. We'll wait till then."

"And what are we supposed to do in the meantime—take cold showers?"

"I don't see why you're in such a hurry, Sara."

"I don't see why you're not."

In truth Ted could not explain the qualms he felt about the prospect of "going all the way" with her. He had grown up with the notion that love and sex were for two completely different kinds of women. While he and his buddies took swaggering pride in their exploits with girls who "went down," none of them would ever have dreamed of marrying anyone who was not a virgin.

And though he dared not admit it even to himself, something subconscious in him wondered why a "nice" girl like Sara Harrison was so eager to make love. And so he welcomed the delay till Visitors' Sunday at her dorm. It would give him more time to reconcile the antitheses of sensuality and love.

Still there was a nagging question in the back of his mind and he searched for ways to broach it delicately.

Sara sensed that he was anxious about something.

"Hey, what's eating you?"

"I don't know. It's just—I wish I'd been the first."

"But you are, Ted. You're the first man I've ever really loved."

"Andrew—are you busy tonight?" Ted asked nervously. "I mean, could you spare me five minutes after the library closes?"

"Sure, Lambros. Want to go downstairs to the Grill for a couple of cheeseburgers?"

"Uh? Well, actually, I'd prefer someplace a little more private."

"We could take the food up to my room."

"That would be great. I've got something special to drink."

"Ah, Lambros, that sounds really interesting."

At a quarter past midnight, Andrew Eliot placed two cheeseburgers on the coffee table in his suite, and Ted produced a bottle from his bookbag.

"Have you ever tasted retsina?" he asked. "It's the Greek national drink. I've brought you some as a kind of gift."

"What for?"

Ted lowered his head and mumbled, "Actually, it's sort of a bribe. I need a favor from you, Andy, a really big favor."

From the embarrassed look on his friend's face, Andrew was sure he was about to be hit for a loan.

"I really don't know how to say this," Ted began, as Andrew poured the retsina. "But whether you say yes or no, swear you'll never tell a soul about this."

"Sure sure, of course. Now spill—you're giving me a heart attack from the tension."

"Andy," Ted started shyly, "I'm in love. . . ."

He stopped again.

"Uh, congratulations," Andrew responded, uncertain of what else to say.

"Thanks, but you see, that's the problem."

"I don't get it, Lambros. *What's* the problem?"

"Promise you won't make any moral judgments?"

"Frankly, I don't think I have any morals that I know of."

Ted looked at Andrew with relief and suddenly blurted, "Listen, could I borrow your room a couple of afternoons a week?"

"That's it? That's what's giving you a brain hemorrhage? When do you need it?"

"Well," he replied, "house parietal rules let you have girls in the room between four and seven. Do you and your roommates need this place in the afternoons?"

"No sweat. Wigglesworth's got crew and then eats at the Varsity Club. Ditto for Newall with tennis. I work out in the IAB. So that leaves you a clear field for whatever you've got in mind."

Ted was suddenly beaming.

"God, Eliot, how can I ever thank you?"

"Well, the occasional bottle of retsina isn't a bad idea. There's only one thing—I'll have to know this girl's name so I can sign her in as my guest. It'll be a little tricky at first, but the super's a good guy."

They established a system that would enable Ted and his inamorata ("an absolute goddess" named Sara Harrison) to enjoy the hospitality of Eliot House. All he had to do was give Andrew a few hours' warning.

Ted was effusive with gratitude and floated out of the room as if on a cloud.

Andrew was left wondering, as that clever Yalie Cole Porter put it, "What is this thing called love?"

He sure as hell didn't know.

The spring belonged to Jason Gilbert.

He finished his initial season of varsity squash undefeated. And went straight on to unseat the current captain for the number-one singles slot on the tennis team. Here, too, he did not lose a match. He then crowned his sophomore achievements by winning both the IC4A and Eastern College titles.

These ultimate exploits made him the first member of The Class to have his picture on the sports page of the more widely circulated version of the *Crimson*, i.e., *The New York Times*.

If he had suffered any psychic damage from the unhappy experience with the Final Clubs, it was in no way apparent—at least to his athletic opponents.

In every American college there is always a figure known as the BMOC—"Big Man on Campus." Harvard prided itself on not recognizing this as a valid designation.

Semantics notwithstanding, at this moment in the drama of undergraduate life, the undisputed hero—or in Shakespeare's words "the observed of all observers"—was indisputably Jason Gilbert, Jr.

Danny Rossi's esteem in the tiny music community could not counteract the chagrin he felt after the humiliating destruction of his piano. He hated Eliot House, and even at times began to resent Master Finley for bringing him to this den of obnoxious pseudo-sophisticates.

His disdain was reciprocated by most of the house members. And he ate almost every meal alone—except when Andrew Eliot would catch sight of him, sit down, and try to cheer him up.

Ted Lambros's growing involvement with Sara demonstrated the validity of the platonic notion that love draws the mind to higher planes. He got straight A's in all his classics courses. Moreover, he no longer felt himself a total alien from campus life. Perhaps because he was spending so many afternoons a week at Eliot House.

Andrew could only sit on the sidelines and marvel at how his classmates were developing. Petals were opening, blossoms emerging. Sophomore year was a glorious awakening for the entire Class.

It had been a time of hope. Of confidence. Of boundless optimism. Almost every member of The Class left Cambridge thinking, We've only half-begun.

When, in truth, it was half-over.

D anny Rossi's second summer at Tanglewood had been even more memorable than his first. Whereas in 1955 his most exalted task was, as he himself put it with self-deprecating humor, "polishing Maestro Munch's baton," in 1956 he actually got to wave it in front of the orchestra.

The white-haired Frenchman had developed a grandfatherly affection for the eager little Californian. And, to the consternation of the other students at the Festival School, gave Danny every opportunity to make "real" music.

When Artur Rubinstein came up to play the *Emperor Concerto,* for example, Munch volunteered Danny to turn the virtuoso's pages during rehearsal.

At the first break, Rubinstein, legendary for his prodigious musical memory, bemusedly demanded to know why the conductor had stuck so familiar a score in front of his face. To which Munch replied with a sly grin that it was for the page turner's benefit. So that Danny Rossi could study the master up close. "The boy is on fire," he added.

"Weren't we all at that age?" Rubinstein smiled.

Moments later he invited Danny to his dressing room, to hear *his* interpretation of the concerto.

Danny began hesitantly. But by the time he had reached the allegro of the third movement, he was too involved to be diffident. His fingers were flying. In fact, he stunned himself by the uncanny ease with which he played at such a frantic tempo.

At the end he looked up, breathless and sweating.

"Too fast, huh?"

The virtuoso nodded, but with admiration in his eyes. "Yes," he acknowledged. "But extremely good nonetheless."

119

"Maybe I was just nervous, but this keyboard made it feel like I was rolling down a hill. It sort of sped me up."

"Do you know why, my boy?" Rubinstein asked. "Since I am not gifted with great size, the Steinway people kindly manufactured this piano with the keys one-eighth smaller. Look again."

Danny marveled at Artur Rubinstein's personal piano. For on it he, who was also not "gifted with great size," could stretch a full thirteenth with ease.

Then the master generously remarked, "Listen, we all know that I don't need any pages turned. So why not stay here and play to your heart's content?"

On another occasion, at an outdoor run-through of Mozart's Overture to *The Marriage of Figaro,* Munch suddenly gave a histrionic sigh of weariness and said, "This Massachusetts weather is too hot and humid for a Frenchman. I need five minutes in the shade."

He then motioned to Danny. "Come here, young man," he said, extending his baton. "I think you know the piece enough to wave this stick in front of these musicians. Take over for a minute and be sure they behave."

With this he left Danny feeling very naked and alone on the podium before the entire Boston Symphony.

Of course the orchestra had several assistant conductors and *répétiteurs* precisely for occasions such as this. And they stood on the sidelines burning with a lot more than summer heat.

He was really high that night. And as soon as he got back to his boarding house, Danny phoned Dr. Landau.

"That's wonderful," the teacher commented with pride. "Your parents must be delighted."

"Yeah," Danny answered half-evasively. "I—uh—would you mind calling Mom and telling her about it?"

"Daniel," Dr. Landau answered gravely, "this melodrama with your father has gone on too long. Look, this is a perfect opportunity to make a gesture of conciliation."

"Dr. Landau, please try to understand. I just can't bring myself to . . ." His voice trailed off.

ANDREW ELIOT'S DIARY

September 29, 1956

Sex.

I had given it a lot of thought all summer as I sweated my guts out at the construction job my father had so considerately arranged to enhance my acquaintance with physical labor. While my roommates, Newall and Wig, were off cruising the better beaches in Europe, the only thing I got to lay all summer was a lot of bricks.

I returned to Harvard for junior year determined to succeed where I had never failed—because I'd never even had the guts to try.

I was going to lose my virginity.

Mike and Dick came home with these incredible tales of trysting the nights away with nymphs of every nationality and cup size.

And yet peer pressure prevented me from asking either of them for advice—or more specifically for a phone number. I'd become the laughingstock of the Porcellian—not to mention Eliot House, the crew and probably even the biddies who served in the dining hall.

In desperation I thought of trying the notorious bars around Scollay Square, but I couldn't work up the courage to go on my own. And besides, the whole idea was kind of sordid.

Who could help me?

The answer became apocalyptically clear the first evening I returned to my library job. For there, grinding away at his usual table, was Ted Lambros.

This time it was Andrew who begged Ted to come to his room for an urgent conversation.

Ted was puzzled, since he had never seen his friend so agitated.

"What's up, Eliot?"

"Uh. How was your vacation, Ted?"

"Not bad, except I only got to see Sara for a couple of weekends. Otherwise it was just business as usual at The Marathon. Anyway, what's your problem?"

Andrew wondered how the hell he could broach it.

"Hey, Lambros, can you keep a secret?" he asked.

"Who're you talking to, Eliot? We have a sacred tenant-landlord relationship."

Andrew opened another beer and took a long swig.

"Uh—you know I've been going to boarding schools since I was eight. The only girls we ever got to see were the ones they trucked in for tea dances and stuff. You know, prissy little ice maidens. . . ."

"Yeah," Ted replied. "I know the type."

"Your high school was coed?"

"Sure, that's one advantage of not having bucks."

"So you must have been pretty young when you—uh—started going out with girls?"

"Yeah, I guess so," he replied, treating the whole subject with an insouciant levity that suggested he was unaware of Andrew's mounting anxiety.

"How old were you when you had your first—you know—experience?"

"Oh, about average," Ted replied. "Maybe a little old, actually. I was almost sixteen."

"Pro or amateur?"

"Oh, come on, Eliot, you don't *pay* for that sort of thing. It was a hot pants little sophomore named Gloria. What about you?"

"What about me?"

"How old were you when you lost it?"

"Ted," Andrew muttered uneasily, "this may kind of shock you. . . ."

"Don't tell me, Eliot—you did it at eleven with your nanny!"

"I only wish. That's what practically happened to Newall. No, what I wanted to tell you is—shit, this is so embarrassing—I still have it."

The instant he confessed, Andrew was frightened that his friend might laugh. But instead, after a moment of reflection, Ted looked at him with genuine sympathy. "Hey, you got problems or something?"

"No—unless you call total fear a problem. I mean, I've had a lot of dates in the past few years, and I think some of them would have . . . cooperated. But I've been too scared to make the move. Because, frankly, Lambros, I'm not sure I have the technique. I mean, I've read all the books—*Love Without Fear, The Ideal Marriage.* But I've obsessed about it for so long that I'm scared of clutching at the crucial moment—if you know what I mean."

Ted put a paternal hand on Andrew's shoulder. "My boy, I think you need what the football team calls a 'practice scrimmage.' "

"Yeah. But I wouldn't want to put you to any trouble."

"Hey, no sweat, Andy. There are plenty of chicks from my high school still around Cambridge. They'd be tickled to go out with a Harvard man—especially a sophisticated guy from Eliot House."

"But, Ted," he responded with frenzy in his voice, "they can't be utter pigs. I mean, I've gotta be seen with them. You know, in the dining room, or on some kind of date."

"No, no. You don't have to wine 'em and dine 'em. You just invite 'em to your room and let nature take its course. And don't worry, the one I have in mind for you is really great-looking."

"Hey, not *too* good-looking. I want to start my career sort of at the bottom and work up. If you know what I mean."

Ted Lambros laughed.

"Andy, Andy, stop being a goddamn puritan. Everything in life doesn't have to be done the hard way. Look, why not meet me in front of Brigham's at twelve-fifteen tomorrow? The little blond ice-cream scooper is a real firecracker."

He stood up and yawned. "Listen, it's getting real late and I've got a nine o'clock. See you tomorrow."

Andrew Eliot sat there shell-shocked. He had not expected things to move so fast. There were a million questions he still wanted to ask.

Outside Brigham's the next day, he greeted Ted with annoyance.

"What the hell kept you? I've been waiting for hours."

"Hey, I'm right on time. I had a class till noon. What's the matter with you? C'mon, let's get the show on the road."

"Wait, wait, wait, Lambros. I've got to know what to do."

Ted answered softly, "Listen, Eliot, just walk inside with me, order a cone, and when no one else is around I'll introduce you to Lorraine."

"Who's Lorraine?"

"She's your passport to paradise, baby. She's a really good kid and just *loves* Harvard guys."

"But, Ted, what exactly do I say?"

"Just give her one of your charming smiles and ask if she'd like to have a drink this afternoon. And Lorraine being Lorraine, she'll say yes."

"What makes you so sure?"

"Because she's never said 'no' to anything in her life."

She came over the moment they reached the counter. Ted had not been lying—the girl was a real looker. As they chatted amicably, she leaned forward and Andrew could not keep from gazing down her carelessly unbuttoned uniform.

Wow, he thought, can this really be happening to me? God, I wish I'd spent more time rereading those manuals last night.

"So, what house are you in?" Lorraine inquired.

"Uh—Eliot," he replied without elaboration. Then he felt Ted's elbow in his ribs and added, "Uh—would you like to come over this afternoon?"

"Sure," she replied. "Parietals start at four, don't they? I'll just meet you at the gate. 'Scuse me now, I got customers getting impatient."

*   *   *

"Well?" asked Ted when they were outside again. "Are you all set now?"

Set? He was about to pass out.

"Lambros," he pleaded, "couldn't you give me just a few tips? I mean about making the first move."

Ted stopped as they were both in the middle of Harvard Square in a sea of noontime students.

"Andy," he said indulgently, "say something casual like, 'Lorraine, why don't we go to the bedroom and fool around?' "

"Isn't that a little crude?"

"Jesus, Eliot, she's not Doris Day! I mean, she really loves to make it with Harvard guys."

"Honestly?"

"Honestly," he repeated. And then as a final gesture he reached into his pocket and put something into Andrew's hand.

"What's that?"

"It's a cultural first," he replied, smiling. "You just got a Trojan from a Greek."

ANDREW ELIOT'S DIARY

September 30, 1956

Had a really terrific day.
I'll never forget Ted Lambros for the favor he did me.
As a matter of fact, I'll never forget Lorraine, either.

D anny Rossi returned to Cambridge in September with a revised view of the world—and himself. Artur Rubinstein had praised his pianistic skills. He'd conducted a real symphony—if only for a minute.

Though he had hardly become a Casanova, his few brief encounters (two, to be precise) had led him to discover a new erogenous zone: the keyboard. He would now not be intimidated even by Brigitte Bardot—as long as there was a Steinway in the room.

To become a triple threat musician, all that remained was for him to start composing seriously. As promised, Walter Piston took him in his seminar and Danny began to write in earnest.

But he was growing ever more impatient to be free of all the trappings of "studenthood." He had had enough of being known as some famous person's pupil, protégé, or favorite. He now bridled at such distinctions. He was prepared to be a great man on his own.

The Composition Seminar disappointed him. For it seemed to consist only of exercises in the style of various past masters. When Danny complained of his frustration at the "limiting" assignments, Professor Piston tried to clarify the logic of the method.

"All great writers, whether they make prose or music, start by imitation. That's what gives a man a sense of style. And only after that can he begin to forge his own. Be patient, Danny. After all, young Mozart wrote at first like pseudo-Haydn, and even Beethoven began by imitating Mozart. Don't be so impulsive, you're in august company."

Danny heard the cautionary words but really didn't listen. Events at Tanglewood that summer had turned his head. While dutifully fulfilling all of Piston's course demands, he started to seek outlets for expressing his own musical personality.

And then the opportunity found him. His phone rang late one afternoon as he was finishing an essay at his desk.

"Is this Danny Rossi?" asked a slightly nervous female voice.

"Yes."

"I'm Maria Pastore, president of the Radcliffe Dance Club. And—I hope you don't think this is presumptuous—the group would like to put on an original ballet this spring. Naturally your name was the first one we all thought of. Please tell me if this is imposing and I won't go on. . . ."

"No, no," Danny encouraged, "I'm very interested."

"You are?" Maria said delightedly.

"Sure," Danny answered. "Who would be the choreographer?"

"Uh, well," Maria responded shyly, "sort of me. I mean, I'm not a total neophyte. I've studied with Martha Graham and—"

"Please," Danny said with exaggerated magnanimity, "we're all just undergraduates. Why don't we have dinner at Eliot and talk it over?"

"Gee, that would be terrific. Should I meet you near the superintendent's office at, say, five-thirty or so?"

"No," Danny answered. "Why not come around five? We can talk things over in my room before we eat."

And inwardly he thought, If this Maria turns out to be a dog, I just won't take her to the dining hall.

"Your room?" Her voice was slightly nervous once again.

"Uh—yes," he answered suavely. "I mean, I've got a piano here and everything. If not, we can meet sometime in Paine Hall. But I should definitely be near a keyboard."

"Oh no, that's okay," Maria Pastore quickly responded, her tone belying her words, "your room would be fine. So I'll see you Wednesday at five. I'm really excited about this. Thanks."

She hung up. And Danny thought, I wonder how excited I'll be.

At precisely 5:00 P.M. on Wednesday, November 14, there was a knock on Danny Rossi's door.

"Come in," he called out as he straightened his tie and then—took a sniff. He had somewhat overdone it with the shaving lotion. The room fairly reeked of Old Spice.

He rushed to the window and raised it a few inches. Then he opened the door.

"Hello," said Maria Pastore.

She was so tall that at first Danny did not even see her face. But what he did perceive was interesting enough for his gaze to linger before moving upward.

She was extremely pretty, too. Long black hair framed her wide, soulful Mediterranean eyes. No question about it, they'd be eating dinner at Eliot that night. And many jaws would drop in admiration.

"Thanks for giving me a chance to talk to you," Maria bubbled with enthusiasm.

"It's my pleasure," Danny Rossi replied gallantly. "Your idea interests me."

"I haven't actually explained it to you yet," she answered shyly.

"Oh," said Danny Rossi. "I mean, the notion of composing a ballet is really attractive. Uh—could I take your coat?"

"No, thanks," Maria responded diffidently, "it's kind of cold in here."

"Oh yeah," said Danny, hurrying to close the window. "I like fresh air. You know, it sort of keeps your head clear."

He motioned for her to sit down. She did so, and throughout their conversation remained bundled up. Danny sensed that it was not merely because of the wintry temperature.

She's shy, he thought. But at least I'll get to see what she's been covering when we get to the dining hall.

"Drink?" he asked.

"No, thank you. It's really not good for dancers."

"I meant just a little drop of sherry." (He believed the undergraduate maxim, "Whisky makes them frisky, but sherry makes them merry.")

"I really don't like alcohol," Maria said in a tone that was almost apologetic.

"Coke?" asked Danny.

"Fine."

As he listened intently to her ideas for a short ballet, Danny wondered whether Maria could sense that he was taking off her clothes as he was gazing at her. But in fact she was so nervous that she barely noticed anything.

It took her half an hour to present her concepts.

She had gone through the *Idylls* of Theocritus, the *Eclogues* of Virgil, and made some general notes from Robert Graves's *Greek Mythology,* gathering enough material for a potential ballet scenario that she would call *Arcadia* ("for example, Apollo and Daphne could be an exciting sequence"). The principal dancers could be shepherds and shepherdesses, and for comic relief there could be a recurring motif of grotesque little satyrs running on and off stage chasing nymphs.

Danny thought the idea was terrific. This was going to be one hell of a stimulating project.

The next day at lunch, some guys he didn't know passed by his table to remark on the extraordinary pulchritude of his dinner date the previous night. Danny smiled with masculine bravado.

Yeah, he thought, the Eliot House dining hall has never seen the likes of her. When certain cruder types came straight out and inquired, "Are you scoring with her, Rossi?" he avoided the whole issue with genteel protectiveness of Miss Pastore's honor.

But the truth was as he walked her all the way back to Radcliffe he had concluded that he probably would never even get to kiss her. She was much too tall. And though the plans they made would bring her to his room on many future afternoons, he stood no chance of making progress.

For she was five foot ten of Snow White—who, of course, was just platonic friends with all the dwarfs.

November 12, 1956

There is a common misconception that preppies are perpetually cool. Calm. Unruffled. Never get ulcers. Never even sweat or get their hair messed up. Well, let me put the lie to that. A preppie hath eyes. He hath hands, organs, passions. If you prick him, he will bleed. And if you hurt him, he may even cry.

Thus it was with my longtime friend and roommate, Michael Wigglesworth, Boston Brahmin, tall and handsome, stroke on the crew and general good guy.

None of this, not even the genuine affection of his teammates and his buddies in the Porc or the admiration of his many friends in Eliot House, could keep his mind intact. When he went home to Fairfield for the weekend, his fiancée calmly informed him that, upon reflection, she'd decided to marry some older guy— who was nearly thirty.

Wig seemed to take all this with stoic equanimity. At least till he got back to school. Then one evening, as he was going through the dinner line, he cheerfully remarked to one of the serving biddies, "I'm going to kill the Christmas turkey."

Since he was giggling at the time, the matrons laughed as well. Then, from inside his baggy, well-worn J. Press jacket, Wig produced a fire ax. And, swinging wildly, he proceeded to chase a turkey—which apparently only he was able to see—around the perimeter of the dining room.

Tables overturned, plates flew in the air. Everybody—tutors, students, Cliffie guests—scattered frantically. Someone called the campus cops, but when they arrived they too were scared shitless. The only guy who had the cool to deal with the situation was senior tutor Whitney Porter. He slowly approached Wig and with unwavering calm asked if Michael was finished with the hatchet.

This innocent question, so ingenuously posed, made Wig

131

stop swinging and take stock. He didn't answer right away. I think he was gradually beginning to realize that there was a lethal weapon in his hand, for a purpose that was not entirely clear to him.

With the same uncanny tranquility, Whitney again asked Michael for the ax.

Wigglesworth was nothing if not polite. He immediately offered the implement (handle first) to the senior tutor, saying, "Yes, sir, Dr. Porter."

By then a couple of doctors from the Health Service had shown up. The medics led Mike off, and, no doubt to their eternal gratitude, Dr. Porter insisted on riding with them to the hospital.

I went to visit him as soon as they would let me. And it really broke my heart to see our Harvard Hercules looking so helpless. And alternating between tears and laughter. The doctor said he would "need a lot of rest." In other words, they really didn't know when—or probably even how—he would get better.

Ten days after Michael Wigglesworth's precipitous departure, Master Finley called Andrew into his office for a chat. It began, as so many of their previous conversations had, with many repetitions of his surname in various tones. The Eliot declarative, the Eliot meditative, the Eliot interrogative. These prefatory invocations once pronounced, he then said, "Eliot, I regard you not only as an eponym but a true epigone."

(Right after the conversation, Andrew sprinted back to his dictionary to discover that he had been praised first for stemming from the family that gave the name to his house, and second for being worthy of that name.)

"Eliot, Eliot," Master Finley repeated, "I am sorely troubled by the fate of Wigglesworth. I have been searching my heart and wondering whether there were signs I should have noticed. But I always regarded him as a veritable Ajax."

Andrew was slightly lost. The only Ajax he knew was a foaming cleanser.

"You know, Eliot," the scholar continued, "Ajax, 'the wall of the Achaians'—second only to Achilles himself."

"Yes," Andrew agreed, "Wig was a real 'wall.' "

"I would see him every morning," the master continued, "as the crew stroked past my window. He looked hale."

"The crew is going to miss him."

"We all shall," said Finley, shaking his silver mane sadly. "We all shall."

The great man's next words were not unexpected.

"Eliot, Eliot," he said.

"Yes, sir?"

"Eliot, Michael's untimely departure leaves us with a space

133

both in our house and in our hearts. And while one cannot find a second Wigglesworth, perhaps Destiny has played a hand in all of this."

He stood up, as if to spread his rhetorical wings.

"Eliot," he continued, "who can be unaware of the tragic events of recent days? As, after Troy fell, countless innocent inhabitants were *iactati aequore toto . . . reliquiae Danaum atque immitis Achilli. . . .*"

Andrew had had enough prep school Latin to realize the master was quoting the *Aeneid.* Was he about to say that Wig's place was going to be filled by a *Trojan* student?

Finley was frantically pacing the room, frequently gazing out onto the river where hale Mike Wigglesworth would never more be seen, when he suddenly whirled and fixed Andrew with a coruscating gaze.

"Eliot," he concluded, "George Keller will be arriving tomorrow evening."

GEORGE KELLER

Something sinister in the tone
Told me my secret must be known:
Word I was in the house alone
Somehow must have gotten abroad,
Word I was in my life alone,
Word I had no one left but God.

ROBERT FROST
CLASS OF 1901

Budapest, October 1956

George's childhood had been dominated by two monsters: Joseph Stalin—and his own father. The only difference between the two was that Stalin terrorized millions, and his father merely terrorized George.

True enough, "Istvan the Terrible," as George often thought of him, had never actually killed or even imprisoned anybody. He was merely a minor official in the Hungarian People's Working Party who used Marxist-Leninist jargon to castigate his son.

"Why does he flagellate me?" George would complain to his sister, Marika. "I'm a better socialist than he is. I mean, I believe in the theory, anyway. And even though I think the party stinks, I've joined for his sake. Why is he so fed up?"

Marika tried to mollify her brother. And comfort him. For, try as he did to deny it, George was genuinely upset by the old man's disapproval.

"Well," she said softly, "he'd like your hair a little shorter. . . ."

"What? Does he want me to shave my skull? I mean, lots of my friends wear Elvis Presley ducktails."

"He doesn't like your friends either, Gyuri."

"I don't know why," said George, shaking his head in consternation. "They're all sons of party members. Some are big

135

shots, too. And they're a lot easier on their children than Father is."

"He just wants you to stay home and study, Gyuri. Be honest, you're out almost every evening."

"You be honest, Marika. I graduated first in my gimnazium class. I'm studying Soviet law—"

At that very moment Istvan Kolozsdi entered the room and, immediately taking command, finished his son's sentence.

"You are at the university because of my party status, *yompetz*, and don't forget it. If you were merely a clever Catholic or Jew, it wouldn't matter how high your grades were. You would be sweeping some provincial street. Be grateful you are the son of a party minister."

"Assistant minister," George corrected him, "in the Farm Collectivization Office."

"You say it as if it were a disgrace, Gyuri."

"Well, it's hardly democratic for a government to force people to farm against their will—"

"We do not force—"

"Please, Father," Gyuri answered with an exasperated sigh, "you're not talking to some naive idiot."

"No, I'm talking to a *yompetz,* a worthless hooligan. And as for that girlfriend of yours—"

"How can you criticize Aniko, Father? The party thinks she's good enough to study pharmacy."

"Still, it hurts my standing when you're seen with her. Aniko's a bad type. She malingers. She sits in cafés in Vaci Ucca listening to Western music."

What really annoys you, George thought, is that I sit right next to her. Last Sunday in the *Kedves* we heard Cole Porter for nearly three hours.

"Father," said George, hoping for reasonable debate instead of a brawl, "if socialist music is so great, why doesn't the *Stalin Cantata* have any good tunes?"

Livid, the government official turned to his daughter. "I won't talk to this *yompetz* anymore. He's a disgrace to our entire family."

"I'll change my name," George said facetiously.

"Please," said the old man, "the sooner the better." He stormed out and slammed the door.

George turned to his sister. "Now what the hell did I do?"

Marika shrugged. She had been the referee in these father-

and-son combats for as long as she could remember. There seemed to have been conflict ever since their mother died—when George was five and she only two and a half.

The old man was never the same after that. And in his fits of bitterness he would vent his anger on his eldest child. While she tried to grow up as quickly as she could to be a mediating force—a mother to her brother and a wife to him.

"Try and understand, George, he's had a very hard life."

"That's no excuse for giving me one. But in a way I understand. He feels trapped in his job. Yes, Marika, even socialist officials harbor ambitions. The Farm Program is an unmitigated disaster. His boss naturally blames him, so who can he let out his frustrations on? Sometimes I wish we had a dog so he could kick it instead of me."

Marika realized that, despite George's angry protestations, at a certain level he genuinely sympathized with his father's disappointment. Yet, the old man had done well for someone who had begun life as an apprentice shoemaker in Kaposvar. Istvan Kolozsdi's greatest misfortune was that he had sired a son whose brilliance would inevitably show how mediocre he really was.

Somewhere in their hearts, the two men knew it. And this made them afraid to love each other.

"I have tremendous news!" called Aniko as she dashed across Muzeum Boulevard to catch George between lectures at the Law Faculty.

"Don't tell me," he smiled, "the pregnancy test was negative."

"That I won't know till Friday," she replied, "but listen to this—the Polish students are striking to support Gomulka—and we're organizing a sympathy march."

"Aniko, the Secret Police will never let you get away with it. Those AVO thugs will beat your brains in. Or else our friendly Russian 'visitors' will."

"Gyuri Kolozsdi, not only will you march with me, but you will carry one of the posters I've spent all morning painting. Now, which one would you like—'Hail Polish youth'? 'Russians get out'?"

George smiled. Wouldn't the sight of him carrying such a placard warm his father's heart? "I'll take that," he said, pointing at "New Leadership for Hungary."

They kissed.

March Fifteenth Square was electric with anticipation. Thousands of demonstrators had crowded onto its grassy turf, carrying posters and flags. There were delegations from factories, schools, and universities. A young actor from the National Theater clambered up the statue of Sándor Petofi and began to declaim the poet's "National Hymn," which had ignited Hungary's 1848 Revolution.

The ever-increasing throng joined in with special vigor when they reached *"Most vagy soha—now or never!"*

For the first time, George began to feel that something important was happening. And he was a part of it.

At last the procession began, led by chanting demonstrators who carried a wreath of red carnations. They began to pour into the main city streets, blocking traffic as they passed. But there was no animosity. Many motorists simply locked their cars and joined the marchers, whose ranks had already been swelled by the shop owners and workers all along the way. Every window, every balcony was filled with families waving encouragement.

As if by magic, Budapest was transformed into a boundless field of red, white, and green. People everywhere had fashioned tricolors of ribbons, cloth—and even paper. When the students took their final turn into Jozsef Bem Square, they could see that the statue at the center was already draped with a huge Hungarian flag, the Soviet coat of arms torn out of its center.

Toward sunset, many students talked about going to demonstrate in front of Parliament. Others proposed an attack on the great statue of Stalin that had for so many years stood in the center of the City Park looking down at Budapest with cast-iron mockery. George and Aniko held hands and let the mainstream carry them back across the river toward Parliament Square.

"What do you think the government will do?" George asked.

"Resign. They have to."

The immensity of the crowd in Parliament Square was almost frightening. Hundreds of thousands—it seemed like millions—were laying siege to the venerable government edifice with its embroidered Gothic pinnacles. All were shouting for the return of the only leader they trusted, Imre Nagy, who had been removed from office by the Russians the year before.

Evening became night and the air grew bitingly cold. But many had made torches of the newspapers and pamphlets they held in their hands and continued to shout for Nagy.

Then suddenly, unexpectedly, a slight figure appeared on a balcony. From the front rows a ripple of voices began to echo and crescendo toward the back. "It's Nagy, it's Nagy!" Somewhat weakly, himself overcome by the emotion of the moment, the deposed leader raised his hand to plead for silence.

"Has he gone mad?" George wondered out loud. "He's waving his hands like a lunatic."

But in an instant all became clear. He was leading the massive throng in the singing of the national anthem. It was a stroke of genius!

After the song ended, Nagy disappeared as swiftly as he had materialized. The crowd—thrilled and elated—now began to break up. Instinctively, they knew no more would happen that night. At least not in Parliament Square.

George and Aniko were halfway back to the university when they heard gunfire. He took her hand and they began to run down toward Muzeum Boulevard. The cobblestone streets swarmed with people, excited, curious, frightened.

When they reached the Muzeum Garden, there were still traces of tear gas in the air. She took out a handkerchief and held it to her face. George's eyes were beginning to burn. A hysterical young girl was shrieking that the Secret Police had massacred defenseless people.

"We're going to kill every one of those bastards!" she sobbed.

"Fat chance," George whispered to Aniko. "I'll believe it when I see my first dead AVO man."

He took her hand and they began to run again.

Less than a block later, they stopped in their tracks, horrified. Above them, strung up by his feet from a lamppost, were the bloody remains of a Secret Police officer. George felt sick.

"Gyuri," said Aniko with a shudder, "we know what they did to *their* prisoners."

On the next block they saw corpses of two more AVO agents.

"God," Aniko pleaded, "I can't bear this anymore."

"Come on, I'll take you home."

"Well, *yompetz,* I see they haven't arrested you yet."

It was nearly 5:00 A.M. Istvan Kolozsdi was seated close to the radio, exhausted, smoking nervously. Marika rushed to embrace her brother.

"Gyuri, we've been hearing such terrible rumors. I feared that something had happened to you."

"Forget rumors, Marika," the patriarch interrupted. "The truth has just been on the news."

"Really?" George said softly. "And what is Radio Budapest's version of tonight's events?"

"There was a small Fascist insurrection, which the police have dealt with severely," said Istvan Kolozsdi. "And where have you been all evening?"

George sat down in a chair opposite his father, leaned forward, and said with a smile, "Listening to Imre Nagy."

"You are mad. Nagy is a nonperson."

"Try telling that to the thousands who cheered him in Parliament Square. And we're going to get him back as party leader."

"And I'm getting my hair back on my head. You're all a bunch of crazy idiots."

"Spoken like a true socialist," said George, as he headed out of the room. "I'm going to sleep. Even lunatics need rest."

Scarcely three hours later, his sister was prodding him. "Wake up, Gyuri. Nagy is named premier! It's just been on the news."

George forced his weary body to get out of bed. He had to see his father's face. Still buttoning his shirt, he shuffled into the sitting room. The old man seemed welded to the spot beside the radio, surrounded by ashtrays spilling over with cigarette butts.

As Marika handed George a cup of black coffee, he asked his father, "Well?"

The patriarch looked up and, without the slightest trace of irony, replied, "You have never heard me say a word against Imre Nagy. In any case, he must have the blessing of Moscow, because he has asked for help from the Soviet troops."

"Now I think *you're* the dreamer, Father." And then, turning to his sister, he said, "When Aniko calls, tell her I've left for the university."

He tossed a jacket over his shoulder and hurried from the house.

In the years that followed, George looked back at this moment and wondered why he had neglected to say more of a farewell. Not to his father. For he was angered by the old man's shameless display of hypocrisy. But why had he not been more affectionate to Marika?

He was never able to console himself with the thought that, on that cold October morning in 1956, he could not have dreamed how far he was going.

The university was a tornado of rumors. After every radio broadcast, people would scurry around the hall like town criers. The exhausted students cheered upon hearing that President Eisenhower had said, "The heart of America goes out to the people of Hungary." They sang to one another, "The whole world is watching!"

But the peak of euphoria came on Tuesday afternoon, when Premier Nagy announced that the evacuation of Soviet troops had begun. George must have knocked down six people as he dashed ecstatically across the room to embrace Aniko.

On the morning of November first, George was rudely awakened by Geza, a fellow law student.

"What the hell—"

And then he noticed something very odd. Scrawny Geza today looked like a circus fat man. George rubbed his eyes in disbelief.

"What the hell has happened to you?" he asked.

"We've got to get out of here," Geza said. "I'm wearing all my clothes—at least everything I could squeeze on—and heading for Vienna."

"Have you lost your mind? The Soviets are gone. Don't you hear Radio Free Europe?"

"Yes, but I also hear my cousin in the village of Gyor. He rang about two hours ago and said there were hundreds of Russian tanks massing at the western border. They're just regrouping to come back."

"Is he sure?"

"Do you want to wait and find out?"

George hesitated, but only for a split second.

"Let me get Aniko," he said.

"Okay, but make it snappy."

She was reluctant.

"What makes you *so* sure the Soviets are coming back?"

"How many reasons do you want?" George answered impatiently. "Look, if Hungary goes independent, that will give the Poles and the Czechs big ideas. Then boom, the Russian empire tumbles like a house of cards."

Her face grew pale. She was frightened by the magnitude of the decision being forced upon her.

"But what about my mother—she can't manage without me."

"She will have to," George replied impassively. He put his arms around her. She was sobbing quietly.

"Let me at least call her," she pleaded.

"Yes. But please be quick."

They started walking. George and Aniko with just the clothing on their backs, Geza wearing his entire wardrobe. As they reached the outskirts of Buda, George saw a phone booth and suddenly thought of his sister.

"Anybody got some change?" he asked.

Aniko pressed a coin into his hand.

"Gyuri," his sister said anxiously, "where are you? Even Father's been concerned."

"Listen," he replied, "I'm in a hurry—"

Just then, Geza stuck his head into the booth and whispered, "Tell her the Voice of America is passing code messages from refugees who make it across."

George nodded.

"Please, Marika, don't ask me any questions. Just listen to the Voice of America. If they say that—" He hesitated once again. "That 'Karl Marx is dead'—that'll mean I'm all right."

"Gyuri, I don't understand. You sound scared."

"I am," he confessed, and then added, "so for God's sake, pray that he does die."

He hung up without another word.

"What about your father?" Aniko asked. "Won't he get into trouble when they learn you've fled the country?"

"Listen, he's a consummate politician, with a genius for self-preservation. He'll be just fine, I assure you."

And in his heart he thought, He turned his back on me during my whole childhood, why should I care what happens to him now?

They plodded on in silence. The only traffic on the road was the occasional ancient truck—nearly always heading toward the western border. Once in a while the trio would get a lift for a few dozen kilometers. The drivers never asked where they were going or why.

It was nearly nightfall when they reached the outskirts of Gyor.

"What do we do now?" George asked Geza. "It's much too cold to sleep outside, and I've barely got a few *forints* in my pocket for food."

"I don't even have enough for a bowl of soup," Aniko added.

Geza merely smiled. "Leave it to me. Do you have the strength to walk another hour?"

"Only if I knew we could get *inside* somewhere," said George. Aniko nodded agreement.

"Tibor Kovacs's parents live in Enese—about ten kilometers from here. He was going to leave with us. His parents would be expecting him."

Aniko gasped. "Don't they know he was shot two nights ago?"

"No," Geza replied, "and there's no point in telling them."

And he began to lead them toward Enese.

In half an hour, they were trudging down an icy country road lit only by moonlight. They had been walking since early morning and were almost too tired to speak.

"Tomorrow would be a good day to try to make it across," said Geza. "It's All Souls' Day. The roads will be filled. Everybody will be going to the cemeteries."

The Kovacs family was glad to welcome friends of their son and did not seem concerned that he was not with them. He had been instructing various groups of the newly formed militia in the use of arms, so that George's fabrication—that Tibor was needed for another few days in Budapest—seemed perfectly plausible.

Dinner was a dream. Unlike the capital city, the villages had plenty of food, and Mrs. Kovacs set before them a feast of chicken and vegetables. There was even a bottle of Tokay.

"I admire you." Mr. Kovacs smiled broadly. "If I were a few years younger, I'd be going, too. For sure as snow will fall tomorrow, the Russians will be back. Everyone I speak to has seen the tanks. They are off the main road, but they are out there in the forests, waiting like hungry bears."

Aniko was offered Tibor's bed. Though inwardly horrified, she knew she had to accept. The two young men curled up by the fire in the main room.

The next morning it was snowing heavily.

Geza looked at George and Aniko. "In this weather, I think the best idea is to try to catch a train to Sopron. From there, we have a long and very sparse border with Austria. If we are lucky, we should be able to walk across tonight."

At midday they thanked the Kovacses and started off, leaving all sorts of encouraging messages for Tibor.

At the outskirts of the village, they got their first shock. The Russian tanks were no longer hiding behind trees. Two of them were squatting right in the center of the road.

"Well?" George asked Geza.

"Don't panic, Gyuri. It's snowing like hell and they don't seem to be paying very close attention. We're not carrying any luggage, so why should they suspect us of anything?"

"You, Geza, look like a walking football in all those clothes," said George. "If you intend to try to bluff your way past those tanks, you'd better strip down."

A sudden look of anxiety crossed Geza's face. He was loath to part with five-sixths of his worldly possessions.

"Let's go around the town and see if we can reach the railroad from the other side," he insisted nervously.

And so they set off.

But there were two more tanks at the farther entrance to the village. They had hiked for more than an hour in the snow to no purpose. George and Aniko stared at Geza. Without a word, he began to unbutton his top jacket. His fingers were trembling—and not merely from the cold.

"Who—who—who'll do the talking?"

"Come on, Geza," George replied, "we've all had at least six years of Russian. Let's just be sure we tell the same story."

"Your accent is the best, George," Geza insisted. "It would be much better if you spoke for us. Besides, when it comes to inventing lies, you're something of a genius."

"All right, comrade," said George, "I'll be our ambassador."

After Geza removed his penultimate suit and buried the rest of his garments in a snowdrift, they started off toward the tanks.

"Stoi! kto idyot?"

A soldier asked them to identify themselves. George took a few steps forward and began to engage him in impeccable Russian.

"We are three students from Eotvos Lorand University, visiting a friend who is ill with glandular fever. We would like to take the train back to Budapest. Do you wish to see our papers?"

The soldier had a whispered conversation with one of his colleagues and then turned back to George.

"That will not be necessary. *Proiditye!*" And he waved them on. They hurried into the village, toward the train station, their hearts pounding.

"Damn," said Geza, pointing to the station up ahead. "They have tanks there too."

"Ignore them," George replied. "I don't think these soldiers know what they're supposed to do, anyway."

He was right. No one stopped them from getting onto the platform, where a very crowded train was about to leave. There was much noise and confusion. All three of them called desperately to various people, "Sopron? Going to Sopron?"

There was shouting and waving from inside the train, which now began slowly to pull out. Geza leapt on board first. George helped Aniko and then clambered on himself. In an instant, they had left the station.

There was not a single empty seat, so they stood in the corridor looking out the window. Each knew what the other two were thinking. In an hour and a half at most they'd be in Sopron. And then the border.

There were startling new additions to the otherwise familiar Hungarian landscape. Russian tanks. Everywhere. All with their guns aimed straight at the train.

They did not exchange a word in the next half-hour.

Then came the shock.

"George," said Geza, sounding as if a noose were around his neck, "do you see where we are?"

George looked beyond the Soviet armor. His heart nearly stopped.

"We're going in the wrong direction! The damn train isn't going to Sopron—it's going back to Budapest!" Aniko grabbed his arm in terror.

The train suddenly halted with a jolt. Aniko fell against George, who kept his balance only because he was holding on to the window rail. The passengers glanced at one another in fear and confusion. George's eyes were fixed on the Russian tanks outside the window.

"You don't think they're going to shoot, do you?" Aniko whispered.

"I wouldn't bet against it," he replied, biting his lip.

Then, suddenly, at the far end of the car, a conductor in a faded blue-gray uniform appeared, trying to weave his way through the crowd. Questions were fired at him from every direction. He cupped his hands and announced:

"We cannot enter Budapest. Repeat, we cannot enter Budapest. The Soviets have surrounded the city and there is fierce shelling." And then the most startling piece of information: "We are turning back. We must go all the way to Sopron."

Geza, George, and Aniko looked at one another. There was jubilation in their eyes. In a few moments, the train started up slowly . . . away from the Soviet stranglehold on Budapest.

The entire journey toward the border seemed to be through a corridor of tanks. When they finally arrived and stepped onto the Sopron station platform, hope permitted them to take one deep breath. So far, so good.

It was now late afternoon.

"Which way is the border?" George asked Geza.

"I don't know," he confessed.

"Well, what the hell do you expect us to do?" he snapped. "Ask some Russian soldier?"

Then it occurred to Aniko. "Isn't there a School of Forestry here? We could ask a student."

She didn't have to finish her thought. In a split second, George had obtained directions from an elderly woman and they were off.

The minute they entered the great hall, a young man in a beret asked, "Do you need ammo, comrade?"

The atmosphere inside the school was actually festive. Dozens of patriots were arming to drive the Russian invaders from their homeland.

They were each given a piece of bread, a cup of cocoa—and a handful of bullets scooped out from a large vat.

"Where are the weapons?" George asked, his mouth stuffed with bread.

"They will come, comrade, they will come."

The three of them went to sit down in a corner and plan their next move. One thing was certain. They had not come all this way to join a doomed rebellion.

"These people are crazy," said Geza, shifting a half-dozen bullets from hand to hand as if they were mixed nuts. "The shells are all of different calibers. I don't see two alike. What are they going to do—spit them at the Russians?"

And then he rose and walked off to seek out geographical orientation.

George and Aniko looked at each other. This was the first time they had been alone in days.

"How do you feel?" he asked her.

"Scared. I hope we can make it."

She clasped his hand.

"Don't worry," he replied. And then after a few minutes inquired, "By the way, what did you tell your mother?"

"I know you'll laugh, but it's the only thing she would've believed." She smiled weakly. "I said we were going off to get married."

He grinned wearily and squeezed her hand.

"Maybe it won't be a lie, Aniko."

"Do you really mean it, George?"

He hesitated for a split second and replied, "Why else did I bring you along?"

Then they both leaned back, silent and exhausted.

A few minutes later she said sadly, "I wonder how it's going in Budapest."

"You must force yourself not to think of these things," he replied.

She nodded. But, unlike him, she could not so easily eradicate her memories.

Geza reappeared. "Austria is a few kilometers' walk through those woods back there. If we left now, we could still get there by nightfall."

George looked at Aniko. She stood up, saying nothing.

It had begun to snow heavily again. Thick, silent chunks of white. All three of them were soon soaked and freezing. Their thin city shoes made it worse than walking barefoot.

But they were not alone. Every few minutes a group or a family with children would pass. Some times they would merely nod. At others, they'd exchange what meager information they possessed. Yes, we think the frontier is in that direction. Yes, we did hear that most of the Border Patrol has deserted. No, we haven't seen any Russian soldiers.

Deep in the forest they would pass bunkers from which submachine guns protruded menacingly. These were Border Guard stations, apparently—hopefully—unoccupied. They just moved on, half-expecting a sudden burst of bullets in the back.

The snow reflected an eerie light. In the distance, they heard a growling dog. They stopped in their tracks, paralyzed.

"Is it the guards?" Geza whispered in a panic.

"How the hell do I know?" George shot back. A second or two later, a man with a German shepherd crossed their path. But that was all he was—just a local peasant out for a stroll with his dog. They pressed forward again.

Less than five minutes later, they were out of the woods. On a hill overlooking what had to be the Austrian border. They could see soldiers in overcoats stopping vehicles at a gate, talking, gesturing for documents, et cetera. Some cars were waved through, others turned away.

"Well, we're here," Geza announced, a tinge of triumph in his exhausted voice.

"Yeah," George commented wryly, "now all we have to do is get past the guards. Anybody know how to fly?"

The next words were spoken in a strange voice.

"Halt—put your hands in the air!"

They whirled and saw two men in uniform behind them. One was holding a machine gun.

Damn—the Border Patrol!

"You weren't intending to go on a picnic in Austria, by some chance?"

Neither George nor Geza nor Aniko answered. They were numb beyond despair. The second officer had a radio, with which he now began to contact headquarters.

Knowing they had nothing to lose, George tried desperate diplomacy.

"Listen, we're all Hungarians. In a few hours, we'll be Russian prisoners. And I mean you guys, too. Why don't we all—"

"Silence!" barked the man with the radio. "We have caught you illegally attempting to cross the frontier."

But the soldier with the gun seemed to be trying to catch

George's eye. Could he be hallucinating—or was the officer tilting his head slightly as if to say, "Run for it"?

Actually, it didn't matter. This was their last chance for freedom and they all instinctively knew it.

He touched Aniko's hand lightly. She understood. And at the same instant they both broke into a run. Geza, equally hungry for survival, dashed to the left as George and Aniko bolted to the right.

They had taken two or three steps before the bullets began whistling through the air. Perhaps the gunner was not really aiming, but George didn't want to find out. He tucked his head down and sprinted and sprinted and sprinted.

George had no idea how long he had been running. He knew only that he still did not feel tired. He flailed on and on in the knee-deep snow until gradually he began to realize there was no more gunfire. In fact, there was no noise at all. Suddenly, he found himself in a vast, empty field of snow.

He felt safe enough to slacken his pace. Only now did he sense that he was exhausted and near collapse. All he could hear was the sound of his own labored breathing. He turned to look at Aniko.

But he saw nothing. No one. Gradually, painfully, he began to comprehend that she was no longer with him. He had been too preoccupied with his own flight to think of her.

Had she tripped and fallen? Lost her way in that blinding snow? Had one of the many bullets struck her?

George started to retrace his steps, wondering if he should call her name. He opened his mouth, but no voice emerged. He was afraid. Afraid to attract attention. And if he kept heading back, the police might get him. As they might already have gotten her. Was there any point to committing suicide?

No, Aniko would want him to go on and save himself. He turned again, trying not to think of the girl who loved him and left everything to be with him.

Moments later, in the distance, he saw—or thought he saw—the outline of a tower against the evening sky. Then he recognized it as a steeple.

They don't have churches like that in Hungary, he realized. This has to be Austria. He set out toward the horizon.

Half an hour later, Gyorgy Kolozsdi staggered into the Austrian town of Neunkirchen. The villagers were celebrating some local festival. As soon as he appeared, they knew who he was. Or at least what he was. A plump, ruddy-faced man approached, pointing a finger at him.

"*Bist du ungarisch?*" he asked.

Even in his state of shock, he knew they were asking him if he was Hungarian. And, more important, they were speaking *German.* He was safe.

Two men came up and helped him sit down on a bench. One had a flask of schnapps. George took a swig. Then suddenly he began to sob.

He felt guilty to be alive.

A small Austrian police van creaked to a halt about fifty feet from where George was sitting. A tall, slender, and totally expressionless officer came up to him.

"*Guten Abend,*" he said quietly. And then gesturing toward his vehicle added, "*mit mir, bitte.*"

George breathed the sigh of a defeated man, rose obediently, and slowly followed his captor. When he climbed wearily inside, his worst fears were confirmed. There were ten or twelve other passengers, all Hungarians like himself.

"Welcome to the West," said a short, wiry man with bushy sideburns, ensconced in a rear seat. George hastened to sit next to him.

"What the hell is going on?" he asked anxiously.

"The Austrians are rounding up strays like us. My name's Sándor, Miklos. Call me Miki. And you—?"

"Kolozsdi, Gyorgy," George replied. And then asked quickly, "Are they taking us back?"

"Don't be silly. I am on my way to Chicago."

"How do you know?"

"Because on this side of the border people are free to go where they want to. Isn't that why you left?"

George thought for a moment and then replied softly, "Yes, I suppose so. But where are we going in this bus?"

"Well, after they pick up a few more fish that slipped through the Soviet nets, they'll take us someplace to snooze. I know a bit of German and I've chatted up the captain."

George was almost tempted to feel relief. But there had been so many disappointments, so many unexpected turns of the screw, that he dared not let his guard down.

As they drove through the night, many of the refugees dozed

off. But George remained awake, gazing intently out the window to catch the names of towns and villages. He wanted to be absolutely certain there were no deviations from the path to freedom.

Just before daybreak they reached Eisenstadt. The van pulled into the crowded parking area of the railroad station—which was bristling with thousands of Hungarian refugees.

"What's happening?" asked George as Miki trotted back from a lightning reconnaissance mission.

"They're organizing trains," he puffed, "to take us to some big abandoned army camp the Russians used during the war."

"I don't like the sound of that," said George.

"Yes," Miki agreed with a wink. "Anything Russian—even without Russians in it—is not for me. I'm going freelance."

"Meaning what?"

"Look, sooner or later they'll have to take these people to Vienna. But I prefer to go right now. Want to join me?"

"Sure. Do you have a map?"

"In here," the little man answered, pointing to his head. "I memorized everything. All we have to do is head north and watch the signs. Okay, let's separate and stroll nonchalantly toward the far exit. When you're sure nobody's looking, slip away and start walking along the main road. We'll rendezvous at the first beerhouse on the right-hand side."

They nodded and quickly parted company. George hurried as inconspicuously as possible to the edge of the station. Then, after whistling his way past the armed guards, he began to stride northward as quickly as he could.

The first tavern was a mere six hundred yards away. The older man was already there, leaning casually against a fading wooden sign that identified the establishment as "Der Wiener Keller."

"It means the Vienna Wine Cellar," explained Miki, pointing to the placard. "It's a sort of weak pun on 'Wein' and 'Wien.' Not sophisticated enough for gentlemen like us. I suggest we move on."

Without another word they set off.

"How's your English?" asked Miki, as they marched briskly.

"I don't know a single word," George replied.

"Oh yes, you're one of those privileged party children who

get to study all those years of Russian. Not very provident of you, was it?"

"No. But I'll start learning English the minute I can buy a book."

"You're walking with one," his fellow refugee replied. "If you pay attention, I will have you speaking good American before we reach Vienna."

"Okay." George smiled. "Start teaching."

"First lesson. Repeat after me, 'I am a cool cat. You are a cool cat. He is a cool cat. She is a —' "

"What does that mean?" George asked.

" 'Cool cat' is a nice compliment meaning 'good person.' Trust me, George, I'm up-to-date from studying all the newspapers. Now stop the questions and start repeating."

After two hours, George was able to make a modicum of idiomatic small talk. He knew how to flatter his future countrymen. To tell them that life in Hungary was "a drag." And that the United States was the hope for the future of all mankind. On the more pragmatic side, he was able to ask where the men's room was.

They slowed somewhat as they crossed the Danube. For they both were acutely aware that, a few hundred kilometers to the east, this same river bisected their native city.

"Do you have family back in Budapest?" George asked.

Miki hesitated. His expression seemed to alter slightly.

"Not anymore," he answered enigmatically. "And you?"

Regretting that he had broached the subject, George responded with the same words: "Not anymore."

And he once more fought to drive the thoughts of Aniko from his mind.

Miki explained that he was going to seek out the major American relief organizations and tell each one of them that he had a sister and brother-in-law in Illinois. He also had a profession. And besides, Charles Lancaster was willing to be his sponsor.

"Who the hell is Charles Lancaster?" asked George.

"My brother-in-law, of course."

" 'Lancaster'?"

"Listen, Gyuri, if your name were Karoly Lukacs, wouldn't you change it to something more familiar to the American ear?"

George agreed. And immediately applied the lesson to his own predicament. "But, Miki, what will they make of 'Gyuri Kolozsdi'?"

"They will make a mess of it, my friend. An American needs an American name."

"Well, what would you suggest?"

" 'Gyorgy' is no problem," answered Miki, clearly enjoying the opportunity to rebaptize an adult. "It simply becomes 'George.' But 'Kolozsdi' must be replaced by something clear and neat."

George searched his mind. For some strange reason, his thoughts returned to that first tavern on the road to freedom— Der Wiener Keller. "How does 'George *Keller*' sound?"

"Very dignified. Very dignified indeed."

At this point they could have taken a tram, but George was loath to leave his new friend.

"Do you think they'll want a simple student? I mean, I have no degree or anything."

"Then you must find something that will make them want you."

"I was studying Soviet law. What good is that in America?"

"Aha—there you have it. You have had a thorough party education. You know Russian almost as a mother tongue. Tell them you want to use this knowledge in the struggle *against* world communism. Tell them you want to go to university to help in this fight."

"Any university in particular?"

"In America, the two best are Harvard and Yale. But you'd better say you want to go to Harvard."

"Why?"

Miki smiled. "Because for a Hungarian, 'Yale' is too hard to pronounce."

They finally parted company on the Ringstrasse.

"Good luck, Georgie."

"Miki, I'll never forget what you've done for me."

Several moments later George discovered an envelope in his pocket. It contained Miki's future address in Highland Park, Illinois. And twenty-five U.S. dollars.

The American Red Cross committee seemed fairly impressed with George's academic background. But instead of receiving an air ticket, he was assigned to barracks on the outskirts of town. This wouldn't do.

George approached a fresh-faced official wearing a Red Cross tag that identified him as:

ALBERT REDDING
English-Deutsch-Français

"Excuse me, Mr. Redding," George said politely. "I would like to go to Harvard."

"Who wouldn't?" The young man laughed. "I got turned down flat. And I was third in my graduating class and editor of the paper. But don't you worry, we've got lots of colleges. You'll finish your studies, I'll promise you that."

But George had a trump card, one of the "key American phrases" Miki had taught him on their march from Eisenstadt to Vienna.

"Mr. Redding," he said with a slight quaver in his voice, "I—I want to be in America . . . for Christmas."

It worked! George could see from the expression on Redding's face that he was moved by this lonely refugee's yearning.

"You're a good fella, you know that?" he said with genuine affection. "Look—give me your name and I'll see what I can do."

Gyorgy Kolozsdi spoke his freshly minted appellation for the first time. "It's Keller. George Keller."

"Well, George," said Albert, "I can't promise anything, but come back and see me tomorrow morning, okay?"

"Okay."

"And if there's anything you need in the meantime—"

"There is," George interrupted this gentle attempt to brush him off. "I understand it is possible to get messages on the Voice of America, yes?"

"Uh, sure. That's not my department, but I could pass it on." He withdrew a pad and pencil from his jacket pocket and George dictated.

"I would simply like it said please that . . . 'Mr. Karl Marx has died.' "

"That's it?"

"Yes, please."

The young man looked up at George and inquired diffidently, "Say, don't they know this behind the Iron Curtain?"

"It may shock some people," George replied. "Anyway, thank you, mister. I will return tomorrow early."

At seven-thirty the next morning, Albert Redding was in a state of shock.

"I dunno," he muttered to George, waving a telegram in his left hand. "Maybe I should have been born Hungarian."

"What is it?"

"I just do not believe this luck," the young man repeated in dismay. "Listen to this: 'To the Field Director, American Red Cross, Vienna—Harvard University has set up a committee to seek out and subsidize one or two qualified refugee students from Hungarian universities. We would appreciate complete details on any potential candidates. Please reply to me with fullest particulars. Signed, Zbigniew K. Brzezinski, Assistant Professor of Government.' "

Redding looked wide-eyed at George. "Do you *believe* that?"

"Who knows? But let us anyway quickly send this person a report about me."

The response came within twenty-four hours. This young refugee was just the sort of candidate they were looking for. The rest was merely bureaucratic detail.

Eight days afterward, George Keller boarded a bus for Munich, where he was placed on an aircraft; twenty-six hours later, he alighted at Newark Airport, USA. He was not at all tired by the long journey. It had allowed him time to memorize more of his newest acquisition, a book called *Thirty Days to a More Powerful Vocabulary*.

Customs at the airport was perfunctory. It had to be. All George possessed were two books, three newspapers, and some clean underwear the Red Cross had given him. As he walked tentatively out of the Immigration area, a pale angular man with a crewcut held out his hand.

"George Keller?"

He nodded, still slightly unfamiliar with his new name.

"I'm Professor Brzezinski. Welcome to America. We've arranged for you to sleep tonight at the New York Harvard Club."

Andrew first met George Keller after lunch in Master Finley's office. Professor Brzezinski had just brought the young refugee over from South Station and made the introductions. He then gave Andrew two hundred dollars and asked him to take George around the Square and fit him out with all the basic clothes he'd need. They would have to be thorough, since the Hungarian didn't even have pajamas. Lest Andrew get the wrong idea, Brzezinski cautioned, "We are on a tight budget, Mr. Eliot. So I think it wise you do most of your shopping at The Coop."

As soon as they reached the Square, George began to read the billboards out loud, and then he eagerly asked, "Do I pronounce these words correctly, Andrew?"

He recited everything from slogans such as "Lucky Strike Means Fine Tobacco" to "Eight Minutes to Park Street" (on the electric sign over the subway). And then he would immediately try to use this verbiage in a sentence like, "What do you think, Andrew? Shall we buy some Lucky Strike? I'm told that it is fine tobacco and it is very good to smoke." Or, "I hear the journey into Park Street, which is known to be the center of Boston city, is eight minutes only from this Harvard Square. Am I correct?"

He then listened with frenetic intensity to whatever nonsense Andrew replied, immediately asking for definitions of words he had not understood.

"Please, George," Andrew begged at last, "I feel like a walking dictionary."

Not that George wasn't grateful. He kept effusively repeating things like, "Andrew, you're a really cool cat."

The preppie wondered where the refugee had picked up slang

like that. But then concluded that it must be a translation from Hungarian.

Inside The Coop, George acted like a child in Santa's storehouse. He had never seen such an array of merchandise in his whole life. What struck him most was the amazing brightness of the colors.

"Back in my home—my former home, I mean to say—all things were gray," he commented. "Also a great big drag."

Despite a gleam in his eyes that made Andrew think he wanted to buy everything in the place, when it came down to selecting the most trivial of items, George was enormously fastidious. They stood in the underwear department and engaged in a long dialectic as to whether the majority of Harvard men wore boxer shorts or "the most cool of them" preferred the jockey type. (Every part of him had to be fashionably American.)

They ran the same investigative gamut when it came to socks and ties. Andrew steered him toward the reps, of course.

With notebooks and similar supplies, it was a good deal easier. George simply picked everything that had the college emblem on it (even the ballpoint pens, strictly a tourist item).

And yet he was a little leery when Andrew explained that Harvard types carried their stuff around in a green bookbag.

"Why green? Is not the official university color this winelike crimson?"

"Yeah," Andrew sputtered, at a loss for words, "but—"

"Then what is the reason you make me buy green?"

"Hey, George, I honestly don't know. It's just an old tradition. I mean, all the cool people—"

"Oh, truthfully?"

"Even Dr. Pusey," Andrew answered, hoping that the President of Harvard would not mind his invoking him in vain.

They spent an aeon in the textbook section. On the train, Brzezinski had helped George work out a schedule of courses that would suit someone with perfect Russian. Still, in addition to his class texts, he bought all sorts of English grammar books and dictionaries. Anything that would advance his crusade to conquer the language.

As they were lugging all their purchases back home to Eliot, George suddenly asked in an incongruous whisper, "We are alone now, Andrew, are we not?"

Dunster Street was empty, so the answer obviously was yes.

"Then we can speak the truth to one another?"

Andrew was totally confused. "I don't understand you, George."

"You can trust me to keep a secret, Andrew," he continued, still half-whispering. "Are you the spy?"

"The what?"

"Please. I am not some naive newborn child. In every university the government has spies."

"Not in America," Andrew answered, trying to sound convincing. For, like someone in a Kafka story, he felt slightly guilty.

"George, do I look like a spy to you?"

"Of course not," he said knowingly. "That is the biggest reason why I suspect you. Please—you won't report this, yes?"

"Hey look," Andrew protested, "I don't report to anybody. I'm just a Harvard undergraduate."

"Is your name really Andrew Eliot?"

"Of course. What do you find so strange in that?"

"Look here," he reasoned, "the dwelling they assign me is called Eliot. You say that is your name also. Do you not find that curious coincidence?"

As patiently as possible, Andrew tried to explain how Harvard buildings got their names from notable alumni of a bygone age. And that his family had been pretty distinguished. Apparently that satisfied George for the moment. In fact, it seemed to lift his mood.

"Then you are an aristocrat?"

"You might say so," Andrew answered candidly. And was pleasantly surprised to find that for some unfathomable reason, this seemed to make George happy.

Then came the horror show.

They had left Eliot at about half past one. It was close to five when they returned.

Fortunately, Andrew was the first to walk into the suite. Something made him glance toward the bedroom, where he saw in panic what they'd interrupted.

The day's events had made him totally forget! It took Andrew half a second to react. First he ordered George to wait in the hall, then he sprinted like a demon to the bedroom door and slammed it shut.

At last, he turned around to see the refugee staring at him, his suspicion now inflamed to paranoia.

"Eliot, what is happening?"

"Nothing, nothing, nothing. Some friends of mine have just been . . . borrowing the place."

As Andrew stood there like a sentry at the bedroom door, both men could hear frantic shuffling inside.

"I don't believe you," George stated angrily, a quaver in his voice. "And I wish to speak to your superiors immediately."

"Hey, wait a minute, Keller, let me explain this, huh?"

He glanced at his brand-new Timex watch and, like a military officer, replied, "Okay, I give you five minutes. Then I phone Brzezinski to get me out of here." He sat down and folded his arms.

Andrew didn't know how to begin. "Look, George, there are these two friends of mine who—" At a loss for words, he stood there making futile gestures in the air.

"So far, no good," Keller said disapprovingly. Then he glanced at his watch again. "Four minutes twenty and I call Brzezinski."

Suddenly he looked up and his expression changed completely. He jumped to his feet and, with a broad smile, said, "Greetings, honey, I am George. What's your name?"

Andrew whirled around and saw that Sara had emerged, a little red-faced.

"I'm Sara Harrison," she said with as much friendly composure as she could muster under the circumstances. "Welcome to Harvard."

George held out his hand. They shook. Then Ted appeared and introduced himself. George was miraculously transformed.

"And so we all are living here?" he asked with newfound optimism.

"Uh—not really," Andrew stammered. "It's just that Ted and Sara have no place to, you know—"

"Please," George said gallantly, "there is no need to explain. We have these housing problems also in Hungary."

"Hey," Ted whispered to Andrew apologetically, "I'm sorry for this little mess-up. But you didn't give us any warning."

"No, no, you guys. It's all my fault. I should have called you when I learned what train he would be coming on."

"No sweat," Ted reassured him. "But look, it's getting late.

I've got to walk Sara back and go to work. Thanks, Eliot, it was great while it lasted."

As Sara kissed Andrew on the cheek and started out, he called, "Hey, you know nothing has to change. I mean, you're welcome to continue . . . visiting."

Sara stuck her head back in. "We'll see." She smiled. "But I think you've got your hands full."

The Eliot House dining hall was the one selected to stay open through the Christmas holidays. To offer nourishment—a flattering term for Central Kitchen fare—to the poor souls who had to stay in Cambridge during the vacation.

These were not the usual men of the house, but rather a potpourri of undergraduates from all over the campus. Many were seniors (of the Class of '57) feverishly working on their honors dissertations. Some were freshmen who lived too far from home and didn't have the wherewithal even for bus fare.

Still, a few were genuine Eliot men, each of whom had a special reason for remaining in arctic Cambridge over Christmas.

Danny Rossi was one of them. He welcomed the liberation from his classwork to plunge fully into composing *Arcadia*. The place was quiet. Not a single raucous shout rose from the snowy courtyard to destroy his concentration. For, wanting to impress Maria, he'd rashly promised that he'd have the whole score done by New Year's Eve.

He worked demonically from dawn to late at night. One theme came magically—the plaintive love song of the shepherds. It was a melody born of his longing for Maria. The rest took sweat to write but gradually the staves were filled.

It was, he thought, the best stuff he had ever done.

This dedication was convenient for another reason. His mother's recent letters had been urging him to come home for the holidays and make peace. Yet, his important first commission gave him a legitimate excuse to continue to avoid facing his father.

Danny spent his Yuletide locked up, psychologically as well as physically. For his obsession with this new ballet helped him to

161

shut out all emotion: the natural desire to spend Christmas with his family, especially his mother. And those feelings for Maria. So lovely. So desirable. So completely unattainable.

Hell, he tried to rationalize, I'll put the pain down on the music paper. Passion can inspire art. But, in this case, his attempt to sublimate passion merely inspired more passion.

◆

George Keller had also chosen to remain in Cambridge. Though Andrew Eliot had kindly invited him to his home, George preferred to stay on monastically and make his rapidly improving English even better.

On Christmas Eve, the dining hall came up with something tasting almost like roast turkey. George Keller did not notice. He sat at the far end of a rectangular table, devouring a vocabulary book. At the other end, his classmate Danny Rossi was intently reading over what he had composed that day.

They were too engrossed to notice each other. Or the fact that each of them was lonely.

Close to midnight, the subconscious child in Danny Rossi reemerged. He put away his score and for some atavistic reason began to improvise Christmas carols on the keyboard.

Since his window had been slightly open, the music floated gently out across the darkened courtyard where it could be heard by George Keller, who was, of course, still madly studying.

The refugee leaned back and closed his eyes. Even in Hungary, he had always been affected by the melody of "Silent Night." Now, a million miles away, he harkened to it echoing faintly in the icy Cambridge air.

And for a moment he remembered things that he had hoped had been suppressed forever.

ANDREW ELIOT'S DIARY

January 18, 1957

This George Keller is driving me insane. Maybe it's the immigrant mentality. In fact, I'm working up a theory that Americans are driven by ambition in direct proportion to how recently they've set foot on these shores.

I mean, I once thought Lambros had a bullet up his ass. But he was born here. It was his father's generation that came over on the boat. But nothing, absolutely nothing, tops the frenzied drive of this Hungarian, barely two months in America. I mean, if he were a locomotive he'd explode, he's stoking his fire so hot.

When I wake up at what for me is the ungodly hour of 8:00 A.M., he's already hard at work, having long since eaten breakfast. Almost every day he tells me with a kind of gleeful pride that he was first man in the dining hall. (Compare this to Newall, who revels in the distinction of never once having gotten up for break-fast in his entire Harvard career.)

George borrowed fifty bucks from me (which he'll pay back as soon as his scholarship money comes through), and bought a portable recorder he takes to every class.

Now in the afternoons he plays back the lectures—and some-times not just once—till he practically knows them by heart. Lots are in Russian. Which may be great for him, but makes me feel like I'm suddenly living in the Kremlin. Needless to say, George has the suite pretty much to himself during the days.

We did have a little problem about Ted and Sara. While George was very understanding of their need for a place to be alone, he insisted that he wouldn't mind if they used my bedroom as long as he could keep studying in the living room.

I had to explain to him very tactfully that *they* would mind very much. George finally agreed to go and sit in the house library from four to six-thirty on the days Ted and Sara are in temporary residence.

Now here's a shocker. I have no idea what time he goes to bed. In fact, I have the sneaking suspicion that the guy doesn't sleep at all! And I had this really weird experience late the other night.

After a hard session of drinking at the Porc, nature obliged me to get up at around 2:00 A.M. As I was standing in the john taking care of my needs, I suddenly heard this ghostly voice emanating from the shower, saying things like, "begin-began-begun, bite-bit-bitten, sing-sang-sung."

I called out to George, but, instead of answering me directly, he simply went on rehearsing his verbs in that tile echo chamber.

Then I pulled back the shower curtain. There he was, naked except for his new à la mode jockey shorts, holding an English grammar. He barely noticed me as he droned on, hammering new words into his head.

I warned him that he'd drive himself to death. To which he replied, "Drive-drove-driven."

I went to the sink, picked up a glass of cold water, and poured it over his head. He shivered and looked at me with comatose astonishment, then ripped the curtain from my hand, slammed it closed, and continued his verbal gymnastics.

"Show-showed-shown, speak-spoke-spoken."

Shit, I thought. He can kill himself for all I care.

I shut the bathroom door behind me so that at least Newall could have some peace, staggered back to my bed, and went to sleep.

Or, as George would have put it, sleep-slept-slept.

"Hello, Dad. It's Jason. I've got some great news."

"I can't hear you, son. There's a terrific racket going on behind you. Where are you calling from?"

"Racket's a good word for it. The whole squash team's in my room. They just voted for next year's varsity captain and for some stupid reason they chose me."

"Son," the elder Gilbert said elatedly, "that's just terrific news. I can't wait to tell your mother. And you know what? I bet you'll be tennis captain, too."

As Jason hung up, he felt a kind of vague, inexplicable sadness. For his dad's last remark had unsettled him. After all, he had been calling to announce a great success. And though his father was obviously delighted, he had concluded with the pretty unsubtle expectation that his son would bring him still more glory. Where would it end?

"Hey, Captain," Newall interrupted giddily, "are you still sober?"

"Yeah." Jason laughed. "Couldn't let my dad think we were all a bunch of drunken bums, which naturally we are."

His teammates roared appreciatively. There were a dozen of them crowded in his little room, plus several hangers-on including Ted and Sara. Andrew Eliot had brought them along to get a glimpse of the more athletic creatures in the Harvard bestiary.

Originally Newall had intended these festivities to be a surprise. But then George Keller had refused to let them use their own room to hold the party. Newall had no alternative but to tell Jason in advance, so they could use his suite.

"How is that dingbat?" Jason asked, while pouring out a Bud. "I bet he's out memorizing the *Encyclopedia Britannica* by now."

"Don't laugh," cautioned Andrew. "Besides studying like a maniac for all his courses, he also reads every inch of *The New York Times*—including real estate and recipes—and writes down every word he doesn't know."

"And that includes the Sunday edition," Newall added, "when the goddamn paper's practically as long as *War and Peace*."

"Well," said Jason, "you gotta admire a guy like that."

"I'll be happy to admire him," Newall retorted, "if only someone else would *room* with him."

Suddenly the members of the squash team started clinking glasses and calling boozily for silence. It was time to toast their newly chosen captain. The most eloquent of them was Tod Anderson, former Andover captain, now number three on the varsity.

Tod raised his glass and spoke a tribute appropriate for such a gathering of jocks. "To our beloved new leader, Jason Gilbert, ace racket-man and incomparable ass-man. May his shots in court drop as often as his shorts in bed."

Just after seven, the final partyers began to disperse, and the squash team, as prearranged, started strolling through the streets of Cambridge toward the Hasty Pudding Club. Thursday was steak night, the best buy in Cambridge for $1.75.

As they trooped down Mount Auburn toward Holyoke Street, the knights of the Harvard Squash Varsity broke into a euphoric variant of the college's most popular fight song:

> With Gilbert in triumph flashing
> Mid the strains of victory
> Poor Eli's brains we are smashing
> Into blue obscurity . . .

They grew only slightly more sedate as they shuffled up the wooden steps of the clubhouse, at number 12, and mounted the stairs, past two centuries of theatrical posters, to the dining room where Newall had reserved a large table for the entire group.

Naturally they put Jason at the head, which cheered him immensely, because his prominent position drew the attention of every other Pudding member's date. To these ordinary mortals' discomfiture, their female guests kept smiling at the man of the hour. And he smiled disarmingly back at them.

At about ten o'clock Jason, Andrew, and Dickie Newall were weaving their way back to Eliot House when something occurred to the captain-elect.

"Hey," he remarked, "I didn't see Anderson at dinner. Did he duck the party or something?"

"C'mon, Jason," Newall responded with liquid lightheartedness, "you know Tod's not a member of the Pudding."

"How come?" asked Jason, surprised that such a popular athlete should not be in the eating society that took almost a third of all upperclassmen.

"Haven't you noticed that Anderson's a Negro?" Newall chided.

"So what?" said Jason.

"Come on, Gilbert," Dickie continued, "the Pudding's not *that* liberal. I mean, we've still got to keep *somebody* out."

Thus, even on the night of such personal triumph, Jason Gilbert was once again reminded that although all Harvard undergraduates are equal, some are more equal than others.

Professor Samuel Eliot Morison was among the most eminent members of the Harvard faculty, and by far the most prolific. Renowned for his many volumes of naval history and his chronicles of Harvard, this distinguished gentleman was also, as his middle name suggests, vaguely related to the Eliot in The Class of '58.

Andrew had been gliding along for almost three years now, flitting like a bee from major to major (English, American studies, even Ec. for a few silly weeks). But now his senior tutor sent him an ultimatum: he had to choose a subject and stick to it. Knowing that he had to graduate from Harvard with a degree in *something*, he was panicked into seeking professional advice.

Gathering his courage, he wrote Professor Morison a note. And was agreeably surprised to receive an immediate invitation to visit the great man in his map-lined office deep in the stacks of Widener.

"What a real pleasure," he remarked as they shook hands. "I see before me living proof that old John Eliot's line is vibrant still. I knew your father when he was an undergraduate and tried to get him to help me a bit with my colonial history. But I guess the banking branch seduced him."

"Yes," Andrew averred politely, "Dad is sort of fond of money."

"Nothing wrong with that," said Morison, "especially since so much Eliot philanthropy has helped to build this college. My own namesake, Samuel Eliot, endowed the first professorship of Greek back in 1814. Tell me, Andrew, what's your major?"

"That's just it, sir. I'm a junior and I still haven't made up my mind."

"What do you think you'll be doing after college?"

"Well, naturally, I'll have to do some military service—"

"The Eliots have long served with honor in the navy," he commented.

"Yes, sir, Admiral Morison," Andrew replied. But did not tell him that that was why he was thinking of the army.

"And after that?"

"I guess Dad expects me to be some sort of banker." After all, he thought, I'm coming into so much dough in four years I'll at least have to visit where the bonds are kept. That's sort of banking, isn't it?

"Well, then," said Morison, "you'll have a fine vocation. Now you ought to choose a major that will give you some enriching avocation. Have you ever thought about the history of your own family?"

"Dad never lets me forget it," Andrew responded with honesty and some discomfort. "I mean, while I was still in diapers he was already lecturing me about our noble heritage. To be frank sir, it's a bit off-putting. I mean, over pablum I was hearing about John Eliot, the Apostle to the Indians, and great-granddad Charles, the famous Harvard President. I was practically smothered by the foliage on our family tree."

"But you've just leapfrogged several centuries," the admiral remarked. "What about the Revolutionary War? Do you know where all the Eliots were during 'the times that tried men's souls'?"

"No, sir. I just assumed they were shooting off their muskets around Bunker Hill."

Now the professor smiled. "Then I think I have some enlightenment for you. The eighteenth century Eliots were splendid diarists. And we have records in their very words of what they saw and did during the Revolution.

"Andrew, I can think of nothing more exciting, especially for an Eliot, than studying what Harvard graduates were up to at that time. It could be a splendid topic for a senior thesis."

At this point Andrew had to confess. "Sir, I think I should tell you that my grades are not exactly at the honors level. They'd never let me write a dissertation."

The great historian smiled.

"Then you can have the essence of true education, Andrew. I'll arrange for you to have tutorial with me, and we'll go through the Eliot diaries together. Grades won't enter into it. Just reading them will be their own reward."

Andrew left Morison's office almost breathless with elation. Now there was a chance that in addition to receiving a diploma, he might even get an education.

D anny Rossi was torn.
At times he desperately wanted
the rehearsals of *Arcadia* to
end, so the damn ballet would be performed and close. Then he
would never have to see Maria again.

At other times he wished the preparations would go on
forever. Six afternoons a week in February and March he had to
sit for several hours at the keyboard as Maria put the ballet on its
feet. Drilling the dancers, demonstrating the movements, and
often coming over to lean on the piano and ask the composer's
advice.

It was that damn blue leotard of hers. No, how could he
blame the garment when what was driving him crazy was the
body it so tantalizingly accentuated.

Perhaps the worst part of all was when they would go out for
a bite afterward to discuss how the ballet was going. She was so
warm and friendly, and their conversations would go on for
hours. Agonizingly, these evenings grew more and more to seem
like dates. Yet Danny knew they weren't.

Once, when she had Asian flu, he went to visit her in the
Infirmary and brought a flower. He sat down by her bed and
tried to cheer her up with silly anecdotes. She laughed a lot and,
when he rose to leave, said, "Thanks for coming, Danny. You're
a pal."

That's all he was, goddammit, just a lousy pal. And yet how
could it be otherwise? She was beautiful and confident—and tall.
And he was none of these.

And worst of all, what pretext could he possibly invent to see
her once the performances had ended?

Opening night finally arrived. All the self-styled Harvard
cognoscenti assembled in Radcliffe's Agassiz Theater to sit in

judgment on Maria Pastore's choreography and Daniel Rossi's score.

Danny was too involved conducting to notice how it was going, although at several points the audience burst into applause. Was it for the music or the dance?

Since most of the performers were abstemious, the party was held in an adjacent rehearsal room, where brackish Kool-Aid punch was served and a few daring souls drank beer.

Harvard theatrical premieres are just like those on Broadway in one respect. The performers all sit up waiting for the reviews. The only difference is that in Cambridge they merely keep vigil for the verdict of the *Crimson*.

At about eleven, someone sprinted in with Sonya Levin's comments for tomorrow's *Crime*. For a journal by implicit policy supercilious, the review began with some pretty enthusiastic remarks about Maria's choreography, which was deemed "dynamic and imaginative, with touches of lighthearted invention."

Then Miss Levin turned her attention to Danny Rossi. Or rather her guns. In her opinion,

> the music, though ambitious and energetic, was, to say
> the least, derivative. Imitation may be the sincerest form
> of flattery, but Stravinsky and Aaron Copland could justi-
> fiably ask Rossi to pay royalties.

To Danny's consternation, this was all being read aloud by the stage manager, who was growing steadily uneasier as he recited.

Danny was stung. Why was this sarcastic *Crimson* smart-ass trying to make herself look good at his expense? Did she have any idea how this would hurt?

He felt a sudden urge to run out of the room. Just as he stood, there was a hand on his shoulder. It was Maria.

"Hey, Danny—"

"Don't bother," he muttered bitterly. He could not turn around and face her. And forgetting he had left his parka folded on a backstage chair, he started slowly out of the room.

As soon as he reached the stairway he quickened his pace. He had to get the hell out of there. To escape all those pitying glances.

When he reached the ground floor he noticed the sign pointing toward the public telephone and remembered his promise to
call Dr. Landau as soon as the performance was over.

Oh, shit, no. How can I repeat those crushing things that
bitch reviewer said? In fact, how could he *ever* call his teacher
now? He was a failure. A conspicuous and public failure. Like
that long-ago day on the high school track.

He pushed open the glass door and walked out into the
cold March night, insensitive to the harsh wind hitting his face.
He was too preoccupied with the thought that this unexpected
turn of events would deprive him of his beloved teacher's
respect.

Danny always knew he would be Landau's last pupil. And he
wanted to be his best.

He could go no farther. He sat down on the stone steps and
put his head in his hands.

"Hey, Rossi, what are you doing there? You'll catch pneumonia."

Maria was standing above him, just outside the door.

"Go away, Pastore. You shouldn't hang around with second-
raters."

Ignoring his words, she came down and sat a step below
him.

"Listen, Danny, I don't care what Sonya says. I think your
music's brilliant."

"Everybody in the college's gonna read that tomorrow
morning. That'll give those bastards in Eliot House a few laughs."

"Don't be silly," she replied. "Most of those preppies can't
read anyway." And then added gently, "I only wish you'd believe
that I hurt just as much as you."

"Why? *You* got good reviews."

"Because I love you."

"You can't," he answered as an unwitting reflex. "You're
much too tall."

She could not help laughing at this absurd reaction.

Then he began to laugh as well. And reached down and drew
her toward him. They kissed.

After a moment Maria gazed at him and smiled. "Now it's
your turn."

"What?"

"I mean, is this a one-way thing or not?"

"No," he answered softly. "I love you too, Maria."

They did not feel the chill wind blow as they continued to embrace.

Harvard spring vacations can mean many things to many people.

Seniors stay in place to finish off their dissertations, which are due the day that classes recommence. The more affluent undergraduates fly off to Bermuda for that fabled rite known as College Week. The program includes sunning, sailing, waterskiing, calypso dancing, and—at least hypothetically—seducing the girls who flock there for most of the same reasons.

Spring normally visits Cambridge in name only. And athletic muscles need the vernal warmth to tone them for the crucial competitions yet to come.

The track team gets to fly to Puerto Rico. Which sounds more exotic than it is. Because, unlike the tourists on the beaches of Bermuda, the harriers get up at 5:00 A.M., go ten miles before breakfast, and then sleep all day until it's time to run again that afternoon. Few have the energy, or even the desire, to seek out señoritas in the evening.

Tennis, golf, and baseball tour the southern states to limber up, competing against some of the local universities. These teams live less ascetically than the runners, and thus have reservoirs of energy for nighttime entertainment. After dinner they strut through the richly landscaped campuses wearing an irresistible lodestone for the lovely southern coeds: sweaters with that noble **H**.

After a hard-earned victory against the University of North Carolina, Jason Gilbert and his teammates were preparing to go out and captivate the female population of Chapel Hill. As they dressed and showered, Dain Oliver, the coach, was offering constructive criticism to his men—including Jason, who, although he'd won, had looked a little sluggish on the court.

"Because I'm *tired*, coach," he was protesting. "All this

traveling and practicing and playing matches isn't really what you'd call a picnic."

"Come on, Gilbert," Dain reprimanded with good humor, "you've been putting too much effort into postgame partying. May I remind you this is not *supposed* to be a holiday?"

"Hey, coach, you do remember that I won today, don't you?"

"Yeah, but you were sleeping on your feet. So shape up, or I'll slap a curfew on you. Do you read me, Gilbert?"

"Yessir. Sorry, mother dear."

As laughter echoed even from the shower room, a graying academic type in suit and tie appeared and asked to have a few words with the coach.

"Who is that guy?" Jason whispered to Newall, who was drying himself at an adjacent locker.

"Probably an FBI man after you, Gilbert," he quipped. "I think you've violated the Mann Act four or five times so far this week."

Before Jason could reply, the coach was calling for the team's attention.

A dozen players in varying states of undress obediently assembled.

Coach Oliver addressed them. "Guys, this gentleman is Rabbi Yavetz, the director of the U.N.C. Hillel Society. He tells me that this evening is the first night of the Passover holiday. And all Jewish players on the team are welcome to attend his service."

"It will be short and festive," the rabbi added in a southern accent. "Just a simple seder with some pretty good food and the songs I hope your granddads taught you."

"Any takers?" asked the coach.

"I'll be glad to come," said sophomore Larry Wexler, new to the team at number seven. "That'll smooth things over with my parents, who were sort of disappointed that I won't be home."

"Anybody else?" Oliver inquired, glancing at Jason Gilbert.

He looked back blandly and replied, "Thanks a lot, but I'm not really . . . interested."

"You're always welcome if you change your mind," the rabbi said. And then turned to Larry Wexler. "I'll send one of our members to the dorm where y'all are staying about half past six."

When the clergyman departed, Newall asked with casual curiosity, "Say, Wexler, what's this holiday for, anyway?"

"It's kind of neat," replied the sophomore. "It celebrates the Jews' exodus from Egypt. You know, when Moses said, 'Let my people go.' "

"Sounds like a colored folks' jamboree," Newall commented.

"Listen," Wexler retorted, "as Disraeli once told an English bigot, 'When my ancestors were reading the Bible yours were still swinging from trees.' "

An hour later, as he was carefully adjusting the knot in his Varsity Club tie, Larry Wexler noticed a reflection in the mirror.

It was Jason—dressed, with uncharacteristic formality, in a sedate blue blazer.

"Hey, Wexler," he said uneasily, "if I go to this thing, will I look like a total asshole? I mean, I don't know what to do."

"No sweat, Gilbert. All you've got to do is sit, listen, and then eat. I'll even turn the pages for you."

They were about four dozen, seated at long tables in a private dining room of the Student Union.

Rabbi Yavetz made some brief introductory remarks.

"In a real sense, Passover is the cardinal holiday on the Jewish calendar. For it fulfills the central commandment of our faith, as put forth in Exodus, Chapter Thirteen—that of reminding our children in every generation that the Lord delivered us from oppression in Egypt."

Jason listened mutely as the celebrants took turns reading from the biblical account and singing psalms of praise. At one point he whispered to Larry, "How come you all know the same tunes?"

"They're from the Top Ten of 5000 B.C. Your ancestors must have been on a very slow camel."

Jason was relieved when the dinner was served. For then the conversation became very much twentieth-century collegiate and he did not feel like an odd man out.

During the meal Larry whispered, "Did any of it mean anything to you—you know, culturally?"

"Sort of," Jason replied, with politeness if not much conviction. For in truth he had not really understood what this ritual had to do with him in 1957.

And yet, before the evening ended, he did.

When the service continued, the rabbi bade everyone rise to

pray for the coming of the Messiah. At this point he added a note of more recent history:

"We are all, of course, aware that the ancient Egyptians were far from the last to try to destroy our people. As recently as Passover 1943, the brave Jews in the Warsaw ghetto, starved and almost without arms, began their last heroic stand against the Nazis who were besieging them.

"This did not happen to our forefathers, it happened to our very own relatives. Uncles, aunts, grandparents—and for some of us, brothers and sisters. It is of them—and the six million others murdered by Hitler—that we think at this moment."

There was a sudden hush.

Jason saw a young man at the first table lower his head and begin to weep silently.

"Did you lose any relatives—over there?" Jason whispered.

Larry Wexler looked at his teammate and answered somberly, "Didn't we all?"

A moment later they were again seated, singing festive songs.

The formalities concluded not long after. They were followed by some unofficial socializing with the attractive coeds, who, enjoined by a double code of hospitality, flocked to welcome the two visitors from Harvard.

At a little before eleven, Larry and Jason were walking through the darkened campus back to their dorm.

"I don't know about you, Gilbert," Larry commented, "but I'm really glad I went. I mean, don't you think it's good to know about our roots?"

"I guess so," Jason Gilbert answered half-aloud. And thought, My own roots seem just to go back to a courthouse twenty years ago. When some accommodating judge gave my father a new, non-Jewish name.

And to secure our future, he mortgaged all our past.

As they walked on, he mused further. I wonder why Dad had to do it. I mean, this guy Wexler's no worse off than I. In fact, he's better. He's got an identity.

Jason returned from the spring tour changed in one official way. After their match against a group of former college all-stars now serving with the Marines in Quantico, Virginia, he had succumbed to the blandishments of a persuasive recruiting officer and signed up for the Platoon Leaders Class.

He had decided that this would be a great way to discharge his military obligation since, unlike the ROTC program, it would meet only during the next two summers. Then, after graduation, he'd go straight into the Marines and serve a two-year stint as an officer. There were even heavy hints that after basic training he might be transferred to Special Services and could spend his tour of duty hitting tennis balls.

But first another battle lay before him. There was Yale to face in May. And the New Haven hordes were out to get revenge.

"**N**o."
"Please."
"No!"

Maria Pastore sat bolt upright, her face flushed.

"Please, Danny, for God's sake, do we have to go through this all the time?"

"Maria, you're being unreasonable."

"No, Danny, you're being cruel and insensitive. Can't you understand I have my principles?"

Danny Rossi could get nowhere with Maria.

Though for the first few weeks they had lived in a kind of paradise for two, alone amid the crowds of Cambridge, they soon encountered serious ethical differences.

Maria was the nicest, kindest, brightest, and most beautiful young woman he had ever met. And she adored him. But the problem was—for reasons he refused to understand, or at any rate accept—she would not sleep with him. In fact, she would permit considerably less than that.

They would embrace and kiss each other passionately while lying on his couch, but whenever he so much as slipped his hand beneath her sweater, all her ardor suddenly turned to rigid panic.

"Please, Danny. Please don't."

"Maria," he reasoned with her patiently, "this is not a fly-by-night affair. We really care for each other. I only want to touch you because I love you."

She stood up, and pulling down her sweater pleaded with him to appreciate her feelings.

"Danny, we're both Catholic. Can't you understand it's wrong to do this sort of thing before you're married?"

"What sort of thing?" he said exasperatedly. "Where is it

written in the Bible that a man can't touch a woman's breasts? In fact, the Song of Songs—"

"Please, Danny," she said quietly, but with obvious inward agony, "you know it isn't that. It would never stop there."

"But I swear to you I won't ask for more."

Maria looked at him, her cheeks red, and said candidly, "Hey look, maybe you think you could break off right in the middle. But I know myself. I know that once we reached that point, *I* couldn't stop."

For a moment this confession elated Danny. "Then in your heart you do want to go all the way?"

She nodded, with a look of shame.

"Danny, I'm a woman. I'm in love with you. And I've got a lot of passion bottled up inside me. But I'm also a religious Catholic. The sisters taught us that to do this is a mortal sin."

"Hey look," he now persisted as if in a university debate. "Can you, an enlightened Radcliffe girl in 1957, tell me you really think you'll burn in hell if you go to bed with someone you love?"

"Before I'm married, yes," she answered without hesitation.

"God, I don't believe this," he responded, running out of patience. And of arguments.

Overcome with dizzying desire to convince this sensual conservative, he said impetuously, "Look, Maria, we'll be married someday. Isn't that enough for you?"

Perhaps she was too upset to notice that he had actually mentioned matrimony. In any case she answered, "Danny, please believe, by everything that's holy, I simply can't forget the way I've been brought up. My priest, my parents, no—I won't evade responsibility and put the blame on them—it's *my* belief. I want to give my husband my virginity."

"Jesus, that's so antiquated. Haven't you read Kinsey? Maybe ten percent of women do that nowadays."

"Danny, I don't care if I'm the last girl on this earth. I'm going to be chaste until my wedding night."

To which, having reached the end of his rhetorical tether, Danny could but answer with a near-involuntary, "Shit."

Then, trying to rein in his own passion, he said, "Okay, okay, let's forget this whole thing and have some dinner."

As he started to put on his tie, he was surprised to hear her answer, "No."

He whirled and barked, "Now what?"

"Danny, let's be honest. Neither of us can go on like this. Because we're starting to get angry with each other. And that means all our tender feelings will inevitably dissipate."

She stood up. As if to put him at a physical as well as moral disadvantage.

"Danny, I really care for you a lot," she said. "But I don't want to see you—"

"Anymore?"

"I don't know," she replied, "but for a while anyway. Look, you've got Tanglewood this summer. I'll be working back in Cleveland. Maybe the separation will do us good. We'll both have time to think."

"But didn't you hear me say I want to marry you?"

She nodded. And then answered softly, "Yes. But I'm not sure you know if you really mean it. That's why we need time apart."

"At least can we write to each other?" Danny asked.

"Please, let's."

Maria then walked to the door and turned. She looked at him silently for a moment and then murmured, "You'll never know how much this hurts me, Danny."

Then she left.

By the spring of 1957 George Keller was as intellectually prepared as anyone in The Class to take courses in the normal language of instruction at Harvard College.

Not unexpectedly, he had chosen to major in government. For Brzezinski had explained how, with his fluent Russian and firsthand knowledge of Iron Curtain politics, he'd be indispensable in Washington.

Among the courses he selected for the spring was Government 180, Principles of International Politics, even though the name of the professor had evoked in him some of his original feelings of paranoia. For the instructor was one William Palmer Eliot—yet another (alleged) relative of his roommate, Andrew.

Still, it was a fateful choice. For Eliot's assistant was a chubby young instructor who spoke English with a foreign accent heavier than George's. His name was Henry Kissinger. And by some uncanny mutual telepathy they gravitated toward each other.

Kissinger, a refugee like George, albeit from wartime Germany, had also been a Harvard undergraduate (and likewise anglicized his first name). He had acquired an uncanny grasp of politics—both in theory and practice. Dr. K. (as he was affectionately known) already directed something called the Harvard International Seminar. And was on the board of what was probably the world's most important political journal, *Foreign Affairs*.

George thought his own cleverness had gotten him Kissinger as section man, only to discover that the teacher had made all the necessary efforts to win *him* for his discussion group. Neither man was disappointed.

Among other things, Kissinger was impressed by George's command of the Russian language. But it was his own burning ambition to be number one at Harvard (and, by extension, in the world) that most made him want to enlist the young Hungarian for his team. For he knew how much his archrival Zbig Brzezinski desperately desired to keep George in his own sphere of influence.

After a section meeting early in the term, he stopped George and said, "Mr. Keller, may I see you for a moment? I would like to add a word or two about your recent essay."

"Certainly," George said politely, suddenly afraid his paper had been less than the original and perceptive analysis he himself considered it.

"Was it all right, Professor?" George asked when the last student had departed. Keen academic strategist, he had astutely bestowed on Kissinger the title of Professor when he knew full well he was a mere instructor. The honoree was clearly flattered. Or at least he smiled broadly.

"Your paper, Mr. Keller, was not just 'all right.' It was absolutely first rate. I've never seen an essay that so perceptively distinguished all the subtleties of the various East European philosophies."

"Thank you, Professor," George replied elatedly.

"I know you are one of our new imports from Hungary. What were you studying in Budapest?"

"Law. Soviet law, of course. Pretty useless, eh?"

"Depends to whom. Personally, for my researches I would welcome someone who was expert in this area and could read Russian easily."

"Well, sir, to be quite above the boards," George replied, "I didn't finish my degree. So you could hardly say I was an expert."

Kissinger's eyes twinkled behind his thick, black-rimmed glasses.

"Perhaps in Hungary you would not qualify as such, but in Cambridge people even with your experience are as rare as hen's teeth—"

"Or snowflakes in July perhaps?" suggested George, to demonstrate his range of English idioms.

"Indeed," Dr. K. replied. "So if you have time, I would like to hire you as a research assistant. The European Study Center pays two dollars an hour, which is pretty good. And there would be the additional incentive of our possibly finding a senior-thesis topic in the work you will be doing."

"Are you intimating that you might personally direct my dissertation?"

"Young man, I'd be insulted if you didn't ask me," Kissinger responded with seductive affability. "So do I take it then that you accept my offer, George? Or do you want to think about it? Maybe talk it over with your faculty adviser? Who is it, that young Polish fellow Brzezinski?"

"It's all right, I'll explain things to Zbig. When shall I start working, Dr. Kissinger?"

"Come to my office after lunch today. And, George, from now on, when we're not in class, please call me Henry."

A nd thus Junior Year concluded. While in the outside world, Eisenhower had been reelected President by his loving U.S. family, one of The Class had been chosen as the minister of millions to the Lord himself. For when the reigning Aga Khan was dying, he unexpectedly chose his grandson, Prince Karim '58, to succeed him as spiritual leader of the millions of Ismaili Moslems.

Many members of The Class saw this as an augury that they too would be blessed by heaven.

George Keller had traveled farthest—both geographically and mentally. After barely seven months, he had truly conquered the English language. Sentence structure bent to his will. Words had become mere pawns in a power play to breach the walls of argument and capture minds.

He now was free to climb the academic mountain. And here he had a magisterial mentor. For if Harvard served him no other purpose, it had brought him close to Henry Kissinger, with whom his mind worked in uncanny synchronicity.

Thus, he was rewarded with the enviable summer job of acting as Dr. K.'s special assistant in organizing the International Seminar and editing its journal, *Confluence*.

The program had gathered several dozen government officials and important intellectuals from both sides of the Iron Curtain for a series of colloquia and public lectures, to make them more sensitive to the new postwar configurations of the global family.

Part of George's duties was to fraternize among the representatives from the Eastern bloc countries and find out what they *really* thought of Harvard, the seminar—and even Kissinger himself.

Despite their initial wariness, they all ultimately succumbed to George's European charm and, at one point or another, spoke far more candidly than they had ever imagined they would in the alien confines of a Western capitalist university.

Of course, nothing in Henry's brief to George suggested that he need go as far as to become physically intimate with any of the participants. This he did on his own initiative.

Perhaps it was something about the sultry Cambridge weather, the sudden stimulation of seeing bevies of non-Radcliffe girls stroll through the Yard in the shortest of shorts and the tightest of T-shirts.

Or perhaps the guilt that had inspired George's self-induced chastity—a kind of subliminal penance—had been absolved by time.

In early August he went to bed with one of Poland's leading journalists. She was nearly forty and a woman of the world. Her comments on George's amorous technique, therefore, carried substantial weight.

"Young man," she whispered, "you are the most expert lover I have ever known—"

George smiled.

"—And the coldest," she quickly added. "You do everything as if you have learned it from a textbook."

"Do you doubt my sincerity?" he asked good-humoredly.

"Of course not," she replied with a sly smile. "I never for a minute believed that you had any. You are their spy, yes?"

"Of course." George grinned. "The director wants me to find out which delegate is the best in bed."

"And?" she inquired saucily.

"If they ever give a Lenin Prize for sex, you would win hands down."

"Ah, George," she cooed, "you talk as elegantly as you screw. You have a great future ahead of you."

"In what field do you think?" he asked, genuinely eager to learn how such a woman of the world viewed him.

"It's obvious," she replied. "There is one profession which needs an equal quantity of your two best talents. I mean, of course, politics."

And she pulled him to her to engage once again in the dialectic of Eros.

◆

Jason Gilbert's march to sporting glory went on unimpeded. He had won the IC4A Tennis Title for the second straight year. And, as if that were not sufficient kudos, his teammates demonstrated the exceptional esteem in which they held him by voting him their captain—as they already had for squash.

Though normally not vindictive, he could not keep himself from sending to his Old Blue headmaster, Mr. Trumbull, the lengthy *Crimson* article that assessed his extraordinary number of sporting achievements to date. And, as the encomium concluded, "Who can dare to speculate what further heights Gilbert will reach with yet another year to go?"

◆

Ted and Sara's love had grown to such intensity that the mere notion of having to spend two months apart became an intolerable prospect. She therefore persuaded her parents to allow her to attend Harvard Summer School and sublet a flat in North Cambridge. Sara's mother was more than slightly dubious about her daughter's sudden passion to take on yet more academic work. But her father, to whom she could confide the fact that mother's suspicions were in fact correct, was generous in his support and helped her win the day.

It was a long and passionate summer (during which they even made love one starry night in Harvard Yard itself, in the quadrangle behind Sever Hall). Parting on Labor Day was a painful wrench. Sara cried the entire week before they had to give up the apartment.

◆

For Danny Rossi, the summer of '57 was a kind of overture to the highest point yet in his musical career.

Munch had booked him to perform with the Boston Symphony on October 12, when he would play Beethoven's Third Piano Concerto. Those trills in the opening movement would have reverberations around the musical world. When he jubilantly called Dr. Landau to tell him the news, he was thrilled to hear that his teacher had been saving money for the plane fare and intended to be present at the concert.

Still, Danny's imminent debut offered far less joy than he had always dreamed it would. For his junior year had taken from him more than it had bestowed. The humiliation of the *Crimson*'s pan for his ballet still haunted him. And then there was the tortured relationship with Maria.

He had hoped their separation through the summer would allow him time to clarify his thoughts and possibly to seduce a few girls at Tanglewood to fortify his masculine self-image. But a sudden tragedy cast a huge pall on everything.

The very night he arrived at Tanglewood, his mother called to tell him that Dr. Landau had suffered a fatal heart attack. In a haze of grief, Danny packed and flew out for his teacher's funeral. At the graveside he cried unashamedly.

When, after the brief service the mourners started to disperse, his mother, whom he had not seen in three long years, implored him to come home. She told Danny it was Dr. Landau's final wish that he be reconciled with his father.

And so the prodigal son returned at last to the house where he had spent such a miserable adolescence.

Arthur Rossi seemed to have changed both inwardly and outwardly. He was subdued now. There were furrows in his face, and he was completely gray at the temples.

For a fugitive instant, Danny felt a pang of remorse. As if his father's outward signs of physical decline had somehow been *his* fault.

But as they stood there facing each other wordlessly for those first awkward moments, Danny forced himself to remember how callously this man had treated him. But he could no longer find it in himself to hate his father. Still, he could not love him, either.

"You're looking well, son."

"You too, Dad."

"It—it's been a long time, hasn't it?"

That was the full extent of what he could say. Danny's long-cherished fantasy of a paternal apology was just that—a figment of his own childish desires.

Thus, with a quiet magnanimity born of grief and newly found indifference, Danny offered his hand to signal that their quarrel was finally at an end. The two even embraced.

"I'm really glad, son," Arthur Rossi murmured. "Now we can all let bygones be bygones."

Yeah, thought Danny, what the hell. It's so unimportant now. The only man who ever acted like a real father to me is dead.

August 8, 1957

All summer I had one foot in the future and the other in the past (don't ask me which I like better).

Since—with any luck—I'll be graduating next June, Father thought it best that I forgo the usual physical labor this year. And instead begin to get acquainted with the family banking business.

Naturally he was in Maine, running things by phone. So he put me into the charge of "good old Johnny Winthrop," an officer quite accurately described by both those adjectives.

"Just keep your eyes and ears open, lad," he explained at the beginning of my very first day. "Watch when I buy, watch when I sell, watch when I hold. You'll quickly get the knack of it. Now why don't you get us both a nice cup of tea?"

Our offices in downtown Boston are just a short walk across the Common from the Historical Society. This is where I did my real learning, as I delved into the diaries of the Reverend Andrew Eliot, Class of 1737, and his son, John, 1772.

They gave me a real sense of our country's (and my family's) history. And also that, give or take a few improvements in the plumbing, Harvard life seems to have been the same since the beginning.

I photostated some juicy tidbits from John Eliot's freshman diary.

Item. September 2, 1768. John leaves for college. Packs his vital gear. Required blue coat, three-cornered hat, and gown. Also fork, spoon, and chamberpot (freshmen had to bring their own).

Item. Dad insists he take Charlestown ferry. Cheapest way. And—most important—Harvard gets the proceeds.

Item. Tuition can be paid in kind, e.g., potatoes or firewood. One guy brought a sheep.

Item. College punch called "flip." Two-thirds beer, molasses, spiked with rum. Served in huge, tall mugs (called "bumpers").

Item. September 6, 1768. Describes wretched food in Commons.

"Each undergraduate receives one pound of meat a day," John wrote. "But since it has no taste at all, one cannot tell what animal it comes from. Now and then there are some greens. On great occasions, dandelions. The butter is unspeakable and several times has been the cause of violent student demonstrations.

"At least we shall not die of thirst. For the supply of cider is unlimited. Each table has large pewter cans which we pass from mouth to mouth, just like the English wassail-bowl."

Except for the presence of cider, this could well have been the description of an Eliot House dinner. Especially their table talk. There's a certain eternal quality to undergraduate bullshit.

Not all was fun and games. As the situation with Britain deteriorated, the campus atmosphere grew tense. There were bloody fights between rebel and loyalist students. And then the war broke out.

In late 1773, just after the Boston Tea Party, there was a violent riot in the dining hall between patriots and Tories. No simple food fight, but a deadly battle. Tutors struggled to halt bloodshed.

One afternoon, I discovered something fascinating. I learned that the British army once intended to wipe Harvard College off the map.

"On the eighteenth of April in seventy-five," as Professor Longfellow's famous poem goes, Paul Revere galloped through the night to alert the citizens of Lexington and Concord that the redcoats were coming.

But another part of their forces was heading toward Cambridge. John Eliot's diary of April 19 tells of the panic at Harvard. For it was well known that the English considered the college "a hotbed of sedition."

Fearing that the enemy might arrive via the great bridge over the Charles River, a group of undergraduates dismantled it so that the British would be unable to cross. They then hid in the bushes to see what would happen.

Just after noon, a horde of troops appeared on the western bank led by Lord Percy himself, splendidly attired, mounted on a beautiful white horse.

When he saw what we—I mean the Harvard guys—had done to thwart him, he was pretty ticked off. But the canny British bastard had brought along some carpenters, who repaired the bridge in less than an hour.

They then marched straight through the center of the town, whose windows all were shuttered tight.

Percy was en route to reinforce the troops already out in Lexington. But he did not know the way. And so he headed for the most likely source of information—Harvard College. He led some of his men right into the center of the Yard and shouted at the seemingly deserted buildings for someone to come out immediately and give him directions.

No one ventured forth. Those undergraduates had guts.

John Eliot and his roommates were peering anxiously through the slats of his shutters, fearing Percy might order his troops to start shooting. And well he might, but first he tried a different ploy. He asked again—in Latin.

Then Tutor Isaac Smith suddenly appeared from Hollis Hall and approached the Englishman.

The students couldn't hear them speak, but saw Smith motion toward Lexington. Percy waved, and all then galloped off.

Almost instantly the tutor was bombarded by shouts of, "grubstreet lobster-loving idiot."

The man was quite bewildered. He was of that breed who can quote all of Cicero and Plato without book, yet can't recall a student's name.

He stuttered that the information had been requested in the king's name. So how could he, as a loyal subject, have refused? He added that Lord Percy planned to honor Harvard with another visit.

The students were outraged. It seems the general had told Tutor Smith they'd have "a glass of good Madeira by the fire" later that night. The idiot didn't realize that by "fire" the redcoat had meant *conflagration*. Some wanted to tar and feather this overeducated simpleton. But, typical of Harvard, everyone proposed a different course of action.

And while they were haranguing one another, Tutor Smith slipped quietly away. He was never seen again.

That evening Paul Revere rode into Cambridge with the awesome news of Lexington and Concord.

Some of the students joined the minutemen who had hastily built barricades on Cambridge Common, preparing for the British to attack.

They never came.

The Brookline militia, led by Isaac Gardner '47, ambushed the approaching redcoats at Watson's Corner. Though Isaac fell, his brave charge made the British scatter, thinking that the route to Cambridge teemed with patriots as fierce as he.

Thanks to men like him, there was no battle fought in Harvard Yard.

That steamy afternoon when I first read John Eliot's words, I couldn't help but wonder how we modern undergraduates would have responded if the university was under siege of arms. What would we do—hurl Frisbees at the enemy?

It was nearly five when I got back from "lunch." I went straight to Mr. Winthrop to apologize. He looked up from his desk and said he hadn't even noticed I was gone.

That is the story of my life.

When The Class of '58 returned to Cambridge for their final year, they all were painfully aware that very little sand remained in the hourglass of their college lives. For in precisely nine months they would be cast from the comfortable womb of Harvard into the cold, harsh world.

Everything seems to speed up at a frighteningly rapid pace. The seniors are like downhill skiers, some of whom are frightened by the gathering momentum and, although the end is manifestly near, still cannot keep their balance.

The Class had thus far had three suicides, all more or less precipitated by the pressures of trying to remain at Harvard. Now in this final year, two more of them would take their lives. But this time out of fear of leaving.

The final act is sad in other ways as well. The cynicism that is so endemic in the first three years turns slowly and surprisingly into nostalgia. Which by June creates an embryonic feeling of regret. Of wasted time. Of chances lost. Of carefree feelings none of them will ever know again.

There are exceptions. Those who can survive this senior crucible are usually the ones most likely to bring glory to The Class.

Not the least of them made his debut as piano soloist with the Bostom Symphony on October 12, 1957.

Yet, the Danny Rossi who walked nervously to the keyboard in the crowded, venerable auditorium was different physically from the bespectacled young man who had left Eliot House the previous spring.

He was no longer wearing glasses.

Not that his vision had improved—although his appearance most dramatically had.

He owed his metamorphosis to the suggestion of an amorous admirer from last summer's Tanglewood Festival staff. Seeing his face under circumstances when he did not need glasses to function, she remarked on the appeal of his piercing gray-green eyes—and what a pity it was that his spectacles hid them from the audience's view. The next day he went out and was fitted for contact lenses.

The minute he appeared on stage of Symphony Hall, Danny could sense how right his inamorata's advice had been. Amid the polite, friendly applause, he could perceive remarks like, "Oh, he's cute."

His performance was almost flawless. He was always passionate. And in the final movement some of his front locks fell across his forehead.

A standing ovation.

He had no notion of how long the public adoration lasted. In fact, Danny was swept up in its tidal wave and had lost all sense of time. He would have stayed on stage forever had not Munch, a friendly arm around his shoulder, led him to the wings.

Shortly after he got to his dressing room, his parents appeared. And, hard upon their heels, new planets that began to spin around the sun of Danny Rossi—journalists.

First the flashbulbs popping at him shaking hands with Munch. Then several with his mom and dad. And then a series with dignitaries of the music world, many of whom had come up from New York.

Finally, even Danny had had enough.

"Hey, guys," he pleaded, "I've just started to feel very tired. As you can imagine, I didn't get too much sleep last night. So can I ask you to pack up and go? I mean, if you've got all you want."

Most of the press was satisfied and started to retreat. But one of the photographers realized that a single commercial picture yet remained untaken.

"Danny," he cried out, "how about one with you kissing your girlfriend?"

Danny glanced toward the corner where Maria, dressed sedately, had been all but hiding. (It had taken weeks of persuasion to get her to go to the concert just as a "friend.") He motioned to her to come forward. But she shook her head.

"No, Danny, please. I don't want to be photographed.

Besides, this is your night. I'm just here as a member of the audience."

Doubly disappointed, for he would have liked the world to see him with a really sexy girl, Danny acquiesced and told the journalists, "She isn't used to this. Another time, okay?"

Reluctantly, the Fourth Estate departed. And the Rossis and Maria headed toward the limousine to drive down to The Ritz, where a suite had been reserved by the Symphony management.

Danny rode to the hotel half in a dream. Cocooned within the leather plushness of the chauffeured car, he inwardly repeated to himself, *I can't believe it, I'm a star. A goddamn star.*

Never having imagined he would be feeling such euphoria, Danny had deliberately requested that his parents keep the party small. For he thought that after the performance he would be consumed with sadness at the absence of the man who was responsible for bringing him so far. But the night's ovation had been so intoxicating that for the moment he could think of no one but himself.

Munch and the concertmaster dropped by for a single glass of champagne and quickly left. They had a matinee the next afternoon and needed to get home to rest. The managing director of the B.S.O. had brought along a most distinguished gentleman who absolutely would not wait even a day to talk to Danny.

The unexpected guest was none other than S. Hurok, the world's most famous concert manager. He told the young pianist not only how much he admired his performance, but that he hoped Danny would consider allowing his office to represent him. He went as far as to promise Danny the chance to play with major orchestras as early as next year.

"But, Mr. Hurok, I'm a total unknown."

"Ah," the old man smiled, "but I am not. And most of all the symphony directors I will contact trust their ears."

"You mean there were some in the audience tonight?"

"No," Hurok smiled, "but Maître Munch thought it might be useful if he had this evening's concert taped. With your permission, I could make very good use of those reels."

"Gosh—"

"Hi, Mr. Hurok," Arthur Rossi interposed. "I'm Danny's dad. If you would like, we could have breakfast in the morning."

Danny shot a withering glance at his father, and then turned back to the impresario. "I'm very flattered, sir. If we could talk some other time—"

"Of course, of course," Hurok said with enthusiastic understanding. "We'll chat again when you're less busy."

He then politely said good night and left with the director. Now there were only four of them. Danny, his parents, and Maria.

"Well," Arthur Rossi jested, smiling at Maria, "here we are, just us Italians." He was avoiding Danny's gaze. For he knew that just a moment earlier he had overstepped the newly redrawn boundaries of their father-son relationship. And he was afraid of Danny's anger.

"With everyone's permission," said Gisela Rossi, "I would like very much to drink a toast to someone who was here tonight only in spirit."

Danny nodded and they raised their glasses.

"To Frank Rossi—" his father began.

And then suddenly stopped himself as he heard his younger son whisper, with supreme self-control, "No, Dad, *not tonight*."

There was a silence. Then Mrs. Rossi murmured, "To the memory of Gustave Landau. Let us pray that God let Danny's music go to heaven tonight so such a fine man could take pride."

They drank somberly.

"That was Danny's teacher," she told Maria.

"I know," she answered softly. "Danny's told me all about how much he—loved him."

There was a sudden pause as no one knew what to say next.

At last Maria spoke again. "I don't want to spoil the party, but it's kind of late. I think I'd better take a taxi home to Radcliffe."

"If you can wait a minute," Danny offered, "I'll be glad to take you and then have the driver drop me back at Eliot."

"No, no," she protested. "I mean, the orchestra's given you this terrific suite. It will be a lot more fun than just a metal bed in a Harvard house."

Maria suddenly felt a tinge of embarrassment at the way she had put her last remark. Would that give the elder Rossis the impression that she'd been in Danny's bedroom?

In any case, before she knew it, Arthur and Gisela had said good night and headed for their own room farther down the corridor.

Danny and Maria stood side by side in the descending elevator, looking straight ahead.

As they were heading for the door, Danny stopped her gently. "Hey, Maria," he whispered, "let's not separate tonight. I want to be with you. I mean, I want to share this special night with someone I really love."

"I'm tired, Danny, honestly I am," she answered softly.

"Maria, listen," Danny pleaded, "come upstairs with me. Let's share that room—and be a couple."

"Danny," she responded tenderly, "I know what all this meant to you. But we really don't belong together. Especially after tonight."

"What do you mean?"

"I saw you change up there. I'm happy for your big success, but you've just entered a whole new world where I don't feel comfortable at all."

He tried not to be angry, but he couldn't help it.

"Is that just another excuse for saying you won't come to bed with me?"

"No," Maria whispered with emotion in her voice, "I saw tonight that there's no room for anybody in your life. The spotlight isn't big enough."

She turned and started walking through the darkened lobby toward the exit.

"Maria, wait!" he called. His voice echoed slightly in the marble hall.

She stopped and said, "Please, Danny, don't say any more. I'll always have the fondest memories of you."

Then she said barely audibly, "Goodbye." And disappeared through the revolving door.

Danny Rossi stood in the deserted lobby on the night of his greatest triumph, rent by feelings of elation and a sense of loss. But finally, there in the darkness, he convinced himself that this was the price he had to pay.

For fame.

Ted and Sara were now totally inseparable. They took almost all the same courses, and their conversations—except when making love—were mainly about the classics.

They even chose congenial topics for their senior theses. Sara got Professor Whitman to direct her essay on Hellenistic Portrayals of Eros—focusing on Apollonius of Rhodes. And Ted got Finley himself to supervise his dissertation, which compared Homer's two great antithetical female characterizations, Helen and Penelope.

Every afternoon they sat opposite each other in Widener Library grinding away, punctuating their assiduity by passing silly notes to each other in Latin or Greek.

At about four o'clock they would join the exodus of jocks who were on their way to practice. Only their field of play was in Andrew's new room.

And yet, since they had returned to Harvard for their senior year, they were both increasingly aware that their entire idyll, like the halcyon days of college, had eventually to reach its conclusion. Or perhaps some sort of consummation.

Ted had applied to Harvard Graduate School in Classics, and Sara was toying with doing the same, although her parents had indicated that they might be willing to subsidize a year of European study.

This was by no means an expression of disapproval of her relationship with Ted. For they had never met him and knew little, if anything, about him.

Sara, on the other hand, had become a regular weekly guest at the Lambros's Sunday dinners and felt almost a part of the family—which was what Mama Lambros prayed each week she would become.

They were not ambivalent about the future, these passionate lovers of the classics and each other. They never discussed marriage. Not because either of them doubted the other's will to wed, but simply because they both took it for granted that their commitment to each other was for life. The ceremony would be just a formality.

They both knew that the Greek words for *man* and *woman* also meant *husband* and *wife*. And thus semantically, as well as spiritually, they were already married.

George returned to Eliot House for his senior year feeling as much or more American and Harvardian than his classmates.

Since his need for study was so great, he had amicably separated from his preppie roommates and moved into a single.

"Now you can keep *yourself* up all night," Newall had jested.

George felt like an artillery officer. He had spent his junior year at Harvard getting his bearings. He had passed the summer taking aim—selecting an ideal senior thesis. After all, who was better suited to write on "The Hungarian Revolution as Portrayed by the Soviet Press"? As Dr. K. strongly hinted, it could be publishable.

He was now ready to use his newly acquired ammunition to eliminate all barriers in his path to political triumph.

But what, in fact, was he after? This was the question Kissinger asked him the afternoon the seminar ended, as they sat in his air-conditioned office sharing congratulatory glasses of iced tea.

"You could be a professor at Harvard," Henry assured him.

"I know." George smiled. "But is that where *your* ambitions stop, Henry?"

With the tables turned, his mentor laughed uneasily and tried to answer with deflecting jocularity.

"Well," he laughed, "I of course would not mind becoming the emperor. Would you?"

"I would not even mind being President," George smiled, "but even you are ineligible for that. There, Henry, we must share similar disappointments. We are fated both of us never to reach the top."

"I beg your pardon, Mr. Keller," Kissinger said, his index

finger raised. "You seem to be under the mistaken illusion that the men in the White House actually run the country. Let me quickly disabuse you. They are mostly quarterbacks who rely heavily on their coach's advice. You and I, George, are both in a position to become indispensable advisers. That would be exciting, don't you think?"

"You mean what attracts you is sort of the power behind the throne?"

"Not exactly. What interests me is what one can achieve with power. Splendid things, believe me."

George nodded, with a grin. He raised his glass and toasted, "More power to you, Henry."

J ason Gilbert returned to Cambridge from a summer of Marine Corps training tanned and fit, more muscular than ever.

As soon as he arrived, he headed over to see Eliot and Newall in their new double, free from the mad Hungarian. There was ice-cold beer and tales of love and war to tell. Newall, in the naval ROTC program, had spent the summer touring the Pacific on an aircraft carrier. Before returning home he went, as he put it, "totally berserk" for a week in Honolulu. Which he gleefully recounted in minute detail.

Jason's summer in the blazing southern sun had been a little different. First there was the drill sergeant who really had it in for all the Ivy League boys. At one point, for some petty infraction, the guy had made him jog around the base in combat boots and full pack for a whole hour in the blazing sun.

"That must have killed you," Eliot remarked while opening a second beer.

"It wasn't all that bad," Jason said casually. "I was in shape, remember. But, of course, I acted like I was about to have a heart attack."

"Good ploy," said Newall. "I hear those Marine types can be sadists anyway."

"I actually felt sorry for the guy," Jason said unexpectedly.

"How come?" Newall asked.

"I kind of understand why he was riding us so hard in camp," he explained, somewhat subdued, " 'cause off the base, life in Virginia isn't all that great if you're not white.

"One Saturday when we were off, the guys went into town to gorge ourselves on ice cream. We were sitting there in Howard

Johnson's when this sergeant happened to pass by. And, asshole that I am, I waved to him to come and join us."

"What's wrong with that?" asked Andrew.

"You won't believe this, but he just stood out there and gave us all the finger. And on Monday we were doing so damn many push-ups we were almost living on the ground."

"I don't get it," Andrew said. "I mean, you guys were only being friendly, weren't you?"

"Of course, but naive Jason Gilbert hadn't clicked that *off* the base, the town of Quantico is segregated like before the Civil War. Can you believe this member of the U.S. military was not *allowed* to have an ice cream in that place with us? That's why he was so pissed off. He thought that we were mocking him."

"No shit," said Newall. "That's amazing in this day and age. Christ, Gilbert, bet that made you happy that you're only Jewish."

Jason, staring at his teammate and supposed friend, deflected the unwitting insult like a skillful boxer. "Newall, I'll forgive that last remark because I know you're congenitally stupid."

The eternal mediator, Andrew Eliot, deftly changed the subject. "Hey, listen, guys, I've got the latest *Freshman Register*. Why don't we check out the new crop and get our bids in early, huh?"

"Sounds good to me," said Newall, happy to move back to neutral ground. "What do you say, old Gilbert? Shall we cast our eyes upon the lovelies of the Class of '61?"

Jason smiled. "At least you're consistent, Newall," he jibed, "always last man off the mark. I did my homework yesterday. The pick of the new talent is Maureen McCabe. And I'm taking her to Norumbega Park tonight."

ANDREW ELIOT'S DIARY

November 24, 1957

We start our college lives, symbolically as well as literally, in the ignominy of the End Zone. But our progress brings us to the happy culmination. In senior year, we get to sit right on the fifty-yard line near the President and the most distinguished alumni, whom the college honors with this pride of place.

Ironically of course, as first-year grads we'll be back in the End Zone come next fall. So a gang of us decided to make this year's Harvard-Yale game into a gigantic farewell blast.

Newall and I contacted some of our old prep school buddies down in New Haven and arranged for floors and couches for us all to sack out on.

We even got a place for Gilbert, who reciprocated by having his sister Julie fix us up with some of her more desirable (and we hoped pliable) girlfriends from Briarcliff.

Julie's Cliff, unlike the one in Cambridge, Mass., is a much more pragmatic ladies' college that puts the emphasis where it belongs—on pulchritude and charm. I mean, brains are okay for a girl in moderation, but the Radcliffe types are so goddamn intellectual—and competitive—that they sometimes make you forget why the Lord created women.

Not that I have anything against Radcliffe. If I ever had a daughter, I'd want her to go there. It's just that when it comes to marriage, I think I'm much better off in the Briar patch.

Julie Gilbert came through with real dishes for Newall and myself. And we fixed her up with our Yale host, Charlie Cushing, a really sweet fellow. Which is a polite way of saying he's got perfect manners but not a brain in his head (I mean, he makes me look like Einstein).

Our seats in Yale Bowl were indeed sensational. We sat on the fifty-yard line with luminaries of the world scattered around us like confetti at a birthday party.

205

Four rows down from me were President Pusey and the deans, politely clapping when our boys did something good (which was not very often).

Ten yards to my left was our Massachusetts senator, Jack Kennedy, and his neat wife, Jackie. They were less sedate than most of the old grads in that distinguished section, shouting their lungs out for Harvard to score against the wild, hypertrophied, and, alas, all-too-competent Yalies.

Unfortunately, not even the strenuous vociferations of a U.S. senator could help our boys that day. Yale steamrolled over us 54–0.

Oh what the hell, I thought, during the postgame festivities back at Branford College, these Yalies have so little to be proud of, let them at least win the goddamn game.

One afternoon in early December, Sara gazed across the pillow and smiled. "Ted, isn't it about time you asked my parents for my hand?"

"And what if they say no?"

"Then we'll just set two fewer places at the wedding party," she replied.

"I don't get it. Do you care what they think or don't you?"

"Oh, nothing will keep me from staying this close to you forever," she answered. And then added with shy sincerity, "But it would make me happy if my father liked you. And I'm sure he will. Mummy wouldn't approve of anybody I brought home."

Ted was understandably nervous. For he wanted very much to please Sara by finding favor with her father. Hence, he spent the days prior to their visit trying to learn as much as he could about the man she so admired.

Who's Who informed him that Philip Harrison was St. Paul's, Harvard '33, a decorated naval officer, and one of the most successful merchant bankers in the country.

Moreover, his name appeared at frequent intervals in *The New York Times* as having paid a visit to advise the current White House resident on some particularly thorny economic issue.

He had sired three sons. But his daughter was the apple of his eye. And to hear Sara tell it, he was the incarnation of every possible virtue.

Boy, thought Ted, if there's anything to this Oedipal business, I haven't got a prayer!

* * *

"I think the blue would be great for Christmas dinner, Ted."

"How about the gray flannel for dinner and saving the blue for church?"

They were scouring Andrew's wardrobe for fashionable holiday regalia to help Ted make the best possible impression.

"Look, Lambros, it doesn't really matter. Old Man Harrison's not gonna judge you by your clothes."

"You mean *your* clothes." Ted smiled. And then asked nervously, "But what about her mother—or don't you think I have a chance with her?"

As a friend, Andrew thought it best to free Ted from all illusions. "No, Lambros, she'd probably like you at her daughter's wedding as a waiter, but definitely not as the groom. I mean, take *all* my clothes—even my damn club tie, if it'll make you feel any better. But I'm afraid you couldn't impress Daisy Harrison unless you had a crown on your head. And that I can't lend you."

"You're doing wonders for my confidence," Ted grumbled.

Andrew leaned over and grabbed his friend by the shoulders. "Hey, hasn't three and a half years of Harvard taught you that it's not *who* you are, it's *what* you are?"

"You can talk, Eliot. You've probably still got all the labels from the *Mayflower* on your suitcase."

"Come on, Ted, I'd trade places with you any day. What good is it that my ancestors came over if I can't even get a date for New Year's Eve? Am I getting through to you?"

"Yeah, I guess. . . ."

"Good. Now pick up your preppie costumes and go snow her parents."

They took the Merchants Limited on the 23rd of December. Though the overheated train was packed with students chattering gaily or bellowing carols and other spiritual ditties like "You Ain't Nothin' but a Hound Dog" and "Blue Suede Shoes," Ted and Sara sat reading quietly, barely exchanging a word.

"Who's meeting us at Greenwich?" Ted finally asked as they pulled out of Stamford.

"Probably one of my brothers. Daddy usually works late before a holiday."

"What are the odds of any of them actually liking me?"

"That's a little too close to call," Sara answered. "I mean,

Phippie and Evan are bound to feel a little jealous of the fact that you're at Harvard and they both got shot down."

"No kidding—not even with all your father's influence?"

"Daddy's not an alchemist," Sara smiled, "and their board scores were far from golden. No, Lambros, you and he will be the only Harvard men at table. Does that make you feel a little better?"

"Yeah," Ted conceded, "it actually does."

Just after eight, when they clambered down onto the dimly lit platform, Sara scanned the crowd of people waiting for the passengers, trying to find one of her brothers. Then suddenly she emitted a squeal of joy.

"Daddy!"

Ted stood motionless as she sprinted into the arms of a tall gentleman in a sheepskin coat, his silver hair illuminated by the headlights from the parking lot behind. After what seemed like several minutes, they approached him arm in arm.

Philip Harrison held out his hand.

"Good to meet you, Ted. Sara's told me a lot about you."

"I hope some of it was good," Ted replied, trying his best to smile. "I'm very grateful to be invited."

They drove along the Merritt Parkway, then down narrow wooded lanes, and turned into the drive of what seemed—compared to Ted's fantasies—a modest white colonial house with green shutters.

Daisy Harrison was at the door to greet them, looking impeccably informal. She kissed her daughter and then turned to their visitor. "You must be Theodore," she said as they shook hands. "We've *so* looked forward to meeting you." She was unable, despite herself, to play the script of conventional politeness with any real conviction.

A few moments later Ted found himself holding a hot toddy in front of a fashionably roaring fire, surrounded by the Harrison clan. It was almost like a *New Yorker* cartoon. They all were wearing countryish Abercrombie & Fitch-style garb, making Ted feel slightly overdressed in his tab collar and Andrew Eliot's three-piece suit.

The two elder brothers seemed friendly enough, although

Phippie's "Hi there" and Evan's "Nice to meet you" were hardly effusive.

Fourteen-year-old Ned's greeting was a good deal warmer. "Gosh, Ted," he chirped, "isn't it awful the way Yale creamed Harvard in football this year!"

This was just the type of dialogue that Ted had mastered by osmosis from his proximity to Eliot House.

"You've got to understand, Neddy," he responded, "we have a kind of social obligation to lose to Yale every so often. I mean, it bolsters their inferiority complex."

This flagrant Harvardian bullshit completely captivated the youngest Harrison.

"Wow," Ned exclaimed, "but isn't losing fifty-four to nothing going a little far?"

"Not at all," Sara interposed. "The boys in New Haven were feeling really insecure this year. I mean, Harvard killed them in the Rhodes Scholarship department."

"Which is a little more important than football," added an amused Philip Harrison '33.

"Actually, Ted," remarked Mrs. Harrison with a sweetness that would put a diabetic into shock, "all my family is Yale. Is yours all Harvard?"

"Absolutely," replied the well-prepared Ted Lambros.

Sara smiled inwardly and thought, The Greeks lead the WASPs one to nothing.

The first night set the pattern for the week that ensued. Mr. Harrison seemed interested and friendly. When they weren't out chasing local debs, the older boys were offhandedly cordial. Young Ned, whose fondest dream was to be admitted to Harvard, was enchanted by his sister's guest. And when Ted actually spent an entire hour helping him work on some Virgil, he would gladly have traded his two elder brothers just to have him in the family.

But then there was Daisy. . . .

One night Ted was awakened by the voices of Mr. and Mrs. Harrison from the adjacent room. The conversation was heated and a few decibels above normal. To his discomfort, he was the subject of the argument—though never once referred to by name.

"But, Philip, his family own a restaurant."

"Daisy, your grandfather drove a milk wagon."

"But he put my father through Yale."

"And he is putting *himself* through Harvard. I don't see what's bothering you. The young man is perfectly—"

"He's common, Philip. Common, common, common. Don't you care at all for your daughter's future?"

"Yes, Daisy," said Mr. Harrison, lowering his voice, "I care very much."

Their conversation then became inaudible, leaving Ted Lambros bewildered in the darkness of his bedroom.

On New Year's morning, which would be their very last before returning to Cambridge, Philip Harrison asked Ted to join him for a walk in the woods.

"I think we should be frank with each other," he began.

"Yes, sir," Ted replied apprehensively.

"I'm not unaware of how my daughter feels about you. But I'm sure you've sensed that Mrs. Harrison is—"

"Dead against it," Ted said quietly.

"Well, that's putting it a bit strongly. Let's say Daisy's a bit reluctant to see Sara commit herself so soon."

"Uh—that's understandable," Ted replied, careful not to say anything disloyal.

They walked a few paces in silence as Ted worked up the courage to ask, "How do *you* feel, sir?"

"Personally, Ted, I think you're a bright, decent, and mature young man. But my opinion should have no bearing on the matter. Sara's told me she loves you and wants to marry you. That's good enough for me."

He paused, then continued slowly, his voice shaking slightly, "My daughter is the most precious thing I have in the world. All I want in life is for her to be happy. . . ."

"I'll do my very best, sir."

"Ted," Mr. Harrison persisted, "I want you to swear that you'll never hurt my little girl."

Ted nodded, almost unable to speak.

"Yes, sir," he said softly, "I promise."

The two stood facing each other. And then, though neither moved, both men embraced in their imagination.

February 2, 1958

Maybe I do have a future as something after all. I could be a matchmaker. At least the one fix-up I have engineered in my life has resulted in marriage.

The ceremony took place this past Saturday at the First Unitarian Church of Syosset, Long Island. The bride—looking lovely—was none other than my buddy Jason Gilbert's sister, Julie. The lucky guy was my old classmate Charlie Cushing, whom I had heretofore regarded as totally useless.

Obviously I was wrong about that, because he had succeeded in getting Julie pregnant the very first time they went to bed together.

Happily, the impending maternity was discovered at a very early stage so that things could be done *comme il faut*. She got her picture in *The New York Times* and Mrs. Gilbert arranged a lavish celebration with such grace—and speed—that her grandchild would be able to arrive "prematurely" without too many local tongues wagging.

Actually, invisible shotgun or not, I think the two of them suit each other. Julie is cute, but she's not exactly Madame Curie. She was probably majoring in husband catching at Briarcliff anyway. And one may say she's graduating with highest honors.

After all, "the Cush," as we affectionately referred to him in prep school, is a real Boston Brahmin, with a pedigree extending back to colonial times. And the Gilberts make up in dynamism what they lack in patina. Jason's dad is a real pioneer in the television industry and flies to Washington almost as often as the Eastern shuttle.

Moreover, if there was any tension on the part of either family because of the circumstances surrounding the nuptials, it was certainly not apparent. They made a handsome couple, and to their delight, old man Gilbert set them up in a very comfortable house in Woodbridge, so the Cush could finish his Yale studies in style.

What totally surprised me was that I kind of choked up at the wedding. I mean, Cush was the first one of our gang to go. Which made me think that maybe someday I might even take the plunge. Although what sensible girl would want to marry me?

Newall and Andrew were squeezed into Jason's Corvette during the swift post-nuptial ride back to Cambridge. Gradually, Andrew began to notice that Jason seemed gloomy. In fact, he had not smiled much during the whole affair.

"Hey, Gilbert," Andrew said as they neared the Hartford Bridge, "you seemed pissed off."

"I am," Jason replied laconically, and accelerated.

"From that I understand you disapprove of the match."

"You might say so," he commented, gritting his teeth.

"On what grounds?" Newall inquired.

"On the grounds that Cushing is the closest thing to a total asshole that I've ever encountered."

"Hey, Jace," Newall remonstrated, "aren't you being a bit severe?"

"Hell no," he answered. "My sister's barely eighteen. Couldn't that dingbat have been a little more careful?"

"Maybe they love each other," Andrew offered, his role in life being to discover silver linings in the cloudiest situations.

"Ah, come on," Jason exploded, punching the dashboard with one hand, "they hardly know each other."

"I think both parents were pleased," Newall suggested.

"Sure," Jason responded. "The one thing they have in common is an allergy to scandal."

"Unless my eyes deceived me," Newall said, "your dad really likes the Cush."

"Yeah," Jason answered sarcastically, "but mostly because his ancestors fought at Bunker Hill."

"So did mine," Newall added. "Is that why you like me, Gilbert?"

"No," he replied, only half-joking. "I don't like you at all, actually."

"**D**anny, I think you're making a very big mistake."

Professor Piston had asked his prize pupil to come by the office to discuss his plans for next year.

"I'm sorry, Professor, but I just can't see going through another year of studying."

"But with Nadia Boulanger, Danny, that is hardly what you call drudgery. One might even say that woman *is* modern music. Remember, most of the major composers of our time have studied at the 'Boulangerie.' "

"But what if I just put it off for, say, a year or so? I mean, Mr. Hurok has got all these fantastic offers for me from major orchestras—"

"Aha, so you're hungry for the sound of applause, Danny," Piston answered knowingly. "I wish you wouldn't be so impetuous. Once you start traveling on that circuit, you'll be caught up in the whirlwind and never slow down again to study."

"But that's a chance I'm willing to take. Anyway, even if this sounds a little arrogant, I think I could start writing on my own."

The music chairman hesitated. But Danny sensed that he was holding back, and forced the issue.

"Do I take it, sir, that you don't think I'm ready as a composer?"

"Well," Piston said slowly, searching for the words that would put it most delicately, "most of the people who went to Nadia, Copland for instance, were already full-blown artists. Yet she brought out something more in them, enriching everything they wrote thereafter. . . ."

"I don't think you quite answered my question," Danny said politely.

"Well," Piston replied, lowering his gaze, "I think a teacher's obligation is to tell the truth. That is an imperative of education."

He paused and then pronounced his verdict.

"Danny, that you are a great pianist everybody knows. And that with the years you'll grow into a fine conductor I have not the slightest doubt. But at this stage, your compositions are still—how can I put it?—raw material. I mean, fine ideas, but without sufficient discipline. That's why I feel so strongly that you spend a year with Nadia."

Danny's ego was jolted. The professor was talking almost like that *Crimson* reviewer.

He looked at Walter Piston and thought inwardly, What good did Boulanger do *you*? Your symphonies aren't *that* great. And when's the last time that an orchestra asked you to be their soloist? No, Walter, I think you're just a little jealous. I'm going to give the Boulangerie a miss.

"I'm sure I've hurt your feelings," Piston said solicitously.

"No, no. Not at all. You told me what you thought, and I appreciate your being honest with me."

"Then will you think about it once again?" the chairman asked.

"Of course," Danny said diplomatically. Then rose and walked from the office.

He could not even wait to get back to his room and so he called New York from a booth in Harvard Square.

"Mr. Hurok, you can book me anyplace on earth as long as the piano's tuned."

"Bravo," the impresario exulted. "I'll fix you one exciting year."

And thus, whether courageous or foolhardy, Danny Rossi had chosen to lead The Class. To be the first to dive from the cozy, amniotic safety of Harvard into the icy, shark-infested waters of the Real World.

L ike the stretto in a fugue, spring term accelerated the tempo of a melody already racing to its conclusion. May seemed to enter even before April ended. Those who had just completed senior theses barely had time to catch their breaths before taking General Examinations.

Some of The Class availed themselves of this, their final opportunity to have a nervous breakdown.

On the afternoon of his General Exams in History and Lit., Norman Gordon of Seattle, Washington, was found wandering on the banks of the Charles—providentially by his own tutor.

"Hey, Norm, did you finish writing this early?"

"No," replied the senior who had kept a straight-A average till now, a manic glow in his eyes. "I've decided that I don't like my major at all. In fact, I'm planning not to graduate. I'm going out west to start a cattle ranch."

"Oh," said the tutor, then gently led him to the Health Department.

And psychiatry picked up where education had left off.

But in a sense young Gordon had succeeded in his unconscious aspiration: he had managed to avoid having to leave the four-walled shelter of a paternal institution.

"It was a brilliant piece of work," said Cedric Whitman, as he met with Sara in Boylston Hall for their last tutorial. "I don't think I'm being indiscreet if I tell you that my view is shared by everyone in the department who read it. Actually, I'd go as far as to say it's got the makings of a doctoral dissertation."

"Thank you." Sara smiled shyly. "But, as you know, I'm not going to graduate school."

"That's a pity," Whitman replied. "You've got a really original mind."

"I think one classicist in the family is enough."

"What do you intend to do then, Sara?"

"Be a wife—and a mother, eventually."

"Does that exclude everything else?"

"Well, I feel I should be helping Ted as much as I can. And it
would be easier if I had some kind of nondemanding job. I'll be
studying shorthand at Katie Gibbs this summer."

Whitman could not fully mask his disappointment.

Sara sensed this and was slightly defensive.

"It isn't that Ted would mind," she offered. "It's just that—"

"Please, Sara," the professor responded, "you don't have to
explain. I understand completely." And inwardly he thought, It's
obvious that Ted *would* mind.

He rose to shake hands and wish her well.

"It's a nice thing to know that you and Ted will still be
around Cambridge. Perhaps we will have a chance to have you
over to the house. In any case, I'll venture a sibylline prediction.
I'd say you'll both soon be wearing a Phi Beta Kappa key."

Whitman's prediction proved accurate. For on May 28, when
America's oldest academic-honor society announced its annually
elected senior members, Ted and Sara were among the chosen.

So was Danny Rossi (no surprise, for he would be graduating
summa), and George Keller, for whom certain of the normal
criteria had been waived. But then his senior thesis had won the
Eliot (sic) Prize as best essay of the year in social sciences. And
Dr. K. had composed a most persuasive letter emphasizing George's
staggering achievements in so short a time.

Jason Gilbert won no academic kudos. But he continued his
distinguished career on the tennis court. He inspired his charges to
trample Yale for the third year in a row. And, as an index of the
relative significance of sport and intellectual achievement, Jason
was elected by a landslide to be senior-class marshal. As such he
would lead their procession on Commencement Day.

He also won the Bingham Prize as the most courageous
athlete.

But the notion of a surfeit when it comes to honors is
unthinkable for Harvard men. And thus to no one's great surprise Jason won a Sheldon Fellowship as well, an award given to

students for specialized achievements. It subsidizes a year of travel—with the proviso that the recipient do no formal studying. Mr. Sheldon knew how to fulfill an undergraduate's fantasy.

Even the Marine Corps was impressed with all the decorations Jason had received and willingly postponed his tour of duty so he could enjoy the Sheldon first.

("Actually, it's a pretty convenient time," his commanding officer jested. "We seem to be between wars at the moment.")

All this heightened prominence brought Jason's name to the attention of some undergraduates who normally would never read the *Crimson* sports page. It even caused an unexpected visitor to knock on his door early one evening.

"Yeah, can I help you?"

"Hey, what brings the Human Dictionary to my room? Run out of words?"

"Don't be derisive," George Keller retorted. "I have come to make a small request of you."

"Me? But, George, I'm just a dumb old jock."

"I know," said Keller with the tiniest of smiles. "That's exactly how you can assist me."

"How?" asked Jason.

"Could you teach me tennis, Gilbert? I'd be most appreciative."

Jason looked somewhat baffled. "Why tennis? And why me?"

"It's obvious," said George. "Last summer proved to me that it is the most—how shall I put it?—socially advantageous sport. And you, of course, are the most skilled practitioner of it at Harvard."

"I'm deeply flattered, Keller. But, unfortunately, I'm committed to beating the shit out of all the guys who'll be gunning for me in the NCAAs next week. I really haven't got the time."

George Keller's look of expectation turned to one of disappointment. "I'd be glad to pay you, Jason. Anything you say."

"It isn't the money. I'd teach you free—"

"When?" George quickly asked.

"Hell, I don't know," said Jason, feeling cornered, "maybe sometime during Graduation Week."

"Sunday the eighth—at five o'clock? I know there is nothing planned for then." The guy knew the entire schedule by heart!

"Okay," Jason capitulated with a sigh. "Do you have a racket?"

"Of course," said George, "and I have balls."

"I knew that without asking," Jason murmured as he shut his door.

George Keller stood there beaming with satisfaction. The sarcasm had escaped even the magniloquent new master of the English language.

◆

Andrew Eliot was already waiting outside the History Department when the General-Exam grades were posted. For one of the rare times of his life off the athletic field, he was perspiring.

A swarm of students rushed forward as the department secretary came out of the chairman's office to pin the results on the bulletin board.

Fortunately, Andrew was tall enough to see over the heads of the mob. What he read astonished him. He walked numbly back to Eliot House and phoned his father.

"What in blazes is the matter, son? It's still expensive-calling hours."

"Dad," Andrew mumbled in a haze, "Dad, I just wanted you to be the first to know. . . ."

The young man hesitated.

"Come on, my boy, speak up. This is costing you a fortune."

"Dad, you won't believe this but—I passed my Generals. I'm going to graduate."

The announcement at first struck Andrew's father speechless.

Finally he said, "Son, that *is* good news. I frankly never thought you'd do it."

June 10, 1958

As a kind of anodyne for the trauma of our symbolic rebirth, Harvard arranges a series of assorted ceremonies for Senior Week, culminating in Thursday morning's sacred laying on of hands.

The Baccalaureate Service on Sunday in Memorial Church was a pretty desultory affair. At least, that's what I heard from one of the guys who actually went. It wasn't exactly a big draw.

Monday's formal dance—for some reason called the Senior Spread—was much better attended. About half The Class filled the Lowell House courtyard, clad in rented white dinner jackets, dancing into the wee hours to the mellow saxophone sounds of Les and Larry Elgart's orchestra.

I guess if it had an educational purpose, which I assume everything at Harvard does, it was to give us a preview of what it would be like to be middle-aged.

The band gave an occasional nod to musical modernity with one or two cha-cha-chas—the current terpsichorean vogue—and also some Elvis tunes. But it was soft and gentle stuff like "Love Me Tender."

Oh yes, we did have dates. I blush to say that Newall and I had a social arrangement with Jason, somewhat analogous to my sartorial-exchange policy with Ted Lambros. We got his hand-me-downs.

But, of course, when you get an ex from Gilbert, they are still in exceptionally fine condition. As Joe Keezer might put it, "hardly worn." The only problem is they still have this vestigial attachment to Jason.

The result being that while he was dancing with this incredible blonde (a tennis journalist he'd picked up at some tournament), Lucy, my so-called date, and Melissa, who was supposed to be with Newall, kept angling to stay in his line of vision in hopes they could scrounge a single dance with our Class Leader.

Needless to say, even with our own considerable charm, Dickie and I didn't get to first base with either of our girls. But at least we had a lovely on our arms, which I suspect was the motivation for a lot of the pairings that evening. I think that Ted and Sara were among the maybe dozen or so couples who were actually involved romantically.

Tomorrow night we have yet another jolly event—for which Gilbert has already obtained me an escort—a moonlight cruise in Boston Harbor. Newall is going to pass on that one since, for some irrational reason, he's afraid he might get seasick. And how would that look the next morning, when he's due to be commissioned as a naval officer?

But as this artificial carnival continues, I keep wondering more and more why no one really seems to be enjoying it.

And I've come to what I think is a profound conclusion. The Class is really *not* a class. I mean, we're not a brotherhood—or anything at all cohesive for that matter.

In fact, the time we spent here was a kind of truce. A cease-fire in the war for fame and power. And in two more days the guns come out again.

Though it had rained intermittently throughout the earlier part of Commencement Week, Harvard's apparent connections in Very High Places succeeded in making Thursday, June 12, 1958, a hot and sunny day, perfect for the university's 322d Commencement Ceremony.

Everyone seemed to be in costume. From the rented black caps and gowns of the undergraduates to the electric pink of the doctoral candidates. Or the eighteenth-century garb of the sheriff of Middlesex County, who rode in on horseback to open the proceedings.

Led by Jason Gilbert and the two other marshals, The Class of '58 marched through the Yard, around University Hall, and into the vast area between Memorial Church and Widener Library. For a few hours every year, rows of wooden seats spring up and this sylvan space is magically transformed into "Tercentenary Theater."

As had been the practice for three centuries, the solemnities began with an oration in Latin—which perhaps sixteen people understood and everybody else pretended to.

This year's speaker, selected two weeks earlier by the Classics Department, was Theodore Lambros of Cambridge, Massachusetts. His speech was entitled "*De optimo genere felicitatis*"—on the noblest form of happiness.

The Latin salutatorian's task is, as the word suggests, to greet the dignitaries present in hierarchical order. First President Pusey, *then* the governor of Massachusetts, deans, pastors, and so forth.

But the crowd is really waiting for the traditional greetings to the Radcliffe girls (who, of course, come at the very end).

Nec vos ommittamus, puellae pulcherrimae
Radcliffianae, quas socias studemus vivendi,
ridendi, bibendi. . . .

Nor shall we overlook you, Most exquisite Radcliffe
maidens, Whom we zealously pursue as companions for
Living, laughing, and quaffing. . . .

Twenty thousand pairs of hands applauded. But none more
vigorously than those of the proud Lambros family.

After all the salutations, the orator is supposed to pronounce
a small homily. And Ted had chosen as his message the fact that
the highest form of happiness was to be found in truly unselfish
friendship toward one's fellow man.

It was not long thereafter that President Pusey bade The
Class of '58 rise to its feet and its representatives mount the
steps of Memorial Church to join "the fellowship of educated
men."

First Marshal Jason Gilbert walked to the podium to accept
the symbolic diploma for all of them.

Sitting near the stage in a section reserved for relatives of the
participants, Jason's father overheard a female voice exclaim, "He
looks just like something out of Scott Fitzgerald."

Mr. Gilbert turned to caution his wife not to speak so loudly.
But in doing so, he realized that Betsy was crying and the compliment had been articulated by another woman sitting in their row.
And he smiled and thought, There's no prouder father in this
whole damn place.

He was not correct, of course. There were nearly a thousand
fathers of The Class of '58 among those present, all of whom were
sharing what they thought was the zenith of euphoria and pride.

Four years earlier, 1,162 young men had entered Harvard
with The Class of '58. Today, 1,031 of them received diplomas.
Just over ten percent had failed to stay the course. In ancient
Roman terms, they had been decimated.

Some who had flunked out along the way might perhaps
come back in a later year and finish their degrees. Still others had
surrendered their ambition to be Harvard men either by giving
up their sanity or taking their own lives. But no one thought of
them today, for this was a time for congratulation, not compassion.

Not even Jason gave a thought to David Davidson, his freshman roommate, who was still resident in Massachusetts Mental
Hospital, undaunted by his temporary setback, still dreaming of
future scentific glory.

Half an hour later, The Class broke into smaller groups to
have luncheon in their houses.

◆

Back at Eliot, Art and Gisela Rossi's meal with Danny would
be simultaneously a farewell. For he'd be leaving the next morning to return to Tanglewood—as soloist this summer. And after
that to Europe to begin the concert tour that Hurok had arranged.

His mother couldn't keep from asking why Maria was not
there. For she had really liked the girl.

Art Rossi was more understanding. "Come on, honey," he
whispered, "she was probably just a passing fancy. Dan's too
young and clever to let himself get hooked so soon."

Danny kept up the charade and smiled. Though inwardly he
was aggrieved that when he'd asked her to be his date "just for
old times' sake," Maria had declined.

◆

George Keller had resigned himself to eating lunch alone on a
courtyard step. Clearly, no one near and dear to him was that day
present. Then Andrew Eliot approached him. "Hey, George," he
said good-naturedly, "do me a favor, huh? Come on over to our
table and talk to some of my stepsisters. I mean, I can't remember
half their names but some of them are cute."

"Thank you, Andrew, that is most cordial. I'd be ravished to
join you."

As George rose to walk to the Eliot family table in the
courtyard of the house called Eliot, with his classmate Andrew of
that same name, the latter whispered to him, "George, your
English is terrific. But don't say 'ravished.' Say my sister—any one
of them—is ravish*ing*."

◆

Later in the afternoon, the separation was complete. They
now divided into a thousand atoms, going off at varied speeds in
differing directions.

Would they ever come together as a unity again?

Had they ever been one?

REAL
─────────────
LIFE
─────────────

Human kind
Cannot bear very much reality.

T.S. ELIOT '10

June 14, 1958

Ted and Sara got married today. I was best man—probably on the grounds that I had been their landlord for so long. ("If this were the Middle Ages, you'd be entitled to *droit du seigneur*," Sara joked.)

It was a simple affair for complex reasons. To begin with, Sara was Episcopal and Ted, of course, Greek Orthodox. Not that the Lambros family was making any sacramental demands, mind you. But Daisy Harrison seemed to have thought it best to have the ceremony on more or less neutral grounds: in Appleton Chapel, at the back of Mem. Church, under the aegis of the distinguished George Lyman Buttrick, Preacher to the University.

This, as I interpreted Daisy's strategy, solved a multitude of problems while preserving at least a shimmer of class.

Naturally she had always dreamed of marrying off her only daughter in Christ Church, Greenwich, that extraordinarily imposing sanctuary built to the glory of God—with considerable help from some local worshippers of Mammon.

But two things had precluded this pomp and ceremony. For one, she was not all that eager to parade her in-laws before *le tout* Greenwich. For another, Sara said she would get married there only over her dead body (which would take some of the joy out of the occasion).

Thus, it boiled down to the intimacy—but unmistakable patina—of Harvard's chapel, the exquisite singing of the University Choir, and, perhaps most important, a short guest list, almost exclusively students.

Let posterity record that I did *not* forget the ring. In fact I guarded it with my life during the twenty-four hours it was in my possession, since it was a Lambros family heirloom from the Old Country.

I stood in a unique position, able to watch both participants and audience, and thus could note the more intense pockets of emotion. It came as no surprise that Mrs. Lambros did most of the crying. And of Sara's entire family, only one person had difficulty holding back the tears. Phil Harrison himself.

I guess I shouldn't have expected Sara's mother to be sentimental. And she wasn't. In fact, she sort of acted as if Ted's family were merely poor relatives one simply had to invite. I heard her remark to Mrs. Lambros, "I hope you appreciate that your son is marrying into one of the oldest families in America."

Daphne translated this to her mother and then gave Mrs. Harrison the response, "Mama says you carry your age very well."

Something may have been lost in translation, but it certainly wasn't love.

For the reception Daisy hired an opulent suite at The Ritz. To add to the ecumenical nature of the occasion, the sparkle she chose was Dom Pérignon, a sort of homage to the Catholic inventor of champagne. Anyway, the blessed bubbles from Dom's discovery filled every glass, and quite soon every head.

I think Mrs. Harrison was surprised by several things that afternoon. The first was that the whole Lambros family came attired in recognizably Western garb (a great deal of it Brooks Brothers via Joe Keezer). According to Sara, she had expected them to show in babushkas, or whatever Greek peasants wear.

Secondly, the grossest behavior of the occasion was, hands down, that of her own elder sons. For Phippie and Ev rather recklessly thought they would take on the mighty imbibers of Eliot House in a sport of which we are clearly the masters.

They found, to their chagrin (and no doubt subsequent headaches), that there is not enough champagne in France, much less Boston, to bring a hollow-legged drinker like Newall to his knees. Even Jason Gilbert, who is always in training, is a veritable sponge when it comes to champers.

Anyway, feeling that my obligations as best man superseded even the rare opportunity of unlimited vintage quaffing, I remained (relatively) sober so I could dislodge my duties to the very end.

This gave me a chance to chat with Old Man Harrison, who, by happy coincidence, was celebrating his Twenty-fifth Harvard Reunion concurrent with our commencement. He said he'd found the whole occasion deeply moving.

I mean, I personally found it impossible even to think of where I might be twenty-five years from now. I'm still confused from one day to the next about what I want to do with my life.

No one knew where they were honeymooning. Except me, of course. For, despite their protestations, I had insisted that the newlyweds take advantage of our family's empty summer house up in Maine. It gave me pleasure to know the place would be used for such a worthwhile purpose.

It would be misleading to assume that I'm always on the giving end with Lambros. In fact, when Sara's bouquet was caught by her cousin Kit from Chicago, she called out to me to take care of her.

I got the message, and happily entertained her for the next few days. And nights.

Weddings do that sort of thing to you.

Danny Rossi could never have imagined that his childhood bouts of asthma would ultimately serve a useful purpose in his musical career.

For while most of his Harvard classmates who did not have student deferments were marching and saluting in fulfillment of their military obligations, he had been declared 4-F. And was therefore free to roam the world and *be saluted* as a rising star.

At a first glance it might have appeared that Hurok had merely booked his young discovery indiscriminately—one might almost say promiscuously—with any orchestra he could. But the veteran concert manager had a very well-thought-out master plan.

He wanted to expose Danny to demanding conductors, sophisticated audiences. To become inured to harsh, critical scrutiny. In short, polish his musical techniques while hardening his psyche.

What the old man didn't realize was that Danny was also a virtuoso with reporters. His press was uniformly favorable.

He captured London playing Brahms with Beecham and the Royal Philharmonic, then flew on to Amsterdam for Mozart with Haitink and the Concertgebouw.

Paris was next, with a solo concert at the Salle Pleyel (Bach, Chopin, plus Couperin and Debussy to please the locals). In *Le Figaro*'s opinion Rossi was *"un nouveau Liszt en miniature"*; *Le Monde* had a similar opinion if a different metaphor: *"pas seulement un géant pour son âge mais un géant de son âge."*

On the evening after Danny's last appearance in Berlin, von Karajan arranged a midnight supper at the Kempinski with the director-general of Deutsche Grammophon Records. The next morning Danny had a five-album contract.

*　　*　　*

"Well," said the young pianist as he sat proudly in Hurok's portrait-laden office, observing the impresario leaf through his folder of reviews. "What do you think?"

The old man raised his glance and smiled. "What I think, my boy, is that you have just done New Haven."

"I beg your pardon?"

"Are you not familiar with the theatrical expression? Whenever a producer wants to open a show in New York, he always tries it out first in a small place like New Haven."

"Are you suggesting that London, Amsterdam, and Paris are 'try-out towns'?"

"I am indeed," Hurok said without blinking. "For New York, every other city on earth is New Haven. When you make it *here* you've really made it."

"When do you think I'll finally be ready for the 'Big Time'?"

"I'll be glad to let you know exactly," the concert manager answered, casually reaching for a document that lay upon his antique desk. "February 15, 1961, with Lenny and the Philharmonic. He suggests you play one of the Beethovens."

"That's another whole year. What do I do till then—besides bite all my nails off?"

"Danny," the impresario said paternally, "am I a booking agent or a nursemaid? You will go out and do more New Havens."

Such was the success of the pre-concert propaganda campaign that the audience filling Carnegie Hall on the night of Danny's New York debut was more predisposed to worship than to judge.

During the lengthy standing ovation at the end of the concert, Bernstein pulled Danny onto the podium and held his hand aloft like a victorious boxer's. Danny was indeed a new world champion. He had won where it counted most.

The reception was held in the sumptuous penthouse of one of the Philharmonic's trustees. Although Danny was now indisputably a major star, by no stretch of his own imagination (or ego) was he the greatest luminary present.

There were famous actors who, just a few years earlier, he would have shyly asked for an autograph. There were other world-renowned musicians, as well as important political figures. Cover girls were as abundant as the uniformed waitresses serving caviar.

And yet, incredibly, they all were flocking around wanting to meet *him*.

Not unexpectedly, he was asked to play. A Steinway grand was wheeled into the center of the living room and its lid propped open.

Danny had anticipated that at this hour of the night, after so arduous an effort, he would not be at his best in some classical piece. He had therefore prepared a little *jeu d'esprit*.

Before sitting down, he made a short speech.

"Ladies and gentlemen," he began, "my thank yous could go on forever. So forgive me if I mention just two people in particular. First Mr. Hurok for having such faith and supporting me all this time—"

"Excuse me, my dear boy," the impresario joked, "it's you who have been supporting me."

"And if Lenny doesn't mind, I'd like to express my gratitude to him at the keyboard."

Danny began with a fortissimo rendition of the piano entrance to the concerto he had played that night. He then quickly switched to a jazz medley of the tunes from Bernstein's *West Side Story*.

The audience was enchanted and would not let him leave the piano.

"What now?" Danny asked ingenuously. "I'm running out of material."

Bernstein smiled and suggested, "Why not do unto others what you just did unto me?"

Danny nodded, sat down again and for nearly half an hour poured forth jazz versions of *My Fair Lady* as well as standards by Cole Porter, Rodgers and Hart, and Irving Berlin. Finally he pleaded exhaustion.

Later in the evening, a dapper executive type waved a business card in front of him and murmured something about doing an album along the lines of that night's improvisations.

Just as the man retreated, an extremely elegant brunette approached Danny and said in dulcet tones, "Mr. Rossi, I very much enjoyed your performance this evening. I hope Jack and I can entice you to come and play for a small group at the White House sometime."

Battle weary and a little high, Danny had at first merely nodded politely and said, "That's very nice. Thanks a lot."

Only after she had gracefully turned and walked off did he realize that he had been talking to the wife of the President of the United States.

ANDREW ELIOT'S DIARY

March 10, 1959

After graduating I expected to find myself metaphorically, but not literally, at sea.

Yet here I am crossing the Atlantic on a ship of the U.S. Navy. Knowing of my family's distinguished record in this branch of the services, I had been determined not to follow where I might stumble in their footsteps.

But when the ninety-day notice suddenly came from the army, I panicked and thought, I don't want to spend the next two years of my life marching around some bog. So I signed up for the navy. I mean, how bad can things be on a ship? At least there's nowhere to hike.

I found out otherwise, however. A sailor's existence can be hell. While my old roomie Newall is an ensign stationed out in San Francisco waiting for a ship full of guys to whom he can bark orders as they cruise the tropics, I thought I'd give myself a real dose of what life without privilege is like. So I'm seeing the navy as a simple white-hat, an enlisted man.

Anyway, after basic I was assigned to the destroyer tender *St. Clare* as an ordinary swabbie. Our task is to escort the USS *Hamilton* as a kind of oceangoing nanny. My initial duties were twofold. First, keeping the *St. Clare* shipshape. In other words, scrubbing decks. And second, acting as a football for our chief petty officer, who somehow took an instant dislike to me. I couldn't figure out why. I never said I was from Harvard or even went to college. (Someone later told me that he thought I was "obnoxiously polite"—whatever that means.)

But the guy was fixated on giving me grief. And when I wasn't doing the many extra tasks he set for me, or standing watch, he would storm into our bunkroom and confiscate as "trash" whatever the hell I was reading.

Once I thought I'd try to get my own back at him.

I indicated at evening mess that I felt like turning in early to read, and hurried back to settle in with . . . the Holy Bible. Sure enough, he barged in a few minutes later and, without even looking, ripped the book from my hands, bellowing, "Sailor, you are polluting your mind!"

And it was then that I indicated, in front of two other guys, that I had been merely enriching my soul with the Scriptures.

All he could manage was, "Oh," replaced the book on my bunk, and marched out.

I had won that battle all right. But unfortunately I lost the war.

After that, the guy rode me day and night. At one point I was so desperate that I thought of going AWOL. But then, of course, we were a thousand miles from the nearest landfall. There are, after all, some advantages to being in the army.

If this was real life, I'd had enough of it. And if I was to survive the navy, I had to get my hands and knees off the deck.

When I was certain that this guy was on another part of the ship, I went to see the first lieutenant to plead for a transfer of duty. I didn't give the real reason, I just said that I felt I might have some other talents that could better serve the navy.

Like what? he inquired.

Like what, indeed? I thought to myself. But off the top of my head I suggested that I had a kind of yen to write. And that seemed to impress him. So, much to my chief petty officer's disappointment at not being able to drive me into leaping off the ship, I've been transferred to our information office.

Here I'm kind of an editor and journalist, writing for the various internal navy newspapers, as well as forwarding the more interesting stories to Washington for wider dissemination.

This has turned out to be a pretty neat job. Except my one chance for a wire-service break was censored by the captain. *I* thought it was a good story. I mean, it had excitement, thrills, surprise, and so forth—even a touch of humor. But somehow the upper echelons didn't see it that way.

Last week when we were just entering the Mediterranean, it was a terribly dark foggy night. (Dramatic start, huh?) And in the perilous obscurity we collided with another ship. No hands were lost, though some repairs would have to be done at the next port of call.

What I found so fascinating was that we had actually collided with our *own* destroyer. I mean, I thought the story had a certain human interest value.

But the captain felt otherwise. He argued that American ships never did that sort of thing.

Assuming it was a journalist's task to report the truth, I pointed out that we had in fact just done so.

At this he blew his top and hurled at me a veritable thesaurus of synonyms for lack of intelligence. His essential message was that the U.S. Navy may make an occasional error, but they sure as hell don't send out a press release.

I will be discharged in one year, three months, eleven days. With any luck it will be honorably.

In any case, it cannot be too soon.

Sara had finished at the top of her class.

Actually, nothing in her previous educational experience gave any hint that she would excel her fellow Radcliffe graduates in the arts of shorthand and typing. But sure enough, at the end of that first summer, she could take down dictation at an admirable 110 words per minute and could type an amazing 75.

"I don't think any further courses could possibly improve your chances in the job market, Sara," counseled Mrs. Holmes, head of the summer course. "With your speeds and educational background, you're more than ready for an executive secretarial position. I suggest you start following up the want ads."

Buoyed by this encouragement, Sara and Ted set about checking the newspapers. There seemed to be so many openings in Cambridge that she could probably find something within walking distance of their apartment on Huron Avenue.

Her first two interviews resulted in firm offers and a real dilemma. The job with the vice-president of the Harvard Trust paid a lavish seventy-eight bucks a week, whereas the University Press had an opening with longer hours offering a mere fifty-five. Yet, it was clear which attracted both husband and wife.

First of all, the Press was closer (you could even slide there in a snowstorm). Secondly, it offered the possibility of advancement ("With your languages, you might move into copy editing fairly soon," Mrs. Norton, the personnel director, had remarked when she saw Sara's initial reaction to the proposed salary).

Perhaps the most attractive dimension, as they both realized, was that it could be a rich source of top-level information about the Classics world. They would be among the first to know who was writing a book on what, and whether it was going to be accepted or rejected. This sort of intelligence might prove invaluable at Ted's job-seeking time.

Graduate school was much more rigorous than he had ever anticipated. To earn a Ph.D., you had to take some brutally difficult seminars in Linguistics, Comparative Grammar, Metrics, Greek and Latin Stylistics, and so forth. Fortunately, he was blessed with a nightly dinner partner with whom he could discuss such esoterica.

From as early as the summer they first lived together, Ted had always insisted on cooking the evening meals. But now, since he believed the chef should have his classical studying finished before entering the kitchen, Sara had the uncomfortable prospect of having to wait till nearly ten o'clock before her husband would begin to prepare their *deipno* (dinner).

This posed some delicate problems of diplomacy. For what sane woman could object to a delicious meal accompanied by choice Greek wine, served with music and soft candlelight by a highly professional waiter—who would then sit down and tell you how much he loved you. And after dinner would join you in bed.

How could a woman tell such a husband that, though the evenings were enchanted, the mornings after she could barely stay awake at her typewriter? Sara therefore concluded that the only way to solve this predicament was to learn the secrets of Lambros cuisine from Mama herself. This way, while Ted was still struggling with Indo-European etymologies, she could be starting dinner.

Thalassa Lambros was flattered by her daughter-in-law's interest and did everything she could to accelerate her culinary education. This included detailed memos, which Sara diligently studied.

By January she was confident enough to arrogate the task of cooking dinner. And none too soon. For Ted would be facing a battery of language exams at the end of the spring semester.

The German requirement was killing him. Dammit, he had often thought, why does *so* much important classical scholarship have to be written in this preposterously difficult language? Here again, Sara, who had taken three years of German in school, was able to help him acquire a feeling for its periodic sentence structure. And by plowing through several articles with him, showed how he could intuit the general meaning of a passage from the classical citations in the text.

After one of these mini-tutorials, he looked at her with unadul-

terated affection and said, "Sara, where the hell would I be
without you?"

"Oh, probably out seducing some attractive graduate student."

"Don't you even joke like that," Ted whispered, reaching
over to caress her.

With Sara's help and encouragement, Ted successfully jumped
all the examination hurdles and began a thesis on Sophocles. As a
reward he was made a teaching fellow in Finley's Humanities
course.

He tossed and turned but still could not get back to sleep.

"Darling, what's the matter?" Sara asked, placing her hand
gently on his shoulder.

"I can't help it, honey. I'm so damned scared about tomorrow."

"Hey," she said soothingly, "it's understandable—the first
class you've ever taught in your life. It would be unnatural if you
weren't nervous."

"I'm not nervous," he replied, "I'm absolutely catatonic." He
sat up on the side of the bed.

"But, darling," she reasoned, "it's only a Hum Two discussion.
The kids will be more frightened than you. Can't you remember
your first freshman section?"

"Yeah, I guess. I was a scared little townie. But they say the
damn undergraduates are getting smarter and smarter. And I keep
having this ridiculous fantasy that some world-famous professor
is going to decide to drop in unannounced tomorrow."

Sara glanced at the alarm clock. It was nearly 5:00 A.M., and
there was no point in trying to talk Ted into going back to sleep.

"Hey, why don't I make some coffee and listen to what you
plan to say? It could be a kind of dress rehearsal."

"Okay," he sighed, relieved to be liberated from the prison
of his bed.

She quickly made two large mugs of Nescafé and they sat
down at the kitchen table.

At seven-thirty she began to laugh.

"What the hell's the matter? What did I do wrong?" Ted
asked anxiously.

"You crazy Greek." She smiled. "You've just talked brilliantly about Homer for nearly two hours. Now, since all you've
got to do is kill fifty minutes, don't you think you're adequately
prepared to confront your first freshmen?"

"Hey," he smiled, "you're some good psychologist."

"Not really. I just happen to know my husband better than he knows himself."

The date, the time, and the place of Ted's first class are indelibly engraved in his memory. On Friday, September 28, 1959, at 10:01 A.M., he entered a discussion room in the Alston Burr Science Building. He unpacked a ridiculous number of books, all with carefully marked passages he could read aloud should he run out of ideas. At 10:05 he wrote his name and office hours on the blackboard and then turned to confront the students.

There were fourteen of them. Ten boys and four girls, their spiral notebooks open and pencils ready to transcribe his every syllable. Jesus, he suddenly thought, they're going to write down what *I* say! Suppose I make some incredible mistake and one of the kids shows it to Finley? Worse still, suppose one of them with a million years of prep-school Classics catches me right here? Anyway, Lambros, it's time to start.

He opened his yellow notepad to his meticulously outlined remarks, took a breath, and looked up. His heart was beating so loud that he half-wondered if they could hear it.

"Uh—just in case somebody thinks he's in a physics class, let me start by saying that this is a Hum Two section and I'm your discussion leader. While I'm taking your names down, you can learn mine. I've written it on the board. It happens to be the Greek word for 'brilliance,' but I'll leave you guys to make up your minds about that after a few weeks."

There was a ripple of laughter. They seemed to like him. He began to warm to the task.

"This course deals with nothing less than the roots of all Western culture, and the two epics ascribed to Homer constitute the first masterpieces of Western literature. As we'll see in the weeks to come, the *Iliad* is the first tragedy, the *Odyssey* our first comedy. . . ."

After that moment he never once looked down at his prepared text. He simply rhapsodized about the greatness of Homer, his style, the oral tradition and early Greek concepts of heroism.

Before he knew it, the class was nearly over.

"Hey," he said with a smile, "I guess I got a little carried away. I should stop here and ask if you have any questions."

A hand shot up in the back row.

"Have you read Homer in Greek, Mr. Lambros?" asked a young, bespectacled Cliffie.

"Yes," Ted answered proudly.

"Could you possibly recite a bit of it in the original, just so we could get a feel of how it sounded?"

Ted smiled. "I'll do my best."

Now, though he had the Oxford texts on the table, he found himself passionately reciting the beginning of the *Iliad* from memory, putting special stress on words they might possibly comprehend—like *heroon* for "heroes" in line four. He reached the crescendo at line seven, emphasizing *dios Achilleus*, "godlike Achilles." Then he paused.

To his utter amazement, the tiny class applauded. The bell rang. Ted felt a sudden surge of relief, elation, and fatigue. He had no idea how it had gone until assorted comments filtered to him as the students left the room.

"God, we lucked out," he heard one say.

"Yeah, this guy is dynamite," said another.

The last thing Ted heard—or thought he did—was a female voice offering the opinion, "He's even better than Finley."

But surely that was the figment of a tired imagination. For John H. Finley, Jr., was one of the greatest teachers in Harvard history.

J ason Gilbert made the first months of his Sheldon Fellowship for traveling a balanced combination of culture and sport. He took part in as many European tournaments as he could, but gave almost as much time to museum going as he did to tennis playing.

Though forbidden by the terms of his award from doing formal academic work, he spent the winter researching a Comparative Study of International Skiing—with special emphasis on the slopes of Austria, France, and Switzerland.

When his enthusiasm for the sport began to defrost, he headed for Paris, city of a million sensuous attractions. He knew no French but was fluent in the international language of charm, and never had to look very far to find a female guide.

Almost within hours he befriended an art student named Martine Pelletier, while she was admiring a Monet in the Jeu de Paume, and he was admiring her legs.

As they strolled the boulevards together, Jason marveled at the Parisian way of life, and stopped to examine the multitude of posters plastered all over the street kiosks advertising cultural offerings. He was struck by one announcement in particular:

Salle Pleyel.
Pour la première fois en France
la jeune sensation américaine
DANIEL
ROSSI
pianiste

"Hey," he said proudly to Martine, "I know that guy. Shall we go and hear him?"

"I would adore it."

And so by a harmonious cadence of fate, Jason Gilbert was present in the auditorium when Danny Rossi made his triumphant Paris debut.

Backstage, Jason and Martine had to push their way through a stampede of reporters and assorted sycophants to get close enough to attract Danny's attention. The star of the evening was delighted to see a classmate, and welcomed Jason's attractive companion in swift, fluent, and courtly French.

Jason proposed that they all go out for dinner, but Danny was committed to a private party to which, unfortunately, he was unable to invite them.

Later that evening, as they were sharing thick onion soup in Les Halles, Martine asked Jason, "I thought this Danny Rossi was your friend."

"What makes you think he isn't?"

"Because he asked me to go to Castels tonight—without you."

"That cocky little runt, he thinks he's God's gift to women."

"No, Jason," she smiled, "*you* are that. He is only God's gift to music."

By late April 1959, Jason had had his fill of the memorabilia of things past and was burning to get back to the tennis courts. Regarding it as a kind of farewell tour, he had booked himself in as many international competitions as he could wangle.

And yet even this aspect of his journey turned out to be educational. For he was learning how very far he was from being the best tennis player in the world. He could never get past a quarter final, and he began to reckon it a minor triumph if he won so much as a single set against a seeded player.

At the Gstaad International Tennis Tournament in mid-July, he had the dubious honor of drawing as his first opponent Australia's Rod Laver. Jason succumbed to the indomitable left-hander in straight sets, but was graceful in defeat.

"Rod," he commented as they shook hands afterward, "it was a real honor to be creamed by you."

"Thanks, Yank. Good on you."

Jason walked slowly off court shaking his head and wondering why he had been so slow that afternoon—or the ball so fast.

A tall young woman with a chestnut ponytail approached him to offer friendly consolation.

"You weren't very lucky today, were you?" Her English had a strange, charming accent.

"I wasn't until now," he replied. "Are you here to play?"

"Yes, I am in the ladies' singles tomorrow afternoon. I was just going to ask if you wanted to join up for the mixed doubles on Friday."

"Why? You've just seen how badly I play."

"I'm not that good either," she answered candidly.

"That means we'll probably both be killed."

"But we could still have fun. Isn't that what really counts?"

"I was brought up to think that winning was all that mattered," Jason said with lighthearted honesty. "But I'm revising my theories. So why not? It would be a pleasure to be defeated in your company. By the way, what's your name?"

"Fanny van der Post," she replied, offering her hand. "I'm a university player from Holland."

"I'm Jason Gilbert, who, as you saw, is barely good enough to be a ball boy for Rod Laver. Can we discuss our court strategy over dinner tonight?"

"Yes," she answered. "I'm staying at the Boo Hotel in Saanen."

"What a coincidence," Jason remarked. "So am I."

"I know. I saw you in the pub last night."

That evening, they drove in Jason's rented VW Beetle to a three-hundred-year-old inn in Chloesterli.

"My God," said Jason, as they sat down, "this place is older than America."

"Jason," Fanny smiled, "almost everything in the world is older than America. Haven't you noticed that?"

"Yeah," he acknowledged, "this whole trip has been kind of a steamroller for my ego. I feel born yesterday and two feet tall."

"I tell you, Jason," she said with a twinkle, "if you really want to learn what it's like to be small, come to Holland. Once upon a time we were a big world power—we even owned Central Park. Now our only claim to fame is that we gave the world Rembrandt and the English word for 'cookie.' "

"Are all the Dutch so self-deprecating?"

"Yes. It's our sly way of being arrogant."

They talked nonstop for hours well into the early morning. By the time they said good night, he knew that this girl was very special.

Fanny had been born on a farm near Groningen during the early years of the Second World War, and had lived through the terrible hunger that devastated her country as the conflict drew to a close. Despite the hardships of her childhood, she had a buoyant good humor and optimism that delighted him.

And although Fanny had ambitions, they were not all-consuming. She was a medical student at Leiden, studying just enough to become a good doctor, and practicing just enough tennis to remain a decent player.

Jason concluded on the basis of this single evening's conversation that Fanny was the most balanced person he had ever met. She was neither an overly cerebral Radcliffe girl battling for a Med School professorship, nor a bubble-headed Long Island deb whose only goal in life was an engagement ring.

Fanny had a talent he had not encountered in all the girls he'd dated in America. She was happy just being herself.

As he sat in the grandstand watching her play that next afternoon, his admiration grew. Not only had she stayed up late the night before a match, but they had shared quite a bit of wine. He was certain that the Florida girl she was facing had been in bed by nine, after drinking a glass of warm milk.

But Fanny was still good enough to make her opponent work for the victory. Her service was strong and accurate and was never broken until the second set, when the gritty American teenager began to wear her down. Fanny lost 5–7, 6–3, 6–1. Jason met her at the gate to the court with a towel and a glass of orange juice.

"Thanks," Fanny puffed, "but I'd really like a nice cold beer. Aggressive little devil, wasn't she?"

"Yeah," replied Jason, "I bet her father would have spanked her if she lost. God, didn't his shouting drive you crazy?"

"No, I never hear anything when I'm playing. Anyway, I enjoyed myself."

They began to walk toward the changing rooms.

"Hey," said Jason, "you could be really great if you worked at it."

"Don't be silly, tennis is a game. If I actually worked at it, it would become a job. Now, where would you like to have dinner tonight?"

"I don't know. Any suggestions?"

"How about going to Rougemont for a fondue? It's my turn to invite you anyway."

That evening they briefly discussed strategy for their doubles game. Since Fanny was shorter (though not by much), she would play net.

"I'm counting on you to keep all the balls from even reaching me in the back court," Jason joked.

"Please don't get your hopes up. I think somewhere in that competitive American brain of yours you imagine we actually have a chance of winning tomorrow."

"Well," Jason conceded, "I confess it was on my mind. The two turkeys we're playing may be worse than we are."

"Nobody in this tournament is worse than we are."

"Gosh, what a partner you are. You're destroying my confidence."

"Nothing could destroy your confidence, Jason." She smiled meaningfully.

They almost won.

Neither of the Spanish couple they were facing was a power hitter, and they actually took the first set with ease. Then gradually their opponents began placing their long, slow shots with greater accuracy, getting them past Fanny and making Jason run himself into exhaustion.

After a marathon battle, he was sweaty and breathless from the sun and the thin Swiss air.

Too tired even to go change, he simply sat on a bench and contemplated his fatigue. Fanny arrived with two paper cups of mineral water and sat down beside him.

"Thank God we lost," she said, wiping his face with a towel. "I don't fancy the idea of another long afternoon like this. But I'll tell you something, Jason. I think we played pretty well together for the first time. Next year we might even lose by a closer score."

"Yeah, but I can't make it next year. I've got another engagement."

"Engagement?" she asked, misunderstanding. "You are engaged to someone?"

"Yeah," he replied, protracting the ambiguity. "My fiancée's name is the United States Marines. I owe them my body for two years starting in September."

"What a waste of a nice body." She smiled. "When are you going back?"

"Oh, I've got another three weeks or so yet," he answered. And then looked her in the eye. "Which I'd like to spend with you—and I don't mean playing tennis."

"I think that could be arranged," she replied.

"I've got my VW," he said. "Where would you like to go?"

"Well, I've always wanted to see Venice."

"Why?" Jason asked.

"Because it's got canals like Amsterdam."

"I can't think of a better reason," he replied.

They took their time, driving first through the mountain roads of Switzerland. Then down into Italy, spending a few days on the banks of Lake Como. And all the time they talked.

Jason soon felt that he knew all her friends intimately and could practically list them by name. And Fanny discovered that her new boyfriend was a lot more complex than the handsome blond tennis player she had first admired across a crowded lobby.

"What kind of American are you?" she asked, as they were picnicking by the lakeside.

"What do you mean?"

"I mean, unless you are a red Indian, your family must have come from somewhere. Is Gilbert an English name?"

"No, it's just made up. When my grandparents came to Ellis Island, they were called Gruenwald."

"German?"

"No. Russian. Russian Jewish, actually."

"Ah, then you are Jewish," she said with apparent interest.

"Well, only vaguely."

"How can one be only vaguely Jewish? It would be like being only vaguely pregnant, wouldn't it?"

"Well, America's a free country. And my father decided that since the religion didn't mean anything to him, he might as well, as he put it, join the mainstream."

"But that's impossible. A Jew cannot be anything but a Jew."

"Why not? You're a Protestant, but couldn't you become Catholic if you wanted to?"

A look of incredulity crossed her face.

"For an intelligent person you make such a naive argument,

Jason. Do you think Hitler would have spared you and your family because you denied your faith?"

He began to grow irritated. What was she driving at?

"Why does everybody invoke Hitler in trying to convince me that I'm Jewish?" he asked.

"My God, Jason," she replied, "don't you realize what the Atlantic Ocean spared you in your childhood? I grew up in the shadow of the Nazis. I saw them take our neighbors away. My family even hid a Jewish girl during the whole war."

"Really?"

She nodded. "Eva Goudsmit. We grew up like sisters. Her parents owned a china factory and were—so they thought—pillars of the Dutch community. But that didn't impress the soldiers who took them off."

"What happened to them?" Jason asked quietly.

"The same thing that happened to millions of Jews all over Europe. After the war, Eva searched and searched. She went to all kinds of agencies, but they could find nothing. All they traced was a distant cousin living in Palestine. So when she finished school she went off to join him. We still keep in touch. In fact, every few summers I go and visit her kibbutz in the Galilee."

That conversation and several others like it in the weeks they spent together crystallized in Jason's mind a firm desire to learn about his heritage. And ironically, he owed this resolution not to another Jew but to a Christian Dutch girl of whom he was growing fonder each day.

He had wanted to drive her all the way back to Amsterdam and take the plane from there. But they both fell so in love with Venice that they lingered till it was nearly time for Jason to report for duty.

Their parting at the airport disconcerted him. After they'd kissed and embraced dozens of times, Jason swore fervently that he would write her at least once a week.

"Please don't feel you have to say these things, Jason. It's been very lovely and I'll always think of you with affection. But we'd both be very silly to think that we'll sit pining for each other for two years."

"Speak for yourself, Fanny," he protested. "I mean, if you felt as strongly for me as I do for you—"

"Jason, you're the nicest man I've ever met. And I've never

felt as close to anyone. Why don't we just see what happens—as long as we have no false illusions."

"Have you read the *Odyssey*, Fanny?"

"Yes, of course. The couple were separated for twenty years."

"So what's twenty-four months compared to that?"

"The *Odyssey*, my love, is a fairy tale."

"Okay, my cynical little Dutch girl," Jason replied, affecting a John Wayne posture to impress her, "you just promise to answer every letter I write and we'll see what happens."

"I promise."

They embraced a final time. He walked off toward his flight. As he reached the door of the plane he looked at the observation gate and saw her standing there.

Even at that distance he could see tears streaming down her cheeks.

D anny Rossi woke up slightly confused at finding himself in a strange, if lavish, hotel room. Because of his packed concert schedule he was used to changing bedrooms as often as pajamas. But he had always been sure of exactly where he was. What country. What city. What orchestra. What hotel.

As he tried to clear the cobwebs from his mind, he perceived five glittering gold statuettes on the dresser just beyond the bed. Then it slowly began to come back to him.

Last night had been the annual Grammy Awards ceremony, honoring the best achievements in the record industry. It had been held at a festive gala in the grand ballroom of the Century Plaza Hotel in Los Angeles. He had flown in just in time to register at the Beverly Wilshire, change into a tux, and hurry down to the limo where two PR toadies were waiting to escort him to the ceremony.

Danny's victory as best classical soloist was not unexpected. After all, the awards are as much for playing the media as playing an instrument. And he had become a master of both.

While it was arguable that his interpretation of the complete Beethoven piano concerti was the best thing put on disk during the previous twelve months, it was indisputable that his publicity campaign was nonpareil.

But what had created the stir last evening was the fact that he had won a second Grammy for best solo *jazz* album. This was the culmination of a pleasant little irony that had begun the night of his debut with the New York Philharmonic, when he had improvised all those show tunes at the party.

The gentleman who had requested an audience did indeed contact him the following day. He turned out to be Edward

Kaiser, president of Columbia Records, and he was absolutely certain that there was a vast "crossover audience" that would lap up Danny's musical trifles like cotton candy.

At first *Rossi on Broadway* had a slow but steady sale based mainly on Danny's gradually growing popularity. But his appearance on the *Ed Sullivan Show* launched him higher than astronaut John Glenn. It accelerated sales from three thousand to seventy-five thousand "units" per week.

The Sullivan broadcast also came at an especially fortuitous time. For the evening it was aired, the Grammy ballots were in the mail to the voters. Earlier, smart money would have picked Count Basie as a surefire winner. But after Ed's monotonal but hyperbolic introduction ("America's great new musical genius"), it was a totally different ball game.

Thus it was that Danny wrote another page of musical history—winning Grammies in both the classical and jazz categories in a single day. Indeed, as Count Basie himself was overheard to remark, he was "a lucky little pecker."

Who knows how many units per week they'd be selling after this!

As Danny put the mosaic of his mind into place, he still could not account for the presence of all the gold statuettes glittering there in dawn's early light.

Where the hell had the others come from?

But that, of course, might be explained once the mystery of why he was in this strange hotel room had been solved.

He heard the sound of water running in the bathroom. Someone was performing morning ablutions. He had clearly shared the room and—from the look of it—the bed with someone the night before. Why was his normally razor-sharp memory in such a haze?

Just then the crystal tones of a female voice sang out, "Good morning, honey."

And making an impeccably coiffed and diaphanously clad entrance from the bathroom, triple Grammy Award winner Carla Atkins appeared.

"Hey, Carla," Danny enthused, "you certainly were a hit last night."

"You weren't too bad yourself, baby," she cooed, creeping under the covers next to him.

"I take it you're not talking about the Grammies?" Danny asked with a smile.

"Hell," Carla laughed in her lower register, "those little statues aren't any good in bed. I think the two of us deserve a special award, don't you?"

"I'm glad you think so," Danny answered candidly. "I just wish I could remember more about my evening with America's greatest vocalist. Did we drink anything?"

"Oh, a little bubbly downstairs. Then when we got up here I broke open a few amies."

"Amies?"

"Yeah, honey. Amyl nitrite. You know, those little pills with the invigorating smell. Don't tell me that was your first time?"

"It was," Danny confessed. "Why can't I remember if I enjoyed it or not?"

"Because, baby, you were higher than a rocket ship. I had to stuff you with downers or you would have danced on the ceiling. Are you interested in some breakfast?"

"Yeah, now that you mention it," Danny replied. "What about five or six eggs and bacon and toast—?"

Carla Atkins smiled. "I get the picture," she said and picked up the phone to room service and ordered breakfast for "a quintet."

"Quintet?" Danny asked after she had hung up.

"Yeah, baby—those little fellahs over there."

And she pointed at the five Grammies shining in a row.

The stewardess offered him champagne.

"No, thank you," Danny said politely.

"But, Mr. Rossi, you should be celebrating your victories," the flight attendant said, smiling invitingly. She was very pretty. "Well, call me if you change your mind—and congratulations."

After lingering for yet another awkward second in the hopes that Danny would ask for her phone number, she went reluctantly off to attend to some of the other stars who were also flying that afternoon in the first-class cabin from Los Angeles to New York.

But Danny was deep in thought. He was racking his brain to reconstruct what had occurred after he had walked into Carla Atkins's hotel room.

Little by little it was coming back to him. First, the thrill of being with the undisputed star of the evening. Then the thrill of being intimate with her. And then the sensation of those pills she had brought out.

Yes, he remembered he had felt a kind of wild exhilaration. His heart beat faster merely in retrospect. They had certainly made him feel . . . vigorous. But then the stuff she used to bring him "down" had really fogged his brain.

And he had forgotten to ask her what *they* were.

ANDREW ELIOT'S DIARY

December 20, 1960

I'm getting married tomorrow. It should be very interesting.

Newall's stuck in Hawaii with the navy and can't make it. But otherwise all my buddies will be there—including Ted and Sara Lambros, and even that nutcase, George Keller.

Kind of because I admire him so, I've asked Jason Gilbert to be my best man. He agreed, but refused to wear his marine uniform, even though it would add flash to the occasion.

Our church ceremony will be followed by a champagne reception at the Beacon Hill Club. After which we'll fly to Barbados for our honeymoon, and then return to New York, where I'll be starting as a trainee with Downs, Winship, Investment Bankers.

I'm sure it will be a joyous experience—especially if I can figure out how this all happened to me so quickly.

From one standpoint, I could say it was parental pressure. Although in our family that doesn't exist. My father merely *suggests* things.

When I was mustered from the navy last summer in time to join everybody up in Maine, he casually remarked that he supposed I'd be getting married one of these days.

To which I dutifully replied that I supposed so. And that sort of concluded the conversation, except for his observation that, "After all, a man shouldn't wait until he's over the hill."

Seeing as there were no more decks to swab or naval reports to file, I was, to tell the truth, at a loss for things to do. Also, spending so much time at sea had only sharpened my desire to get more involved with the female sex. And I suppose marriage is as involved as you can get.

Up until this year I had the romantic notion that getting married had something to do with love. But then, of course, having been isolated—first by Harvard and then by the vast ocean—I had no real idea what life was all about.

Matter of fact, love is one of the few subjects on which my father had such strong feelings that he actually expressed them in a four-letter word. We were out fishing on the lake a few days later and I mentioned how touched I had been at Ted and Sara's wedding. And how they were my ideal of what a loving couple should be.

Dad looked at me with eyebrow raised and said, "Andrew, don't you know love is . . . *bosh?*"

I can't pretend that I didn't hear stronger language in the navy, but never from my father's lips. He then patiently explained that when he was a boy the best marriages were not made in heaven, but over lunch at the club. Pity that sort of thing was going out of style.

For example, his classmate, Lyman Pierce, chairman of Boston Metropolitan, had "an absolutely smashing daughter," to whom, in the good old days, he would have arranged a splendid betrothal for me.

I allowed that I was in no way averse to meeting smashing women and would be glad to call this lady up as long as it was on a friendly basis—and without obligation.

To which my father replied that I wouldn't regret it. And returned to his fishing.

I had no great expectations when I dialed Faith Pierce at the Wildlife Preservation Fund, where she was a full-time volunteer. I assumed she would be a vapid, overprivileged, snobbish Brahmin. Well, she may have been a lot of those things, but she wasn't vapid. And what absolutely amazed me when we met was that she was so *good-looking.*

I mean, she was one of the prettiest girls I'd ever seen. I thought she gave Marilyn Monroe a fair run for her money (except that *she* had more money).

What's more, I liked her. She was that rare creature among the so-called bluebloods—a real enthusiast. Every activity to her was "a fun thing." Whether it was tossing a football on the banks of the Charles, having a gourmet meal at Maître Jacques, or sex before marriage. Moreover, all her previous life could be subsumed under that same description.

Her mummy and daddy hadn't gotten along too well. But when they divorced and she was sent to boarding school at the age of six, it turned out to be "a fun thing." Likewise the finishing school in Switzerland, where she picked up a terrific French accent—and one or two words to say with it.

Skiing, sailing, riding, and sex (previously mentioned, I guess) also came under that category.

And she's a terrific gardener.

I would describe our courtship as whirlwind—and I have no doubt how she would term it. In any case, we seemed to know so many people in common that I feared the only thing that would keep us from marrying would be some kind of incest by association.

For the record, I'm not marrying Faith simply because our mutual fathers and mothers are fairly berserk about the whole idea.

Knowing his deeply held views, I would never admit it to my dad, but secretly—I'm still a romantic.

And I'm marrying Faith Pierce because she said something that no one has ever said to me in my entire life.

Just before I proposed, she whispered, "I think I love you, Andrew."

One morning in late spring of '62, Danny Rossi woke up alone. Not merely alone in bed, but feeling a pervasive emptiness in his entire life.

How could this be? he asked himself. Here I am in my new Fifth Avenue duplex overlooking Central Park. In a minute a butler is going to walk through that door with my breakfast on a silver tray. He'll also be bringing this morning's mail, which will contain invitations to at least a dozen parties all over the world. And I suddenly feel unhappy.

Unhappy? What a ridiculous thought. I'm the critics' darling. I think if I sneezed during a concert they'd write it up as an exciting new interpretation of whatever I was playing. I can't even walk from here to Hurok's office without people calling out friendly greetings or asking for autographs.

Unhappy? There isn't an orchestra in the world that wouldn't die to have me as a soloist. And now the commissions for symphonic compositions are starting to come in. Everybody seems to want me for my talent, as well as my personality—not to mention the innumerable lovelies who want me for my body.

So why, with the platinum winter sun streaming brightly through the windows of my fantastic apartment, do I feel worse than I ever did when I was stuck in that lousy little practice room in my parents' cellar?

This was not, in fact, the first time he had had such thoughts. But now they seemed to be coming more frequently.

What made matters worse, he had no official engagements for the day. No concerts, no rehearsals, not even an appointment with his hair stylist.

This, of course, had been on his own insistence. Because he wanted to devote the day to composing the orchestral suite commissioned by the St. Louis Symphony. And yet now the prospect of being alone with sheafs of empty music paper depressed him.

What could possibly be causing this melancholy?

After breakfast he put on jeans and a Beethoven sweatshirt (the gift of an adoring fan) and climbed to his studio on the upper floor. There on his piano, where he had left it late the previous night, was his unfinished composition. And on an easy chair nearby, a magazine he had leafed through to relax and let his sleeping pill take effect.

Perhaps just to avoid sitting down to work, he ambled over and picked it up again. It was the *Harvard Alumni Bulletin* that he had left open the previous evening at the Class Notes section.

Why is it, he asked himself, only the boring guys write in their "achievements"? And what the hell makes them think that their marriages or even the birth of a kid would be of any possible interest to anybody else?

Yet, despite his indifference, he sank once again into the chair and reread the list of new matrimonies and parenthoods that had been so somniferous the night before.

Then, alone in his magnificent penthouse studio, almost involuntarily he made a confession to himself. This isn't boring, really. It's an account of all the joys in life that I've been missing. I mean, applause is heady stuff. But how long does it last? Five, ten minutes at the most. When everything is over I still come home and no one's here except the staff. Sure it's fun when I bring a woman back. But after all the physical excitement we don't *talk*. I mean, it sometimes makes me feel more lonely.

I want a wife, I think.

I know I want a wife. But someone genuine I can share my life with—and my thoughts. And most of all—if this is possible—a woman who might like me for myself and not that phony PR image my publicity machine has manufactured.

Come to think of it, who in my life has ever loved me for myself?

Only . . . Maria.

God, he had been stupid, letting his one real chance for a relationship slip through his fingers. And for the worst possible reason: because Maria did not act like every other woman and offer her body to the altar of his ego.

How long had it been since he'd last seen her? Two years?

Three years? By now she'd graduated from Radcliffe, probably married some nice Catholic guy, and was raising kids. Yeah, someone that fantastic doesn't sit around and wait for Danny Rossi to call back. No, she's got too much sense.

Now he knew exactly why he was depressed. And also that there was nothing he could do about it.

Or was there?

Maria would be, say, twenty-three or twenty-four at most. Not every woman's married by that age. Maybe she went to graduate school. Who the hell knows—maybe she even became a nun.

Funny, he had always kept her Cleveland phone number. A semiconscious reminder that he had never surrendered hope.

He took a deep breath and dialed.

Her mother answered.

"May I speak to Maria Pastore, please?" he asked nervously.

"Oh, she doesn't live at home anymore—"

Danny's heart sank. He was, as he had feared, too late.

"—But I could give you the number of her apartment. May I ask who's calling?"

"Uh—it's, uh—it's Daniel Rossi."

"Oh my," she responded. "I knew the voice was familiar. We've been following your career with enormous admiration."

"Thanks. Uh—is Maria well?"

"Yes. She's teaching dance at a girls' school and enjoys it very much. She's there now."

"Could you give me the address?" Danny interrupted.

"Certainly," Mrs. Pastore replied, "but I'd be glad to pass on a message."

"No, please. In fact, I'd be grateful if you didn't say I called. I'd sort of like to . . . surprise her."

◆

"One-two-three-plié. Now fourth position, girls. Tuck in at the back, please."

Maria was leading a ballet class of a dozen or so ten-year-olds at the Sherwood School for Girls. She was so involved that she barely perceived the studio door opening behind her. Yet something made her gaze into the mirror and see the reflection of a once-familiar figure.

She was astonished. Incredulous. But before turning around

she had enough presence to tell her charges, "Keep repeating those movements, girls. Laurie, you count the beats."

She then about-faced and walked to greet her visitor.

"Hello, Danny."

"Hello, Maria."

They were both distinctly uneasy.

"Uh—are you in town for a concert? I must have missed it in the papers."

"No, Maria, I flew out especially to see you."

That stopped the conversation cold.

For several moments they stared at each other mutely while behind them ten-year-old Laurie counted cadence for the little dancers.

"Did you hear me, Maria?" Danny said softly.

"Yes. It's just that I don't know what to think. I mean, why after all this time—?"

Rather than answer her question, Danny asked the more urgent one that had been burning in his brain during the entire flight to Cleveland.

"Has some lucky guy nabbed you yet, Maria?"

"Well, I've been sort of going with this architect. . . ."

"Is it serious?"

"Well, he wants to marry me."

"Do you ever think about me anymore?"

She paused and then replied, "Yes."

"Well, that makes two of us. You've been on my mind."

"When do you have the time, Danny?" she asked with gentle sarcasm. "Your love affairs are so public I can read about them at supermarket checkout counters without even buying the paper."

"That's somebody else. The real Danny Rossi is still in love with you. All he wants is a wife named Maria and lots of kids. Maybe half-a-dozen cute little dancers like those girls over there."

She looked at him quizzically.

"Why me?"

"Maria, it would take a hell of a long time to explain."

"Could you give me a brief outline in twenty-five words or less?"

Danny knew that if he could not sway her now, he would never have another chance.

"Maria," he said earnestly, "I know the last time you saw me I was drunk with applause. I won't lie to you and say that I don't like it anymore. But I've realized it isn't enough. My concerts may be packed, but my life is incredibly empty. Am I making any sense?"

"You still haven't answered my original question. Why me?"

"This is kind of hard to explain, but since I've become—I guess *famous* is the word—everybody I meet says they love me. And I don't believe a goddamn word of it. The only person I ever came close to trusting was you. I know you understand that I put on my cocky little show because deep down I don't think that anybody could really care."

He paused and looked at her.

"That's slightly more than twenty-five words," she replied softly.

"How much do you believe?"

Her answer was barely audible because she was on the verge of tears.

"Everything," she said.

Though he never told a soul, it was the only educational experience that Jason ever enjoyed more than Harvard. The twenty-one-week course at the Marine Basic School in Quantico, Virginia, offered instruction in such unacademic subjects as leadership, techniques of military instruction, map reading, infantry tactics, and weapons, as well as the history and traditions of the corps. In addition, there was first aid, combat intelligence, vertical development operations, tank and amphibious operations, and, his favorite of all, physical training and conditioning.

While the majority of the other college graduates were either fainting or groaning, or praying for it to end, Jason grew more elated with every pull-up, push-up, sit-up—and every mile he ran. He actually *loved* the obstacle course and spent some of his rare free moments trying to perfect his technique in negotiating it. His rifle became even more familiar to him than a tennis racket.

Though he had been far from an outstanding student in college, he was determined to finish number one in *this* class.

In the final week they took written examinations in military knowledge and skills, as well as practical tests in land navigation and techniques of military instruction. While Jason scored well in these, he was counting on the more sportslike contests to win him a gold medal.

He qualified with extremely high scores in rifle and pistol marksmanship, but was still outshot by half-a-dozen country boys who'd used firearms all their lives. Still, he led everyone in the physical-fitness tests. And that was some consolation for his overall finish in fifth place.

Second Lieutenant Jason Gilbert, USMC, took advantage of

his first leave to write a long letter to Fanny explaining the reason for his silence. She answered briefly but warmly.

> I was really surprised to hear from you. Maybe the *Odyssey* is not such a fairy tale after all.
>
> Now it's my turn to plead for your patience as I have my qualifying exams to study for. Afterward, when I'm working in a clinic, I'll have time to write.
>
> Love, F.
>
> P.S. Did I mention that I miss you?

At Christmastime he deliberately wore his dress uniform (blue jacket, gold buttons rising to the neck, white hat) to make the maximum impression on his mom and dad.

Unfortunately, his impressively costumed arrival was upset by a more somber event.

When Jason made his grand entrance, he found his father, mother, and sister all sitting at the dining-room table. Julie was leaning forward, her head in her hands. The cries of baby Samantha were audible from another room.

The elegant marine officer was, to say the least, disappointed when his father greeted him with a desultory glance and a "Hi, son, you're just in time."

He kissed his mother and as he sat down at the table asked, "Hey, what's going on?"

"Charles and Julie are having a bit of trouble," she replied.

"Trouble?" his father suddenly bellowed. "The son of a bitch has left her! He just upped and walked out. Abandoning your wife and one-year-old child is hardly what I call adult behavior."

"Well, I never thought Charlie was much of an adult," Jason commented. "What was his reason?"

"He said he doesn't like being married," Julie wailed. "He said he never wanted to get married."

"I could have told you that and saved you a lot of grief," Jason remarked. "You were both too young."

"Stop being so holier-than-thou, Jason," his father bristled.

"Okay, I'm sorry," he answered softly. And added, "Hey, Julie, I'm really sorry that you got involved with that preppie idiot."

She reacted to her brother's expression of condolence with a fresh burst of tears.

"Well, I can see it's hardly going to be a very merry Christmas," Jason commented, getting up and starting to pace the floor.

Just then, Jenny the housekeeper entered the room and, spying the younger Gilbert, exclaimed, "Why, Mr. Jason, don't you look snazzy!"

The holiday dinner was a pretty grim affair. By now the elder Gilbert had gotten over the initial shock of his daughter's failure to live up to parental expectations, and had begun to concentrate on the traditional source of his pride.

"You mean to tell me you thought basic training was *fun*, Jason?" he marveled.

"In a way, but I'm afraid I overdid it. My C.O. wants me to stay on and be in charge of one of the fitness programs."

"What's wrong with that?"

"Well, I really don't relish the prospect of another year and a half in Quantico. But still there's a chance they'll let me go to a few tennis tournaments. Anyway I'm a lot better off than Andrew who I hear is swabbing decks on a destroyer."

"I'll never understand why he didn't become an officer," Mr. Gilbert remarked.

"I can. The Eliots have always been big shots in the navy— admirals and stuff. He probably felt he had too much to live up to. That's why, compared to him, I'm sort of at an advantage when it comes to my career."

"How so?" inquired his father, who was now president of the second largest electronics corporation in the world.

"Because, unlike Andrew, who's hanging from a precarious limb of the great family tree, we're all just one generation out of the ghetto."

"That's a rather unattractive way of putting it," his father remarked. To the best of Jason Gilbert, Sr.'s knowledge, this was the first time the word *ghetto* had ever been pronounced in their home. It made him uncomfortable and it seemed especially inappropriate at Christmas dinner.

He shifted to a more festive topic. "Have you heard from that Dutch girlfriend of yours recently?"

"Not as recently as I'd like," Jason answered. "In fact, with your permission, Dad, I'd like to call her up after dinner."

"By all means," replied Jason Gilbert, Sr., relieved to be looking forward again, away from the not-sufficiently-distant past.

Jason was mustered early from the Marine Corps in August 1961 so that he could get up north in time to enter Harvard Law School.

He had spent his tour of duty first as an instructor in the Basic School, then, primarily because he looked so perfect in his uniform, as an O.S.O. (officer selection officer). His assignment had been to tour campuses and induce undergraduates to follow his own path to military glory by joining the Platoon Leaders Class—or, failing that, at least the marines.

Jason inwardly likened these recruitment expeditions to a fishing contest. And, competitive as always, he was determined to come home with the biggest catch. He was pleased, if not surprised, to learn from his commanding officer that he had won this challenge as well.

Still, he was relieved to be out of the military and eager to tackle the law.

He was also eager to see Fanny. For their correspondence had continued unabated throughout the nearly twenty-four months that they had not seen each other.

But the marines would not grant him a few extra weeks so he could visit the woman he was certain he wanted to marry. That reunion would have to stand the test of yet another academic year.

More letters. More phone calls. But a lot less patience.

There is an old saying about the experience of Harvard Law School: in the first year they scare you to death. In the second they work you to death. And in the third they bore you to death.

The two years of military service that separated Jason from most of his classmates helped him when it came to confronting the terrifying Law School professors. They were nowhere near as frightening as many drill sergeants. And if he was unable to give a magnificent answer in, say, contracts class, the teacher's sneer was a lot more benign than having to do a hundred push-ups.

He also benefited from the fact that some of The Class of '58 who had gotten student deferments were now seniors and more than willing to help their undergraduate hero.

"You should go in for trial law," advised Gary McVeagh. "With your looks, you could snow the female jurors without opening your mouth. And they'd take care of the men. You'd never lose."

"Nah," contradicted Seymour Herscher, "he should go in for divorce law. They'll all come flocking to him hoping to get Jason as part of the settlement."

But Jason already had a game plan. He and his dad had discussed it for years.

First, if he could manage to keep up with these superbrains in the Law School, he would try to get a clerkship. From there it would be a few years of general practice with a prestigious New York or Washington firm. All of which would serve as a springboard for his ultimate ambition—politics.

"Jason," the elder Gilbert had once jested, "I'm so sure you'll succeed, I'd be willing to invest in a house in Washington right .now."

But these juvenile career fantasies were supplanted by a newer and better dream that sustained Jason through the grim series of practice exams in January, and the spring tension when the real finals were approaching.

It was the thought that, pass or fail, he would at last be reunited with that lovely Dutch girl whose picture smiled at him from his desk.

He had not lived like a total monk in the two-and-a-half-year interval since he had last seen Fanny. But the girls with whom he had casual dates only reminded him of how different his relationship with her was.

And though she never said anything in her letters, he somehow sensed that she too was merely marking time till they could be together again.

For this reason Jason welcomed the advent of exams with enthusiasm. While most of his classmates grew sicker and more panicked with every test, he regarded the filling of each bluebook as another leaf in the passport that would take him through the gates of the Law School. And into the arms of his beloved.

*   *   *

During the long flight to Amsterdam, Jason was nervous about seeing her again. It had been so long. Had he just embellished the wonder of their relationship in the desperate boredom of military routine? Would their meeting at Schiphol Airport be an anticlimax?

He knew when he saw her just beyond the customs gate that it was not. When they kissed, he felt the same stirring.

They spent the first few days at her parents' farm, where he savored the warmth and closeness of the van der Post family. Her brother, who was studying in The Hague, and her married sister—not to mention assorted cousins and aunts—came by to meet Fanny's American friend.

The night before they left, he was standing in front of the fireplace in the main room of the farmhouse looking at the photographs on the mantelpiece.

"It's amazing," he exclaimed, "I've met all of these people in less than a week."

And then he stopped in front of the snapshot of a dark-haired girl.

"Except her."

"That's Eva," said Mrs. van der Post. "I suppose Fanny has told you about her."

"Yes," Jason replied.

"She's a wonderful girl," added Fanny's father. "Always a little sad, but that's understandable."

Fanny took Jason to visit the Anne Frank house at Prinsengracht 263, in the shadow of the Westerkerk. To give him a graphic demonstration of what his co-religionists had experienced during the Second World War.

He stood there silently, glancing at the cramped garret where the young Dutch girl and her family hid from the occupying troops for more than a year before being dragged off to their deaths.

"All through this, she never lost her humanity," Fanny remarked. "You should read her diary. Despite everything, she believed people were really basically good at heart. And they took such a person—an innocent little girl—to the gas chambers just because she was Jewish."

The story was not totally new to Jason. For Anne Frank's

diary had been dramatized into a successful Broadway play, which he knew his parents had seen.

In retrospect, he wondered why they had not discussed it at any length with him and his sister. Could they have possibly believed that it had *nothing* to do with them?

And then they drove to Venice to resume their love affair where it had left off three years earlier.

"Fanny, do you think we're the first couple to make love in a gondola?"

"No, my darling, we're about a thousand years late."

"Well, we're the first to make *great* love."

Their joy and passion had not changed. Fanny had the unique gift of making Jason see the laughter in the world. But now there was something more to their relationship.

Jason had known many women and had at times been captivated, even infatuated. But what he felt for Fanny was completely different. Never before had he wanted to give so much of himself. Not only sensuality but tenderness. He longed to shelter her, to take care of her.

And she, the strong independent doctor, could let herself become a child again and revel in the warmth of his protectiveness.

But when the amorous initiative was hers, she made him feel he could be vulnerable. And for the first time he experienced a woman's love not merely fired by his strength.

Thus they were parent, child, lover, and friend to each other. A completeness too miraculous to lose.

Their holiday was all too brief and once again they were about to part.

"I'll fly back as soon as my last exam is over in June," he promised.

"What'll I do until then?" she asked forlornly.

"Come on, it's not that long. Our last separation was nearly three years."

"Yes," she replied wistfully. "But then I had no idea how much I loved you."

Jason looked at her. "Fanny, I have a confession to make."

"What?" she asked, slightly off balance.

"Yesterday afternoon when I wanted to go off by myself, there was a reason." He reached into his pocket and withdrew a small velvet box. "If it fits any one of your fingers, then I think we should get married."

"Jason," she smiled, "if it fits one of my toes we will get married."

The future bride and groom embraced.

Andrew met George Keller at the Trailways Bus Station in Bangor. They used the drive back to the Eliot retreat in Seal Harbor to get up to date.

"You look pale, George. Haven't you been outside all summer?"

"I'm a graduate student, not a lifeguard, Andrew. And I must finish my dissertation by next spring."

"What's the urgency?"

"Because I want to get my degree next June."

"What'll you do after that?"

"I don't know yet."

"So what's the rush?"

"You wouldn't understand. But I must keep to my schedule. Anyway, I'm grateful for your enticing me up for the weekend."

"Weekend? I thought you were staying the whole week."

"No no no. I must get back to my writing."

"Okay," Andrew capitulated. "But if I see you scribble so much as a postcard in the next two days, I'll punch you out. Agreed?"

"Under protest." The scholar smiled. "Anyway, old boy, how's marriage?"

"Oh, let me tell you, Keller, it's a fun thing. You ought to try it."

"All in due time, Andrew. But first I must—"

"Don't even say it," his classmate interrupted. "I forbid you to mention your thesis all weekend. And—uh—if you could manage to keep the conversation general, it'd be nice for Faith. I mean, she's a great kid, but academics is not her strong point."

The lovely Mrs. Andrew Eliot waved to them from the edge of the dock as they approached. Even the otherwise preoccupied

George Keller could not help noticing how good she looked in a bikini. And how it felt when she gave him a welcoming hug.

Faith then led both men to the terrace where a large pitcher of martinis awaited.

"I've been looking forward to having a real talk with you ever since we met at the wedding," Faith remarked as she handed George a glass. "Andrew says you have a brilliant mind."

"Andrew flatters me."

"I know." She giggled. "He flatters me, too. But I like it."

George then presented her with a gift-wrapped package.

"Oh, you shouldn't have," she exclaimed as she tore it open. And then with slightly forced gaiety added, "Oh—a book. Look, Andrew, George brought me a book."

"That's great," her husband remarked. And turning to their guest added, "Faith really likes books. What is it, dear?"

"It looks exciting," she replied and held up the cover.

It was *The Necessity of Choice,* by Henry Kissinger.

"What's it about, George?" she asked.

"The U.S.–Soviet 'missile gap.' It is unquestionably the most important work on the subject to date."

"It's by one of George's professors," Andrew explained.

"A very great man," George quickly added. "He's my thesis adviser and, from the moment I arrived in America, he's acted *in loco parentis.*"

"You mean kind of crazy?" Faith inquired.

The reply seemed like a non sequitur to George. And so he added, "He mentions me in the preface. May I read it to you?"

"Oh, this is exciting," Faith gushed, as she handed him the tome. "I've never known anyone who was in a book before."

George quickly found the page and read aloud, " 'Gratitude for the advice and insight of my student and friend George Keller cannot be adequately expressed.' "

"Gosh," Andrew commented, "he actually calls you his friend. That's terrific."

"Yes. And he's not only made me his head section man in Gov. 180, but he's even arranged for me to have a piece in *Foreign Affairs.*"

"Oh, George." Faith smiled. "That sounds very naughty."

George was charmed by her delightful sense of humor.

"Eliot," he smiled, "you're a really lucky man."

*   *   *

"Well, Faith," Andrew asked when he returned from driving George to his bus, "what do you think of old George? A mad genius, huh?"

"He's quite attractive," she replied thoughtfully. "But something about him worries me. I mean, I can't exactly put my finger on it. But I think it's the way he talks. Have you noticed that he has no foreign accent at all?"

"Sure. That's what's so fantastic about him."

"Andrew, don't be naive. If a foreign person doesn't have a foreign accent that means he's trying to hide something. I think your ex-roommate just might be a spy."

"A spy? Who the heck could he be spying for?"

"I don't know. The enemy. Maybe even the Democrats."

From the "Milestones" section of *Time* magazine, January 12, 1963:

T he only prenuptial promise Maria had extracted from Danny was that he would drastically cut down his frenetic touring so that they could take roots somewhere and build a domestic existence.

Though at first he was reluctant to give up the polyglot murmurs of adulation that gave him such pleasure, the offer from Philadelphia had come as a kind of miraculous solution.

They bought a spacious Tudor home on an acre and a half in Bryn Mawr. It was large enough to transform the entire top floor into a studio for Danny. And a light airy room for Maria, where he insisted on installing a barre, but which she wanted to become a nursery as soon as possible.

They spent their wedding night in the downtown Cleveland Sheraton, where Gene Pastore had thrown a lavish reception.

Throughout the celebration, Danny was strangely subdued— although he tried not to show it. For he was preoccupied with the fact that, having earned the reputation of being an international Don Juan, he might not live up to it on the one occasion that really mattered.

Not unexpectedly, he was coerced by the wedding guests into playing the piano. To his mind, it proved an ominous harbinger. For though he delighted them with a complete rendition of *Rossi on Broadway,* he was perhaps the only person in the room who noticed he was not performing as well as usual.

Perhaps it was the champagne. He had been sipping a little all evening to calm his nerves, even though he knew it was not a good idea. As an ironclad rule, he never drank anything stronger than Coke before a concert. He might take a Miltown or a phenobarb if he was especially nervous. But it was too late for that.

Now that he was slightly boozy, he wondered if he hadn't been sabotaging himself. For he would soon have to enter the bedroom of the sexiest girl he had ever known, *who had waited all her life for this moment.*

There were "his" and "hers" bathrooms in the bridal suite. As Danny brushed his teeth (long and slowly), he looked in the mirror and saw the face of a frightened adolescent.

Could he go through with it? Of course, he told himself. Come on, don't make a big deal out of all this. Besides, she's a virgin. Even if you're not at your very best, how could she know?

Danny looked at himself again. And his own expression told him that he couldn't walk into the bedroom and face Maria.

Not alone, anyway.

He unzipped a pocket in his toilet kit and stood half-a-dozen small bottles of pills on the shelf above the sink. They ranged in effect, as he'd often joked to himself, from *largo e pianissimo* (tranquilizers) to *allegro e presto* (stimulants for when he was tired from a long flight).

Thank God for medical science, he thought, reaching for a jar marked "Meth." He poured one into his sweaty left palm, closed the cap, and returned the pharmacopoeia to its hiding place.

A playful voice called from the bedroom, "Danny, are you still here, or have I been abandoned on my wedding night?"

"I'll be right with you, darling," he replied, hoping his tone had not betrayed any nervousness.

He crushed the tablet in his palm in hopes of speeding its effectiveness, and swallowed it with a glass of water.

Almost instantly his mood lightened. Though his heart beat

faster, it was no longer with fear. He put on his robe and started slowly toward the bedroom.

She was waiting for him, her face beaming.

"Oh, Danny," she said tenderly, "I know we're going to be so happy together."

"I know it too, darling," he replied, and climbed in beside her.

Until that moment, Danny Rossi had never given a performance, either musical or otherwise, that was not impassioned and flawless. That night was no exception.

But it had been very, very close.

Fanny and Jason were now too excited to rely on letters. Their feelings were so intense that they had to express them through the more dynamic medium of the telephone. What started as a weekly ritual soon became almost a daily one. The bills were astronomical.

"It would be cheaper if one of us flew over to be with the other," he remarked.

"I agree, Jason. But you can't take your exams here and I can't take mine there. So if you can control yourself for another few months, we'll be together so long you'll get tired of me."

"I'll never get tired of you."

"That's what they all say," she joked. "I sometimes wish we were just living together and not having to go through all this ceremony business."

"Fanny, you're going to live in Boston. This is *still* a puritan town. Besides, I want to sign you to a lifetime contract so there's no possible chance of your getting away."

"I like the sound of that," she replied.

The wedding would be in July at her family's church in Groningen. Since Fanny had planned to visit Eva again that summer, it was decided that she would go in late spring—as soon as she had qualified.

On May 15 she called Jason to say, "Goodbye for three weeks." Since her "sister" Eva's kibbutz in the Galilee was a pretty spartan establishment, communication would be all but impossible.

"I think they've got about three phones in the whole place," Fanny remarked. "So I don't think they'd appreciate our babbling all the time. Do you think you can bear not speaking for twenty-one days?"

"No," said Jason.

"Then think about meeting me in Israel as soon as your last exam is over. It's about time you saw the land of your forefathers, anyway."

"I just may, if I grow desperate enough," he replied. "Hey—I almost forgot to ask you, how did your orals go?"

"Fine," she replied modestly.

"Then you're a real doctor. Congratulations! Why aren't you excited?"

"Because," she replied with affection, "I'm about to become something a lot more important—your wife."

Those words were burned in fire in the memory of Jason Gilbert. For they were the last he ever heard spoken by Fanny van der Post.

Ten days later, he was awakened at 6:00 A.M. by a phone call from Amsterdam. It was her brother, Anton.

"Jason," he said, his voice quavering, "I'm afraid I've some terrible news about Fanny."

"Has she been in an accident?"

"Yes. Well, not exactly. She's been killed."

Jason sat up, his heart pounding frantically.

"How? What happened?"

"I don't know all the details," he stammered. "Eva just called and said that there was a terrorist attack. Their kibbutz is very close to the border. Apparently some Arabs crossed over in the night and threw hand grenades into the children's dormitory. Fanny was seeing to a sick little girl and—" He broke down and sobbed.

At first Jason was numb. "I can't believe it," he murmured to himself. "I just can't believe this is really happening."

In the twenty-six sheltered years of his life he had never known anything remotely resembling tragedy. And now it had struck him like a bullet in the soul.

"Eva says she was very brave, Jason. She threw herself on one of the grenades to protect the children."

Jason did not know what to say. Or think. Or do. He sensed that at any time the tears would come. And the rage explode within him. Now he was simply frozen with shock. Then he realized that he had to say something to her brother.

"Anton," he whispered, "I can't tell you how sorry I am."

"We are sorry for you, too, Jason," he replied. "You and Fanny loved each other so much."

He then added in a voice that was barely audible, "We thought you might like to come to the funeral."

The funeral. Oh God, the thought of it brought a dull ache. Yet another harsh fact to make him understand that Fanny was really dead. That he would never hear her voice again. Never see her alive.

But he had been asked a question. Did he wish to attend the ceremony in which the body of his beloved would be lowered into the ground and covered with earth?

"Yes, Anton. Yes, of course," he replied, his voice as weak as a reed in the wind. "When's the service?"

"Well, it was to be as soon as we could all get there. But, of course, if you're coming we'll wait for you."

"I don't understand," said Jason. "Isn't the funeral in Holland?"

"No," Anton replied. "The family has had other thoughts. You know we're quite religious and have very strong ties with the Bible and the Holy Land. Since Fanny died . . . where she did . . . we thought she should be buried in the Protestant cemetery in Jerusalem."

"Oh."

"Maybe that's too long a journey for you," Anton said gently.

"Don't be silly," Jason answered quietly. "I'm going to call the airlines as soon as they open and get the first plane out. I'll call you back and let you know when I'll be arriving."

Ever since he had first met Fanny, he had kept his passport near him should the need to see her become unbearable. So all he had to do was pack a suitcase, find a flight, and go.

He had an exam that morning for which he had done weeks of preparation, and since his flight to Israel left JFK that evening, he could have taken it.

But nothing mattered anymore. He didn't give a damn about anything.

He went to a travel agent in the Square, got his ticket, and spent the rest of the day wandering aimlessly around Cambridge. The sun was shining, and students, laughing happily, were heading toward the riverside to picnic.

Their laughter put him in a silent rage. How can they smile

and walk the streets as if life is just the same as it was yesterday? How can the goddamn sun dare shine so brightly? The whole damn world should stop and weep.

At four he flew from Boston, transferred to Idlewild, and walked across the parkways to where El Al Airlines had their check-in. His parents met him there.

"Jason," his mother cried, "this is so horrible."

"Is there anything we can do?" his father asked.

"I don't think so," Jason answered distractedly.

A lithe young man with black curly hair, wearing a half-open shirt and carrying a walkie-talkie, came up to them and in a slightly accented voice asked, "Are you all three passengers?"

"No," said Jason, "only me."

"Then I'm afraid those other people have to go," he said politely. "Only passengers allowed here. For security reasons."

This upset the elder Gilbert. "Look at this terminal," he complained, as he reluctantly began to leave. "There are policemen everywhere, and at least a dozen types like that fellow. This must be the most dangerous airline in the world."

Before Jason could respond, the security agent turned and addressed them. "Excuse me, but I think we are the *safest* airline in the world because we take the most precautions."

"Do you always eavesdrop on other people's conversations?" Jason's father snapped.

"Only when I'm at work, sir. It's part of the job."

Unchastened, Mr. Gilbert turned to his son and said, "Promise me you'll take an American airline back."

"Dad, please, I'd be grateful if I could just be left alone."

"Yes, son," he said quietly. "Of course."

They embraced their son and quickly left.

Jason sighed as he watched the two female security officials carefully empty the contents of his little overnight bag—three shirts, some underwear, two ties, a toilet kit—onto the bench and meticulously examine them. One even checked his tubes of toothpaste and shaving cream.

Finally they repacked it, far more neatly than he himself had done.

"Can I go now?" he asked, trying to suppress his impatience.

"Yes, sir," replied the young woman, "right to that booth. For the body search."

The flight was long and crowded. Children chased one another up and down the aisles. Old bearded men—and a few young bearded men—paced up and back as well, no doubt meditating on some vital point of the Talmud or a passage in the Prophets.

Inexplicably, Jason got up and walked with them. He wondered at the various faces that he saw among the passengers. Besides the stereotyped patriarchs straight from the pages of the Old Testament, there were tanned and muscular young men. He sensed that many of those open-shirted athletic types were security guards. There were also faces black as any Negro he had ever seen. (He learned later they were Yemenites.)

But what struck him most was that he also recognized himself. For here and there were blond and blue-eyed passengers conversing rapidly in Hebrew.

They were all different. Yet they were all Jews. And he was among them.

Fourteen hours later, when the pilot announced they were beginning their final approach to Tel Aviv airport, Jason perceived sobs among the people sitting near him. In fact, they were audible from many corners of the plane. And when they disembarked, walking across the tarmac past rows of heavily armed soldiers, he saw an old man bend and kiss the earth.

Jason noticed that the passengers felt such emotion at having arrived in this hot and muggy place that they could express it only by one of two extremes. Tears or laughter. He himself was too stunned to feel anything.

The customs officer who stamped his passport smiled and said, "Welcome home."

Instinctively Jason replied, "I'm just a tourist, sir."

"Yes," said the officer, "but you're a Jew. And you have come home."

Having no baggage to pick up, he walked directly past customs to the sliding doors. They opened into an ecstatic mob of shouting people, greeting their arriving relatives in a babel of languages.

He stood on tiptoe and caught sight of Anton van der Post

waiting off to the side with a fat, balding, middle-aged man. He hurried over to them.

The only conversation they could manage without crying was an exchange of platitudes.

"How was the flight?"

"Fine, Anton. How are your parents taking it?"

"All right, considering. Oh, this gentleman is Yossi Ron, the secretary of the kibbutz."

Jason and the elder man shook hands.

"Shalom, Mr. Gilbert," he said. "I can't tell you how sorry I am. . . ."

He, too, was at a loss for words. They climbed silently into an old kibbutz truck and began to drive.

About an hour later they ascended a steep hill as the road bent to the right. Jerusalem came into view, its peach-white stone shimmering in the early morning sun.

Then Anton spoke for the first time in the entire journey. "We thought she would want to be buried with your ring, Jason. Is that all right?"

He nodded. And in a sudden rush of grief, his thoughts collided with the awful truth of what had brought him to this so-called holy place.

She was buried in a simple ceremony behind the towering trees of the Protestant cemetery on Emek Refaim.

A delegation had driven down from the kibbutz during the night and now were gathered at the graveside. They all were tanned and open-shirted. Jason felt slightly out-of-place in his dark suit and tie. Standing in the first row with his parents were Anton, his arm around his mother, and a short, dark-haired Israeli girl clinging to Mr. van der Post's hand. Clearly, this must be Eva Goudsmit.

The faces of the Dutch visitors were etched with pain. The kibbutzniks wept openly at the loss of a friend.

But she was only that to them. They could never dream what Fanny had meant to Jason Gilbert. When they lowered the coffin into the grave, something inside him was buried with her.

His grief was too deep for tears.

As the service ended and the mourners began to leave, he and

Eva were drawn instinctively to each other. No introductions were necessary.

"Fanny spoke of you often," she said in a hoarse voice. "If anyone deserved a happy life it was she. I should have been the one to die in that explosion."

"That's the way *I* feel too," Jason murmured. They continued walking, passed through the cemetery gate, and turned right. When they reached the Bethlehem Road he said, "I'd like to see where it happened."

"You mean the kibbutz?" she asked.

He nodded.

"You can come back on the bus with us this afternoon."

"No," he replied, "I want to be with her family until they leave in the morning. I'll rent a car and drive up to the Galilee on my own."

"I'll tell Yossi to make some arrangements for you. How long will you be staying?"

Jason Gilbert looked up as the rooftops of the Old City came into view, and answered, "I don't know."

At 5:00 A.M. the next day, Jason drove the three people who would have been his in-laws to their flight home.

Though they exchanged promises to keep in touch, both parties understood that there would be little, if any, contact. Because they had lost the person who linked their lives.

With a map spread out on the empty seat beside him, Jason proceeded northward. First along the Mediterranean coast, the blue sea on his left. Then east after Caesarea, through Nazareth, and across the Galilee until he reached the sea where two millennia ago Christ had walked upon the water. He then turned north again, the Jordan River on his right, through Kiryat Shmona.

By noon he reached the gates of Vered Ha-Galil, drove in, and parked his car.

Except for the lush greenery and flowers, the place reminded him of a small army installation. For it was ringed with barbed wire. Only when he looked out over the Jordan did he feel a sense of its tranquility.

The kibbutz seemed deserted. He glanced at his watch and understood why. It was lunchtime. The dining room had to be in the single large structure standing at the edge of the bungalows.

Inside, there was a din of animated conversation. He scanned the tables and soon found Eva, dressed like everyone else, in a T-shirt and shorts.

"Hello, Jason," she said softly. "Are you hungry?"

It was only then he realized that he hadn't had anything since a cup of coffee in Jerusalem six hours earlier. The food was simple—home-grown vegetables, cheese, and *leben*, a kind of yoghurt.

Eva introduced him to the kibbutzniks sitting nearby, all of whom expressed a welcome tempered with condolences.

"I'd like to see where it happened," Jason said.

"It's siesta time now," said Ruthie, one of the children's counselors. "Can you wait till four?"

"I suppose so."

After lunch Eva walked with him along rows of identical wooden huts toward the *srif* where he would be staying.

"You'll be sleeping in Dov Levi's bunk," she remarked.

"Where's he going to sleep?"

"Dov's away on *miluim*—army-reserve duty. He'll be gone another three weeks."

"Oh, I don't think I'll be staying that long."

Eva looked up at him and asked, "Are you in a hurry to get back to something?"

"No," he conceded, "not really."

Jason kicked off his shoes, lay back on top of the creaky metal bed, and pondered the events of the past seventy-two hours.

Earlier that week he had been strolling the Harvard Law School campus in the company of his friends, his thoughts preoccupied with marriage, exams, his future political career. Now here he was alone in the so-called land of his forefathers with absolutely no meaning to his life.

At last he dozed off into a troubled sleep. The next thing he knew he was being prodded gently by Yossi. He was with a broad-shouldered man of about forty, whom he introduced as Aryeh, the kibbutz security officer.

Jason quickly shook the sleep from his head and joined them to walk across toward the children's quarters.

"It seems kind of strange to me," he said as they neared the dormitory. "Why do you have all the kids sleep in one place? Wouldn't they be safer with their parents?"

"It's part of kibbutz philosophy," Yossi explained. "The

young children are brought up together to give them a feeling of comradeship. They don't lack for love. They see their parents every day."

The long rectangular nursery had two rows of beds, and walls decorated with some of the youngsters' artwork. There were no visible signs of any destruction. The damage obviously had been quickly repaired.

"So it was here?" Jason asked quietly.

"Yes," Aryeh acknowledged, pain in his voice, puffing at a cheap cigarette. "A little girl had tonsillitis and Fanny was taking care of her when. . . ."

"Don't you have guards here? I mean, you're so damn close to the border."

"Everyone in the kibbutz does a night a month walking the perimeter of the land. But there's so much area to cover that if the *Fedayeen* are patient, as these fellows obviously were, they can wait for the patrol to go by, cut the wires, do their nasty business, and escape."

"You mean you didn't catch any of them?"

"No," Aryeh answered wearily. "The explosions made so much confusion—they also set off flares by the water tower. And we first had to think of our wounded. Besides Fanny, there were three children injured. By the time I organized a search party, they had gotten too big a lead on us and gone back across the border."

"Why didn't you keep chasing them?"

"The army took over. We just have to be sure we stop them next time."

"You mean, you know they'll be back?"

"Either them or their cousins. They'll keep trying to drive us away until we convince them that this is our home."

Jason asked to be left alone. The two men nodded.

He relived the scene of the terrorists smashing through the screen door and lobbing their grenades at the sleeping children. Reflexively he reached for the pistol he had once worn on his hip to shoot at the attackers. Rage exploded inside him. Anger with *himself.*

I should have been here to protect them, he thought. To protect *her.* If I had, she would still be alive.

◆

Something was keeping Jason in Vered Ha-Galil. Superficially, he told himself, the hard physical labor was the only anodyne for his all-pervasive grief. And the evening discussions with the kibbutzniks were a catharsis for his troubled soul.

A week after his arrival, he managed to get through to the United States on the telephone in the main hall. The connection was weak and he had to shout. His father reported that he had spoken to the Harvard Law School dean and explained the circumstances. Jason would be allowed to make up the exams he had missed during the following spring.

"When are you coming home, Jason?"

"I'm not sure, Dad. I'm not sure about a lot of things."

The kibbutz was one of the oldest in the country. It had been established by visionary Jews who had left Europe before the deluge, believing that they, like every other people, should have a homeland. In fact, they believed Palestine had always been their homeland. And their idealism inspired them to lead what they hoped would be a mass return.

"If you think these buildings are primitive," Yossi remarked one evening after dinner, "imagine how it was when the older folks came. Living in tents all year round, plowing fields without a tractor."

"It must have been intolerable," Jason commented.

"Uncomfortable yes, but not intolerable. Most relished every minute of it, even the freezing rain. Because, like the land it was falling on, this rain was for *them*.

"World War Two brought us more. First, those who got out ahead of the murder squads. And later, the survivors of the camps. Some of them are still around here working a full day in the fields next to youngsters like you."

Jason had already noticed the blue numbers tattooed on their forearms, which they made no attempt to hide.

Eva's cousin, Jan Goudsmit, had escaped the gas chamber and reached Palestine on one of the many illegal boats. But he was caught and interned by the British as an alien.

"Can you imagine them trying to tell a man he doesn't belong in his own country?" Yossi laughed. "Anyway, they locked Goudsmit in another camp. Not as bad as the Germans, mind you. The British didn't mistreat them. But the barbed wire was the same. He escaped in time to fight in the War of

Independence. That's where he and I met up. We were sharing the same rifle."

"You what?" asked Jason.

"You hear me, my American friend. We had one rifle for two people. And, believe me, we didn't have very many bullets, so the second man always kept an accurate count. Anyway, when it was over I brought Jan home with me."

"That's how I found him," Eva joined in. "Once he had a fixed address, he gave his name to HIAS, which was trying to unite survivors. Their Netherlands committee got us in contact."

"It must have been tough to leave the country you grew up in," Jason offered. "I mean, learning a new language and all that stuff."

"Yes," Eva acknowledged, "it wasn't an easy decision. I was so fond of the van der Posts. But curiously, it was they who convinced me."

"Don't you ever get homesick?" Jason asked, instantly regretting his poor choice of adjective.

"I do get nostalgic for Amsterdam," Eva acknowledged. "It's one of the loveliest cities in the world. I went back a few times to see Fanny. But by the time Jan died he had convinced me there was only one place a Jew could ever be at home."

"As a patriotic American," Jason said, "I take exception to that."

"You mean as an ostrich," Yossi interposed. "Tell me, Jason, how many years have Jews lived in America?"

"If I can recall my grade-school history, Peter Stuyvesant let a few into New Amsterdam in the early 1700s."

"Well, don't be so quick to draw conclusions, my boy," Yossi responded. "Jews lived in Germany for more than twice as long as that. And they were just as successful—"

"—And just as integrated," Eva quickly added.

"—That is, until that mad housepainter decided they were infecting Aryan society and should be exterminated. Then suddenly the fact that Heine was a Jew and Einstein was a Jew and most of their orchestras playing Mendelssohn were Jews meant nothing. They had to destroy us. And they almost did."

Jason sat quietly for a moment and tried to tell himself that this was merely the propaganda that every visitor to Israel received.

Besides, he'd been brought up to think that there was another way the Jews could save themselves from the pogroms and persecutions of their long and painful history. His father's way. Assimilation.

And yet, after the first week of orange picking by day and debates throughout the night, he still felt no desire to leave. In fact, it was only when reminded that Dov Levi would be returning from reserve duty and would want his bed back that Jason realized he had to make some sort of plans.

"Listen," Yossi reasoned, "I'm not asking you to spend your lifetime here. But if you want to stay the summer, I can put you in a bungalow with six or seven other volunteers. What do you say?"

"I think that's fine," said Jason.

He sat down and wrote his parents:

> Dear Mom and Dad,
>
> I'm sorry I've been so uncommunicative since our phone call, but my whole world has suddenly fallen apart.
>
> Next month was supposed to be the wedding. I feel such aching sadness that the only solace I can find is staying near the place she died.
>
> Also, I need time to think about what I want to do with the rest of my life. Losing Fanny has changed me a great deal. I seem somehow to feel less of the ambition I once had to go out and become a big "success"—whatever that means.
>
> The attitude on this kibbutz is catching. Sure, some of the young men want to be doctors or professors. But when most of them have finished their studies they'll come back and share what they've learned with the community.
>
> It's curious that among all the people I've met here, there's not one whose aim in life is to be famous. They just want to live in peace and quiet and take pleasure from the real joys of life. Like hard work. And kids. And friendship.
>
> I wish I could say that my mind is tranquil, but it isn't. Grief is not the only thing I feel. There's something primitive in me still crying out for vengeance. I know that's wrong, but I can't exorcise these feelings yet.

So I've decided to spend the summer as a volunteer working side by side with the rest of the kibbutzniks.

Since I can handle firearms I'll also take a regular turn at guard duty. And if a terrorist is crazy enough to try to attack this place again, he'll sorely regret it.

Anyway, thanks for letting me work all this out for myself.

Your loving son,
Jason

From the *Harvard Alumni Bulletin* of June 1963:

Theodore Lambros received his Ph.D. in Classics at mid-year's. The Harvard University Press will publish his revised dissertation, under the title of *Tlemosyne: The Tragic Hero in Sophocles*. This fall he will join the Classics Faculty as an Instructor.

ANDREW ELIOT'S DIARY

June 25, 1963

I called up Lambros to congratulate him on fulfilling his dream—making it to the faculty of Harvard. This in addition to getting a book accepted for publication. The guy's an absolute rocket.

He kind of downplayed it, telling me that an instructorship is not that big a thing, and that the real challenge is whether or not they give you tenure. But the guy's in such a hurry. I know he's going to make it all the way. I just wish he wouldn't be so overanxious.

Then Sara took the phone to congratulate *me*.

I protested that credit ought to go to Faith. I mean, all I did was get home on time from the office one evening to sort of start things going. She carried little Andy for nine months.

Sara was keen to discuss diapers and breast-feeding and all kinds of maternal stuff. Which leads me to believe that she and Ted have got procreative inclinations. It makes sense. He's reached the point in his life where he can be proud of what he's accomplished. And that's the time to start a family.

When Faith was preg, we splurged and bought a big house outside Stamford. It's an easy commute for me. Indeed, since I'm now involved in IPO's—otherwise known as underwriting—at Downs, Winship, I can sometimes use the commuting time to arm-twist an old school or college buddy from another institution on the Street into joining us in financing a new issue.

I've learned a good deal about banking in the past few years. There is some technical stuff but a lot depends on getting along with other preppies over lunch at their Wall Street clubs.

There's nothing difficult for me in that, and so I've not been kicked out yet. In fact, just the other day, one of the vice-presidents told me to "keep up the good work."

I don't know how I can possibly improve, unless I have two lunches a day.

I like marriage. It's not only enjoyable, it's efficient from the point of view of time and motion. All the bachelors in my office are preoccupied with where their next date is coming from. While I know that after a hard day of being likable, when I get off the train and drive eleven minutes, there'll be a great-looking blonde waiting to greet me with the driest martini in Connecticut. I mean, you can't get any closer to bliss than that, can you?

Naturally, we go to all the Harvard football games, following the whole ritual from tailgate picnics before to cocktail parties after. Sometimes I even stay in New York after work and watch films of the previous Saturday's game at the Harvard Club. And then sit around with the guys discussing what we did wrong.

Faith doesn't mind. She's a great kid that way.

Actually, I dream of taking my son along to the game someday. He'll be the Harvard Class of '84.

I know that the most interesting thing that's happened to me in my whole life is becoming a father.

Of course, there's not much for me to do yet. In fact, we've got this great English nanny, so there's not much for Faith to do, either. But I really look forward to talking to Andy, teaching him how to swim and play ball, and having him—for a while at least, I hope—look up to me with respect.

And I'll try to spare him all the pressures of the "Eliot tradition."

I talk to him already. Sometimes I sneak into his room when the nanny's not around and say stupid things like, "Hey, old buddy, why don't we two slip down to Cronin's for a few beers?"

I think he smiles at this, so maybe he understands more than I imagine.

All in all, my life seems to be "a fun thing."

I'm bullish on the future.

On the first Sunday in July, the kibbutz volunteers arrived at Vered Ha-Galil, and Jason moved into the small barracks that had been set aside for them. They were from Scandinavia, France, and England, as well as the United States and Canada. Almost all were younger than he. And surprisingly, many were Christian.

They rose at 5:00 A.M. and, with few complaints, worked in the orange groves till 8:00. Then after breakfast when the others returned to the fields, they went to the classroom for elementary language instruction. Even though he felt like their grandfather, Jason tagged along.

But in the evenings while the others partied, he would work alone in the kibbutz garage repairing and tuning their vehicles. What had once been a pleasant hobby was now a necessary activity. To keep him from thinking.

Since the kibbutz was not a religious one, on the Sabbath they piled the volunteers into their ramshackle bus and bounced them over the countryside on endless excursions.

As one of the English teachers, Eva was in charge of the descriptive aspects of these expeditions. One was to the mountain fortress of Masada, overlooking the Dead Sea. Here, in the first century A.D., a small band of Jewish Zealots withstood a two-year siege by the Roman legions. And when they were finally on the verge of defeat, chose to take their own lives rather than become slaves.

Eva gave her little explanatory briefing, while all about them archaeologists—including hundreds of summer volunteers—continued to excavate the site.

"This remnant of old Israel," she began, "has become a

rallying symbol for us. It shows our determination never again to surrender to an oppressor."

Jason looked over the stone walls at the plain below and imagined what it must have been like for the outnumbered Zealots to see the heavily armed enemy swarming below them. God, they had courage, he thought.

But then, they had nowhere to go.

If Masada had been uplifting, their next tour was devastating.

They visited Yad Va-Shem, the memorial in Jerusalem dedicated to the six million victims of the Holocaust.

On the floor of the darkened building were plaques naming the many concentration camps in which the victims had perished. The magnitude of the catastrophe was almost too monstrous to contemplate.

The flame burning in eternal commemoration of those wretched martyrs seemed pitifully small. Yet indestructibly bright.

Eva dwelt on this theme during the solemn bus ride home.

"Compared to the many who died, there are few of us here to keep that flame alive," she said. "I don't think anyone can understand what this country means until they have seen what we saw today."

The Sea of Galilee glowed with the rays of the setting sun as the bus journey neared its conclusion. For nearly an hour all had ridden in total silence. Then Jonathan, an American volunteer, spoke out.

"Eva, something's always bothered me. Whenever I try to discuss the Holocaust with my gentile friends back home, they always ask the same question— Why did they go so passively to the gas chambers? Why didn't they fight back?"

There was a slight stirring among the passengers in the bus as they strained forward to hear how Eva would reply.

"There were some who fought, Jonathan. Like the brave resisters in the Warsaw ghetto who gave the Nazis a battle to the very end. But it is true that not enough were like that. And there is an explanation.

"When the world found out—and believe me, everyone, including your own President Roosevelt, knew—that Hitler meant to destroy all the Jews of Europe, countries did not throw open their gates and offer them sanctuary. On the contrary, I could tell you terrible stories about shiploads of escapees being turned away and sent back to Germany.

"And when the Jews realized that there was nowhere in the world they could go, a great many despaired. They had no will to fight because they had nothing to fight *for*."

There was silence for a moment. Then a young Danish girl raised her hand and asked, "Do you think it is possible such a thing could happen again?"

"No," Eva replied. "Never. And what makes me so sure is what you see outside the window. The Jews at last have a country of their own."

"That was quite a speech you gave," Jason remarked to Eva as they were strolling after dinner. It was a late-summer evening, the air heavy with the scent of flowers.

"Did it make sense to you?" she asked.

"Yes," he replied. "In fact, it was very upsetting."

"Which part?" she asked.

"Well, your intimation that a Jew will never be fully accepted anywhere but here. That's not what I've been brought up to believe."

"Forgive me," she replied, "but my family was as Dutch as yours is American. Still when the war came, it was amazing how quickly we became Jews and aliens."

"My father thinks otherwise."

She looked up at him and said with quiet fervor, "Then your father has learned nothing from the history of his people." And she quickly added, "I'm sorry if that sounded impolite."

"That's okay," he answered sincerely. "But I grew up believing that America is special. A place where everyone really is equal—like it says in our Constitution."

"Do you still believe that?"

"Sort of," he said, temporarily forgetting some of the minor setbacks he'd experienced because of his heritage.

"May I ask you something?"

"Sure."

"Could you ever be elected President of the United States?"

He hesitated and then replied, "No."

She smiled. "The difference is—you *could* be elected President of Israel."

*   *   *

By the middle of August, Jason had a rudimentary knowledge of the Hebrew language. He also had a collection of increasingly urgent letters from his parents inquiring when exactly he
intended to return. He could not reply because he was still unable
to decipher his own emotions.

Did he, in fact, want to go back to law school at all? Did he
want to leave Israel?

Finally, he came to a decision. He waited up past midnight,
when there was a better chance of getting a clear connection to
the States, and phoned his parents.

"Look," he explained, trying to sound both cheerful and
rational, "I think I'd like to hold off going back to school for a
while."

"Son," his father pleaded, "you've never let me down before.
Can't you pull yourself together and get over this? You've got a
brilliant life ahead of you."

"Look, Dad," he answered patiently, "I'm a grown-up now.
I'm making decisions for myself."

"Jason, this isn't fair. I gave you the best of everything."

"Dad, you did give me the best. But I'm not sure you gave
me everything."

When he hung up and walked out of the secretary's office, he
saw Eva seated at one of the long tables in the empty dining hall.
He went over and sat down next to her.

"Want a lemonade?" she asked.

"I'd prefer a beer."

She got him a bottle from the kitchen and sat down again.
"So who won?"

"It was a split decision," Jason replied. "Let's just say we
both lost."

"Are you staying?"

"For the next year, anyway. I mean, I might as well finish
learning the language, right? Maybe I'll become the George Keller
of Israel."

"I don't understand," she said. "What is a George Keller?"

"A crazy Hungarian and my Harvard classmate."

"From what you've told me so far, all your Harvard classmates are crazy."

"That's true," he smiled back, "and the proof of it is that

here I am, First Marshal of my class, potential U.S. senator, picking oranges in the north of a little Middle Eastern country."

"On the contrary," said Eva lightheartedly, "that proves you're the only sane one."

For the first time in his life Jason Gilbert became an academic grind.

With Eva's help he found the most intensive Hebrew-teaching *Ulpan* in the country. It was at Tel Aviv University, intended for high-powered professionals who needed to master the language quickly.

There were four hours of instruction in the morning, a lunch break, and then another four in the afternoon. After which he would run on the university track, then go back to his room in Beit Brodetsky and study until he could keep awake no longer. The only rest he took was from nine to nine-thirty to watch *Mabat,* the news broadcast on television.

After a month and a half of this self-inflicted torture, he was heartened to find that he could actually understand what was happening in the outside world.

S ara Lambros was awakened by muffled sounds from the other room. She squinted sleepily at the bedside clock. It was just after 6:00 A.M.

"Ted, what the hell are you doing?"

"Getting dressed, honey. Sorry I disturbed you."

"Do you know what the time is?"

"Yeah, I'd better hurry."

"But where are you going at this hour?"

"The Square. Gotta get to the newsstand before any of the students are up."

"What on earth for?"

Ted came back into the bedroom. He was unshaven, dressed sloppily in a grungy army-surplus jacket with a woolen cap.

"Are you going out like that? You look like a bum."

"Great, Sara. That's the whole point. It's absolutely crucial that nobody recognizes me buying the *Confy Guide*."

Sara sat up laughing.

"Is that it? Come on, Ted. You know everybody on the faculty reads it."

"I know, I know. But have you ever actually seen one in a professor's hands?"

"No. And I'll be damned if I can figure out how they get a hold of it. I've a strong suspicion they might send their wives. And I'll gladly shill for you during my lunch hour."

"God, no, I can't wait that long. I've gotta know the verdict. I'm going now."

He kissed her quickly on the cheek and headed out. As he strode rapidly toward Harvard Square he began to sweat. After all, this was September, the first day of the new term. And he was dressed for the middle of winter.

Out of the corner of his eye he could see the huge pile of shiny black-covered magazines. They had probably just been delivered. First he glanced left and right to make sure the coast was clear. Then he casually picked up a *New York Times* and swiftly snatched a copy of *The Harvard Crimson Confidential Guide to Student Courses*, immediately burying it in the paper. Having carried the exact change in his hand, he quickly paid and was off.

Unable to bear the tension of the journey home, he hastened around the kiosk into one of the telephone booths. He pulled out the magazine, his fingers nervously groping for the classics evaluations.

First he looked at Greek A. It was an auspicious start: "Dr. Lambros is a marvelous guide through the intricacies of this difficult language. He makes what could be a boring task an absolute delight."

Then Latin 2A: "Students taking this course will be well advised to opt for Dr. Lambros's section. He is arguably the liveliest teacher in the department."

He closed the book, shoved it back into the *Times,* and let out an inner whoop of joy. By that afternoon everybody at Harvard would have—just as clandestinely—read those student critiques.

He was made in the shade. If there had been any doubt of his being promoted to assistant professor that spring, this would dispel it. All those hours he'd spent in preparation had not been in vain.

Wait till Sara sees this.

He left the phone booth and began a homeward sprint. Suddenly a familiar voice hailed him.

"Theodore."

He skidded to a stop and whirled to see that it was John Finley, who—what rotten luck—was probably taking his early-morning constitutional.

"Uh—hello, Professor Finley. I—uh—was just jogging on the river to get fit for the new term."

"Splendid, splendid," the great man replied. "Don't let me interrupt you."

"Thanks, sir," Ted blurted and whirled again to escape.

"Oh, and, Ted," Finley called after him, "congratulations on your marvelous reviews."

November 23, 1963

I don't think I'll ever be the same after yesterday. The newspapers are calling what happened in Dallas a "Greek tragedy," but to me it's an American tragedy. In fact, it's something I feel so closely that I would almost call it a death in the family.

I think everybody—rich and poor, black and white, but especially those of us who had so identified with him because he was young and a Harvard man—is stunned by Jack Kennedy's assassination.

Here we were just getting set for the upcoming Harvard-Yale game, half-expecting the President himself to show up at the last minute in an army helicopter, and the next thing we know he's dead.

I'm not alone in looking up to him as some kind of gallant knight. He had a kind of aura that changed the atmosphere of the whole country. He made us feel proud. Dynamic. Full of hope. It looked like the beginning of a new and glorious chapter in our history.

But what really shakes me is that he was killed for no apparent reason. Here was a guy whose ship had been torpedoed in the war and who not only survived but saved one of his crewmen as well. If he had died defending some principle, it might have at least made some sense.

I think from today my whole generation will change its outlook on life. I doubt if success can mean the same to any of them.

Look—Kennedy won every prize. The sweet fruition of an earthly crown. And yet they'll bury him with fully half a life still left unlived.

D anny Rossi was in Tanglewood when he learned that
Maria had given birth to a
girl.

He was, of course, planning to be at her bedside and had
merely flown off for twenty-four hours to conduct a single concert.
But little Sylvie (they had discussed names in advance) decided to
arrive early.

Mr. and Mrs. Pastore were already with Maria when Danny
entered the hospital room bearing armfuls of flowers.

He exchanged hugs with them, kissed the glowing mother,
whispered a few affectionate words in her ear, and hurried to the
neonatal ward to peer through the large glass pane at his new
daughter.

At first he could not find her. By an unconscious reflex his
eyes kept glancing at the cots with blue blankets. At last a helpful
nurse picked Sylvie up and brought her to the window. Now he
could see traces of Maria—and of himself—in her features.

"Even better than creating a symphony, eh, Mr. Rossi?"

It was their obstetrician, who happened to be passing by on
his rounds.

"Oh yes," Danny quickly agreed as he shook the doctor's
hand. "Thanks for everything. Maria says you were great."

"My pleasure. And don't worry, you'll get used to it."

"What?"

"Having a daughter. Most men secretly want boys—at least
the first time. But I know Sylvie will bring you a great deal of
happiness."

Danny thought about the doctor's words and felt relieved.
During the flight home he had been unable to suppress the tinges
of disappointment that Maria had not produced a son. He had

hoped for an heir to continue the musical tradition he was establishing. After all, there were so few world-class women pianists. And the only time a female got to lead musicians was when twirling a baton. He had not considered that a girl might become a prima ballerina.

Sylvie was christened three weeks later and the Rossis had two hundred guests to their home for a champagne brunch. The Philadelphia papers published large photographs of their orchestra's popular associate director with his lovely wife and new child. Danny was exhilarated. Being a father seemed to elevate him to a new status.

Yet, something puzzled him. Maria didn't want a nanny. The most she would agree to was a nurse for the first few weeks. After that, she wanted to raise Sylvie on her own.

"Danny, I've spent the last nine months reading books about child care. I don't want some starched-apron biddy telling me I don't know how to be a mother."

"But you'll be exhausted."

"Not if you help a little."

"Sure," he smiled, "but I've got a helluva concert schedule."

"You act as if you're a slave to your own fate. I mean, you don't have to make *so* many guest appearances all over the place, do you?"

How could he make her understand?

"Maria, darling, you know that old chestnut about music being an international language? Well, nowadays it's an international business. I have to do a certain amount of traveling—just to keep up my contacts."

Maria looked at him. Her face grew flushed.

"Danny, I thought marriage would change you. And then when it didn't, I thought at least being a father would. Why the hell can't you grow up?"

"What are you talking about?"

"Why do you keep buzzing around the world like a bee from flower to flower? Do you still need that much adulation? If I'm not enough, there are plenty of local women to worship you."

Danny did not feel compelled to justify the lifestyle of an artist.

"Maria, I assume this whole outburst is just the product of postpartum depression."

Then, realizing he had wounded her, Danny came over and knelt by her side.

"Hey, that was shitty of me to say. Please forgive me. I really love you, Maria. Don't you believe that?"

She nodded. "I just wish it were *only* me."

Scarcely five months later, Maria was pregnant again. And the following year gave birth to a second daughter.

This time, Danny was in New York when she went into labor and made it to the hospital before the child arrived.

By January 1964 Jason had completed his six months of language training in the *Ulpan*. Having exercised the utmost discipline, using English only to write weekly letters to his parents, he found himself reasonably fluent in Hebrew.

The elder Gilberts had exerted frequent epistolary pressure on him to come home for Christmas. Jason had demurred, arguing that his course did not break for anything but the Jewish holidays in September. Now he once again avoided the possibility of returning to the States, even for a short visit, by saying that he was about to undertake "a very important job."

He discussed it with Eva and Yossi—in Hebrew—on his first visit to the kibbutz since the summer.

"I'm going to join the army," he announced.

"Good," the kibbutz secretary exclaimed. "They can use an experienced man like you."

Eva said nothing.

Yossi noticed the stern expression on her face and asked, "What's the matter, aren't you pleased with his decision?"

"I'm glad he's staying," she replied. "But I've a feeling he's doing it for the wrong reason."

"And what may that be?" Jason inquired.

"As a personal vendetta—to revenge Fanny's death."

"I don't care what his reasons are," Yossi retorted defensively. "Besides, doesn't the Bible allow us an eye for an eye?"

"That's primitive and you know it," Eva countered. "It's a metaphor, not to be taken literally."

"The Arabs take it literally," Yossi interposed.

"Hey, let's cut the polemics. Do I have your blessings to enlist or not?" Jason asked.

"Not mine," Eva stated adamantly.

"Well, you have mine," Yossi countered, "and that of your whole kibbutz."

"But I'm not a member of the kibbutz," Jason replied.

"You will be after this week's meeting," the secretary responded. "That is, if you want to."

"Yes. I want very much to belong."

Though it was winter, Jason spent the next weeks in punishing, self-imposed, pre-basic training: getting up early to run in the freezing rain, lifting weights in the primitive kibbutz exercise room, and then running again before dinner.

He spent a lot of time talking to Eva, trying to convince her that his dedication was sincere. And pleading with her to make him less ignorant about the country's history. Sometimes, at night, their conversation tentatively approached the personal.

He asked about her childhood. How it had been during the war with Fanny's family. How she had been able to recover from the trauma of the Holocaust and the discovery that her parents had been slaughtered.

She told him how shattered she had been by the news of her parents' fate. Still, she now felt she had been luckier than most. During the war, she had been blessed with the loving protection of the van der Post family. And afterward the establishment of Israel meant that her children would never suffer as she had.

Her talk of children led Jason to ask hesitantly why she was not married. At first she told him that like so many others, she had emerged from the Holocaust with her emotions deadened. But Jason sensed she was hiding something. And one night Eva told him the truth.

When she was in the army she had known a young officer named Mordechai. They had become very close. He was killed during his last month of active duty. And not by enemy fire, but during a training exercise with live ammunition.

"*I'm* going to come back," Jason assured her, assuaging a fear she had not even dared articulate.

"Oh, I know you will," she said, unconvincingly. "Nobody gets killed working in a clothing depot."

"What makes you think I'm joining the Quartermaster Corps?" he asked.

"I told you," she replied. "I've been in the army. Most

recruits go in at eighteen. A man like you is considered practically senile. You'll be lucky if they don't make you check handbags at the cinemas."

"I was a U.S. Marine," he said, smiling. "I finished training with the fifth highest grade in my battalion. Want to make a bet?"

"You'd lose," she smiled, "because you're about to encounter the best thing in Israel—its army. And the very worst—its bureaucracy."

On a raw February day, Jason Gilbert stepped off the bus at the Kelet, the army induction center just outside Tel Aviv. The camp was large and sprawling, consisting of corrugated-roofed huts, occasional eucalyptus trees, and a series of tents.

Up north at the local army office, he had enlisted for the mid-winter induction and passed a series of preliminary mental and medical tests.

Now he stood on line with another member of the kibbutz, eighteen-year-old Tuvia Ben-Ami, who was manifestly nervous. Not about the army as much as being away from home for the first time.

"Keep calm, Tuvi," said Jason, pointing at the long line of adolescents waiting to be processed. "You're going to find a lot of new friends in this kindergarten."

When the recruits were assigned to small groups, the young kibbutznik practically held on to Jason's belt to ensure they would not be separated.

Then they all went to the "butcher's shop" to have their hair mercilessly sheared. For some of the urban Casanovas, it was the trauma of their lives. Jason had to laugh as he watched them suppress tears as their Elvis-like plumage dropped to the floor.

He in turn simply sat down and let the army lawnmower relandscape his locks.

Then it was time for the dog tags. The dispensing officer suggested that Jason consider changing his name to something more biblical and more patriotic.

"In Hellenistic times, when the Jews all aspired to be sophisticated Greeks, every Jacob changed his name to Jason. Think about that, soldier."

After donning their khakis, they were led by their supervising corporal to the tents where they would be staying for the next three days.

Tuvia whispered to Jason, "You can tell who are kibbutzniks, and who are soft boys from the cities, just by the way they look at the sleeping bags. I think some of them expected feather beds."

After dinner they strolled through the camp to look at the recruiting huts where they would be interviewed for special units. Over one shack a sign boasted THE BRAVE TO THE PARATROOPS.

"That's where I'll be at dawn tomorrow," said Jason.

"You and a thousand others," replied Tuvia, "including me. *Everybody* wants to earn his red beret. And stupid as it sounds, I've got a better chance than you."

"Oh yes? What was your grade at the medical exam last month?"

"Ninety-one," Tuvia answered proudly.

"Well, I got ninety-seven," Jason retorted confidently. "That's the highest they give. And when I asked them about the other three points, they said that Superman isn't Jewish."

"Listen," Tuvia smiled, "even if he were, he couldn't get into the Israeli Paratroops. Because he's too old."

By seven the next morning there were already long lines outside the huts of the elite brigades.

Jason passed his time by doing stretching exercises. At last he was admitted to the tent of the paratroop recruiting officer, a wiry, dark-haired man in his middle thirties.

His first words were hardly encouraging: "Beat it, Yankee. I admire your initiative, but you're over the hill."

"I'm only twenty-seven and I've got two years' military experience."

"Twenty-seven means ten years of you that I've already lost. Send in the next candidate."

Jason folded his arms. "With due respect, I'm not leaving until I get a physical test."

The interviewer stood and leaned his hands on the desk. "Listen, you'd drop dead if you even looked at our training course. Now do I have to throw you out myself?"

"I'm afraid so, sir."

"Fine," he replied, quickly reaching over and grasping Jason's collar with a cross-armed grip.

Instinctively the ex-marine broke the hold with an upward

motion of his clasped hands and then proceeded to pin the officer down onto his desk.

"Please sir," said Jason with extreme politeness. "I beg you to reconsider."

"All right," he gasped, "you'll get a try."

After Jason had left, the interviewer sat rubbing his bruises and wondering whether he should call the Military Police.

No, he thought, let the arrogant bastard collapse on the hills.

"Next!" he shouted hoarsely.

Jason was walking slowly toward the test course when he heard footsteps behind him. He turned and saw that it was Tuvia.

"Well," Jason smiled, "I see you made it, too. Was he rough on you?"

"Not at all. He took one look at my papers, saw we were from the same kibbutz and signed me on. What was all that noise I heard in there?"

"Just two Jews settling a difference of opinion." Jason grinned modestly.

It was only two kilometers but it was all uphill. The candidates had to run in groups of four—carrying telephone poles.

Tuvia contrived to be in the same quartet as Jason. But, as they were ascending the final incline, one of their number collapsed and fell to his knees. The other three men stopped dead in their tracks, barely able to hold the huge pole aloft.

"Come on," Jason encouraged, "you can do it. Just four hundred meters to go."

"I can't," gasped the recruit.

"You've got to," Jason barked. "You'll mess it up for the rest of us. On your goddamn feet!" His tone—more like that of a commanding officer—shocked the young boy into getting up again.

They completed the course and dropped their gigantic burden to the ground, where it sank a few inches into the mid-winter mud.

Jason and Tuvia, who had done most of the lifting for the other two, struggled for breath and massaged their arms.

One of the recruiting officers approached them. "Not bad," he said. And then he pointed to the boy who'd fallen. "You'd better go back to the infantry, son. The others can stay on for further testing."

He looked at Jason. "Okay, grandpa," he grinned, "are you ready to go again?"

"Right away?" Jason asked, quickly masking his incredulity. "Uh, sure, as soon as you like. The same course?"

"Yes, the same course. The same log. But this time with me on top."

At the end of two hours they were, like Gideon's army, a small but select group.

"All right," the officer barked. "If you thought today was difficult, I suggest you try another brigade. This was child's play compared to what's coming. So think it over. You may save yourself a nervous breakdown. Dismissed."

Jason and Tuvia staggered back to their tent and flopped down onto their mattresses.

"You were the gutsiest one out there," Tuvia said. "I saw the officers watching you. They were smiling like hell. You were so great that I'm going to share my most precious possession with you."

Jason felt something being forced into his hand. He looked. It was half a bar of Swiss chocolate.

Twenty-four hours later, candidates for the Paratroop Brigade were loaded into a bus to be taken to the base at Tel Noff. During the journey, a man moved down the aisle and stopped in front of Jason. It was the paratroop recruiting officer.

"Hello, grandpa," he said. "I'm surprised to see you're still with us. But I warn you, you won't stop running for the next six months."

"That's okay, sir," Jason replied.

"And another thing, don't call me 'sir.' My name is Zvi."

All Jason remembered of the next six months was that he even ran in his dreams.

On his first twenty-four-hour leave, he hitched a ride to Vered Ha-Galil. He was happy to see Eva, who understood that what he needed most was sleep.

When he finally awoke she had some news for him.

"Your father's been phoning. I told him where you were, and he sounded distraught. He made me promise to have you call the moment I saw you."

Jason got up, went to the kibbutz phone, and called his father collect.

"Look, son," the elder Gilbert remonstrated, "I've been pretty patient with you, but this army business is going a bit too far. I want you to get back where you belong. That's an order."

"Father, I only take orders from my commanding officer. As far as being where I belong, that's a personal matter."

"What about your career? What about everything you trained for at Harvard?"

"Father, if Harvard taught me one thing, it was to find my own set of values. I feel needed here. I feel useful. I feel good. What the hell else is there in life?"

"Jason, I want you to promise me to see a psychiatrist."

"I'll tell you what, Dad. I'll visit a shrink if you'll visit Israel. Then we'll all sit down and decide which of us is crazy."

"All right, Jason, I don't want to argue anymore. Just promise you'll call whenever you can."

"Sure, Dad. I promise. Love to Mom."

"We miss you, son. We really miss you."

"Me too, Dad," he answered softly.

Jason was among the fifty percent who survived the ordeal and received their wings and red berets.

He immediately entered the advanced course, mastering techniques of helicopter assaults and learning every inch of the country's topography. Not from a map. During the next six months, he covered every inch of the Holy Land on foot. He began to enjoy sleeping in the open air.

After that he spent a week at the kibbutz, taking long walks with Eva, and writing a lengthy letter to his parents. Then he entered the Officers' Candidate School near Petach Tikva. There, the only thing he learned that he did not already know was the Israeli principle of leadership, which could be summed up in two words: "Follow me." Officers lead all missions from the front.

Eva and Yossi came to the graduation ceremony and saw Jason parade by the chief of staff and salute. Standing right next to the commander was Zvi, his original recruiting officer. As Jason passed, he was whispering something into the general's ear.

"I guess the nickname's going to stick," Jason said when he joined them later. "Now everybody calls me *saba*—'grandpa.' "

*   *   *

As they were driving back to the kibbutz, Yossi asked Jason how he intended to spend his ten days of freedom before active duty.

"I want to go back and look at every inch of ground I marched over," he replied. "Only this time I want to do it with a car . . . and a guide."

"The Bible is the best thing for that," Yossi offered.

"I know," said Jason. And then added shyly, "but I was hoping Eva would be my tour leader."

In the days that followed, they covered four thousand years of history. From King Solomon's mines deep in the Sinai, up through the stark desert of the Negev to Beersheba, home of Abraham, Isaac, and Jacob.

Then to Ein Gedi, the lowest point on earth, where they swam—or rather floated—in the buoyant, salty Dead Sea. Then up through Qumran, in whose caves the Dead Sea Scrolls were discovered. And Jericho, whose walls had tumbled to the blasts of Joshua's trumpets, and whose balsam gardens had been given as a gift by Anthony to Cleopatra.

And finally, Jerusalem, the city conquered by King David ten centuries before Christ, and still the spiritual capital of the world.

Its very stones exuded a kind of holiness that even Jason could somehow feel. They were not able to visit the remains of the holy Temple of Solomon as it was on the Jordanian side of the divided city.

"We'll get to see it some day," Eva said, "when there's peace."

"Will we live that long?" asked Jason.

"*I* intend to," Eva replied. And then added, "And even if I don't, my children will."

During the entire journey, Jason and Eva had slept within a few feet of each other. First outdoors in the Negev, now in a cheap hostel. Yet, their only physical contact was when he helped her climb a rock or a monument.

Spending days and nights in such spiritual proximity had created a bond between them. And yet their friendship remained platonic.

Toward the end of their first day in Jerusalem, Jason told Eva he was going to the YMCA on King George Street to try to pick up a game of tennis. She said she would take a walk and meet him later for dinner.

It did not occur to her that he had not brought a racket along. She herself was too preoccupied with wanting to make a personal visit.

The afternoon shadows were lengthening as she entered the cemetery on Emek Refaim and walked slowly toward the area where her childhood friend was buried. A hundred yards from the grave she stopped short.

Jason was already there, standing motionless, his head bowed. Even from a distance she could see he was crying.

She turned and walked silently off, deferring her grief to his.

F rom the "Class Notes" section of the *Harvard Alumni Bulletin* of October 1965:

1958

Born: to **Theodore Lambros** and **Sara Harrison Lambros** (Radcliffe '58), a son, Theodore Junior, on September 6, 1965. Lambros has recently been promoted to Assistant Professor of Classics at Harvard.

October 12, 1965

Ironic, isn't it? Just as Ted and Sara, my Ideal Couple, are reaching new heights of marital bliss with the birth of their first child, I am becoming a statistic.

Much to the delight and profit of the legal profession, Faith and I are divorcing.

Although it isn't in anger, it is with what you might call a lot of deeply held indifference. It seems that she never really thought that being married to me was "a fun thing." Our lawyers are citing "irreconcilable differences," but that's because the fact that Faith finds being out here "an utter bore" is not sufficient grounds for divorce.

Actually, I can't see how she could say her life in the country was dull. She was having so many affairs that her schedule must have bordered on the hectic.

When I first started to suspect that she was branching out into the realm of extramarital dalliance, I was worried what my friends would think. I shouldn't have. She was having flings with almost all of them.

In some ways I wish I had never found any of this out. Because frankly, I didn't realize anything was really wrong. I mean, our weekends were pleasant enough. And she seemed to be enjoying herself. But, unfortunately, one of my buddies at The Lunch Club thought it his duty as a fellow Harvardman to let me know, in so many words, that I was the laughing stock of southern Connecticut.

On that all-too-short train ride home, I tried to figure out a way to broach the whole thing with Faith. But when she met me at the door, I didn't have the guts to confront her.

Hell, I kept telling myself, maybe it isn't true. And so I went through the motions of drinks and dinner and going to bed. Still, I was awake all night, my heart pounding, wondering what to do.

Finally I understood what was behind my Hamlet-like hesitation. It was not really any doubt of her infidelity. I noticed in retrospect how cozy she had been with so many of the guys at the club during those weekend dances.

What was shaking me to the core was the fact that I knew I'd be losing the children.

I mean, no matter how promiscuous you prove the woman to be, the court inevitably gives her custody. And I can't bear the thought of not being able to come back at night and hear little Andy shout, "Daddy's home" as if I were king of the universe. Or to be there when Lizzie speaks her first sentence.

Not only have they given meaning to my life, but I've discovered that being a father is actually something I do pretty well.

I grew so desperate thinking about all this, that at around 4:00 A.M. I had the wild notion of grabbing both kids and rushing off in the car somewhere. But, of course, that wouldn't have solved anything.

The next morning I called in sick (which was not a total lie), so I could have it all out with Faith. She didn't deny anything. I actually think she wanted me to know. She certainly said a very quick "yes" when I asked her whether she wanted a divorce.

I inquired when it was exactly that she had discovered she didn't love me anymore. She replied that she *never* actually had been in love with me but had, at one time, merely *thought* she was.

Now, having discovered that she was wrong, she deemed it best that we separate. I told her it was pretty irresponsible to have two kids with a guy she didn't really like.

To which she retorted, "That's what I can't stand about you, Andrew. You're such a sentimental drip."

She asked if I wouldn't mind packing a bag and moving out that morning, as she had a very busy day. I retorted that I damn well did mind, and I would stay until Andy got home from nursery school so I could talk to him. She told me to suit myself as long as I was out of the house by dinnertime.

As I mindlessly threw some shirts and ties together in a suitcase, I wondered how the hell you explain to a four-year-old why Daddy is going away. I know you're not supposed to lie to kids. But saying, "Mummy doesn't love me," seemed hardly conducive to the health of his psyche.

By the time the nanny brought him home, I had cooked up a

story about having to live in New York to be nearer my work. That he shouldn't worry, I would be out to see him and Lizzie every weekend. And I was sure we could still spend the summer together in Maine. Or at least part of it.

I watched the expression on his little face when I recounted this fiction. And I could see that he understood the truth. It broke my heart. Even at four, my son was disappointed that I couldn't be totally honest with him.

"Can I come with you, Daddy?" he pleaded.

My entire soul ached to steal him. But I told him he'd miss school. And his friends. And now he had to be a good boy and take care of his baby sister.

He promised and—I suspect, to make it easier on me—didn't cry as he watched me toss my bag into the car to drive to New York. He just stood at the doorway and quietly waved.

Kids are smarter than we think. Which is why we end up hurting them so much.

When the Pulitzer Prizes for 1967 were announced, there was particular joy in the Harvard University news office. While it was hardly novel that two Harvard men won awards in the same year, it was rare—if not a first—that two members of the same class were simultaneously honored.

This was a nice little tidbit they could get out over the wires. For the year's prizewinner for poetry was Stuart Kingsley '58, and the recipient for music the already much-honored Danny Rossi of the same rich vintage.

In fact, the two classmates had not known each other at college. Stuart Kingsley spent his years at Harvard as an almost-invisible figure in Adams House. His powerful verse in the *Advocate* occasionally elicited praise from the reviewers of the *Crimson*.

Indeed, until the morning he received the phone call from the Pulitzer Committee, Stuart had continued to live in relative obscurity. He and his wife, Nina (Bryn Mawr '61), and their two kids lived in a high-ceilinged, slightly seedy apartment on Riverside Drive near Columbia, where he taught creative writing.

What excited Stu almost as much as the prize itself was the prospect of finally meeting his illustrious classmate at the award ceremony.

"Think of it, Nina," he enthused, "I might actually get my picture taken with Danny Rossi."

But then to his chagrin, Stuart learned that there was no Pulitzer award ceremony. That phone call and your picture in *The New York Times* was *it*.

"What the hell," Nina said to dispel her husband's disappointment. "I'll throw you the biggest damn party you've ever seen. Taylor's New York State champagne will flow like seltzer."

He hugged her. "Thanks, I'd like that. I don't think I've ever really been the subject of a party."

"Listen honey, if you want to meet Danny Rossi so badly, I'll gladly invite him."

"Yeah," he replied with a sardonic smile, "I'm sure he'd love to come."

Nina grabbed him by the shoulders. "Now you listen to me, kid. I haven't seen this *Savanarola* ballet Rossi's won for, but I'm sure it didn't hurt that it was choreographed by George Balanchine. Anyway, it would have to be damn good to be on a level with your *Collected Poems*. So if you don't mind my saying it, the honor would be his."

"It doesn't matter, Nina. In New York it isn't so much talent that matters as image. And Danny's got so much charisma. . . ."

"Oh, for God's sake, Stu, that's just hype from a press agent's office. Frankly, the only thing Rossi's got over you is a few locks of flashy red hair."

"Yeah," Stu smiled, "and a few million bucks. I'm telling you the guy's a real star."

Nina looked at him with indulgent affection. "You know why I love you so much, Stu? Because you're the only genius I know who suffers from the opposite of megalomania."

"Thanks, honey," he replied, gathering up his notes and stuffing them into his briefcase. "But you'd better cut this ego-boosting short, or I'll be late for my four-o'clock seminar. See you around seven. We can throw a party just for us."

When he returned, she had a surprise for him.

"Really, Nina? Are you serious?"

"Yes, my dearest. You are actually having lunch with your 'charismatic' classmate at one tomorrow in the Russian Tea Room. By the way, you may be stunned to learn he's looking forward to meeting *you*."

"How did you reach him?"

"Oh, I just had an apocalyptic notion. I left a message with the Hurok office and about ten minutes later he called back."

"Nina, you're terrific. It will be some occasion."

"Yes, Stuart," she said lovingly. "For him."

*   *   *

The Russian Tea Room, on Fifty-seventh Street, scarcely an octave's distance from Carnegie Hall, is a favorite New York haunt of the international music and literary set. Until this afternoon, Stuart Kingsley had known it only by reputation. Now he stood nervously at the entrance, scanning the tables to catch sight of Danny Rossi.

At one point he nodded to what he thought was an old friend. The balding, bespectacled chap gave him the most tenuous of acknowledgments and then turned away. It took another second for Stuart to realize that he had mistakenly greeted Woody Allen.

He did not commit the same gaffe when he perceived Rudolf Nureyev holding forth to a table of worshipful balletomanes. He merely smiled inwardly at the prospect of being so close to such living legends.

At last he spied his classmate. When their glances met, Danny waved him over to a corner booth, its table covered with yards of music paper.

"I see you don't like to waste even a second," Stuart remarked jovially as they shook hands.

"No, you're right. I have an unfortunate tendency to overcommit myself. And you can't deliver a 'July Fourth Suite' on Christmas Eve, can you?"

After Danny ordered *blinis* for them both, they ran the gamut of do-you-know, and discovered they had many friends in common among the artistic community of The Class.

"Do you get up from Philadelphia very often?" Stuart asked.

"At least once a week, unfortunately. It's gotten so that I've had to rent a studio in the Carnegie Hall Apartments."

"Must be kind of hard on your wife," Stuart offered, unable to imagine having to spend a single day away from his beloved Nina.

"Yeah," Danny replied, "but Maria's pretty involved with the kids." He then quickly changed the subject. "You know, I was almost as happy for your prize as I was for mine. I've always admired your stuff."

"You've read my poetry?"

"Stuart," Danny answered with a smile, "you publish regularly in the *New Yorker*. That's my favorite airplane reading. So I don't think I've ever missed a poem you've had in there."

"My wife's not going to believe this," Stuart murmured half under his breath. And then aloud, "What are you writing at the moment, Danny? I mean besides what we're using for a tablecloth."

"That's just it, Stuart. I'm staring to feel somewhat hemmed in on the composition front. That's why this whole meeting with you is a kind of kismet. Have you ever thought of writing lyrics for a musical?"

"Do you want to know something?" Stuart confessed. "It's not only been my secret dream, I've actually been playing around with a specific idea for a couple of years. It's based on a kind of highbrow book, though."

"Nothing wrong with that," Danny responded warmly. "I wouldn't be interested in doing another *Hello, Dolly!* What masterpiece of world literature do you have in mind?"

"Would you believe James Joyce's *Ulysses?*"

"Wow, that's a sensational idea. But do you think it's really do-able?"

"Listen," Stu answered, his creative juices now really flowing, "I'm so steeped in that damn book that if you had the time I could lay the libretto right out on this table. But I suppose you've got a fiendishly busy schedule."

Danny stood up in the middle of Stu's apology and said casually, "Order us some more coffee while I go reorchestrate my agenda."

All afternoon Danny listened spellbound as his classmate cascaded with ideas. Naturally, they couldn't cram Joyce's whole epic novel into two hours of stage time. But they could concentrate on the "Nighttown" episode, when the protagonist, Leopold Bloom, wanders through various exotic parts of the city.

There were infinite possibilities for musical invention. Only one significant change was needed. In Stuart's words, "Our only concession to commercialism."

All they would have to do was translate the locale from Joyce's Dublin to New York. Stuart even had exciting ideas for specific scenes and songs. But it was growing late and they'd have to put this off for a second meeting.

"I think we're already a little pregnant, Stuart," he commented. "If you're free tomorrow, I'll be glad to stay over in New York so we can keep going."

"I've got no classes. What time do you want to start?" Stuart responded eagerly.

"Well, if you can make it to my studio as early as, say, eight, I'll provide lots of cups of disgusting but strong Nescafé."

"You're on," said Stu as he stood up. He glanced at his watch. "Gosh, it's nearly five o'clock. Nina'll think I've been hit by a bus. I'd better call and tell her I'm okay."

"Is it really that late?" asked Danny. "I'd better scramble, or I'll have one hell of an angry guest waiting outside my apartment."

After their second meeting the two were ecstatic.

They had worked through the day, even chatting as they munched the sandwiches Danny ordered from the Carnegie Deli.

After eight hours of feverish symbiotic creativity, they had not only a broad outline of both acts, but at least half-a-dozen song suggestions and a place pinpointed for a ballet sequence.

Most of all, they shared the common euphoria that when the curtain fell on Bloom parting with young Stephen Dedalus, there would not be a dry eye in the house. Or a single prize they wouldn't win.

Danny suggested that if they spent a lot of concentrated time together, they could finish the whole thing very quickly. He proposed they rent adjacent houses on Martha's Vineyard for the summer. Then they could bring their families along and—if they could snare a producer—have the show ready to go into rehearsal just after Christmas.

There was only one difficulty. And Stuart approached it with some diffidence.

"Uh, Dan, a house on the Vineyard is—uh—a little out of my budget."

"No sweat. With what we've got already, I'm sure we can find a producer willing to give us a healthy advance. But first we've got to get somebody to represent the property. Do you have an agent?"

"Poets don't have agents, Danny. I'm just lucky to have a wife who's not afraid to talk on the phone."

"Then why don't I ask around and see who's supposed to be the best for Broadway. That okay with you?"

"Sure."

"Good. Hey—I've got to really sprint. As the Mad Hatter put it, 'I'm late for a very important date.'"

It was the White Rabbit, thought Stuart Kingsley. But he didn't dare contradict his senior partner.

The next evening, as Stuart and Nina were conscientiously studying an LP of Danny's *Savanarola* ballet, the phone rang. It was the composer himself.

"Hey, Stuart," he said, slightly out of breath, "I'm rushing to catch a plane, so I've got to talk quickly. Ever heard of Harvey Madison?"

"No. Who's he?"

"My informants tell me he's the best theatrical agent in New York. I mean, a guy in Hurok's office said he isn't even ten percent of a human being."

"That's good?" Stu responded with astonishment.

"Good? It's incredible. What you need to negotiate for you is an absolutely heartless shit. And this guy Madison makes Attila the Hun look like Saint Francis of Assisi. What do you think?"

"Well," the poet confessed, "I've always had a soft spot for Saint Francis. But you're the guy that knows the business."

"Great," Danny said, quickly signing off. "I'll call Harvey at his house right now so he can start beating the drums. See you, Stu."

Summer on Martha's Vineyard is always glorious. But if you are the author of a show in progress that is destined for Broadway, it becomes the Island of the Blessed.

Stuart and Nina were invited to numerous star-studded barbecues, celebrity clambakes, and glittering soirées.

Of course, had he been merely a Pulitzer Prize-winning poet, he might not have merited inclusion on the "A-List." But he was also living in one of the most luxurious houses in Vineyard Haven, a sure sign that his balance sheet scanned as well as his verses.

Actually, he had Harvey Madison to thank for his good fortune. For it was their new agent who had set up the fateful meeting with Edgar Waldorf, undisputed king of Broadway producers. It had taken place at the only possible venue for such an encounter—over lunch at '21'.

Stuart, Harvey, and Danny had been waiting for twenty minutes when the rotund, flamboyantly clad producer made his

grand entrance. Before he even sat down, he looked at the composer and lyricist and stated emphatically, "I *love* it."

Stuart was somewhat confused. "But, Mr. Waldorf, we haven't
said a word yet. I mean—"

His polite response was strangled in mid-sentence by the
strong under-the-table grip of Harvey Madison, who then
interposed, "What Edgar means is he adores the concept."

"No, what I adore is the chemistry of the authors. When
Harvey called me about this, I literally frissoned right there in
my office. The thought of two Harvard Pulitzer Prize winners
writing for Broadway is absolutely fab-u-lous. By the way, have
you thought of a title yet?"

Edgar had diplomatically used the plural but was really di-
recting his question to Danny, whom he knew to be worth a lot
of candle power on the marquee.

"Well," the composer replied, "as you know, we've based it
on Joyce's *Ulysses,* just changing the locale to New York—"

"I love it. I love it," Edgar murmured like a countermelody.

"Now, the novel is, in turn, based on Homer's *Odyssey,*"
Danny continued. "And since the essence of our piece is the hero's
trip around the city, we thought we'd call it *Manhattan Odyssey.*"

Edgar pondered for a moment, and popped a shrimp into his
mouth before replying.

"It's good, it's good. My only question is—is it *too* good?"

"How can anything possibly be too good?" Stuart naively
inquired.

"I mean relatively speaking," Edgar responded, deftly back-
tracking. "After all, your average Broadway audience didn't go to
Harvard. I don't think I could fill the theater with enough people
who know what the word *Odyssey* means."

"Please, Mr. Waldorf," Danny disagreed, "it's a common
term in the English language."

At which point Harvey Madison felt it opportune to refocus
the conversation.

"Hey, guys, Edgar's got a sensational idea for a title. Just
wait till you hear it."

The spherical producer waited until the spotlights of all gazes
shone upon him. And then uttered, "Rejoice!"

"What?" asked Danny Rossi.

"Don't you get it? The author's name is James Joyce. We are

bringing his property back. So it's *re*-Joyce. Of course, we'll add an exclamation point after it. And that's it. Fab-u-lous, huh?"

Danny and Stuart exchanged incredulous glances.

"I think it's absolutely brilliant," offered Harvey Madison, instinctively accustomed to praising anything uttered by a potential source of income. "What do you boys think?"

"You might as well call it *Hello, Molly!*" Danny Rossi commented sardonically.

"I like *Manhattan Odyssey*," Stuart said quietly.

"But you just heard Edgar Waldorf—" Harvey Madison interrupted.

"I like *Manhattan Odyssey*, too," Danny echoed.

Then, from an unexpected quarter, came the rather surprising panegyric, "I think *Manhattan Odyssey* is absolutely fabulous. And I, Edgar Waldorf, will be honored to present it."

The producer then proceeded to elicit schedules from the authors, so that he could plan rehearsals, arrange a tour, and book a theater. Hearing that the boys could complete the work this summer if they could be isolated on Martha's Vineyard, he magnanimously offered Stuart the use of his own unhumble abode on that island.

"Oh, I couldn't, Mr. Waldorf."

"Please, Mr. Kingsley, I insist. Besides, that will help me write the place off for taxes."

Then, without having read a word or heard a note, he went straight to the heart of the matter.

"Who're we going to get to star?"

"I think Zero Mostel would be great as Bloom," Danny offered.

"Not great," replied Waldorf. "Fab-u-lous. His agent's a ballbreaker, but I'll get to work on that monster this afternoon. Oh God, will Zero bring in the theater parties!"

In the midst of his own self-induced rapture, he suddenly chastised himself, "But—"

"But what?" Harvey Madison asked anxiously.

"Zero is great for the party crowd. But we need another name that will draw the out-of-towners. Someone with broader appeal. Is there a woman's part in this thing?"

"Haven't you read it, Mr. Waldorf?" Stuart Kingsley inquired.

"Yeah, sure. I mean, a college girl in my office did me a kind of summary."

"Then you might remember that Bloom's wife, Molly, is a rather important role," said Danny Rossi, muzzling his impatience.

"Of course, of course, a great role," the producer agreed enthusiastically. "So what about Theora Hamilton?"

"Unbelievable," Harvey ejaculated. "That's a genius idea, Edgar. But do you think she'd share the marquee with Zero?"

"You leave that to me," boasted the producer, snapping his fingers. "The First Lady of the American musical theater owes Edgar Waldorf a favor or two, and I'm going to call in my marker."

"Isn't that great, boys?" Harvey bubbled to the authors. "Mostel and Hamilton. Or maybe it'll have to be Hamilton and Mostel. Anyway, they'll be lining up for tickets from here to Hoboken."

"To be honest," Stuart confessed shyly, "I don't think I've ever seen her."

"You'd remember if you had," Danny remarked. "She's got tits like the Goodyear zeppelin. Unfortunately, her talent does not extend as far as her mammaries."

Edgar Waldorf turned ingenuously to Danny Rossi and inquired, "Am I to infer that you do not respect the vocal gifts of Miss Theora Hamilton?"

"I couldn't possibly," Danny replied quietly. "She doesn't have any. Look, Mr. Waldorf, Stuart and I want to write a good show, a classy show, and, yes, a commercial show. But if you have so little faith in our ability to attract an audience without giving them—please excuse my pun—gross titillation, then I think we'd better find another producer."

Harvey Madison coughed uneasily.

But Edgar Waldorf shifted gears as smoothly as a Rolls-Royce.

"Please, Mr. Rossi, let us forget the female lead for the moment and concentrate on what really matters in this enterprise—your two genius talents."

And then he raised his hand in benediction.

"Go, boys. Go off to Martha's Vineyard and create exquisiteness that will dazzle Broadway and that limey bastard from *The New York Times*. Write your masterpiece. Mr. Madison and I will work out the vulgar details."

As he backed off from the table, Edgar bent in what almost

seemed like a curtsy and said, "You boys are giving me the honor of my life."

He then turned and exited to the flourish of invisible trumpets.

Soon thereafter, Harvey Madison departed, leaving the two authors to revel in their success.

"Hey," said Stu, "I've gotta call Nina. Can you wait and we'll walk uptown together?"

"Sorry," Danny replied. "I've got an important matinee in twenty minutes."

"I didn't know you were performing today."

Danny grinned.

"Strictly chamber music, Stu. See the cover of this month's *Vogue?*"

"Not my style of magazine," he replied, still not tuned in to his partner's wavelength.

"Well, check it out at your local newsstand, my friend. She's the guest of honor at my studio this afternoon."

"Oh," said Stuart Kingsley.

E xcept for the occasional cocktail parties, the junior and
senior members of the Harvard
Classics Department almost never socialized. It was not merely a
question of age differences, but the almost Calvinistic distinction
between those who had tenure and those who did not.

Assistant Professor Ted Lambros was therefore surprised when
Cedric Whitman invited him to lunch at the Faculty Club, even
though, as both he and Sara agreed, he was the most humane
humanist they had ever known.

After they ordered, the senior professor cleared his throat
and said, "Ted, I got a phone call from Bill Foster, the new
chairman at Berkeley. His department very much admires your
book and wonders if you'd be interested in their tenure opening
in Greek literature?"

Ted did not know how to respond. For he could not sense
precisely what lay behind the question. Was it an intimation that
he was not going to be granted tenure at Harvard?

"I—uh—I guess I should be very flattered."

"I should say," Whitman replied. "Berkeley's got one of the
best departments in the world. They've certainly got some
very distinguished scholars. Pragmatically speaking, their salaries
are extremely generous. I took the liberty of telling Bill to write
you directly. That'll mean at least a nice invitation to go to
California and lecture."

Ted felt like Aeschylus' famous description of Agamemnon
"struck deep with a mortal blow." But he summoned the courage
to ask.

"Cedric, is this Harvard's way of saying they won't renew
my contract? Please be frank, I can take it."

"Ted," said Whitman without hesitation, "I can't speak for

the whole department. You know that John and I admire you enormously. And naturally, we'd like to keep you here. But this will ultimately come down to a vote, and heaven knows how the historians and archaeologists and people who are less familiar with your work might stand. If you got a formal offer from Berkeley, it might stimulate the uncommitted into feeling more possessive."

"So you think I should at least go out there?"

"Take it from a veteran," his mentor smiled, "an academic never gives up a free trip to anywhere halfway decent. And to California, well, *res ipsa loquitur*."

Sara was delighted to see him.

"What a nice surprise," she said as she skipped down the stone steps of the University Press and saw her husband. He kissed her perfunctorily but could suppress his fears no longer.

"Cedric had some pretty gloomy words at lunch."

"They're not renewing you?"

"That's the bitch of it," he answered with frustration. "He evaded the whole Harvard issue. All he said was that Berkeley wants me for a tenure job."

"Berkeley's got a fantastic classics department," she replied.

Ted's heart stopped. This was not what he had hoped to hear.

"So you think it's the ax, huh?" he asked mournfully. When she did not reply, he added, "I really thought I had a shot at tenure here."

"Hell, so did I," she answered honestly. "But you know how their system works. They almost never bring up someone through the ranks. They sort of send them off and see what kind of a reputation they build up. And if they grow, they pluck them back."

"But it's in California," Ted complained.

"So what? Can't we survive three thousand miles away from Harvard?"

Two nights later, Bill Foster called and formally tendered the invitation to lecture. They agreed on a date close to Harvard's Easter vacation.

"We don't usually do this," he added, "but we'd like to

include your wife as well. The folks at U.C. Press would like to meet her."

"Uh—that's great," said Ted, while inwardly he thought, They know all about me. I'm like a baseball player being traded. They've gone over my hitting and fielding—and probably even my team spirit. It intensified the feeling that, in some way, he had failed.

On the last Sunday in March, Ted and Sara, having left their son in the care of his doting grandparents, boarded the late-afternoon flight to San Francisco.

"Isn't this exciting?" Sara bubbled as they fastened their seat belts. "Our first free trip, courtesy of your brain."

Ted looked at his watch three hours later. They had barely crossed half the continent.

"This is ridiculous," he said. "I mean, where the hell is this place? It's incredibly far from civilization."

"Ted," she chided affectionately, "stay loose. You may just discover something wonderful about the world."

"Like what?"

"Like the life of the mind does not cease at the borders of Massachusetts."

As they disembarked in San Francisco, they were met by a middle-aged academic and a younger colleague holding, as a sign of identification, a copy of Lambros on Sophocles. Ted's mood, which had changed from glum to numb during the last few hours of the journey, lifted at this gesture of respect.

Bill Foster greeted them warmly and introduced Joachim Meyer, a papyrologist, recently transplanted from Heidelberg to California. They were both enormously cordial and in the baggage area insisted on carrying the suitcases out to their car.

Though it was early evening Berkeley's main street was swarming with activity.

"I seem to see a lot of hippies," Ted observed with a tinge of disapproval.

"I can hear some nice music," said Sara.

Bill Foster picked up on Ted's remark.

"Don't get the wrong impression, Ted. These students may walk around in jeans instead of tweeds, but they're the brightest kids you'll ever meet. They drive you crazy with their penetrating questions. Keeps you intellectually on your toes. We'll visit some classes if you like."

"Yes," Ted replied, "I'd like that."

"I'd enjoy that too," Sara chimed in.

"*Ach ja,*" Meyer said cordially. "I know you are an enthusiast for Hellenistic poetry, Sara."

Just then they reached the end of the avenue and Bill Foster announced, "Meyer and I will drop you at the new Faculty Club. I suggest, if you aren't too tired, that you stroll down Telegraph Avenue and have a beer at some place like Larry Blake's. Just sort of get a feel of the place at night."

"They're super people, don't you think?" asked Sara as they were unpacking a few moments later. "I mean so easygoing and friendly. You'd never guess from the way he talks that Meyer was a full professor at thirty-one. And for a German he seems very un-Teutonic. Maybe they've California'd him up."

"Come on," said Ted, "they're just romancing us. You notice that they even knew about your undergraduate thesis."

"I noticed and I *liked* it," Sara answered. "Don't you enjoy being seduced?"

"Well, I'm not seduced yet," Ted replied dourly.

"Well, keep an open mind, and let's check out Telegraph Avenue."

At first it appeared that nothing was going to please him. Not the lively streets, the bookshops, or the colorful minstrels with their guitars. But after merely one block, Sara perceived that one aspect of this vibrant place had finally caught her husband's interest.

"Aha," she smiled, "at least you dig some of the scenery."

"What are you talking about?"

"We've just passed six girls without bras and you enjoyed half-a-dozen healthy gawks, Dr. Lambros. And don't tell me I'm wrong, because I've been watching your face."

"You are wrong," said Ted, tight-lipped. "There were at least seven." And he smiled, at last.

Because of the three-hour time difference, they awoke extremely early and assumed they would be first in the Faculty Club dining room. They were mistaken.

For there was already someone seated at a corner table

spooning some species of breakfast flakes with one hand, and with the other holding an Oxford Classical text.

"Do you see what I see?" Sara whispered. "We are sharing this entire dining room with the Regius Professor of Greek at Oxford."

"Jesus, you're right. It's Cameron Wylie. What the hell is he doing here?"

"Same as we," Sara smiled, "eating breakfast. Also, isn't he giving this year's Sather lectures?"

"Hey, that's right. Something on Homer and Aeschylus. Do you think we'll get a chance to hear him?"

"Why don't you go over, introduce yourself, and ask?"

"I can't," Ted protested, suddenly timid. "I mean, he's such a great man."

"Come on, you blustering Greek. What's happened to your usual bravado? Or would you prefer I went as your emissary?"

"No, no, no, I'll be all right. I just don't know how to begin," Ted answered, rising reluctantly.

"Try 'hello.' That's a time-honored opener."

"Yeah," Ted countered laconically, his sense of humor completely dampened by his sudden social insecurity.

He listened nervously to the sound of his own steps as they traversed the floor of the empty dining room.

"Excuse me, Professor Wylie, I hope I'm not disturbing you, but I just wanted to say how much I admire your work. I thought your article on the *Oresteia* in last year's *JHS* was the best thing ever written on Aeschylus."

"Thank you," said the Englishman with undisguised pleasure. "Won't you join me?"

"Actually, my wife and I were wondering if you wouldn't join us. She's over there."

"Ah yes, I couldn't help but notice her when you walked in. Thank you, I'd be delighted." He stood, picked up his bowl and his Oxford text, and followed Ted to their table.

"Professor Wylie, this is my wife, Sara. Oh, and I forgot to mention I'm Theodore Lambros."

"Hello," said the Englishman as he shook Sara's hand and sat down. Then he turned to Ted. "I say, you're not the Sophocles man, are you?"

"Actually, yes," Ted answered, near vertiginous at the recognition. "I'm out here to give a lecture."

"I thought your book was first-rate," Wylie continued. "Blew a lot of dust off Sophoclean scholarship. I've put it on the Oxford Mods list already. Actually, I was delighted to see someone with your surname write a book on Sophocles. It seemed so appropriate."

Ted could not understand the connection but was loath to appear obtuse before so august a scholar. Sara leapt into the breach and sacrificed herself on the altar of naïveté.

"I'm afraid I don't follow you, sir," she said respectfully.

The don was happy to expound. "Why, as your husband knows, a chap called Lampros was Sophocles' dance and music teacher."

"What a coincidence," replied Sara, genuinely charmed by this amusing tidbit. Then she posed the question she knew Ted burned to ask: "Could you tell me the source for that?"

"Oh, a veritable cornucopia," replied the Regius Professor. "Athenaeus I.20, references in the *vita* and a few other bits and pieces. Must have been a good man, this Lampros. Aristoxenus ranks him with Pindar. Of course, there's that fragment of Phrynichus which is too silly to take seriously. Are you a Hellenist as well, Mrs. Lambros?"

"Not professionally," Sara answered shyly.

"My wife's a bit modest. She's got a *magna* in classics from Harvard."

"Splendid." And then he asked Ted, "What will you be speaking on?"

"Oh, I'm just trying out a few random ideas I've been germinating about Euripides' influence on Lampros's prize pupil."

"I very much look forward to hearing it. When's your talk?"

For a split second Ted hesitated. He was not sure he wanted so great a scholar to sit in judgment on his inchoate new theories.

Sara, on the other hand, had no such qualms. "It's tomorrow at five in Dwinelle Hall," she said.

The Englishman withdrew a fountain pen and a little Oxford diary to note the particulars.

Just then Bill Foster appeared. "Well, I see our two visiting classicists have met each other already," he said breezily.

"Three," The Englishman corrected him with an admonitory finger. "The Lambroses are both *lamproi.*"

After which the elder statesman rose, took his book (which happened to be his own edition of Thucydides), and wandered off toward the library.

*   *   *

As Bill Foster gave them a comprehensive walking tour of the campus, Ted had to admit to himself that it was beautiful. But still, the campanile and the late-nineteenth-century Spanish-style buildings somehow did not seem what a *university* should be like. He had always associated the pursuit of higher learning with Georgian architecture—like the grand towers of Lowell or Eliot House.

The library was undeniably impressive (and boasted shuttlebus service—colloquially known as the Gutenberg Express—direct to the Stanford University library). And all these quiet, solid structures stood in vivid contrast to the frenetic kaleidoscope of student activities concentrated—like the ancient Athenian agora—at a single, tumultuous spot in Sproul Plaza, between the Administration building and the Student Union.

After visiting an animated Latin class, the trio squeezed into a tiny health-food restaurant for a whole-earth lunch.

But something was obsessing Ted.

"What kind of a guy is Cameron Wylie?" he asked Bill, trying to act nonchalant.

"A tiger and a pussycat. He's been absolutely terrific with our undergraduates. But when it comes to professors, he doesn't suffer fools gladly. Last week, for example, when Hans-Peter Ziemssen came to lecture, Wylie made absolute mincemeat of him in the question period."

"Oh Jesus," muttered Ted.

He spent the next few hours in a blur of fear. Sara made him run through his entire lecture just for her. After which she said in all sincerity, "You're ready, champ, you really are."

"So was Daniel when he went into the lions' den."

"Read your Bible, honey. They didn't eat him, if you recall."

By the time he entered the lecture hall, Ted had resigned himself to what the Fates would bring.

There were about a hundred people scattered in the auditorium. To him they all seemed faceless, with three exceptions. Cameron Wylie and—two collie dogs. Dogs?

"Are you all set?" Bill Foster whispered.

"I think so. But, Bill, those uh—canine visitors? Is that—?"

"Oh, it's usual at Berkeley." Foster smiled. "Don't worry. In fact, they're some of my most attentive students."

He then mounted the podium and introduced today's guest speaker.

The applause was polite.

All alone now, Ted began by conjuring a striking picture.

"Imagine Sophocles—an established playwright already in his forties, who had even defeated the great Aeschylus in dramatic competition—sitting in the theater of Dionysus, watching the maiden production of a new young author named Euripides. . . ."

The audience was in his hands. For his words had transported them back to fifth-century B.C. Athens. They felt as if they were going to hear about *living* playwrights. And indeed, when Ted Lambros spoke of them, the Greek tragedians were very much alive.

As he concluded, he glanced at the clock on the far wall. He had lectured for exactly forty-nine minutes. Perfect timing. The applause was universal—and palpably genuine. Even the two dogs seemed to approve.

Bill Foster went up to shake his hand and whispered, "Absolutely brilliant, Ted. Do you think you have the strength for a question or two?"

Ted was trapped, knowing that if he refused, it would reveal a kind of academic pusillanimity.

Like a nightmare coming true, the first hand raised was that of Cameron Wylie. Well, thought Ted, it can't be any worse than all the questions I've dreamed up myself.

The Englishman stood up. "Professor Lambros, your remarks are most stimulating. But I was wondering if you saw any significant Euripidean influence in the *Antigone?*"

Blood began to flow again in Ted's veins. Wylie had actually thrown a compliment and not a javelin.

"Of course, chronologically it's possible. But I don't share any of the nineteenth-century Jebbsean romanticized views of *Antigone.*"

"Quite right, quite right," Wylie concurred. "The romantic interpretations are all silly nonsense—and have no basis in the text."

As Wylie sat down with an approving smile, Ted recognized a frizzy-haired girl in the back row, frantically waving her hand.

She rose and began to declaim. "I think we're all missing the point here. Like I mean, how are the guys you've been discussing relevant to *now?* I mean, I haven't heard the word *politics* mentioned once. I mean like, what was these Greeks' position on free speech?"

The audience groaned. Ted heard an "Oh shit" from somewhere in the crowd.

Bill Foster motioned to him that he could ignore the question if he wished. But Ted was high on approbation, and chose to address himself to the student's query.

"To begin with," he observed, "since every Greek drama was performed for the entire population of the *polis,* it was inherently political. The relevant issues of the day were so important to them that their comic poets spoke of nothing else. And there were no restrictions on what Aristophanes and company could say—that's the Greek notion of *parrhesia.* In a sense, their theater is an abiding testimony to the democracy they helped invent."

The questioner was stunned. First by the fact that Ted had taken her seriously—for she had intended to stir up a little intellectual anarchy—and second by the quality of his answer.

"You're cool, Professor," she mumbled and sat down.

Bill Foster stood, glowing with pleasure.

"On that stirring note," he announced, "I'd like to thank Professor Lambros for a marvelous talk which was both logical and philological."

Ted felt triumphant.

The reception in their honor was held at the Fosters' house in the Berkeley Hills. Everyone who was anyone in academia in the Bay Area seemed to be there, not to mention a certain distinguished professor from Oxford.

The mood was festive and the talk was all of Ted.

"I hear your lecture was even more exciting than our last student riot," Sally Foster joked. "I'm sorry I had to miss it. But somebody had to stay here and prepare the goodies. And Bill insisted that my tacos would entice you to come to Berkeley."

"I'm already enticed," said Sara Lambros, smiling happily.

Sensing that her casual remark had made Ted slightly uneasy, Sally quickly added, "Of course, I'm not supposed to say that sort of thing, am I? I always put my foot in my mouth. Anyway, Ted, I'm under strict orders to see that you keep circulating among the various literary lights."

And there was indeed a high-voltage group of San Francisco intellectuals. Ted noticed Sara in animated conversation with a character who looked amazingly like the beat poet Allen Ginsberg. And on second glance, it *was* Ginsberg.

Ted had to meet the author of *Howl,* the radical ululation in verse that had generated so much literary controversy in his undergraduate days. As he approached, he heard Ginsberg describing some personal apocalyptic experience.

"Looking through the window at the sky, suddenly it seemed that I saw into the depths of the universe. The sky suddenly seemed very *ancient.* And this was the very ancient place that Blake was talking about, the sweet golden clime. I suddenly realized that *this* existence was *it*! Do you dig me, Sara?"

"Hi, honey," Ted smiled, "hope I'm not interrupting."

"Not at all," she answered and then introduced her husband to the bearded bard.

"Say, I hear you guys may be moving west," said Ginsberg. "I hope you do—the sense of *prana*'s real strong out here."

Just then they were interrupted by Bill Foster.

"Sorry to break in, Allen, but Dean Rothschmidt is desperate to have a few words with Ted before he goes."

"That's cool. I'll be glad to continue fascinating Ted's old lady."

The Dean of Humanities wanted to express his admiration of Ted's lecture and ask if he could drop by his office at ten the next morning.

As Ted was returning to Sara, Cameron Wylie cornered him.

"I must say, Professor Lambros, your lecture was absolutely first-rate. I look forward to reading it in print. And I do hope we'll have the pleasure of hearing you at Oxford sometime."

"That would be a great honor," Ted replied.

"Well, when you get your next sabbatical I'll be happy to make some arrangements. In any case, I do hope we'll stay in touch."

A bolt suddenly struck the lightning rod of Ted's ambition.

Two days earlier, Cameron Wylie had spoken highly of his Sophocles book. This evening he was admiring the talk he had just delivered. Might not a letter from the Regius Professor of Greek at Oxford, repeating those same sentiments, tip the precarious balance at Harvard in Ted's favor?

In any case, he could lose nothing by seizing this most propitious moment.

"Professor Wylie, I—uh—I was wondering if I could ask you a rather special favor. . . ."

"Certainly," the don answered amiably.

"I—uh—I'll be coming up for tenure at Harvard next year, and I was wondering if you'd be willing to write on my behalf."

"Well, I've already composed rather a panegyric for the Berkeley people. I wouldn't mind saying the same sort of thing to Harvard. I won't ask why you would choose to endure the cold Cambridge winters. In any case, it's past my bedtime and I must be off. Please say good night to Sara for me. She's chatting with a rather hirsute character and I wouldn't want to catch his fleas."

He turned and marched off.

Ted smiled with elation. Within his chest the fires of aspiration burned brightly.

"You were fantastic, Ted. This was the proudest day of my life. You snowed everybody."

As they headed toward their room at the Faculty Club, Ted could hardly wait to tell her his good news. "Even old Cameron Wylie seemed pretty impressed," he remarked casually.

"I know. I overheard him telling two or three people."

He closed the door behind them and leaned against it. "Hey, Mrs. Lambros, what if I told you that we might not have to leave Cambridge?"

"I don't get it," Sara answered, a little off balance.

"Listen," Ted confided with intensity, "Wylie's going to write to Harvard for me. Don't you think a letter from him would boost me up into tenure heaven?"

Sara hesitated. She had been so elated this evening, so enchanted by the whole Berkeley experience, that this "good" news actually came as a disappointment. A double disappointment, in fact. Because in her heart she sensed that Harvard had already made up its mind and nothing could change it.

"Ted," she replied with difficulty, "I don't know how to say this without hurting your feelings. But all Wylie's letter can do is say you're a good scholar and a great teacher."

"Well, Jesus, isn't that all there is to it? I mean, I don't also have to run a four-minute mile, do I?"

Sara sighed. "Hey look, they don't need a letter from Oxford to tell them what they already know. Face it, they're not just judging you as a scholar. They're voting to let you into their club for the next thirty-five years."

"Are you trying to suggest they don't like me?"

"Oh, they like you all right. The question is, do they like you *enough?*"

"Shit," Ted said, half to himself, his euphoria suddenly tumbling into an abyss of desperation. "Now I don't know what the hell to do."

Sara put her arms around him. "Ted, if it'll help any in this existential dilemma, I want you to know that you've always got tenure with me."

They kissed.

"Ted," Dean Rothschmidt began the next morning, "Berkeley's got a tenured slot in Greek Lit. and you're our unanimous first choice. We'd be willing to start you at ten thousand a year."

Ted wondered if Rothschmidt knew that he was offering him nearly three thousand more than he was currently earning at Harvard. On second thought, of course he did. And that was enough to buy a hell of a nice new car.

"And naturally we'd pay all your moving costs from the East," Bill Foster quickly added.

"I—I'm very flattered," Ted replied.

The pitch was not over. Rothschmidt had further blandishment. "I don't know if Sara will recall, with all that madness at Bill's last night, but the gray-haired gentleman she spoke with briefly was Jed Roper, head of the U.C. Press. He's prepared to offer her a junior editorship—salary to be negotiated."

"Gosh," Ted remarked, "she'll be thrilled." And then he added as casually as possible, "I assume I'll be getting a formal offer in writing."

"Naturally," the dean replied, "but it's just a bureaucratic formality. I can promise you this is a firm offer."

This time *he* took Whitman to lunch at the Faculty Club.

"Cedric, if there still is any enthusiasm for my being kept at Harvard, I think I've got some new ammunition."

His mentor seemed pleased at what Ted reported. "Well, I think this strengthens your case considerably. I'll ask the chairman to call Wylie for his letter so we can bring up your tenure at the next departmental meeting."

My tenure, thought Ted. I actually heard him say my tenure.

The formal vote took place twenty-four days later. The department had for their consideration Ted's bibliography (four articles, five reviews), his book on Sophocles (and the critiques of it, which ranged from "solid" to "monumental"), and various letters of recommendation, some from experts in the field whose names Ted would never know. But one certainly from the Regius Professor at Oxford.

Ted and Sara waited nervously in the Huron Avenue apartment. It was nail-biting time. They knew the meeting had begun at four, and yet by five-thirty there was still no word.

"What do you think?" Ted asked. "Is it a good sign or a bad sign?"

"For the last time, Lambros," Sara said firmly, "I don't know what the hell is going on. But you have my fervent conviction both as wife and classicist that you truly deserve tenure at Harvard."

"If the gods are just," he quickly added.

"Right." She nodded. "But remember, in academia *there are no gods*—just professors. Quirky, flawed, capricious human beings."

The phone rang.

Ted grabbed it.

It was Whitman. His voice betrayed nothing.

"Cedric, please, put me out of my misery. How did they vote?"

"I can't go into details, Ted, but I can tell you it was very, very close. I'm sorry, you didn't make it."

Ted Lambros lost the carefully polished Harvard veneer he had worked a decade to acquire, and repeated aloud what he had said ten years earlier when the college had denied him a full scholarship.

"Shit."

Sara was immediately at her husband's side, her arms around him consolingly.

He would not hang up till he asked one final burning question.

"Cedric," he said as calmly as possible, "may I just know the pretext—uh—I mean the grounds—I mean, in general terms, what lost it for me?"

"It's hard to pinpoint, but there was some talk about 'waiting for a second Big Book.' "

"Oh," Ted responded, thinking bitterly, there are one or two tenured guys who still haven't written their *first* big book. But he said nothing more.

"Ted," Whitman continued with compassion in his voice, "Anne and I want you to come to dinner tonight. It's not the end of the world. It's not the end of anything, really. So will you come?"

"Dinner tonight?" Ted repeated distractedly.

Sara was strenuously nodding her head.

"Uh, thanks Cedric. What time would you like us?"

It was a warm spring night and Sara insisted that they walk the mile or so to the Whitmans' house. She knew Ted needed time to gain some equilibrium.

"Ted," Sara said as he shuffled dejectedly, "I know there are at least a dozen four-letter words going around in your head, and I think for the sake of sanity you ought to shout them right out here in the street. God knows, I want to scream too. I mean, you got screwed."

"No. I got *royally* screwed. I mean, a bunch of uptight bastards just played lions and Christians with my career. I feel like kicking in their goddamn mahogany doors and beating the shit out of all of them."

Sara smiled. "Not their wives too, I hope."

"No, of course not," he snapped.

And then, realizing the childishness of his outburst, he began to laugh.

They both giggled for a block until suddenly Ted's laughter turned into sobs. He buried his head on Sara's shoulder as she tried to comfort him.

"Oh God, Sara," he wept, "I feel so stupid. But I wanted it so bad. So goddamn bad."

"I know," she whispered tenderly. "I know."

For Stuart and Nina it was the greatest summer of their lives. Every morning he would get on his bike and pedal over to the Rossi house, often passing Maria and her two girls in the station wagon on their way to enjoy Edgar Waldorf's stretch of private beach with Nina and the boys.

Stu would return in the early evening, at once exhausted and overstimulated, grab Nina by the hand, and take her for a long walk by the sea.

"How's the great classical composer at writing show tunes?" she asked during one of their promenades.

"Oh, the guy's so fantastically versatile he could write a rondo with his left hand and ragtime with his right. But he doesn't pander."

"What do you mean?"

"I mean he doesn't underestimate the intelligence of his audience. Some of his melodies are—you know—pretty complex."

"I thought the secret of success on Broadway was simplicity," Nina remarked.

"Don't worry, hon, he isn't writing *Wozzeck*."

"This is exciting. I mean, I know your words are terrific. But I'd really like to hear what Danny's done with them. Apparently, Maria tells me, he hasn't even played anything for her."

"Well, every artist's temperament is different, I guess," said Stuart, picking up a bit of driftwood and hurling it out across the water.

"And every marriage, too," Nina added. "Do you think they're happy?"

"Hey, honey," Stuart cautioned, "I'm his lyricist, not his shrink. I just know he's a good working partner."

*   *   *

On Labor Day weekend, Edgar Waldorf flew in with Harvey Madison to hear the fruits of his young geniuses' summer toil.

Ever munificent, he arrived laden with presents for the Kingsley sons, the Rossi daughters, and the authors' wives. As far as "the boys" were concerned, *they* would have to have something for *him*.

After a huge Italian dinner, the two visitors, the artists, and their wives repaired to the living room for the first hearing of the score to *Manhattan Odyssey*.

As Danny sat at the piano, Stuart narrated, here and there injecting a bit of dialogue to show how deftly he had made Joyce theatrically viable. And then he would introduce the songs. His lyrics were ingeniously set. The music was muscular, the rhythms bold.

After the lively octet in Bella Cohen's fabled brothel, the privileged little audience broke into applause. Then Danny proudly commented, "You don't hear many Broadway scores with songs written in five."

"What's five?" asked Edgar Waldorf.

"It's a kind of tricky rhythm, five-four. Never mind what it is—as long as you like what you hear."

"Like it?" Edgar exclaimed. "I love it, I love it. Maybe five symbolizes the number of years we're going to run SRO."

"Why stop at five? Why not six or seven?" interposed Harvey Madison, unable to resist the agent's impulse to up the ante.

The authors together sang the final duet between Bloom and Stephen, his surrogate son. Then they looked to their families and arbiters for judgment.

At first there was reverential silence.

"Well, Nina?" Stuart asked his wife impatiently. "Would you buy a ticket to this thing?"

"I think I'd go every night," she responded, exultant at the ingenuity of her husband's work.

"Did it get *my* wife's approval?" Danny asked.

"Not that I'm a professional critic," Maria began shyly, "but I honestly think that's the best musical score I've ever heard—by anybody."

Edgar Waldorf rose to his feet to make an announcement. "Ladies and gentlemen—and geniuses—it has been my humble honor to listen to the first playing of what is undoubtedly the most fabulous musical ever to sweep Broadway off its feet."

He then turned to the authors. "My only question is—what are you guys going to do with the ten million bucks this is going to earn you?"

"Nine," Harvey Madison quickly corrected, professional even in jest.

Now it was the men's turn to walk the beach.

Edgar had to complete the financing. He hoped the tape he was bringing back to New York would do the trick. But they still needed to discuss the director and the stars.

Having so admired Jerome Robbins's work on *West Side Story,* Danny wanted him to direct and choreograph their show.

Stuart enthusiastically agreed.

But Edgar, obsessed with the British origins of the *Times* critic, plumped for Sir John Chalcott, whose recent work at the Old Vic had been so well received.

"After all," the producer reasoned, "we are dealing with one of the great classics of the English language. Why not put it in the hands of someone who is accustomed to dealing with the immortals?"

" 'Immortal' can be a synonym for 'dead,' " Danny Rossi commented.

"Please, Daniel," Edgar retorted, "I've got a gut feeling on this. I think Sir John's name would add even more class value."

After another quarter of a mile, he succeeded in twisting their arms.

Then the talk got around to principals. They started with passionate unanimity. Not only did they all agree on Zero Mostel, but the star himself had already consented merely on the basis of the novel.

Casting the female lead proved more difficult. Danny had what he thought was a sensational idea. He had written the role of Molly—who is a professional singer even in Joyce's book—for someone with real vocal ability. So he proposed what was to his mind the supreme voice of their time: Joan Sutherland.

"An opera singer in a Broadway show?" Edgar Waldorf cringed. "Besides, she'd never do it."

"First of all," said Danny, "I got to know her when I conducted *Lucia* at La Scala. She's a terrific lady. And she's got the courage to take on new challenges."

"Look," reasoned the ever-reasonable Edgar Waldorf, "I would be the last person to knock Miss Sutherland's talent, but opera and Broadway don't seem to mix."

"What about Ezio Pinza in *South Pacific?*" asked Stuart.

"A fluke, a fluke," said Waldorf. "Besides, what made that show was Mary Martin. And anyway we can't afford Sutherland. No, I say we've got to go with someone used to doing eight shows a week. Someone who's a proven draw—magnetic, vibrant, exciting—"

"And also big tits, maybe?" Danny asked facetiously.

"That wouldn't hurt either," said the producer, trying to act ingenuous.

Danny Rossi stopped walking, put his hands on his hips, and stood like a small colossus in the sand of Martha's Vineyard.

"Listen, Edgar, I would rather die than have Theora Hamilton in a show of mine. I have my principles."

"That goes for me as well," Stuart added.

"Easy, boys, easy. Nobody's going to compromise anybody's principles here," mediated Harvey Madison. "There are a million talented ladies in the American theater and I'm sure we can come up with someone who meets everyone's specifications. Now, why don't we all start back? It's already a half-hour past cocktail time."

When the quartet returned, Maria Rossi, busy lighting a charcoal fire with Nina Kingsley, looked up and asked, "Well, gentlemen, did you settle all your problems?"

"Absolutely," said Harvey Madison. "The great minds are all in sync."

And there in the growing twilight on that lonely beach, Edgar Waldorf proclaimed, "It gives me great pleasure to tell you that *Manhattan Odyssey,* under the direction of Sir John Chalcott, will begin rehearsals on December twenty-sixth. And commence its pre-Broadway engagement at the Schubert Theater in Boston on February seventh.

"By the time it opens in New York on March twenty-fourth, it will undoubtedly be sold out for a year. Since not only is it geniusly written, but it will also have the incredible one-two punch of Mr. Zero Mostel—" He paused for effect. "And Miss Theora Hamilton."

The authors' wives shot startled glances at their husbands, whose expressions were strangely resigned.

Chitchat continued during the barbecue. Then they all left the beach quickly to sit silently in front of the television. And admire the pitching virtuosity of Sandy Koufax keeping the ball away from every single batter of the San Francisco Giants.

"How did he convince you?" Maria asked as they were driving home.

"I'm not sure myself," Danny confessed. "I mean, he used so much sophistry that my head is still spinning. I felt like General Custer. Every time I fended off one of Edgar's attacks, he was behind me with another tomahawk."

"But, Danny," Maria insisted, "you're the artists. Surely you and Stuart should have the last word."

"I did have the last word." He smiled sardonically. "It's just that Edgar had a few thousand arguments *after* my last word. All of a sudden Zero wasn't enough to sell tickets to anybody. He was a ham. The audience had enough of him after *Fiddler*. His arguments were endless.

"According to Edgar, the only thing that could possibly save us would be the mammiferous presence of the untalented Theora Hamilton. Look, I'll just cut down her role so she won't be an utter embarrassment to us."

"But couldn't you have agreed on anybody else?"

Danny looked at her sheepishly and confessed, "Edgar seems to be finding resistance to James Joyce among his investors. And it would be hard to find another female star whose husband is willing to put up half a million bucks if we give his wife the role."

"Aha," said Maria, with a mixture of surprise and disappointment. "Well, they say that Broadway plays always rise like Venus from a sea of compromises."

"Yeah," said Danny, now unable to hide his frustration, "but this is the last compromise. The very last."

Within mere hours of Ted Lambros's rejection for tenure at Harvard, communications began to pour in from every important university center of the United States.

Some were simply to express condolences. Others to inquire if it were really true. The subtext being that if Lambros had been shot down, there might be a possibility for *them* at Harvard. But perhaps the most astounding calls were from those who presumed to know the secrets of that fateful afternoon's proceedings.

When Ted and Sara returned from the Whitmans', he had passed beyond depression into a kind of postmortem euphoria. A paradoxical feeling of being "high" on disappointment.

Walt Hewlett from the University of Texas called to convey the inside dope. "Teddie, I know the guys who screwed you were the 'garbologists.' " This was Walt's term for archaeologists, whom he viewed as mere rummagers in the trash cans of ancient civilizations.

"What makes you so sure, Walt?"

"Listen, those guys have an incredible animosity for anything written in a book. They only trust pornographic graffiti scrawled on Roman urinals. So I guess you'll be going to Berkeley, huh?"

Ted was stupefied. He had no idea that everybody in the world of classics knew everything.

"I'm not sure," he answered cagily. For today's experience had taught him a great lesson in the laws of the academic jungle. "Hey, Walter old friend, I'm really touched that you called. But it's past midnight. And just because I don't have tenure doesn't mean I can skip my nine-o'clock class tomorrow."

He hung up and looked at Sara, who, by now, was also

giggly. "This is a farce, Ted. We should take the receiver off the hook and go to bed."

That instant the telephone rang yet again.

It was Bill Foster from Berkeley.

This was not a voice Ted had hoped to hear after midnight, when he was tired and semi-sloshed. But mercifully Bill did all the talking.

"Listen, Ted, I know it's late back there, so I'll make it short. We really want you here and look forward to getting your written acceptance so we can list you on our prospectus."

"Thanks, Bill," Ted answered, trying to sound both sober and sincere. And having difficulty doing either.

The next day was the most painful of Ted's life. Not only because he had a terrible hangover. But because somehow he had to muster the courage to walk into Boylston Hall. To go to the Classics office. To say good morning to the secretary, as if nothing were different.

And, still worse, to have to confront the senior professors and exchange bland cordialities, suppressing all the curiosity—and violent anger—he felt inside.

As he entered the Yard and passed John Harvard's statue, he was even anxious about running into John Finley, fearing that his idol might resent him now that he was a "failure."

But he realized that he had to go through the motions of normalcy. He could not sulk like Achilles in his tent. Certainly not, especially since he was no longer a great hero—at least in Harvard's eyes. He had been blackballed. Rejected from the club.

From nine to ten he walked like a somnambulist through Elementary Greek. And then deliberately tried to preserve the numbness he felt as he went to pick up his mail in the department office.

Mercifully, no one else was there, so all he had to do was exchange perfunctory salutations with the secretary. Ted could not help but marvel at her ability to camouflage her awareness—for she really *did* know everything—of yesterday's events. It was, he joked inwardly, a quality that departmental secretaries probably shared with undertakers. They had to keep an affable demeanor in the midst of catastrophe.

But on the way to his eleven-o'clock lecture, the adrenaline began to flow in him again. What the hell, he thought, I'm not going to give these kids a bum deal just because those bastards kicked me where it hurts.

Fortunately, he had a subject he could dig into—Euripides' tragedy *Hippolytus*. He could speak about the injustice of the gods.

Ted took the podium and gave one of the most stirring lectures of his life.

The students applauded—a rare occurrence in the middle of a semester.

Screw the garbologists. I'd like to see those fogies set a class on fire like that. No, dammit, they may have crumpled my career like a paper cup, but they won't crush me.

His son greeted him at the door. Here, Ted thought, is at least one guy who still thinks I'm terrific.

He kissed Sara, and while she prepared dinner, went through the ritual of putting his son to bed. The high point was Ted's off-key rendition of "*Nani to moro mou, nani,*" a Greek lullaby.

Then he sat down at the kitchen table with Sara and gradually removed the mental armor he had worn all day.

"Do you feel wretchedly terrible, or just terribly wretched?" she asked gently.

"Well, I got through the first day of being a nonperson without punching anybody or throwing myself into the Charles."

"That's good," she said, smiling.

The telephone rang.

"I'm sorry, Ted, I forgot to take it off the hook when we sat down. Let me get rid of whoever it is."

But Sara did not hang up immediately. "It's Robbie Walton," she called out. "I think you should speak to him. He's really upset for you."

Ted nodded and went to the phone. When Rob, the first graduate student whose thesis he had directed, had left Harvard to begin an instructorship at Canterbury College, he had vowed eternal gratitude.

"How could Harvard do this to you?" Rob said with anguish.

"Listen, it's the breaks of the game. Let this be a lesson to all of us."

"Anyway, I'll bet you've got a million alternatives. At least you deserve to."

"I've got a couple," Ted answered noncommittally. "How are things at Canterbury, Rob?"

"Not bad. Some of the kids are really bright—and the place is unbelievably gorgeous. The Classics Department is a little quiet, though. I mean, they haven't got anybody like Ted Lambros."

"Maybe that's because they haven't asked," Ted replied, only half in jest.

"You mean you'd actually consider coming up here?"

"Frankly, at this point, I'm not really sure what I want. I'm gonna just play it by ear for a while."

Suddenly Robbie grew excited.

"Hey, listen, if you're at all serious about Canterbury, I'll tell the dean first thing in the morning. My God, he'll go bananas!"

"Well," Ted answered casually, "it might be interesting to see what would happen if you mentioned it. Thanks, Rob."

"What kind of Machiavellian mischief are you up to now?" Sara asked when he sat down again.

"Honey, that little maneuver is called keeping your options open."

"I'd call it dirty pool."

"Sara, haven't you learned by now? 'Dirty' is the only way to play the academic game."

Robbie called two days later. He was exultant. "I knew it," he effused. "I gave your book to Tony Thatcher—he's Dean of Humanities—and it really turned him on. He told me to arrange a date with you for a guest lecture. How's Wednesday the fourteenth?"

"Fine," Ted replied, trying to underplay his satisfaction, "that sounds fine."

In the next few days Ted devoured all the information he could obtain about Canterbury College. Founded in 1772, it was one of the oldest colleges in America. And unlike Harvard and Yale, which acquired their names from mere commoners, it had a noble cachet. The college was established on the order of Gilbert Sheldon, Archbishop of Canterbury under King George III, to train ministers for the colonies.

But to Sara, Canterbury had always been merely a football rival from the wilds of Vermont. Though she had heard how pretty its campus was, she had never heard particular praise for its classics department.

If she had dared to speak with total candor, Sara would have confessed that she actually liked Berkeley even better than Harvard. But the idea of going to Canterbury seemed to lift Ted's spirit so. After all, here he would be the undisputed king of the mountain. Sara's only misgivings—unspoken, of course—were about having to live on that mountain.

After a leisurely afternoon drive, they checked in at the rustic but elegant Windsor Arms and went immediately to sit on its front porch to gaze at the fairyland spread out before them. Directly ahead, across the lush town green, stood Hillier Library, its white Georgian tower stretching proudly toward a cloudless sky.

"Gosh, Sara, it's even more imposing than Eliot House, isn't it?"

"No," she replied, "but it is beautiful."

Just then Robbie arrived and greeted them effusively. He was wearing an orange blazer, white button-down shirt, and rep tie.

"I've been designated your official guide," he said. "We've got plenty of time for a thorough tour and a cup of tea before your lecture."

Rob was an ardent convert to the Canterbury way of life.

"Breathe that air," he urged. "It's the purest stuff you've ever had in your lungs. No city pollution out here."

"No city, either," Sara added matter-of-factly.

Later, as they neared Canterbury Hall, Robbie grew uneasy. "Uh—Ted, I—uh—I hope you don't mind if there isn't a huge crowd."

"That's okay. I'd be happy to talk just to you and Sara."

"You may well," Rob mumbled, now patently embarrassed. "I mean, I announced your talk to my own classes, but they didn't get the posters up till kinda late."

"How late?" Ted inquired.

"Uh—this morning, I'm afraid," Robbie replied as they reached the main entrance of the building.

Sara Lambros began to think dark thoughts.

The large lecture room was sprinkled with fewer than two dozen people. Ted had difficulty masking his disappointment.

"Don't worry," Rob whispered, "the dean and provost are out there—and that's what really counts."

"What about members of the department?"

"Oh sure," Rob answered quickly, "a couple of them are here too."

Both Ted and Sara knew what this meant. Some of the professors—who needed no poster to inform them of this occasion—had chosen to boycott his talk.

Though his former student was warmly eloquent in introducing Ted, Sara could not help but wonder why the department hadn't chosen someone senior to present him. He was, after all, the author of what the *American Journal of Philology* had praised as the most important Sophoclean book of the decade.

Ignoring the emptiness of the auditorium, Ted gave his lecture with quiet confidence.

At the end, the happy few clapped energetically.

An elegant gentleman with graying temples was the first to offer his hand.

"I'm Tony Thatcher, Dean of Humanities," he said, "and I very much enjoyed your presentation. Could we have breakfast at, say, eight tomorrow?"

"Fine," Ted replied.

He then turned to answer a few student questions, after which Robbie introduced a youngish academic with horn-rimmed glasses and Clark Gable mustache.

"Ted, this is our Latinist and chairman, Henry Dunster. He'll be taking you to dinner."

"How do you do, Professor Lambros," said Dunster in a deep baritone that sounded like it had its own echo chamber. "I suppose you could use a nice dry martini about now."

"Thanks," said Ted, trying to ignore the fact that the chairman had not offered even the most perfunctory compliment about his lecture. "I'll get Rob and Sara."

"No, Rob won't be joining us," Dunster intoned. "I thought an intimate dinner would be best for you to meet the senior colleagues. Incidentally, Ken Bunting had a conflicting commitment and couldn't make it. But I know he'll want to chat with you."

As he ushered the two guests of honor out of the auditorium, Sara could not help feeling a twinge of pity for Robbie.

*   *   *

They entered the candlelit restaurant of the Windsor Arms, where, at a corner table, the rest of the Classics Department's senior faculty were waiting.

"Ah, Professor Lambros," murmured Dunster, "you've brought the department out in force."

The three other full professors stood as they approached. Dunster made the introductions.

"Professor and Mrs. Lambros, this is Graham Foley, our archaeologist. . . ."

A balding spheroid rose and shook hands wordlessly.

"And Digby Hendrickson, our historian."

A lithe little man cracked the first smile of the evening. "Hi there, call me Digby. May I call you Ted and Jane?"

"If you'd like," Ted smiled back diplomatically, "but my wife's name is actually Sara."

"And this," quoth Dunster in conclusion, pointing to a tall, middle-aged preppie with straight flaxen hair combed down across his forehead, "is our missing Hellenist, Ken Bunting."

"Sorry I couldn't make your lecture, Lambros," he apologized. "But, of course, I'll probably read it when it's published, won't I?"

"I don't know," said Sara, who had quickly analyzed the situation. "It was just a few ideas that Ted put together. It would need a lot of working up."

At first Ted was astonished at his wife's downplaying of his scholarship. This feeling quickly changed to gratitude when he beheld the warm response her understatement had evoked in Canterbury's Hellenist.

"Indeed," said Bunting. "All this precipitance to get things in print—that's rather rife at Harvard, isn't it?"

"Uh—I suppose so."

"Shall we order, then?" said Chairman Dunster. "Do I hear martinis all around?"

His colleagues were unanimously in favor, although the archaeologist merely nodded his assent.

By seven-thirty all that had been served were large cocktails and small talk. Sara tried to keep herself and Ted sober by buttering bread sticks, thickly spreading the cheese dip on Ritz crackers, and dropping unsubtle hints like, "I hear the salmon's very good here. What would you recommend we *eat*, Professor Dunster?"

Ted's mind was working feverishly, trying to determine where the power base lay in this group. In preparation for his visit, he had read every article the Canterbury department members had produced. It hadn't taken that long. He decided to address their Greek scholar on his most important article, "The Symbolism of Homer's Catalogue of Ships."

"Professor Bunting, I was intrigued by your piece in *TAPA* on the end of *Iliad* Two. Your theory about the Attic contingent was—"

At this point the mellifluous voice of Chairman Dunster interrupted with the welcome announcement, "Mademoiselle is here to transcribe our dinner selections."

Sara Lambros inwardly sang hallelujah.

Suddenly, the silent archaeologist rose and totally dumbfounded Ted and Sara by articulating several syllables.

"It's past my bedtime," he announced to no one in particular. " 'Night, all. Thanks for the free booze." Then immediately reverting to his prior muteness, he nodded at the guests of honor and departed.

"He's lying." Dunster sneered. "He's just going home to watch the tube. Can you imagine," he inquired of Sara Lambros, "that man watches television?"

"Many people do," she answered noncommittally.

"Does your husband have a predilection for that medium?" he probed.

"Oh, we don't own a set," she answered blandly. Thinking, Let him call it poverty or snobbery as long as he approves.

Two further hours passed without a single reference to a Greek or Latin author. Ted was trying desperately to comprehend it all. But he remembered Sara's words: "It's a club, you're being judged to join a club."

"Do you play tennis, Lambros?" Bunting of the thousand ships inquired.

"Oh," Ted lied, "a bit. Actually, I'm trying to improve my game." And made a mental note that if he ever got this job, he'd have one of Sara's brothers give him lessons.

"Old Bunting here's the glory of our whole department," piped Digby the historian. "He was IC4A runner-up in fifty-six.

In fact, he had a big match today—against a new instructor from the Government Department." And then turning to his semi-champion colleague he inquired, "Didya whip him, Ken?"

Professor Bunting nodded modestly. "Six–four, five–seven, six–three, six–one. It took so long it almost made me late for dinner."

"Whoopee," Digby trumpeted, "we'll drink to that."

But as they toasted Kenneth Bunting for this minor tennis triumph, Sara brooded, You pompous jock. Couldn't you have put your match off to come hear my husband's lecture?

Later when they were alone, Ted finally allowed himself to say what they had both been thinking all through dinner.

"Christ, what shits they are."

"Hey, look, Ted," Sara answered, slightly giddy from the whole experience, "there are shits at Harvard too. But these were such a bunch of *little* shits."

She woke at dawn to find her husband staring out the window.

"What's the matter, honey?" Sara asked solicitously. "Did it all get to you?"

"No," he answered quietly, still staring at the town green, "it's just the opposite."

"You mean you're pleased at how they mauled you yesterday?"

"No, it's this place. It takes my breath away. I think we could be really happy here."

"Who are we going to *talk* to?" she asked plaintively. "The trees? The babbling brooks say more than that autistic archaeologist!"

He lowered his head. "Those student questions yesterday were pretty good."

She did not react.

"The library's fantastic. . . ."

She still did not respond.

"This place has got some really fine departments. French, for instance. And that Lipton guy in Physics worked on the atomic bomb—"

"Hey, Ted," she interrupted gently, "you don't have to use sophistry with me. This place does have a sense of history. And I know something in you still can't face the world without the epaulets of 'Ivy League' on your shoulders. It's something I can't understand, but I'll have to accept."

"It's a nice location, Sara."

"Yeah, just a three-hour drive from Harvard . . ."

"Two and a half," he said softly.

The breakfast room looked like an orange grove. At every table, couples varying from middle-age to old sat monochromatically garbed. The gentlemen wore orange blazers, their ladies all had Canterbury scarves.

"Is this some kind of reunion?" Ted asked Tony Thatcher as he sat down to breakfast with the dean.

"No," Thatcher answered, "it's like this all year 'round. The old grads don't just come up for the football games—they're always making 'sentimental journeys.' "

"I can appreciate their feelings," Ted remarked.

"I'm glad," the dean replied, "because I'd like to see you here at Canterbury."

"I take it from your use of the first-person singular that there isn't unanimity in the department."

"I don't think they'd even vote unanimously on a raise in salary. Frankly, what we need is a cohesive force—a solid academic who has both feet on the ground. I want Canterbury to be the number-one small college in the country. Even better than Dartmouth or Amherst. And we can't accomplish that without attracting men of your caliber. So I have the provost's authority to offer you an associate professorship on tenure-track."

"What's tenure-track?"

"It means after a year the job is permanent. How does that sound to you?"

"To be honest, the thought of a probationary period is a bit unsettling."

"It's really a formality," the dean replied in reassuring tones. "Besides, the men who count up here know what we've got in you."

"Ted, I'll make the best of it. I really will."

As they were driving home Sara reiterated in so many words that she had married him for better or worse. And having said for the last time that Berkeley was better and Canterbury worse, she would learn to love the great outdoors.

"Sara," Ted replied, to reassure himself as much as her, "we're going to return in triumph someday. I'm going to use the peace and quiet to write a Euripides book that's so damn good that Harvard'll come begging on its knees to ask me back. Remember how the Romans groveled to Coriolanus after kicking him out."

"Yeah," she retorted. "But the guy still ended up with a knife in his back."

"Touché." Ted smiled. "Why did I marry such a clever woman?"

"Because you wanted clever children," she said, smiling back.

But inwardly she brooded, If you really respected my intelligence, you'd be taking my advice.

Jason Gilbert made two important decisions that were to affect the rest of his life. He had come to realize that everything he had done in the previous two and a half years signified a commitment to defend the land of his forefathers. This meant he would stay there and grow roots.

And yet his loneliness weighed heavily on him. Watching the young kibbutz children playing made him long to be a father. But he was not sure that he had a whole heart to offer. He was still angry. And still mourning.

Nonetheless, whenever he was back on leave, he and Eva would sit in the huge, empty dining hall and talk until the early hours of the morning. These were the times when Jason felt most human.

Late one evening he confessed to her, "I don't know what I'll do when you get married. Who'll stay up and listen to me bitch about the world?"

"I've been thinking the same thing," she answered shyly. "Since you've been here, I've had, as you might say, a shoulder to cry on."

"But you never actually cry."

"It was just a manner of speaking."

"Sure. Like my saying, 'You're the one person in this place who holds my hand.' Just a metaphor."

"Yes. We are both . . . metaphors."

Their glances met.

"I'd like to really hold your hand," he said.

"And I would like really to cry on your shoulder."

They put their arms around each other.

"Eva, I really care for you. I want to say I love you. But I honestly don't know if I'm still capable of love."

"I feel the same, Jason. But we could try."
Then they kissed.

The ceremony took place at Vered Ha-Galil at the beginning
of a one-month leave granted Jason upon his reenlistment. The
kibbutzniks rejoiced that the couple had chosen to remain among
them, even though for long periods of time Jason would be
involved in army duty at various—mostly secret—areas of the
country.

For Jason the kibbutz had replaced his family. His estrange-
ment from his parents was now almost complete. Eva asked him
to invite them to their wedding. But he refused. Instead, the night
before, he sat up in their new quarters—a two-room *srif* with the
added luxuries of a small fridge, hot plate, and black-and-white
television—and wrote his parents a letter.

> Dear Mom and Dad,
>
> I am getting married tomorrow. To Eva Goudsmit,
> the girl hidden by Fanny's family during the Holocaust.
> It's to her I owe my understanding of what Israel means.
>
> Under normal circumstances I would have invited
> you. But I know how deeply you disapprove of the direc-
> tion my life has taken, and tomorrow's vows only sanctify
> what I suppose you regard as a rebellion.
>
> I followed your game plan for the first twenty-four
> years of my life, barely noticing the little compromises I
> had to make along the way, as I'm sure you barely notice
> yours. I know you meant well. You wanted your children
> not to suffer from the stigma of being Jewish.
>
> And that's exactly what I want for *my* children.
>
> Here, being a Jew is an honor and not a handicap.
> My children may grow up in some danger, but they will
> never grow up in shame.
>
> I will always appreciate everything you gave me while
> I was growing up. Now that I *have* grown up, even if you
> don't agree with my beliefs, please respect my right to live
> by them.
>
> Your loving son,
> Jason

Their honeymoon, subsidized by the kibbutz, was spent in Eilat, the southernmost point of Israel, at the tip of the Negev. The Red Sea port was founded by King Solomon to ship out the ore from his mines. And was where he welcomed the Queen of Sheba.

Jason taught Eva how to skin-dive. And they spent the mornings among the multicolored underwater coral.

At night they walked hand in hand from the cheap (but expensive) shish kebab joints to the tinsel (and even more expensive) discotheques.

But they were both happy.

"This must be what the French Riviera is like," Eva said one night as they were walking on the shore.

"More or less," Jason replied, not wanting to shatter his bride's illusions. "The only difference is here, if you go for too long a swim you can end up in Saudi Arabia."

"Yes," she acknowledged, "the Arabs are kind of close, aren't they?"

"They must think the same about us. But their children and ours will probably play together."

"I hope so," Eva said tenderly. "I mean, I hope we have a lot of children."

It would be a good marriage and a strong one. Because it was without any illusions. They cared about the same things. About the same people. About each other. Their love was anointed with tears of abiding grief. And, at the same time, strengthened by a common loss.

During the following year, the Arab guns on the mountains of the Golan Heights incessantly shelled the kibbutzim in northern Israel. From the Jordanian and Lebanese borders, terrorist infiltrators were increasingly successful in crossing over, striking at non-military targets, and murdering civilians. Women in a crowded marketplace on Friday morning. Children in a school playground.

The outraged Israeli population was demanding action, not merely reaction. If they couldn't keep the *Fedayeen* out, let them do something to stop them before they got in. Orders came down for an elite group of paratroopers to begin acts of reprisal.

Jason Gilbert was part of an operation that spent weeks rehearsing for the strike across the border.

The night before, they slept in a field a few hundred yards from the Jordanian frontier. At first light they jumped into their vehicles and sped toward the hilltop village of Samua, which Intelligence informed them was a base for *El-Fatah* commandos. A quarter of a mile from the village, they dismounted and continued the rest of the climb on foot, rifles in hand.

Israeli aircraft appeared overhead. They flew beyond Samua to bomb and distract the Jordanian regulars and keep them away from the operation.

When they were less than a hundred yards from the village, Jason broke into a run and signaled his men to begin shooting to create confusion. As they worked their way up the steep slope, guns appeared at the windows and began returning the fire.

The soldier at Jason's immediate right was struck in the chest and fell backward. For a moment Jason was frozen, watching the red blood stain the shirt of the man he knew merely as Avi.

It was the first time he had ever seen someone wounded in battle. He continued to stare. It was only when the medical officer rushing toward them waved him on that Jason turned and started up the hill again, his anger inflamed.

As he charged, he pulled a grenade from his belt, withdrew the pin, and hurled it toward the center of the village. It exploded on a rooftop.

By the time the paratroops entered Samua, the terrorists had fled, leaving behind them a few aged and confused inhabitants. The Israelis quickly searched the houses and herded the frightened villagers down the slopes.

A flare was set off to signal that Samua was now empty. With lightning speed, Jason and the explosives experts began to set charges to the houses. Ten minutes later, the Israeli raiding party had regrouped 250 yards below. One of the engineers detonated the first charge. In quick succession the stone houses were blown into the air.

Seventeen minutes later, they were all back across the border. Jason was riding in a half-track with Yoram Zahavi, their chief in command.

"Well," said Yoram, "Operation Samua is a total success."

Jason turned to him and said bitterly, "Try telling that to Avi's parents."

The officer nodded, shook his head, and answered Jason softly, "Listen, *saba,* war isn't like a football match. You can never win by a shutout."

There were more operations like Samua, but the Israelis still could not stem the rising tide of terrorist infiltrations.

In fact, from early 1967 onward, the guerrilla strikes became bolder and more savage. The shelling from the Golan Heights of the kibbutzim in the Huleh Valley grew more intense than ever.

On the southern front, Cairo Radio was broadcasting the voice of Egyptian leader Nasser shrieking, "A hundred million Arabs are living for the day when the imperialist Israelis will be driven into the sea."

At the end of May 1967, Captain Jason Gilbert was home with Eva celebrating the birth of their first child—a son they named Joshua in memory of her father—when the radio announced a general mobilization. All reserve troops were being called up.

During the next twenty-four hours, the Voice of Israel poured forth an endless flow of seeming nonsense, like, "Chocolate ice cream must go on the birthday cake," "Giraffes like watermelon," "Mickey Mouse can't swim." These were the code signals telling the citizen-soldiers where to report with their weapons.

Nasser had massed a hundred thousand men armed with Soviet equipment, as well as a thousand tanks, in the Sinai Peninsula on Israel's southern border.

War was inevitable. The only question was whether Israel could survive it.

Since 1956, Egypt and Israel had been separated by small token units of the United Nations Emergency Force, scattered along the frontier. Nasser ordered the UNEF units out of his way. When they withdrew, nothing but sand stood between the two countries.

The King of Jordan put his own army under the Egyptian high command and contingents arrived from other Arab countries.

Israel was now confronted by over a quarter of a million troops, two thousand tanks, and seven hundred aircraft. The country was menaced on three borders. Its fourth frontier was the sea. And that was where the Arabs intended to drive them.

With the odds so heavily stacked against them and all the

nations of the world preaching restraint but doing nothing to enforce it, they were totally on their own.

Jason Gilbert's platoon of the 54th Paratroop Battalion had been mobilized for over a week, camping in an olive grove near Tel Shahar.

On the order of Battalion Command, they did endless stretcher training to practice the rapid evacuation of the wounded. This was hardly an encouraging exercise. Nor was the fact that so many of his men had portable radios and could keep abreast of the worsening situation. The British and American Embassies advised their staffs to leave Israel.

As darkness fell each evening, Jason would try to lift the morale of his soldiers. But as the days drew on and the tension mounted, he was less and less convincing. Especially since he himself knew so little of what was happening.

Finally, on the evening of June 4, he received a communiqué: *Prepare to move men tomorrow at 0600.* It did not say where.

When he told this to his platoon, they were actually heartened. At last they would be doing *something* other than waiting to be bombed out of existence.

"Try and get some sleep, guys," Jason said. "We're going to have a job to do tomorrow."

As the men disbanded and started toward their sleeping bags, a young reservist in a skullcap approached Jason and, withdrawing a small blue leather book from his breast pocket, asked politely, "*Saba*, would it be all right if I prayed instead of sleeping?"

"Okay, Baruch," Jason said. "Maybe God is listening tonight. But what prayers can you say the night before—before an attack?"

"The Psalms are always appropriate, *saba*. You know, 'Out of the depths I cried unto Thee, Thou answered me with great deliverance.' "

"Yeah," Jason smiled wanly, "just be sure you ask for a three-pronged deliverance."

The young soldier nodded and walked off to a quiet corner where he would not disturb his sleeping comrades. And began to chant the Psalms very softly. Over and over.

Jason lay down in his sleeping bag and wondered if he would ever see his wife and son again.

At dawn on Monday, June 5, the buses arrived. They were the same rickety vehicles on which some of these men rode to work in Tel Aviv. Today they were taking them down toward the

Sinai. To an air base deep in the Negev where a fleet of Sikorsky helicopters was waiting.

As they left the buses, the soldiers glanced nervously toward the sky, instinctively sensing that hostilities had begun. And, being so close to the border, fearing an attack by the Egyptian Air Force.

Jason was in the midst of reassembling his men and dividing them into groups of eight for each chopper, when a senior officer called him over for a moment. He came sprinting back, his face beaming.

"I've got a pretty interesting announcement, guys," he called out. "It appears that at 0745 hours this morning, our planes undertook a preemptive strike against enemy airfields. There is no longer such a thing as the Egyptian Air Force. The skies belong to Israel. Now it's up to us to take the ground."

Before the men could cheer, a young soldier raised his hand. It was Baruch. Pointing to his little prayer book, he shouted exultantly, "You see, *saba*, God *was* listening!"

There were no agnostics in the Israeli Army that morning.

"Okay," Jason said, "here's our agenda. We're all moving out. The tanks, the infantry, everybody. We're going right across the Canal to visit the pyramids. There's only one little job we have to do first. The Egyptians are really dug in at Um Katef—the front door of Sinai. The tanks can't get close enough, so it's our job to clear them the hell out. Now there's not enough room for everybody, so I'll take volunteers."

Every hand shot up. And even when he had picked his troops, extra men pushed themselves onto the helicopters.

As soon as it was fully dark, they began to land in the dunes north of the Egyptian stronghold. The choppers went back and forth ferrying troops like businessmen in a subway rush-hour. The last few landings were under heavy fire from the fortress.

By prearrangement, the men split into an attack force and a cover group. Jason led his soldiers toward the Egyptian guns, firing rifles, Uzis, and bazookas as they advanced.

Suddenly one of their own rockets hit an ammunition convoy. It exploded, causing devastation on both sides. By the light of the flaming tower, Jason counted five motionless bodies and dozens of wounded comrades. He ordered his men to stop their advance and wait for the stretchers to come up. Then they performed in earnest the exercises they had done so many times in practice.

At last he picked up his gun and went back to the inhuman job of killing. For the sake of peace.

By the end of the first day the threat of annihilation no longer existed. For the Jordanian and Syrian air forces had suffered the same fate as the Egyptian. The Southern Command was on its way toward the Suez Canal almost unimpeded.

Though Israel was fighting a war on three fronts, it did not have three armies. Its single fighting force had to fire to the north as well as to the south. Thus, as soon as the exhausted 54th Paratroop Battalion had cleared the way for the capture of the Sinai, they drove northward where the battle for the Golan Heights was raging.

And all the while they were traveling, a fierce hand-to-hand battle was under way for the ultimate prize—Jerusalem.

When they reached the Golan on Wednesday morning they were greeted by news that paratroops had recaptured the Old City. And were at the holiest of Jewish shrines—the Temple Wall.

Meanwhile, Jason's battalion captured the Syrian position east of Dar Bashiya. The big guns that had for years been pounding the northern kibbutzim were finally silenced.

Six days after it started, the war was over. And the face of Israel had changed. In the south it had the entire Sinai Desert as a protective buffer. It controlled all the territory to the west down to the River Jordan, giving it a defensible frontier. And in the north, Israelis were now on the Golan Heights, threatening Syria instead of vice versa.

It was a success in every way but one. It did not bring peace.

On September 1, the Arab Summit Conference at Khartoum passed three resolutions: no negotiations with Israel, no recognition of Israel, no peace with Israel.

Jason Gilbert, rocking his son in his arms, remarked to his wife, "They could have added no *rest* for Israel, either."

Even as he spoke, the shellshocked and defeated Arabs were planning a new kind of war against their enemy. A campaign of terror and sabotage. They created the PLO, whose stated aim was the "national liberation" of the people who had never been a nation.

*   *   *

No measures seemed to prevent these new terrorists from entering Israeli territory. They could slip across the Jordan River, hide in caves, do their mischief, and either return or travel north and vanish across the Lebanese border. At first the Israeli Army tried the retaliatory raids that had proven moderately effective before the war. Now they were of no avail.

They sealed off the Jordan with a fence of minefields. They even raked the paths so that early-morning patrols could tell if anyone had passed through during the night. But like the hydra serpent of Greek mythology, every time one head was cut off, the invaders seemed to grow two more.

To deal with this problem the best commandos of every unit were recruited for a supreme counterterrorist force known as *Sayaret Matkal,* the General Staff Reconnaissance Unit.

Jason was determined to be part of this group. He drove to headquarters prepared to fight the same "you're too old" battle he had fought five years earlier.

But when he met the interviewing officer he realized it was not necessary. For it was none other than Zvi Doron, whom he had so persuasively "convinced" in the paratroop-recruitment shack. This time the two men laughed for a few minutes until Zvi voiced his single qualm about Jason's desire to join.

"Listen, *saba,* I know you can do this job physically. But you're a father and a husband now. And this is not really the kind of job that makes for happy marriages. To begin with, you'll be away a lot. For another thing, you won't be able to talk to your wife about any of our operations. Believe me, I saw enough divorces in para reconnaissance."

"Look," Jason answered, "I'm not in Israel to pick oranges. I stayed here to do a job. And as long as I can still be useful, I'll run any risk that's necessary. Now will you take me?"

"Only if you promise to talk it over with your wife."

"That's a deal."

Eva understood him too well even to argue. She knew she had married a man with fire in his soul. And in a sense, it was that fire which warmed their marriage. She would not stand in his way. She merely extracted from him the futile promise that he wouldn't take any unnecessary chances.

After all, he was a family man with a wife and son. And a second child due in four months.

George Keller could almost have been working in the Museum of Modern Art. Every morning for the past four years, since Labor Day 1963 to be precise, he had been going to 30 Rockefeller Plaza, in New York City, passing various security procedures and ultimately taking an elevator to the fifty-sixth floor. There he would enter portals marked simply "Room 5600."

On the way to his luxurious office, he would walk down corridors lined with Renoirs, Picassos, Cézannes, and van Goghs. Not to mention equally priceless statuary. For he was in the midst of one of the finest private art collections in the world.

It was at this rarefied height that Governor Nelson Rockefeller and his brothers had their base of operations, each maintaining a wing devoted to his various interests, patronage, philanthropy, politics, and combinations thereof.

On Henry Kissinger's recommendation, George had been hired to join the staff writing memoranda on international affairs for the governor. As Henry put it, "You would be laying the groundwork for the foreign policy of the Rockefeller presidency."

If he had any doubts about leaving Harvard, they were dispelled by the knowledge that scarcely a year out of graduate school he was already earning the equivalent of a full professor's salary.

He had not lacked for attractive offers. With each summer he spent helping to organize the Harvard International Seminar, his responsibilities had grown in proportion to his rise in Kissinger's esteem. By the time he received his Ph.D. in government, he was the co-editor of *Confluence*, the seminar's flagship publication.

Henry was fiercely loyal to his protégés and never hesitated to include George in the strategy for his own advancement. This was not out of uncritical affection. George was clearly an asset, for both his academic brilliance and his innate feeling for diplomacy. It was, if not an alliance of equals, at least a genuine partnership.

Naturally Harvard had wanted George to stay on. The department chairman even called in Kissinger to discuss how they could persuade the young scholar to remain in the academic ranks. His adviser countered that George was a strong-willed man.

"I sense his aspirations lie in Washington and not in Cambridge," Henry offered. "But I will do my best."

Kissinger did not exert undue pressure on George to remain at Harvard. For he himself had more use for soldiers to man the advance guard of his own career. Hence, by placing George with his long-time patrons, the Rockefellers, he had an ally he could count on in the "real world."

In June 1963, George Keller not only received his doctorate but—and perhaps of greater importance—took the oath of fealty to the U.S. Constitution. Thus officially becoming a proud and patriotic American.

The granting of his citizenship was to him a kind of late-arriving birth certificate. By this time he had not only secured his future, he had all but suppressed his past.

It was almost as if he had never been Hungarian. Or had never had a father or a mother. Or a sister. Or a fiancée named Aniko. Only once in a great while did he have a nightmare about being lost in a blinding snow storm, not being able to find his way home. He had even conscientiously avoided reading the Hungarian press, except when it was absolutely necessary for his course work. He was like Athena in Greek mythology, sprung full-grown from the forehead of Zeus. Only in George's case his creator was Henry Kissinger.

And so George Keller set out for New York—in some eyes the greatest city in the world. But, in his view, merely a suburb of Washington.

His philosophy in acquiring a new wardrobe was based on the personal theory that if a garment was tailor-made it had to be better. He found out who had been the late President Kennedy's tailor and ordered several new suits in every "distinguished" color.

In fact, he became something of a sartorial proselytizer. He would even chide Andrew, whom he occasionally met at the New York Harvard Club either for lunch or squash, "Eliot, I can't for

the life of me fathom why you still buy off the rack. After all,
you're an up-and-coming banker."

"I'm only just a trainee," his classmate would counter affably.
"Besides, we New England Yankees are indoctrinated to be thrifty."

He did not mention, nor did George with his impeccable
sense of tact, that two years before, upon turning twenty-five,
Andrew had come into a trust fund of several million dollars.

There were other advantages to working for the Rockefeller
organization. For example, access to unobtainable concert and
theater tickets. Not to mention bright, pulchritudinous young
women who also worked in Room 5600.

George enthusiastically took advantage of all these opportunities. He reveled in the glittering first nights at the opera and
important theatrical events. He had house seats when Fonteyn
and Nureyev first danced the young Russian's version of *Swan
Lake* in America. Indeed, when Danny Rossi played the Bartok
Second Piano Concerto with the New York Philharmonic, George
was sitting in the Rockefeller family box with Sally Bates, the
governor's charming and beautiful assistant for urban affairs.

As Danny strode on stage, George could not keep himself
from whispering to Sally, "This is like old home week for me.
Bartok is Hungarian. And Rossi is a Harvardman. He and I were
classmates."

"Do you know him personally?" she inquired, most impressed.

"We were both in Eliot House," George replied evasively.

"Oh, that's exciting. Can we go backstage and meet him
afterward?"

"Uh—I don't think we should," he backtracked as suavely as
possible. "I mean, Danny's always exhausted after he performs.
Some other time."

The normally staid atmosphere of Room 5600 seemed electrified during those days in 1964 when Nelson Rockefeller was
making his bid for the Republican presidential nomination. Kissinger
was there so often that George wondered how he managed to
teach his classes.

Nominally, Henry was on the Rockefeller staff as foreign
policy adviser. But he delegated to George the drafting of the
position papers, while he himself huddled in the inner sanctuary
with Rocky to discuss the strategy of the campaign.

George went along with the entourage to the Republican Convention in San Francisco. And even after their patron lost the nomination to Barry Goldwater, he stayed on to assist Kissinger in writing the foreign-policy planks of the party platform.

On Election Night, George and Henry stood in a corner of the subdued hotel ballroom watching each return increase the magnitude of their candidate's crushing defeat at the hands of Lyndon Johnson.

"Well, Henry, I guess that's the end of the ball game."

"Not at all, George, not at all."

"What do you mean? They're swamping us nearly two to one."

"Not *us*," Kissinger replied. "Only Senator Goldwater. Just remember the Democrats will also need expert advice."

Inwardly George thought his old teacher was merely putting up a brave front. Kissinger would be relegated to the classroom just as he would be to Room 5600.

And yet, three years later, while Lyndon Johnson stood helplessly mired in the pernicious swamps of the Vietnam war, a chubby, bespectacled Harvard government professor presented himself in the office of Secretary of Defense Robert McNamara. The academic offered to relay secret messages via certain French contacts to Ho Chi Minh, the North Vietnamese leader.

The Pentagon was impressed. And, to the surprise of many, but certainly not to the professor, they agreed to make Henry Kissinger their secret envoy.

Of course, George ultimately guessed what games the master strategist was playing by interpreting the "slips" that Kissinger would make in their conversations.

Once when they were chatting about food, Henry said, "I had the most superb *coquilles* at Prunier the other night."

"Where's that?" inquired George.

"Oh, Paris," he answered quite offhandedly. "I was over for a few hours to . . . give a paper."

George sifted for the nuggets of truth. Clearly, Kissinger was now involved in some kind of covert negotiations on behalf of the U.S. government.

But he still could not grasp why a Democratic administration should choose a relatively unknown professor who had actually worked against them in the previous campaign. Didn't they have contacts of their own? Why Henry?

When Kissinger's role finally became public knowledge, George dared to ask what made him think his audacious offer would even be taken seriously.

"Well," Henry replied, "I could fob you off with a quote from Clausewitz *On War*. But if you want the unvarnished truth, I just thought I'd give it a shot. There were only two possible answers, so I had a fifty-fifty chance."

"Oh," said George Keller in monosyllabic awe. And thought, This man is a genius.

In direct contrast to the sophisticated Realpolitik of George's mentor was the naive sentimentality of his first Harvard roommate. Often, at lunch, Andrew would seek George's diagnosis of the malady that was infecting the nation. In early June 1968, he was absolutely distraught.

"George, what's happening to this country? I mean, has the war drained off all our sanity? Why are we killing each other? It's barely two months since they shot Martin Luther King—and now Bobby Kennedy. Can you explain any of this madness?"

George replied with cool academic detachment, "I think these are all signs that the Republicans will win in November."

But whatever Kissinger was doing on those secret Paris journeys, it was clearly not enough. The Vietnam conflict grew worse. Among its casualties was Lyndon Johnson himself, who, worn down by the onslaught of protests, chose not to seek reelection. Thus leaving the bombing to an unscarred and less-heartsick leader.

In a sense, LBJ was handing the presidency to Richard Nixon. For this canny politician did not need the advice of brilliant strategists like Kissinger and his young assistant Keller. Common sense told him that a simple promise to end the war would sweep him into office.

And it did.

It also swept George out of Rockefeller Center. His disappointment at the thought of not being able to see those Renoirs and van Goghs every morning was somewhat mitigated by the fact that, although his new working quarters would be cramped and airless, they were at least well located.

In the White House basement, fifty yards from the National Security Adviser, Henry Kissinger.

B roadway musicals are never better than on the first day of rehearsal. This is the moment when the authors themselves read through the play, singing the lyrics in their fresh, unadulterated form.

When Stu and Danny finished their two-man show, the cast clapped enthusiastically. Sir John Chalcott, the director, rose to make some inaugural remarks.

"I think all of us here recognize what a superbly written piece of theater we've just heard. It is our duty as professionals to live up to the authors' intentions. All our efforts in the next six weeks will be bent in that direction."

Polite applause.

Zero Mostel now stood up. "This is not your ordinary Broadway dreck. I honestly think James Joyce would have respected what Stu and Danny have done. And, guys—we're going to knock our kishkes out for you."

More applause.

Sir John turned to the leading lady and inquired, "Miss Hamilton, would you care to say a word or two?"

She did.

Honoring her director by affecting what she thought was an English accent, she remarked, "Can either Mr. Kingsley or the celebrated Mr. Rossi explain to me why Mr. Mostel gets to sing the final number?"

This was hardly what Sir John had expected. But his cast did not seem at all surprised. They merely turned to hear the authors' explanation.

Danny got up from the piano and took a few steps toward the table around which the cast was gathered.

"Look, Miss Hamilton, this is our concept. Stu and I want to emphasize Joyce's theme of Stephen looking for his lost father and Bloom for his dead son. We feel the real emotional pull is between the two of them."

"But surely, Mr. Rossi, the novel itself ends with Molly's soliloquy. Why are you mutilating a classic for what I assume is the sake of Mr. Mostel's ego?"

Before Danny could reply, the male lead offered a laconic comment.

"Bullshit."

In an accent now more aristocratic than ever, Theora Hamilton turned to her costar and said sternly, "Mr. Mostel, such vulgarity is unworthy of the professional you aspire to be."

To which Zero simply replied, "Bullshit."

Sir John Chalcott rose again.

"Miss Hamilton, ladies and gentlemen, I'm sure none of us here is unfamiliar with Joyce's masterpiece. And for that very reason we can appreciate how ingeniously our authors have captured its spirit. You do, after all, have a musical version of the soliloquy when you sing 'Roses and Fire and Sunset' in the penultimate scene. I think the slight modification of putting Zero's duet last works better for the *stage*. Call it justifiable artistic license."

"I still think I should sing a reprise just before the curtain," she replied. "After all, whom are the public flocking to see if not Theora Hamilton?"

To which Zero Mostel answered, "Zero Mostel."

The First Lady of the American musical theater turned again to her costar and said, in an accent by no means English, "Bullshit."

Rehearsals had begun.

Six weeks later, prior to leaving for Boston they did a run-through in New York. Afterward Edgar Waldorf reported that the group of invited professionals had all been laudatory about the project. Some indeed had confessed to being moved to tears by the lovely duet that concluded the play.

Danny and Stuart embraced warmly.

"Just think," the poet enthused, "we'll be starting our triumphal march in the shadow of Harvard Yard. Doesn't that give it an extra kick?"

"Yeah, it really does."

"Hey," Stuart suggested, "do you and Maria want to take the train up with me and Nina? We could all hold each other's hands."

"Thanks, but Maria's going to stay in Philly. She gets sort of nervous at these things. I'm going home over the weekend to conduct two concerts and I'll fly up Sunday night. We can meet for a drink in my suite at The Ritz."

"Great. But listen, Danny. I know I've told you before but, as Hamlet says, I want to engrave this on the tablets of your memory. I'll always be grateful that you chose me to collaborate with you—"

"Stu, you're enormously talented—"

"Please, Danny, you could have had any lyricist you wanted, but you gave a shot to a guy with no track record. Don't think I'll ever forget your generosity."

"Hey, Stuart, now it's my turn. This whole thing has been a joy. We're not just partners anymore. We're almost brothers."

It is an invariable rule in the theater that musicals are never written. They are rewritten.

"That's what tryout towns like New Haven and Boston are for," Edgar explained to Danny and Stu. "Bostonians are as sophisticated as New Yorkers—but more tolerant. They appreciate the fact that we're there to cut and trim and polish. Even the critics can give you a useful tip or two."

"Suppose a show is perfect?" Stuart asked tongue-in-cheek.

"Then we just make it *more* perfect. Even *My Fair Lady* polished all its diamonds on the road. And, boys, let me tell you, this show is a thousand times better."

Manhattan Odyssey opened its Boston run on February 12, 1968. The initial reviews were not quite as enthusiastic as Edgar Waldorf had predicted. Indeed, they were not very good. To be more precise, they were scathing.

The only "useful tip" the *Boston Globe* could offer was that "this unmitigated disaster should fold its tents as quickly as possible and creep away in the night." The critic found the words pretentious and the score incongruous. The other papers were even more disparaging.

Danny was in shock. These were the first hostile reviews he'd received since the Harvard *Crimson* panned *Arcadia*.

When she heard of the catastrophic reception, Maria offered to fly up and give him support.

"No," he told her on the phone, "I have a feeling we're going to be working night and day. You'd be better off out of the line of fire."

"Danny," she said reassuringly, "this has happened to a lot of out-of-town shows before. You've got plenty of time to fix whatever is wrong."

"Yeah. Besides, I think the Boston critics are being a little bit snobbish. I'll wait and see what *Variety* has to say. That's the only opinion I really trust."

Variety, the respected publication of the snow-business world speaks unvarnished truths in its own unique idiom. And, from its opening headline, "No Cause to ReJoyce," it was an unmitigated pan.

Danny quickly skipped over the unfavorable comments about Stuart's words, Sir John's staging, the stars' heroic efforts to overcome the feeble material, and shot right to the paragraph that addressed itself specifically to his work.

> On the cleffing side, Rossi is clearly out of his element. He seems to write noise, not tunes. His material is distinctly unhummable. He seems allergic to melody, which may be chic in his longhair circles, but it's not likely to send the average play-goer stampeding to the wickets.
>
> In short, *Manhattan Odyssey* is going to need mucho work to make it on the Main Stem.

As he sat there in the quiet splendor of his suite at The Ritz, Danny read the review several times, still unable to dispel his incredulity.

Why were the critics so vicious? That music was the best he had ever written. He was sure of it. At least, until this moment.

There was a knock at his door. He glanced quickly at his watch. It was twenty minutes past midnight. But, as his New York friends had often reminded him, when a show is out of town it's like an obstetrics ward. There is no night and no day.

His nocturnal visitor was Edgar Waldorf, their no-longer-ebullient producer.

"Did I wake you, Dan?"

"No, I was just about to jump out the window."

"Then you've seen *Variety*?"

"Yeah."

Edgar flopped onto a couch and breathed a histrionic sigh.

"You know, Dan, we've got trouble."

"Edgar, I'm aware we have problems. But isn't that what out-of-town tryouts are for?"

"Stu has got to be replaced," he replied quickly. "I mean, he has big talent, a huge talent. But he's too inexperienced. He's never worked under the gun like this."

Danny did not know how to react. His friend and college classmate—a fine and intelligent writer—was going to be summarily fired.

He brooded silently for a moment, and then said softly, "He's a sensitive guy, this'll kill him. . . ."

"No," the producer replied. "He's a big boy. He'll live to write another day. And when we save the show he'll have royalties to live very well. But right now we need to play doctor—somebody who writes great, funny, and *fast*."

"Uh, who'd you have in mind?" said Danny, dreading what might now become of Stuart's elegant dialogue.

"My wife is calling New York to see who's available."

"But Stu'll still stay on as lyricist. . . ."

"God knows, we still need work there, too," Edgar commented, a perceptible tinge of uneasiness in his voice. And then quickly added, "Stu's back in New York. I don't want him on the lyrics, either."

"Dammit, Edgar, the least you could have done is let *me* tell him! Aren't you being a bit brutal?"

"It's not me who's brutal, Dan, it's the business. Broadway is strictly sink or swim, either one night or ten years! It's a goddamn war between the artists and *The New York Times*!"

"Okay, okay, I'm getting the idea," Danny acquiesced. "But who'm I gonna work with on the lyrics?"

Edgar now took a prodigiously deep breath. It was as if the entire hotel suite had suddenly become an oxygen tent. He squirmed, clutched his heart, and in his most mellifluous lower register said, "Daniel, we have to talk about the music, too."

"What about it?"

"It's terrific, sensational, brilliant. It's just maybe a little *too* brilliant."

"Meaning what?"

"Well, not everybody can appreciate such quality. I mean—you've read the reviews."

No, thought Danny Rossi, *this can't be happening. He doesn't want to fire me!*

"We need some songs," Edgar explained. "You know, tunes."

"I've read *Variety,* Edgar. I'll simplify the stuff. I'll write catchy melodies." Panic had gripped him, and his tone of voice had involuntarily become a plea, a supplication.

"Danny, you're a classical composer. God knows, you may be a modern Mozart!"

He seized the feeble compliment to use as a weapon for his own survival. "That's just the point, Edgar. Mozart could write in any style—from Requiem Mass to 'Twinkle, Twinkle, Little Star.' "

"Yeah," replied the producer. "But he's not available. And listen, baby, you need help."

There was a frightening pause. What was this ignoramus going to propose?

"You've gotta understand there's nothing personal about this, Dan. It's for the show. We've gotta do this to save the show. Ever hear of Leon Tashkenian?"

Indeed, to his ineffable distress, Danny had. Tashkenian was known among his serious musical friends as "*Trash*-canian." A two-bit, Tin Pan Alley hack!

"He writes *shit,* Edgar, pure unadulterated shit!"

"I don't give a damn what you call it," Edgar retorted. "Leon's got it and we need it. Do you hear me? Does reality ever pierce your magnificent ego? Like the fields need manure, this show *needs* some shit!"

Daniel Rossi was choking with rage and humiliation.

"Edgar, I know my rights under the Dramatists Guild contract. You can't bring in a new composer without my consent. And I hereby refuse to consent."

"Okay, Mr. Rossi," Waldorf said calmly, "I know my rights, too. This show sucks. Your music is putrid. The people hate it. So if you don't want the helping hand of Mr. Leon Tashkenian, you have a simple alternative. You can die in Boston and be buried in your beloved Harvard Yard. Because if you say 'no Leon,' I'll go right over to the theater and post the notice."

He stormed out in a melodramatic huff, knowing Danny was already vanquished.

In fact, Edgar went straight to the downstairs telephone to call Leon Tashkenian, who had already been working in a suite at the Statler since early that morning.

Danny swallowed a tranquilizer, which seemed to have no effect. Then he began to seek consolation from every possible source. First, his agent, Harvey Madison, who had been expecting a call and who was quick to reassure his distinguished client that during a long battle with Edgar Waldorf earlier that evening, he had preserved Danny's integrity in every way. Leon Tashkenian would receive no billing whatsoever.

"Listen, Dan," Harvey philosophized, "this is how every Broadway show gets on. It's patched together with a dozen different *shmatas* from a dozen different people. And if you're exceptionally lucky, the critics decide it's silk and not the same old toilet paper."

Danny was seething with betrayal.

"Harv, you haven't got a shred of integrity," he shouted.

"Danny, wake up. In the theater, 'integrity' is what closes on Saturday night. Stop playing Goody Two-Shoes and be grateful Tashkenian was willing to ghost for you. Look, we'll talk, babe. As soon as the new stuff is in, I'll fly up to Beantown and we'll have a quiet meal and a good heart-to-heart. Stay loose."

As he slammed down the phone, Danny thought of getting drunk. But then suddenly realized that, for all his moral indignation, he had forgotten the devoted Stuart Kingsley, now so brutally banished.

He dialed New York. Nina said her husband could not come to the phone.

"Danny, you're a ruthless, cold-hearted bastard," she hissed. "Is there anything or anyone you won't sell out? He thought you were his friend. God knows he would have protected you—"

"Nina—"

"I hope this show goes down the sewer and you with it. That's where you all belong!"

"Please, Nina, let me speak to Stuart. *Please*."

There was a slight pause. She then replied with subdued fury, "He's in Hartford, Danny."

"What the hell's he doing in—?" But it dawned on him before he had finished his sentence. "You mean the sanitarium?"

"Yes."

"What happened?"

"He got knifed in the back by his friend."

"I mean, what did he do?"

"Washed down a few dozen pills with a bottle of scotch. Luckily, I came home early—"

"Thank God. Nina, I—"

"Oh, console yourself, Daniel. The doctors understand his case completely—"

"Good," said Danny, genuinely relieved.

"—They think he'll probably succeed next time."

Mercifully, Danny had to be away from Boston for the next few days. First he conducted a pair of concerts in Los Angeles, then took the Red Eye straight to New York. He arrived at 6:00 A.M., caught some sleep in the dressing room, swallowed two "*allegro vivaces*" for stimulation and went out to rehearse for three hours.

That evening he performed Schoenberg's complex piano concerto to such rapturous applause that he had to play an encore.

Danny's choice—a complete musical contrast—revealed that Boston was very much on his mind. He played Mozart's Variations in C (K 265). Otherwise known as "Twinkle, Twinkle, Little Star."

He finally got back to Boston at twenty-five to one. As he entered his suite at the Ritz, the phone was ringing.

"Yes?" he said, sighing wearily.

"Welcome home, Danny, are you free?" It was Edgar.

"Hey, I'm dog tired. Can't we speak in the morning?"

"No, we've got a rehearsal call for eleven and I want to get the parts copied."

"What parts?"

"Leon's new material. Can we come up?"

Oh no, did he actually have to *meet* his nemesis?

"Edgar, you don't need my approval. I've already capitulated. I know it's terrible without even having to hear it. . . ."

"Then let Leon play it and maybe you'll change your mind. You might even have a suggestion or two."

Daniel Rossi was a quick study. He now, as it were, knew

the score. Although he had waived his right to veto additional music by Leon Tashkenian, he had retained one privilege, empty gesture though it might be.

Contractually, he could still remove his name from the whole enterprise. And, what the hell, wasn't that something? Didn't his name lend class to the marquee? Didn't his reputation as a serious musician ensure some kind of respect on the part of the reviewers? Edgar *still* had to stroke him.

"All right. But this has got to be as brief as possible."

"It'll be the Minute Waltz," Edgar blurted. And immediately hung up.

Danny barely had the time to swallow an "Allegro" when he heard a knock. He opened the door with trepidation. There stood a bizarre couple. Elegant, melon-shaped Edgar Waldorf and a youngish, swarthy man with Brillo hair. The latter was garbed in black corduroy, save for a white shirt open amply enough to allow an unobstructed view of a gold medallion nestling in a field of fleecy muscularity.

"Hi." Leon Tashkenian smiled, offering his hand.

"Bollinger," said Edgar Waldorf, offering a magnum of champagne.

Danny said nothing. Never squander ammunition in a siege. As the two men entered the room, a waiter suddenly appeared behind them, bearing a tray of three chilled glasses. He retrieved the bottle and proceeded to open and disgorge its contents.

"You played really great tonight," Tashkenian remarked.

"Thanks," Danny muttered sarcastically, taking it as typical showbiz bullshit. "Were you in New York today?"

"No. But you were live on WGBH."

"Oh."

"Let's all drink up," Edgar interposed, foisting champagne glasses into the two composers' hands. He then raised his own goblet in an emotional toast: "To the Show."

Leon lifted his glass but did not drink. Danny merely gulped it and sat down.

"Okay, let's see what you've done," he said, reaching out toward Tashkenian's sheaf of papers.

"Let him play it," Edgar insisted.

"I can read music," Danny snapped.

"I would expect no less of a Harvard graduate, Daniel," Edgar replied. "But, unfortunately, I am educationally deprived.

Besides, I like Leon's delivery. C'mon, Lee, give out with the material." And then turning to Danny, he editorialized, "It's fabulous! Fab-u-lous!"

Boom-bam, boom-boom-bam! Leon played like a mad woodman trying mightily to fell a Steinway.

Danny raised his hand. "Okay. I've heard enough."

"Wait, wait," Edgar protested, "he's just warming up."

Danny capitulated with a sigh and turned to refill his glass.

Gradually through the din a few sounds became intelligible. The tonic, the relative minor, the second, the dominant seventh. Could he have expected anything better than the most hackneyed, overused chord sequence in pop music?

There had been moments in Danny's life when he had dreamed of becoming Beethoven. Now he merely longed to be deaf. For, among his many virtues, Leon Tashkenian had the voice of a ruptured hyena.

Now and then, Danny could discern a word or two of text. There was something about "Mars," suggesting that the rhyme "stars" could not be far behind. And it arrived, just as surely as "crying" followed "flying." At last, on the very brink of a vocal orgasm, Leon screeched "above," harmonized by an E major seventh.

The end was near—and so damn predictable—that Danny had all he could do to keep from groaning the inevitable concluding wordlet, "love."

By this point, Edgar was pirouetting around the room. He rushed over to Tashkenian, kissed him on the cheek, and announced, "He loves it, Danny *loves* it!"

Sweating and gasping for breath, Leon looked up at the Renaissance man of modern music.

"What do you think, Mr. Rossi?" he asked like a nervous neophyte.

"Leon, it gives the word *crap* a new dimension."

"He's kidding, he's kidding." Edgar laughed nervously.

"He's not," said the young man at the piano, quietly but with less diffidence. And then, turning to Danny, he inquired, "Could I have some more specific criticism?"

"Specifically, Leon, I object to the clichéd use of 'one-six-four-five-one.' "

"A cliché is what you make of it, Mr. Rossi," Leon replied. "Richard Rodgers used it beautifully in 'Blue Moon.' "

"You're not Richard Rodgers—and that mindless sequence of notes isn't music."

Tashkenian was young, but he was aware of his own worth, especially at this moment. After this latest barrage of insults, he owed the maestro no more deference.

"Look, Rossi, I've got better things to do than sit here and be abused by a pretentious, overrated asshole like you. I know damn well my chord progressions are familiar. But that's the name of the game. The clichés make 'em think it's something they've heard before. They're half-remembering it even before they hear it. And that means they can hum it at intermission. And *that,* in the musical theater, spells success. You don't have anything against success, do you?"

At this point, however, Edgar Waldorf felt impelled to defend the star who was providing his show with light if not heat.

"Mr. Rossi is one of the great composers of our time," he said.

But Tashkenian had gone too far to back down.

"Of what?" he sneered. And then turned to Danny. "You're not even that good at classical. I mean, at Juilliard we studied the last movement of your pseudo-Stravinsky *Savanarola* ballet—as an example of heavy-handed orchestration. You're nothing but an Ivy League con man."

As suddenly as he started, Leon stopped, gripped with fear at what he'd allowed himself to say.

Danny could say nothing. Because some pellets of truth in Leon's wild shotgun rage had hit home.

They simply stood there, glaring at each other, both frightened at who might explode next.

Curiously, it was Leon Tashkenian. He began to cry. He reached into his pocket for a handkerchief, wiped his cheeks, and then said quietly, "I'm sorry, Mr. Rossi. I spoke out of turn."

Danny did not know how to respond.

"Come on," Edgar pleaded, "he said he was sorry."

"I really didn't mean what I said," Tashkenian added meekly.

Danny concluded that magnanimity would be his only way of saving face. "Forget it, Leon, we've got a show to think about."

Edgar Waldorf rose like a phoenix from his sofa of despair.

"Oh God, I love you both. You are two beautiful human beings."

By some miracle, both men avoided his passionate lunges. He then took Leon's lead sheets and handed them to Danny.

"Here, schmaltz 'em up with your classical virtuosity."

"What?"

"You gotta play these tunes to the cast tomorrow morning."

What new humiliation was this? Was he to "schmaltz" up Leon's musical guano as this cheap hack looked on gloating?

"Why do *I* have to play it?"

"Because it's supposed to be your stuff, Dan."

"They don't know about Leon?"

Edgar shook his head emphatically. "And they never will."

Danny was speechless. He turned to the young man, whose eyes were still red with tears, and asked, "You really don't want any credit?"

Leon smiled shyly. "It's part of the business, Mr. Rossi. I'm sure you'd do the same for me."

"They're humming! Do you hear me, Danny? They're *humming!*"

Edgar Waldorf was phoning from the manager's office of the Shubert Theatre. It was the first intermission after Leon's numbers had gone into the show. They had even added a reprise of "The Stars Are Not Enough," which Theora Hamilton would now sing just before the curtain fell (Sir John Chalcott, who had threatened to resign if this change were effected, was at that moment on a flight back to London).

Danny had not been able to bring himself to go to the theater for fear of—he knew not what. Hearing the new songs fail? Or, worse perhaps, hearing them succeed?

"And, Danny," Edgar continued to enthuse, "I smell success. We've got a winner! Trust Edgar Waldorf, we've got a smasheroo!"

Toward the midnight hour, there was a sensuous tap-tap-tapping at his hotel door.

It was the distinguished—and heretofore coolly distant—leading lady. Miss Theora Hamilton was carrying a bottle of showbiz soda water, otherwise known as champagne.

"Mr. Rossi," she cooed, "I've come to toast a genius. That new ballad you wrote for me is a classic. I could see tears in their eyes as the curtain fell."

Danny had never taken much heed of her opinions, but he had always entertained some interest in her breasts. He was pleased to see that she had not neglected to bring them along.

"Well, may I enter, or do we have to drink this in the hallway?"

"Madame," said Danny with a gallant bow, *"je vous en prie."*

And so the legendary Theora wafted in. First bottle, then breasts, then the heart that lay passionately within. They all were his that night.

Yes, music hath charms. Even if it is by Leon Tashkenian.

On the night of the New York opening, Danny had his driver bring Maria from Philadelphia directly to the theater. While she went in to watch the performance, Danny and Edgar paced nervously in the empty lobby. Every time they perceived laughter or applause they exchanged glances and mumbled something like, "Do you think they liked it?"

During the ride to the party, Danny anxiously asked Maria what she thought.

"Well, frankly, the original version was a little more to my taste. But the audience seemed to like it and I guess that's what's important."

"No, it's only what the critics think that counts."

"I looked everywhere," she said, "but I didn't see Stuart and Nina."

"They were both too nervous," Danny improvised. "In fact, I don't think they'll even come to the reception. They'll probably just sit at home and watch the television critics."

By eleven-thirty, almost all the important reviews were in. The networks had been unanimously favorable. All complimented Stuart Kingsley's literate book (Edgar's wife, who had stepped in when Neil Simon declined the rewriting task, went graciously unbilled). And all remarked on Danny Rossi's "sinewy, melodic score" (CBS-TV). It now seemed a foregone conclusion that the *Times* would come through with a rave.

And it did. In fact, Edgar was on the bandstand at that very moment, tearfully reading the words that would make them all rich and famous forever.

"It's a Valentine!" he shrieked, waving a yellow sheet of paper above his head, "an unadulterated Valentine! Listen to his goddamn headline—'Melody Makes a Mighty Return to Broadway.' "

The crowd of actors, investors, and Beautiful People broke into cheers. Edgar raised his hand to plead for silence. At last, they quieted down to hear more. Only the tinkle of glasses was audible, occasionally punctuated by melodramatic female sighs and appreciative whispers.

Meanwhile, Edgar read on from the sacred document.

"Tonight, at the Shubert Theatre, Daniel Rossi confirmed beyond doubt that he is master of every musical form. What better demonstration of the enormous range of a composer than the comparison of his complex, powerful, nearly atonal *Savanarola* ballet with the dulcet and unabashedly simple melodies from *Manhattan Odyssey*. Certain to become standards are gems like, 'This Evening, Like All the Other Evenings,' and, especially, 'The Stars Are Not Enough.'

"Poet Stuart Kingsley has also shown that he has a magical gift for the theater. . . ."

Immediately after the definitive critic's closing salvo ("I hope it runs forever"), the band broke into "The Stars Are Not Enough." And everyone, young and old, drunk and sober, began to vocalize. Except Danny Rossi.

As the guests sang chorus after chorus, Maria leaned over and whispered in her husband's ear.

"It's really lovely, Danny."

He kissed her on the cheek. Not to acknowledge what she had naively intended as a compliment, but because there were photographers watching.

The following March, at the Tony Award ceremonies, *Manhattan Odyssey* was chosen as Best Musical of the year. Not unexpectedly, Danny Rossi was named Best Composer. Accepting the prize on behalf of Stuart Kingsley, who had won for Best Lyrics, Edgar Waldorf gave a touching little speech about Stu's teaching commitments making it impossible for him to attend.

In a frantic round of bidding, MGM carried away the screen rights for a record sum of nearly seven million dollars.

Not long thereafter, Danny Rossi's picture appeared on the cover of *Time*.

*   *   *

For a long while Danny felt ashamed about the secret *Manhattan Odyssey* humiliation. Though only two other people in the world knew, he harbored an inner sense of failure.

Yet, the soul has remarkable powers of regeneration. As years passed, and the number of different recorded versions neared two hundred, Danny gradually began to believe that he actually *had* composed "The Stars Are Not Enough."

And, what the hell, given half a chance, he probably could have.

May 15, 1968

Practically living as I do at the New York Harvard Club, I was probably the first guy outside of Cambridge to see a copy of the *Decennial Report,* which chronicles our class's progress in the first ten years since graduation.

I note a tendency of the less successful guys to write longer histories than their more shining counterparts.

I mean, one character goes on for paragraphs in tedious detail about his uneventful army service, his choice of wife, what his kids both weighed at birth, and so forth. Also how challenging life is in Daddy's shoe-manufacturing business ("We've had to move our operations from New England to Puerto Rico and are now exploring the possibility of relocating in the Far East").

The only thing he doesn't talk about at length is his divorce. *That's* where I might have found something to empathize with. Anyway, it's clear to see through the thick clouds of his verbosity that he's trying to disguise a life of quiet desperation. He concludes with the philosophical observation, "If the shoe fits, you've got to wear it."

In other words, he's taken four whole pages to inform us that he's on his way to being a successful failure.

On the other hand, Danny Rossi merely lists the dates of his marriage and his daughters' births, the things he's written, and the prizes he's won. That's all. He didn't even offer a pithy conclusion like "I've been very lucky," or "I owe it all to eating Wheaties," or some such.

And yet who hasn't seen his face in all the papers and read at least a half dozen stories that all but deify him?

I bet a lot of guys who thought he was a weenie are now boasting to their wives and kids that they were buddies with him in the college days. I confess that I even exaggerate my passing friendship with him, too.

Ted Lambros's entry was also brief and to the point. He and Sara had enjoyed the decade at Harvard. He was gratified that his Sophocles book had received favorable reviews, and he and his family were looking forward to the new challenge of living and teaching at Canterbury.

Neither Jason Gilbert nor George Keller sent in a response, both for reasons I well understood. Jason, with whom I'm still in touch by letter, has been through a hell of a lot.

And George is just the same old paranoid, suspicious nut. He didn't even vouchsafe any of the meager information he gives me when we have lunch.

Unlike a lot of my classmates, I thought I'd try to be honest in my capsule history.

My two years in the navy got a sentence, and I didn't glorify them. Then I simply noted that after seven years at Downs, Winship, I'd been elected a vice-president.

Then I said that the greatest joy I've had is watching my children grow. And the greatest disappointment that my marriage didn't work.

I don't think many people bothered reading my entry, but I didn't give much away.

I didn't mention that I'm really not that much of a success in investment banking. I owe my promotion to the fact that a couple of buddies and I helped float Kintex, which grew to be the world's largest producer of The Pill. And hence took off like a wild rocket. (Sheer luck—or was it a subconscious way of regretting that I had allowed myself to have children with such an unfit mother?)

I didn't say that though there are thousands of new singles' bars sprouting all over First Avenue for so-called successful guys like me to meet fairly neat women, my life is desperately lonely.

I spend every weekend trying to reconnect with my kids (Andy now seven, Lizzie four), to little avail. Faith seems to have given up sex in favor of booze—and her face shows it. Apparently the only time she sobers up is when she's telling the kids what a bastard I am. And I only have a couple of hours on Saturdays to try to counter this calumny.

My one solace still seems to come from Harvard. Though I've bought a fancy pad in a new high-rise on East Sixty-first Street, I spend most of my time playing squash at the H-Club and socializing with the guys. I help the Schools Committee recruit good men for "the age that is waiting before." I'm even thinking of running for the Alumni Council—which would give me a nice pretext to go up and walk in the Yard again.

In short, I'm no happier than the garrulous shoe salesman. On the other hand, I think I hide it a little better.

Ted Lambros prepared himself for his new life at Canterbury with typical enthusiasm. He spent the summer of '68 packing books and notes, improving his old lectures, and—most important—taking tennis lessons at Soldier's Field.

As they were settling into the ramshackle house they had rented from the college on North Windsor Street, Sara cautioned him, "You know, honey, if you actually beat Bunting, he'll never vote for you."

"Hey," he replied jocularly, "you're speaking to the great tactician. I've got to be just good enough for him to want to keep me as a sparring partner—or whatever they call it."

But there was more than the tennis vote to worry them. The department had three other senior classicists—and also influential wives.

Naturally, there had to be a separate dinner with each couple. Henry Dunster made the first move and invited them. The present Mrs. D. was Henry's third, and there was every indication that she might not be the last. Predictably, he made a sort-of-pass at Sara. Which did not flatter her at all.

"I mean, he wasn't vulgar," she complained to Ted as they drove home, "it's that he was so ludicrously tentative. He wasn't even man enough to be an honest flirt. God, what a creep."

Ted reached over and took Sara's hand.

"One down," he whispered, "three to go."

The next hurdle on this steeplechase to tenure was a dinner with the Hendricksons—Digby, the historian, and his loving wife, Amelia. Theirs was indeed a marriage of true minds, for they thought as one. They shared a love of hiking, mountaineering,

389

and a fervid paranoia that everyone in the department was out to steal Digby's history courses.

"I think it's awful," Sara commented, "but in a way their jealousy is understandable. History, after all, is the foundation of the classics."

Digby took her point and ran with it a little further.

"Not just the foundation, Sara, it's the whole shebang. Literature is nice, but what the heck, when all is said and done it's only words. History is facts."

"I'll buy that," said Ted Lambros, specialist in literature, clouding his mind and swallowing his pride.

Sara had already started action on the distaff front. In fact, her "friendship" with Ken Bunting's wife had blossomed into weekly soup-and-sandwich luncheon dates at The Huntsman.

Dotty was a self-styled social arbiter who neatly pigeonholed the Canterbury wives into one of two categories: "real class" or "no class." And Sara Lambros of the New York banking Harrisons was certainly genuine cream, not Reddi-Whip. And since Dotty was, as she put it, a blueblood from Seattle, she regarded Sara as a soulmate.

The only difference was their marriages.

"Tell me," Dotty asked in furtive tones, "what's it like being married to, you know, a Latin type?"

Trying mightily to keep a straight face, Sara patiently explained that Greeks, though dark and—to some eyes, perhaps—a little swarthy, weren't quite the same as "Latins." Still, she understood the interrogatory innuendo and replied that she assumed all men were basically alike.

"You mean, you've known a lot?" asked Dotty Bunting, titillated and intrigued.

"No," Sara answered calmly, "I just mean—you know—they have the same equipment."

Dotty Bunting turned a vivid crimson.

Sara quickly changed the subject and sought Dotty's counsel on the "real class" children's dentists in the area.

One thing was clear. If Mrs. Bunting had a vote, Sara certainly would have it. It remained to be seen what influence she had on her husband. And that could be determined only when the two couples actually met for dinner. Again, consistent with traditional collegiality, the Buntings asked the new arrivals to their home.

The conversation, as anticipated, was tennis-oriented. Bunting jocularly accused Ted of dodging his innumerable invitations to "come and hit a few." Ted volleyed back that he'd been so involved in setting up the house and starting courses that his game was far too rusty to give Bunting even token competition.

"Oh, I'm sure he's only being modest, Sara," Dotty Bunting gushed. "I bet he even played for the varsity."

"No, no, no," Ted protested, "I wasn't nearly good enough. Tennis is one of the few sports Harvard actually is not bad in."

"Yes," Ken allowed, "it was a Harvard guy who beat me for the IC4A title back in fifty-six."

Unwittingly, Ted had reopened the most painful wound in Bunting's sporting memories. Ken now began to hemorrhage verbally.

"I really should have won it. But that Jason Gilbert was such a crafty New York type. He had all sorts of sneaky little shots."

"I never thought of New York people as particularly 'crafty,'" Sara said ingenuously. "I mean, I'm from Manhattan too."

"Of course, Sara," Bunting quickly said apologetically. "But Gilbert—which was probably not his name for very long—was one of those, you know, Jewy characters."

There was an awkward pause. Sara held back to let her husband speak up in defense of their Harvard classmate.

Then, seeing that Ted was having trouble finding an appropriate response, Sara mentioned casually, "Jason was The Class of '58, with Ted and me."

"Oh," said Dotty Bunting. "Did you know him?"

"Not very well," Sara replied, "but he dated a few girls from my dorm. He was very good-looking."

"Oh," said Dotty, wanting to hear more.

"Say," Ken interrupted, "whatever happened to old Jason? His name seems to have disappeared from the pages of *Tennis World.*"

"The last I heard, he'd gone to live in Israel," Ted answered.

"Indeed?" Bunting smiled. "He should be very happy there."

Ted looked at Sara, his glance imploring her advice on what to say. This time, she too was at a loss. The best she could come up with was, "This dessert is marvelous. You *must* give me the recipe."

*   *   *

Left for last because they seemed the toughest nuts to crack
were Foley, the stone-faced archaeologist, and his equally impene-
trable wife. Sara made countless attempts to fix a time with them.
But they always seemed to have some previous engagement. At
last, she verbally threw up her hands and said, "Please, name *any*
night you're free. It's fine with us."

"I'm sorry, dear," Mrs. Foley said cheerfully, "we're busy
then."

Sara hung up politely and turned to Ted. "What the hell,
we've got three out of four. That ought to do it."

Collegiality aside, Ted grew more and more to love the
Canterbury way of life. He was pleased that Sara seemed to be
adapting to rusticity as well as coming to appreciate the rich
classics section of Hillier Library. She read all the latest journals
from cover to cover and would even brief him over dinner on
what was new in the ancient world.

The students were enthusiastic, and he felt the same toward
them. And, of course, it didn't hurt Ted's ego that his course in
Greek drama drew the largest crowd in the department.

Raves for his teaching soon reached the office of the dean.
And Tony Thatcher thought it now opportune to sound out all
the classicists about Ted's tenure. He elicited affirmative responses
from the Hellenist, the Latinist, and the historian. And from the
archaeologist he even got a nod.

All would have come off without the slightest hitch had it
not been for the affair with young Chris Jastrow.

In certain circumstances it might have been a touching sight—a
muscular Adonis in an orange crew-necked sweater emblazoned
with a C, sleeping like a mighty lion in the sun.

Unfortunately, this was in the middle of Ted's Latin class.
And he was anything but touched.

"Wake up, Jastrow!" he snapped.

Christopher Jastrow slowly raised his handsome head and
looked at Ted with half-open lids.

"Yes, sir, Professor," he mumbled with exaggerated deference.
And removed his feet from the desk in front of him.

"I'm sorry to interrupt your siesta. But would you be kind
enough to conjugate *voco* in the present passive?"

"*Voco?*"

"Yes, *voco*," Ted repeated. "As you may recall, it's first conjugation. And I'd like to hear you go through it in the present passive."

There was a slight pause.

"I'm afraid I didn't get today's assignment, sir."

"What you're saying is that you weren't here last time and didn't bother to ask anybody what to prepare."

"Well—"

"Mr. Jastrow, I want to see you in my office this afternoon between four and five."

"I'm sorry, I can't make it, sir," he answered courteously. "I've got practice."

"Listen," Ted warned sternly, "I don't care if you've got a meeting with the President of the United States. You show up between four and five today—or else."

And even though there was some ten minutes remaining, he could not continue teaching.

"Class dismissed," he said, fuming.

As the students filed slowly toward the front and out the door, sophomore Tom Herman stopped at Ted's desk and spoke sympathetically.

"Excuse me, Professor Lambros, would you be offended if I said something?"

"Tom," Ted answered, "nothing you could say could possibly offend me any more than Jastrow's attitude."

"Well, that's just it, sir," Herman said diffidently. "Maybe you don't know who he is."

"I read the college paper," Ted replied. "I know Jastrow's our first-string quarterback. But I'm still going to bounce him from the class if he doesn't start working."

"Sir, with due respect, you can't do that. I mean, without him we can't win the Ivy title."

Having spoken out bravely, he turned and quickly left the classroom.

Ted sat in his Canterbury office from four till half-past five that afternoon. Several students dropped by, some to question points that genuinely puzzled them. Some merely to gain points with him.

But Chris Jastrow was not one of them.

Ted threw on his (Harvard) scarf and coat and started down
the hallway. He noticed that the Classics Department was still
open and Leona, the secretary, was typing. He stuck his head
inside.

"Hi, Lee, have you got time to do a short note for me?"

"Sure." She smiled, then quickly rolled a fresh sheet of statio-
nery into the typewriter and said, "Fire away."

"To Anthony Thatcher, Dean of Humanities: Christopher
Jastrow '69 is currently failing intermediate Latin. His attitude is
insouciant bordering on the arrogant. Barring some unforeseen
miracle, there is no possibility of his being kept in the course past
midterm. Yours truly, et cetera."

Ted dictated this in one cathartic burst, his head in his hands.
When he glanced up he noticed that Leona looked uneasy.

"Yes, I *know* who he is. But this is the Ivy League, we've got
standards to maintain." And as she typed the envelope he added,
as if to absolve her of complicity, "I'll put it under the dean's
door myself."

He had no classes the next day, and so took full advantage of
the rich facilities of the Canterbury Library to further his research.

He emerged after spending nearly eight hours abstracting the
entire Fondation Hardt volume on Euripides, his green bookbag
heavy with valuable copies of European journals that he—and
Sara—would devour over the weekend.

Something made him glance up the hill at Canterbury Hall.
There was no light on in the department office. What the hell, he
thought, I might as well pick up my mail.

In addition to the routine correspondence there was a hand-
addressed letter from the Department of Athletics.

Dear Ted:
I'd be grateful if you could drop by as soon as possible.
I'm usually in my office till at least 7:30 P.M.

Your friend,
Chet Bigelow
(Head Football Coach)

He had half-expected this. Glancing at his watch he saw
there was still time to put this presumptuous bastard in his place
tonight. He marched off toward the gym.

*   *   *

Chet Bigelow's rugged features looked like they had been the model for the phalanx of trophies lined up on the desk that separated the two men.

"Well then, Professor," he began, "I understand our boy Jastrow's having difficulty with your Latin course. Perhaps you don't realize the pressure our men are under during the season."

"Frankly, Mr. Bigelow, that's none of my concern. In fact, what puzzles me is why Jastrow's taking Latin in the first place."

"Why, Prof, you surely know the college rules as well as I. A guy's gotta fill a foreign-language requirement to graduate. Right?"

"But why Latin? Why in the world did you have your precious quarterback take an ancient language that is probably twice as difficult as any modern one?"

"It's not hard if you've got the right teacher," Bigelow explained.

"What?"

"Most of your classics boys have been terrific to us over the years," Chet reminisced. "I mean, Henry Dunster's absolutely fantastic. And, of course, we've played ball with him, too."

"Coach Bigelow, I'm afraid you're losing me."

"All right, Teddie, lemme put it another way. If you suddenly got a lot more students taking Latin, you'd have to hire a lot more *teachers*. Am I right?"

"I don't like your insinuation," Ted said with disgust.

"Just what do you imagine I'm insinuating, Prof?"

"Naturally, I'm just a dimwit from Harvard. But it seems to me you're suggesting that if the football team increases our enrollments by sending us warm bodies, we should be so grateful that we should let them sail through without doing any work."

There was a pause. The coach stared silently at Ted. And then he smiled.

"You clearly know the game, Professor. Now I suggest you go out and play by the rules. For, from what I gather, you do not yet have tenure at this place. And just like we need a good season, *you* need a good season."

Ted stood up.

"If you want a war, Coach," he whispered, "you're gonna get one. Tomorrow's the midterm exam. And if Jastrow flunks, he'll be out on his ass."

"Have it your way, Teddie. Just remember you're dealing with a man who's undefeated in six seasons."

At the exam next morning, Jastrow did not appear at all. As soon as it was over, Ted Lambros stormed over to Barnes Hall and requested an audience with the Dean of Humanities.

"Tony, I'm sorry to barge in on you like this."

"That's all right," the dean replied. "In fact, you might say your visit has been heralded."

"Coach Bigelow?"

He nodded. "Yes, Chet's a bit overprotective of his boys. Anyway, sit down and tell me about it."

Thatcher listened as Ted went on like a prosecuting attorney. A frown gradually appeared on his face. There was a moment of silence before he commented, "Look, Ted, I don't think flunking Jastrow's the most prudent way of handling this."

"Do you see any alternative?"

The dean turned his chair ninety degrees and gazed out over Windsor Green. "Well," he mused, "as John Milton so eloquently put it, 'They also serve who only stand and wait.' " He then swiveled back and looked at Ted.

"Milton was *blind* when he wrote that. But I'm not."

Dean Thatcher gave this response careful thought, then smiled benignly.

"Ted, I want to talk to you for a moment off the record. You know how highly I regard you. And I feel you're at the start of an extremely promising academic career."

"What could this possibly have to do with my professional future?"

The administrator replied, unblinking, "Everything."

"Can you explain that, please?"

"Listen," the dean replied patiently, "you don't seem to understand. If Jastrow can't play, *my* head's right there on the block with yours."

"Why? You're a full professor. You've got tenure."

"I've also got three kids and a mortgage. They could freeze my salary forever. You've got to realize that Canterbury alumni are a very powerful group. And they feel pretty strongly about this place."

"And its football team," Ted added sarcastically.

"Yes, dammit, and its football team!" the dean shot back

with exasperation. "Can't you fathom that every time we beat Yale or Dartmouth, our grads interpret it as a sign that we're superior in other ways as well? And let me tell you, the Monday after one of those victories, checks pour in like manna from heaven. An undefeated season can literally mean millions of dollars. And I'm not going to sit by and let a sanctimonious punk like you mess up the system. I mean, you don't seem particularly grateful to be here."

"Why should I be grateful, dammit?" Ted retorted. "I've already published more than the rest of the department put together."

The dean shook his head. "You amaze me. You still have no idea what it takes to get ahead in the academic world."

"I'm a good teacher and I've written an important book. I should think that would suffice."

Tony Thatcher grinned. "It didn't suffice for Harvard, did it? I mean, they didn't seem to want to make a professor out of a Cambridge townie. And, frankly, neither do some of our boys."

Ted had been in street fights. He had been kicked and punched and bruised. But now he felt inwardly lacerated. While he had already seen that a provincial place like Canterbury judged him on social grounds, he never would permit himself to think that his rejection at Harvard had been on anything other than academic criteria.

But he was suddenly uncertain about everything. He didn't know whether to stay or leave. And so he remained frozen in his chair awaiting—fearing—what Thatcher would say next.

Finally, the dean addressed him in soft, paternal tones. "Ted, let me tell you what's going to happen. You're going to pass Chris Jastrow. And he, in turn, is going to pass for innumerable touchdowns—to the delight of our generous alumni. Now, of course, you and I are aware that the boy doesn't know the first thing about Latin. But we also know that in the scheme of things, it isn't all that important. What matters is that nobody rocks the boat. That way, everybody's future is brighter—including yours."

He rose and held out his hand in amical valediction.

"I'm sorry," Ted said quietly, "but you still haven't convinced me."

"Professor Lambros," the dean responded cordially, "let me leave you with one little thought. If we should deny you tenure at the end of this year, you might not find another teaching job anywhere. . . ."

"That's a crock."

"No, that's a fact. Because no matter how much you've published, the dean of wherever you apply is going to check with us for a character reference. You know, to find out if you're "collegial.'" He paused and then added almost in a whisper, "Need I say more?"

"No," Ted answered, barely able to hear his own voice.

Sara was livid.

"They can't do this to you. It's cruel, it's barbaric—and it's totally unethical."

"You're right. But it's also frighteningly possible."

He was sitting on their dilapidated couch utterly bereft of confidence. Sara had never seen him so shaken.

She sat down and put her arms around him. "Ted, Canterbury's not the end of the world. There are other schools that would kill to get you, even if these guys here say you're a total shit."

He lowered his head for several minutes.

At last he spoke. "Suppose they're not bluffing? Suppose Tony Thatcher does have the power to blacklist me? What then?"

Sara Lambros thought for a moment and carefully weighed every syllable of her reply.

"Ted, I love you because you're brave and good and honest. And I'll stick by you no matter what happens. Isn't that enough?"

He raised his head and looked at her. "I can't lie to you, Sara. I've never been so scared in all my life."

Before either of them could say another word, their little son burst joyfully into the room. "Daddy, Daddy," he chirped and ran to his father's arms. "Jamie Emerson tried to beat me up again."

"Again?" Ted asked bemusedly, as he continued to embrace his son.

"Yeah," said the boy, "but this time I did what you told me. I punched him right back in the belly. It made him cry."

Ted smiled and thought to himself, At least there's one fighter in the family.

*   *   *

They barely spoke at dinner. Sara assumed her husband was just emotionally spent and was thankful for the respite. She was somewhat surprised when he stood up and reached for his parka.

"Where're you going?" she asked.

"I don't know, I thought I'd walk to Canterbury Hall. It's such a nice place when nobody's around. I want to grade those exams tonight—so I can exorcise this whole business."

"Good idea," she answered, sensing that he had regained some confidence. "I can sit here and abstract one or two pieces from *Wege zu Euripides.*"

He kissed her on the forehead. "Sara, you are the Tenth Muse."

"Thanks, sport, but I'm happy just being plain Mrs. Lambros. Now go off, do your homework, and come back to my loving arms."

He sat in his tiny office and looked out over Windsor Green. A preview of snows to come had powdered its broad surface, which glowed softly in the moonlight. Now and then students passed, and the air was so still he could hear their laughter from afar.

The bell tolling ten o'clock admonished him to complete his task. He turned back to the pile of bluebooks on his desk and set about transcribing the results for submission to the dean's office. They hadn't been bad. A handful of A's, two C's, and the rest varying shades of B. All in all, something a language teacher could take pride in.

Of course, there was the no-show of a certain football player. But that was quite another matter.

It took him less than two minutes to enter the grades. Now only the space following Christopher Jastrow '69 remained—like the new snow outside—fresh, clean, and unsullied. Blank.

What should it be—F, Incomplete, or ABX (meaning absent from the exam)? Any of these would put the quietus on the little bastard's football career.

He sat there, staring at the paper, writing nothing.

At first he had no notion of what he was going to do. But then gradually it dawned on him that he had left the house and gone to his lonely, underheated cubicle for a definite reason. To get away from Sara. To elude the beacon of her conscience.

Sara was unable to understand the kind of fear that gripped

him. Her family had status, substance, and security. He still felt like an immigrant, desperately needing roots in his new country. Perhaps her forebears had made compromises in generations past. But they were buried deeply now in the unshakable foundation of her respectability.

It was such a little thing to do. In years to come he would resent acting out of false bravado. This was not ancient Athens. He was not Socrates. So why the hell should he drink hemlock for some small-time football star? What lofty principle would be served by failing Jastrow?

No, he told himself. Our whole future's at stake. This is for self-preservation.

He took his pen and in the space by Jastrow's name hastily scribbled—"C."

And en route home he dropped the grades in Barnes Hall.

As he entered, he could hear Sara in the bedroom speaking to someone on the telephone. At this hour?

He walked to the open door. She was so engrossed in conversation that she didn't notice his arrival.

"I just don't know what else to do," she was saying plaintively. "This is such a blow for Ted, and I can't seem to help him. . . ."

She paused to listen. He still did not signal his presence.

"Oh would you?" she then said eagerly. "I think that might really help."

Who is she talking to? With whom is she sharing our most intimate secrets?

"I'm home, Sara," he said quietly.

She looked up, smiled, and then immediately ended her phone call. "Oh, the man of the house just entered. Thanks for everything. I'll call you in the morning." And she quickly hung up and hurried over to kiss him. "How do you feel, darling? Can I get you a bite of something?"

"I wouldn't mind a beer," Ted answered tersely.

As they headed for the kitchen, he asked calmly but with an unmistakable edge of disapproval, "With what member of the community were you sharing our little moral crisis?"

"Oh, Ted, I'm so glad I don't have to wait to tell you. I've just had a long talk with Daddy."

She opened the fridge, took out two beers, and handed one to him.

"Why did he have to know about this?" Ted asked.

"Because I thought he could help, and he can. He knows Whitney Vanderbilt—who's as heavy a Canterbury alumnus as there is. Daddy's sure he can get him to step in and help us out. Isn't that great?"

Ted felt his anger mounting.

"So you went running to Daddy with *our* problem. *My* problem, to be precise. I find that slightly disloyal, to say the least."

She was stunned.

"Disloyal? For God's sake, Ted, you were suicidal when you left here. I would have done anything to help you—even strangle Tony Thatcher with my bare hands. I don't see why you're not overjoyed that my father actually has the power to help us. . . ."

Her voice trailed off as she began to realize how furious he was.

"Sara, you shouldn't have done this without asking me. I mean, am I or am I not the man in the family?"

"What the hell does this have to do with gender? Do you want to go down in flames just to preserve your masculine ego?"

Ted exploded. "Goddamn you, Sara!" And slammed his beer bottle so violently on the kitchen counter that it shattered.

Before either of them could speak, frightened sobs and shouts of "Mommy!" began to emanate from little Ted's bedroom.

For another moment they just glared at each other. Finally she whispered, "I'd better go to him."

It took Sara nearly twenty minutes to lull her fearful six-year-old back to sleep. When she returned to the kitchen she saw that Ted had cleaned up and disposed of the broken glass. She walked into the living room. He was seated, facing the fire, a glass of scotch in his hand. He did not turn when he heard her approach.

"Do you want to talk?" she asked calmly.

Still with his back to her, he said tersely, "I gave Jastrow a C."

By now she had guessed as much. And knew she had to suppress—or at least postpone—her anger.

"Ted," she began softly, "it was for you to decide. I just wish you'd trusted me enough to share the pain of compromise."

He sat like a statue, unresponsive.

"Look, I said I'd stick by you. And if staying at Canterbury means that much to you, we'll pay the price. We can be happy anywhere as long as we keep together."

"You think I was a coward, don't you?" he murmured.

"No, Ted," she answered. "I was just as scared as you. I shouldn't have tried to make you into some Sophoclean hero. I mean, life is full of compromises, and what you did is pretty minuscule in the scheme of things."

He still did not turn. She walked up behind him and placed her hands gently at the base of his neck. Her touch brought a surge of comfort.

"Sara," he whispered, "I sat there all evening wondering what the hell to do about it. And then something said to me that bucking the system would be like King Lear raging against the winds. It would have meant risking everything we worked for, everything we want to do. . . ."

"It's over now, Ted," she said softly, "so just forget it."

"You know I can't. I never will." He paused, then added, "And you won't either."

Inwardly she knew that he was right.

The National Security Council had existed, at least in name, since 1947. But it was only after 1969—when Richard Nixon named Henry A. Kissinger to lead this advisory group—that it began to impinge upon and gradually usurp some of the powers of the Department of State.

Most of this was attributable to Kissinger's brilliance and resourcefulness. But he also benefited from what, in geopolitical terms, might be called first-strike capability at access to the President.

The Secretary of State has his headquarters in an imposing building on Twenty-first Street and Virginia Avenue, but the head of the NSC works out of a windowless warren in the bowels of the White House itself. Thus, though William Rogers may have had the cabinet post and trappings of office, Henry Kissinger had the President's ear.

To assist in building a power base in the National Security Council, Henry had brought along several of his Harvard students, many of whom he had long been grooming. Of these, George Keller was by far the most gifted. And, paradoxically, had the hardest time being cleared for security.

No Kafka victim was ever grilled as relentlessly as George was questioned by the FBI. It was all polite, of course. But, as the agents kept emphasizing, when you are checking someone for the highest security level, the fate of the nation lies in your thoroughness.

First he had filled out an exhaustive written questionnaire asking his name, any former names, and all the addresses he had ever lived at since he was born. Also the sources of all the income he had ever earned. Moreover, they demanded as many names as possible of Americans who could testify to his loyalty. George

offered Kissinger, Professor Finley, and Andrew Eliot. All of
whom, he later learned, were personally visited by the Bureau.

But during his oral interview, when questions were repeated
again and again by the two agents, he began to grow upset.

"Gentlemen, I must have told you a dozen times. I can't be
sure that I didn't live in one place or another when I was two
years old. I hope you can appreciate that."

"We do, sir," the senior FBI man said tonelessly. "But I
hope you appreciate the sensitive position you're in. When a
candidate still has relatives back there the possibility for blackmail can't be ignored. And you still have—what, Dr. Keller,—a
father—?"

"And a sister," George quickly repeated for the millionth
time. "And as I told you gentlemen, I haven't seen them since
October 1956."

"Still, you are aware that your father is a high official in the
Hungarian People's Government, are you not?"

"I only know what I read in the papers," George replied.
"And that, gentlemen, is part of my duties as an East European
area expert. Yes, it's true that Istvan Kolozsdi" (he was unable to
pronounce the words *my father*) "has been kicked upstairs, as
you might put it. But the jobs he has held are absolutely
insignificant."

"And yet he is, after all, a Deputy Assistant Secretary of the
Party," countered the senior agent.

George laughed derisively. "You could be too, sir. In Hungary
they hand that title around like candy."

"Then what you're saying is that your father is not that
important. Is that so, Dr. Keller?"

"Precisely. He's what you might call a successful failure."

Some of the queries were not unexpected.

"What do you think of communism?" gave George the opportunity for an eloquent tirade against the various Marxist re-
gimes of Eastern Europe. A speech that, he sensed, considerably
impressed his interviewers.

And yet, even after an entire day of talking, one question
startled him.

"Do you love your father, Dr. Keller?"

George suddenly grew tense. Inexplicably, he was at a loss for words.

"Do you love your father?" the agent repeated.

George groped for a suitable response: "He stands for a repressive political system, one which I have dedicated my life to opposing. I cannot but loathe such an individual."

The FBI men shifted impatiently in their chairs. The senior officer then commented, "Dr. Keller, we asked you a personal question and you gave us a political answer. Now I know it's getting late and we've been here a long time. But if you don't mind, sir, I'd like to hear you address yourself to that question again. Do you love your father?"

Why was he having such trouble giving them a simple "no"?

"Look," he said in a confidential tone, "can I say something off the record?"

"Please feel free, sir."

"The truth is, I hate that man. He treated me like a dog from the day I was born. I detest Istvan Kolozsdi as a human being. Now, if I can answer on the record—please. I have no affection whatsoever for my father. Is that clear enough for you, gentlemen?"

"Yes, Dr. Keller. I think that about wraps it up. Thank you for your patience."

After they left, George fell into a sudden depression. Not really worrying about his security clearance. Kissinger had forewarned him that the FBI was pretty severe with foreign-born candidates.

No, it was that last question. He had thought that he no longer had any feelings at all for his father. But never had he been obliged to testify on record, "I swear I do *not* love my father."

Was it totally true?

A long-forgotten childhood memory suddenly surfaced from his psyche, catching him completely unaware.

"Why are you crying, Father—is it for Mama?"

"Yes, boy. To love someone is terrible. It brings such pain."

"But, Father, I love you."

"Then you're a little fool. Get out and let me be."

♦

Most of the staff of the National Security Council was headquartered in large, airy, colonial-style rooms on the second floor of the Executive Office Building, an historic structure within the White House compound. ("It's like being on campus again," George remarked to an assistant.)

The little rooms along the NSC corridor contained bright young specialists in diplomacy, defense, and various geographical areas of the world. They toiled long hours in the service of their country and their own advancement.

But George was singled out from the very beginning. He was given office space—though little of it—right in the White House basement, where his boss could hale him into conference at all times of the day. And even well into the night.

He was also only steps away from the two most vital scenes of governmental deliberations, the Oval Office and the Situation Room, that airless cubicle sometimes referred to as "a sauna for world crises."

Though George's twenty-five-thousand-dollar salary was somewhat less than he had received in New York, he was still able to rent a small apartment in Town Square Towers, a few minutes drive from the White House—especially at 7:00 A.M., when he usually arrived.

Even Kissinger's influence did not extend to getting parking places. Therefore, as a junior aide, George had to leave his car in the government lot beneath the Washington Monument, then walk north and cross Constitution Avenue to reach the White House gate.

Actually, it was a rare occasion in his long and busy day that he got to see some of the other NSC staffers who worked across the way in the EOB. For Henry made enormous demands of his team. His insatiable appetite for information of all sorts was such that they rarely had the chance to leave their desks, even to go downstairs to the cafeteria for lunch.

No one worked later than Kissinger himself. And George made sure that he never left his office until Henry passed by and wished him good night.

George had no social life at all. Indeed, the entire staff in the EOB worked themselves to such exhaustion that they barely had the strength to drive home. There were many burnouts even among the whiz kids in their middle twenties.

One of George's tasks was assisting Kissinger to recruit bright, new faces—which would very shortly become pale, tired faces—for the National Security Council staff.

Early that first spring, he interviewed a young graduate of Georgetown for a job in the Latin American section. She had excellent qualifications: an honors degree in Spanish and Portuguese, as well as several letters from Republican party officials reminding the White House boys how important a Washington lawyer her father was.

George was nonetheless determined to grill her severely. He felt too strong a loyalty to Kissinger to allow party politics to impinge upon the important work they were doing. If this girl turned out to be some flighty social type, they would farm her out to some senator's office.

The fact that Catherine Fitzgerald was blond and attractive confirmed his prejudgment that an empty-headed debutante was being foisted on them. But then she genuinely confounded him. Not merely with her credentials and obvious intelligence, but with her experience as well. She had spent two years with the Peace Corps in Latin America, and had worked three summers during college for a bank in São Paulo to perfect her Portuguese.

George's evaluation was positive, and Catherine Fitzgerald was hired to work for the National Security Council.

After that, he passed her occasionally in the corridors while following up something for Henry with people in the EOB. But otherwise he gave her no thought. He was too immersed with helping Kissinger solve the jigsaw puzzle called world politics.

That is, until late one icy winter evening, when he left the West Wing of the White House and was heading for the gate. He glanced over to check whose office lights were still on in the EOB and caught sight of her emerging from the entrance.

"Miss Fitzgerald," he said jokingly, "don't tell me that you're going home so early?"

"Oh hi, Dr. Keller." She sighed wearily. "You know that actually isn't a joke. This is the first time I've left the office before midnight."

"I'll be sure to tell the boss," said George.

"Don't bother. I'm not bucking for promotion," she replied. "I only wish he'd hire one or two more aides for my department. Some people around here think South America is just a suburb of Mexico."

George smiled. "Is your car parked over by the Monument?"

She nodded.

"So's mine. I'll walk you over. We can protect each other from the muggers."

Crossing Constitution Avenue, George looked at Cathy and a surprising thought occurred to him.

This person is a girl. She's not bad-looking. No, in fact, she's fairly pretty. And I haven't even had a social conversation since I've been in Washington. With so many hours of hard work behind him, his conscience allowed him to ask if she would like to have a drink.

"Fine," she replied, "but only if it's coffee."

George then suggested several spots in fashionable George-town that he'd heard of and wanted to check out.

"Oh no," she answered pleasantly, "I don't feel up to facing the *jeunesse dorée* of Washington. Why don't we just drive to my place and have coffee there?"

"Okay," George replied. "You lead and I'll follow."

She lived alone on South Royal Street in Old Town Alexandria—an attractive three-room walk-up.

As she fussed with an espresso machine, George studied the posters on her wall. They were mostly colorful souvenirs from her Latin American travels. Except for one, which piqued his curiosity.

"Say, Cathy," he asked, pointing to the large white-and-blue placard that had pride of place over her sofa, "is that some kind of joke?"

"Oh, you mean my antinuclear artwork?" she responded blithely. "No, I was actually pretty active in the antiwar movement in college. I was even in a couple of big marches."

"Then I don't understand—"

"What? How I got the NSC job? Or why I wanted it?"

"Both, I guess."

"Well," she said, sitting down beside him and handing him a cup, "to begin with, this is a free country and I'm not ashamed to say I think we're wrong to be in Vietnam. On the other hand, I obviously don't advocate the violent overthrow of the government, or I wouldn't have gotten security clearance. Ergo, you might say I'm an idealist who wants to work for change within the system."

"Very noble," George responded. "Are there many others like you in the NSC corridor?"

"One or two." She smiled. "But I'm certainly not going to name any names to 'Kissinger's shadow.' "

She stopped herself, suddenly embarrassed.

"Is that what they call me—'Kissinger's shadow'?"

"Well, you two are pretty inseparable. I suppose it's just a little jealousy on the part of those of us who work across the tracks. I mean, somebody mentioned that you were probably the youngest guy with an actual office in the White House."

"What else do they say?" George coaxed.

"You're putting me on the spot. Can't we change the subject?"

"Yes, but only if you let me guess what the other staffers think of me. My intuition says they consider me conceited, arrogant, and ruthless."

He looked at her for a response.

"No comment," she pleaded.

"You don't have to, because it's true. I am all of those things."

"I don't believe you." Cathy smiled. "I think that somewhere underneath that stuffed shirt of yours there beats the heart of Santa Claus."

"Thanks for the leap of faith," said George.

"Actually, I think the boss is that way too. Henry just likes to make tough noises. That's why you two get on so well. It's probably your European backgrounds."

"What do you know about my background?"

"What everybody knows, I guess. I mean, we're sworn to secrecy about government affairs, so what else can we use for gossip if not our colleagues' private lives?"

"But I don't have a private life," George retorted.

"Too bad. You could probably make some girl extremely happy."

"I doubt it. I'm the least romantic person in Washington."

"But you're probably the most brilliant. I've read your articles in *Foreign Affairs* and—though I disagree with most of your conclusions—they're amazingly astute."

"I'm flattered." He touched her on the shoulder lightly and inquired, "Have you got anyone to make you happy?"

"Not at this moment. No."

"May I apply for the position?"

"You may," she smiled. "But then I'll have to interview you."

"How about dinner Friday night?"

She nodded. "That's great. I'll try to finish by nine. Is that okay?"

"That's fine," said George. "It's somewhat early for me, but I'm really looking forward to it."

"**K**ala *Christouyina!*"
"Merry Christmas!"
The Lambros clan had much to celebrate in December of 1968 as they all crowded around the festive table at the family home in Cambridge.

One week earlier Ted had received the official word of his promotion to tenure—effective July first of next year. Unbelievably, the departmental vote had been unanimous.

Indeed, Ted had been so conspicuously successful in his teaching that enrollments for his courses in the winter term were immense. And if this trend continued, the deanery might vote another junior slot so that the department could expand.

Little Ted seemed totally adjusted to the change of schools and even started to excel at peewee hockey. To top it off, Sara had convinced Evelyn Ungar, Director of the Harvard University Press, to let her do some freelance classics editing by mail.

Alumni contributions had reached new heights, due in no small part to the magnificent achievements of Canterbury's undefeated football team. In the season finale, they crushed Dartmouth, their traditional rival, 33–0. Chris Jastrow was named first-string Ivy quarterback and looked likely to be drafted by the pros. Even Tony Thatcher was elevated to Dean of the College. So Ted had friends in high places.

O tidings of comfort and joy!

As soon as Ted and Sara returned to Windsor, they began to look for a house. And to take lessons in cross-country skiing. The omnipresent whiteness gave the campus an aura of enchantment.

After a few weeks of searching, they found a solid old place on Barrington Road with a magnificent view of the mountains. It needed fixing up, but then, as Ted rationalized, this activity would be an outlet for some of his wife's creative energies.

411

For, though she never complained, slipping and sliding down icy winter paths was not exactly *summa felicitas* for Sara Lambros. She began to toy with the idea of graduate school, studying the Harvard catalog to work out courses she could squeeze into a weekly forty-eight-hour visit to Cambridge.

Ted did not discourage her. Yet, at the same time, he did not disguise the fact that he felt her absence, even for so short a time, might have a negative effect on little Teddy.

But then Sara was soon heavily involved in refurbishing the house.

With all this nesting, hibernating, growing roots in snow and so forth, it was natural that the couple wanted to increase and multiply. ("Teddie would enjoy a little sister, don't you think?") And yet each month brought only disappointment.

"Damn," Sara would exclaim. "I'm really sorry, Ted."

"Hey look," he would reply. "Maybe we just screwed up on the calculations. Stay loose. Be patient, honey."

"I will," she'd answer, with a wan smile. "Just promise that you won't lose patience with me."

He took her in his arms.

"Listen, for another kid like Teddie, I'd gladly wait a dozen years."

His words were comforting, but with each succeeding lunar cycle seemed to be spoken with a little less conviction.

When Ted wrote Cameron Wylie to report the good news of his tenure, the Regius Professor's reply included more encouragement to visit Oxford.

Though he had been but newly elevated, Ted was bold enough to ask the college for leave of absence. As he argued in his letter, a break from teaching would allow him to complete his research on Euripides. This, he subtly implied, would bring further glory to the college. The response of the executive committee that adjudicated his petition was quite unexpected.

"Lambros," said the provost, as they questioned him *in camera*, "we're prepared to grant your rather premature petition, if you'll agree to give us something in return."

"Sure, anything," said Ted, secure in the awareness that, with tenure guaranteed, he could not be bounced even if he ultimately reneged.

"If we let you go to Oxford," said an elder member of the committee, "we'd expect on your return that you'd take on the chairmanship of classics—for at least five years."

Ted could hardly credit what he had heard. Were they actually requesting that he accept the leadership of his department as a favor? How quickly academic decorations now were rushing to be pinned upon his chest.

And yet he knew enough not to reveal excessive eagerness.

"Well, I'll commit to three," he answered with a smile. "And we can haggle after that."

"You've got a deal, Professor Lambros," said the provost. "I think the college has a rising star in you."

October 16, 1969

Yesterday was "Moratorium Day." All over the country there were protests against the war in Vietnam.

No one was surprised that there were demonstrations in Washington, New York, and Berkeley. But what astonished a lot of hard-liners were the gatherings in such unlikely places as Pittsburgh, Minneapolis, and Denver.

And what really staggered people was the antiwar march—of all places—on *Wall Street*.

I worked as hard as hell trying to encourage people from the financial community to find the guts to join our noontime walk for peace. I spent the better part of a week making phone calls to all sorts of executives, trying to convince them that the war was wrong not only morally but economically. (The latter argument was very helpful.) I got a lot of curses and hang-ups, but I also got a lot of recruits.

Still, in my wildest dreams, I never imagined that we'd amass a crowd of nearly ten thousand. Someone was quoted in today's *Times* as saying it was the largest demonstration ever staged on the Street.

It was a clear, sunny day, and as we strode along, most of us wearing black armbands, above us a skywriting plane spelled out "For Peace." Our journey ended at old Trinity Church, whose pews were soon filled to overflow. There, one after another, nearly a hundred of the most important corporate executives in the country rose to the stone pulpit to take turns reciting the names of the boys killed in Southeast Asia.

Among the readers were several former cabinet members and an amazing number of partners in the big investment banks. These guys, I think, were the bravest. Because the companies whose shares they traded were directly involved in the war.

414

For some unknown reason—maybe my last name—I was asked to be one of the readers. It was an honor that made me sick at heart.

Of course, today was the aftermath. My old competitive spirit took pleasure to see in the morning paper that our Wall Street rally had outdrawn the one in Central Park. I hope the jeans-and-guitar crowd hears about this and realizes that we gray-flannel guys have consciences too.

Then I got to the office and the heat began. Most of the partners of Downs, Winship, were far from pleased by my activities. The day before, they had told me—some in not so many words—that I was an unpatriotic bastard, disloyal to my country as well as to them. I took their opprobrium as politely as I could, figuring it would dissipate in a few days.

But I didn't expect the phone call that came at exactly nine-thirty. The blast of "You blathering idiot!" nearly blew my ear off. It was Dad.

For the better part of twenty minutes he ranted on, barely pausing for breath. About what a fool I was. Did I not realize, he asked, what damage "shenanigans" like yesterday's march could cause? Was I not literate enough to read that my own trust portfolio had several thousand shares of Oxyco, most of whose business relied on defense contracts?

I couldn't reply to any of this because he wouldn't stop talking long enough to let me do so. But finally he asked me something that was not rhetorical.

Did I not think I had disgraced the Eliot name?

Usually he grinds me into the ground with this sort of question, but this time I had an answer.

Was the Reverend Andrew Eliot disloyal to King George in 1776? Or did *he* follow the course his conscience dictated?

This kind of stopped Dad in his tracks.

He clearly could not think of how to react. So after a minute I reminded him, "That's what the Revolution was all about, Dad." I then politely said goodbye and hung up.

It was the first time in my entire life that I stood up to him and had the last word.

Andrew's was far from an isolated case. The conflict in Vietnam was tearing America apart on every level. Hawks against doves, rich against poor, parents against their children.

And it put a near-unbearable strain on the relations between George Keller and Catherine Fitzgerald.

On October 15, 1969, she had dared to take the day off to join the Washington protest march. And when she saw George the next evening, Cathy had "forgotten" to remove the black armband from her coat.

"Would madam care to check her wrap?" asked the maître d' as he showed them to a table in Sans Souci.

"Yes," George quickly answered.

"No, thank you," she politely overruled him. "I'm still feeling a bit chilly."

And she kept the garment draped over her shoulder, with the offending sleeve as conspicuous as possible.

"Cathy," said George nervously. "Do you know what the hell you're doing?"

"Yes," she replied. "Do you? Look, if you want to date me, you have to take my principles too. They come with the package."

"But people are staring," he whispered. "Important people."

"Don't be paranoid, George. I only wish they were. This restaurant is closer to the seat of power than the White House gates."

He shook his head in consternation.

"Can't we even have a truce at the dinner table?"

"I'm certainly not in favor of belligerence." She smiled. "So I'll compromise for once and put you out of your misery."

With that, she took the sleeve of her coat and slowly began to tear the armband from it.

Anyone who had not noticed it before now knew it had been there. Especially since Cathy handed it across the table to George, with an innocent smile.

"Here, Dr. Keller, use it as you see fit."

Now, having made her point, she considerately changed the conversation to an issue of mutual interest. Was Henry Kissinger going to marry Nancy Maginnes or not?

"Why do I put up with you?" he asked, only half-jokingly, as they were driving home.

"Because, to paraphrase one of your heroes, Senator Goldwater, 'in your heart you know I'm right.' "

"But it's common knowledge that I don't have a heart," he replied.

"I disagree. It's well hidden, but it's there. Which is why *I* put up with you."

Catherine Fitzgerald was not alone among the junior *and* senior members of the National Security Council who were trying to persuade the government to veer from what they regarded as a suicidal course.

Naturally, being "Kissinger's shadow," George not only held opposing views but was actively involved in the escalation of hostilities. Nixon still wanted a victory, and his inner circle was determined to give him one. They would spare no effort. And no bombs.

"Can't you convince Henry that this is folly?" Cathy asked George one evening.

"Can't you forget about the war even when we're in bed?" he retorted.

"No, I can't. Please George, I know he respects your opinion."

"I can't make him end it just like that."

"You could try," she said softly. And then added, "It's going to get even worse, isn't it?"

"I don't know."

"You do, too. But you just don't trust me. Why? I'm not some undercover agent. Can't you level with me?"

"Cathy, I swear I don't know any more than you do."

"Would you tell me if you did?"

"What do you think?" he asked, kissing her again.

On April 20, 1970, President Nixon announced that 150,000 American troops would be withdrawn from South Vietnam the following spring. The doves took heart.

Two days later, Nixon began a series of secret meetings with Kissinger and a few trusted aides. To discuss *widening* the war by invading neutral Cambodia, to destroy the enemy's supply depots.

George was proud to be one of those whom Kissinger regarded as trustworthy enough to include in these strategy sessions. His pride increased when he realized that not even the Secretary of Defense was present.

Nixon was in an angry mood. "The damn North Vietnamese are romping in Cambodia. We've got to move boldly to show them and the Russians that we can hang tough."

"Not everybody in the State Department would agree with you, Mr. President," George dared to comment respectfully.

"Jerks," murmured Nixon.

On Sunday, April 26, 1970, the President decided to commit thirty-two thousand American troops to the invasion of Cambodia. In his own words: "Knock them all out." Plans were finalized with the military in Southeast Asia without the knowledge of several key cabinet members.

That same afternoon, the National Security Council met to debate the merits of a possible Cambodian invasion. Only a few of them knew that the decision had already been made. The attack was set to begin forty-eight hours later.

Kissinger "objectively" presented the argument to his assembled staff.

"We have a very stark choice," he began gravely. "We could permit North Vietnam to overrun Cambodia. Or we could commit troops and try to stop them. A successful attack might be a step toward achieving an honorable peace. Any comments?"

Many speakers had deep misgivings about this potential escalation.

Though she was by far the most junior person present, Catherine Fitzgerald bravely raised her hand. "With due respect, I think if the government goes ahead with this invasion, every campus in America will explode."

Kissinger answered her calmly. "Our decision must not be swayed by a group of rootless, self-indulgent adolescents with no sense of political realities."

Catherine could not stop herself from responding, "Isn't that a bit harsh, Dr. Kissinger?"

"Perhaps that was an overgeneralization. I beg your pardon, Miss Fitzgerald."

The debate grew more heated and even less conclusive.

"I'm glad you called Henry on that antistudent remark," George said, as they were sharing a bottle of white wine in her apartment that evening. "But I think if you weren't so pretty you wouldn't have gotten away with it."

She brushed off the compliment and remarked, "You were certainly quiet today."

"I don't think I had anything to add," he replied evasively. "Besides, everybody knows where I stand."

"Yes. Right behind Kissinger. The point is, where does *he* stand?"

"I don't know," George lied.

Though the President did not announce it officially till the evening of April 30, the National Security Council was informed of the U.S. invasion of Cambodia on April 28.

There was outrage among some of the members, who realized that the entire debate on Sunday had been nothing but a charade. Several senior members stormed into Henry's office and immediately resigned.

But the disaffection was even more widespread among the younger aides, some of whom cut off promising government careers to quit in protest.

Catherine Fitzgerald was among the first to leave. And after delivering a strongly worded letter to one of Kissinger's secretaries, she marched ten paces down the corridor to the office of George Keller.

"You bastard!" she exploded before he had even shut the door. "You ruthless, heartless bastard! You have no respect for anything or anyone. You and that Svengali of yours trifle with human lives—"

"Cathy, please calm down—"

"No, let me finish, George. Because today I'm walking out of the White House and out of your life."

"Cathy, be reasonable. I'm not responsible—"

"But you *knew*! You knew and you didn't even trust me enough to tell me."

"Well, I was right, judging by this hysterical reaction," George countered.

"It isn't hysterical—dammit. It's *human*. In all your great assimilation of English words, George, did you ever really learn the meaning of *that* word?"

Before he could reply, she disappeared.

He sat motionless at his desk for several minutes, mulling over what had happened.

I suppose it was inevitable, he rationalized. Anyway, we couldn't have gone on much longer fighting our own private war.

Maybe Henry's right. Women should only be a hobby.

Six days later, after four students were killed at Kent State University in a protest demonstration, a taxi driver appeared at George Keller's home, bearing a battered suitcase.

Inside he found a pile of shirts, ties, and other clothes that he had left at Cathy's place. There was also a page onto which she had neatly pasted newspaper photographs of the four victims.

Her message was simple and direct: "These are *your* children, Dr. Keller."

If Alice found her Wonderland by entering the looking glass, Ted Lambros first spied his as he was peering through the dusty windows of a British Rail carriage as it slowed down just before Oxford station.

On that same chilly autumn day, Cameron Wylie took the Lambros trio on a walking tour of a university which had been conducting classes more than three full centuries before Columbus found America. Some of the original colleges, like Merton and St. Edmund's Hall, still had portions from the late 1260s. And there was also a vestige of the Middle Ages in Exeter, Oriel, and "New" College.

Magdalen, a relative newcomer from the fifteenth century, was Oxford's jewel, with its exquisite gardens bordering the river Cherwell. It even had a deer park, which made little Ted feel like he was in a fairy tale.

And finally, Christ Church, dominated by the huge octagonal Tom Tower built by Christopher Wren (an imitation of which adorned Harvard's Dunster House). This was Wylie's college, where he had arranged temporary Common Room privileges for Ted.

"What do you think, kiddo?" Ted asked his son, as they stood in the Great Quadrangle.

"It's all so old, Daddy."

"That's the best atmosphere for getting new ideas," Sara commented.

"Quite right," said the Regius Professor.

They then proceeded in his Morris Minor to the small terraced house in Addison Crescent that was to be their lodgings for the year.

Confronted with the fading greens and browns and tired

furniture, the only comment Sara could manage was, "Oh, Professor Wylie, it's so quaint."

"All credit to my wife," he answered gallantly. "Heather tracked it down. You have no notion of how grotty so many flats are here in Oxford. She's filled the fridge with some basics, just to tide you over till she drops in tomorrow morning. Now I must take my leave, I've got a pile of galleys to correct."

Sara cooked eggs and sausages for dinner, sang young Ted to sleep, and then descended to the sitting room.

"It's cold as hell in here," she commented.

"All three of these electric bars are blazing," Ted replied and pointed to the orange-glowing fireplace.

"That looks like a dilapidated toaster." Sara frowned. "And it's just about as warm."

"Come on, honey," Ted cajoled, "where's your sense of adventure?"

"Frozen," Sara answered, as she opened up the sherry Mrs. Wylie had thoughtfully provided for them. "Couldn't Heather have found us someplace that had central heating?"

"Hey look," Ted reasoned, "I'll grant this isn't Buckingham Palace, but it's only a couple of minutes from Teddie's school, and we can walk right into town." And then he noticed. "Hey, why have you got your hat and gloves on? Are you going somewhere?"

"Yeah. To bed. I'm not a polar bear."

The next morning Ted met Wylie at the entrance to the Bodleian and the professor introduced him to an elderly librarian who then made Ted recite the ancient "Readers' Oath" aloud.

"I hereby undertake not to remove from the Library, or to mark, deface, or injure in any way, any volume, document, or other object belonging to it or in its custody; not to bring into the Library or kindle therein any fire or flame. . . ."

Of course, no books could be borrowed from this hallowed repository. Even Oliver Cromwell himself, when he was ruler of the land, was not allowed this privilege.

So for most of his daily work Ted used the collection at the Ashmolean Museum. Here each morning he would pass imposing Greek statuary on his way to the stuffy room that housed the classics of the classics—and indeed some of the men who'd written them.

One afternoon that first week he bought himself a Christ Church scarf on Broad Street. He wanted to be just as Oxonian, or more, as anyone in Oxford.

Several times a week he lunched in College with Cameron— they were now on a first-name basis. Here he met not only scholars in his field but luminaries from the other disciplines as well.

It was soon clear to all the classicists from other colleges that this young American was Wylie's special protégé. And, therefore, on the evening of Ted's lecture to the Philological Society, they came ready to attack.

The talk was splendid. By far the best he'd ever given. And Wylie leapt to his feet and trumpeted, "I think that the Society has just heard a most distinguished presentation. And if Professor Lambros is not too fatigued, perhaps he'd entertain one or two questions."

Four hands shot up, all brandishing invisible knives.

The "inquiries" were really probes to see if Ted had substance as a scholar. But, like Horatius at the bridge, he staunchly held them off, decapitating Tarquin after Tarquin. And with it all he never lost his winsome smile.

The warm applause was but a tiny index of his victory. For nearly every don attending waited patiently to shake his hand— and offer invitations to have lunch with *them*.

Several hours later, Ted and Sara were walking homeward, arm in arm, intoxicated by his triumph.

"*Onoma tou Theou,*" she rhapsodized in loving imitation of his mother. "You were unbelievable. I wish the guys at Harvard could have heard you here tonight."

"Don't worry," Ted replied, with newly bolstered self-assurance, "they'll hear about it soon enough."

By January, when Hilary term began, Ted Lambros was almost a fixture on the Oxford scene. So much so that the head of the University Press always tried to sit near him at High Table, to win his next book for OUP.

Wylie, who was himself revising the Oxford edition of Euripides, offered a special seminar for graduates as well as postgraduates on the *Alcestis*. And he asked Ted to collaborate with him.

In retrospect, there was an element of irony in the choice of play. For Euripides' heroine nobly sacrifices herself to save her husband, and thereby perpetuates their marriage. Whereas the seminar itself led to the death knell of Ted's relationship with Sara.

Perhaps it was inevitable. For his great success at Oxford had aroused in him a wild cerebral ecstasy. He felt intellectually priapic.

The object of his affection—or, as he unconsciously considered it, the prize for his achievements—was an auburn-haired, nineteen-year-old undergraduate named Felicity Hendon.

Two things made her conspicuous at the seminar. First, her splendid command of Greek, which was exceptional even by Oxford's high standards. And then her body, whose slender sensuality was noticeable even beneath her loosely flowing—and short—academic gown. Ted had difficulty taking his eyes off her legs.

Felicity had come to Oxford to make intimate acquaintance with the noblest minds. In truth, her initial reason for taking the seminar was to attempt to seduce the Regius Professor himself.

Yet, there was Ted. An academic old enough to qualify as "senior" in her estimation, but who still possessed what she acknowledged as the vestiges of youthful vigor.

And with it all, Ted thought *he* was seducing *her*.

The whole adventure started with an unpretentious gathering to which Felicity and Jane, her roommate, asked the nine students and two teachers from the seminar. Like almost every Oxford invitation, it implicitly excluded wives.

Sara had grown used to this inequity, though she continued to resent it. She knew Ted enjoyed visiting those High Tables at the different colleges. Especially when they were black-tie evenings. He, who once would cringe at fastening his bow tie to go out and wait on tables, now was thrilled to don the very same cravat to go to academic dinners with his penguin-suited fellow Fellows.

And Sara did derive some pleasure from the fact that Ted was having fun. Besides, she knew he would reciprocate next year when they returned to Canterbury and she started working for a doctorate at Harvard.

Though students at St. Hilda's College, the two girls lived in a small rented flat on Gresham Road. That February evening the festivities began with cheap white wine, then changed to even cheaper red to grace the execrable food the hostesses imagined was a gourmet meal.

Cameron was the first to leave. His relationship with Heather was notorious in Oxford. They were most unfashionably faithful to each other. And so he always departed for home as early as good manners would allow. The students disappeared by casual attrition—for studies, assignations, pot, or simply sleep.

At a little after ten, a hood in motorcycle gear materialized. Ted's anxiety turned quickly to relief when he discovered it was Janie's boyfriend Nick, a third-year student reading medicine at Trinity. She hurried for her helmet and they zoomed off toward The Perch for one quick drink before repairing to his rooms.

Ted and Felicity were alone.

He looked at her and wondered if she sensed his hunger for that youthful body.

"I'll help clear up," he offered gallantly.

"Thanks."

For an instant, he felt panicked and uncertain. Ted was suddenly aware that he had not touched another woman for nearly a decade.

How do you start this sort of thing?

As she was piling dirty dishes in the sink, he moved behind her and tentatively placed his arms around her waist. She took his hands and moved them up to clasp her breasts. Then, without further words, she turned and joined him in a fiery embrace.

Ted got home after midnight. As he slipped into bed, Sara stirred and murmured, "How did it go, honey?"

"Not bad," he answered quietly. She fell asleep again.

He remained awake for a long time and pondered the significance of what he had begun that night.

The next day at breakfast—and at many meals thereafter—Ted kept wondering if it showed. Could Sara, who understood him so well, read his face, deciphering the hieroglyphics of his guilt?

He felt noblesse oblige to show her amorous attention. He tried making love to her with increased ardor. But gradually he grew resentful of this obligation to display connubial affection.

Sure, Sara deserved respect. She was a loyal wife. The mother of his son. And a true friend. *But she was not exciting.* Not merely now, when she had let herself put on some weight. But as far as he recalled, she had never been that sensual.

Perhaps that was what had so drawn him to Felicity. She awakened in him dormant feelings he had thought forever gone. She was dynamic. Not just physically, but intellectually.

And there was something else, although Ted did not realize it at first. The greatest thrill of all was that it was . . . illicit.

After a while, he reassured himself that Sara had not noticed anything. Still, her very presence was an inconvenience. Assignations with Felicity had to be scheduled for afternoons or early evenings. Only rarely could they meet at night.

Once he fabricated yet another college banquet. And Sara, faithful, trusting (boring), never even checked. Even her naive passivity started to annoy him.

Felicity kept urging him to spend a weekend with her. But what pretext could he find? Oxford functions seemed to shut down automatically on Saturday and Sunday.

Then Fate flashed him an amber light, suggesting he go forward—but with caution.

Philip Harrison '33, currently a high executive of the U.S. International Banking Commission, arrived in London on a ten-day visit for the government. Generous as usual, he took a suite at Claridge's next to his own, so that his daughter, son-in-law, and beloved grandson could enjoy a break from academic tedium.

As soon as her father had announced his visit, Sara began to check the theater listings in *The Times*. While her husband looked for a plausible excuse to free himself to spend the weekend driving through the romantic villages of Gloucestershire.

Then he and Felicity could spend entire evenings in one of the historic Cotswold inns. And make some history themselves.

Sara Lambros was happy to be staying at Claridge's. Not that she particularly enjoyed elegant hotels, but quite simply because she reveled in the central heating.

And the warmth of her father's love.

Philip Harrison could not help mentioning that his daughter looked pale. Her fire, he thought, was burning low. Indeed, it seemed as if her pilot light was all but extinguished. Sara blamed the frigid Oxford weather. And yet how could she explain the fact that Ted looked radiant?

She argued that hard work obviously agreed with him. She recounted his triumph with the Philological Society and little Ted's success at the local primary school. Now he'd taken up soccer.

"You're a real little jock, aren't you?" his grandfather said, smiling affectionately.

"And he's not too bad at Latin either," Sara added proudly. "The English really start them early."

"I guess they're still culturally more advanced than we are," her father observed. "Their theater certainly is. I had to resort to my contacts at the Embassy just to get us four seats to Olivier's *Othello*."

"Oh, Daddy, I've been dying to see it. When are we going?"

"The best I could do was the Saturday matinee."

"Oh gosh," Ted responded anxiously, "Saturday's gonna be a problem for me. You know I've almost finished the first draft of my Euripides book. . . ."

"Yes, Sara told me. Congratulations."

"Well, Cameron Wylie called me last night and said he wanted to spend the whole weekend going over it with me. I didn't even have a chance to mention it to Sara."

"Oh, Daddy," little Ted complained, "I like it here in London."

"Well, you can stay with Mummy and Grandpa," he reassured his son. And then turned to Mr. Harrison. "I'm really sorry, but it was an opportunity I just couldn't pass up. Don't you agree, honey?"

Though deeply hurt, she was forced to play the reluctant accomplice.

"I guess Ted's right," she said loyally. "How long will you be gone?"

"Oh, don't worry, I'll be back in London in time for dinner Sunday night."

The seven-hundred-year-old George Inn in the Cotswold town of Winchcombe was once used by pilgrims to St. Kenelm's tomb.

This weekend it was playing host to a twentieth-century couple on an extremely secular journey.

"What do you think?" Felicity asked, as she unpacked a small bottle of vodka and began to pour it into the hotel glasses.

"It's sort of a medieval version of a motel," he answered.

Ted felt decidedly uneasy. Winchcombe was a relatively short drive from Oxford and someone might chance to see them. And more importantly the early pangs of conscience he had felt now blossomed into full-fledged qualms.

He could not silence an inner voice that kept reiterating, Lambros, what you're doing's called adultery. And it's a sin. You have a wife and kid. And what about those sacred vows you took?

Ah yes, but that was long ago. And in another country. And besides, the wench has changed. And dammit, the times have changed as well.

"Ted, where are you?"

Felicity's voice shattered his ethical reverie. And for the first time he became aware that her hands were exploring intimate areas of his anatomy.

"Are you having second thoughts—or cold feet?" she inquired coquettishly.

"Neither," he replied, to convince her if not himself.

"Hey," she coaxed. "Then will you take your clothes off and give me a little proof of your enthusiasm?"

Zippers glided open. She stood enticingly before him, Aphrodite in a medieval inn.

He could think of nothing else as she now beckoned him to bed.

They drove back Sunday afternoon and reached Oxford just as darkness was approaching. And it was not merely chance that made him choose the Folly Bridge for her to drop him, so he could wend his way discreetly homeward in the dusk.

For throughout their wildly carnal weekend, whenever the ecstasy abated, Ted had been unable to fight off the demons of remorse. Despite inward invocations of the New Morality, his conscience was still rooted firmly in the fifties. And he already felt that he would have to pay a price for his brief moment of adventure.

But he never dreamed that it would be so soon.

The moment he opened the door of Addison Crescent, he found the incarnation of the Furies waiting for him.

"You left the house unlocked," said Cameron Wylie, his face half in shadows.

"Yeah," said Ted distractedly. "Uh—I'm sorry I kept you waiting, but I didn't know you were coming—"

"Nor did I," the Regius Professor answered, traces of displeasure in his voice. "I tried ringing you, then came round to leave a note. But then I saw the door was open and I assumed you'd be arriving about now. So I waited."

There was a sudden silence. And then Wylie burst out angrily, "You bloody fool. You bloody, stupid fool."

"I'm sorry, Professor, I don't understand," Ted stammered, instinctively demoting himself back to pupil's status.

"I don't care about your morals, Lambros. I just gave you credit for more common sense. I'll grant adultery's as popular at Oxford as any place on earth. But most of those who practice it don't play with undergraduates. That girl's nearly half your age."

The sanctimonious dressing-down began to anger Ted. He gathered courage for a quiet counterattack.

"Is that what you came to see me about?"

"No," Wylie responded, "that was just my prologue. Sara rang me, wanting to speak to you."

Oh shit, he thought. I knew I should have telephoned.

"She was very apologetic," Wylie continued. "But it was an emergency."

Ted suddenly grew anxious. "Did something happen to her father?"

"No," Cameron replied. "It's your son. He was taken very ill. They rushed him into hospital. When Sara phoned she was at her wit's end."

A shiver chilled Ted to the core. "Is he—alive?" He looked at Wylie, his eyes pleading for an answer.

"He'll be all right. You've missed the worst of it. Fortunately, she had her father there."

"Where is he? Where's my son?"

"At the children's hospital in Paddington Green."

Though Ted wanted to bolt from the room, something kept him frozen to the spot. "Does Sara have any idea where I've been?"

"No," answered the professor. "I hardly thought it appropriate." He paused, then added, "I'll leave that to you."

It was Sunday and the trains to London crept like pious snails. And all the way Ted thought, Suppose he dies before I get there.

He who gave no thought to Christ from one Easter to the
next, now started to converse with Him. To negotiate for little
Ted's survival. Please, Lord, I'll pay the price. Take anything from
me, but let him live.

His morbid thoughts were not relieved as he rushed through
the portals of the hospital. It was bare and ill-lit and, to Ted,
seemed ominously empty.

He found Sara and her father on the second floor outside the
Lewis Carroll ward.

"Is he all right?" Ted quickly asked.

"Yes," she answered. "Didn't Wylie tell you everything?"

"No," he replied.

Sara began to recount the story at breakneck speed. As if she
had to get it out as quickly as she could. For her own catharsis.

"He woke up last night with an incredibly high fever—"

"Over a hundred and five," her father added, as he too
relived the painful moments. "Thank God when we got him here
the doctor on duty knew exactly what it was. She put him—"

"She?" Ted intruded with atavistic disapproval. And then
immediately apologized. "Sorry I stopped you. Please tell me
what's wrong."

"Viral pneumonia," Philip Harrison announced. "Calm down,
Ted. The big crisis is behind us."

Damn, he inwardly berated himself. And I wasn't there.

Just then Dr. Rama Chatterjee appeared in the distance.

"Here she comes," said Sara. "Maybe we can see Teddie
now."

Ted's confidence in female physicians was not enhanced by
the discovery that this one was Indian.

"He's sleeping comfortably," the doctor said with a smile as
she approached, and then addressed the new arrival. "You must
be Professor Lambros. He was asking for you."

"I want to see him now," Ted demanded. "And after that I
want to see the head of your department."

"You can do both at once," said Dr. Chatterjee good-naturedly.
"I'm the Chief of Pediatrics."

In the days that followed, Sara rarely left her son's side. She
even slept next to him on a folding bed the hospital provided.

Ted also spent most of the daylight hours at the hospital. He
and Sara would sit in the same glass cubicle and each in turn

engage their son in conversation. But they rarely talked to each other.

She seemed emotionless. But Ted assumed it was merely a way of hiding her anxiety about their sick child. He had already convinced himself that her preoccupation had made her oblivious to the difficulty she had had in reaching him the previous Sunday.

When visiting hours ended, Ted and his father-in-law would have dinner and then stroll on the perimeter of Hyde Park.

They quickly exhausted topics of mutual interest. So one evening Ted delivered a monologue about how he'd been knifed at Harvard, an incident that in his own imagination had acquired the mythic magnitude of the assassination of Julius Caesar.

Mr. Harrison merely indicated interest by punctuating Ted's harangues with "hmm's" and "ah's."

The moment they returned to Claridge's, the Harvard Overseer said good night and hastened to his room.

Early Friday morning a large Daimler arrived for Mr. Philip Harrison.

It would be a long day for him. He and Ted would take Sara and his grandchild from Paddington Green to the John Radcliffe Infirmary in Oxford. He would then have to hurry back to Heathrow and catch the last plane to Geneva.

He was, after all, on a mission for the government of the United States, and could put off his obligations no longer.

Dr. Vivian Stone was waiting for them at the Radcliffe and saw to it that the young patient was installed as quickly as possible in a comfortable bed.

Looking at Sara's haggard face, the pediatrician remarked, "Rama Chatterjee told me you've been camping out with little Ted all week. I suggest you go home and get a proper night's sleep, Mrs. Lambros. We don't want two patients on our hands."

When they were back at Addison Crescent, it dawned on Ted that he and Sara had not really talked privately since the whole thing had begun. He had attributed her silence to fatigue and worry, but still he felt impelled to reestablish their lines of communication.

"Thank God he's all right," he remarked, choosing the least abrasive comment to open conversation.

Sara did not reply. She had her back to him and was unpacking.

"It must have been deadly for you. I mean being on your own like that. It was lucky Dad was in London."

She whirled around, her face flushed with anger. "He's not your father, dammit!" she snapped. "And I'm sick of having to be civil to you for his sake. I'm going to the hospital now. When I get back I want you out of here. And I don't mean just you, I mean your clothes and every one of your academic books. Just be damn sure you don't take any of *mine*."

"Sara, what's all this?"

"Listen," she answered bitterly, "I've stood by you for twelve years. Caring for you. Doing half your research. Keeping together the pieces of your fragile confidence. I've listened, I've sympathized. I've practically turned myself into a human handkerchief for you to cry into—"

"Sara—"

"No, dammit, Lambros, let me finish. I didn't mind any of it, I didn't even mind having to be both parents to our son—as long as I thought I meant something to you. But then you had to choose Oxford—the biggest small town on earth—to slap me in the face. My God, *everybody* knows you were screwing that little tramp! And if that wasn't humiliation enough, you had to flaunt it right in front of my father!"

Ted had never heard her speak with such fury.

"Sara, please don't blow this out of proportion. Except for this one . . . indiscretion, I've always been completely faithful to you. I mean, that girl didn't mean a damn thing to me. Look, I was wrong. I made a mistake. It could happen to almost anybody."

"Ted, I could've possibly accepted your 'indiscretion,' as you so fastidiously put it, if our marriage were really solid. But you simply don't love me anymore. Let's stop pretending. We haven't had a real marriage for a long time."

"Are you saying that you want a divorce?"

"Yes. The sooner the better."

"What about the little guy? We can't do this to him. It isn't fair."

"Look, Ted, he's not so little anymore. And he can sense what's happening to us. So don't give me that old junk about staying together for the children's sake."

"Sara," he replied forcefully, "I refuse to allow you to do this."

"You refuse?" She looked at him with quiet outrage. "Whatever you may think, I'm neither your puppet nor your pet. So, to put it into the decent obscurity of a learned tongue, *apage te, tuas res habeto!*"

She knew she had succeeded in bruising him. The crowning blow was her reciting the Roman formula for divorce, which, as they both knew, was what the *man* should say to the *woman*.

It was just after teatime when Ted rang the bell on Gresham Road. Felicity was pleased to see him, but somewhat surprised by the suitcases he had brought along.

"You look like you're packed to leave town. Are you?"

"No," Ted replied self-consciously. "I'm afraid Sara's kicked me out. Could you put me up for the night?"

"Yes," she grinned, "I suppose we have room for you and your books."

But once he was inside, she quickly spelled out the limits of his tenure.

"Listen, Ted, I'm happy to help you out with your little difficulty. But I hope you don't plan to stay for any length of time."

"Do you think you can tolerate my presence for, say, a couple of weeks?" he asked, affecting his most charming smile.

"Oh please, Ted," she replied, "two or three *days* at the most."

"That's fairly cold comfort. I mean, after all, your roommate Janie and her motorcyclist—"

"Yes, but that's different," Felicity explained.

"Why?"

"Because I hate messy situations."

At the hospital the next morning they tried not to say anything that would worry their recuperating son.

But when they left his room at lunchtime Sara said coolly, "Let's go where we can talk in private."

Short-sighted despair made him believe that there was still a possibility for reconciliation. He was quickly disabused.

She simply wanted to outline the terms of their divorce. It was only his emotional exhaustion—compounded by the fatigue of sleeping on Felicity's couch—that kept him from protesting that she seemed to be talking *at* him rather than to him. For she was not negotiating or discussing. She was dictating the conditions.

Sara did not want alimony. She felt that he should pay a fair share of child support. Even this would be reasonable, since there was no tuition to pay. She intended to keep Teddie in the same state school next year.

"You want to stay in Oxford?"

"Yes," she replied coolly. "And anyway that's no longer your business."

"Excuse me, Sara," he said resentfully. "I'm not going to let you keep my son an ocean away from me. Besides, what the hell are you going to do here?"

"What do most people do at Oxford if they're not working in the car factories?" she replied sarcastically. "As outrageous as it may seem, I'm going to start a degree. I do have a Radcliffe *magna* from the Dark Ages, you may recall. You can visit little Ted at Christmas and in the summer."

"Do you have any idea what a transatlantic ticket costs, Sara?"

"Relax. I'll be spending Christmas with my family in Connecticut. And before we say another word, let's get one thing straight. I won't allow him to become a psychological cripple because of this. I'll never say a nasty word about you. You have my word of honor. And I'll see to it that you spend as much time together as possible."

"And suppose I try to fight you in court?" he asked, trying a bit of poker playing.

"Don't waste the effort," she replied unemotionally. "My father's lawyers will grind you into moussaka meat."

Ted Lambros drank his way back across the Atlantic. The pretext for his inebriation was intellectually motivated. It was based on the famous line in Virgil, *Varium et mutabile semper femina.* Or, as he loosely translated it, "All women are unpredictable bitches."

August 6, 1970

Ted called me today with the incredible news that he and Sara are splitting.

God, there's no future for matrimony if those two can't make it together. He didn't offer any details on the phone, but I suppose I'll hear the blow-by-blow when he comes up here next weekend. (I had to invite the poor guy. He sounded so lonely.)

Ted has no idea what anguish he's in for. Divorce is bad under any circumstances. Although they say it's worst for the kids, I personally feel that it's the fathers who suffer most.

In addition to my weekend rights—which are pretty useless now that both of them are at boarding school—I only really get to spend time with my son and daughter during the summer months.

And parenthood, I've discovered, is simply not a part-time job. It's more like being a trapeze artist. Once you let go of the swing, you fall and there's no way you can get back up.

I spend the winter months trying to plan each summer day so it will be interesting for Andy and Lizzie. I map out excursions we can take—like trips to Canada—and contact other parents in the area whose kids we can have over. But at best I become a head counselor with the purely honorific title, "Dad."

Young as he is, Andy already says his generation's disgusted with our involvement in Vietnam. And for some reason he seems to blame it on me. You'd think I was personally dropping napalm on innocent civilians.

"The guys at school all say it's Wall Street's war," he says. As if I were Wall Street, instead of just a minor bank official.

I try to make him understand that I'm on his side. That I'd actually helped organize an important antiwar march. All he replies is, "That's a lot of crap."

When I tell him not to use that sort of language, he retorts

435

that since *I* do, I'm a hypocrite like my whole generation (now I'm a whole generation!).

I think deep down he misses me and is just playing macho to pretend he doesn't really need a father.

I try my best to pierce the armor of his hostility, but one summer month in Maine is simply not enough. I can't convince him that I care.

Lizzie is also a problem. She mopes a lot, disappears for walks and won't let me come along. Now and then I try to chat with her, but she resents me too. At least her reasons are more personal and less political than Andy's.

"If you really loved us, you and Mom wouldn't have busted up. I hate my boarding school. It's kind of like an orphanage with fancy uniforms. I don't think more than five girls in my class still have both parents."

After several talks like this, I fought like hell to get Faith to allow me to have custody of Lizzie so she could have some semblance of a home and go to day school.

But Faith being Faith she still won't relent. I can't see why she's so hostile. After all, she's engaged to marry some tycoon from San Francisco (good luck to the poor bastard).

In my longing to get the kids back, I've thought of getting married again. But I haven't met anyone who makes me confident enough to risk a second plunge.

Ted told me on the phone that though it hurt, he imagined it was for the best. He doesn't know how wrong he is.

It's not just that he's lost a wife. And not just that he's lost his son—which I can promise is for sure.

He's lost the only thing that gives some sense to all the other things we do in life.

It was late January 1973. George Keller stood on the steps outside the Georgetown Law Center.

At the stroke of noon, students began to pour out of the building. Among them was Catherine Fitzgerald, whom he diffidently approached.

"Cathy—"

"Goodbye, George," she answered, turning away.

"Wait, please. Can't we just talk for a few minutes?"

"I'm not in the mood for even sixty seconds of prevarication, Dr. Keller."

She started to walk off briskly.

He hurried to catch up with her.

"Please, Cathy," he said urgently. "If America and North Vietnam can make peace, why can't we?"

She whirled and demanded, "George, now that you and Henry have your cease-fire, you're international heroes. Why bother with the one person in the world who still thinks you're a worm?"

"Precisely because you're the only person who matters to me."

"Do you really expect me to believe that bullshit?"

"I would hope you would at least give me a chance to convince you. I mean, you're practically a lawyer. Even criminals are entitled to speak in their own defense. Will you have coffee with me?"

She sighed. "All right, but just one cup."

"How did you know where to find me?" she asked. "Are you bugging my phone?"

He shook his head in consternation. "Give me a break, Cathy. I asked one of your old friends at NSC."

"If they were friends of mine they should also have told you I didn't want to see you."

Like his diplomatic mentor, George was an indefatigable negotiator.

"Look, Cathy." He began a new tack. "I know I've been callous. Dishonest, even. But I've learned my lesson, really I have. All these lonely months I've done nothing but castigate myself for not trusting you."

"To be honest," she replied, in a tone that was for the first time not hostile, "you barely even trust yourself. That's your problem, George."

"Aren't you willing to believe a person can change in three years?"

"I'd have to see it to believe it," she replied.

"Will you at least let me try to show you?" he pleaded.

She drained her coffee quickly and stood up. "Listen, I've got some important exams to study for. If you're really serious, call me early next month and I can meet you without worrying about torts and contracts."

"Fair enough," he replied. "Can I walk you to the library?"

"I think it would be better if you didn't. You and Henry are still pretty much persona non grata on campus."

They began to see each other again. First at weekly intervals—both of them guarding their emotions. But gradually, Cathy had to acknowledge to herself that George was making a genuine effort to right the wrongs of their earlier relationship.

For the first time, he spoke openly about his childhood. About what it meant to leave a country that he loved. About arriving in a strange new land without a relative or friend, barely able to say ten words in the language. About his desperate yearning to *fit in*. It was, however, a selective disclosure. For he only briefly mentioned that he had "a pretty poor" relationship with his father. And did not mention Aniko at all.

To make her understand his instinctive caution when dealing with others, he told of his first, bewildering days in America. Of being in constant fear. And his still latent paranoia that there were spies everywhere.

In short, he told the truth—if not the whole truth. And his partial candor enabled Cathy to let herself care once more.

"Who's your best friend, George?" she asked as they were taking a Sunday-afternoon stroll.

"I don't know," he replied offhandedly. "I guess I've never had one really."

"Not even as a child?"

"No, I was always a lone wolf. I'm just not gregarious."

She paused and then said gently, "You know, it's a paradox. We've been lovers for a long time now but we're not friends yet. At least, you don't regard me as one."

"Of course, I do," he protested.

"You'd make a lousy witness, Dr. Keller. You've just changed your testimony under my cross-examination. You started out by saying you didn't have a best friend."

"What am I?" he asked good-humoredly. "A guinea pig for your courtroom technique?"

"No, George, you're *my* friend. And I want to be yours."

"Cathy, you're the most wonderful girl I've ever met. I just can't fathom why you care so much for an iceberg like me."

"To begin with, you've got an electrifying mind. You also happen to be a very attractive man. And, most of all, you bring out something in me that wants to make you happy."

He stopped walking and put his arms around her. "Cathy," he said affectionately, "I love you."

"No," she whispered. "You don't yet. But you will."

Cathy graduated from law school that June and passed the Maryland Bar exam, which would enable her to practice in Washington, D.C., six months thereafter. Despite lucrative and interesting offers ranging from government work to private industry (women professionals were very much in demand in 1973), she chose to join the consumer advocates colloquially known as Nader's Raiders.

"Why do you want to work with such a cockeyed organization?" George asked in a tone midway between amusement and amazement. "I mean, you could so easily get a job in the Attorney General's office."

"Look, George," she explained, "despite being Washington born and bred, I'm still an optimist. But I'm not crazy enough anymore to think I can improve things on a global scale. My quixotic days ended when I left NSC. At least with Ralph's group we can do some tangible good, and sometimes I can actually see the faces of the people I help."

"It's amazing," he said with affectionate admiration, "you're the most idealistic person I've ever met."

"Well, you're the most pragmatic."

"That's what makes us a good match. We're like Jack Sprat."

"Except that they were married," she replied.

"No comment." He smiled.

"You don't have to," she answered knowingly. "One morning you're going to wake up, realize what an asset I'd be for your career, and ask me."

"Is that how you think I base all my decisions?"

"Yes. And that's probably the only thing that would keep you from asking me."

"What?"

"The fact that I actually know what makes you tick."

Success illumined Danny Rossi like a halo. He was rich and famous. His life overflowed with praise, his den with trophies—and his bed with beauties. He had everything a man could want.

Except a marriage.

One evening in the early spring of 1973 when his chauffeur met him at the airport, Danny urged him to drive as quickly as he could to Bryn Mawr. He rushed into the house to announce his latest coup: he had been offered the directorship of the Los Angeles Philharmonic. In fact, the orchestra wanted him so badly that they had agreed to his keeping the Philadelphia job as well. He would be a transcontinental conductor.

"That's super, Daddy," Sylvie cried. "Does it mean we'll be moving out to California?"

"Well, it might be good to get away from the snow and ice. But we'll really have to let your mom decide."

He looked at Maria. She was stone-faced. And said nothing.

"Hey, what's the matter, darling?" he asked at dinner, when the kids were gone.

"Danny," she said slowly, "we've got to talk."

"You mean about California?"

"No. About 'Miss Rona.' "

"Who?"

"Please, Danny, don't play the ingenue. Her column is syndicated even in a hick town like Philadelphia."

"Well, what slimy rumor is she spreading now?"

"Oh, nothing scandalous," Maria replied sarcastically. "Just a little tidbit about a 'famous composer-pianist whispering sweet nothings to Raquel Welch at a Malibu restaurant.' "

"Do you really believe that kind of crap?"

"The only thing I'm not sure of is whether that item came from her press agent or yours."

"Wait a minute—"

"No, maestro," she retorted. "This time you listen. All these years I've tried to look the other way because I felt it was somehow my fault. I mean that you have to have your little affairs because I was inexperienced and couldn't satisfy you. But why do you have to do it so damn *publicly*? You've already proved your manhood to the whole world—why haven't you proved it to yourself?"

There was a pause. Then Danny asked calmly, "What suddenly brought this on?"

"It's not sudden. I've just finally reached the end of my very long rope."

"Maria, we've been through this before. I've never claimed to be a Boy Scout. But I still think I'm a good husband. I mean, I take care of you and the kids, don't I?"

"Every way but emotionally. Your daughters are starved for attention, which I can only assume you haven't noticed. And I dread the moment they first see your name in a gossip column."

Danny had two concerts to conduct the next day, so he tried to mollify her. "Darling, you know there's only one person in the world I really love, don't you?"

"Of course," she retorted. "Yourself." And then added wearily, "Look, I simply can't take it anymore."

There was another pause. "Are you asking for a divorce?"

She grew angry again. "That's what any woman in her right mind would want, isn't it? But we're Catholic—at least *I* still am. And besides, it would devastate the girls."

"So where does that leave us?"

"In separate bedrooms," she replied.

He looked at her incredulously. "You can't be serious. You don't mean that our sex life is over?"

"With each other, anyway."

Her innuendo threw Danny off balance. "Do you mean you intend to have affairs?"

"Can you give me one good reason why I shouldn't?"

He was about to say, You're a wife and mother. But then, he was a husband and father. Still, he was furious. "Maria, you can't do this to me. You can't."

"Danny, whether I can or I can't is not for you to judge. And whether I do or I don't is not for you to know."

By the spring of 1972, Jason Gilbert had taken part in so many operations of *Sayaret Matkal* that Zvi insisted he take a sabbatical to "relearn what normal life is all about."

He went back to the kibbutz and finally began to get close to his two sons, Joshua, now five, and three-year-old Ben.

He discovered that he could derive joy from family life and even from tinkering in the garage.

"What are you doing to that truck, Daddy? Is it very broken?"

Jason looked up from under the hood to greet his firstborn.

"It isn't really broken at all, Josh. I'm doing what in America is called 'souping it up.' "

The little boy laughed. "That sounds so funny—feeding soup to a machine."

"No, *chabibi*. It's just a way of saying 'make it go faster.' Want a lesson?"

"Yes, please."

Jason lifted the boy high into the air and held him over the exposed entrails of the vehicle. "See that? It's what's known as a carburetor—*m'ayed*. It mixes the air and the gas. . . ."

For the next three afternoons, Jason lovingly introduced his elder son to the arcana of automotive engineering.

As he joked to Eva, "He'll be the youngest hot-rodder in the Galilee."

Since his own childhood instruction had been by an array of professionals, Jason took particular pleasure in being his sons' tutor for everything.

With Josh as his "assistant professor," he taught the younger one how to swim in the communal pool.

443

"Keep kicking, Ben, you're doing great. Pretty soon you'll be a regular fish."

"I'm not a fish, Daddy, I'm a little boy."

Eva sat in the shade of a nearby tree, smiling with satisfaction, praying that this idyllic summer would never end.

Sometimes she would cook a simple dinner for the two of them in their bungalow. And they would share some of the red wine from the lot Yossi had obtained in a trade for oranges with a nearby *moshav*. Marriage and motherhood had wrought a profound change in Eva. She was more relaxed than she had ever been in her life. She smiled. She even dared to feel happy.

In mid-July Isaac Stern, the violinist, came up to Vered Ha-Galil and gave a concert in the dining hall. He also left several of his latest LPs for the kibbutz library.

When Eva borrowed one of them to play on their hi-fi, Jason noticed that the Mendelssohn Violin Concerto had been recorded with the Philadelphia Orchestra under the baton of Daniel Rossi.

This evoked a torrent of reminiscences about the college days.

Eva reached over and took his hand. "Are you feeling slightly homesick, my love?"

"Yeah, now and then," he confessed. "For stupid things like the World Series, the Super Bowl—even the Harvard-Yale game. I'm going to take you to one of *those* someday, Eva. It would be a nice change—it's a fight to the death where nobody dies."

"When shall we go? I can pack in fifteen minutes."

"When there's peace," he replied. "Then I'll take all four of us over to visit Harvard—"

"And Disneyland, I hope."

"Naturally. We'll hit all the cultural high spots." And he repeated his proviso, "When there's peace."

"I think we'll be too old to travel by then, Jason."

"You're a pessimist, darling."

"No, I'm a realist. That's why I want you to give me at least a tentative date."

"Okay, okay. I'm First Marshal of The Class. I'll *have* to go to my Twenty-fifth Reunion."

"When is that?"

"Oh, just eleven years."

"Good." She smiled. Her lack of irony surprised him.

"You mean you don't mind waiting that long?"

"No. It's perfect. That's exactly one year before Josh goes into the army."

"You've thought that far ahead?"

She nodded. "Every Israeli mother works that out the day her son is born. Ben has another fourteen years."

They were both silent for a moment, trying to assimilate the awesome significance of knowing exactly when their little children would have to go to war.

Jason then rose and took her gently in his arms.

"Darling, when I finally go back to the *Sayaret*, remember this conversation. I want our boys to be able to play with tennis rackets, not rifles."

"I'd like my husband to do that, too."

Since Zvi had not given him a deadline, Jason planned on staying away from active duty for six months. But this halcyon period lasted less than ninety days.

On the morning of September 5, 1972, eight Black September terrorists broke into the quarters of the Israeli team in the Olympic village in Munich, killing two athletes and holding nine others hostage.

After the first sketchy announcement on the radio, Jason was already racing back to the unit. He knew it was a crisis that needed the *Sayaret*'s expertise.

A group was gradually assembled and prepared to fly out. But Moshe Dayan's request to allow the Israeli commandos to rescue their countrymen was refused by the German authorities. The *Bereitschaftspolizei* could—and would—handle this crisis themselves.

When the news came that the German rescue assault had failed and all Israeli hostages had been killed, the entire *Sayaret* was filled with despair and rage.

Only Zvi's supreme self-control enabled him to speak calmly. "We will find out which terrorists planned this. And we will exact revenge on every last one of them."

To which Jason responded simply, "I'm coming back to work."

It did not take long for the Intelligence Service to discover the identities of those who had organized the Munich Massacre. One of the chief engineers had been Abu Youssef, El-Fatah's chief intelligence officer and Yasser Arafat's closest deputy. The Secret Service had even located the apartment in Beirut from which he was currently operating.

Zvi and his fellow officers began to map out a plan to get him. The unit would also take advantage of its brief presence in the Lebanese capital to settle some other scores against the terrorists who had killed so many Israeli citizens.

On the night of April 10, Jason was one of several dozen men who boarded a patrol boat that sped up the Mediterranean coast and dropped anchor off the shore of Beirut. They were dressed as typical tourists on a night out in the "Riviera" of the Middle East.

They climbed into rubber dinghies and headed quietly toward a darkened beach club where the Secret Service had left rented cars for them. Then they set off to their assigned destinations.

Jason began to drive toward Rue Khaled Ben Al Walid. He parked near the building which photographs had identified as Abu Youssef's residence.

Five of them got out of the car and walked inside. The apartment was on the third floor, defended by two armed men whom Jason and Uri, another commando, planned to dispatch before they could make any noise.

They weren't fast enough. One of the guards managed to get off a shot before hitting the ground. By the time the commandos had smashed through the entrance, the terrorist leader had barricaded himself in the bedroom.

Jason and the others splintered the door with a hail of machine-gun fire. When they stepped inside, they found that their bullets had killed Abu Youssef—and fatally wounded his wife.

Jason had barely reacted to this sight when Uri called out, "Police cars coming."

"All right," he replied, quickly rifling the terrorist chief's desk and grabbing what documents he could. "Let's get the hell out of here."

As they sprinted down the stairs, an old woman stuck her head out of an apartment door. A startled commando fired and she crumpled to the ground.

Out in the street, they tossed hand grenades to distract the arriving gendarmes, leapt into their car, and sped toward the seafront.

The other men were already back at the beach. When they

caught sight of Jason's group they waved, ran toward the water's edge, and clambered into the rubber boats. Jason and his men quickly followed and began rowing furiously out to sea.

A few hours later they were back at the *Sayaret* headquarters in the heart of Israel.

One of the other squad leaders was reporting that he had blown up part of the terrorists' headquarters and shot several defenders in the process. A second unit had hit other PLO buildings, including a bomb-making workshop.

But it was the results of Jason's assignment that most concerned Zvi.

"Well, *saba,*" he asked anxiously, "how did you do?"

Jason replied slowly and deliberately, "We killed the guy who planned the Munich Massacre."

"Congratulations—"

"But we also killed a few innocent people."

He then fell silent.

"*Saba,* we are in a war. When the air force bombs a military target, even if they score a direct hit, it's inevitable that civilians are affected."

"Yeah, but the bombers are thousands of feet up in the clouds. They don't have to see any faces."

Zvi grabbed him by the shoulders and said firmly, "Listen to me. You're a soldier defending your country. These men killed Israelis and were planning to kill more. You probably saved hundreds of lives. Maybe thousands. You should be proud."

Jason merely shook his head, walked out of the building, climbed into his car, and drove north to the kibbutz.

It was early morning when he arrived, and the children were on their way to the schoolhouse. His young sons saw him and rushed to embrace him.

As he held them tightly and kissed them, he thought, You two are the only justification for going on in this killing business. Maybe when you grow up, the world will have finally come to its senses.

Two weeks later, Zvi called Jason into his office. He was relaxed and smiling. "I've got an operation I think you'll actually enjoy."

"I doubt it," Jason replied sarcastically.

"No, really. This should appeal to the Harvard man in you.

It involves going to America. Our government is concerned with Israel's deteriorating image, especially among the young people— the so-called New Left. We need a few eloquent spokesmen to tour campuses and maybe even speak to Jewish groups to bolster morale."

"I'm not much of an orator," Jason replied.

"But you still have a lovely American accent. That would help. Also, I remember when we first met you used to have a certain charm."

" 'Used to' is right."

"Anyway, you can take Eva to Jerusalem with you for the week the Foreign Office needs to brief you. Look at it as a holiday, *saba*. Maybe a little vacation with your wife will help you find some of that long-lost charm."

As they walked the streets of Jerusalem, Eva recalled that when Jason had first come to Israel, they had been able to visit only half of it.

"That's something you could mention in your talks," she suggested. "When Jordan held the Old City, they not only kept the Jews from their holy places, they actually used our synagogues as stables. The world has got to give us credit for ensuring freedom of religion here."

"Eva, the world doesn't give us credit for anything."

"Well, I feel proud anyway," she insisted.

"Good." He smiled. "Then maybe you can go and give my speeches for me."

Jason arrived in New York at the end of May. It was the first time in nearly ten years that he had set foot on American soil. And it felt good. At least some of it, anyway. He was in the land of his birth, a place he had missed desperately at times. But it was also the home of his parents, who were now a mere ten-cent phone call away.

He had spent his last few days with Eva agonizing over what to do about them, and had reached no satisfactory conclusion. She felt he should drive out to Long Island and see them. So much more could be accomplished in a face-to-face confrontation. They could look into his eyes and perceive his commitment. That could change everything.

But it was easier for her to say than for him to do. He knew he had caused his parents heartache. And whatever the rights or wrongs of his actions, he still felt guilty.

Yet, one thing Eva told him gnawed at his consciousness: "You'll never make peace with yourself until you make peace with them. One way or another, you have to free yourself or you'll never grow up."

"But I'm nearly forty years old," he had protested.

"All the more reason for you to become a full-fledged adult," she had replied.

Still, Jason sat in his hotel room that afternoon unable to pick up the phone. Instead, he put on his newly acquired summer-weight suit and went out for a walk. He told himself that he was ambling up Fifth Avenue merely to stare in shop windows at all the luxuries no Israeli could afford. Yet, when he reached Forty-fourth Street, he knew that what had drawn him there was the Harvard Club.

He hadn't paid his dues for years, but he talked his way in by fabricating the excuse that he would be meeting Andrew Eliot upstairs in the gym.

He took the elevator to the fifth floor and checked the squash-reservations book for that afternoon. Sure enough, at 5:00 P.M. there was a court assigned to "A. Eliot '58." He glanced at his watch—only twenty minutes to wait.

Andrew could not believe his eyes. He was ecstatic.

"My God, Gilbert. You haven't changed at all. I mean, the rest of us are losing hair and growing paunches and you look like a goddamn freshman. What's your secret?"

"Try active duty in the army for ten years, Eliot."

"No, thanks. I'd rather be safe and fat. Want to play a little squash? You can have my court and my opponent, who's just an overweight stockbroker."

"Thanks. I'd love to—if you can get me some gear."

"No sweat, old buddy," Andrew replied jauntily. "Then can we have dinner afterward?"

"Doesn't your wife expect you home?" Jason inquired.

"Not exactly. But that's another story."

June 2, 1973

It was really great to see Jason Gilbert again after all these years. And also a bit disconcerting.

On the one hand, the guy has barely changed physically. He still looks like a twenty-year-old athlete, making me feel more like a middle-aged slob than I already do.

And yet there was something strangely different about him. I search for the appropriate adjective, but the only thing I can come up with is "somber." While he's obviously happily married and adores his kids, he seems to have lost something of his old joie de vivre. I mean, he smiles a lot when we talk about the escapades of the past. But he never laughs. Nothing seems to amuse him *now*.

Of course, I'm aware that he's been through a great deal these past few years—most of which he avoided talking about. I mean, when your fiancée is murdered and you've been in the thick of a real shooting war, that's certainly reason enough to be somber. But I sensed there was something more bothering him, and I tried my best to dig it out. At one point he said, "I'm really lost, Andy."

That kind of shook me. Because if there was anyone in The Class whom I thought knew what he was doing and why, it was Jason. I mean, he'd dedicated himself to a cause and sacrificed a lot of the glittering prizes that would have come his way if he had stayed in the American rat race. After all, he was the best rat in our whole damn pack.

I got a glimpse of what was weighing heavy on him when I told him how the press—and even the man in the street—admired the exploits of the Israeli Army in the Six Day War. It was kind of a David and Goliath that really captured the American imagination.

To which he replied that the media must have glorified it. Because no matter how much you believe in what you're fighting for, it's a terrible thing to take another person's life. He was having trouble living with the awareness that there were probably kids in the world he himself had orphaned.

I replied that it must be pretty hard to be a soldier if you have thoughts like that.

He looked at me with a sadness in his eyes that I'd never seen before and said softly, "It's impossible to be a soldier and a complete human being."

Up till then, I was convinced that I and our other classmates were feeling the weight of the world—stalled careers, mortgages, divorces, custody fights, rebelling kids—and all the stuff of which middle-age crises are made.

But, unlike the rest of us, still in hot pursuit of fame and fortune, all Jason wants to do in life is be a human being.

And he's far from certain he can do it.

During his first week in New York, Jason had to face twelve different audiences, ranging from a few political leaders to more than a thousand Friends of Israel at a luncheon in the Biltmore Hotel.

There were more than just "Friends" at the gathering. During the question period, several New Left sympathizers attacked him vehemently for representing an "imperialist nation." He calmly replied that, far from aspiring to empire, Israel wanted only to be a democratic country just like any other. And—in his personal opinion—would surely relinquish territory in exchange for the Arabs' acknowledgment of her right to exist.

For a long while afterward, crowds clustered around the podium. Talking to him. Shaking his hand. Wishing him well. Finally, there was only one couple left.

He was standing face to face with his father and mother.

Each of them was afraid to say the first words. But the glances they exchanged spoke eloquently. Of admiration and affection on their part. Of relief and love on his. Of the passionate desire for a reconciliation on both sides.

"Hello, Mom, Dad. It's . . . good to see you."

"You look wonderful, Jason," his mother said softly.

"Yeah," he replied. "I guess danger agrees with me. You guys look pretty good yourselves. How's Julie?"

"She's fine," his father answered. "She's in California. Married a lawyer from Santa Barbara."

"Is she happy?"

"Actually, she and Samantha will be moving back this summer. When the divorce is final."

"Again?"

His father nodded. "Julie hasn't changed." He then added hoarsely, "We . . . we've missed you very much, son."

Jason hopped off the platform and put his arms around his parents. For a long moment they held this triangular embrace.

"Do you have time to come out to the house?" his mother asked.

"Sure, I'd really like to."

The next evening at dinner he showed his parents pictures of Eva and their two grandsons. They were very moved just to see them and delighted that his marriage was so successful.

"Can we keep any of these?" his mother asked.

"Keep them all," Jason offered. And then confessed, "Actually, I brought them for you."

Just after eleven, his mother pleaded tiredness and excused herself, leaving Jason and his father alone for the first time in ten years.

Jason was the first to speak. "Dad, I know how much I must have hurt you and Mom—"

"No," his father interrupted. "If there are going to be any apologies, let me go first. I was wrong not to respect your convictions."

"Please, Dad."

"No, let me finish. You've taught me a lesson about our heritage. I realize that it's possible to be one-hundred-percent American and at the same time still be a Jew. The Six Day War was a catalyst for a lot of people like me. There was such a sudden outburst of pride. . . ." He paused.

Jason did not know what to say. His father's voice lowered as he continued.

"Then, of course, I knew you were in the thick of it and I was worried as hell." He raised his head. "Oh God, son, I'm glad you made it through so we could have this talk."

The two embraced.

Eva and the boys were waiting when his plane landed in Tel Aviv. As they hugged and kissed, little Ben asked, "Daddy, did you bring us any presents?"

"You bet I did, Benjy. But the best one will be coming here in October."

"What's that?"

"A grandma and a grandpa."

"Come on in," Richard Nixon called to George Keller. "You can use a little exercise."

It was a hot day in August 1973, at the Western White House, in San Clemente, California. The President was conferring with Kissinger as they sat waist deep in the shallow end of the swimming pool. George Keller was seated nearby, taking notes as Henry called them out. ("Be sure I call Pompidou at 0700 GMT.")

Nixon again repeated his invitation to George.

"I'm afraid I can't, Mr. President, thank you," George replied awkwardly. "In fact, I didn't even bring a suit along."

At which Nixon turned to Kissinger and joked, "Henry, don't tell me this boy of yours can't swim."

"Oh, he most certainly can, Mr. President. In fact, he couldn't have gotten his college diploma without being able to swim fifty yards."

Dr. K. always scrupulously avoided saying the word *Harvard* unless absolutely necessary. Nixon had a phobia about that institution, dating from the time he was on Joe McCarthy's investigating committee (and in fact, its president, Derek Bok, was on the current White House "enemies list").

"Well, okay," the President replied. "But, George, I want you to promise me you'll do a few laps before dinner. I need my team to be in tip-top shape."

"Yes, sir, Mr. President," he replied. "Now if you'll excuse me, I've got to go back to my room and type up some of these memos."

George dutifully gathered up his papers, zipped them into an attaché case, and strode to the guest cottage where the various White House aides were billeted.

He could not have been at his desk for more than five minutes when Kissinger, wearing a terrycloth robe, entered without even knocking.

"George," he said excitedly, "you won't believe what the President just did."

"Is it good or bad?"

"Well, that depends on your vantage point, my boy," said Kissinger, a smile beginning to cross his face. "He's just asked me to become Secretary of State."

"Gosh, Henry, congratulations."

"Listen, can I use your phone? I'd like to call my parents and tell them."

At 11:06 A.M. on September 22, in the East Room of the White House, Dr. Henry A. Kissinger took the oath of office and assumed the duties of the fifty-sixth American Secretary of State.

George Keller was privileged to be among the few nonmedia people present at the swearing-in. For he was joining the new Secretary as a Special Assistant.

Kissinger's short remarks of gratitude were spoken from the heart. "There is no other country in the world where it is conceivable that a man of my origin could be standing here next to the President of the United States. . . ."

George could not keep from hoping that America would also offer unlimited opportunity to a man of *his* origin.

"Henry, can I have a few seconds of your time?"

The new Secretary of State looked up from his desk and replied affably, "Certainly, George. What unsolvable new crisis do you wish to bring to my attention?"

"It's not a crisis exactly, it's more of a puzzle. You know I've always been liaising with Andreyev at the Russian Embassy—"

"Of course. Our best friend with the enemy."

"Well, he's invited me to lunch at Sans Souci."

"Good." Kissinger smiled. "At least we're still salvaging a few meals from what's left of détente."

"Seriously, Henry," George responded, "he wants to introduce me to their new Cultural Attaché."

"Ah yes," Kissinger replied with his near-photographic memory. "Fellow named Yakushkin."

George nodded. "What do you think he wants?"

"That, my dear boy, is precisely what I expect you to find out. But will you take a word of advice from your old professor?"

"Certainly," said George.

"Try their *aiguillettes de canard*. They cook them in cassis."

It is a Washington paradox. Under other circumstances it might be decried as giving aid and comfort—and in this case, haute cuisine—to the enemy. But in America's capital city they call it "gastronomic diplomacy."

Some of the President's men, like Haldeman and Ehrlichman, were regular clients of the Sans Souci, by far the best restaurant within walking distance of the White House. And they were fully accustomed to seeing high government officials (and even middle-rankers like George) sit down to dine with representatives of the nation that was supposed to be their mortal enemy.

This was not the first such meal in George Keller's government experience. Though he could not fathom why, the Russian Embassy seemed to have taken a particular liking to him. At first he thought it was because of his fluency in their language. And yet all their conversations were held in English. And not even in hushed tones.

Still, always following the ground rules, he would furnish the FBI with a "Memorandum of Conversation" detailing the topics covered in each dialogue he had.

Far from arousing suspicion, the esteem in which the Soviets seemed to hold George actually raised his stature. For there were strategists at the State Department and the CIA who thought he might one day be useful in sniffing out a potential Communist defector.

It was a nice day, so George walked across Pennsylvania Avenue and down 17th Street to the restaurant.

Andreyev, middle-aged and bald, in a typical shapeless gray Russian suit, waved him over to the table, where a younger man, wearing a blue blazer and striped tie, rose to shake his hand.

"Dmitri Yakushkin, this is George Keller," said Andreyev. He then added jocularly, "Be nice to him. He knows more about Eastern Europe than we do."

"I'll be on my best behavior," said the diplomat in impeccable English.

George could not help but think, My God, his accent is almost as good as mine.

"What would you prefer to drink," Andreyev asked, "Bloody Mary or champagne cocktail?"

"Since they have excellent Russian vodka here, I'll have a Bloody Mary."

Andreyev raised three fingers to the Maître d', who simply nodded, having no need for further elucidation.

The conversation was extremely cordial and exceptionally superficial. George sat there waiting for the hidden zinger.

Yet, when the *crème brûlée* arrived, Yakushkin was asking him whether he ever went back to Hungary, which was now feasible since he was a U.S. citizen. And other trivialities.

George discoursed perfunctorily—but not too chauvinistically—about the pleasures of living in a capitalist society and how much he enjoyed the social life in Washington, which was a veritable cornucopia of lovely women. As Dmitri would soon find out.

At this juncture, he thought he saw a sparkle in the young man's eyes. Perhaps he's a candidate, George mused. Perhaps he's asking in an oblique way how well a former Communist could live if he went to the other side.

This, at least, was the only conclusion he could offer in the Memorandum of Conversation he dictated to his secretary when he returned from lunch.

Sometime after three o'clock, the Secretary of State peeked his head through George's door and asked, "Well?"

"You were right, Henry. The duck was absolutely great."

Five days later, Yakushkin called George at his office "just to touch base" and confirm how much he had enjoyed their meeting. In fact, he wanted to invite George to dinner.

They set a date and a gastronomic venue—the Russians' favorite restaurant, appropriately called La Rive Gauche, on Wisconsin Avenue. According to the State Department in-jokes, this was the most exclusive place in Washington. For its clientele was made up almost entirely of CIA and KGB agents watching one another watching other people.

Again, the chat was casual. But this time the beverage was vintage Bordeaux—and plenty of it. Each of them sat nonchalantly, trying to make out that they were just a little drunker than they really were.

"George," Dmitri said casually, "this city's so expensive. Do they pay you a good salary at State?"

"Not bad," said George, and added almost as an afterthought, "thirty-six thousand per."

"How much is that in rubles?" the young Russian asked.

"I really don't know," George responded with a smile.

"To be honest," the diplomat laughed, "I'm not so sure myself. But anyway, between the two of us, I'd rather get my pay in dollars, eh?"

"That's the only thing they take in America," George replied, sensing that they were approaching a topic of some importance.

George casually lobbed the ball into the Russian's court.

"Tell me, Dmitri, can you make ends meet on your salary?"

There was a pause. The two chess players eyed each other, and the Russian said in candor, "Frankly, that was just what I was going to ask you."

And George thought, What an ass. He's trying to recruit *me.* Do the Russians think I'm such a patsy?

Still, he had to keep his cool.

"I'm fine for money, Dmitri," he responded casually. "My needs are very simple."

"Yes," the Soviet concurred, a tinge of mystery in his voice, "you seem to lack for nothing. So is there no way we can . . . help you?"

George knew that he had to play along.

"That's most considerate," he said almost facetiously. "But why should your embassy want to help a person like myself?"

"Because you were brought up a Marxist and because perhaps you sometimes have nostalgia—"

"Never."

"I don't mean for the system, but for the old country. Don't you feel the slightest bit deracinated?"

"I'm an American," George Keller answered firmly.

Dmitri pondered his reaction for a moment, reached into his pocket, and withdrew two thin silver canisters.

"Cigar?" he asked. "They're Havanas. We bring them over in our diplomatic pouch. I bet you've never had one, eh?"

"No, thanks," George said politely. "I don't smoke."

He wanted the FBI observers to note that he would not even touch a Communist cigar.

Yakushkin lit up and started blowing little rings.

"Dr. Keller," he started with deliberate slowness, "I have some information that may be of interest to you."

The Russian's sudden change of tone made George uncomfortable.

"I'm always glad to receive information from the Russian Embassy," he replied with nervous humor.

"It's about the status of your father," said the diplomat. "I thought you might like to know that—"

"I know my father's risen in the party," George interrupted with annoyance.

"I mean the status of his health."

"Is he ill?"

"He has lung cancer."

"Oh," George said gravely. "I'm sorry to hear that."

"It will no doubt be very painful," the Russian added.

"What do you mean 'painful'?"

"Look," Dmitri began with fraternal consolation, "you're an expert on East European affairs and you know the level of hospital facilities in Hungary. We don't have the abundant supply of medication that you have in the West. So it's not clear how long he'll live. It could be one year. It could be several months. . . ."

Yakushkin sighed like a world-weary physician.

"George, this wretched arms race sometimes makes humanitarian concerns a secondary matter. If your father were in America, he would be so much more comfortable. You are so far ahead of us in—what's the word?—analgesics."

"I'm sure Party officials don't lack for Western medicine, Dmitri."

"True," the Russian conceded. "But as you and I know, your father's rank is not that high. . . ."

He paused and blew another Cuban smoke ring.

"I don't see what all this has to do with me," George protested quietly.

"Well," Dmitri said with a little smile, "a father is a father. I mean, if I were in your place I would want to help him. At least to die peacefully. It's possible I could be in a position to help him."

"Then do so."

There was a pause, like the rest period between rounds of a fight.

Yakushkin replied simply, "It doesn't work that way."

"What the hell are you driving at?"

Dmitri refilled George's wine glass and then spoke in friendly, reassuring tones.

"Please, Keller, if you think I'm going to ask you to commit espionage, you're sorely mistaken."

"But you do want me to do something," George insisted.

"Yes. Something perfectly legal. It is simply a matter of unblocking the logjam of your government's bureaucracy. We have been trying for months now to obtain a piece of equipment—"

"Which, I suppose, you would like me to steal," George interrupted.

"No, no. This is a small device that we are trying to buy. Do you hear me? *Buy.* It is merely a gadget for enhancing photographic images from weather satellites. There's no hanky-panky here, but your Department of Commerce just won't get off the fence."

"And you want me to push them?"

" 'Push' is too strong a word," the diplomat replied. "I would prefer to say 'gently nudge.' Look, all I want you to do is satisfy yourself that the Taylor RX-80 is of no military value. Take your time and give me a buzz when you've checked it out. Anyway, I've had a very pleasant evening."

"Yes," George replied, trying to keep his psychic equilibrium. "Thanks very much."

In his Memorandum of Conversation to the FBI referring to his second meeting with Dmitri Yakushkin, Cultural Attaché at the Soviet Embassy, George Keller wrote succinctly:

I tried to recruit him. He tried to recruit me.

Game ended in a scoreless tie.

G.K.

But in fact, in the days that followed, George was haunted by thoughts of the father whom he hated. And by thoughts of that same father lying in agony in a Budapest hospital. Whom he could no longer hate.

After three days and nights he was still in an anguished quandary. The thought even occurred to him that the Russians might be bluffing. For all he knew, his father might be hale and hearty in some elegant resort for Party officials. How could he be sure?

Dmitri Yakushkin had anticipated this. On the fourth morning, when George went downstairs to get the mail, he found a large manila envelope that had been delivered by hand.

It contained two chest X-rays and a short note from the diplomat:

> Dear George,
>   I thought these might be of interest.
>
>   D.

September 30, 1973

I'm scared that something's terribly wrong with George Keller. He called me this afternoon and asked me, since I'm active in alumni affairs, whether I knew any good doctors in the Washington area.

I was puzzled for several reasons. Why did he ask me, a layman? And why didn't he ask some friends of his who live in his area?

He explained that it was something really serious and had to be kept confidential. Of course, I said that I would try to help him but I'd need some details, like exactly what *kind* of doctor he was looking for.

At first he gave a very strange answer. He needed someone "very trustworthy."

This made me think that George might be having some kind of nervous breakdown. I mean, I know those high-security guys are under tremendous pressure.

But, no. What he wanted was the name of the best *oncologist* within driving distance of Washington.

This really upset me. Why did he need a cancer specialist? I didn't feel I had the right to ask.

I just told him I'd make some discreet inquiries among my medical friends and call him back. Then he quickly insisted that *he*'d call *me*.

At this point the operator interrupted to say that his three minutes were up. He shoved in some more coins just to say he'd call the next day at exactly the same time.

Naturally, I immediately contacted the alumni office and asked one of my old buddies who works there to have the computer try to find what George needed (without using any names, of course). I soon found out that a classmate, Peter Ryder, was now a professor of oncology at Johns Hopkins, in nearby Baltimore.

Though I was worried about his health, something else also disturbed me.

Why did he call from a pay phone?

P eter Ryder, Professor of Oncology at Johns Hopkins Medical School, startled George by
his greeting.

"*Kak pozhivias?*" he said.

"I don't understand. Why are you speaking Russian to me?"

"Gosh," said the tall, balding physician, unable to conceal
his disappointment, "don't you remember me? I sat right next to
you in Slavic 168. But I guess in those days you were too busy
listening to the lecture to notice anything else, huh?"

"Uh, I suppose so," George said distractedly. "Do you think
we could go somewhere private and talk?"

"Yes, of course. You said you had some X-rays. We can look
at them in my office."

George clutched the manila envelope as he followed the
white-coated specialist down the corridor. Even when the door
to Ryder's office was closed, he would not relinquish the
photographs.

"Doctor," he said in confidential tones, "there's something I
must explain to you first."

"Please call me Pete," he insisted.

"Well, Pete, you know that I work for the State Department.
These X-rays are of a security nature."

"I don't follow you, George."

"They are of a high-ranking Communist leader and were
smuggled out under great secrecy. I need to be sure that there will
be no written report of this conversation. And I won't be able to
explain why I need the information."

"That's okay," Ryder replied. "I'm savvy enough to guess it's
important for you guys to know how healthy the big shots on the
other side are. Anyway, you can count on my discretion."

He pinned the X-rays to his lighted cabinet. And immediately said, "I don't understand why you had to come to an oncologist."

"What do you mean?"

"I mean any med student could see what's wrong. See that black mark on the apex—that's the upper lobe—on the left lung? That's a very large malignancy. This patient has very little time to live—several months at most." He then turned to George and asked, "Isn't that what you wanted to know?"

George hesitated and then asked, "Is it possible for you to tell me if the patient is in any . . . distress?"

"I can make a pretty accurate conjecture," Ryder answered and turned back to the photograph. "The carcinoma seems to be impinging on the lorachial plexus of nerves. This would cause severe pain in the upper chest at that point and radiate down the arm as well."

George was momentarily at a loss for further questions.

"Is there anything else I can tell you?" the physician asked.

"Uh—yes. Just some theoretical information, if you would, please—uh—Pete. If this person were your patient, how would you go about treating him?"

"Well, there's zero chance of actually reversing the disease, but we could perhaps prolong life with X-ray treatment and some of the new drugs like Adriamycine, cisplatin, and Cytoxan. These could be used singly or in combination."

"Would they ease the pain?" George asked.

"In many cases. If not, we have a whole pharmacopoeia of narcotics and sedatives."

"So it's possible that even a person as sick as this could . . . die in peace?" George asked.

"I'd like to think that's a very important part of my job," Ryder said gently.

"Thank you very much, Pete," George mumbled, and tried to keep his wits about him to make a nonchalant exit.

"Not at all," his classmate replied. "But could I ask you a question? I mean, you can count on my complete discretion."

"What?"

"Is it Brezhnev?"

"I'm sorry," George replied softly. "I can't tell you."

George asked his secretary to get Stephen Webster of the Commerce Department on the phone. He was a technology expert fresh out of MIT who had recently introduced himself to George at a party. And who, like all ambitious young men arriving in Washington, was eager to curry favor with his superiors.

"Gee, Dr. Keller," he said cheerfully. "It's a pleasant surprise hearing your voice. How can I help you?"

"Steve," he began casually, "this is really a very small matter. Are you familiar with this RX-80 business?"

"You mean the Taylor photographic filter?" the scientist inquired, anxious to show he was on top of things.

"Yes. Could you explain to a layman like me just what the thing does?"

"Sure. We're using it on weather satellites to sharpen our pictures and prevent guys like you from getting caught in the rain without an umbrella."

"Sounds pretty innocuous to me," George replied. "That's the reason some of us at State were wondering why you guys are sitting on it. Could it possibly serve any military purpose?"

"Well," Webster replied, "almost anything could. It depends how you use it. I mean, theoretically, a clearer satellite image might help you aim a missile better."

"So which way are you guys going to go on this?"

"Listen, Dr. Keller, I'm practically one step above the office boy. If you want my opinion, it probably depends on what State decides."

"Do you mean Kissinger?"

"Could I possibly mean anyone else?"

"Thanks, Steve. By the way, do you play tennis?"

"A little," he replied eagerly.

"Then I'll call you sometime next week and maybe we could hit a few balls."

This time it was George's turn to invite Yakushkin to dinner. He chose Cantina d'Italia, another elegant Washington restaurant favored by the Russians for détente dinners. As soon as they ordered, he got right to the point.

"Dmitri, I've done some preliminary explorations with Commerce and it does appear we could possibly speed along your government's request for that little filter."

"That's wonderful news," said the young diplomat, smiling broadly. "I'm extremely grateful to you. And if there's any way I can ever reciprocate . . ."

George tried to glance around in a nonfurtive way to see if they were within earshot of the other guests.

But Yakushkin knew what was on his mind and immediately remarked, "You know, you wouldn't recognize your native city, George. Budapest has modern skyscrapers now, modern hospitals with the best facilities and advanced medications. . . ."

"The very best?"

"I'll wager they've got any drug you have in the West. Try and stump me if you can."

He had made it easy for George, who had, of course, memorized the relevant pharmacology.

"How about Adriamycine, cisplatin, and Cytoxan, for example?"

"Certainly obtainable when the circumstances call for them."

"I'm very impressed," said George.

And both gamesmen knew it was time to switch to other topics.

In his capacity as Assistant Secretary of State for East European Affairs, George would prepare a series of policy memos, consistent with his boss's political philosophy, but written by himself and given to Kissinger in a pile at the end of each week.

By now he was so adept at doing this that he could even reproduce Henry's distinctive turns of phrase. That Friday the heap of correspondence to various departments and bureaus included a brief memo to a middle-ranking office at the Department of Commerce:

> There seems no point in holding up the sale of the Taylor RX-80. Its military value is tenuous at best. Besides, we might as well sell to them and get the money before they steal it.
>
> Yours,
> HAK.

George briefed the Secretary of State on the contents of what he had placed before him.

They were mostly policy directives, notes to various think-tanks to be sure their area studies were on target. And one or two miscellaneous notes, like a memo to DOD about security precautions at an upcoming arms-trade show. Also a note to DOC about an innocuous camera device the Soviets want to buy.

"Who did you check it out with to be sure it was 'innocuous'?" Kissinger asked.

"Oh, an MIT whiz kid at Commerce named Webster," George replied casually.

"I don't think I know him. Is he new?"

George nodded. "But I looked into him. Apparently, nobody knows more than he does about this filter."

"Do you think I ought to have a word with him myself?"

George's mind raced frantically. "Uh—I don't think you need to in this case."

"I suppose you're right. You always do a thorough job, George. Okay, you go home while I sign these."

"Thanks, Henry."

His boss looked up. "Have a good weekend, George. Don't work too hard."

Henry Kissinger remained at his desk for another two and a half hours. During which time he executed sixty-five different directives, including all the documents given him by George Keller.

Jason Gilbert's parents did not go to Israel as planned in early October 1973. Because, as the country was at a standstill for Yom Kippur—the sacred day of atonement—the Egyptian and Syrian armies attacked in force.

Israel was caught completely off guard and, for several days, hovered on the brink of annihilation.

By the time news of the simultaneous attacks on the frontiers reached central command, Egyptian tanks had crossed the Suez Canal and were slaughtering the forces manning the southernmost lookout points. It seemed as if they would reach Tel Aviv without resistance.

The north was even worse. There hundreds of Syrian tanks had smashed across and were only a few hours from the population centers.

The handful of Israeli troops on duty dug in to slow the onslaught, knowing that the cost would be great, but equally aware that they had no alternative.

As the radio broke the silence of the holy day with frantic code messages to mobilize the nation's reserves, Jason received a call at the kibbutz.

"What the hell's going on?" he demanded anxiously.

"Listen, *saba*, don't ask questions. It's chaos in central HQ. We're mobilizing like mad, but meanwhile we've got to slow the Syrians down. Get as many men as you can up to the Heights and reinforce them until we can get more armor through. Hurry the hell up to Nafa and report to General Eytan. He'll give you a command."

"Of whom?" Jason snapped.

"Of whoever's still living, dammit! Now get going."

*   *   *

Jason and five other kibbutzniks took one of their trucks and started north up the bumpy road, stopping every few miles to pick up other soldiers headed for the front. Some of them were still in jeans and sweatshirts, carrying only their weapons and ammunition. They said almost nothing during the ride.

But the Syrians had gotten to Nafa before them, and forced General Eytan to retreat.

The kibbutzniks found him in an improvised camp right by the roadside. Jason was stunned by the number of soldiers dead and wounded. The live and the quick were in short supply. Only a handful of reservists had been able to muster.

Among the half-dozen officers being briefed by Eytan, Jason recognized another member of the elite *Sayaret Matkal*, Yoni Netanyahu. The two nodded at each other as they listened to the commander's litany of disaster.

"The Barak Armored Brigade is almost completely demolished. We're outnumbered and outmatched. They've got the latest Russian T-62s. But we've still got to hold them till our own armor gets here. Try and organize your men and drill them with the antitank rocket launchers. And don't waste ammunition!"

"How long till we get reinforcements?" Jason asked.

"God knows," Eytan replied. "But all we have now is what you see here."

"So, we'll do it," said Yoni Netanyahu with almost mystical conviction. "We'll be like Gideon's army."

"I think even Gideon had more men than we do," Jason quipped with what could only be called gallows humor.

As the meeting dispersed, the two young officers walked off together toward the small group of reservists waiting nervously for their orders.

"I know you're a pretty good man with motors, Jason," Yoni remarked. "Do you think you could oversee the repair of some of our less-battered tanks?"

"I guess so. But what the hell good is it? Even if I get them to work, we'll still be outnumbered fifty to one."

"Well," Yoni said confidently, "that reduces our tactical options to only one. If they've got the armor, all we have is the timing. Have your tanks ready to attack by 0600 hours tomorrow."

"Attack?" Jason retorted incredulously. "You must really believe in God, Yoni."

"Ask me when all this is over. Meanwhile, I'll be praying that you get those tanks operational."

"You know, Yoni, where I come from we'd say that you play guts ball. It means—"

"I know what it means," the young commander replied. "I'm going to college in America when this damn thing is over. Your alma mater, in fact."

"No shit," replied Jason. "Do you mean I'm up here in the valley of the shadow of death with another Harvard man?"

"Future Harvard man," Yoni replied. "Now shake ass and get me some tanks."

It was early evening in Washington when the first news of the Arab assault reached the White House.

Nixon asked Kissinger to brief him on the situation. He in turn called George and ordered him to gather as much intelligence as he could from the Pentagon and the Israeli ambassador.

"Awright, guys, give me the numbers," the President demanded before the two men even sat down.

Kissinger pointed to George, who had a sheaf of documents.

"The scope of it all is pretty staggering, Mr. President," he began.

"Cut out the Harvard commentary, George," Nixon snapped, "and just give me the damn numbers."

"Well," he continued, "the Egyptian Army is one of the largest in the world. They've got at least eight hundred thousand troops. We're not sure how many have already crossed the Canal."

"What do the Israelis have to hold them off?"

"I think we can safely assume the Egyptians have already destroyed any resistance," Kissinger said solemnly.

"And in the north?" the President asked.

"Well, the Syrians have some fourteen hundred tanks—" George began.

"I've heard enough," Nixon interrupted with a wave of his hand. "We're talking about a massacre, aren't we? I mean, this is the Alamo, right?"

Kissinger answered analytically, "George hasn't gotten to the most important aspect. The Russians have armed Egypt and Syria to the teeth. Besides the old SAM missile systems, they've got hundreds of new portable SAM-7s."

"They're antiaircraft launchers that can be used by ground forces," George offered.

"I won't sit and watch the Soviets turn the Middle East into their own country club!" Nixon pounded his fist on the desk. "We've got to upgrade the Israeli armory. I want you guys to tell Defense to get the supply line going."

"Mr. President," Kissinger cautioned, "a massive rearming of Israel is not going to please certain members of Congress."

"Neither would the sight of Brezhnev drinking vodka in Tel Aviv. Now start the ball rolling and we can debate later."

As they left the Oval Office, George could not help whispering to Kissinger, "I didn't think Nixon liked Jews that much."

"He doesn't. But he hates the Russians more."

"Well, Henry, I'd better get on the phone. I've got a lot of generals to convince this morning."

"Let me deal with the Secretary of Defense, George. Schlesinger needs special handling."

"Okay. But if things get rough you can always sing a few Harvard songs in his ear."

Henry smiled and patted his protégé on the back. "Let's meet in the Situation Room at five o'clock. By then we'll have a better picture of where Israel stands."

"You mean *if* it's still standing," George replied.

After haranguing the mechanics mercilessly, Jason had provided Yoni with a dozen tanks that could at least move. The young paratroop officer had immediately set off to counterattack the Syrian tanks.

Meanwhile, Jason led a small group of young and panicky soldiers in trying to recapture the Nafa camp. As they were nearing their objective, three huge Russian-made Ilyushin helicopters packed with enemy troops appeared on the horizon.

"Listen, guys," Jason shouted urgently, "the key element is surprise. Catch them before they get their bearings. As soon as they touch down, start firing and scare the shit out of them."

His men nodded wordlessly.

The minute the first chopper hit the ground, Jason called out, "Follow me!" and led the charge, firing as he ran.

The first Syrians to land returned their fire, killing several Israelis. But Jason continued to rush forward. Still in motion, he pulled a grenade from his belt and hurled it toward the disembarking commandos. It exploded near the helicopter and created a panic. The enemy began to scatter in every direction.

Yet these were elite Syrian troops, and some stood their ground, poised for hand-to-hand combat.

Though Jason had long trained for this kind of fighting, this was the first time he had done it with his life at stake. The first time he could see the faces of the men who would be his victims—or his killers.

At last the Israelis prevailed. The other two helicopters were frightened off. The ground was strewn with the dead and dying of both sides.

Seeing his shirt drenched in scarlet, Jason thought he had

been wounded. He then realized it was the blood of the men he had fought—and dispatched.

One of his soldiers came up and said, "We nailed thirty of them, *saba*. I don't think they'll try to take Nafa again."

"How many did we lose?"

"Four," the soldier replied. "And two or three are pretty badly cut up. I've radioed for the medics."

Jason nodded numbly and looked off into the horizon.

Slowly the tide of battle turned.

At long last, their ranks were swelled with mobilized troops and they began to advance into Syria, ultimately regrouping within artillery range of Damascus.

By Saturday, October 13—one week after Yom Kippur—the Syrian front was quiet enough to allow some of the Israeli troops to be transferred to the Sinai, where the battle was still fierce.

Jason boarded a helicopter, saw Yoni, and sat down next to him.

"Hey," he joked wearily, "I'll bet you a beer I've slept less than you in the past week."

"I haven't slept at all," replied the younger officer.

"Sorry I asked," Jason said. "I got a magnificent two hours last night. I owe you a brew."

"I won't forget it," Yoni smiled.

And they flew off to join the fighting in the Sinai.

They had courage to spare. The only thing they were running out of was ammunition.

Richard Nixon had ordered George Keller to appear immediately in his office. "Goddammit," he fumed, "the Russians are pouring arms into Egypt and Syria. What's happened to our airlift?"

"Apparently the Pentagon is arguing about whether we should use private or government planes. Some protocol thing, sir."

The President rose and leaned on his desk angrily. "Listen, Keller, you get right on the phone and tell them to use every damn plane we have. I want that equipment in the air. And I want it now!"

On the eleven-o'clock news that evening, State Department spokesman Dr. George Keller appeared at a brief press conference announcing that the first transport planes with weapons for the Israelis were now en route to Tel Aviv.

Fifteen days after the war had begun, Henry Kissinger and George Keller boarded a plane to Moscow to work out a cease-fire between Israel and Egypt, which went into effect on the following day. President Sadat of Egypt showed his gratitude for these efforts by establishing a new and direct relationship with Washington.

Historians will long argue over which side won the Yom Kippur War. But without question, the victor in the battle for world prestige was Henry Kissinger.

George Keller's conscience ached. What was originally a small subterfuge had been magnified in his mind into an act of high treason. He was too frightened to discuss it with anyone—including Cathy.

Though he scoured every science magazine for mentions of the RX-80, nothing he read gave the slightest suggestion that it could be of strategic advantage.

Nevertheless, George lived in constant fear that his actions would be discovered. And he knew it would do him no good to plead humanitarianism. When you are a government official, you must let your father die if he's on the other side.

He had received no word of Istvan Kolozsdi's fate. He had been afraid to contact Yakushkin at the Russian Embassy, lest observers begin to think they were getting a little too chummy.

George tried to assuage his guilt pangs by convincing himself that he had done nothing legally wrong. And that with the amount of paperwork flowing between State, the Pentagon, Commerce, and the Oval Office, the chances of detection were nil. Only then was he able to get a night's sleep.

But world events constantly rekindled the spark of fear in him. No less a figure than Willy Brandt, Chancellor of West Germany, had to resign in May 1974, when his close aide was exposed as a Communist spy.

George sometimes imagined he was being followed—and he had long suspected that his home phone was tapped. Even while accompanying Kissinger on his Middle East shuttle jaunts he did not feel secure. He could not trust the phones at the King David Hotel in Jerusalem or at the Nile Hilton in Cairo.

*　　*　　*

Late one afternoon, after a long and fruitless day of negotiation with the Syrian authorities, the Secretary of State was flying back to Israel.

Kissinger signalled to George to come and sit by him. "Listen, my boy," he said confidentially, "I'm under a lot of pressure from back home. Certain factions in Washington think I'm spending too much time out here and neglecting other business. They don't seem to understand that I can't be in twenty places at once. So I'm going to have to put more responsibility on those young shoulders of yours."

"What did you have in mind?"

"As you know, the President plans to tour the Middle East and then go on to Russia. I could do with a trustworthy advance man to lay the groundwork in Moscow. And, George, there's no one I trust more than you."

"You flatter me, Henry."

"I have to," the Secretary joked, "otherwise you wouldn't work for me. The pay's too low. Anyway, I want you to fly to Paris tomorrow morning. Brent Scowcroft and Al Haig will meet you there in three days and you can go on together to Moscow."

"Fine," George replied, genuinely pleased to have such prestigious responsibility. "But, Henry, what am I supposed to do while I'm waiting for them?"

Kissinger's reply shook George as if turbulence had struck the plane.

"Go to Budapest."

He did not know how to react.

"Listen," the Secretary of State continued in a soft voice, "your father hasn't got very long to live. I think you should make peace with him."

"How did you know?" he asked (And how much? he wondered).

"It's my job to know. You can pull the same trick I used when I first went to Peking. Check into the Crillon, fake a cold, then quietly slip out to the airport. It's only a two-hour flight. You can go and come back and no one will be the wiser."

George was still searching for words. All he could manage was to stammer, "I—don't know what to say."

"Don't say anything," Kissinger replied, patting him on the arm. "It's the least I owe you for the years you've helped me."

As the air-force plane began its final approach to Ben Gurion

Airport, George thought, How can I tell him I don't want to go? How can I tell him that I have nothing to say to my father before he dies?

I can't. Because it's not true. I do want to see him one last time. I have to.

Customs in Budapest was perfunctory. Except that the officer questioning George took a long look at his red diplomatic passport before saying, "Welcome home, Dr. Keller."

It was a strange feeling being back in his native city. Though it was brighter—and the stores fuller—than during those dark days when he had fled, it seemed relatively unchanged. Rakoczi Street was like it always was. Here and there an ultramodern structure stood comfortably beside the old.

The terrace of the Hilton—a Hilton Hotel in Budapest! —looked out toward the ancient spires of St. Stephen's Church. The huge Duma Intercontinental, where George was staying, was a concrete imitation of any new American hotel.

He checked in quickly, washed, and changed his shirt. And braced himself for the meeting that had brought him here.

Before George left Jerusalem, Kissinger had given him complete details on where his father was receiving treatment—even the phone number.

Now, he asked himself, should I call the hospital and say I'm here? Or should I just show up? My God, the shock of it might kill him then and there. No, it would make better sense to phone one of the doctors, announce his presence, and solicit advice.

In a matter of minutes he was speaking to Dr. Tamas Rozsa, chief of medical services at the People's Municipal Hospital.

After the physician had repeated for the third time what an honor it would be to receive a visit from him, George finally exacted precise details of Istvan Kolozsdi's condition.

"Ah, what is there to say," Rozsa answered philosophically. "There's so little one can do in cases such as his—"

"Did you give him medication?" George interrupted forcefully.

"Yes. Yes, of course. The very newest—right out of Switzerland."

"Is he in pain?" George asked.

"He is and he isn't."

"Can you explain that?"

"It's quite simple, Dr. Keller. If we drug him so strongly that he feels nothing at all, then he is comatose and cannot communicate. Of course, at night we help him to sleep comfortably."

"So, in other words, in order to speak he'll have to forgo some of the painkillers?"

"I'm sure your father will want it that way," said Dr. Rozsa. "When he awakes I'll inform him that you're here, and ring you back. That should be about five this afternoon."

"Is anybody with him now?" George asked.

"Of course. Mrs. Donath practically sleeps in the hospital."

"Who's she?"

"Comrade Kolozsdi's daughter. Your sister, Dr. Keller."

"Oh," said George, as he slowly let down the receiver. And thought, I've got a second confrontation here in Budapest.

He now had several hours to kill and summoned the courage to go out and look at the city of his birth. To revisit all the places he had known when he was Gyorgy Kolozsdi.

His first entry into Budapest was like that of a swimmer into ice-cold water. But once he was actually *in* it and in motion, he began to feel warm and good and exhilarated. He reveled in the sound of his mother tongue being spoken everywhere.

Oh God, he thought, it must be fifty thousand English words ago that I felt so at home.

But his euphoria ended when it neared five o'clock. He returned to the hotel to wait for Dr. Rozsa's phone call.

It came at about quarter to six.

"He's awake now and I told him you were here," the doctor said.

"And?"

"He wants to see you. Grab a taxi and come over right away."

George snatched his raincoat and hurried down to find a cab.

It was the evening rush hour and even the modern traffic underpass on Kossuth Lajos Street could not ease the traffic jam sufficiently. The ride seemed endless.

George walked slowly up the hospital stairs trying to calm his beating heart.

The building was someone's idea of modern—amorphous glass and drab stone. It did not appear to be bustling like an American hospital.

He walked up to an old, fat lady perched behind a desk and softly stated his purpose. She responded quickly, lifted the receiver, and an instant later Dr. Tamas Rozsa, a jowly little man, appeared and greeted George obsequiously.

As they marched briskly down the halls toward his father's private room ("Very rare in Socialist states, I assure you"), Dr. Rozsa gave a tedious account of how the hospital was only partially completed. And how much he envied all the medical technology the Western powers had developed.

What the hell does this guy want, thought George, a handout? Maybe he thinks I can just tell Congress to send him a few million bucks' worth of equipment.

As they turned down a narrow, dimly lighted corridor, George spotted the far-off silhouette of a woman sitting by herself.

His instinct told him that this should be his sister, Marika. But she was three years younger than he. The person sitting there looked positively middle-aged.

As they drew nearer, she glanced up at George.

The eyes, he thought. Those are my sister's eyes in an old woman's face.

"Marika?" he said tentatively. "It's me. Gyuri."

The woman kept staring at him, her eyes like lasers.

"Marika, aren't you going to speak to me?"

They both remained silent for a moment. At last, she responded with quiet anger. "You should not have come. You don't belong here anymore. I told the doctors not to let you in."

George looked at Dr. Rozsa, who nodded. "Yes," he affirmed, "Mrs. Donath was very much against it. It was your father who insisted."

Marika turned her face away.

"Shall we go in now?" Dr. Rozsa asked.

George nodded. For his vocal cords were paralyzed.

He stood for a moment after they entered the room, looking at the frail, white-clad form on a pile of pillows.

The old man sensed his presence and rasped out, "Is that you, Gyuri?" The question was punctuated with a racking cough.

"It's me," said George, still motionless.

"Come closer to the bed. Don't be afraid. Death is not catching."

George started forward nervously.

"I'll leave you two alone," said Dr. Rozsa, making his retreat.

"Sit down," the patriarch commanded, motioning his bony finger at a wooden chair placed near the bed.

George silently obeyed.

He had not yet dared to look his father in the face. He had somehow managed to avoid making visual contact. But now their gazes met and locked.

Istvan Kolozsdi still had the same stern visage, albeit emaciated and extremely pale. George stared at him and thought, This is the demon I've been afraid of all my life. Look at him. So small and frail.

He listened as his father breathed with difficulty.

"Gyuri, do you have children?" he asked.

"No, Father."

"Then who will come and comfort you when you're lying as I am?"

"I guess I'll get married one of these days," George replied. And wondered, Is that why he wants to see me—to make sure I find a wife?

There was an uneasy silence.

"How are you feeling, Father?"

"Not as good as I will when it's all over," answered the old man, and gave a laugh that made him wince with pain. "Listen, Gyuri," he continued, "I'm glad to have this chance to talk. Because there is something I want to tell you. . . ."

He paused to draw strength and breath.

"On second thought," he contradicted, "I don't have to tell you. Just open that drawer." He pointed to the gray bedside table. "Open it, Gyuri."

George leaned over to obey his father's order.

Inside he found a tangled mass of newspaper clippings in several languages. Some were yellowing, some torn.

"Look. Look at them," the old man prompted.

There were articles from the world press about *him*. About George. There was even—God knows how it had gotten there—a profile published last year in the *International Herald Tribune*. He was dumbfounded.

"What do you see?" asked the patriarch.

"I see a lot of old rubbish, Father," George answered, trying to make light of it. "What do you see?"

Making a supreme effort, the old man lifted himself onto his elbows and leaned toward George. "I see *you*, Gyuri. I see your face in every paper in the world. Do you know what you have done to me?"

George had painfully anticipated this question.

"Father, I—I—"

"No," the old man interrupted. "You don't understand at all. You're a big shot in the world."

"On the wrong side," George said deprecatingly.

"My boy, in politics there's no wrong side. There is only the winning side. You have the makings of a master politician, Gyuri. Kissinger will eventually stumble and—you'll become the Secretary of State!"

"That's wishful thinking." George smiled, trying to retain his composure. He could hardly believe that for the first time in his life Istvan Kolozsdi had praised him.

"You're twice as smart as Kissinger," the old man insisted. "And what's more, you aren't a Jew. I'm sorry I won't be around to see the rest."

George felt tears welling in his eyes. He tried to fight them back by attempting lighthearted banter.

"I thought you were a dedicated Socialist," he said with a smile.

The old man emitted a sandpaper laugh.

"Ah, Gyuri, there's only one philosophy that rules the world—success."

He took a long lingering look at George and said, beaming, "Welcome home, my son."

Twenty minutes later, George Keller left his father's room, gently closing the door. Marika was still seated there, impassive. He sat down next to her.

"Look, you have every right to be angry with me," he said nervously. "There's so much to explain. All this time I should have written—"

"You should have done a lot of things," she said mechanically.

"I know. I know."

"Do you, Gyuri? Did you ever think what you were doing when you abandoned us? Did you ever even try to find out how father was? Or me? Or even Aniko?"

He suddenly grew cold. As frozen as he had been that wintry day so many years ago. All this time, whenever he had thought about those moments—or whenever dreams compelled him to remember—he'd felt a piercing shame. The only consolation had been that it was his private secret. But now he realized that other people knew. How?

"I tried to find her," George protested helplessly.

"You *left* her! You left her bleeding there to die."

"Where—where is she buried?"

"In a shabby municipal flat."

George was stunned and incredulous. "Are you saying she's alive?"

"Barely, Gyuri. Just barely."

"What does she do?"

"She sits," Marika answered. "That is all she is able to do."

"How can I find her?"

"No, Gyuri, you've caused her enough pain. And I won't let you hurt her anymore."

"Please, Marika, I have to see her. I have to. I want to help her."

She shook her head and quietly concluded the conversation. "You should have done that eighteen years ago."

She turned her back and would not speak to him again.

The next morning when he arrived at the hospital, George Keller was informed that his father had died peacefully in his sleep during the night.

He took the first flight back to Paris. He had never felt more lonely in his life.

The moment he cleared customs at Washington's Dulles Airport, George picked up the phone and called Catherine Fitzgerald at the Nader office.

"Hi, how was the trip? The papers said you did well in Moscow."

"It's a long story," he replied. "Right now I need an urgent favor from you."

"The sound of that worries me, Dr. Keller. You never do anything without an ulterior motive. What exactly is it you're after?"

"A wife," George replied.

There was sudden silence at the other end of the wire.

"Is this some kind of joke?"

"You know I have no sense of humor. Now, will you marry me?"

"I won't say yes unless you name a specific time and place."

"How's Friday noon at the clerk's office at the Municipal Center on E Street?"

"If you're even one minute late," she warned playfully, "I promise you I'll walk."

"And if you're late," he retorted, "I promise you I'll wait. Now do we have a deal?"

"Let's say we've had a successful negotiation," she replied. And before hanging up, added with sudden tenderness, "George, I *do* love you."

After the wedding, Cathy permitted her parents to give them a small reception at the family home in McLean, Virginia. There were several of Cathy's old friends from school, a few Nader's Raiders, some of her father's law partners and their wives. George invited only one couple—Henry and Nancy Kissinger.

The Secretary of State proposed a witty toast that utterly disarmed and enchanted the bride, who had spent the preceding night dreading the thought of seeing her old nemesis.

"I hope we can be friends now," Henry smiled as he kissed Cathy.

"Dammit," she replied happily, "it's true what they say about you, Henry. Your charm is irresistible."

"I hope you hear that, Nancy," quipped the Secretary to *his* new bride.

For a Republican working in Washington, D.C., late July 1974 was hardly a time for honeymoons. Though Cathy moved into George's townhouse right after the wedding, she barely saw him. And then only very late at night.

For now it became increasingly clear that because of the Watergate scandal, Nixon was going to have to resign from office.

While Henry Kissinger metaphorically—and sometimes literally—held the tormented President's hand, George helped Al Haig set the White House in order.

If his wedding had lacked confetti, it was more than made up for by the mass of shredded paper emanating from the Executive

Mansion late those evenings as George "deep-sixed" documents that various members of the "Palace Guard" brought in to him.

George destroyed the material so quickly that he didn't have a second to determine what he was being given. He simply stuffed it into burn bags to be carted off.

Cathy was awake when he arrived home one morning at three o'clock.

"I don't know whether to offer you a nightcap or breakfast," she joked. "If it were anyone else, I'd think there was another woman."

"Hell, it's like a deathwatch over there, Cath. Al Haig feels it's only a question of time."

"Why doesn't Nixon just quit and put everybody—especially the country—out of its misery?"

George looked at her.

"It's a helluva decision," he said softly.

"Yes, but he's got a helluva lot to answer for."

"So does every politician," George responded. "We've all got some kind of skeleton in our closet."

"Not you, Georgie," she said, embracing him. "You're still a high-minded public servant, aren't you?"

"Of course," he answered, trying to seem jocular.

"Then why not quit while you're ahead? When Nixon goes, let's go too."

"Don't be silly, Cathy. Now's the time the Administration needs me most."

He didn't add that it was a rare opportunity to make a quantum leap ahead in his career.

"Ah," she said, kissing him on the cheek, "my patriotic husband."

At eleven-thirty on the morning of August 9, Henry Kissinger buzzed George to come into his office. The White House Chief of Staff was also present.

"Morning, Al," said George, cheerily doing his best to imitate a military salute.

Haig merely nodded somberly in the direction of the Secretary of State, who was seated at his desk holding a small piece of white paper.

"Oh," George said solemnly, "is that it?"

Kissinger nodded and handed George the document, which read simply:

> Dear Mr. Secretary,
>   I hereby resign the office of President of the United States.
>
>   Yours truly,
>   Richard M. Nixon

George scanned it several times and looked at Haig.

"Where's the President now?" he asked.

"Strictly speaking," Kissinger replied, "at this moment there is no President."

Haig concurred. "Yeah. Just think, George. Right now the three most powerful guys in the United States—and by consequence the world—are standing together in the same room. Does it feel good?"

"I'm not sure," he replied noncommittally. But it did, in fact, feel very good.

"Anyway," said Kissinger, rising from his chair, "unless we want to rule as a triumvirate, we'd better head for Gerry's swearing in."

◆

Gerald Ford had spent the majority of his adult life as a contented congressman from Michigan. He had never aspired to the White House. And yet now he had become the most powerful leader in the Western world, in a tension-filled atmosphere he did not really relish.

The responsibility of office did not weigh too heavily on Ford. He could meet that challenge. But he couldn't bear the cutthroat competition among his aides for access to his ear.

Old football player that he was, he could recognize a tackle trying to break through to reach the quarterback. And he knew he had to clear the field to give himself some running room.

Obviously, Kissinger had to remain for continuity—and for the nation's image in the world.

Yet, despite the fact that Haig insisted that the new President badly "needed him," Ford wanted to get at least this Nixon courtier away from Washington. Happily he found a glittering pretext.

He got Al Haig appointed Supreme Commander of the NATO Forces—thereby transferring him to Brussels. He would remain in the White House just long enough to help in the negotiations for the Nixon pardon.

Then, to establish his own global stature, Ford set off with Kissinger to meet Brezhnev at a summit meeting. Naturally, George Keller was in tow. And he was so conspicuously effective that during the long flight home on *Air Force One,* the President invited him to his quarters.

"What did you talk about?" Kissinger asked with a scintilla of jealousy as he returned to his seat.

"You won't believe this, Henry," he replied. "It was about football."

"But, George, you don't know the first thing about the game."

"Listen, Henry, if there's one thing I learned at Harvard, it was how to pretend that I always know what I'm talking about."

George and Cathy Keller quickly became the most popular young couple on the Washington social scene.

And George soon discovered that his wife had a remarkable gift for "party politics." She could initiate a dialogue for him with anyone, and was especially adept at dealing with the Fourth Estate. The press "discovered" the up-and-coming Dr. Keller and wrote admiringly.

There was only one difficulty. George could not adapt to marriage.

There weren't parties every night, and sometimes he would come home from the office and have no one to talk to but Cathy. He would discourse knowledgeably about the issues of the day. But he was really talking *at* her.

Marriage vows did not make him less guarded with his emotions. He could give, but he couldn't *share.* He could make love, but he couldn't make her feel loved.

Still she was undaunted, patiently waiting. Surely he would ultimately master the art of intimacy, the way he had every other challenge in his life.

But in the meanwhile she had her own life to live. George had his career, but Cathy had a cause.

Three years earlier, Congress had approved the 27th Amendment to the Constitution, prohibiting sex discrimination against women. If it could be ratified by two-thirds of the states, the equality of male and female would become the law of the land.

Cathy wanted to pack her bags and join the pro-ERA bandwagon to barnstorm the uncommitted states.

"Catherine, this is ridiculous," George complained. "You're the last person in the world who needs an equal-rights amendment. You're strong, you're independent, you're a gifted lawyer. My God, if you'd apply yourself, you could become a Supreme Court judge."

"But, George, isn't 'altruism' in that vast vocabulary of yours? I'm not doing this for me. I want to stand up for the millions of people who are doing a man's job and getting a woman's pay."

"Cathy, you're starting to talk like a pamphlet."

"Well, it's only fair, George. Most of your dinner conversation is like an interdepartmental memo. Do you think it's fascinating just because it's about someplace like Afghanistan?"

"Are you accusing me of being boring?"

"No. I'm just accusing you of thinking that all that matters in the world is what goes on in your office." She sighed in exasperation. "Can't you appreciate anybody else's commitment?"

George switched to a more personal plea. "Look, what really bothers me most is that we'll be separated."

"I couldn't agree more," she said, and added sarcastically, "So why don't you take a vacation and come on the road with me?"

His best arguments could not dissuade her. In the end, she even convinced him to drive her to the airport.

Cathy lost count of the number of speeches she made. Paradoxically, she often found the women harder to convince than the men. Most of them were actually frightened of losing their "second class" status. But she could empathize with their feelings; they had been so inculcated to be subordinate that they were afraid of being unable to stand on their own. Her job was to give them the courage of their own worthiness. And it was damn tiring.

In the space of three months, she and her fellow crusaders harangued, debated, and cajoled their way across Illinois, Oklahoma, and Florida in a heroic—if losing—effort.

Although they regularly spoke by telephone, she and George did not see each other till Memorial Day weekend, when they were Andrew's guests at the Eliot summer house in Maine.

As they were flying back to Washington, Cathy remarked, "Your old roommate is lovely. Why isn't a guy like that married again?"

"I'm afraid he lacks confidence," George replied.

"I noticed. But I don't see why. I mean, he's so kind and considerate. And he's got a great sense of humor. I think what he needs is a good woman to straighten him out."

"That would take a lot of doing, Cathy. Do you know anybody up to the job?"

"There must be dozens of women," she replied. "I mean, I could do it." She smiled at him. "But of course I'm spoken for."

"Lucky me." He smiled back, taking her hand.

"You're right, darling. I'm glad you finally noticed."

Late one afternoon in November 1975, George was alone in his office, dictating comments on an area report, when Kissinger opened the door.

"What's the matter, Henry? You look a little upset."

"Well," said the Secretary, as he sat down in an easy chair, "to tell the truth, I am a bit depressed."

"Why?"

"It's the view of Mr. Ford that one man should not be both Secretary of State and National Security Advisor."

"But you've done both jobs brilliantly."

"Yes, I thought so, too. But he wants me to resign the NSC. Frankly, I think it will undermine the perception of my position."

"I'm sorry, Henry," George said with genuine sympathy. "But it's not as if you've fallen from power completely."

"No, you're right. In fact, it may make it easier for me to operate, since I have such a good relationship with my successor."

"Who's the new Security Adviser?"

Kissinger looked poker-faced at his one-time Harvard tutee and answered, "You."

November 3, 1975

I saw my former roommate's picture in *The New York Times* today.

George Keller's been appointed to succeed Kissinger as the head of the National Security Council. He's moving back into the West Wing of the White House, where he'll be able to knock on the President's door anytime he wants and really get to turn the steering wheel of government.

On the seven-o'clock news tonight some pundits were speculating that George is being groomed for something even bigger.

Rumor has it that Gerry Ford would be more comfortable with someone he himself selected as Secretary of State. They say if he's reelected—which looks likely—he'll bring in a fresh new team, starring George. What a coup! He's really got the world by the tail. Fame, power—and a terrific wife. Some guys have all the luck.

Something occurred to me. If I phoned George at the White House, would he still take my call?

Telegrams and letters poured into the White House congratulating George on his appointment. At the end of the day, his secretary handed him two overflowing shopping bags so that he could read them with Cathy.

"I'll look silly walking in the White House parking lot like this," he protested mildly.

And then he thought, Hell, I'll enjoy every minute of it. My car is parked *inside* the presidential compound now.

Cathy greeted him on the doorstep. "I've prepared a celebration feast," she said, hugging him.

"Who's coming?" he inquired.

"Nobody. Now, are you ready for a drink?"

"Absolutely."

As she pulled him toward the living room, she whispered, "I've got a surprise for you. It's something I've been saving for a long time. Look."

She pointed to the coffee table, where she had placed two glasses and a bottle of—

"Hungarian champagne!" George gaped. "Where did you get *that* stuff?"

"It wasn't easy, let me tell you."

They got a little drunk, picked at the food, made love in the living room, and then got drunker still.

"Hey," Cathy murmured, "you certainly brought home a load of telegrams."

"I didn't know I had so many friends."

"Don't worry, love. Now that you're one step from the Oval Office, you'll discover a *lot* of brand-new pals. Ah, come on, let's open some and see who wants to get in good with you."

They giggled and then started reading.

Naturally, the governor of every state had cabled. Likewise the mayors of important cities. Democrats no less than Republicans. In fact, anyone who harbored aspirations of a diplomatic or political nature.

And even several major personalities from Hollywood.

"Well, one thing's sure," Cathy grinned, "I won't let you travel on your own from now on. Some of these are pretty close to propositions."

George was savoring it all. Because he knew this was only the beginning. The best was yet to come.

"Hey," she hailed him boozily. "This one's a little screwy. Who the hell is 'Michael Saunders from the good old days'?"

George was puzzled. "Let me see it."

He studied the telegram and gradually the message became clear.

QUITE A LONG ROAD FROM THE WIENER KELLER EH OLD BOY?
YOUR FIRST ENGLISH TEACHER MIKI WISHES YOU SUCCESS. IF
YOU'RE EVER IN CHICAGO LOOK ME UP.

MICHAEL SAUNDERS FROM THE GOOD OLD DAYS

"Does that mean anything to you?" his wife inquired.

"Not anymore," he answered, crumpling the paper and tossing it into the fire.

Such was that happy Garden-state
While man there walked without a mate:
After a place so pure and sweet,
What other help could yet be meet!
But 'twas beyond a mortal's share
To wander solitary there:
Two paradises 'twere in one,
To live in Paradise alone.

In the third year of his rebache-lored life, Ted Lambros thought of himself as the embodiment of Andrew Marvell's famous lines. Indeed, he told himself, the poet was unconsciously setting forth the formula for academic success. A professor on his own can really get a lot of work done.

Immediately upon his return to Canterbury, Ted had sold the home on Barrington Road and moved into an apartment at the top of Marlborough House, the best faculty accommodation available.

His triennium as chairman of the Classics Department had been singularly impressive. Enrollments had increased, the number of majors had doubled, and he had even managed to goad his colleagues into publishing a word or two. He had also succeeded in winning tenure for his former student Robbie Walton, the young man who had gotten him to Canterbury in the first place. Lambros always paid his professional debts.

It is arguable whether Ted had been an angry young man, but it was beyond doubt that he was a furious middle-aged one. He was fueled by rage to toil night and day, *serenas noctes vigilare*, as Lucretius put it.

As soon as he could free himself from paperwork, he would go back to Marlborough House, wolf down a defrosted dinner of dubious nutritional value, and immediately head for his desk.

After the initial hours of intense concentration, he would pour himself a little retsina. Gradually the ingestion of modern Greece's national drink began to illuminate ancient Greece's greatest playwright. Ted's research on Euripides took on a Dionysian cast. And he was determined to uncover all the enigmatic author's secrets.

He had no social life to speak of. In fact, he refused all invitations, except if he was fairly certain that a high administrator might attend. For the rumor had it that when Tony Thatcher's term was up, Ted Lambros would be his successor.

In his persistent anger, he still avoided women. That is, emotionally. There were the biological necessities—which now were easier to satisfy at Canterbury. In addition to the usual supply of cast-off first wives, and the young, attractive Europeans whom the college brought over to teach elementary languages, the seventies saw a new influx of mature women.

The government was making a lot of noise about Affirmative Action hiring at senior-faculty levels. And so the administration diligently searched for such rare females lest they risk losing federal subsidies.

Among the bevy of these new profs were several who were not loath to engage in a liaison without sentiment. Especially with Ted Lambros. And not merely because he was attractive. No, these women were just as ambitious as their male counterparts. And just as eager to advance their careers.

Lambros was important. Lambros sat on many a committee. And, one fine spring day—as predicted—Theodore Lambros was named Dean of Canterbury College.

When Ted got back home after receiving the big news, a voice within him suddenly wanted to call out, "Hey, Sara, I'm the goddamn Dean!"

But, of course, no one was there. He lived alone. Determinedly alone. And thought he had convinced himself that he liked it better that way.

Yet, he now had a strangely hollow feeling. Sara had always been there when things were bad, to help him share the hurt.

Now he realized that he needed her to share the joy as well. For otherwise it had no meaning in this empty room.

The Dean of Canterbury College is saluted everywhere on campus. But once at home, he loses both his scepter and his crown and becomes an ordinary human being. With ordinary needs.

He'd been a husband and a father once. And now, in this moment of triumph, he realized how he missed the flesh-and-blood dimensions of his life.

One Saturday, two or three weeks earlier, Rob and his wife had forced Ted to go ice skating with them, hoping that the exercise would lift his mood. They had not imagined it would have the opposite effect.

For all Ted saw around him at the rink were fathers and their skating children. Fathers and their children holding hands. Fathers picking up and comforting little ones who'd fallen on the ice.

He longed to put his arms around his son again. And, painful to admit, he also longed for Sara.

Sometimes, late in the night, he'd wake with pangs of loneliness. His only cure was to get up, sit at his desk, and dull the ache with work. He was emotionally dead.

The only part of him he kept alive—by intravenous shots of research—was his intellect. He was close to finishing that goddamn book that would be his academic passport to a brave new world.

So, if the price of this was solitude, then he would make the most of it.

Only once during this entire time did he succumb to emotion. One evening in the second term that he was dean, his brother, Alex, called to tell him that their father had just died.

He stood there in the cemetery, his arms around his mother and his sister. And he wept.

From across the grave, Alex whispered, "You made him very proud, Teddie. You were the glory of his life."

Ted could only nod.

That night he returned to Canterbury, sat down at his desk, and started working again.

The telephone rang. It was Sara.

"Ted," she said softly, "why didn't you call me? I would have flown over for the funeral."

"How did you find out?" he asked numbly.

"Someone from the Harvard Department rang me. I'm very sorry. He was a wonderful man."

"He loved you, too," Ted answered. And then, taking advantage of this moment, added, "It's a pity he saw so little of his eldest grandchild."

"He saw him just this Christmas," Sara countered gently, "and you know I write your parents every month. And send them pictures. Anyway, if you'd only called I would have taken little Ted to the funeral. I think it would have been important for him."

"How is he?"

"Pretty upset by the news, but otherwise okay. He's top of the class in Latin."

Ted felt a desperate need to keep her talking on the phone. "How's your own work coming?"

"Not bad. I've had my first article accepted by *HSCP*."

"Congratulations. What's it on?"

"Apollonius. Sort of a distillation of my senior essay."

"Good. I look forward to reading it. How's your thesis coming?"

"Well, with any luck I'll finish it by the end of spring. Cameron is reading the first chapter and Francis James the second."

"You mean the new tutor at Balliol? Tell him I liked his book on Propertius. What are you writing on, anyway?"

"I really bit off more than I could chew." Sara laughed. "My topic is nothing less than 'Callimachus and Latin Poetry.' "

"Well," Ted joked, "that's sent many a strong man to an early grave. Uh—no antifeminism implied. I guess I should have said 'person.' I still have trouble getting used to the new terminology."

He ransacked his mind for topics that would keep the conversation going.

"Then you think you'll get your degree in June?"

"I hope so."

"Then I guess you'll be coming home, huh?"

"I'm not really sure, Ted. Anyway, I think this is something we should discuss face to face when you come over next month."

"I'm really looking forward to it," he replied.

"So is Teddie," she replied softly. "If it fits my schedule, we'll try to meet you at the airport."

"Thanks for calling, Sara. It was really good to hear your voice."

He hung up and thought, I only wish I could see your face.

◆

"I can't believe it," Ted remarked, "the kid talks with an English accent."

"What do you expect?" Sara asked. "He's lived here most of his life."

They were sitting in the (now redecorated) living room in Addison Crescent, drinking iced coffee.

"He also didn't seem very friendly to me," Ted commented. "I mean, all I got was a fleeting 'hello, Daddy.' And then he disappeared."

"Your son has priorities." Sara smiled. "And this afternoon is a crucial cricket match against Saint George's School."

Ted had to laugh. "The son of a Cambridge townie is playing cricket? The next thing I'll hear is that he's got a knighthood."

"Oh, I doubt if that'll be for a few years."

He took a swig of coffee. "Have you decided when you're moving back, yet?"

"Not for another year at least."

"Shit."

"Please, Ted. I've got several good reasons, I assure you."

"Give me one."

"I want Teddie to finish his education here. He's doing so well the headmaster is certain if we let him go the whole route here, he'll breeze into any college in the world."

"Come on, Sara. I thought the one thing we still agreed on was that he would go to Harvard."

"That ought to be his decision—when the time comes. Anyway, you've still got quite a few years to give him a good sales pitch."

They were both silent for a moment.

"You said you had other reasons for wanting to stay."

"Well, I've been offered a classics tutorship at Somerville College."

"Professional congratulations and personal objections," he responded.

"Since when do you have the right to object to anything I do?" she asked, more bemused than angry.

He paused and then continued with great difficulty. "What I mean is—I miss you. I miss being married to you, and I was wondering if . . . if maybe you had any vestigial feelings of regret."

"Of course I have regrets, Ted. The day our divorce became final was the bleakest of my life."

"Then do you think there's a chance that we might—you know—give it another try?"

She looked at him with sadness, and simply shook her head.

Perhaps he should have suspected that there was someone in her life when she offered to let him stay with young Ted in Addison Crescent for the month of July while she was on vacation. Especially since she was so vague about her plans.

All she would vouchsafe was that she was going to Greece to "visit the places I've been writing about."

"Who with?" he had bravely asked.

"Oh," she had replied evasively, "several million Greeks."

But it did not take Ted long to discover who his ex-wife's traveling companion was. For his son's conversations were liberally sprinkled with references to "Francis." And unless he was alluding to the famous talking mule from the movies of Ted's childhood, it had to be Francis James, classics tutor at Balliol.

"I'd like to meet that guy someday," Ted said, at the *n*th mention of his name.

"Oh, you'd really like him," his son replied. "He's an absolutely smashing chap."

My God, he thought, my son really is an Englishman.

That July, Ted tried to be a father. He sat through countless cricket matches. Got a lot of theater tickets. And made numerous attempts at conversation over dinner.

But a gap as wide as the Atlantic separated them.

The young man was polite, good-natured, and friendly. Yet, the only thing they could discuss was distant plans for higher education. Ted tried to sell his son on Harvard.

"Teddie, there's something I've gotta explain to you. Going to Harvard is an experience that changes your life. I mean, it certainly did mine."

The young man looked at his father and said, "Frankly, I rather like my life the way it is."

Ted Lambros had spent the month with someone who bore his name but in all other ways was someone else's child.

At the end of July, a tanned Sara returned from Greece with an equally bronzed Francis James and announced that they had decided to get married.

To Ted's chagrin, the first congratulation came in the form of a spontaneous "Super!" from his son, who rushed to throw his arms around the tall, bespectacled classics tutor.

Trying to mask his chagrin, Ted offered his hand and his congratulations to Francis.

"Thank you," the Englishman responded. And added with warm sincerity, "I've always been one of your great admirers. If those articles you've been publishing are anything to go by, your Euripides book is going to be magnificent. How close are you to finishing?"

"I sent off the manuscript to Harvard last week," said Ted, feeling strangely hollow at announcing the accomplishment.

"Mummy says it's absolutely brilliant," young Ted interjected.

Ah, his father thought, at least the kid still respects me.

And then his son concluded, "I'm dying to hear what you think of it, Francis."

Ted now realized that there was nothing to keep him in Oxford. He took the next morning's plane to Boston and went up to Canterbury to await the verdict of the Harvard University Press.

It did not take long. In fact, that very weekend Cedric Whitman called him, bursting with enthusiasm. He had been designated First Reader for the Press and he could neither maintain his anonymity nor restrain his admiration.

"Cedric," Ted inquired tactfully, "while we're exchanging confidences, may I ask you who the other reader is?"

"Someone who admires you almost as much as I do—the newly emeritus Professor of Greek at Oxford."

"Cameron Wylie?" Ted asked, his elation dissipating.

"The very same," Whitman answered. "And I can't imagine his report will be less favorable than mine."

I can, thought Ted as he hung up.

He spent the next week playing dawn-to-dusk tennis with any professor, undergraduate, or groundskeeper he could lay his hands on. He could not bear the tension.

And then a hand-addressed envelope with an Oxford postmark at last arrived. He dared not open it in the presence of the department secretary. Instead, he rushed to the men's room, locked himself in one of the booths, and tore it open.

He read it several times and then began to howl at the top of his voice.

A few moments later, Robbie Walton, summoned by the secretary, arrived to see what was wrong.

"Rob," cried Ted, still in the confines of his narrow kingdom, "I'm made in the shade. Cameron Wylie still thinks I'm a bastard, but he loves my Euripides book!"

"Hey," said Rob with amusement, "if you'll come out of there, I'll buy you a drink."

Danny Rossi began to grow tired. Not of music. And certainly not of the applause that seemed to surround him quadraphonically both on and off stage. Nor was he weary of the unending parade of women who presented themselves for his sexual signature.

No, what he felt was fatigue in its most literal sense. His forty-year-old body was weary. He found himself growing short of breath at the mildest physical activity.

Danny had never been an athlete, but several times when he was in Hollywood homes and invited to take a dip, he found that he could barely swim one length of the pool. If he were still at Harvard, he joked to himself, he would not be able to last the requisite fifty yards. And he increasingly found himself going to bed merely to sleep.

He finally decided to consult a noted internist in Beverly Hills.

After a full workup, during which every inch of him was probed and every bodily fluid analyzed, he sat down across the glass-and-chrome desk in Dr. Standish Whitney's office.

"Give it to me, Stan." Danny smiled uneasily. "Am I going to die?"

"Yes," the doctor replied poker-faced. Then immediately added, "But not for at least another thirty or forty years."

"Then why am I always so goddamn tired?" Danny asked.

"For one thing, Danny, any guy with a love life as active as yours would be worn out. Although let me quickly say that no one ever died from too much sex. On the other hand, you do other things besides screw. You compose. You conduct. You play and—I presume—you must spend some time rehearsing. Also, if an airline pilot traveled as much as you, he'd be grounded. Are you reading me?"

"Yes, Stan."

"You're giving your system a lot of wear and tear. Do you think you could cut down on any of your activities?"

"No," Danny answered candidly. "I not only *want* to do all the things I do, I *have* to do them. I know that may sound strange—"

"Not at all," the doctor interrupted. "This is L.A.—paradise for the compulsives. You're not the first patient I've seen who wants to die young and leave a beautiful corpse."

"Correction," Danny retorted. "I don't want to die young. I just want to keep on *living* young. Isn't there anything you prescribe for your other 'compulsives'? I mean, I assume they don't slow down either."

"No," Dr. Whitney answered, "but they come to me at least once a week for a little booster shot."

"What's in it?"

"Oh, megavitamins mostly. Plus a little of this and a little of that to lift you up and mellow you out. If you'd like, we could try a series and see if it helps."

Danny felt like Ponce de León when he caught sight of the Fountain of Youth. "Any reason why we can't start right now?"

"None at all," Dr. Whitney said with a smile. And rose to go and mix his potion.

Danny was a born-again workaholic.

During the next month he felt like a teenager. He breezed through his frenetic schedule of work and play. He could once again go from conducting an evening concert to an amorous rendezvous. Then go back to his home in Bel-Air and practice the piano for several hours.

In fact, the only problem was that, on the few occasions when he actually wanted to sleep, he felt too stimulated. For this the good Dr. Whitney kindly prescribed some soothing phenothiazine.

During the past year or so, his relationship with Maria had gradually evolved from silent antagonism to a kind of entente cordiale. Whenever he was in Philadelphia they play-acted happy couple for the outside world and loving parents for their daughters. What went on in his Hollywood Hills "bachelor pad" was, of course, never discussed.

Now that the girls were at school, Maria resolved to build a life for herself. To find something real to do behind the facade of their cardboard marriage.

For a thirty-eight-year-old former dance teacher, the schoolhouse doors were bolted shut. There was no way to pick up where she had left off. And she was painfully aware that although she had brains and a good education, she had no particular skill to offer the job market. Some of her suburban friends worked for various charities. But that seemed to Maria to have too much of a social aspect to be genuinely satisfying.

She did agree to help out with the annual auction to raise money for the local PBS television station. After all, having spent so much time in studios with Danny, she felt she had absorbed some knowledge of how television worked. At least she might be able to contribute a suggestion or two.

Being the wife of the city's symphony conductor, Maria was something of a minor celebrity. And the officials at the station tried to persuade her to appear on camera to attract contributions from viewers.

She was coaxed by Terence Moran, the charming, prematurely white-haired president of the station.

"I can't," she protested. "I'd be a nervous wreck."

"Please, Mrs. Rossi," he insisted. "All you'd have to do is stand in front of one of the tables and say a few words about the objects on it."

"I'm sorry, Mr. Moran. My voice would freeze. You'd either have to superimpose the dialogue or do a voice-over yourself."

The youthful executive smiled. "I'll accept that compromise," he said.

"You will?" said Maria, slightly taken aback.

"Sure. You just stand there and point to the items and I'll describe them from off-camera. Is it a deal?"

"No, not yet," Maria replied anxiously. "I'd have to know your director's shooting plans."

"Mrs. Rossi," Moran responded affably, "I'm so keen to get you on even for a split second that I'll let you literally call the shots."

"Okay," she relented. "I guess I can't get out of it now. If you must show me, let it be in a wide establishing shot in front of the table. But I want your word of honor that the minute you begin to describe the merchandise, you'll zoom in close and get me out of frame."

"It's a deal," Moran replied. "And I'm very impressed."

"With what? My stubbornness?"

"No. You seem to have more camera expertise than my directors."

"You don't have to keep flattering me, Mr. Moran. I've already said I'd do it. Anyway, I've spent about a million hours with Danny in TV studios. To keep from overdosing on coffee and doughnuts, I locked myself in the control booth and sort of picked up what all those buttons meant by osmosis."

"Well," he quipped, "as Plato said, 'Osmosis is the best teacher.' Or was it Aristotle?"

"I think it was Terry Moran," smiled Maria Rossi.

"You looked wonderful even in the millisecond-long shot, Mrs. Rossi. And we got good prices for everything on your table," the station president commented as they drank sugary tea from paper cups in the Green Room.

"I'm still glad it's over," she said, sighing. "I absolutely loathe being on camera."

"But you do enjoy the control board, don't you?"

"Oh, that's always fun. I love to look at the bank of monitors and try to imagine which camera I'd use if I were the director. It's nice and safe when it's only a game."

"Have you ever thought of actually doing it?"

"Oh, I daydream sometimes. But then I also fantasize about doing a pas de deux with Nureyev. Anyway, thanks for accommodating my idiosyncrasies."

She rose to put on her coat, but Moran motioned her to sit down. "Mrs. Rossi, I'm sorry I can't speak for Rudolf—who I'm sure would be delighted to know you're interested—but I can speak for this station. Would you like a job?"

"You mean, a real job?"

"That's the only kind we have around here. I mean—nothing high-powered to start with. But we can always use an extra assistant director. And you already have enough know-how for that."

Maria was tempted, but diffident. "I'm not in the union," she protested meekly.

"Neither is this station." Moran smiled. "Now, are you interested?"

"You're doing this just because I'm Danny Rossi's wife."

"Frankly, that's your only liability. Because if things don't work out I'll have to fire you. And then I'll be in trouble, won't I?"

"No," Maria answered cheerfully. "But if I can get home in time to have dinner with the girls, I'll give it a try."

"No problem," he replied. "Oh—I haven't told you the bad news, though. The salary is pretty laughable."

"That's all right, Mr. Moran. I could use some laughs."

Ted was awakened late one night by a call from Walter Hewlett, professor at Texas and best-informed gossip in the world of classics.

"Lambros, I've just heard something sensational and I wanted you to be the first to know."

"Oh God, Walt, what could possibly be so important at two in the morning?"

"It's Dieter Hartshorn—"

"What about that pedantic German?"

"Then you know—?"

"Yeah. The guy Harvard just hired for the Greek chair."

"Then you *don't* know—listen. Rudi Richter just called from Munich. Hartshorn's been killed in a crash on the Autobahn. I mean, this news hasn't even reached the papers yet, baby."

"Christ, Walt, you're gloating like a ghoul."

"Hey, Lambros, do I have to spell it out for you? Harvard now has *no* Eliot Professor of Greek. And the chances are—if you drive carefully—the job's going to be *yours*. Sleep on that, amigo."

As Ted hung up, he could not help but think, This is not good news at all.

It's fantastic news.

A decent interval after the tragic death of Dieter Hartshorn, the Harvard Classics Department circulated a small announcement to the effect that applications were being solicited for the Eliot Professorship of Greek.

In earlier days they would simply have made a few phone calls, perhaps written some letters, and then sat down and voted a successor. But now federal legislation required all universities to

507

advertise their available positions, offering Equal Opportunity for advancement to men and women of all races and creeds.

Naturally, with such a prestigious chair, the public notice was merely a formality to comply with the dictates of Washington. In practice, the system still worked in its time-honored way. The department met and made a short list of the most eminent Greek scholars in the world. And, since his book was causing a stir even in manuscript, Theodore Lambros's name was among the leaders.

Again in compliance with the Equal-Opportunity directives, he would, like all other candidates, be required to visit Harvard and deliver a lecture.

"I know this is silly," Cedric Whitman apologized on the phone. "After all, we've known you for years and heard you speak. But to follow the new rules *au pied de la lettre* you'll have to give that obligatory 'tryout' talk."

"That's okay," he responded, already mentally packing his bags for the triumphal return to Cambridge.

They then set a date for the lecture. Officially it would be an audition, but, at least in Ted's mind, it would be his inaugural address.

◆

"Among the many publications of tonight's speaker, two stand out in particular: *Tlemosyne,* a brilliant study of the Sophoclean tragic hero, and *The Poet of Paradox,* his forthcoming analysis of Euripidean drama, which I have had the great pleasure of reading in manuscript.

"Tonight he will unravel the complexities of Euripides' final play, *Iphigenia at Aulis.* It gives me enormous pleasure to present Professor Theodore Lambros."

Ted rose, shook Whitman's hand, and placed his notes on the lectern. As he adjusted the microphone, he glanced out at the spectators. And could not help thinking that he had never seen Boylston Hall so full.

Had his scholarly reputation preceded him? Or was it common knowledge that tonight's audience would be getting a sneak preview of the next Eliot Professor of Greek?

He felt extraordinarily relaxed under what should have been extremely trying circumstances. For he had rehearsed this moment so many times in dreams it was already second nature.

The more he spoke, the less he had recourse to his notes. He began to look out into the audience, skillfully making eye contact with the more important people present, who included no less a dignitary than Derek Bok, the President of Harvard University.

He had just begun to discuss the bold visual symbolism in Clytemnestra's entrance carrying the infant Orestes, when he suddenly lost his breath.

Perhaps the audience, enraptured by his dramatic presentation, did not notice. But Ted himself had seen a vision that shook him.

Could it be possible—or was he merely imagining that his former wife, Sara, was standing at the back, leaning against a post?

Though inwardly panicked, his powerful sense of survival enabled him to find his place in the manuscript and—albeit in a somewhat subdued voice—continue reading his lecture.

But he was keenly aware that his sudden shift of style and tone had broken the enchanted atmosphere.

And now he could not control a desperate urge to get the damn talk over with.

Maybe, he thought, if I reassure myself she isn't really there, I can get back in gear. So, as he turned to his final page, he glanced beyond the farthest row.

Sara *was* right there. And looking more beautiful than ever.

But why? Why the hell is my ex-wife, who ought to be in Oxford, here in Boylston Hall?

And then with thoughts swifter than light, he exhorted himself like a Homeric hero. Get loose, goddammit, Lambros. Pull yourself together. This is your last chance to get everything you want in life.

And heroically, he did. He took a breath, slowed himself, ignored the final written paragraphs, and raised his head to paraphrase them. His concluding words were greeted with admiring applause.

Before they left, the President and deans came over to shake his hand. Then, while the senior members of the Classics Department waited discreetly in the back of the room, Sara approached the podium to greet her former husband.

"That was great, Ted," she said warmly. "You've done a lot of terrific work on that last chapter."

"Hey, I don't get it," he responded, trying to seem nonchalant. "Shouldn't you be in England teaching?"

"Yes," she answered. And then added with a curious admixture of timidity and pride, "But Harvard's invited me to apply for the chair. "I'm giving a seminar on Hellenistic poetry tomorrow morning."

He was incredulous. "They've asked you to apply for the Eliot Professorship?"

She nodded. "I know it's silly. Clearly it'll go to you. I mean, just on your publications."

"They flew you all the way over just on the basis of three articles?"

"Four, actually. And my book."

"Book?"

"Yes, Oxford liked my thesis and the Press is bringing it out this spring. Apparently the Harvard Search Committee's seen a copy."

"Oh," said Ted, the wind knocked from his sails, "congratulations."

"You'd better go now," she said gently. "All the bigwigs want to wine and dine you."

"Yeah," he said distractedly. "Uh—nice seeing you."

The post-lecture reception for Ted was in a private room at the Faculty Club. He knew that it was a social gauntlet he had to run, both to remind his old friends and to convince those who had once rejected him that he was charming, learned, and collegial. That year at Oxford seemed to have enhanced his status—and improved his dinner conversation.

At a late point in the evening Norris Carpenter, the leading Latinist, thought he'd enjoy a bit of Schadenfreude at the candidate's expense.

"Tell me, Professor Lambros," he inquired with a Cheshire grin, "what do you think of Dr. James's book?"

"You mean F.K. James on Propertius?"

"No, no. I mean the former Mrs. Lambros on Callimachus."

"Well, I haven't seen it yet, Professor Carpenter. I mean it's just in galleys, isn't it?"

"Oh yes," the Latinist continued mischievously. "But such a penetrating work must have taken years of research. She must have, as it were, begun it under your principate. In any case, she sheds some fascinating new light on the relationship between Hellenistic Greek and early Latin poetry."

"I'm looking forward to reading it," Ted said politely, as he twisted inwardly from Carpenter's sadistic verbal stilettos.

He spent the next day wandering aimlessly around Cambridge. The Square itself had been concreted beyond recognition since his college days. But the Yard had the same magical aura.

At four o'clock Cedric called him at the family home. He got to the point without delay.

"They've offered it to Sara."

"Oh," Ted gasped, as his blood ran cold. "Is her book really that good?"

"Yes," Cedric acknowledged, "it's a tremendous piece of work. But just as important, she was the right person at the right time."

"You mean she's a woman."

"Look, Ted," the senior professor explained, "I'll grant that the Dean's office is anxious to comply with the Fair-Employment legislation. But, frankly, it came down to weighing the merits of two equally gifted people—"

"Please, Cedric," Ted implored, "you don't have to explain. The bottom line is that she's in and I'm out."

"I'm sorry, Ted. I understand what a blow this is for you," Whitman said softly as he hung up the phone.

Do you, Cedric? Do you understand what it's like to work forty years of your goddamn life with only one goal? To give up everything, to resist any human involvements that might detract from your work? Do you understand what it means to sacrifice your youth *for nothing*?

And can you possibly imagine what it means to have waited since childhood for the doors of Harvard to unlock for you? And now to know they never will.

For the moment, what Ted wanted most to do was get extremely drunk.

He sat alone at a corner table in the back of The Marathon and had one of the waiters make sure that his glass was perpetually filled.

Every now and then his brother, Alex, would come over and insist, "Come on, Teddie, you'll be sick if you don't eat something."

"But that's the point, Lexi. I'm trying to get sick. To get my body in the same condition as my soul."

By nine, when he was becoming comfortably blotto, a voice interrupted his lachrymose inebriation.

"May I sit down, Ted?"

It was the last person he wanted to see at that moment—Sara.

"Oho, congratulations on your new appointment, Dr. James. I guess the best man won, huh?"

She sat down and chided softly, "Sober up enough to listen to me, Ted." She paused briefly. "I'm not going to take it."

"What?"

"I just called the chairman and told him that, having thought it over, I can't accept."

"But why, Sara?" Ted asked, gesticulating broadly. "It's the top of the academic world—the goddamn tippy-top."

"For you," she answered gently. "Ted, when I saw you up there on the podium last night, I knew you were in your own special heaven. I couldn't deny you that."

"You're either crazy or just playing some cruel-revenge joke. I mean, *nobody* turns down the Eliot Professorship at Harvard."

"I just did," she responded, still not raising her voice.

"Why the hell did you let them go to all the trouble and expense if you weren't serious about it?"

"To be frank, I've been asking myself the same thing all day."

"And—?"

"I think it was to prove to myself that I was really worth something as a scholar. I have an ego and I wanted to see if I could really make it in the big leagues."

"Well, you certainly did, baby—if you'll pardon the pun— with a vengeance. I still don't understand why you're handing back the crown jewels."

"Because after the initial excitement wore off, I realized I'd be doing the wrong thing. Look, my career isn't the be-all and end-all of my life. I want to make my second shot at matrimony work. I mean, the libraries close at ten o'clock, but marriage goes on twenty-four hours a day. Especially a good one."

He did not comment. At least not right away. He was trying, in his slightly woozy state, to piece out what all this meant.

"Hey, Lambros, cheer up," she whispered kindly. "I'm sure they'll offer it to you."

He looked across the table at his ex-wife.

"You know, I actually believe you'd be happy if I got it. Considering what a shit I was, I don't see how you can feel that way."

"All I feel is a kind of residual sadness," she said softly. "I mean, we had some very happy years together."

Ted felt a knot in his stomach as he replied, "They were the happiest years of my life."

She nodded in melancholy empathy. As if they were mourning a mutual friend.

They sat silently for several moments more. Then Sara, growing uneasy, rose to leave.

"It's getting late. I should be going—"

"No, wait just one second," he pleaded, motioning her to sit down.

He had something important to say. And if he didn't tell her now, he would never have another chance.

"Sara, I'm really sorry for what I did to us. And if you can believe this, I'd give up anything—including Harvard—if we could still be together."

He looked longingly at her, waiting for her response.

At first she said nothing.

"Do you believe me?" he asked again.

"Yes," she answered quietly. "But it's a little late now."

Sara rose again and whispered, "Good night, Ted."

Then she leaned over, kissed him on the forehead, and started out. Leaving him alone at the top of the world.

Jason Gilbert's parents flew over to Israel in the spring of 1974. First they stayed a week on the kibbutz getting to know—and love—their grandchildren and daughter-in-law.

Then Jason and Eva showed them every inch of the country from the Golan Heights to Sharm El-Sheikh in the occupied Sinai. They spent their final five days in Jerusalem, which Mrs. Gilbert pronounced the most beautiful city in the world.

"They're lovely people," said Eva after they had waved good-bye to his parents at Ben Gurion Airport.

"Do you think they enjoyed themselves?"

"I think if there's a state beyond ecstasy, they're in it," she replied. "What pleased me most was this morning when your father kissed the boys, he didn't say goodbye, he said *shalom*. I bet anything they'll come back again next year."

Eva was right. The Gilberts returned in the spring of 1975 and again in 1976. The third time, they even brought Julie—who, being "between husbands," was keen to test the myth of Israeli machismo.

Jason was an instructor now. Not exactly a sedentary job in the most elite of the special units, but less dangerous than the work he had done in the past.

It was his task to go to the enlistment center outside Tel Aviv and determine which of the eager young recruits would be fit enough mentally and physically for the impossible demands of *Sayaret Matkal*. He was under the direct command of Yoni Netanyahu, who had been much decorated for his bravery in the Yom Kippur war.

Yoni had spent one year at Harvard and was trying to engineer the opportunity to complete his B.A. He and Jason sat many a summer evening reminiscing about familiar Cambridge landmarks like the Square, Widener Library, Elsie's, and running paths along the Charles River.

These conversations awakened in Jason a longing to visit the one place in his life where he had led an uncomplicated and happy existence.

He and Eva discussed it. What if they went to the States for a year after he completed his present army contract? If they'd accept him at the advanced age of thirty-nine, he could finish his law degree and then set up practice in Israel representing U.S. firms.

"What do you think, Eva?" he asked. "Would the kids enjoy it?"

"I know their father would." She smiled indulgently. "And I've heard so much about Harvard all these years, I'm practically homesick for it myself. Go on, write the letters."

Even after being AWOL for so many years, Jason had no trouble being readmitted to the Law School. Especially since the Assistant Dean of Admissions was now Tod Anderson, with whom, in his previous life, he had been a carefree jock.

As a postscript to his letter of acceptance, Tod added, "You may be a major over there, Gilbert, but to me you're still my captain. Squash captain, that is." To which he appended a P.P.S., "I've been working on my game a lot and I think I can finally whip you now."

Jason was admitted as a third-year law student for the 1976–1977 academic year. He and Eva planned to take the boys over in mid-July and leave them with his parents while they searched for an apartment in Cambridge.

In May 1976 he left the *Sayaret* and active army service. Now all he owed Israel was a month of reserve duty every year until he was fifty-five.

When he said goodbye to his young commanding officer, Yoni could not help betraying a bit of envy.

"Think of me when you're jogging on the Charles, *saba*, and send me a few postcards from Cambridge."

The two laughed and parted.

*   *   *

Then, on the 27th of June, everything changed.

Air France flight 139 from Tel Aviv to Paris was hijacked after it stopped to take on passengers in Athens.

But this was not—even by Palestinian standards—a routine terrorist operation.

Landing once to refuel in Libya, it then proceeded to Entebbe, in Uganda. There, the 256 passengers were herded into the old terminal at Kampala airport. And made hostages.

The following day, the captors made known their demands. They wanted fifty-three of their comrades—forty of whom were sitting in Israeli jails—handed over, along with several million dollars.

It had always been Israel's policy not to negotiate with terrorists. But the families of the passengers besieged the cabinet offices in Jerusalem, pleading for an exchange that would save the lives of their loved ones. The government wavered.

Under normal circumstances such a crisis would have been immediately handed over to the antiterrorist section. But this time the hostages were five thousand miles away. Unreachable by any military rescue operation. Or so it seemed.

Minutes after the first radio broadcast of the terrorists' demands, Jason walked into the classroom where Eva was teaching the three-year-olds how to tell time. He motioned her to step outside.

"I'm going," he said tersely.

"Where?"

"Back to the unit."

"You're crazy. They can't do anything. And besides, you're retired."

"I can't explain it, Eva," he said urgently. "It's just that I've spent half my life chasing some of those murderers who are sitting in jail. If we hand them back, that'll destroy everything we've accomplished. The world will become a terrorist playground."

Tears began to well up in her eyes.

"Jason, you're the only thing I've loved that I haven't lost. Haven't you sacrificed enough of your life? Your children need a father, not a hero. . . ."

And then she paused, realizing that no words could stop him. Already feeling the ache of his absence even as he stood before her.

"Why, Jason?" she asked. "Why does it always have to be you?"

"It's something I learned from you, Eva," he replied softly. "The whole reason this country exists is to protect our people *everywhere*."

Eva cried softly against his chest, realizing she'd made *too* good a Jew of him. His love for Israel now transcended even what he felt for his own family.

And so she let him go. Not even telling him that she was pregnant again.

"Get the hell out of here, *saba*. This is young men's work."

"C'mon, Yoni," Jason insisted, "if there's an operation, I want to be part of it."

"Look, I'm not saying there is. So far, the government thinks it's much too risky. To be perfectly frank, we haven't been able to come up with a game plan that'll have even a fifty-fifty chance of working."

"Then why not at least let me in on the skull sessions? For God's sake, I'm not too old to think."

Their argument was interrupted by Major General Zvi Doron, former head of *Sayaret*, now chief of intelligence of the entire Defense Forces.

"Hey, guys," he barked, "this is no time to bicker. What are you doing here, Gilbert?"

"I'm reporting for duty, Zvi."

"Look," Yoni said sternly, "we're up against a wall and we're wasting precious time. So I'm going to give you sixty seconds to convince me why the sentries shouldn't throw you out. Now talk fast."

"Okay," he began, desperately searching for an argument. "When you picked a team to capture Adolf Eichmann, you deliberately chose concentration-camp survivors. Because there's no one braver or less compromising than a victim with a chance for revenge."

He paused and then added, "I'm a victim too. Those animals killed the first woman I ever loved. And there's no one in this unit who would give more to spare others from living with that kind of pain."

Jason unashamedly wiped his cheeks with his sleeve. And then concluded, "Besides, you still haven't got a better soldier than me."

Zvi and Yoni looked at each other, still uncertain.

Finally the commander spoke. "Listen, this whole operation is crazy. If they let us do it, maybe we need a lunatic like Gilbert."

While the *Sayaret* was thrashing out a battle plan, the Israeli government was still trying to negotiate with the hijackers—at least to stall for time.

After another forty-eight hours, the non-Israeli passengers were released and flown to France, where they told a harrowing story. As in the Nazi concentration camps, there had been a "selection"—and the Israeli hostages had been placed in a room separated from the others.

The cabinet was under mounting public pressure to accede to the demands of the terrorists and save a hundred innocent lives. As they hovered on the brink of capitulation, they received a visit from Major General Zvi Doron, who informed them that his staff had come up with a plan for liberating the hostages by force. He explained it in detail and the ministers agreed to think it over.

Meanwhile, Doron went back to rehearse the landing at Entebbe.

Since Israeli architects had helped to build the old Ugandan air terminal, they had detailed blueprints and were able to build a full-scale mockup. And, based on the evidence gained from those released in Paris, they were able to pinpoint where the hostages were being kept.

As one of the veterans present, Jason joined in the discussion of logistics. They could not fly a large force so great a distance, therefore everything would depend on the element of surprise.

Their huge Hercules C-130 transport planes were slow but at least had the range to get there. Still, how the hell could they free the hostages and get them on board before the entire country descended upon them?

In their thoroughness they watched home movies of Idi Amin, the Ugandan leader, riding around Kampala in his long black Mercedes.

"That's what we need," Jason urged. "If we can just make the guards think it might be Amin arriving, we can buy fifteen or twenty valuable seconds until they find out otherwise."

"Good idea," said Zvi. And then turning to his adjutant he said, "Find us a Mercedes."

They planned on taking a two-hundred-man strike force, and a few jeeps and land rovers, divided among three transport planes. A fourth Hercules would serve as a flying hospital. For they estimated ten to fifty casualties—if they were successful.

Late that afternoon, the adjutant arrived with the only Mercedes he could find. It was a white diesel model that coughed and sputtered like an asthmatic horse.

"We can't use that wreck," Zvi said. "Even if we paint it, that damn knocking motor will give us away before we start."

"Listen," Yoni suggested, "why not let Gilbert try to give it an overhaul? He's not too old to fix motors."

"Thanks, sweetheart," Jason said sardonically. "Get me some tools and I'll make that thing as quiet as the fanciest limousine."

He sweated all evening and through the night tuning the ancient vehicle. Then he supervised some of the other commandos spraying it black. But it still needed some spare parts, a list of which he gave to Yoni.

"Do you expect us to send to Germany for this stuff?" the younger officer asked.

"I expect quicker thinking than that from a Harvard man," Jason retorted. "Find some Mercedes taxis and *steal* the parts."

Yoni smiled and went off to select the most likely car thieves among his men.

On Friday the unit held a full dress rehearsal in their model of the old terminal. It took sixty-seven minutes by the stopwatch, to go from imaginary touchdown to evacuation and takeoff.

"Not good enough," Yoni said to his weary soldiers. "If we don't get this down to under an hour, we don't move."

They took a break for a dinner of C-rations and ran through it again. This time it was 59:30.

After the exercise Yoni gathered his men and made a short announcement.

"The terrorists' ultimatum expires tomorrow evening. That's

when they say they'll start shooting the hostages. We've got to get there before it happens. The trouble is, the cabinet won't be voting on our plan till tomorrow morning. So we've got to start the operation and hope they'll radio us to go ahead. Obviously, nobody leaves the base. All the phone lines have been cut. Now try to get some sleep."

The young soldiers disbanded and started toward the adjoining room where they had their sleeping bags. Only Jason remained to speak to Yoni.

"Thanks for your help," Yoni said, "I'm really glad you came along."

"But why aren't you letting me onto the plane?"

"Look," Yoni said quietly. "The average age of these boys is about twenty-three. You're almost forty. Even the greatest athletes slow down by then. They lose that crucial split second of reaction time."

"But I can hold my own, Yoni. I know it. I want to go, even if it's just to service the motors."

"Look, *saba*, this is too serious to let emotions creep in. You're staying here. And that's final."

Jason nodded silently and left the room. He walked out of the *Sayaret* building and, benefiting from years of experience at eluding detection, slipped by the guards and disappeared into the night.

Operation Thunderbolt began just after noon on Saturday, July 3.

First the medical equipment was loaded. Then the military vehicles. Then the black Mercedes. Finally, the men clambered aboard for the five-thousand-mile rescue mission that could not afford to be less than perfect.

Four Hercules "Hippos" lumbered down the runway and into the air heading south. Their plan was to stop for final refueling at Sharm El-Sheikh, the southernmost point of Israeli territory. That would give them maximum possible range.

The pilots' cardinal objectives were to avoid detection by Arab radar and take extraordinary measures to conserve fuel. For the latter purpose they flew so low that the gusts from the desert shook the planes ceaselessly. And when they landed in Sharm El-Sheikh, after only a half-hour in the air, some of the assault force were overwhelmed by air sickness. One man had even fainted.

The minute they hit the airport runway and began to taxi, Yoni ordered the doctors to do something about the men whose stomachs had failed before their courage had been tested.

One of the medics shook his head and murmured, "We should have given out Dramamine pills. That was an oversight."

Let's hope it's our only one, Yoni thought as he leapt from the aircraft onto the tarmac to confer with Zvi, who was riding in the second plane. At that very moment, the cabinet was meeting to decide whether to give them the green light.

Zvi also had sick men in his aircraft.

"I think we're going to have to leave Yoav here in Sharm," he said. "He's much too ill."

"What was his assignment?" Zvi asked.

"He was supposed to drive the Mercedes," said a voice that belonged to neither of them.

And from behind the huge wheels of the C-130 Jason Gilbert appeared wearing a belt of hand grenades, his Kaletchnikov strapped to his shoulder.

"*Saba*, what the hell!" Zvi snapped.

"Listen," Jason said with quiet urgency, "I've been driving all night. You shouldn't have left me behind in the first place. Now you've got to take me."

Yoni and Zvi exchanged glances. The older man made an instant decision.

"Take Yoav off. Get on board, Jason."

At 1530 hours they took off from Sharm El-Sheikh, heading straight down the middle of the Red Sea between Egypt and Saudi Arabia.

Below them they spied Russian naval vessels—doubtless equipped with radar. The four planes descended practically to sea level, acting more like flying fish than aircraft.

A quarter of an hour later, a simple message came through on their radio.

"All systems are *go*. We're now cutting all radio contact. Call us when you're on your way home."

Yoni walked out of the cockpit and said quietly to the men, "The operation's on. We've got seven hours to pass the time and then forty-five minutes to do the best we've ever done. Check your gear and try to get some sleep."

One member of the assault force, dressed in an elaborate

military costume to masquerade as Idi Amin, handed Jason a tube
of deep brown stage makeup.

"Here, *saba* . If you're supposed to be my driver you've got
to look the part. Smear it in your hair, too. I don't think there are
any blond Ugandans."

Jason nodded and took the greasepaint.

"This is the hardest part," said his comrade, "the waiting, I
mean."

"I'm used to it. I once sat outdoors for three days and nights
staking out a PLO big shot."

"Yes, but how far were you from the Israeli border?" the
young man asked.

"About eight miles."

"This is a thousand times as far."

"I didn't say I wasn't scared," Jason said.

"Want a paperback?" the commando asked.

"What have you got?"

"I can lend you *The Guns of Navarone*."

"You're kidding." He laughed. "At this point you're better
off reading the Bible."

"No, *saba,* right now this is more inspirational."

Jason sighed and reached into his breast pocket.

"What are you doing?" the young soldier asked.

"Just looking at some pictures."

"Of the airport?"

"No. My family."

Six and a half hours later they were over Kenya, flying in the
darkness. In a few minutes more they would be over Lake Victo-
ria and descending toward Entebbe airport. Zero hour was
approaching.

Yoni walked around the plane, checking the readiness of his
men. He stopped and peeked through the Mercedes window,
where a blackfaced Jason was checking his pistol. He looked up
as his friend approached. "I'm gonna make sure nobody takes my
parking spot," Jason smiled. "Are your boys nervous?"

"No more than you," answered Yoni, "or me. Good luck,
saba. Let's do the job, huh?"

The timing thus far had been perfect. The first aircraft arrived just as a scheduled British cargo flight was radioing the
Entebbe control tower for permission to land. The lead Hercules

followed right on the limey's tail and touched ground scarcely a hundred yards behind it. At first they headed toward the new terminal, then casually swung left, dropping mobile landing lights so the three other aircraft could easily follow. So far, no one had noticed them. They taxied to a dark corner of the field and began to disembark.

A dozen commandos jumped out and quickly set up a ramp for Jason's Mercedes. It purred as he drove it down and started toward the building where the hostages were imprisoned.

A pair of land rovers with troops followed close behind, within sight of the control tower. Suddenly two Ugandan soldiers stepped into the road to identify the occupants of the car. Yoni and another commando dropped them both with silencer-pistols.

"We'd better go the rest of the way on foot," Yoni whispered.

They got out of their cars and raced toward the terminal. Seconds later, they broke into the hall where the hostages were lying on the floor trying to sleep. It was fully lit so that the guards could watch the captives. That also made it easier for the rescuers.

One of the terrorists realized what was happening and opened fire. He was killed instantly. Two others who had been on the opposite side rushed in, guns blazing.

Frightened by the sudden noise, some hostages jumped to their feet. A commando with a loudspeaker barked out instructions in Hebrew and English.

"We are the Israeli Army. Get down. Get down."

At this point Jason appeared at the doorway, his gun drawn.

A frightened old woman looked at him and asked, "Are you really our boys?"

"Yes," he snapped. "Get down."

"God must have sent you," she exclaimed and immediately obeyed.

Suddenly Jason noticed a suspicious-looking character trying to move behind the hostages.

He called out in Hebrew, "Is he one of us?"

A woman who was being used as a shield bravely cried out, "No, it's one of them." And broke away from her captor's grip.

The terrorist quickly withdrew a grenade and unpinned it. Jason aimed his pistol and fired. As the man fell, the grenade rolled from his hand. Instinctively Jason was already rushing forward. In a single motion he scooped it up and lobbed it into a corner, where it exploded, harming no one.

Yoni was racing through the hall to see if every guard had been eliminated. From outside they could hear fierce gunfire as the other units were battling the Ugandan soldiers.

Yoni grabbed the loudspeaker and called out, "Everybody listen. We've got planes waiting. Start moving as quickly as you can. There are soldiers outside to protect you. We've got jeeps for anyone who can't walk. Let's go!"

The dazed captives obeyed meekly. Too numb to rejoice, too shocked to believe that they weren't dreaming.

As the evacuation began, Ugandan soldiers were shooting wildly from atop the control tower. Through the wall of commandos who had formed to protect the hostages, Jason carried an aged victim who had been struck in the crossfire. He reached the plane and hoisted the man to the medics waiting at the door. Then he pulled himself aboard. Doctors were already working on other casualties.

As Jason was helping settle the old man on a mattress, he heard a soldier holding a walkie-talkie blurt out an anguished, "Oh no!"

"What's the matter?" he shouted.

"It's Yoni—Yoni's been hit!"

Jason was electrified. He grabbed a rifle, rushed to the door of the plane, leapt onto the tarmac, and began to run back toward the terminal. In the distance he could see them lifting Yoni onto a stretcher. A hail of bullets was still coming from the control tower.

As soon as he was in range, he stopped and began to return their fire. His only thought was that whoever had shot Yoni had to pay for it.

From a distance he heard Zvi's voice calling urgently.

"Gilbert, everyone's on board, we're moving out!"

Heedless, Jason continued shooting. A figure stumbled from the tower. He had hit one of the snipers.

Zvi shouted again, "Gilbert, get back here. That's an order!"

Still, Jason kept firing in wild anger until his ammunition was exhausted. The roar of the first Hercules taking off suddenly brought him to his senses. He hurled his rifle to the ground, turned, and began to sprint toward the nearest aircraft.

It was then that the bullet struck him, ripping through his right shoulder blade and into his chest.

He staggered but refused to fall. He would not let his fellow soldiers risk their lives to rescue him. He reached the door of the plane and they pulled him in. When one of the commandos gasped at the sight of his chest, he knew that he was hurt badly.

But he still didn't feel anything.

As the doctor slashed his shirt, he heard the plane door slam and heard somebody call out, "We've done it. We're going home."

Jason looked at the doctor, whose face was ashen.

"Is it true?" he asked. "Did we really pull it off?"

"Relax, *saba,* don't strain yourself. Yes, we got all but one of the hostages. It's not a success. It's a miracle."

The plane taxied faster and in another moment was off Ugandan territory. Mission accomplished.

Jason refused to be silent. He sensed that he had very little time and he still had questions to ask. And things to say.

"Is Yoni dead?" he asked.

The doctor nodded.

"Shit. He was the best of us. The bravest guy I ever knew."

"That's why he would have thought it was worth it, *saba.*" Zvi was now at Jason's side.

"Yeah." Jason smiled, dizzy from loss of blood. "There are no shutouts in war, huh?"

"Jason, don't tire yourself."

"Don't kid me, Zvi. I'll have plenty of time to rest." He was speaking slower and slower. "I just want . . . to be sure that Eva knows . . . that I'm sorry I had to do this to her . . . and the boys. Tell them I love them, Zvi. . . ."

His commanding officer was unable to speak. He simply nodded his head.

"And tell them one more thing." Jason gasped. "Say I've found peace. I've finally . . . found peace."

His head lolled to one side. The doctor placed a hand on Jason's carotid artery. He could not find a pulse.

"He was a very brave soldier," Zvi said softly. "Some of the boys said he threw back a live grenade. He still was quick as an athlete on his feet—"

Zvi's voice broke. He turned away and walked to the back of the plane.

They flew on in triumph. And in sorrow.

Jason Gilbert, Sr., rose as usual at six o'clock on the morning of July 4th and took a quick dip in the pool. He then put on his robe and returned to the house to shave and prepare for the guests who would be coming to their annual Independence Day barbecue.

He sat down in his dressing room and turned on his television to watch the news. There were already reports of the incredible Israeli commando raid.

The commentator was saying that it was an exploit that would go down in military history. Not only because of the distance involved, but because of the brilliant planning that had saved all but one of the hostages at the cost of only two soldiers' lives.

Mr. Gilbert smiled. Incredible, he thought. Jason was right. Israel will do anything to protect its own. He must be very proud this morning.

There was a live interview with Chaim Herzog, the Israeli ambassador to the UN. He explained the wider meaning of what his country had done.

"There is an alternative to surrendering to terrorism and blackmail. This is a common enemy to all civilized countries. For these people obey no human decencies. We are proud. Not only because we saved over a hundred innocent people—but because of the significance of our act for the cause of human freedom."

"Hear, hear," murmured Jason Gilbert, Sr., and went in to shave.

At about eleven o'clock his friends began to arrive. At twelve-thirty, when he was putting the first hamburgers onto the big outdoor grill, Jenny, the housekeeper, shouted that he had a long-distance call.

Damn, he thought. Doesn't my staff even take July Fourth off?

He picked up the phone in the kitchen amid the clutter of plates and glasses, intending to make short work of the employee who was disturbing his holiday.

As soon as he heard Eva's voice, he knew. After listening quietly for a few minutes, he promised to call her back later in the day, and then hung up.

The ashen look on his face startled everyone.

"What's the matter, darling?" his wife asked.

He took her aside and whispered. She was too stunned at first to cry. Then he took a deep breath, determined not to break down until he could convey what had happened. He called for everyone's attention.

"I suppose by now you've all heard about the Israeli rescue at Entebbe."

There were expressions of admiration among his guests.

"Those men did what no other country in the world would even attempt. And they did it because they were alone. That can make people very brave. I'm especially proud . . ." he continued with great difficulty, "because Jason was one of those soldiers . . ."

His friends began to murmur.

". . . and one of those who were killed."

July 5, 1976

We get our *New York Times* a day late up here in Maine so I didn't learn the terrible news until today. Last night on TV there were some pictures of the Israeli hostages arriving back at Tel Aviv airport and the tumultuous welcome they received. There were no shots of the commandos who pulled off the incredible rescue mission because evidently they're a top-secret group and can't be photographed.

Since July is my custody month with the kids, I pretty much had my hands full planning the fireworks display and just trying to be a father. Besides, the whole thing had such a fairy-tale aspect that I never imagined anyone I knew could possibly have been associated with it.

I certainly never dreamed that one of the two officers killed was my friend Jason Gilbert. He obviously wasn't famous enough for any of the networks to mention him by name. But when the army released his picture, it was printed in the *Times* of July 5th. That's when Dickie Newall called me from New York, knowing that I couldn't have seen my copy yet.

My first reaction was disbelief. Not Jason, I thought. Nothing could happen to him. If for no other reason than because he was basically so good.

I needed time to pull myself together before facing the kids. So I told them to go to the village for lunch. I took a boat and rowed out to the middle of the lake.

When I got about as far away from shore as I could, I pulled in the oars and just floated. I tried to make myself confront the truth of what I'd just learned.

And what hit me hardest was how damn unfair it was. Because if there's an Almighty before whom you have to justify your existence on this earth, Jason had the greatest reason for living of anyone I ever knew.

I wanted to cry, but the tears wouldn't come. So I just sat

there and tried to make sense of things, wondering what Jason would want me to do.

When I finally rowed back, I called his parents on Long Island. The housekeeper said that they had left for Israel on the previous night's plane. To attend the funeral. Then I thought maybe I should go too. But when I asked, she told me that it had been scheduled for today. Apparently it's Jewish tradition to have the burial very quickly. So as I was prattling mindlessly on the phone, they were probably lowering him into the ground. I thanked the lady and hung up.

When the kids got back in the early afternoon, I sat Andy and Lizzie down on the porch and tried to tell them about my old buddy. I guess they already knew him by name because everybody from Harvard remembers Jason as the great jock. And whenever two guys in The Class got to reminiscing, his name always came up. They listened patiently while I told them about my friend's heroism, but I could see it was no more real to them than a John Wayne film.

I tried to make them understand that he had sacrificed himself for a cause. They still remained fairly impassive.

I also explained that it was that way in this country too before Vietnam. People went to fight to defend their principles. And then I tried to bring it closer to home by saying that was why our own ancestors fought the British in 1776.

Andy doesn't like it when I mention this sort of thing. In fact, he was pretty unreceptive to my whole sermon.

He told me that I was incapable of getting into my head that the world has got to outgrow war. That *no* violence is ever justified.

Okay, I wasn't going to press the point. I figured it was just a stage he was going through. What the hell does a spoiled teenager know about principles anyway?

Even Lizzie was getting a little impatient. So I concluded our talk by saying I had to go into town and buy some more fireworks.

This suddenly awakened Andy's interest. He asked if we were making July Fourth a two-day holiday.

I replied that this was something special.

We were going to set off some flares tonight in memory of Jason Gilbert.

George Keller spent his first month as the President's Special Advisor for National Security Affairs almost literally up in the air. He accompanied President Ford and Secretary Kissinger (with a gaggle of reporters) on voyages to Peking, Indonesia, and the Philippines. Cathy, of course, understood that these were not the sort of trips you could take your wife on. So she busied herself working in the ERA campaign headquarters and debachelorizing George's townhouse.

As soon as he returned, Kissinger swooped him up again into an air-force jet heading for Russia to make a last-ditch effort at saving the SALT negotiations.

In their absence, the congressional attacks on Kissinger escalated. Ever sensitive to public criticism, the Secretary of State was in despair. One day George overheard Henry talking to Washington on the secure American Embassy phone in Moscow.

"Mr. President, with due respect, if I have so drastically lost the confidence of my countrymen, then I am prepared to tender my resignation."

George sat with bated breath, wondering how Gerald Ford was reacting to Henry's latest histrionic offer to step down. Someday, he thought, they're going to call his bluff and he'll be out. And somebody else will be Secretary of State.

Maybe me.

◆

From February on, Washington began to focus increasingly on domestic affairs. For Gerald Ford this meant currying public favor for the upcoming election in November while holding off the threat from Ronald Reagan to usurp the Republican nomination.

George Keller's problem was even more literally domestic.

Cathy wanted to start a family. While he argued that they had plenty of time, she countered with a reminder that she wasn't getting any younger.

"Don't you have the urge to be a father?" she coaxed.

"I'd be a lousy one. I'm much too selfish to give a kid the time."

"Aha, then you've actually thought about it."

"Yes, a bit."

In fact, he had thought about it more than just a little. From the moment they were married he had been aware that Cathy aspired to motherhood.

All their friends had children. Even Andrew Eliot, who had jokingly remarked, "You ought to try it, Keller. I mean, if I can do it anyone can."

Yet, something visceral in him recoiled at the prospect. Cathy sensed his misgivings and wanted to believe that they were caused by his own abrasive relationship with his father. So she tried to reassure him that, if anything, he would overcompensate to his child.

To some extent she was right. But that was only part of it. Deep within him was an avenging fury warning that he was too guilty to deserve to be a parent.

◆

Kissinger and George were sitting in the wings during the second debate between President Ford and his Democratic opponent, Jimmy Carter, on October 6, 1976.

They winced when Ford fumbled with the ill-considered statement that Eastern Europe was "not under Soviet domination."

At this point Henry leaned over and whispered sarcastically, "Nice briefing job you did, Dr. Keller."

George shook his head. The moment the debate ended he asked Kissinger, "What do you think?"

The Secretary of State replied, "I think that unless there's an immediate revolution in Poland, we're all out of a job."

Kissinger was right. On Election Day, the voters of America sent Jimmy Carter to the White House and Gerald Ford to the golf courses of Palm Springs. Washington would now be a Democratic town—at least for the next four years. And those closely

allied with the Republican cause like George Keller had no place
in it. Ironically, George's office would be taken over by his first
Harvard patron, Zbigniew Brzezinski. (He wondered fleetingly if
he hadn't chosen the wrong horse.)

Cathy was secretly delighted at the turn of events, since she
hated her native city. And she was jealous of her husband's
mistress, politics.

After his initial disappointment, George started looking for a
new career. He rejected invitations from several universities to
teach government and several publishing houses to write a book
about his White House experiences. As far as he was concerned,
they were by no means over.

Instead, he opted to become an international trade consultant
to the powerful New York investment firm of Pierson Hancock.
The potential remuneration was beyond his wildest dreams.

As he joked to Cathy, "Now I'm worse than a capitalist. I'm
a plutocrat."

She smiled and thought, wouldn't it be nice if you became a
parent, too. And with maternity in mind, she convinced her
husband that they should live in the country.

George at last acceded and they bought a Tudor house in
Darien, Connecticut. It meant a lot of commuting for him each
day, but at least he got to read the papers thoroughly before
arriving at his office. To discover what was happening in the
world that he no longer helped to run.

Two years after moving up from Washington, he had more
money than he knew what to do with. And his wife had the same
plethora of empty time.

Despite George's urging, she did not take the New York Bar
exam and seek a job with a metropolitan law firm. Instead, she
qualified in Connecticut and took a one-day-a-week lectureship
at nearby Bridgeport University Law School.

George pretended to ignore the significance of her desire to
remain at home. And Cathy's sadness was compounded by a
growing bitterness that he didn't trust her enough to believe she
was taking The Pill. Such lack of confidence is hardly conducive
to a good marriage. And indeed, theirs was fast becoming a very
unhappy one.

George sensed her increasing discontent and, instead of confronting it, deliberately fashioned a lifestyle that managed to

avoid the issue. He began to work later and later—and come home drunker and drunker.

The New Haven Railroad may have been falling to pieces, but the scotch in its club cars still held many a commuter together. Or at least gave George that illusion.

Suburbia without children was stultifying. All of Cathy's contemporaries were busily involved in the activities of their offsprings' lives, and at lunch discussed little else. Thus, she felt like a double outcast. An alien among mothers, and a stranger to her own husband.

"Are you happy, George?" she asked one evening, as she was ferrying him from the train station.

"What kind of question is that?" he asked, slurring his words slightly.

"I mean, aren't you sick of pretending that everything's okay between us? Don't you hate having to travel all the way out here just for boring old me?"

"Not at all. Get a lot of work done on the train. . . ."

"Come on, George, you're not that drunk. Why don't we discuss our so-called marriage?"

"What's there to discuss? You want a divorce? You can have a divorce. You're still a good-looking girl. Find a brand-new husband in no time."

Cathy felt too upset to be angry. She pulled into the parking lot of a shopping center, so that she could concentrate on this crucial conversation without crashing into a tree.

She then turned and asked him straight out, "So that's it, then—it's over?"

He looked at her and, in one of his rare expressions of true feelings, said, "You know I really don't want to make you unhappy."

"I thought it was I who was making you miserable."

"No, Cathy. No. No. No."

"Then what is it, George? What's come between us?"

He stared straight ahead for a moment, then half-buried his face in his hands and said softly, "My life is shit."

"In what way?" she asked quietly.

"In every way. I'm taking it out on you because I'm miserable doing what I'm doing. It's like running on a treadmill. I'm going nowhere. I'm forty-two years old and already a burned-out case."

"That's not true, George," she said sincerely. "You're brilliant. Your best years are still ahead."

He shook his head. "No, you can't make me believe that. Somewhere along the line I missed my chance. Things are never going to be much different than they are right now."

She put her hand on his shoulder. "George, what we need isn't a divorce, it's a second honeymoon."

He gazed at her, and consciously reaffirmed what he had always known subliminally. She was the best thing that had ever happened to him.

"Do you think we have a chance?"

"As you boys say on Wall Street, George," she smiled, "I'm still bullish about our future. All you need is a little 'sabbatical' to give you a chance to get a second wind."

"A sabbatical—from what?"

"From your unquenchable and temporarily frustrated ambition, my love."

The Kellers' grand tour of Europe was not quite the total holiday that Cathy had wanted. But it was enough to rekindle hope for the future of their relationship.

To begin with, she taught George his first lesson in how to enjoy life. To take satisfaction from what he had already accomplished.

For in every country they visited, high government officials welcomed them in royal fashion. And it bolstered George's ego to see himself still respected, even though he was out of office.

In fact, his political antennae proved to be shrewder than ever. In London, he and Cathy dined with Mrs. Margaret Thatcher, M.P., who would be leading the Conservative Party in the next general election. She complimented George's views on geopolitics, and Cathy's hat.

The same was true in Germany and in France, where the newly installed foreign minister, Jean François-Poncet, entertained them in his home—a Gallic rarity.

Their final stop was Brussels. While Cathy was out doing some last-minute shopping, George had lunch with his old colleague from the NSC days, Alexander Haig, now Supreme Allied Commander in Europe. With his usual candor, the general pronounced his judgment on the current White House occupant.

"Carter's really messing up. His foreign policy is a disaster. It's an experiment in obsequiousness. We've got to behave like the superpower we are. That's the only way to make the Soviets respect us. I tell you, George, Carter'll be a sitting duck in 1980."

"Who do you think we'll run against him?"

Haig replied with a sly grin, "Well, I've been thinking of giving it a shot."

"That's great," George responded with shining enthusiasm. "I'll help you any way I can."

"Thanks. And I'll tell you something—if I make it, my Secretary of State is sitting right here at this table."

"I'm very flattered."

"Come on, Keller," said Haig, "can you name anyone more qualified?"

"No, frankly," George responded mischievously.

He could have flown home without a plane.

If in the 1960s Danny Rossi had become a household name, in the late 1970s he became a household face. His charismatic visage was now beamed regularly into millions of homes, thanks to an enormously successful—and prizewinning—series of musical documentaries made for Public Television.

First there was a baker's dozen of programs on the instruments of the orchestra. This was followed by a history of the symphony. Both, of course, had book tie-ins, and to the many strings on his bow Danny now added that of bestselling author.

"Maria, I've got to talk to you seriously about Danny." They were sitting in Terry Moran's office at the station.

In the three years she had been working for WHYY-TV, Maria had risen from assistant director to full-fledged producer. And it was rumored that the station president would soon elevate her to program director.

Their glass of sherry together on Friday afternoons had now become a weekly ritual. They would go over various crises and indulge in fantasies of what they could do if only they had a bigger budget.

"I feel I have the right to say this," Terry continued, "because now you're not some neophyte. And to put it bluntly, I feel Danny's being unfaithful. To Philadelphia, I mean—and us. Look, I can understand why he'd want to film his first series at KCET in L.A. He directs the Philharmonic there, and there's a huge pool of TV talent in Tinseltown. But why the hell did he have to do his history of the symphony in New York?"

"Terry, you can't imagine the pressure they put on him at

WNET. Besides, I think Lenny Bernstein was working behind the scenes."

Moran slammed his desk. "But dammit, man for man, our orchestra's as good as theirs, if not better. That series earned a fortune for the supplying station, and we could really use the dough. Most of all, I feel Danny should show some allegiance to the city that first made him a conductor. Don't you agree?"

"Terry, this isn't fair. You're putting me on the spot."

"Maria, you've known me long enough to realize I play fair and square. I'm not talking to Danny Rossi's wife, I'm complaining to my business partner. Objectively speaking, don't you think he should do his next TV project here?"

"Objectively speaking, yes. But I—" She grew self-conscious and could not continue her sentence. Though in the past months she had received more genuine warmth and support from Terry, she still felt an atavistic loyalty to the man who was legally her husband.

"I mean, from all those interviews I read in the papers, you and he make those big career decisions together." Moran hesitated and then added, "Or shouldn't I believe what I read?"

Maria grew reticent and wondered what *else* he had been reading in the press.

Actually, there had been times, after a long session in the cutting room, when she had almost felt brave enough to speak to Terry of her domestic unhappiness. After all, he had already confided in her. She knew about his divorce, which had shaken his staunchly Catholic parents. And how badly he missed his children.

These long conversations had made her realize that they were both reluctant to leave because neither had any real home to go to.

Still, she had been too shy to initiate the conversation, assuming—perhaps hoping—that sooner or later Terry would broach the subject.

And now here they were perilously close to trespassing on the most intimate details of her personal life.

"Why so silent?" he inquired amicably. "Or are you thinking of the best approach to catch Mr. Rossi in our butterfly net?"

"I'll be frank," Maria began. "I'm a bit reluctant to broach this with Danny because it kind of blurs the lines of demarcation between our separate work and our . . . marriage."

She hesitated. And then suddenly added, "Hey look, on second thought, I agree about his loyalty to Philadelphia. I'll bring up the idea of his doing a series for us, if we can come up with a concept."

"Well, Maria, you've got the creative brain. What do you think Danny Rossi should do for a television encore?"

Instinctively she knew. "Well, if I can say so, he *is* one of the best pianists of his generation—"

"The *very* best," Moran interrupted.

"Anyway, I would think he'd be the perfect person to do the history of keyboard music."

"Something like 'from harpsichord to synthesizer,' " Terry replied, kindled by the notion. "I think that's absolutely fantastic. If you snare him, I'll squeeze every penny from our budget to give him the lushest deal this station ever offered."

Maria nodded and stood up. "Of course, he'll probably say no," she said quietly.

"Well, if he does, I'll love you all the same."

To her surprise, the idea excited Danny. "I'd have only two ironclad conditions," he said. "First, the tapings have got to be tailored to fit the days I'm already committed to being in Philly."

"Obviously," she agreed.

"And second, I want you to be the producer."

"Why me?" she asked, somewhat taken aback. "Wouldn't that be uncomfortable?"

"Hey listen," he replied, "if we're going to match the level of the other series, I've got to have the best possible studio team. And you are without question the savviest producer they have."

"Have you been reading my clippings?"

"No, I've been running some of your videotapes late at night. I think your work's terrific."

"All right, Rossi," she replied, unable to mask her delight. "But I warn you—you play temperamental artist with me and I'll shoot the whole damn thing from your bad side."

"Okay, boss." He smiled. And then added, "Hey, we could tout this thing as coming 'from the team that brought you *Arcadia*.' "

*   *   *

Maria lay awake that night wondering what was on Danny's mind. She hadn't thought her argument was that persuasive. To be honest, however good their studio facilities now were, they were still no match for New York or L.A. And was that quip about *Arcadia* anything but a casual joke?

They had been so happy in those Harvard days, their collaboration animated by their passion.

"How does he do it?" an astounded Terry Moran exclaimed, as they sat side by side in the control booth.

"Well," Maria answered proudly, "he knows the keyboard repertoire backwards and forwards. And, as you can see, he loves to drive himself."

Even she had not been able to persuade Danny to devote a full day for taping each of the thirteen episodes. To the amazement of the crew, who had never seen such prodigious energy, he insisted on doing three hour-long programs in a single day—and night—session.

"God, where does he get the strength?" wondered the engineer. "I mean, I sit here at the end of the day with my face melting on the control board. And he's out there talking and playing like some virtuoso Peter Pan."

"Yes," Maria agreed thoughtfully, "there is a bit of the Peter Pan in him."

But there was more than that. There was Dr. Whitney's cocktail, too. In fact, Danny could no longer fly on merely one weekly injection. So the doctor had provided him with capsules that included, among other things, Methadrine to tide him over.

The second program of that session, an hour on Chopin, was musically and verbally flawless. With typical Rossi bravado, he'd left the hardest segment for the very end: an introduction to that keyboard acrobat, Franz Liszt.

Danny was munching a sandwich in his dressing room when Maria poked her head in.

"Mr. Rossi," she said, "I don't think you could possibly top that one. Why don't we wrap and do Liszt next time?"

"No way, Madame Producer. I want to finish this taping with a tour de force."

"Aren't you tired at all?"

"A bit," he confessed. "But when I see camera one light up, it'll turn me right on."

"I bet you wish Liszt were still alive, Danny." She smiled. "I somehow think you'd like to see his face when you outdo him at his own cadenzas."

He rose, walked over, and kissed her on the cheek. "See you on the floor in fifteen."

Danny showered, changed clothes, redid his makeup, and walked down to appear punctually at 8:30 P.M. for his third and final taping of the day.

The first half-hour went with metronomic perfection. Danny sketched Liszt's childhood in Hungary; his father's early pressure on the boy; his debut at the age of nine; his lessons with, among others, Salieri—Mozart's nemesis—and Czerny—Beethoven's greatest pupil—who so admired the young boy's talent that he refused any fee for his lessons.

Watching his face on the monitor in the control room, Maria could not help but feel that at this moment her husband was thinking of his own teacher, Dr. Landau.

And so it continued, with colorful accounts of the great pianist's conquests first of Paris, then of London—all before he was sixteen.

"It was at this point," Danny commented, "that the young musician began to feel the strain of his endless schedule of travel and concertizing. He was, one may say, a jet-setter before the invention of jets. In fact, it was scarcely yet the age of the railroad. And it took its toll.

"When he went with his father to the seashore to recuperate, the elder Liszt, also weakened by their travels, contracted typhoid and passed away. His final words to his son were, '*Je crains pour toi les femmes*,' roughly translated, 'I'm worried about what women might do to your music. . . .' "

Staring intently at the monitor, Maria suddenly felt her heart beat faster. Could he possibly be talking to her? Could he be saying in public what he was afraid to say in private? That he had wasted his youth on empty promiscuity. But at last was changing . . . growing up? She now realized why he had left *this* program till last. For he knew that—perhaps for the first time in his life—he would be speaking from the heart.

They stopped for technical reasons, tape changes, and even one or two muffed lines. Thus, it was well after ten by the time they reached the most difficult part of the broadcast.

Danny was explaining how Liszt deliberately created music so difficult that only he himself could play it. And in fact, when his pieces were published, he had to revise and simplify the music for the hands of normal mortals.

It had been Danny's devilish inspiration that, at this point in the program, he would play from the original manuscripts to show how the great man himself might have sounded.

Knowing what a challenge lay ahead for her husband, Maria called a ten-minute break, during which she made the crew double-check everything. She wanted no mechanical foul-ups, lest a perfect performance by Danny require a retake because of some technical failure. She also wanted to give him a breather to gather strength at this late hour of the evening.

At last they resumed.

"Rolling, Danny. Anytime you're ready," came his wife's voice through the loudspeaker in the studio.

They began the sequence with a relaxed medium shot of the pianist explaining what he was about to do. The camera then reverse-zoomed slowly into a long shot of him sitting down at the keyboard. Then, at the most dramatic moment, they would move in over his shoulder for a close-up of his hands.

At 10:45 P.M., Daniel Rossi attacked Franz Liszt. And was beaten back.

He had chosen as his first example the soloist's entry in the E-flat concerto. But for some reason—which he ascribed to fatigue—his left hand kept slipping in tempo as he raced the length of the keyboard.

After three unsuccessful retakes, Maria called through the mike, "Hey, Danny, it's after eleven. Why don't you knock off and finish it first thing in the morning when you're fresh?"

"No, no," he protested, "I want to wrap this damn series tonight. Just give me a short break."

"Take five, everyone."

Danny returned to his dressing room and immediately reached into his makeup kit for one of Dr. Whitney's "megavitamins." He then sat down, looked at his reflection framed by a dozen light bulbs, and tried to take deep breaths to relax.

And then he saw it. The thumb and forefinger of his left hand were trembling involuntarily.

At first he thought it was a mere reflex, a compulsion to drum the damn Liszt fingering into his system. But no, even with a conscious effort, he couldn't stop the shaking—except by covering it with his right hand.

He tried to reassure himself that this was merely tiredness. He had, after all, been working for nearly ten hours. But it was not with any real sense of confidence in his own explanation that he once again appeared on the studio floor.

On the way from his dressing room, he had hit upon a subterfuge that would at least get him through this night's ordeal. For if he indeed had a problem (which he kept telling himself he did not), he wasn't about to share it with the taping crew of the Philadelphia Public Television station.

"Hey, Maria," he called, "can I see you for a second?"

She hurried to him.

"Listen," he whispered to her, "could you have the director change his shot plan a little?"

"Sure. What do you want?"

Danny then motioned with his right hand. "What if, when he pulls back as I start to play, he pans around and shoots me from the top of the piano? That would be a pretty dramatic shot."

"Maybe," said Maria. "But I don't think he'd be able to get your hands in from that angle. Isn't the whole point the fact that you're doing these really difficult fingerings that only Liszt could manage?"

Danny sighed wearily.

"Of course. Yes. You're right. But between you and me, I'm exhausted. I'm not so sure I can get through the stuff without having to stop a million times. This way, if I mess up, we can always overlay the sound with some of the practice cassettes I've made."

"But, Danny," she pleaded, "that seems like such a shame. I mean, I know you can do it. I've heard you in the studio at home. Why don't we just wait until tomorrow?"

"Maria," he said sternly, "this is the way I want to do it. Now help me, *please*."

To the consternation of the director, the taping was completed with the camera shooting down on Danny's face.

And so it did not take in Danny's hands, as once again his left failed to keep pace with the right. None of the crew noticed this subtle discrepancy. But Danny did.

ANDREW ELIOT'S DIARY

I don't know how I could have dreamed it was a good sign.

When Andy got back east from spending Christmas with his mom and her tycoon in San Francisco, he called my office and asked if we could meet for lunch. I thought, Hallelujah the millennium, my son wants to make friends with me. This was especially encouraging since next September he'll be starting college. And I'm hoping to persuade him to choose Harvard.

Gauchely I suppose, I asked him if he wanted to eat at the Harvard Club. He turned thumbs down on that because it was "bourgeois." I should have known then that bad news was in the offing.

I met him at a health-food place in Greenwich Village, where, as we ate a lot of sprouts and leaves, I tried to bridge the chasm separating us with all the loving words I could think of. But, as ever, it was he who was the one conveying truth to me.

He brought up next year. I quickly assured him that if he didn't want to go to Harvard I honestly wouldn't mind. He could go to any college in the world and I would gladly pay the tuition.

He looked at me as if I were a man from Mars. And then patiently explained that American education wasn't relevant to anything. In his view, the whole Western world was decadent. And the only solution was to cultivate our spirits.

I told him I'd back him up in whatever he'd decided.

To which he replied that he strongly doubted it, since his decision was to drop out of the whole family.

I then said something like, "I don't get it, Andy."

He then revealed that his name was no longer Andrew, but Gyanananda (I had to ask him to spell it), which is Hindi for "seeker of happiness and knowledge." I tried to take this all with good humor and offered that he would be the first Eliot of that name.

He explained that he was no longer an Eliot. That he was opting out of everything my rotten generation stood for. And was going to spend his life in meditation. For this he did not want, nor did he need, any of the so-called Eliot money.

When I asked him how he planned to live, he replied simply that I wouldn't understand. I then explained that my question was not philosophical, but practical. For example, *where* would he be living?

In the footsteps of his guru, he replied. At the moment this prophet was presiding over an ashram in San Francisco, but was getting intimations from his *karma* to return to India. I then asked him what he was going to use for money. He replied that he had no use for it. I asked, still more specifically, how he planned to eat. He said that he would beg like the rest of the swami's followers.

I proposed that, since I was a generous soul, he start his begging with me. He refused. Because he sensed I would use it as a string to tie him and he wanted to "fly untrammeled."

He then got up, wished me peace, and started to go. I pleaded with him to give me some sort of address, somewhere to get in touch with him. He said that I could never be capable of being in touch with him unless I divested myself of all material things and learned to meditate. All of which he knew I would never consider.

Before he left, he offered me some parting words of wisdom—a kind of benediction.

He said that he forgave me for everything. For being an unenlightened, bourgeois, and insensitive father. He bore me no malice since he understood that I was a victim of my own upbringing.

He then walked away, stopped, lifted his hand in valediction, and repeated, "Peace."

I know that he's a minor and I possibly could call the cops and have him grabbed for psychiatric observation. But I know he'd wriggle out and only hate me more (if that's possible).

And so I sat there looking at my plate of foliage and thought, How did I screw up like this?

"I'm afraid I have some bad news for you, Mr. Rossi."

Danny was sitting in the Park Avenue office of Dr. Brice Weisman, a world-renowned neurologist. Having taken enormous pains to ensure confidentiality, he had arranged a thorough examination. Though the doctor was about to put a name—and perhaps a fate—to it, Danny had known there was something physically wrong with him from that horrible moment in the studio when his left hand suddenly rebelled, refusing to obey the brain that had been its absolute master for forty years.

The following day he had returned to the television studio with the rehearsal tapes he had made at home. Then he, Maria, and a single engineer superimposed them at the crucial moment in the previous night's taping when his hand had failed him.

Though Maria was his accomplice in this bit of deception so uncharacteristic of Danny, he had not confided in her completely. He had simply pleaded a busy schedule, impatience, and even television economy for this bit of electronic trickery.

"After all," he had joked, "I'm dubbing myself. It's not as if I had to sneak in Vladimir Horowitz."

The only thing that made Maria suspect something more serious was Danny's persistent questioning about whether the engineer was "a trustworthy guy." Did he realize how many times he asked her? What was bothering him?

Indeed, that was what had brought Danny to Dr. Weisman's office.

At first the neurologist merely listened impassively as Danny offered his own explanation as to why his left hand occasionally trembled. And that night, as well as in practice sessions thereafter, had seemed to be disobeying his mind.

545

"I mean, clearly it's fatigue, Doctor. I suppose it could be nerves, too. I drive myself very hard. But obviously, as you can see from all those little movements you asked me to do—touching my fingers and all that—there's nothing wrong with me physically."

"I'm afraid there *is,* Mr. Rossi."

"Oh."

"I can detect a peripheral tremor in your left hand. There's also some discernible bradykinesia—meaning it moves slightly slower than your right. All of this indicates basal ganglia dysfunction. In other words, some kind of damage to the motor area of your brain."

"You mean a tumor?" Danny asked, his fear exacerbating the tremor in his hand.

"No," the doctor said calmly, "your CT scan shows no evidence of one."

"God, that's a relief," Danny sighed. "Then how can we fix this damn thing so I can get back to work?"

Weisman paused and then answered softly, "Mr. Rossi, I would be less than honest if I told you we could 'fix' your condition. In fact, we can only hope that it progresses very gently."

"You mean it might spread to my other hand as well?"

"Theoretically, that's possible. But when someone as young as you presents this sort of unilateral tremor, it usually remains on that one side. And, you may be relieved to know, the loss of function is very, very gradual."

"But you're a doctor, dammit. Why the hell can't you cure this sort of thing?"

"Mr. Rossi, much of the working of the brain is still a mystery to us. At this stage of our knowledge, the best we can offer are medications that mask the symptoms. But I assure you, we can hide a tremor as small as yours for many years."

"Will these drugs let me play the piano?" he asked.

Dr. Weisman took off his glasses and began wiping them with his tie. Not that they really needed cleaning. But this way Daniel Rossi's face would be out of focus when he told him the worst.

And he began with a kind of verbal anesthetic.

"Mr. Rossi, may I tell you, I've always admired you as an artist. And what I find most remarkable about your talent—and what will help you in what I know is going to be a difficult situation—is your versatility."

He paused and then consigned Danny Rossi to a living death.

"I'm afraid you won't be able to play concerts anymore, Mr. Rossi."

"Not at all?"

"No. But your right hand is fine and very likely to remain so. You'll be able to continue conducting with no problem."

Danny did not reply.

"And the best consolation I can offer is something I learned from one of your own TV programs. Giants like Bach, Mozart, and Beethoven all started as performers, but are remembered today only because of what they wrote. You can throw the energy you once spent at the keyboard into composition."

Danny hid his face with his hands and began to sob more intensely than he had at any time in his life.

Dr. Weisman could not offer any further comfort. For he had no inkling of what his words would elicit from his patient's psyche.

Danny suddenly leapt to his feet and began to pace the room. Then he shouted from the depths of his grief, addressing the neurologist almost as if his diagnosis had been an act of hostility. "You don't understand, Doctor. I'm a great pianist. I'm a truly great pianist. . . ."

"I'm aware of that," Weisman replied softly.

"But you don't get my point," Danny retorted. "I'm not that brilliant a conductor. And at best my composing is second-rate, derivative. I know myself. I can't do any better."

"Mr. Rossi, I think you're being much too harsh on yourself."

"No, goddammit, I'm being honest. The only thing I'm any good at is playing the piano. You're taking away from me the one thing in the world that I can really do well."

"Please understand," the doctor responded, "I'm not taking it away from you. You have a physical disorder."

"But what the hell caused it?" Danny demanded furiously.

"It could be any one of a number of things. You could have been born with this condition, which has only now surfaced. It can also be the result of diseases like encephalitis. It's even been known to be induced by certain medications. . . ."

"What sort of medications?"

"I don't think that would apply in your case, Mr. Rossi. I've looked very carefully at the list of drugs you gave me."

"But I lied, Dr. Weisman. I omitted a few. I mean, with my

schedule I've come to rely on all sorts of stimulants to get me up for performances. Can they have caused this?"

"Conceivably. Is there anything else that you've neglected to mention?"

Danny now let out a feral roar. "Jesus—I'm going to murder that fucking Dr. Whitney!"

"Not the notorious Beverly Hills 'Dr. Feelgood'?"

"You mean you know him?" Danny asked.

"Only from the damage I've seen in the patients his 'cocktails' have brought to my office. Tell me, did his 'vitamins' make it difficult for you to sleep?"

"Yes. But he prescribed—"

"Phenothiazine?"

Danny nodded mutely.

"And how long has this been going on?"

"Two–three years. Could that have—"

The neurologist shook his head in frustration. "That man should really have had his license revoked. But I'm afraid he's got too many powerful patients protecting him."

"Why did he do this to me?" Danny shouted again in frantic despair.

Dr. Weisman's answer was somewhat sterner than his previous remarks.

"In honesty, I don't think you can blame it all on the wretched Dr. Whitney. In my experience, his clients have been at least marginally aware of what they were getting into. And you are a highly intelligent man."

Daniel Rossi walked the twenty blocks to the Hurok office in a kind of trance. He had not learned anything he hadn't already known subconsciously. For long before he'd heard the dread pronouncement he had sensed the catastrophe the doctor had confirmed.

But at this moment he was shocked beyond feeling. And he would take advantage of this temporary numbness to perform the painful act the doctor's diagnosis now required.

His abdication from the keyboard.

As soon as they were alone Danny told Hurok that he'd done an agonizing reappraisal of his life, his lifestyle, and what he had accomplished. In balance, he'd decided that he should be spending more time on composition.

After all, he reasoned, who remembers Mozart as a pianist—or even Liszt? But what they wrote abides forever.

"Also, I think I owe it to Maria and the girls to spend more time at home. I mean, before I know it they'll be grown up and gone. And I won't ever have enjoyed them."

Hurok listened patiently and did not interrupt his virtuoso. Perhaps he was consoling himself with the thought that many great performers in the past had opted for a premature retirement. And then, after a few years' absence from the intoxication of applause, had returned and concertized more actively than ever.

"Danny, I respect your decision," he began. "I won't try to disguise the fact that I'm distressed—because you have so many wonderful years ahead of you. All I'll ask is that you finish out the two or three commitments left on this year's program. Is that reasonable?"

Danny hesitated for a minute. After all Hurok's kindness to him, the impresario at least deserved the truth.

And yet Danny could not bring himself to tell it.

"I'm really sorry," he said softly. "But I have to stop immediately. Of course, I'll write to all the orchestras concerned and give them my apologies. You might—" He hesitated. "You might invent a kind of sickness for me. Hepatitis maybe."

"I wouldn't like to do that," Hurok answered. "All my life I've tried to be above board in my dealings, and it's much too late for me to change. I'll just look through my schedules and see if I can fill your dates with artists of your caliber."

With an undisguised look of sadness on his face, he began to shuffle through his papers. Suddenly he gave a wistful little chuckle.

"What is it?" asked Danny.

"I've already found one pianist whom I can substitute for you in Amsterdam—young Artur Rubinstein, age eighty-eight!"

Fearing he would be unable to retain his composure much longer, Danny stood up to leave.

"Thanks, Mr. Hurok. Thank you for everything."

"Look, Danny, I hope we'll stay in touch. In any case, I'll be at the premiere of your first symphony."

"Thanks."

He turned to go. The old man then called out to him as an afterthought, "Danny, if it's facing audiences that's the problem, you could still record. Look at Glenn Gould and Horowitz. There are so many brilliant performances still locked up inside you."

Danny simply nodded and walked out. He could not say to Mr. Hurok that the pianists he had named still had the use of both their hands.

At 2:00 A.M. Danny was sitting at home in the near-total darkness of his third-floor studio. A gentle voice interrupted his solitary anguish. It was like a small candle at the end of a long shadowy cave.

"What's wrong, Danny?" Maria asked. She was in her night-gown and bathrobe.

"What makes you think there's anything wrong?"

"Well, for one thing, you're sitting in the dark, so you're obviously not writing. For another, I haven't heard any real music for hours. I mean, that's unless you consider a million repetitions of 'Twinkle, Twinkle, Little Star' real music."

"Mozart wrote a whole series of variations on that tune," he replied without conviction.

"Yes, I know. It's a favorite encore of yours. But I don't hear any variations, Danny. That's why I've come up. You know I've never interrupted you before."

"Thanks. I'd appreciate it if you stuck to that policy."

"I'm not leaving until you tell me what's wrong."

"Nothing's wrong. Just leave me alone, please."

He was inwardly glad that she disobeyed him and came over to kneel by his chair.

But when she reached out to take his hands, he withdrew them quickly.

"Danny, for the love of God, I can see you're going through hell. I know you need me now, darling, and I'm here. I want to help."

"You can't help me, Maria," he answered bitterly. "Nobody can."

For the moment he could say no more.

"It's your left hand, isn't it? Look, I've known something was wrong since that evening in the studio. I've passed your bedroom late at night and seen you sitting by the lamp, just staring at it with a kind of panic."

"There's nothing wrong with my left hand," he answered coldly.

"I've seen it tremble at dinner, Danny. And I've watched you try to hide it. Don't you think you should see a doctor?"

"I have."

"And?"

He did not respond verbally. Instead he began to weep.

She put her arms around him.

"Oh, Maria," he sobbed, "I can't play the piano anymore."

And then he told her everything. His tragic journey that had begun at Dr. Whitney's and ended with Dr. Weisman.

When he'd finished the story, for a long time they did nothing but cry in each other's arms.

Finally she dried her own tears and grabbed him firmly by the shoulders.

"Now you listen to me, Daniel Rossi. As terrible as this thing is, it isn't fatal. You'll still have a career. You'll still be involved in music. And most important, you'll still be alive to be with your family. And most especially with me.

"I didn't marry you because you could outplay Liszt. I didn't marry you because you were a star. I married you because I loved you and I believed you when you once said that you needed me. Danny, darling, we can get through this together." Maria kept holding him as he leaned on her shoulder, sobbing softly.

And, unlike all those audiences that clap and then go home, she would always be there.

She stood up and took his hand. "Come on, Rossi, let's get some sleep."

They descended the stairway arm in arm. And when they reached the second floor, she did not let go. Instead she drew him down the corridor.

"Your bedroom?" he asked.

"No, Danny. *Our* bedroom."

May 11, 1978

It was ego-crushing time today. The *Twentieth Anniversary Report* of The Class arrived.

There were some surprises. Although, of course, I read about it last year in the papers, it was still amazing to read Danny Rossi's entry and to see confirmed that he has actually retired from the piano. I'm in awe at the courage it must have taken for him to turn his back on all that public adoration. He's also given up conducting in Los Angeles. And will base all his activities in Philadelphia.

Although one of the reasons he gave was that he wanted to compose more, it was evident that his primary motivation was his wish to spend more time with his wife and kids. As he put it, they're what really matter in this life.

I'm awed by the guy's humanity. The way he's put his values into focus.

On the gloomy side, in addition to the handful of deaths announced, I've noticed that a lot of long-term marriages have lately broken up. As if one of the partners couldn't shift his or her gears into the third decade.

I guess the Eisenhower marriages remained unchanged by the Democratic Camelot that JFK created. But probably—to keep on with the metaphor—the Nixon years made couples listen to the tapes of their relationships. To face the truth about themselves and leave.

On the bright side, several of our classmates have kids who're freshmen.

On the dark side, my son isn't one of them. Or maybe I should say my former son, since I haven't heard from him at all.

Even after all this time, whenever I pick up my mail, I pray that maybe there's a letter or a card from him. Or something. And if I see a longhaired hippie begging on the street I always give the guy at least a buck or two, hoping that wherever Andy is, somebody else's father will be generous to him.

I can't let myself believe that I've lost him forever.

Naturally, in my own report I didn't mention that my kid's disowned me. I simply said that I was tired of Wall Street and, in looking for a change, lucked out. I've been asked by the director of the new Campaign for Harvard College to come up to Cambridge and join the team that's trying to raise three hundred and fifty million for our alma mater.

Needless to say, when Frank Harvey called me with that offer, I jumped at the chance. Not only to leave the concrete capital of all my sorrows, but to start life anew in the only place I've ever been happy.

Basically, my job involves contacting members of our Class, reestablishing our old rapport, and, after due ingratiation, getting them to cough up big for Harvard.

Since I really believe in what I'm doing, I don't look at it as selling. It's more akin to missionary work. As an added bonus, I've been put on the committee that's planning our big Twenty-fifth Reunion (June 5, 1983)! It's said to be a high point of our lives—and I'm entrusted to make sure it is.

Naturally, I spoke to Lizzie before giving Harvard my consent. She's growing up to be a super person—I guess no thanks to me. Although the fact that Mummy lives so far away has, I think, been a help. I see her several times a month and feel we're getting closer now.

Being a romantic (like her dad), she keeps urging me to find a wife. I kind of make a joke of it. But every morning when I look at that one lonely toothbrush in the glass, I know she's right.

Maybe being back at Harvard I'll regain my confidence.

But then I'm not sure I ever had any.

Alexander Haig did not win the Republican nomination in 1980. But Ronald Reagan, who did, and was subsequently elected President, chose him as Secretary of State.

Haig, then head of United Technologies in Hartford, immediately called his fellow Connecticut resident, George Keller, and offered him the government's second-highest foreign-policy position—Deputy Secretary of State.

"How soon could you start, old buddy?" Haig asked.

"Well, anytime," said George elatedly. "But Reagan doesn't even take office till January."

"Yeah, but I'm going to need you before then to prepare for my confirmation hearing with the Foreign Relations Committee. There are some guerrillas in the senatorial jungle who've been waiting years to take a shot at me."

Haig was not exaggerating. For his examination lasted five days. Questions were fired at him from every angle. All the ghosts of Watergate were unearthed. Not to mention Vietnam, Cambodia, the NSC wiretaps, Chile, the CIA, and the Nixon pardon.

As he sat beside his future boss, occasionally whispering a word or two, George felt the sleeping demons in him start to wake. During his own upcoming confirmation hearing, would some hostile senator or young ambitious congressman discover his little "favor" for the Russians long ago?

But his worries turned out to be in vain. Since the committee vented so much spleen at Haig, all residual anti-Nixon animus was spent. George was not only eloquent and poised but witty. And approved by unanimous vote.

*　　　*　　　*

The Haig-Keller foreign-policy team started strongly and impressively, fulfilling Reagan's promise to put new muscle into the American leadership.

And yet, paradoxically, George found the Secretary of State to be somewhat insecure in private. At the end of one long work session, George felt comfortable enough to broach the matter.

"Al, what's eating you?"

"George," he replied, welcoming the opportunity to unburden himself, "how can I run foreign policy when I never get to see Reagan alone? There are always a half-dozen of his California cronies putting their two cents in. I swear if this keeps up I'll offer him my resignation."

"That's a very Kissingeresque gesture." George smiled.

"Yeah." Al grinned. "And it always worked for Henry."

Haig made his move the following week after a White House luncheon for the Prime Minister of Japan. He asked the President for five "completely private" minutes of his time.

Reagan threw his arm warmly around Haig's shoulder. "Al, I'd be glad to give you ten."

As George stood watching the two men walk around the White House lawn, Dwight Bevington, the National Security Adviser, was suddenly at his shoulder.

"Say, George," he said with bonhomie, "if your boss is trying an end run, he's wasting his time. Besides, we all know who the real brains are at State. In fact, I think you and I should try to make our contacts closer."

Before George could reply, the Secretary returned, a broad smile on his face.

"I don't know what it is about Ronnie," beamed Haig, as they were riding together back to State, "but he sure can make a guy feel good. He dismissed my offer to resign and promised we'd have direct communication. Say, I saw that Bevington was buttonholing you. Digging for anything?"

"In vain," George said calmly.

"Good man. You know I'm counting on your loyalty, old buddy."

George Keller was now certain that his boss's days were numbered. And he began positioning himself to jump ship before it sank.

He started having occasional lunches with Bevington just to offer him the benefit of his own experience. But he always reported the meetings to his boss.

He was never overtly disloyal to Alexander Haig. Possibly because events moved so swiftly that he didn't have the chance.

♦

Desperate to prove his effectiveness to the Reagan administration, the Secretary of State found a rare opportunity in the spring of 1982.

Argentine troops invaded the Falkland Islands. And to protect their tiny colonial outpost, Britain sent a huge armada steaming toward a military confrontation in the South Atlantic.

Haig got the President's approval to attempt to avert bloodshed by a Kissinger-like shuttle between London and Buenos Aires.

He woke George in the middle of the night and told him to be at Andrews Air Force Base at 0600 hours.

From then on, there was no day and no night for the two diplomats. They snatched what sleep they could in the jet ferrying them back and forth between England and Argentina, through endless time zones, from frustration to frustration.

Then, just before the British attacked, Haig miraculously convinced Argentina's General Galtieri to withdraw his troops and negotiate. It looked like a real coup.

As they were fastening their seat belts for the long ride home, George congratulated his boss, "Al, I think you won a big one."

But just as the plane door was shutting, a messenger arrived with a letter from Prime Minister Costa Mendez.

"Aren't you going to read it?" George asked.

"I don't have to," Haig said with a weary sigh. "I know it's my death warrant."

Indeed, the execution of Alexander Haig had taken place while he was still in the air.

An unnamed White House source said the administration saw his fruitless mission as mere "grandstanding." The press took the cue and began to quote various authoritative sources that "Haig is going to go, and go quickly."

George Keller had more frequent lunches with Dwight Bevington.

*   *   *

He was sitting at his desk polishing a lengthy telex to Phil Habib, then shuttling between Damascus and Jerusalem, when his secretary buzzed.

"Dr. Keller, there's a phone call from Thomas Leighton."

"You mean *The New York Times* reporter?"

"I think so, sir."

"Well, put him on."

If this was indeed *the* Thomas Leighton, investigative journalist and author of a highly praised book about Russia, it was a favorable signal.

The journalist had possibly been tipped that George was in the wings to succeed Haig. And, like his Harvard mentor, George intended to play the press like a piano.

"Thank you for taking my call, Dr. Keller. I'd like to ask a favor. I'm on leave from the *Times* to write a book about your former boss, Henry Kissinger."

"Is it a snow job or a hatchet job?"

"I hope it'll be an honest job," the reporter replied. "I won't say I haven't heard some nasty things about him. That's why, if you let me have a couple hours of your time, I might get a more balanced picture."

"I see your point," George said, thinking that it would be nice to have such an important journalist on his future team. "Suppose we meet for lunch sometime next week. Is Wednesday good for you?"

"It's fine," said Leighton.

"Let's meet at Sans Souci at twelve."

The first thing that struck him was the reporter's youth. He looked less like a Pulitzer Prize winner than a candidate for the *Crimson*. When George said this to Leighton, he confessed, "Well, actually I did write for the *Crime*. I was Class of '64."

They chatted cordially about their college experiences. Then the journalist got down to business.

"As I'm sure you know, not everybody views Kissinger as a knight in shining armor."

"No," George concurred. "But that's the price you pay when you wield power. What sort of mud are they throwing at Henry?"

"Well, everything from 'war criminal' to 'ruthless manipulator,' and lots in between. You'd be surprised, he had a reputation even at Harvard."

"Yes." George smiled. "I was his student."

"I know that, too. I also know you deserve your nickname of being 'Kissinger's shadow.' Isn't it true that you were as privy as any man alive to every significant decision he ever made?"

"That's a slight exaggeration," George replied, trying to affect humility. And then joked, "I mean, he didn't take me into his confidence about marrying Nancy. Anyway, what's the thrust of your book?"

"I get the impression that your boss was—how can I put it?—sort of amoral. That he played the game of world politics with human beings as pawns."

"That's rather brutal," George interrupted.

"Which is why I want to hear your side of it," Leighton responded. "I'll give you a few examples. Some insiders I've interviewed say he deliberately withheld arms from the Israelis during the Yom Kippur war to 'soften' them into a better negotiating mood."

"I bet I know who told you that one," George said with irritation.

"No comment. I always protect my sources. Anyway, I've done some digging on my own and found that he was not averse to doing curious favors if it could help him win a point."

"Could you be more specific?"

"Well, this may seem a small thing, but I think it's typical of how he operated. Back in 1973, he okayed the sale to Russia of a sophisticated filter for satellite photography. I'm told Commerce had been sort of leery about letting them have it."

George's blood froze. He could barely listen to the rest.

"It's my theory that Henry was trading for something. Now, what I'd like to know from you is—what did *he* get in return?"

George Keller had often testified before senatorial committees. He knew that the ironclad rule for any witness confronted with a startling question was to *wait*. And then answer as simply and directly as possible.

"I think you're going up a blind alley on this one, Tom," he said quietly.

"I'm positive I'm not."

"What makes you so sure?"

"The expression on your face, Dr. Keller."

Leighton paused for a moment and then said politely, "Are you willing to talk about it?"

George's mind was in turmoil. He had to quash this story or his whole life would be ruined.

What could he trade this guy? A great deal, he decided quickly.

All he had to do to save himself, was . . . sell out Kissinger.

"Listen, Tom," he said as casually as possible, "it's a nice day. Why don't we go for a walk?"

First George did some off-the-record bargaining. Without explaining why, he simply offered to exchange the insignificant filter story for whatever other information Leighton would request.

"Can I trust you, Tom?"

"I've got a reputation," the journalist replied. "I've never betrayed my sources. And I never will."

"I believe you," George said.

He *had* to.

On June 25, the ax fell. Ronald Reagan called Alexander Haig into the Oval Office and gave him an envelope. It contained a letter accepting the Secretary's resignation. Now all Haig had to do was formally resign.

The word in Washington was that Keller was going to get the job. The *Washington Post* went as far as to call him "the best appointment Reagan could possibly make."

Dozens of reporters now kept vigil around his home, waiting for the moment when the new cabinet appointee and his wife would step outside to be photographed in triumph.

The major wire services had done their research and prepared a profile. The saga of the teenager who fled Communist oppression and had risen to the top. Only in America, et cetera.

Inside, George and Cathy were rooted by the telephone. They dared not speak to each other. All Cathy had said the entire evening—at regular intervals—was that she would love him even if he was not made Secretary of State.

He wanted desperately to take a drink, but she forbade him even a drop.

"You've got to keep your wits about you, George. There'll be plenty of time for booze after this thing's over, one way or another."

The phone rang. It was Henry Kissinger.

"Tell me, Mr. Secretary," he said jovially, "will you still speak to me when you're appointed?"

George was breathless with excitement.

"What do you know, Henry?" he asked quickly.

"Only what I read in the papers. Just be sure to mention me in your acceptance speech, eh?"

At ten minutes before midnight, the phone rang again.

"This is it," George said to Cathy as he walked over, took a deep breath, and picked up the receiver.

"Yes?"

"George?" It was Caspar Weinberger, Secretary of Defense—and Harvard '38. The omen was good.

"Hi, Cap," George said weakly.

"Listen, George, the President's done a lot of thinking about State—" He paused and then announced as gently as possible, "He's decided to go with Shultz."

"Oh."

Seeing his devastated expression, Cathy grabbed his arm.

"I hope you understand there's nothing personal," the Defense Secretary continued. "It's just that Ron feels more comfortable with—you know—the California boys. And I know that Shultz wants you to stay on as Deputy."

George did not know what to say.

Weinberger tried to assuage his disappointment.

"Hey, Keller," he said buoyantly, "how old are you? Forty-six—forty-seven? You're too young to be where you are already, for heaven's sake. If Reagan wins another term, I'm sure he'll go with you."

"Yes, Cap. Thanks."

George hung up and looked at Cathy.

"I lost," he said softly.

"You didn't lose, George," she said with deep emotion. "You just haven't won yet."

November 17, 1982

One of the joys of being a reunion organizer as well as fundraiser is that I get to go to a lot of interesting places I would never normally be allowed into.

The White House, for instance.

Now, obviously the Reunion Committee wanted George Keller to lecture as part of the week's events. Being his oldest Harvard friend, I was deputized to enlist him.

My first surprise when I called on the Department of State was that I got right through to him. My second was that he invited me to Washington for lunch. My third was that we would be eating not in some posh Washington bistro but at the White House Mess, so he could give me a short tour of the presidential premises.

It was fascinating. I even got to see the famous Situation Room, which was a real thrill because it was so disappointing. I mean, it's just a windowless cubicle with a table and some chairs. To think that so many of recent history's most portentous decisions have been made in this glorified phone booth!

It was here that George asked me to sit down and chat about what had brought me all the way to Washington.

I asked him how he felt about Harvard.

He responded by asking me how they felt about him. Specifically, did the faculty still regard him as a Kissinger hatchet man?

I replied as tactfully as I could that, though they had come down on him and Henry pretty hard during the war, that was now nearly ten years ago. Besides, we were all dying for him to speak to The Class. You know, tell them what it's like to cross swords with Brezhnev and those guys.

"You're a big hero to all of us," I told him. "There's no ambivalence about that."

He smiled.

I then asked him if he was planning to come to the reunion anyway.

He confessed that he had been hesitant, afraid he'd hardly know anybody.

I countered by saying that now everybody knows *him*. Besides, most of the people I'd seen had changed so much physically, guys probably wouldn't recognize their own roommates. I mean, Newall, for example, was balding and twenty pounds heavier.

I didn't tell him that Dickie had also been having a little drinking problem of late (kind of drowning his middle-aged sorrows).

Anyway, I pressed on with my mission to persuade him to appear. And, after a little more flattery, he at last smiled okay.

He even complimented me on my negotiating powers. And said he'd give me a job anytime.

A little while later, he walked me to the White House gate, where a cab was waiting to take me to the airport.

I grinned from ear to ear all the way back to Boston. I, Andrew Eliot, had achieved a diplomatic coup with one of the world's great diplomats.

W hen he returned to his office, George Keller had an unexpected visitor—his wife.

She was seated on the couch, clutching a sheaf of long printed paper.

"What a pleasant surprise."

She waited to reply until he had closed the door. "You bloody traitorous bastard!"

"What's the matter?" he asked calmly.

"Why the hell did you collaborate with that mudslinger Tom Leighton?"

"Catherine, I don't know what's got into you. The man's an important journalist for *The New York Times*. And I had lunch with him—once."

"Come off it, Keller. A friend of mine from *Newsweek* just sent me these excerpts they're printing from his book. The guy's really vicious. And it's obvious to me that the 'source close to Kissinger' he keeps quoting could only have been you."

"Cathy, I swear—"

"George, I can't take any more of your lies. You know I never had much love for Henry, but he was like a second father to you. And that book is an absolute defamation. Don't you have *any* loyalties?"

"Catherine, you're jumping to conclusions based on no evidence whatsoever. Can't we discuss this at home?"

"No, George, I won't be there. I'm leaving you."

"Just because you think I talked to some ambitious reporter?"

"No, George. Because this proves to me how stupid I was to ever think I could change you. You're a selfish bastard who can't give love and isn't even trusting enough to take it. *Now,* have I given you sufficient reasons?"

563

"Please, Cathy, may I have a chance to explain my side of this?"

"On one condition."

"Name it."

"You can have sixty minutes to present your case. But if I'm not convinced, you'll sign papers for a Mexican divorce."

"You mean you've already seen a lawyer?"

"No, my sweet," she replied. "You're so involved with yourself you forget I *am* a lawyer."

ANDREW ELIOT'S DIARY

December 2, 1982

I'm getting married again.

It's not a decision I've taken lightly. But after seventeen years of miserable bachelorhood I've come to understand why Noah's Ark was not a singles' cruise.

I've been fighting the prospect ever since my initial marital catastrophe. The only trouble is, I get lonely—especially around Christmastime. So I've finally resolved to get remarried. And by the time The Class gathers in June, I want to be able to trumpet the great news.

Now all I have to do is find a wife.

The possibilities are rich and various.

First, there's Laura Hartley, whom I saw a lot of in New York. Of course, she's probably too high-powered for me, being managing editor of a famous women's magazine. I admire career girls and Laura sure is dynamic. It's probably why, at thirty-nine, she hasn't gotten married yet. I mean, she's so dedicated to her job that sometimes when we're in bed she leaps out to write down an idea for a column or a feature. And this can sometimes spoil the mood.

There are also a couple of other small problems.

First, she doesn't eat.

Not that she's overweight. On the contrary, Laura's like a toothpick in boots. She's on a perpetual diet of coffee and sugarless chewing gum. I don't know how she survives, but it's kind of rough on me since I have to gobble a sandwich when she isn't looking.

The second difficulty is that she smokes. Not just occasionally, but an endless chain of unfiltered cigarettes that pretty well fog up her apartment. And with her near-emaciation and the low visibility, it is sometimes hard to know if she's actually there.

Still I thought she was a definite candidate until I moved up to Boston.

This city is a real mecca for nubilities. To begin with, Beacon Hill is populated with clones of Faith—newer, turbo-charged models, you might say. Yet, I seem to have a Pavlovian aversion to female preppies. So I keep my distance from the deb set. Especially since there are so many other possibilities.

Like Cora Avery. She's probably one of the most glowing examples of young womanhood in the whole United States. I met her while jogging along the Charles one afternoon. It was clear even despite her floppy sweatsuit that she had an absolutely amazing figure. I was able to keep up with her just long enough to get her phone number. And we started going out.

On our first date I learned that she was a gym teacher at Brookline High. And a marathon runner. And a skier. And a long-distance swimmer. For relaxation she did aerobic dancing.

Naturally she wanted to recruit me for all these invigorating activities, and initially I went along. The fact that every muscle in my body ached was compensated by the fact that she could give a really great massage.

For a while there I thought we really had something going. But when I started staying overnight at her place I began to get cold feet. Literally. She'd shake me at 5:00 A.M., make me down a cocktail of megavitamins, and drag me out to jog. None of Boston's notoriously inclement weather could deter her. Like a mailman, neither snow nor rain nor sleet nor gloom of night could keep her from her appointed rounds. We'd get back at around seven, and instead of letting me tumble into a bath or back to bed, we had to spend another half-hour lifting weights. By the time I got to the office I was a wreck.

But she was a great kid and liked me a lot. She'd often call and suggest we spend a lunch hour together. Unfortunately, this was always at the Harvard pool. Where, after quickly downing a can of Nutrament, she would entice me into the water and I would wearily paddle while she churned her daily mile.

Even my friends remarked that I'd never looked better in my life. And I know if I married Cora I'd probably live to be at least a hundred.

But then there are a couple of drawbacks.

I was beginning to get so tired in the evenings that when she returned from dance class feeling all romantic, I was simply too exhausted to do anything but snooze. She began to think I was not interested in her body. In truth, I was obsessed by her body. It was my own that was the problem.

At the end of next semester she plans to move to Hawaii, where there are better facilities to train for the triathlon (a combination of swimming, biking, and marathoning).

So, time is running out.

The reason I'm having trouble deciding is that new opportunities present themselves at every turn.

There's Roz, a divorcee who lives in Weston. She's bright, well read, and (for a change) a terrific cook. She's constantly asking me out to the house, which is where I find the single obstacle. Or rather, multiple one. Her five kids loathe me. And I guess they'd have to be included in a connubial arrangement.

There are lots of other candidates too. But none of them seems to be quite right.

Perhaps it's my fault. I guess my expectations are too high. I'd like to marry someone who enjoys sitting quietly (without doing push-ups) and chatting about everything from politics to children. A woman who enjoys reading the same books and discussing them.

Most of all, I'd like to find someone as lonely as I. Who wants a hand to hold and a grown-up person to love. Maybe that's too much to ask.

But I'll keep looking.

From the "Milestones" section of *Time* magazine, January 4, 1983:

DIVORCED. **George Keller**, 47, Deputy Secretary of State, and **Catherine Fitzgerald Keller**, 39, political activist; on grounds of irreconcilable differences; after nine years of marriage; no children.

THE

REUNION

JUNE 5–9, 1983

We shall not cease from exploration
And the end of all our exploring
Will be to arrive where we started
And know the place for the first time.

T.S. ELIOT '10

They began to gather on Sunday, June 5. Advance reservations indicated that over six hundred members of The Class would be coming from every state and even Europe and Asia. Registration was at the Freshman Union, where they had all embarked on their great journey twenty-nine years earlier.

But who were these strange people—balding, bespectacled, overweight, and shy? How had they come to usurp the hall reserved for the firebrands of The Class of '58? The only clue was the badges that they wore on their lapels.

Paradoxically, most of them were more frightened at the prospect of their return to Harvard than when they first arrived as undergraduates. For now there was one conspicuous item missing from their spiritual luggage—unbounded faith in their potential.

They were no longer like astronauts striding to the launch pad full of hope, ready to fly to the moon and beyond. They were most of them weary travelers whose horizons ended at the office parking lot.

And for all their glittering achievements, their triumphal entries into the pages of *Who's Who,* they knew they had suffered the irreparable loss of what was once their most precious gift. Their youth.

The Class of '58 had come home as grown-ups. The great expectations that once had burned in them had been replaced by ghosts of old ambitions.

The secret word was *compromise.* Nobody said it outright, but they all could sense it. Yet somehow it was comforting to see that everyone had aged. They had weathered all the storms of harsh reality, and here were seeking shelter in a place where they had once believed no rain could ever fall on *them.*

They were gazing at one another. Some too timid to approach the old acquaintances they thought they recognized—but were too far away to read the badges.

And yet how different from the looks they had exchanged while waiting on line for that first dinner in their freshman year. They all were adversaries then. Independent, trusting only in themselves. The Union air had been suffused with feelings of omniscience and infallibility.

But now they treated one another with a new affection. There were no hierarchies. They were meeting for the first time as fellow human beings. For they were not there to worship. The Class had gathered to commune.

Gradually they could allow themselves to laugh. And talk of football games and college pranks. The good old times when Ike was in the White House and all was right with the world.

The reunion had begun.

The week officially began with a Thanksgiving and Memorial Service at nine-thirty the next morning.

Considering how few had attended the Baccalaureate Service at graduation in 1958, it was remarkable how many were present in Mem. Church that balmy morning of June 6, 1983.

They all had studied the immense red book, the glorious compendium of their collective achievements. But the entries that had captured everyone's imagination were the dead. Eminence is no protection in a highway accident. Cancer does not hold a Harvard graduate in awe.

Perhaps they knew that this was the reason they had really come. To be with classmates once again at the midway point in their lives. And though the service was to honor the departed, in so doing, they were all acknowledging their own mortality.

The church was filled only with members of The Class, their families, and—their survivors. Classmates led the service.

At one point the Reverend Lyle Guttu '58 offered some brief comments.

He emphasized that fear of death is universal. But what lies beneath that fear is the terror of *insignificance*. Of not being remembered, not counting.

"That is why we are gathered, for ourselves, as much as any other. That is why this building is here, to honor the sacrifice of Harvard sons who died in struggles to defend the dignity of man."

He then commented on some of the deaths. One classmate had drowned while attempting to save a child. Another had been executed for leading an abortive revolt against the oppressive regime in Haiti. Yet another gave up his life to save more than a hundred hostages.

573

And finally he stated, "Quiet heroism or youthful idealism, or both? What do we know? That life without heroism and idealism is not worth living—or that either can be fatal? We are here to remember our classmates. They are not nameless. They are known. They were ours, and shall ever be."

At this point, another member of The Class rose to read the names of the departed.

As he finished, the bells of Memorial Church began to toll. Once for every name. The dull knelling profoundly shook those standing in the vast white-paneled church.

Forty years of vibrant life reduced to the reverberation of a single bell.

We will all come to this.

June 6, 1983

I had been looking forward to the Memorial Service with fear and trembling. I didn't think I would be able to keep my emotions in check. And I'm sure I couldn't have, if I hadn't had the responsibility of taking care of a young son. Not my own, of course (I don't have one anymore).

The handsome, blond sixteen-year-old standing next to me was Jason's oldest boy, Joshua, whom I'd invited to be present when we honored his father.

While all about him tears were unashamedly flowing, he remained straight-backed and impassive. In fact, the only time he even opened his mouth was for the first hymn, "The God of Abraham Praise."

I was amazed that he even knew the tune. Although I realized why, as soon as I caught the sound of his softly singing voice. While all of us were chanting the church text, he was singing it—in Hebrew. He told me later that it was a traditional Jewish prayer that, I guess, we Christians had appropriated.

He asked if this was especially for his father.

I answered that it was all for his father. Which, at least from my standpoint, was true.

To add to my aching sadness, I could see some classmates looking at Josh and thinking he was probably my son.

Afterward, I introduced him to as many of Jason's buddies as I could find (there were so many). Every one of them had something wonderful to say to him about his father. I could see that this moved him deeply, and he was struggling manfully not to break down.

As I put him on the train to visit his grandparents, I told him I hoped that he'd come back to Boston someday.

He replied that it was his dream to go to Harvard—like his father. But, of course, he had to do his army service first.

I waited till the train pulled out, thinking how proud Jason would be of the way his son was growing up.

Then I went and had a cup of coffee, since I had to meet another train in half an hour. My date for the reunion.

Just as everyone predicted, this occasion is incredibly emotional—and it had only just begun. Thank heavens I had someone I love to share it with. And who loves me, I think.

Ever since Andy left "the Western world," Lizzie and I have grown much closer. Somewhere along the line she realized I was trying hard as hell to be a loving father. And she started to reciprocate.

Now and then I take her to a football game. Sometimes I drive down to her school—right in the middle of the week—and we go out for a good dinner. She tells me her problems. About the "creepy" men who love her and the "groovy" ones she's trying to attract.

I started offering advice. And, to my astonishment, she *likes* it.

I knew that something good was happening when suddenly her grades, which had been good but not fantastic, started really picking up. In fact, she's gotten acceptances from all the colleges she applied to: Swarthmore, Yale—and Harvard.

Who knows, maybe she'll opt to go to Cambridge, even with her father on the scene. And generations of invisible ancestors looking down. My Lizzie is a plucky girl and I'm really proud of her.

It's nice to know I'll have her hand to hold.

Cynics might argue that the Reunion Memorial Service was merely to remind Harvard men that, although *they* are mortal, the University abideth forever.

At any rate, the rest of the week was dedicated to the impressive demonstration of how much Harvard had done for them. And—with their financial munificence—would be doing for the ages to come.

First, President Derek Bok and Dean Theodore Lambros '58 led a symposium, "The Future of Harvard." Their message was that while most American universities were preparing for the twenty-first century, Harvard, with its greater vision, was already looking forward to the twenty-*second*.

Indeed, in one of his many witty responses during the question period, Dean Lambros said that it would not be Harvard's policy "to grant tenure to computers."

The alumni were suitably impressed. And—especially those with teenage children about to apply to college—extremely deferential.

June 6, 1983

You'd never recognize Ted Lambros. He's preppier than I am. And boy, has he got self-assurance when he speaks. But he's got every reason to be confident. After all, he's really made it in the world.

His new wife, Abbie, is a terrific gal. I ought to know, since she's a distant relative. In fact, she was working with me on the Harvard Fund Drive when Ted met her.

Since she was, to put it politely, in the suburbs of forty, our family had kind of given up on Ab's chances of settling down. But Lambros really swept her off her feet. Now they're living in a big house on Brattle Street.

And I think they'll be good for each other. I mean, Ab's a great hostess. They have everybody who's anybody in Boston at their parties.

Pretty reliable sources have informed me that Ted recently rejected an offer to become the president of Princeton. This leads me to suspect that Harvard's given him some heavy hints that he might ultimately move into our own presidential mansion. The thought of it excites me almost as much as I expect it does Ted.

And it's amazing how obsequious some of the reunion guys were to this man who, in our college days, they scarcely knew was in The Class.

I've got to make this claim for myself, and my diaries bear me out.

I always knew that Lambros was a winner.

George Keller's lecture on foreign policy filled the amphitheater to overflowing.

In the space of less than forty-five minutes, he made pithy observations on all the troubled areas of international relations. From nuclear disarmament to whom the White House backed in Central America and why. From the labyrinthine mysteries of Middle Eastern governments' behavior to a brief character analysis of the new Kremlin leaders.

It was a masterful, pointillistic painting of the whole world's politics.

During the question period, one of the alumni asked George what he thought of Tom Leighton's new book, *The Prince of Darkness,* which makes allegations about Henry Kissinger's ruthlessness in matters like the Cambodia invasion, Nixon's pardon, and even the wiretapping of his own staff.

George looked visibly outraged at the mention of this attack on the man to whom he owed so much. And he rose to the occasion with an eloquent defense of his old mentor.

As The Class began to applaud, someone in the back shouted, "What about the Vietnam war, Dr. Keller?"

"What about it, sir?" George answered quietly.

"How can you and Kissinger justify the fact that you strung out those negotiations at the cost of so many lives on both sides?"

He responded calmly, "That isn't true. Our aim in Paris was to bring the conflict to the speediest possible conclusion—to *save* lives."

But the man was not satisfied.

"What about the Christmas saturation bombing when you destroyed targets like the Bach Mai hospital?"

The audience began to grow distinctly uncomfortable. George remained unruffled.

"Sir, that bombing was necessary and, I think, justified because it proved to North Vietnam that we meant business. Hitting that hospital was just a tragic mistake."

"But don't you think the whole damn war was a mistake?"

George seemed more puzzled than provoked. "I don't understand why you pose your questions with such urgency when we're talking of events that are now history."

Then the man asked, "Do you have children, Dr. Keller?"

"No," George replied.

"Well, maybe if you did, like me, and if your only son was killed in Southeast Asia—for reasons that you still can't understand—even ten years later you'd ask these sorts of questions too."

There was a collective gasp in the auditorium.

George was silent for a moment and then answered softly.

"I'm truly sorry for engaging in dialectic on a subject that's so real a tragedy for you. I think I speak for our whole class in saying that we in some small way share your loss."

"What about the guilt, Dr. Keller? Can you really sleep at night with all that on your conscience?"

George remained poised. Then, after a few minutes of silence, said impassively, "I think we should end the seminar here."

There was no applause. People were too upset.

The man who'd asked the questions simply walked away, his arm around his wife.

ANDREW ELIOT'S DIARY

June 7, 1983

George's schedule was so tight that I had to rush him straight to the airport to make the five o'clock back to Washington. He sat mutely as I zoomed down Storrow Drive. He had clearly been shell-shocked by that guy's explosion.

I tried to buck him up by telling him how brilliant his whole lecture was. That didn't seem to comfort him.

I had driven so fast that we arrived a little early, so we had a few moments to chat in the American Airlines VIP lounge. George ordered a double scotch for each of us. When he saw that I didn't touch my drink, he appropriated it as well. He was incredibly depressed.

In a curious way, I felt slightly responsible. Because I had lured him up to the reunion with the promise of adulation. And here he was going away with the dispiriting impression that "the people at Harvard still hate me." I tried to reassure him that the opposite was true. His classmates all looked up to him. I, for one, particularly admired him.

That made him laugh bitterly and reply that lots of people admired him, but nobody really liked him. Again, I can remember his exact words: "I have a talent for success maybe, but not for friendship."

I suggested that perhaps he was still feeling bruised from the divorce. He disagreed. And, after ordering yet another scotch, he told me that he felt his marriage had failed for the same reasons he couldn't make friends at college. He was too selfish.

At that point he looked at his watch, stood up—without apparent difficulty—and we walked together toward his flight. We stood at the gate for a few seconds before he started back to where he helped rule the world. He then said something that will haunt me for the rest of my life: "Andrew, when you write about me in that diary of yours—never say that I'm a lucky man."

It is a tradition of Harvard reunions that the outstanding musician of The Class is invited to conduct at least a portion of a Boston Pops' concert. In 1964, for example, Leonard Bernstein '39 conducted an evening of his own music. In 1983, the same honor was accorded to Daniel Rossi '58.

The huge organ pipes above the stage of Symphony Hall were festively decked with pink and silver pennants, the massive auditorium packed exclusively with members of The Class.

As he stood in the wings, elegant in tails and perfectly coiffed (even wearing a bit of stage makeup, lest he be thought anything but a perpetual Wunderkind), Danny was suddenly struck by a strange realization.

This was the most important audience he would ever face in his entire life.

All he could remember in this brief flickering of eternity was that during his Harvard years—despite his musical successes—he had been all but disregarded. He had not been athletic. He had not been gregarious. He had not even, at first, been a success with the opposite sex. He had been a wonk.

And after a quarter of a century he still resented the ruthless massacre of his piano.

Now the wheel had come full circle. All those who had persecuted, derided, and ignored him were out there waiting.

He walked on stage.

There was a hush as he mounted the podium, bowed slowly, then turned and raised his baton.

First he led a suite from his *Savanarola* ballet. Admittedly, this was a bit esoteric for some. But it was Danny Rossi's music and they still respected it.

Then he got to what they were waiting for: a medley from *Manhattan Odyssey*. And every time he modulated to a different tune they clapped and sang along.

The biggest ovation was, of course, for "The Stars Are Not Enough"—if not quite a legitimate offspring of The Class, at least an adopted child.

When it was over, he turned and faced them. They were on their feet now, all of them. Cheering and applauding.

Then the first shout came.

"Play the piano, Danny!"

It soon became a tidal wave of chanting, "Play! Play!"

At first he tried to brush it off nonchalantly with a wave of his right hand. But they wouldn't stop.

The one thing they admired most in him was no longer his to give.

And suddenly he sensed he could not hold back the tears. So he quickly whirled to the musicians and signaled them to begin the concluding medley of Harvard football songs.

> With Crimson in triumph flashing
> Mid the strains of victory . . .

Danny had covered his retreat by invoking something they worshipped more than him—Harvard.

June 8, 1983

I'm the only person in The Class who knows Danny Rossi's secret.

I learned it by sheer chance.

The chairman of the Class Campaign had deputized me to "shake up that prima donna Rossi" and make him come up with some sort of contribution.

For, despite our importuning, Danny had resisted giving us even the tiniest donation. And since the Alumni Office has almost as much financial info on our classmates as the IRS, we knew that he was worth several million bucks.

The boys searched high and low for someone who knew Rossi well enough to make one final pitch before our class gift would be announced at the Commencement Ceremony. The fact that I was chosen shows how few close friends he had at Harvard.

Unlike the rest of us, Danny didn't bunk out in the dorms for old times' sake. Instead, he and his wife stayed at The Ritz, which is where we met after last night's concert.

He looked much paler than he did on stage. And even thinner. At first I thought it was just fatigue and the emotion of the evening. He and Maria sat side by side while I tried to make a heartfelt pitch.

Did he feel gratitude to Harvard for his great success, I asked. He answered no. Then what about some bond of friendship or general affection for the place? He answered no to that as well. But then I shifted to another tactic from the "Harvard Guide to Raising Funds." Did he feel warmly about some *department* or activity?

I suggested maybe music or the orchestra. Maybe a prize for composition or performance. Something that was down his alley. He was cordial, but the answer still was no.

This kind of threw me, and I almost lost my cool. Then I

asked earnestly if there was *anything* he cared enough about to want to support.

At this point he exchanged glances with Maria.

Then she asked me very softly not to misunderstand. Danny was a very caring person. But their life was not exactly what it seemed across the footlights. They had in fact talked a lot about a possible gift to Harvard. But they wanted it to be something meaningful to them.

I sensed they were opening up. And at the same time I felt a kind of tension in the room.

Danny then inquired if he could direct his gift to the Med School. I asked him what he had in mind.

Then Maria said they would consider endowing a chair in neurology. One that specifically researched motor dysfunctions.

I was speechless. Did the Rossis realize that a Med School professorship cost a million bucks? Danny said he did. And would donate it on a single condition—that it be anonymous. Totally anonymous.

Now I was really staggered. Why would this guy be so generous and yet want no recognition at all? In fact, I asked them straight out: it was such a noble thing—why did they want it to go unacknowledged?

He glanced at Maria again. They seemed to be thinking as one.

Then, slowly and hesitantly at first, Danny began to tell me the real reason he had given up the piano. He was suffering from a physical handicap. Neurological damage that made him unable to control his left hand.

Just hearing this made me sick at heart. I could scarcely bear to listen.

But Danny tried to make light of it. He joked that their contribution was not really unselfish at all. In fact it was kind of a bet he was placing that some smart Harvard researcher would come up with a cure for his condition "before our Fiftieth reunion." Then he promised to entertain The Class at the keyboard for as long as they wanted to listen.

I said I'd be in the front row for that concert. Then I didn't know what else to say.

As I got up to take my leave, Maria walked me to the door, touched my shoulder, and murmured, "Andrew, thank you for being such a good person."

* * *

Downstairs, I found a private phone and called Frank Harvey, our Chairman.

I told him I had good news and bad news. The bad was that Rossi didn't come through. The good was that I ran into a classmate in the hotel bar who was willing to cough up a million bucks for the Med School—anonymously.

At first Frank didn't believe me. He kept asking if this character was sober. And if *I* was sober.

When I convinced him that a banker's check would be in his hands before the end of the week, he almost did somersaults over the phone.

That put our class gift over the eight-million mark. And, as he put it, made me "the hero of the day."

I hung up and ambled homeward thinking, I'm no hero. Danny is the guy with guts. He needs courage just to wake up every morning and face what's happened to him.

I had always looked at him as the exception to the rule. But now I realize that *everybody* pays a price for his success.

On the afternoon of Commencement Day, the various Harvard classes assembled in the Yard to march into Tercentenary Theater for their annual meeting. They were headed by President Derek Bok, with Dean Theodore Lambros, resplendent in his crimson robes, a step behind. They in turn were followed by batallions of the various classes, several thousand strong.

Those having their Twenty-fifth and Fiftieth reunions had the pride of place. And some of their representatives were honored for various reasons by being asked to sit—wearing top hats and morning coats—on the podium.

Both George Keller and Daniel Rossi had been invited, but respectfully declined. Andrew Eliot was likewise honored for his service to the University Fund Raising Campaign—and sat unobtrusively in a corner of the stage.

Also attending, to represent the Class of '33 (the Fiftieth) was Philip Harrison, former Secretary of the Treasury and Ted's erstwhile father-in-law.

As the old man climbed the steps, Ted rose to greet him, offering his hand.

"Ah, Dean Lambros," the old man said tonelessly, "congratulations. I'm very pleased to see you've gotten everything you've always wanted."

He then walked to his seat. Because, in truth, that is all they had left to say to each other.

During the ceremony, the gifts of the various classes were announced. Franklin Harvey rose to proclaim that the sum donated by the Twenty-fifth Reunion was a record $8.6 million.

There was an audible gasp.

But Frank raised his hand to postpone any further jubilation until he could add an important comment.

"Needless to say, we feel gratitude to the entire Class. But, if I may, I'd like to single out one individual who's worked closely with me on this entire campaign for the past five years.

"It's not just that he's done yeoman service in raising funds. It's more than that. His kindness and selflessness demonstrate the best of what a man can offer to the university and to his friends.

"I'd like this individual to stand, so we can show him our appreciation." He turned and motioned to the honorand, saying, "Mr. Andrew Eliot."

Andrew was stunned. No one had ever applauded him before. Not even his kids when they were young.

He stood up shyly, lost in the unfamiliarity of public appreciation. Pleased. Surprised. And overcome by this display of real affection.

For, though he had not known it—and perhaps still did not understand—he was, in *human* terms, the best man in The Class.

June 9, 1983

I had to leave early to get Lizzie to the five-o'clock train. I was happy she had been there to see her dad acknowledged—deservedly or not—as someone whom the guys respected.

It had been the best day of my life. That is, until I got back to my apartment.

There were two stern-looking characters in drab suits waiting outside my door. The taller of them asked politely if I was Andrew Eliot.

As I nodded, both reached in their pockets and produced IDs. They were from the Secret Service.

The minute we got inside, they started firing questions in subdued tones.

Did I know George Keller?

Of course.

When had I seen him last?

Day before yesterday at the airport.

How would I describe his mood?

He seemed troubled, a bit depressed.

Any particular reason that I knew of?

There was, of course, his divorce. They knew about that. Then there was the matter of the guy at his lecture attacking him.

My heart was starting to beat fast. I asked them what the hell was going on.

They handed me a letter. It read:

> My dear Andrew,
>   You have always been so kind to me that I dare to ask you to serve as my executor.
>   I have a bank account and some stocks and bonds. Please see that these get to my sister in Hungary.

You are all the good things that I never was or could
be. Thanks.

George

The two agents then sat me down and explained that I was
about to be privy to a government secret.

George had committed suicide last night.

I was stunned. And instantly felt guilty for letting him
get on that plane.

They emphasized that his death would be announced as
having occurred from natural causes. Not merely to avoid government scandal, but out of respect for a loyal public servant. Weighed
down by the pressures of his job, George had probably succumbed to despair in a moment of weakness.

Funeral arrangements were being made. By a special Executive
order George would be buried in Arlington National Cemetery
(they emphasized what a rare honor this was for a civilian). Did I
know anyone who should be informed?

What could I say? They probably should contact his ex-wife.
She might want to attend. I could think of no one else.

They suggested that it might be better if I were the one to tell
Cathy and gave me her number in New York.

They left me to my anguish and confusion. I finally gathered
the courage to pick up the phone.

Cathy seemed very pleased to hear my voice. Until I got
around to the reason I was calling. Without my telling her she
guessed that it had been by his own hand.

She was silent for a moment. And then apologized for not
being able to cry. She said she had always been afraid he might do
something like this. And in a very soft voice she thanked me for
having tried to be George's friend.

All I could answer was that I wished I'd been a better friend.

She replied that she wished she could have been a better wife.
But it was impossible for George to accept love. From anyone.

I told her about his being buried at Arlington, which made
him a sort of American hero. That probably would have meant a
great deal to George. She agreed, but said the price was too high.

Then I asked if she wanted to attend the funeral. She said
yes, but sounded anxious. I told her that, if she wanted, I'd fly to
New York so we could travel to Washington together. She said

she really would like that. I was glad she accepted. I would need her company too.

After we hung up I asked myself why the hell George had done it. He had so much to live for.

I guess he just didn't know how to be happy.

That's the one thing they can't teach you at Harvard.

When Commencement Day was over, The Class of '58 returned to the Union one final time. Although champagne was served, the mood was curiously subdued.

After this reunion, they would probably never meet together as a class again—at least not in such numbers. They would spend the next decades reading obituaries of the men who had started out in 1954 as rivals and today were leaving Harvard as brothers.

This was the beginning of the end. They had met once more and just had time enough to learn that they liked one another.

And to say goodbye.